Robert Barr (16 September 1849 – 21 October 1912) was a Scottish-Canadian short story writer and novelist. Robert Barr was born in Barony, Lanark, Scotland to Robert Barr and Jane Watson. In 1854, he emigrated with his parents to Upper Canada at the age of four years old. His family settled on a farm near the village of Muirkirk. Barr assisted his father with his job as a carpenter, and developed a sound work ethic. Robert Barr then worked as a steel smelter for a number of years before he was educated at Toronto Normal School in 1873 to train as a teacher. After graduating Toronto Normal School, Barr became a teacher, and eventually headmaster/principal of the Central School of Windsor, Ontario in 1874. While Barr worked as head master of the Central School of Windsor, Ontario, he began to contribute short stories—often based on personal experiences, and recorded his work. On August 1876, when he was 27, Robert Barr married Ontario-born Eva Bennett, who was 21. (Source: Wikipedia)

Literary works:

"The Face And The Mask" (1894)
In the Midst of Alarms (1894, 1900, 1912)
From Whose Bourne (1896)
One Day's Courtship (1896)
Revenge!
The Strong Arm
A Woman Intervenes (1896)
Tekla: A Romance of Love and War (1898)
Jennie Baxter, Journalist (1899)
The Unchanging East (1900)
The Victors (1901)
A Prince of Good Fellows (1902)
Over The Border: A Romance (1903)
The O'Ruddy, A Romance, with Stephen Crane (1903)

THE STRONG ARM, JENNIE BAXTER, JOURNALIST & IN THE MIDST OF ALARMS

A NOVEL

ROBERT BARR

PRINCE CLASSICS

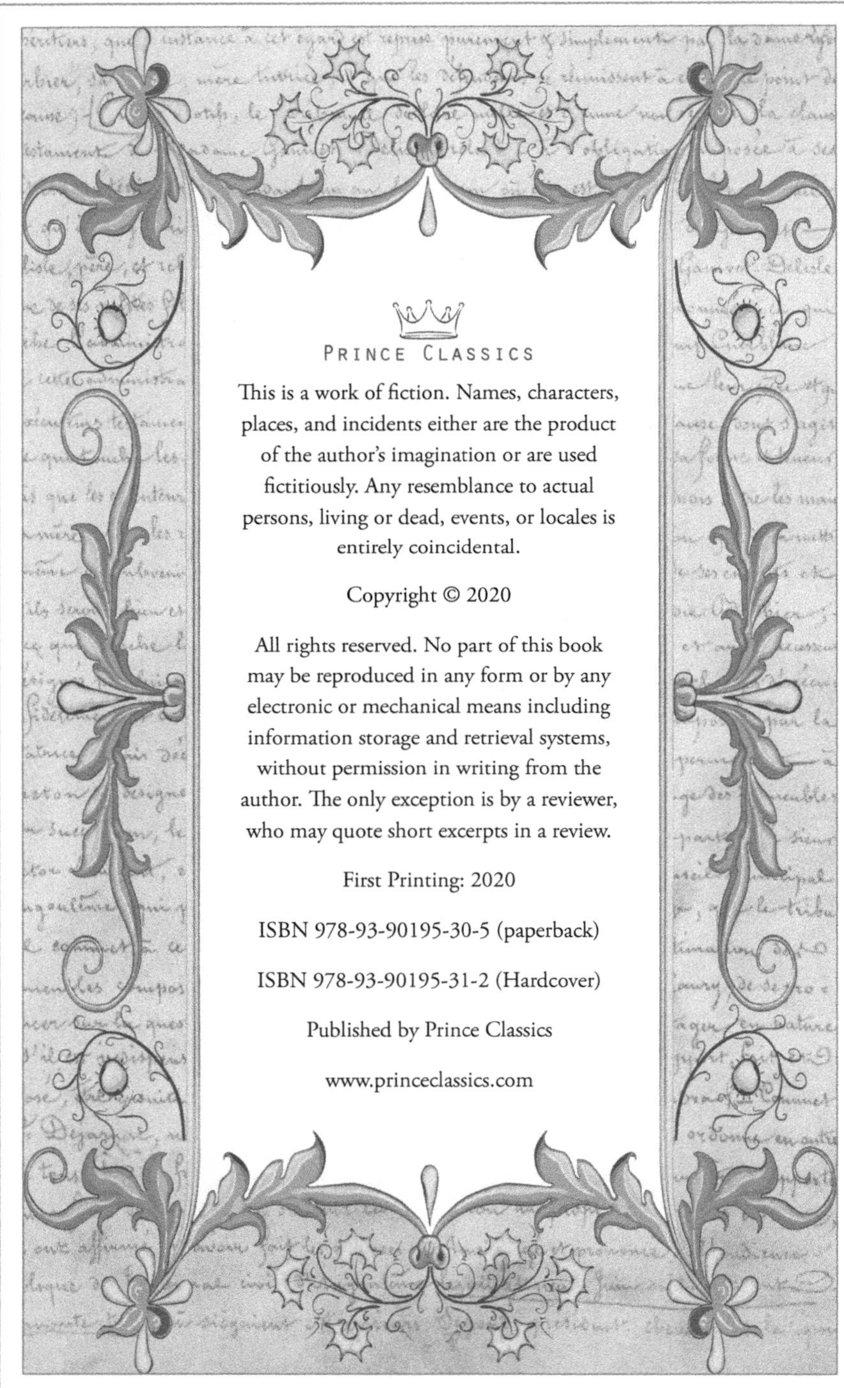

PRINCE CLASSICS

First Printing: 2020

ISBN 978-93-90195-30-5 (paperback)

ISBN 978-93-90195-31-2 (Hardcover)

Published by Prince Classics

www.princeclassics.com

Contents

THE STRONG ARM,
JENNIE BAXTER, JOURNALIST
&
IN THE MIDST OF ALARMS
A NOVEL

THE STRONG ARM

CHAPTER I. – THE BEAUTIFUL JAILER OF GUDENFELS

The aged Emir Soldan sat in his tent and smiled; the crafty Oriental smile of an experienced man, deeply grounded in the wisdom of this world. He knew that there was incipient rebellion in his camp; that the young commanders under him thought their leader was becoming too old for the fray; caution overmastering courage. Here were these dogs of unbelievers setting their unhallowed feet on the sacred soil of Syria, and the Emir, instead of dashing against them, counselled coolness and prudence. Therefore impatience disintegrated the camp and resentment threatened discipline. When at last the murmurs could be no longer ignored the Emir gathered his impetuous young men together in his tent, and thus addressed them.

"It may well be that I am growing too old for the active field; it may be that, having met before this German boar who leads his herd of swine, I am fearful of risking my remnant of life against him, but I have ever been an indulgent general, and am now loath to let my inaction stand against your chance of distinction. Go you therefore forth against him, and the man who brings me this boar's head shall not lack his reward."

The young men loudly cheered this decision and brandished their weapons aloft, while the old man smiled upon them and added:

"When you are bringing confusion to the camp of the unbelievers, I shall remain in my tent and meditate on the sayings of the Prophet, praying him to keep you a good spear's length from the German's broad sword, which he is the habit of wielding with his two hands."

The young Saracens went forth with much shouting, a gay prancing of the horses underneath them and a marvellous flourishing of spears above them, but they learned more wisdom in their half hour's communion with the German than the Emir, in a long life of counselling, had been able to bestow upon them. The two-handed sword they now met for the first time, and the acquaintance brought little joy to them. Count Herbert, the leader of the invaders, did no shouting, but reserved his breath for other purposes. He spurred his horse among them, and his foes went down around him as a thicket melts away before the well-swung axe of a stalwart woodman. The Saracens had little fear of death, but mutilation was another thing, for they knew that they would spend eternity in Paradise, shaped as they had left this earth, and while a spear's thrust or a wound from an arrow, or even the gash left by a short sword may be concealed by celestial robes, how is a man to comport himself in the Land of the Blest who is compelled to carry his head under his arm, or who is split from crown to midriff by an outlandish weapon that falls irresistible as the wrath of Allah! Again and again they threw themselves with disastrous bravery against the invading horde, and after each encounter they came back with lessened ranks and a more chastened spirit than when they had set forth. When at last, another counsel of war was held, the young men kept silence and waited for the smiling Emir to speak.

"If you are satisfied that there are other things to think of in war than the giving and taking of blows I am prepared to meet this German, not on his own terms but on my own. Perhaps, however, you wish to try conclusions with him again?"

The deep silence which followed this inquiry seemed to indicate that no such desire animated the Emir's listeners, and the old man smiled benignly upon his audience and went on.

"There must be no more disputing of my authority, either expressed or by implication. I am now prepared to go forth against him taking with me forty lancers."

Instantly there was a protest against this; the number was inadequate, they said.

"In his fortieth year our Prophet came to a momentous decision," continued the Emir, unheeding the interruption, "and I take a spear with me for every year of the Prophet's life, trusting that Allah will add to our number, at the prophet's intervention, should such an augmentation prove necessary. Get together then the forty oldest men under my command. Let them cumber themselves with nothing in the way of offence except one tall spear each, and see that every man is provided with water and dates for twenty days' sustenance of horse and man in the desert."

The Emir smiled as he placed special emphasis on the word "oldest," and the young men departed abashed to obey his orders.

Next morning Count Herbert von Schonburg saw near his camp by the water-holes a small group of horsemen standing motionless in the desert, their lances erect, butt downward, resting on the sand, the little company looking like an oasis of leafless poplars. The Count was instantly astride his Arab charger, at the head of his men, ready to meet whatever came, but on this occasion the enemy made no effort to bring on a battle, but remained silent and stationary, differing greatly from the hordes that had preceded it.

"Well," cried the impatient Count, "if Mahomet will not come to the mountain, the mountain for once will oblige him."

He gave the word to charge, and put spurs to his horse, causing instant animation in the band of Saracens, who fled before him as rapidly as the Germans advanced. It is needless to dwell on the project of the Emir, who simply followed the example of the desert mirages he had so often witnessed in wonder. Never did the Germans come within touch of their foes, always visible, but not to be overtaken. When at last Count Herbert was convinced that his horses were no match for the fleet steeds of his opponents he discovered that he and his band were hopelessly lost in the arid and pathless desert, the spears of the seemingly phantom host ever quivering before him in the tremulous heated air against the cloudless horizon. Now all his energies were bent toward finding the way that led to the camp by the water-holes, but sense of locality seemed to have left him, and the ghostly company which hung so persistently on his flanks gave no indication of direction, but merely followed as before they had fled. One by one the Count's soldiers succumbed, and when at last the forty spears hedged him round the Emir approached a prisoner incapable of action. The useless sword which hung from his saddle was taken, and water was given to the exhausted man and his dying horse.

When the Emir Soldan and his forty followers rode into camp with their prisoner there was a jubilant outcry, and the demand was made that the foreign dog be instantly decapitated, but the Emir smiled and, holding up his hand, said soothingly:

"Softly, softly, true followers of the only Prophet. Those who neglected to remove his head while his good sword guarded it, shall not now possess themselves of it, when that sword is in my hands."

And against this there could be no protest, for the prisoner belonged to the Emir alone, and was to be dealt with as the captor ordained.

When the Count had recovered speech, and was able to hold himself as a man should, the Emir summoned him, and they had a conference together in Soldan's tent.

"Western barbarian," said the Emir, speaking in that common tongue made up of languages Asiatic and European, a strange mixture by means of which invaders and invaded communicated with each other, "who are you and from what benighted land do you come?"

"I am Count Herbert von Schonburg. My castle overlooks the Rhine in Germany."

"What is the Rhine? A province of which you are the ruler?"

"No, your Highness, it is a river; a lordly stream that never diminishes, but flows unceasingly between green vine-clad hills; would that I had some of the vintage therefore to cheer me in my captivity and remove the taste of this brackish water!"

"In the name of the Prophet, then, why did you leave it?"

"Indeed, your Highness, I have often asked myself that question of late and found but insufficient answer."

"If I give you back your sword, which not I, but the demon Thirst captured from you, will you pledge me your word that you will draw it no more against those of my faith, but will return to your own land, safe escort being afforded you to the great sea where you can take ship?"

"As I have fought for ten years, and have come no nearer Jerusalem than where I now stand, I am content to give you my word in exchange for my sword, and the escort you promise."

And thus it came about that Count Herbert von Schonburg, although still a young man, relinquished all thought of conquering the Holy Land, and found himself one evening, after a long march, gazing on the placid bosom of the broad Rhine, which he had not seen since he bade good-bye to it, a boy of twenty-one, then as warlike and ambitious, as now, he was peace loving and tired of strife. The very air of the Rhine valley breathed rest and quiet, and Herbert, with a deep sigh, welcomed the thought of a life passed in comforting uneventfulness.

"Conrad," he said to his one follower, "I will encamp here for the night. Ride on down the Rhine, I beg of you, and cross the river where you may, that you may announce my coming some time before I arrive. My father is an old man, and I am the last of the race, so I do not wish to come unexpectedly on him; therefore break to him with caution the fact that I am in the neighbourhood, for hearing nothing from me all these years it is like to happen he believes me dead."

Conrad rode down the path by the river and disappeared while his master, after seeing to the welfare of his horse, threw himself down in a thicket and slept the untroubled sleep of the seasoned soldier. It was daylight when he was awakened by the tramp of horses. Starting to his feet, he was confronted by a grizzled warrior with half a dozen men at his back, and at first the Count thought himself again a prisoner, but the friendliness of the officer soon set all doubts at rest.

"Are you Count Herbert von Schonburg?" asked the intruder.

"Yes. Who are you?"

"I am Richart, custodian of Castle Gudenfels, and commander of the small forces possessed by her Ladyship, Countess von Falkenstein. I have to acquaint you with the fact that your servant and messenger has been captured. Your castle of Schonburg is besieged, and Conrad, unaware, rode straight into custody. This coming to the ears of my lady the Countess, she directed me to intercept you if possible, so that you might not share the fate of your servant, and offer to you the hospitality of Gudenfels Castle until such time as you had determined what to do in relation to the siege of your own."

"I give my warmest thanks to the Countess for her thoughtfulness. Is her husband the Count then dead?"

"It is the young Countess von Falkenstein whose orders I carry. Her father and mother are both dead, and her Ladyship, their only child, now holds Gudenfels."

"What, that little girl? She was but a child when I left the Rhine."

"Her Ladyship is a woman of nineteen now."

"And how long has my father been besieged?"

"Alas! it grieves me to state that your father, Count von Schonburg, has also passed away. He has been dead these two years."

The young man bowed his head and crossed himself. For a long time he rode in silence, meditating upon this unwelcome intelligence, grieved to think that such a desolate home-coming awaited him.

"Who, then, holds my castle against the besiegers?"

"The custodian Heinrich has stubbornly stood siege since the Count, your father, died, saying he carries out the orders of his lord until the return of the son."

"Ah! if Heinrich is in command then is the castle safe," cried the young man, with enthusiasm. "He is a born warrior and first taught me the use of the broad-sword. Who besieges us? The Archbishop of Mayence? He was ever a turbulent prelate and held spite against our house."

Richart shifted uneasily in his saddle, and for the moment did not answer. Then he said, with hesitation:

"I think the Archbishop regards the siege with favour, but I know little of the matter. My Lady, the Countess, will possess you with full information."

Count Herbert looked with astonishment upon the custodian of Castle Gudenfels. Here was a contest going on at his very doors, even if on the opposite side of the river, and yet a veteran knew nothing of the contest. But they were now at the frowning gates of Castle Gudenfels, with its lofty square pinnacled tower, and the curiosity of the young Count was dimmed by the admiration he felt for this great stronghold as he gazed upward at it. An instant later he with his escort passed through the gateway and stood in the courtyard of the castle. When he had dismounted the Count said to Richart:

"I have travelled far, and am not in fit state to be presented to a lady. Indeed, now that I am here, I dread the meeting. I have seen nothing of women for ten years, and knew little of them before I left the Rhine. Take me, I beg of you, to a room where I may make some preparation other than the camp has heretofore afforded, and bring me, if you can, a few garments with which to replenish this faded, torn and dusty apparel."

"My Lord, you will find everything you wish in the rooms allotted to you. Surmising your needs, I gave orders to that effect before I left the castle."

"That was thoughtful of you, Richart, and I shall not forget it."

The Custodian without replying led his guest up one stair and then another. The two traversed a long passage until they came to an open door. Richart standing aside, bowed low, and entreated his lordship to enter. Count Herbert passed into a large room from which a doorway led into a smaller apartment which the young man saw was fitted as a bedroom. The rooms hung high over the Rhine, but the view of the river was impeded by the numerous heavy iron bars which formed a formidable lattice-work before the windows. The Count was about to thank his conductor for providing so sumptuously for him, but, turning, he was amazed to see Richart outside with breathless eagerness draw shut the strong door that led to the passage from which he had entered, and a moment later, Herbert heard the ominous sound of stout bolts being shot into their sockets. He stood for a moment gazing blankly now at the bolted door, now at the barred window, and then slowly there came to him the knowledge which would have enlightened a more suspicious man long before—that he was a prisoner in the grim fortress of Gudenfels. Casting his mind backward over the events of the morning, he now saw a dozen sinister warnings that had heretofore escaped him. If a friendly invitation had been intended, what need of the numerous guard of armed men sent to escort him? Why had Richart hesitated when certain questions were asked him? Count Herbert paced up and down the long room, reviewing with clouded brow the events of the past few hours, beginning with the glorious freedom of the open hillside in the early dawn and ending with these impregnable stone walls that now environed him. He was a man slow to anger, but resentment once aroused, burned in his heart with a steady fervour that was unquenchable. He stopped at last in his aimless pacing, raised his clinched fist toward the timbered ceiling, and cursed the Countess von Falkenstein. In his striding to and fro the silence had been broken by the clank of his sword on the stone floor, and he now smiled grimly as he realised that they had not dared to deprive him of his formidable weapon; they had caged the lion from the distant desert without having had the courage to clip his claws. The Count drew his broadsword and swung it hissing through the air, measuring its reach with reference to the walls on either hand, then, satisfying himself that he had free play, he took up a position before the door and stood there motionless as the statue of a war-god. "Now, by the Cross I fought for," he muttered to himself, "the first man who sets foot across this threshold enters the chamber of death."

He remained thus, leaning with folded arms on the hilt of his long sword, whose point rested on the flags of the floor, and at last his patience was rewarded. He heard the rattle of the bolts outside, and a tense eagerness thrilled his stalwart frame. The door came cautiously inward for a space of perhaps two feet and was then brought to a stand by the tightening links of a stout chain, fastened one end to the door, the other to the outer wall. Through the space that thus gave a view of the wide outer passage the Count saw Richart stand with pale face, well back at a safe distance in the centre of the hall. Two men-at-arms held a position behind their master.

"My Lord," began Richart in trembling voice, "her Ladyship, the Countess, desires——"

"Open the door, you cringing Judas!" interrupted the stern command of the count; "open the door and set me as free as your villainy found me. I hold no parley with a traitor."

"My Lord, I implore you to listen. No harm is intended you, and my Lady, the Countess, asks of you a conference touching——"

The heavy sword swung in the air and came down upon the chain with a force that made the stout oaken door shudder. Scattering sparks cast a momentary glow of red on the whitened cheeks of the startled onlookers. The edge of the sword clove the upper circumference of an iron link, leaving the severed ends gleaming like burnished silver, but the chain still held. Again and again the sword fell, but never twice in the same spot, anger adding strength to the blows, but subtracting skill.

"My Lord! my Lord!" beseeched Richart, "restrain your fury. You cannot escape from this strong castle even though you sever the chain."

"I'll trust my sword for that," muttered the prisoner between his set teeth.

There now rang out on the conflict a new voice; the voice of a woman, clear and commanding, the tones instinct with that inborn quality of imperious authority which expects and usually obtains instant obedience.

"Close the door, Richart," cried the unseen lady. The servitor made a motion to obey, but the swoop of the sword seemed to paralyse him where he stood. He cast a beseeching look at his mistress, which said as plainly as words: "You are ordering me to my death." The Count, his weapon high in mid-air, suddenly swerved it from its course, for there appeared across the opening a woman's hand and arm, white and shapely, fleecy lace falling away in dainty folds from the rounded contour of the arm. The small, firm hand grasped bravely the almost severed chain and the next instant the door was drawn shut, the bolts clanking into their places. Count Herbert, paused, leaning on his sword, gazing bewildered at the closed door.

"Ye gods of war!" he cried; "never have I seen before such cool courage as that!"

For a long time the Count walked up and down the spacious room, stopping now and then at the window to peer through the iron grille at the rapid current of the river far below, the noble stream as typical of freedom as were the bars that crossed his vision, of captivity. It seemed that the authorities of the castle had abandoned all thought of further communication with their truculent prisoner. Finally he entered the inner room and flung himself down, booted and spurred as he was, upon the couch, and, his sword for a bedmate, slept. The day was far spent when he awoke, and his first sensation was that of gnawing hunger, for he was a healthy man. His next, that he had heard in his sleep the cautious drawing of bolts, as if his enemies purposed to project themselves surreptitiously in upon him, taking him at a disadvantage. He sat upright, his sword ready for action, and listened intently. The silence was profound, and as the Count sat breathless, the stillness seemed to be emphasised rather than disturbed by a long-drawn sigh which sent a thrill of superstitious fear through the stalwart frame of the young man, for he well knew that the Rhine was infested with spirits animated by evil intentions toward human beings, and against such spirits his sword was but as a willow wand. He remembered with renewed awe that this castle stood only a few leagues above the Lurlei rocks where a nymph of unearthly beauty lured men to their destruction, and the knight crossed himself as a protection against all such. Gathering courage from this devout act, and abandoning his useless weapon, he tiptoed to the door that led to the larger apartment, and there found his worst anticipations realised. With her back against the closed outer door stood a Siren of the Rhine, and, as if to show how futile is the support of the Evil One in a crisis, her very lips were pallid with fear and her blue eyes were wide with apprehension, as they met those of the Count von Schonburg. Her hair, the colour of ripe yellow wheat, rose from her smooth white forehead and descended in a thick braid that almost reached to the floor. She was dressed in the humble garb of a serving maiden, the square bit of lace on her crown of fair hair and the apron she wore, as spotless as new fallen snow. In her hand she held a tray which supported a loaf of bread and a huge flagon brimming with wine. On seeing the Count, her quick breathing stopped for the moment and she dropped a low courtesy.

"My Lord," she said, but there came a catch in her throat, and she could speak no further.

Seeing that he had to deal with no spirit, but with an inhabitant of the world he knew and did not fear, there arose a strange exultation in the heart of the Count as he looked upon this fair representative of his own country. For ten years he had seen no woman, and now a sudden sense of what he had lost overwhelmed him, his own breath coming quicker as the realisation of this impressed itself upon him. He strode rapidly toward her, and she seemed to shrink into the wall at his approach, wild fear springing into her eyes, but he merely took the laden tray from her trembling hands and placed it upon a bench. Then raising the flagon to his lips, he drank a full half of its contents before withdrawing it. A deep sigh of satisfaction followed, and he said, somewhat shamefacedly:

"Forgive my hurried greed, maiden, but the thirst of the desert seems to be in my throat, and the good wine reminds me that I am a German."

"It was brought for your use," replied the girl, demurely, "and I am gratified that it meets your commendation, my Lord."

"And so also do you, my girl. What is your name and who are you?"

"I am called Beatrix, my Lord, a serving-maid of this castle, the daughter of the woodman Wilhelm, and, alas! that it should be so, for the present your jailer."

"If I quarrelled as little with my detention, as I see I am like to do with my keeper, I fear captivity would hold me long in thrall. Are the men in the castle such cravens then that they bestow so unwelcome a task upon a woman?"

"The men are no cravens, my Lord, but this castle is at war with yours, and for each man there is a post. A woman would be less missed if so brave a warrior as Count von Schonburg thought fit to war upon us."

"But a woman makes war upon me, Beatrix. What am I to do? Surrender humbly?"

"Brave men have done so before now and will again, my Lord, where women are concerned. At least," added Beatrix, blushing and casting down her eyes, "I have been so informed."

"And small blame to them," cried the count, with enthusiasm. "I swear to you, my girl, that if women warriors were like the woodman's daughter, I would cast away all arms except these with which to enclasp her."

And he stretched out his hands, taking a step nearer, while she shrank in alarm from him.

"My Lord, I am but an humble messenger, and I beg of you to listen to what I am asked to say. My Lady, the Countess, has commissioned me to tell you that—"

A startling malediction of the Countess that accorded ill with the scarlet cross emblazoned on the young man's breast, interrupted the girl.

"I hold no traffic with the Countess," he cried. "She has treacherously laid me by the heels, coming as I did from battling for the Cross that she doubtless professes to regard as sacred."

"It was because she feared you, my Lord. These years back tales of your valour in the Holy Land have come to the Rhine, and now you return to find your house at war with hers. What was she to do? The chances stood even with only your underling in command; judge then what her fate must be with your strong sword thrown in the balance against her. All's fair in war, said those who counselled her. What would you have done in such an extremity, my Lord?"

"What would I have done? I would have met my enemy sword in hand and talked with him or fought with him as best suited his inclination."

"But a lady cannot meet you, sword in hand, my Lord."

The Count paused in the walk he had begun when the injustice of his usage impressed itself once more upon him. He looked admiringly at the girl.

"That is most true, Beatrix. I had forgotten. Still, I should not have been met with cozenry. Here came I from starvation in the wilderness, thirst in the desert, and from the stress of the battle-field, back to mine own land with my heart full of yearning love for it and for all within its boundaries. I came even from prison, captured in fair fight, by an untaught heathen, whose men lay slain by my hand, yet with the nobility of a true warrior, he asked neither ransom nor hostage, but handed back my sword, saying, 'Go in peace.' That in a heathen land! but no sooner does my foot rest on this Christian soil than I am met by false smiles and lying tongues, and my welcome to a neighbour's house is the clank of the inthrust bolt."

"Oh, it was a shameful act and not to be defended," cried the girl, with moist eyes and quivering lip, the sympathetic reverberation of her voice again arresting the impatient steps of the young man, causing him to pause and view her with a feeling that he could not understand, and which he found some difficulty in controlling. Suddenly all desire for restraint left him, he sprang forward, clasped the girl in his arms and drew her into the middle of the room, where she could not give the signal that might open the door.

"My Lord! my Lord!" she cried in terror, struggling without avail to free herself.

"You said all's fair in war and saying so, gave but half the proverb, which adds, all's fair in love as well, and maiden, nymph of the woodland, so rapidly does a man learn that which he has never been taught, I proclaim with confidence that I love thee."

"A diffident and gentle lover you prove yourself!" she gasped with rising indignation, holding him from her.

"Indeed, my girl, there was little of diffidence or gentleness in my warring, and my wooing is like to have a touch of the same quality. It is useless to struggle for I have thee firm, so take to yourself some of that gentleness you recommend to me."

He strove to kiss her, but Beatrix held her head far from him, her open palm pressed against the red cross that glowed upon his breast, keeping him thus at arm's length.

"Count von Schonburg, what is the treachery of any other compared with yours? You came heedlessly into this castle, suspecting as you say, no danger: I came within this room to do you service, knowing my peril, but trusting to the honour of a true soldier of the Cross, and this is my reward! First tear from your breast this sacred emblem, valorous assaulter of a defenceless woman, for it should be worn by none but stainless gentlemen."

Count Herbert's arms relaxed, and his hands dropped listless to his sides.

"By my sword," he said, "they taught you invective in the forest. You are free. Go."

The girl made no motion to profit by her newly acquired liberty, but stood there, glancing sideways at him who scowled menacingly at her.

When at last she spoke, she said, shyly: "I have not yet fulfilled my mission."

"Fulfil it then in the fiend's name and begone."

"Will you consent to see my Lady the Countess?"

"No."

"Will you promise not to make war upon her if you are released?"

"No."

"If, in spite of your boorishness, she sets you free, what will you do?"

"I will rally my followers to my banner, scatter the forces that surround my castle, then demolish this prison trap."

"Am I in truth to carry such answers to the Countess?"

"You are to do as best pleases you, now and forever."

"I am but a simple serving-maid, and know nothing of high questions of state, yet it seems to me such replies do not oil prison bolts, and believe me, I grieve to see you thus detained."

"I am grateful for your consideration. Is your embassy completed?"

The girl, her eyes on the stone floor, paused long before replying, then said, giving no warning of a change of subject, and still not raising her eyes to his:

"You took me by surprise; I am not used to being handled roughly; you forget the distance between your station and mine, you being a noble of the Empire, and I but a serving-maid; if, in my anger, I spoke in a manner unbecoming one so humble, I do beseech that your Lordship pardon me."

"Now by the Cross to which you appealed, how long will you stand chattering there? Think you I am made of adamant, and not of flesh and blood? My garments are tattered at best, I would in woman's company they were finer, and this cross of Genoa red hangs to my tunic, but by a few frail threads. Beware, therefore, that I tear it not from my breast as you advised, and cast it from me."

Beatrix lifted one frightened glance to the young man's face and saw standing on his brow great drops of sweat. His right hand grasped the upper portion of the velvet cross, partly detached from his doublet, and he lookedloweringly upon her. Swiftly she smote the door twice with her hand and instantly the portal opened as far as the chain would allow it. Count Herbert noticed that in the interval, three other chains had been added to the one that formerly had baffled his sword. The girl, like a woodland pigeon, darted underneath the lower chain, and although the prisoner took a rapid step forward, the door, with greater speed, closed and was bolted.

The Count had requested the girl to be gone, and surely should have been contented now that she had withdrawn herself, yet so shifty a thing is human nature, that no sooner were his commands obeyed than he began to bewail their fulfilment. He accused himself of being a double fool, first, for not holding her when he had her; and secondly, having allowed her to depart, he bemoaned the fact that he had acted rudely to her, and thus had probably made her return impossible. His prison seemed inexpressibly dreary lacking her presence. Once or twice he called out her name, but the echoing empty walls alone replied.

For the first time in his life the heavy sleep of the camp deserted him, and in his dreams he pursued a phantom woman, who continually dissolved in his grasp, now laughingly, now in anger.

The morning found him deeply depressed, and he thought the unaccustomed restraints of a prison were having their effect on the spirits of a man heretofore free. He sat silently on the bench watching the door.

At last, to his great joy, he heard the rattle of bolts being withdrawn. The door opened slowly to the small extent allowed by the chains, but no one entered and the Count sat still, concealed from the view of whoever stood without.

"My Lord Count," came the sweet tones of the girl and the listener with joy, fancied he detected in it a suggestion of apprehension, doubtless caused by the fact that the room seemed deserted. "My Lord Count, I have brought your breakfast; will you not come and receive it?"

Herbert rose slowly and came within range of his jailer's vision. The girl stood in the hall, a repast that would have tempted an epicure arrayed on the wooden trencher she held in her hands.

"Beatrix, come in," he said.

"I fear that in stooping, some portion of this burden may fall. Will you not take the trencher?"

The young man stepped to the opening and, taking the tray from her, placed it on the bench as he had previously done; then repeated his invitation.

"You were displeased with my company before, my Lord, and I am loath again to offend."

"Beatrix, I beg you to enter. I have something to say to you."

"Stout chains bar not words, my Lord. Speak and I shall listen."

"What I have to say, is for your ear alone."

"Then are the conditions perfect for such converse, my Lord. No guard stands within this hall."

The Count sighed deeply, turned and sat again on the bench, burying his face in his hands. The maiden having given excellent reasons why she should not enter, thus satisfying her sense of logic, now set logic at defiance, slipped under the lowest chain and stood within the room, and, so that there might be no accusation that she did things by halves, closed the door leaning her back against it. The knight looked up at her and saw that she too had rested but indifferently. Her lovely eyes half veiled, showed traces of weeping, and there was a wistful expression in her face that touched him tenderly, and made him long for her; nevertheless he kept a rigid government upon himself, and sat there regarding her, she flushing, slightly under his scrutiny, not daring to return his ardent gaze.

"Beatrix," he said slowly, "I have acted towards you like a boor and a ruffian, as indeed I am; but let this plead for me, that I have ever been used to the roughness of the camp, bereft of gentler influences. I ask your forgiveness."

"There is nothing to forgive. You are a noble of the Empire, and I but a lowly serving-maid."

"Nay, that cuts me to the heart, and is my bitterest condemnation. A true man were courteous to high and low alike. Now, indeed, you overwhelm me with shame, maiden of the woodlands."

"Such was not my intention, my Lord. I hold you truly noble in nature as well as in rank, otherwise I stood not here."

"Beatrix, does any woodlander come from the forest to the castle walls and there give signal intended for you alone?"

"Oh, no, my Lord."

"Perhaps you have kindly preference for some one within this stronghold?"

"You forget, my Lord, that the castle is ruled by a lady, and that the preference you indicate would accord ill with her womanly government."

"In truth I know little of woman's rule, but given such, I suppose the case would stand as you say. The Countess then frowns upon lovers' meetings."

"How could it be otherwise?"

"Have you told her of—of yesterday?"

"You mean of your refusal to come to terms with her? Yes, my Lord."

"I mean nothing of the kind, Beatrix."

"No one outside this room has been told aught to your disadvantage, my Lord," said the girl blushing rose-red.

"Then she suspects nothing?"

"Suspects nothing of what, my Lord?"

"That I love you, Beatrix."

The girl caught her breath, and seemed about to fly, but gathering courage, remained, and said speaking hurriedly and in some confusion: "As I did not suspect it myself I see not how my Lady should have made any such surmise, but indeed it may be so, for she chided me bitterly for remaining so long with you, and made me weep with her keen censure; yet am I here now against her express wish and command, but that is because of my strong sympathy for you and my belief that the Countess has wrongfully treated you."

"I care nothing for the opinion of that harridan, except that it may bring harsh usage to you; but Beatrix, I have told you bluntly of my love for you, answer me as honestly."

"My Lord, you spoke just now of a woodlander—"

"Ah, there is one then. Indeed, I feared as much, for there can be none on all the Rhine as beautiful or as good as you."

"There are many woodlanders, my Lord, and many women more beautiful than I. What I was about to say was that I would rather be the wife of the poorest forester, and lived in the roughest hut on the hillside, than dwell otherwise in the grandest castle on the Rhine."

"Surely, surely. But you shall dwell in my castle of Schonburg as my most honoured wife, if you but will it so."

"Then, my Lord, I must bid you beware of what you propose. Your wife must be chosen from the highest in the land, and not from the lowliest. It is not fitting that you should endeavour to raise a serving-maid to the position of Countess von Schonburg. You would lose caste among your equals, and bring unhappiness upon us both."

Count Herbert grasped his sword and lifting it, cried angrily: "By the Cross I serve, the man who refuses to greet my wife as he would greet the Empress, shall feel the weight of this blade."

"You cannot kill a whisper with a sword, my Lord."

"I can kill the whisperer."

"That can you not, my Lord, for the whisperer will be a woman."

"Then out upon them, we will have no traffic with them. I have lived too long away from the petty restrictions of civilisation to be bound down by them now, for I come from a region where a man's sword and not his rank preserved his life." As he spoke he again raised his huge weapon aloft, but now held it by the blade so that it stood out against the bright window like a black cross of iron, and his voice rang forth defiantly: "With that blade I won my honour; by the symbol of its hilt I hope to obtain my soul's salvation, on both united I swear to be to you a true lover and a loyal husband."

With swift motion the girl covered her face with her hands and Herbert saw the crystal drops trickle between her fingers. For long she could not speak and then mastering her emotion, she said brokenly:

"I cannot accept, I cannot now accept. I can take no advantage of a helpless prisoner. At midnight I shall come and set you free, thus my act may atone for the great wrong of your imprisonment; atone partially if not wholly. When you are at liberty, if you wish to forget your words, which I can never do, then am I amply repaid that my poor presence called them forth. If you remember them, and demand of the Countess that I stand as hostage for peace, she is scarce likely to deny you, for she loves not war. But know that nothing you have said is to be held against you, for I would have you leave this castle as free as when you entered it. And now, my Lord, farewell."

Before the unready man could make motion to prevent her, she had opened the door and was gone, leaving it open, thus compelling the prisoner to be his own jailer and close it, for he had no wish now to leave the castle alone when he had been promised such guidance.

The night seemed to Count Herbert the longest he had ever spent, as he sat on the bench, listening for the withdrawing of the bolts; if indeed they were in their sockets, which he doubted. At last the door was pushed softly open, and bending under the chain, he stood in the outside hall, peering through the darkness, to catch sight of his conductor. A great window of stained glass occupied the southern end of the hall, and against it fell the rays of the full moon now high in the heavens, filling the dim and lofty apartment with a coloured radiance resembling his visions of the half tones of fairyland. Like a shadow stood the cloaked figure of the girl, who timidly placed her small hand in his great palm, and that touch gave a thrill of reality to the mysticism of the time and the place. He grasped it closely, fearing it might fade away from him as it had done in his dream. She led him silently by another way from that by which he had entered, and together they passed through a small doorway that communicated with a narrow circular stair which wound round and round downwards until they came to another door at the bottom, which let them out in the moonlight at the foot of a turret.

"Beatrix," whispered the young man, "I am not going to demand you of the Countess. I shall not be indebted to her for my wife. You must come with me now."

"No, no," cried the girl shrinking from him, "I cannot go with you thus surreptitiously, and no one but you and me must ever learn that I led you from the castle. You shall come for me as a lord should for his lady, as if he thought her worthy of him."

"Indeed, that do I. Worthy? It is I who am unworthy, but made more worthy I hope in that you care for me."

From where they stood the knight saw the moonlight fall on his own castle of Schonburg, the rays seeming to transform the grey stone into the whitest of marble, the four towers standing outlined against the blue of the cloudless sky. The silver river of romance, flowed silently at its feet reflecting again the snowy purity of the reality in an inverted quivering watery vision. All the young man's affection for the home he had not seen for years seemed to blend with his love for the girl standing there in the moonlight. Gently he drew her to him, and kissed her unresisting lips.

"Woodland maiden," he said tenderly, "here at the edge of the forest is your rightful home and not in this grim castle, and here will I woo thee again, being now a free man."

"Indeed," said the girl with a laugh in which a sob and a sigh intermingled, "it is but scanty freedom I have brought to you; an exchange of silken fetters for iron chains."

His arms still around her, he unloosed the ribbon that held in thrall the thick braid of golden hair, and parting the clustering strands speedily encompassed her in a cloak of misty fragrance that seemed as unsubstantial as the moonlight that glittered through its meshes. He stood back the better to admire the picture he seemed to have created.

"My darling," he cried, "you are no woodland woman, but the very spirit of the forest herself. You are so beautiful, I dare not leave you here to the mercies of this demon, who, finding me gone, may revenge herself on you. If before she dared to censure you, what may she not do now that you have set me free? Curse her that she stands for a moment between my love and me."

He raised his clenched fist and shook it at the tower above him, and seemed about to break forth in new maledictions against the lady, when Beatrix, clasping her hands cried in terror:

"No, no, Herbert, you have said enough. How can you pretend to love me when implacable hatred lies so near to your affection. You must forgive the Countess. Oh, Herbert, Herbert, what more could I do to atone? I have withdrawn my forces from around your castle; I have set you free and your path to Schonburg lies unobstructed. Even now your underling, thinking himself victorious, is preparing an expedition against me, and nothing but your word stands, between me and instant attack. Ponder, I beseech of you, on my position. War, not of my seeking, was bequeathed to me, and a woman who cannot fight must trust to her advisers, and thus may do what her own heart revolts against. They told me that if I made you prisoner I could stop the war, and thus I consented to that act of treachery for which you so justly condemn me."

"Beatrix," cried her amazed lover, "what madness has come over you?"

"No madness touched me, Herbert, until I met you, and I sometimes think that you have brought back with you the eastern sorcery of which I have heard—at least such may perhaps make excuse for my unmaidenly behaviour. Herbert, I am Beatrix of Gudenfels, Countess von Falkenstein, who is and ever will be, if you refuse to pardon her, a most unhappy woman."

"No woodland maiden, but the Countess! The Countess von Falkenstein!" murmured her lover more to himself than to, his eager listener, the lines on his perplexed brow showing that he was endeavouring to adjust the real and the ideal in his slow brain.

"A Countess, Herbert, who will joyfully exchange the privileges of her station for the dear preference shown to the serving-maid."

A smile came to the lips of Von Schonburg as he held out his hands, in which the Countess placed her own.

"My Lady Beatrix," he said, "how can I refuse my pardon for the first encroachment on my liberty, now that you have made me your prisoner for life?"

"Indeed, my captured lord," cried the girl, "you are but now coming to a true sense of your predicament. I marvelled that you felt so resentful about the first offence, when the second was so much more serious. Am I then forgiven for both?"

It seemed that she was, and the Count insisted on returning to his captivity, and coming forth the next day, freed by her commands, whereupon, in the presence of all her vassals, he swore allegiance to her with such deference that her advisers said to her that she must now see they had been right in counselling his imprisonment. Prison, they said, had a wonderfully quieting effect upon even the most truculent, the Count being quickly subdued when he saw his sword-play had but little effect on the chain. The Countess graciously acknowledged that events had indeed proved the wisdom of their course, and said it was not to be wondered at that men should know the disposition of a turbulent man, better than an inexperienced woman could know it.

And thus was the feud between Gudenfels and Schonburg happily ended, and Count Herbert came from the Crusades to find two castles waiting for him instead of one as he had expected, with what he had reason to prize above everything else, a wife as well.

CHAPTER II. – THE REVENGE OF THE OUTLAW

The position of Count Herbert when, at the age of thirty-one he took up his residence in the ancient castle of his line, was a most enviable one. His marriage with Beatrix, Countess von Falkenstein, had added the lustre of a ruling family to the prestige of his own, and the renown of his valour in the East had lost nothing in transit from the shores of the Mediterranean to the banks of the Rhine. The Counts of Schonburg had ever been the most conservative in counsel and the most radical in the fray, and thus Herbert on returning, found himself, without seeking the honor, regarded by common consent as leader of the nobility whose castles bordered the renowned river. The Emperor, as was usually the case when these imperial figure-heads were elected by the three archbishops and their four colleagues, was a nonentity, who made no attempt to govern a turbulent land that so many were willing to govern for him. His majesty left sword and sceptre to those who cared for such baubles, and employed himself in banding together the most notable company of meistersingers that Germany had ever listened to. But although harmony reigned in Frankfort, the capital, there was much lack of it along the Rhine, and the man with the swiftest and heaviest sword, usually accumulated the greatest amount of property, movable and otherwise.

Among the truculent nobles who terrorised the country side, none was held In greater awe than Baron von Wiethoff, whose Schloss occupied a promontory Some distance up the stream from Castle Schonburg, on the same side of the river. Public opinion condemned the Baron, not because he exacted tribute from the merchants who sailed down the Rhine, for such collections were universally regarded as a legitimate source of revenue, but because he was in the habit of killing the goose that laid the golden egg, which action was looked upon with disfavour by those who resided between Schloss Wiethoff and Cologne, as interfering with their right to exist, for a merchant, although well-plucked, is still of advantage to those in whose hands he falls, if life and some of his goods are left to him. Whereas, when cleft from scalp to midriff by the Baron's long sword, he became of no value either to himself or to others. While many nobles were satisfied with levying a scant five or ten per cent on a voyager's belongings, the Baron rarely rested contented until he had acquired the full hundred, and, the merchant objecting, von Wiethoff would usually order him hanged or decapitated, although at times when he was in good humour he was wont to confer honour upon the trading classes by despatching the grumbling seller of goods with his own weapon, which created less joy in the commercial community than the Baron seemed to expect. Thus navigation on the swift current of the Rhine began to languish, for there was little profit in the transit of goods from Mayence to Cologne if the whole consignment stood in jeopardy and the owner's life as well, so the merchants got into the habit of carrying their gear overland on the backs of mules, thus putting the nobility to great inconvenience in scouring the forests, endeavouring to intercept the caravans. The nobility, with that stern sense of justice which has ever characterised the higher classes, placed the blame of this diversion of traffic from its natural channel not upon the merchants but upon the Baron, where undoubtedly it rightly belonged, and although, when they came upon an overland company which was seeking to avoid them, they gathered in an extra percentage of the goods to repay in a measure the greater difficulty they had in their woodland search, they always informed the merchants with much politeness, that, when river traffic was resumed, they would be pleased to revert to the original exaction, which the traders, not without reason pointed out was of little avail to them as long as Baron von Wiethoff was permitted to confiscate the whole.

In their endeavours to resuscitate the navigation interests of the Rhine, several expeditions had been formed against the Baron, but his castle was strong, and there were so many conflicting interests among those who attacked him that he had always come out victorious, and after each onslaught the merchants suffered more severely than before.

Affairs were in this unsatisfactory condition when Count Herbert of Schonburg returned from the Holy Land, the fame of his deeds upon him, and married Beatrix of Gudenfels. Although the nobles of the Upper Rhine held aloof from all contest with the savage Baron of Schloss Wiethoff, his exactions not interfering with their incomes, many of those further down the river offered their services to Count Herbert, if he would consent to lead them against the Baron, but the Count pleaded that he was still a stranger in his own country, having so recently returned from his ten contentious years in Syria, therefore he begged time to study the novel conditions confronting him before giving an answer to their proposal.

The Count learned that the previous attacks made upon Schloss Wiethoff had been conducted with but indifferent generalship, and that failure had been richly earned by desertions from the attacking force, each noble thinking himself justified in withdrawing himself and his men, when offended, or when the conduct of affairs displeased him, so von Schonburg informed the second deputation which waited on him, that he was more accustomed to depend on himself than on the aid of others, and that if any quarrel arose between Castle Schonburg and Schloss Wiethoff, the Count would endeavour to settle the dispute with his own sword, which reply greatly encouraged the Baron when he heard of it, for he wished to try conclusions with the newcomer, and made no secret of his disbelief in the latter's Saracenic exploits, saying the Count had returned when there was none left of the band he took with him, and had, therefore, with much wisdom, left himself free from contradiction.

There was some disappointment up and down the Rhine when time passed and the Count made no warlike move. It was well known that the Countess was much averse to war, notwithstanding the fact that she was indebted to war for her stalwart husband, and her peaceful nature was held to excuse the non-combative life lived by the Count, although there were others who gave it as their opinion that the Count was really afraid of the Baron, who daily became more and more obnoxious as there seemed to be less and less to fear. Such boldness did the Baron achieve that he even organised a slight raid upon the estate of Gudenfels which belonged to the Count's wife, but still Herbert of Schonburg did not venture from the security of his castle, greatly to the disappointment and the disgust of his neighbours, for there are on earth no people who love a fight more dearly than do those who reside along the banks of the placid Rhine.

At last an heir was born to Castle Schonburg, and the rejoicings throughout all the district governed by the Count were general and enthusiastic. Bonfires were lit on the heights and the noble river glowed red under the illumination at night. The boy who had arrived at the castle was said to give promise of having all the beauty of his mother and all the strength of his father, which was admitted by everybody to be a desirable combination, although some shook their heads and said they hoped that with strength there would come greater courage than the Count appeared to possess. Nevertheless, the Count had still some who believed in him, notwithstanding his long period of inaction, and these said that on the night the boy was born, and word was brought to him in the great hall that mother and child were well, the cloud that had its habitual resting-place on the Count's brow lifted and his lordship took down from its place his great broadsword, rubbed from its blade the dust and the rust that had collected, swung the huge weapon hissing through the air, and heaved a deep sigh, as one who had come to the end of a period of restraint.

The boy was just one month old on the night that there was a thunderous knocking at the gate of Schloss Wiethoff. The Baron hastily buckled on his armour and was soon at the head of his men eager to repel the invader. In a marvellously short space of time there was a contest in progress at the gates which would have delighted the heart of the most quarrelsome noble from Mayence to Cologne. The attacking party which appeared in large force before the gate, attempted to batter in the oaken leaves of the portal, but the Baron was always prepared for such visitors, and the heavy timbers that were heaved against the oak made little impression, while von Wiethoff roared defiance from the top of the wall that surrounded the castle and what was more to the purpose, showered down stones and arrows on the besiegers, grievously thinning their ranks. The Baron, with creditable ingenuity, had constructed above the inside of the gate a scaffolding, on the top of which was piled a mountain of huge stones. This scaffold was arranged in such a way that a man pulling a lever caused it to collapse, thus piling the stones instantly against the inside of the gate, rendering it impregnable against assault by battering rams. The Baron was always jubilant when his neighbours attempted to force the gate, for he was afforded much amusement at small expense to himself, and he cared little for the damage the front door received, as he had built his castle not for ornament but for his own protection. He was a man with an amazing vocabulary, and as he stood on the wall shaking his mailed fist at the intruders he poured forth upon them invective more personal than complimentary.

While thus engaged, rejoicing over the repulse of the besiegers, for the attack was evidently losing its vigour, he was amazed to note a sudden illumination of the forest-covered hill which he was facing. The attacking party rallied with a yell when the light struck them, and the Baron, looking hastily over his shoulder to learn the source of the ruddy glow on the trees, saw with dismay that his castle was on fire and that Count Herbert followed by his men had possession of the battlements to the rear, while the courtyard swarmed with soldiers, who had evidently scaled the low wall along the river front from rafts or boats.

"Surrender!" cried Count Herbert, advancing along the wall. "Your castle is taken, and will be a heap of ruins within the hour."

"Then may you be buried beneath them," roared the Baron, springing to the attack.

Although the Baron was a younger man than his antagonist, it was soon proven that his sword play was not equal to that of the Count, and the broadsword fight on the battlements in the light of the flaming stronghold, was of short duration, watched breathlessly as it was by men of both parties above and below. Twice the Baron's guard was broken, and the third time, such was the terrific impact of iron on iron, that the Baron's weapon was struck from his benumbed hands and fell glittering through the air to the ground outside the walls. The Count paused in his onslaught, refraining from striking a disarmed man, but again demanding his submission. The Baron cast one glance at his burning house, saw that it was doomed, then, with a movement as reckless as it was unexpected, took the terrific leap from the wall top to the ground, alighting on his feet near his fallen sword which he speedily recovered. For an instant the Count hovered on the brink to follow him, but the swift thought of his wife and child restrained him, and he feared a broken limb in the fall, leaving him thus at the mercy of his enemy. The moment for decision was short enough, but the years of regret for this hesitation were many and long. There were a hundred men before the walls to intercept the Baron, and it seemed useless to jeopardise life or limb in taking the leap, so the Count contented himself by giving the loud command: "Seize that man and bind him."

It was an order easy to give and easy to obey had there been a dozen men below as brave as their captain, or even one as brave, as stalwart and as skilful; but the Baron struck sturdily around him and mowed his way through the throng as effectually as a reaper with a sickle clears a path for himself in the standing corn. Before Herbert realised what was happening, the Baron was safe in the obscurity of the forest.

The Count of Schonburg was not a man to do things by halves, even though upon the occasion of this attack he allowed the Baron to slip through his fingers. When the ruins of the Schloss cooled, he caused them to be removed and flung stone by stone into the river, leaving not a vestige of the castle that had so long been a terror to the district, holding that if the lair were destroyed the wolf would not return. In this the Count proved but partly right. Baron von Wiethoff renounced his order, and became an outlaw, gathering round him in the forest all the turbulent characters, not in regular service elsewhere, publishing along the Rhine by means of prisoners he took and then released that as the nobility seemed to object to his preying upon the merchants, he would endeavour to amend his ways and would harry instead such castles as fell into his hands. Thus Baron von Wiethoff became known as the Outlaw of the Hundsrück, and being as intrepid as he was merciless, soon made the Rhenish nobility withdraw attention from other people's quarrels in order to bestow strict surveillance upon their own. It is possible that if the dwellers along the river had realised at first the kind of neighbour that had been produced by burning out the Baron, they might, by combination have hunted him down in the widespread forests of the Hundsrück, but as the years went on, the Outlaw acquired such knowledge of the interminable mazes of this wilderness, that it is doubtful whether all the troops in the Empire could have brought his band to bay. The outlaws always fled before a superior force, and always massacred an inferior one, and like the lightning, no man could predict where the next stroke would fall. On one occasion he even threatened the walled town of Coblentz, and the citizens compounded with him, saying they had no quarrel with any but the surrounding nobles, which expression the thrifty burghers regretted when Count Herbert marched his men through their streets and for every coin they, had paid the Outlaw, exacted ten.

The boy of Castle Schonburg was three years old, when he was allowed to play on the battlements, sporting with a wooden sword and imagining himself as great a warrior as his father had ever been. He was a brave little fellow whom nothing could frighten but the stories his nurse told him of the gnomes and goblins who infested the Rhine, and he longed for the time when he would be a man and wear a real sword. One day just before he had completed his fourth year, a man came slinking out of the forest to the foot of the wall, for the watch was now slack as the Outlaw had not been heard of for months, and then was far away in the direction of Mayence. The nurse was holding a most absorbing conversation with the man-at-arms, who should, instead, have been pacing up and down the terrace while she should have been watching her charge. The man outside gave a low whistle which attracted the attention of the child and then beckoned him to come further along the wall until he had passed the west tower.

"Well, little coward," said the man, "I did not think you would have the courage to come so far away from the women."

"I am not a coward," answered the lad, stoutly, "and I do not care about the women at all."

"Your father was a coward."

"He is not. He is the bravest man in the world."

"He did not dare to jump off the wall after the Baron."

"He will cut the Baron in pieces if he ever comes near our castle."

"Yet he dared not jump as the Baron did."

"The Baron was afraid of my father; that's why he jumped."

"Not so. It was your father who feared to follow him, though he had a sword and the Baron had none. You are all cowards in Castle Schonburg. I don't believe you have the courage to jump even though I held out my arms to catch you, but if you do I will give you the sword I wear."

The little boy had climbed on the parapet, and now stood hovering on the brink of the precipice, his childish heart palpitating through fear of the chasm before him, yet beneath its beatings was an insistent command to prove his impugned courage. For some moments there was deep silence, the man below gazing aloft and holding up his hands. At last he lowered his outstretched arms and said in a sneering tone:

"Good-bye, craven son of a craven race. You dare not jump."

The lad, with a cry of despair, precipitated himself into the empty air and came fluttering down like a wounded bird, to fall insensible into the arms that for the moment saved him from death or mutilation. An instant later there was a shriek from the negligent nurse, and the man-at-arms ran along the battlements, a bolt on his cross-bow which he feared to launch at the flying abductor, for in the speeding of it he might slay the heir of Schonburg. By the time the castle was aroused and the gates thrown open to pour forth searchers, the man had disappeared into the forest, and in its depths all trace of young Wilhelm was lost. Some days after, the Count von Schonburg came upon the deserted camp of the outlaws, and found there evidences, not necessary to be here set down, that his son had been murdered. Imposing secrecy on his followers, so that the Countess might still retain her unshaken belief that not even an outlaw would harm a little child, the Count returned to his castle to make preparations for a complete and final campaign of extinction against the scourge of the Hundsrück, but the Outlaw had withdrawn his men far from the scene of his latest successful exploit and the Count never came up with him.

Years passed on and the silver came quickly to Count Herbert's hair, he attributing the change to the hardships endured in the East, but all knowing well the cause sprang from his belief in his son's death. The rapid procession of years made little impression on the beauty of the Countess, who, although grieving for the absence of her boy, never regarded him as lost but always looked for his return. "If he were dead," she often said to her husband, "I should know it in my heart; I should know the day, the hour and the moment."

This belief the Count strove to encourage, although none knew better than he how baseless it was. Beatrix, with a mother's fondness, kept little Wilhelm's room as it had been when he left it, his toys in their places, and his bed prepared for him, allowing no one else to share the task she had allotted to herself. She seemed to keep no count of the years, nor to realise that if her son returned he would return as a young man and not as a child. To the mind of Beatrix he seemed always her boy of four.

When seventeen years had elapsed after the abduction of the heir of Schonburg, there came a rumour that the Outlaw of Hundsrück was again at his depredations in the neighbourhood of Coblentz. He was at this time a man of forty-two, and if he imagined that the long interval had led to any forgetting on the part of the Count von Schonburg, a most unpleasant surprise awaited him. The Count divided his forces equally between his two castles of Schonburg and Gudenfels situated on the west bank and the east bank respectively. If either castle were attacked, arrangements were made for getting word to the other, when the men in that other would cross the Rhine and fall upon the rear of the invaders, hemming them thus between two fires. The Count therefore awaited with complacency whatever assault the Outlaw cared to deliver.

It was expected that the attack would be made in the night, which was the usual time selected for these surprise parties that kept life from stagnating along the Rhine, but to the amazement of the Count the onslaught came in broad daylight, which seemed to indicate that the Outlaw had gathered boldness with years. The Count from the battlements scanned his opponents and saw that they were led, not by the Outlaw in person, but by a young man who evidently held his life lightly, so recklessly did he risk it. He was ever in the thick of the fray, dealing sword strokes with a lavish generosity which soon kindled a deep respect for him in the breasts of his adversaries. The Count had not waited for the battering in of his gates but had sent out his men to meet the enemy in the open, which was rash generalship, had he not known that the men of Gudenfels were hurrying round to the rear of the outlaws. Crossbowmen lined the battlements ready to cover the retreat of the defenders of the castle, should they meet a reverse, but now they stood in silence, holding their shafts, for in the mêslée there was a danger of destroying friend as well as foe. But in spite of the superb leadership of the young captain, the outlaws, seemingly panic-stricken, when there was no particular reason, deserted their commander in a body and fled in spite of his frantic efforts to rally them. The young man found himself surrounded, and, after a brave defence, overpowered. When the Gudenfels men came up, there was none to oppose them, the leader of the enemy being within the gates of Schonburg, bound, bleeding and a prisoner. The attacking outlaws were nowhere to be seen.

The youthful captive, unkempt as he was, appeared in the great hall of the castle before its grey-headed commander, seated in his chair of state.

"You are the leader of this unwarranted incursion?" said the Count, sternly, as he looked upon the pinioned lad.

"Warranted or unwarranted, I was the leader."

"Who are you?"

"I am Wilhelm, only son of the Outlaw of Hundsrück."

"The only son," murmured the Count, more to himself than to his auditors, the lines hardening round his firm mouth. For some moments there was a deep silence in the large room, then the Count spoke in a voice that had no touch of mercy in it:

"You will be taken to a dungeon and your wounds cared for. Seven days from now, at this hour, you will appear again before me, at which time just sentence will be passed upon you, after I hear what you have to say in your own defence."

"You may hear that now, my Lord. I besieged your castle and would perhaps have taken it, had I not a pack of cowardly dogs at my heels. I am now in your power, and although you talk glibly of justice, I know well what I may expect at your hands. Your delay of a week is the mere pretence of a hypocrite, who wishes to give colour of legality to an act already decided upon. I do not fear you now, and shall not fear you then, so spare your physicians unnecessary trouble, and give the word to your executioner."

"Take him away, attend to his wounds, and guard him strictly. Seven days from now when I call for him; see to it that you can produce him."

Elsa, niece of the Outlaw, watched anxiously for the return of her cousin from the long prepared for expedition. She had the utmost confidence in his bravery and the most earnest belief in his success, yet she watched for the home-coming of the warriors with an anxious heart. Perhaps a messenger would arrive telling of the capture of the castle; perhaps all would return with news of defeat, but for what actually happened the girl was entirely unprepared. That the whole company, practically unscathed, should march into camp with the astounding news that their leader had been captured and that they had retreated without striking a blow on his behalf, seemed to her so monstrous, that her first thought was fear of the retribution which would fall on the deserters when her uncle realised the full import of the tidings. She looked with apprehension at his forbidding face and was amazed to see something almost approaching a smile part his thin lips.

"The attack has failed, then. I fear I sent out a leader incompetent and too young. We must make haste to remove our camp or the victorious Count, emboldened by success, may carry the war into the forest." With this amazing proclamation the Outlaw turned and walked to his hut followed by his niece, bewildered as one entangled in the mazes of a dream. When they were alone together, the girl spoke.

"Uncle, has madness overcome you?"

"I was never saner than now, nor happier, for years of waiting are approaching their culmination."

"Has, then, all valour left your heart?"

"Your question will be answered when next I lead my band."

"When next you lead it? Where will you lead it?"

"Probably in the vicinity of Mayence, toward which place we are about to journey."

"Is it possible that you retreat from here without attempting the rescue of your son, now in the hands of your lifelong enemy?"

"All things are possible in an existence like ours. The boy would assault the castle; he has failed and has allowed himself to be taken. It is the fortune of war and I shall not waste a man in attempting his rescue."

Elsa stood for a moment gazing in dismay at her uncle, whose shifty eyes evaded all encounter with hers, then she strode to the wall, took down a sword and turned without a word to the door. The Outlaw sprang between her and the exit.

"What are you about to do?" he cried.

"I am about to rally all who are not cowards round me, then at their head, I shall attack Castle Schonburg and set Wilhelm free or share his fate."

The Outlaw stood for a few moments, his back against the door of the hut, gazing in sullen anger at the girl, seemingly at a loss to know how she should be dealt with. At last his brow cleared and he spoke: "Is your interest in Wilhelm due entirely to the fact that you are cousins?"

A quick flush overspread the girl's fair cheeks with colour and her eyes sought the floor of the hut. The point of the sword she held lowered until it rested on the stone flags, and she swayed slightly, leaning against its hilt, while the keen eyes of her uncle regarded her critically. She said in a voice little above a whisper, contrasting strongly with her determined tone of a moment before:

"My interest is due to our relationship alone."

"Has no word of love passed between you?"

"Oh, no, no. Why do you ask me such a question?"

"Because on the answer given depends whether or not I shall entrust you with knowledge regarding him. Swear to me by the Three Kings of Cologne that you will tell to none what I will now impart to you."

"I swear," said Elsa, raising her right hand, and holding aloft the sword with it.

"Wilhelm is not my son, nor is he kin to either of us, but is the heir of the greatest enemy of our house, Count Herbert of Schonburg. I lured him from his father's home as a child and now send him back as a man. Some time later I shall acquaint the Count with the fact that the young man he captured is his only son."

The girl looked at her uncle, her eyes wide with horror.

"It is your purpose then that the father shall execute his own son?"

The Outlaw shrugged his shoulders.

"The result lies not with me, but with the Count. He was once a crusader and the teaching of his master is to the effect that the measure he metes to others, the same shall be meted to him, if I remember aright the tenets of his faith. Count Herbert wreaking vengeance upon my supposed son, is really bringing destruction upon his own, which seems but justice. If he show mercy to me and mine, he is bestowing the blessed balm thereof on himself and his house. In this imperfect world, few events are ordered with such admirable equity as the capture of young Lord Wilhelm, by that haughty and bloodthirsty warrior, his father. Let us then await with patience the outcome, taking care not to interfere with the designs of Providence."

"The design comes not from God but from the evil one himself."

"It is within the power of the Deity to overturn even the best plans of the fiend, if it be His will. Let us see to it that we do not intervene between two such ghostly potentates, remembering that we are but puny creatures, liable to err."

"The plot is of your making, secretly held, all these years, with unrelenting malignity. The devil himself is not wicked enough to send an innocent, loyal lad to his doom in his own mother's house, with his father as his executioner. Oh, uncle, uncle, repent and make reparation before it is too late."

"Let the Count repent and make reparation. I have now nothing to do with the matter. As I have said, if the Count is merciful, he is like to be glad of it later in his life; if he is revengeful, visiting the sin of the father on the son, innocent, I think you called him, then he deserves what his own hand deals out to himself. But we have talked too much already. I ask you to remember your oath, for I have told you this so that you will not bring ridicule upon me by a womanish appeal to my own men, who would but laugh at you in any case and think me a dotard in allowing women overmuch to say in the camp. Get you back to your women, for we move camp instantly. Even if I were to relent, as you term it, the time is past, for Wilhelm is either dangling from the walls of Castle Schonburg or he is pardoned, and all that we could do would be of little avail. Prepare you then instantly for our journey."

Elsa, with a sigh, went slowly to the women's quarters, her oath, the most terrible that may be taken on the Rhine, weighing heavily upon her. Resolving not to break it, yet determined in some way to save Wilhelm, the girl spent the first part of the journey in revolving plans of escape, for she found as the cavalcade progressed that her uncle did not trust entirely to the binding qualities of the oath she had taken, but had her closely watched as well. As the expedition progressed farther and farther south in the direction of Mayence, vigilance was relaxed, and on the evening of the second day, when a camp had been selected for the night, Elsa escaped and hurried eastward through the forest until she came to the Rhine, which was to be her guide to the castle of Schonburg. The windings of the river made the return longer than the direct journey through the wilderness had been, and in addition to this, Elsa was compelled to circumambulate the numerous castles, climbing the hills to avoid them, fearing capture and delay, so it was not until the sun was declining on the sixth day after the assault on the castle that she stood, weary and tattered and unkempt, before the closed gates of Schonburg, and beat feebly with her small hand against the oak, crying for admittance. The guard of the gate, seeing through the small lattice but a single dishevelled woman standing there, anticipating treachery, refused to open the little door in the large leaf until his captain was summoned, who, after some parley, allowed the girl to enter the courtyard.

"What do you want?" asked the captain, curtly.

She asked instead of answered:

"Is your prisoner still alive?"

"The son of the Outlaw? Yes, but he would be a confident prophet who would predict as much for him at this hour to-morrow."

"Take me, I beg of you, to the Countess."

"That is as it may be. Who are you and what is your business with her?"

"I shall reveal myself to her Ladyship, and to her will state the object of my coming."

"Your object is plain enough. You are some tatterdemalion of the forest come to beg the life of your lover, who hangs to-morrow, or I am a heathen Saracen."

"I do beseech you, tell the Countess that a miserable woman craves permission to speak with her."

What success might have attended her petition is uncertain, but the problem was solved by the appearance of the Countess herself on the terrace above them, which ran the length of the castle on its western side. The lady leaned over the parapet and watched with evident curiosity the strange scene in the courtyard below, the captain and his men in a ring around the maiden of the forest, who occupying the centre of the circle, peered now in one face, now in another, as if searching for some trace of sympathy in the stolid countenances of the warriors all about her. Before the captain could reply, his lady addressed him.

"Whom have you there, Conrad?"

It seemed as if the unready captain would get no word said, for again before he had made answer the girl spoke to the Countess.

"I do implore your Ladyship to grant me speech with you."

The Countess looked down doubtfully upon the supplicant, evidently prejudiced by her rags and wildly straying hair. The captain cleared his throat and opened his mouth, but the girl eagerly forestalled him.

"Turn me not away, my Lady, because I come in unhandsome guise, for I have travelled far through forest and over rock, climbing hills and skirting the river's brink to be where I am. The reluctant wilderness, impeding me, has enviously torn my garments, leaving me thus ashamed before you, but, dear Lady, let not that work to my despite. Grant my petition and my prayer shall ever be that the dearest wish of your own heart go not unsatisfied."

"Alas!" said the Countess, with a deep sigh, "my dearest wish gives little promise of fulfilment."

Conrad, seeing that the lady thought of her lost son, frowned angrily, and in low growling tones bade the girl have a care what she said, but Elsa was not to be silenced and spoke impetuously.

"Oh, Countess, the good we do often returns to us tenfold; mercy calls forth mercy. An acorn planted produces an oak; cruelty sown leaves us cruelty to reap. It is not beyond imagination that the soothing of my bruised heart may bring balm to your own."

"Take the girl to the east room, Conrad, and let her await me there," said the Countess.

"With a guard, your Ladyship?"

"Without a guard, Conrad."

"Pardon me, my Lady, but I distrust her. She may have designs against you."

The Countess had little acquaintance with fear. She smiled at the anxious captain and said:

"Her only desire is to reach my heart, Conrad."

"God grant it may not be with a dagger," grumbled the captain, as he made haste to obey the commands of the lady.

When the Countess entered the room in which Elsa stood, her first question was an inquiry regarding her visitor's name and station, the telling of which seemed but an indifferent introduction for the girl, who could not help noting that the Countess shrank, involuntarily from her when she heard the Outlaw mentioned.

"Our house has little cause to confer favour on any kin of the Outlaw of Hundsrück," the lady said at last.

"I do not ask for favour, my Lady. I have come to give your revenge completeness, if it is revenge you seek. The young man now imprisoned in Schonburg is so little esteemed by my uncle that not a single blow has been struck on his behalf. If the Count thinks to hurt the Outlaw by executing Wilhelm, he will be gravely in error, for my uncle and his men regard the captive so lightly that they have gone beyond Mayence without even making an effort toward his rescue. As for me, my uncle bestows upon me such affection as he is capable of, and would be more grieved should I die, than if any other of his kin were taken from him. Release Wilhelm and I will gladly take his place, content to receive such punishment as his Lordship, the Count, considers should be imposed on a relative of the Outlaw."

"What you ask is impossible. The innocent should not suffer for the guilty."

"My Lady, the innocent have suffered for others since the world began, and will continue to do so till it ends. Our only hope of entering Heaven comes through Him who was free from sin being condemned in our stead. I do beseech your Ladyship to let me take the place of Wilhelm."

"You love this young man," said the Countess, seating herself, and regarding the girl with the intent interest which women, whose own love affair has prospered, feel when they are confronted with an incident that reminds them of their youth.

"Not otherwise than as a friend and dear companion, my Lady," replied Elsa, blushing. "When he was a little boy and I a baby, he carried me about in his arms, and since that time we have been comrades together."

"Comradeship stands for much, my girl," said the Countess, in kindly manner, "but it rarely leads one friend willingly to accept death for another. I have not seen this young man whom you would so gladly liberate; the dealing with prisoners is a matter concerning my husband alone; I never interfere, but if I should now break this rule because you have travelled so far, and are so anxious touching the prisoner's welfare, would you be willing to accept my conditions?"

"Yes, my Lady, so that his life were saved."

"He is a comely young man doubtless, and there are some beautiful women within this castle; would it content you if he were married to one of my women, and so escaped with life?"

A sudden pallor overspread the girl's face, and she clasped her hands nervously together. Tears welled into her eyes, and she stood thus for a few moments unable to speak. At last she murmured, with some difficulty:

"Wilhelm can care nothing for any here, not having beheld them, and it would be wrong to coerce a man in such extremity. I would rather die for him, that he might owe his life to me."

"But he would live to marry some one else."

"If I were happy in heaven, why should I begrudge Wilhelm's happiness on earth?"

"Ah, why, indeed, Elsa? And yet you disclaim with a sigh. Be assured that I shall do everything in my power to save your lover, and that not at the expense of your own life or happiness. Now come with me, for I would have you arrayed in garments more suited to your youth and your beauty, that you may not be ashamed when you meet this most fascinating prisoner, for such he must be, when you willingly risk so much for his sake."

The Countess, after conducting the girl to the women's apartments, sought her husband, but found to her dismay that he showed little sign of concurrence with her sympathetic views regarding the fate of the prisoner. It was soon evident to her that Count Herbert had determined upon the young man's destruction, and that there was some concealed reason for this obdurate conclusion which the Count did not care to disclose. Herbert von Schonburg was thoroughly convinced that his son was dead, mutilated beyond recognition by the Outlaw of Hundsrück, yet this he would not tell to Beatrix, his wife, who cherished the unshaken belief that the boy still lived and would be restored to her before she died. The Count for years had waited for his revenge, and even though his wife now pleaded that he forego it, the Master of Schonburg was in no mind to comply, though he said little in answer to her persuading. The incoming of Elsa to the castle merely convinced him that some trick was meditated on the part of the Outlaw, and the sentimental consideration urged by the Countess had small weight with him. He gave a curt order to his captain to double his guards around the stronghold, and relax no vigilance until the case of the prisoner had been finally dealt with. He refused permission for Elsa to see her cousin, even in the presence of witnesses, as he was certain that her coming was for the purpose of communicating to him some message from the Outlaw, the news of whose alleged withdrawal he did not believe.

"With the country at peace, the Outlaw has instigated, and his son has executed, an attack upon this castle. The penalty is death. To-morrow I shall hear what he has to say in his defence, and shall deliver judgment, I hope, justly. If his kinswoman wishes to see him, she may come to his trial, and then will be in a position to testify to her uncle that sentence has been pronounced in accordance with the law that rules the Rhine provinces. If she has communication to make to her cousin, let it be made in the Judgment Hall in the presence of all therein."

The Countess, with sinking heart, left her husband, having the tact not to press upon him too strongly the claims of mercy as well as of justice. She knew that his kind nature would come to the assistance of her own suing, and deeply regretted that the time for milder influences to prevail was so short. In a brief conference with Elsa, she endeavoured to prepare the girl's mind for a disastrous ending of her hopes.

Some minutes before the hour set for Wilhelm's trial, the Countess Beatrix, followed by Elsa, entered the Judgment Hall to find the Count seated moodily in the great chair at one end of the long room, in whose ample inclosure many an important state conference had been held, each of the forefathers of the present owner being seated in turn as president of the assemblage. Some thought of this seemed to oppress the Count's mind, for seated here with set purpose to extinguish his enemy's line, the remembrance that his own race died with him was not likely to be banished. The Countess brought Elsa forward and in a whisper urged her to plead for her kinsman before his judge. The girl's eloquence brought tears to the eyes of Beatrix, but the Count's impassive face was sphinx-like in its settled gloom. Only once during the appeal did he speak, and that was when Elsa offered herself as a sacrifice to his revenge, then he said, curtly:

"We do not war against women. You are as free to go as you were to come, but you must not return."

A dull fear began to chill the girl's heart and to check her earnest pleading: She felt that her words were making no impression on the silent man seated before her, and this knowledge brought weak hesitation to her tongue and faltering to her speech. In despair she wrung her hands and cried: "Oh, my Lord, my Lord, think of your own son held at the mercy of an enemy. Think of him as a young man just the age of your prisoner, at a time when life is sweetest to him! Think, think, I beg of you——"

The Count roused himself like a lion who had been disturbed, and cried in a voice that resounded hoarsely from the rafters of the arched roof, startling the Countess with the unaccustomed fierceness of its tone:

"Yes, I will think of him—of my only son in the clutch of his bitter foe, and I thank you for reminding me of him, little as I have for these long years needed spur to my remembrance. Bring in the prisoner."

When Wilhelm was brought in, heavy manacles on his wrists, walking between the men who guarded him, Elsa looked from judge to culprit, and her heart leaped with joy. Surely such blindness could not strike this whole concourse that some one within that hall would not see that, here confronted, stood father and son, on the face of one a frown of anger, on the face of the other a frown of defiance, expressions almost identical, the only difference being the thirty years that divided their ages. For a few moments the young man did not distinguish Elsa in the throng, then a glad cry of recognition escaped him, and the cloud cleared from his face as if a burst of sunshine had penetrated the sombre-coloured windows and had thrown its illuminating halo around his head. He spoke impetuously, leaning forward:

"Elsa, Elsa, how came you here?" then, a shadow of concern crossing his countenance, "you are not a prisoner, I trust?"

"No, no, Wilhelm, I am here to beseech the clemency of the Count—"

"Not for me!" exclaimed the prisoner, defiantly, drawing himself up proudly: "not for me, Elsa. You must never ask favour from a robber and a coward like, Count von Schonburg, brave only in his own Judgment Hall."

"Oh, Wilhelm, Wilhelm, have a care what you say, or you will break my heart. And your proclamation is far from true. The Count is a brave man who has time and again proved himself so, and my only hope is that he will prove as merciful as he is undoubtedly courageous. Join your prayers with mine, Wilhelm, and beg for mercy rather than justice."

"I beg from no man, either mercy or justice. I am here, my Lord Count, ready to receive whatever you care to bestow, and I ask you to make the waiting brief for the sake of the women present, for I am I sure the beautiful, white-haired lady there dislikes this traffic in men's lives as much as does my fair-haired cousin."

"Oh, my lord Count, do not heed what he says; his words but show the recklessness of youth; hold them not against him."

"Indeed I mean each word I say, and had I iron in my hand instead of round my wrists, his Lordship would not sit so calmly facing me."

Elsa, seeing how little she had accomplished with either man began to weep helplessly, and the Count, who had not interrupted the colloquy, listening unmoved to the contumely heaped upon him by the prisoner, now said to the girl:

"Have you finished your questioning?"

Receiving no answer, he said to the prisoner after a pause:

"Why did you move against this castle?"

"Because I hoped to take it, burn it, and hang or behead its owner."

"Oh, Wilhelm, Wilhelm!" wailed the girl.

"And, having failed, what do you expect?"

"To be hanged, or beheaded, depending on whether your Lordship is the more expert with a cord or with an axe."

"You called me a coward, and I might have retorted that in doing so you took advantage of your position as prisoner, but setting that aside, and speaking as man to man, what ground have you for such an accusation?"

"We cannot speak as man to man, for I am bound and you are free, but touching the question of your cowardice, I have heard it said by those who took part in the defence of my father's castle, when you attacked it and destroyed it, commanding a vastly superior force, my father leaped from the wall and dared you to follow him. For a moment, they told me, it seemed that you would accept the challenge, but you contented yourself with calling on others to do what you feared to do yourself, and thus my father, meeting no opposition from a man of his own rank, was compelled to destroy the unfortunate serfs who stood in his way and, so cut out a path to safety. In refusing to accept the plunge he took, you branded yourself a coward, and once a toward always a coward."

"Oh, Wilhelm," cried Elsa, in deep distress at the young man's lack of diplomacy, while she could not but admire his ill-timed boldness, "speak not so to the Count, for I am sure what you say is not true."

"Indeed," growled Captain Conrad, "the young villain is more crafty than we gave him credit for. Instead of a rope he will have a challenge from the Count, and so die honourably like a man, in place of being strangled like the dog he is."

"Dear Wilhelm, for my sake, do not persist in this course, but throw yourself on the mercy of the Count. Why retail here the irresponsible gossip of a camp, which I am sure contains not a word of truth, so far as the Count is concerned."

Herbert of Schonburg held up his hand for silence, and made confession with evident difficulty.

"What the young man says with harshness is true in semblance, if not strictly so in action. For the moment, thinking of my wife and child, I hesitated, and when the hesitation was gone the opportunity was gone with it. My punishment has been severe; by that moment's cowardice, I am now a childless man, and therefore perhaps value my life less highly than I held it at the time we speak of. Hear then, your sentence: You will be taken to the top of the wall, the iron removed from your wrists, and your sword placed in your hand. You will then leap from that wall, and if you are unhurt, I will leap after you. Should your sword serve you as well as your father's served him, you will be free of the forest, and this girl is at liberty to accompany you. I ask her now to betake herself to the field outside the gate, there to await the result of our contest."

At this there was an outcry on the part of Countess Beatrix, who protested against her husband placing himself in this unnecessary jeopardy, but the Count was firm and would permit no interference with his sentence. Elsa was in despair at the unaccountable blindness of all concerned, not knowing that the Count was convinced his son was dead, and that the Countess thought continually of her boy as a child of four, taking no account of the years that had passed, although her reason, had she applied reason to that which touched her affections only, would have told her, he must now be a stalwart young man and not the little lad she had last held in her arms. For a moment Elsa wavered in her allegiance to the oath she had taken, but she saw against the wall the great crucifix which had been placed there by the first crusader who had returned to the castle from the holy wars and she breathed a prayer as she passed it, that the heir of this stubborn house might not be cut off in his youth through the sightless rancour that seemed to pervade it.

The Count tried to persuade his weeping wife not to accompany him to the walls, but she would not be left behind, and so, telling Conrad to keep close watch upon her, in case that in her despair she might attempt to harm herself, his lordship led the way to the battlements.

Wilhelm, at first jubilant that he was allowed to take part in a sword contest rather than an execution, paused for a moment as he came to the courtyard, and looked about him in a dazed manner, once or twice drawing his hand across his eyes, as if to perfect his vision. Some seeing him thus stricken silent and thoughtful, surmised that the young man was like to prove more courageous in word than in action; others imagined that the sudden coming from the semi-gloom of the castle interior into the bright light dazzled him. The party climbed the flight of stone steps which led far upward to the platform edged by the parapet from which the spring was to be made. The young man walked up and down the promenade, unheeding those around him, seeming like one in a dream, groping for something he failed to find. The onlookers watched him curiously, wondering at his change of demeanour.

Suddenly he dropped his sword on the stones at his feet, held up his hands and cried aloud:

"I have jumped from here before—when I was a lad—a baby almost—I remember it all now—where am I—when was I here before—where is my wooden sword—and where is Conrad, who made it—Conrad, where are you?"

The captain was the first to realise what had happened. He stepped hurriedly forward, scrutinising his late prisoner, the light of recognition, in his eyes.

"It is the young master," he shouted. "My Lord Count, this is no kinsman of the Outlaw, but your own son, a man grown."

The Count stood amazed, as incapable of motion as a statue of stone; the countess, gazing with dreamy eyes, seemed trying to adjust her inward vision of the lad of four with the outward reality of the man of twenty-one. In the silence rose the clear sweet voice of Elsa without the walls, her face upturned like a painting of the Madonna, her hands clasped in front of her.

"Dear Virgin Mother in Heaven, I thank thee that my prayer was not unheard, and bear me witness that I have kept my oath—I have kept my oath, and may Thy intervention show a proud and sinful people the blackness of revenge."

Count Herbert, rousing himself from his stupor, appealed loudly to the girl.

"Woman, is this indeed my son, and, if so, why did you not speak before we came to such extremity?"

"I cannot answer. I have sworn an oath. If you would learn who stands beside you, send a messenger to the Outlaw, saying you have killed him, as indeed you purposed doing," then stretching out her arms, she said, with faltering voice: "Wilhelm, farewell," and turning, fled toward the forest.

"Elsa, Elsa, come back!" the young man cried, foot on the parapet, but the girl paid no heed to his commanding summons, merely waving her hand without looking over her shoulder.

"Elsa!"

The name rang out so thrillingly strange that its reverberation instantly arrested the flying footsteps of the girl. Instinctively she knew it was the voice of a man falling rapidly through the air. She turned in time to see Wilhelm strike the ground, the impetus precipitating him prone on his face, where he lay motionless. The cry of horror from the battlements was echoed by her own as she sped swiftly toward him. The young man sprang to his feet as she approached and caught her breathless in his arms.

"Ah, Elsa," he said, tenderly, "forgive me the fright I gave you, but I knew of old your fleetness of foot, and if the forest once encircled you, how was I ever to find you?"

The girl made no effort to escape from her imprisonment, and showed little desire to exchange the embrace she endured for that of the forest.

"Though I should blush to say it, Wilhelm, I fear I am easily found, when you are the searcher."

"Then let old Schloss Schonburg claim you, Elsa, that the walls which beheld a son go forth, may see a son and daughter return."

CHAPTER III. – A CITY OF FEAR

The Countess Beatrix von Schonburg warmly welcomed her lost son and her newly-found daughter. The belief of Beatrix in Wilhelm's ultimate return had never wavered during all the long years of his absence, and although she had to translate her dream of the child of four into a reality that included a stalwart young man of twenty-one, the readjustment was speedily accomplished. Before a week had passed it seemed to her delighted heart that the boy had never left the castle. The Countess had liked Elsa from the first moment when she saw her, ragged, unkempt and forlorn, among the lowering, suspicious men-at-arms in the courtyard, and now that she knew the dangers and the privations the girl had braved for the sake of Wilhelm, the affectionate heart of Beatrix found ample room for the motherless Elsa.

With the Count, the process of mental reconstruction was slower, not only on account of his former conviction that his son was dead, but also because of the deep distrust in which he held the Outlaw. He said little, as was his custom, but often sat with brooding brows, intently regarding his son, gloomy doubt casting a shadow over his stern countenance. Might not this be a well-laid plot on the part of the Outlaw to make revenge complete by placing a von Weithoff in the halls of Schonburg as master of that ancient stronghold? The circumstances in which identity was disclosed, although sufficient to convince every one else in the castle, appeared at times to the Count but the stronger evidence of the Outlaw's craft and subtlety. If the young man were actually the son of von Weithoff, then undoubtedly the Outlaw had run great risk of having him hanged forthwith, but on the other hand, the prize to be gained, comprising as it did two notable castles and two wide domains, was a stake worth playing high for, and a stake which appealed strongly to a houseless, landless man, with not even a name worth leaving to his son. Thus, while the Countess lavished her affection on young Wilhelm, noticing nothing of her husband's distraction in this excessive happiness, Count Herbert sat alone in the lofty Knight's Hall, his elbows resting on the table before him, his head buried in his hands, ruminating on the strange transformation that had taken place, endeavouring to weigh the evidence pro and con with the impartial mind of an outsider, becoming the more bewildered the deeper he penetrated into the mystery.

It was in this despondent attitude that Elsa found him a few days after the leap from the wall that had caused her return to Schonburg, a willing captive. The Count did not look up when she entered, and the girl stood for a few moments in silence near him. At last she spoke in a low voice, hesitating slightly, nevertheless going with incisive directness into the very heart of the problem that baffled Count Herbert.

"My Lord, you do not believe that Wilhelm is indeed your son."

The master of Schonburg raised his head slowly and looked searchingly into the frank face of the girl, gloomy distrust reflected from his own countenance.

"Were you sent by your uncle to allay my suspicion?

"No, my Lord. I thought that a hint of the truth being given, Nature would come to the assistance of mutual recognition. Such has been the case between my lady and her son, but I see that you are still unconvinced."

"For my sins, I know something of the wickedness of this world, a knowledge from which her purity has protected the Countess. You believe that Wilhelm is my son?"

"I have never said so, my Lord."

"What you did say was that you had taken an oath. You are too young and doubtless too innocent to be a party to any plot, but you may have been the tool of an unscrupulous man, who knew the oath would be broken when the strain of a strong affection was brought to bear upon it."

"Yet, my Lord, I kept my oath, although I saw my—my—"

The girl hesitated and blushed, but finally spoke up bravely:

"I saw my lover led to his destruction. If Wilhelm is my cousin, then did his father take a desperate chance in trusting first, to my escape from the camp, and second to my perjury. You endow him with more than human foresight, my Lord."

"He builded on your love for Wilhelm, which he had seen growing under his eye before either you or the lad had suspicion of its existence. I know the man, and he is a match for Satan, his master."

"But Satan has been discomfited ere now by the angels of light, and even by holy men, if legend tells truly. I have little knowledge of the world, as you have said, but the case appears to me one of the simplest. If my uncle wished the bitterest revenge on you, what could be more terrible than cause you to be the executioner of your own son? The vengeance, however, to be complete, depends on his being able to place before you incontrovertible proof that you were the father of the victim. Send, therefore, a messenger to him, one from Gudenfels, who knows nothing of what has happened in this castle of Schonburg, and who is therefore unable to disclose, even if forced to confess, that Wilhelm is alive. Let the messenger inform my uncle that his son is no more, which is true enough, and then await the Outlaw's reply. And meanwhile let me venture to warn you, my Lord, that it would be well to conceal your disbelief from Wilhelm, for he is high-spirited, and if he gets but an inkling that you distrust him, he will depart; for not all your possessions will hold your son if he once learns that you doubt him, so you are like to find yourself childless again, if your present mood masters you much longer."

The Count drew a deep sigh, then roused himself and seemed to shake off the influence that enchained him.

"Thank you, my girl," he cried, with something of the old ring in his voice, "I shall do as you advise, and if this embassy results as you say, you will ever find your staunchest friend in me."

He held out his hand to Elsa, and departed to his other castle of Gudenfels on the opposite side of the Rhine. From thence he sent a messenger who had no knowledge of what was happening in Schonburg.

When at last the messenger returned from the Outlaw's camp, he brought with him a wailing woman and grim tidings that he feared to deliver.

Thrice his lordship demanded his account, the last time with such sternness that the messenger quailed before him.

"My Lord," he stammered at last, "a frightful thing has taken place—would that I had died before it was told to me. The young man your lordship hanged was no other than——'

"Well, why do you pause? You were going to say he was my own son. What proof does the Outlaw offer that such was indeed the case?"

"Alas! my Lord, the proof seems clear enough. Here with me is young Lord Wilhelm's nurse, whose first neglect led to his abduction, and who fled to the forest after him, and was never found. She followed him to the Outlaw's camp, and was there kept prisoner by him until she was at last given charge of the lad, under oath that she would teach him to forget who he was, the fierce Outlaw threatening death to both woman and child were his orders disobeyed. She has come willingly with me hoping to suffer death now that one she loved more than son has died through her first fault."

Then to the amazement of the pallid messenger the Count laughed aloud and called for Wilhelm, who, when he was brought, clasped the trembling old woman in his arms, overjoyed to see her again and eager to learn news of the camp. How was the stout Gottlieb? Had the messenger seen Captain Heinrich? and so on.

"Indeed, my young Lord," answered the overjoyed woman "there was such turmoil in the camp that I was glad to be quit of it with unbroken bones. When the Outlaw proclaimed that you were hanged, there was instant rebellion among his followers, who thought that your capture was merely a trick to be speedily amended, being intended to form a laughing matter to your discomfiture when you returned. They swore they would have torn down Schonburg with their bare hands rather than have left you in jeopardy, had they known their retreat imperilled your life."

"The brave lads!" cried the young man in a glow of enthusiasm, "and here have I been maligning them for cowards! What was the outcome?"

"That I do not know, my Lord, being glad to escape from the ruffians with unfractured head."

The result of the embassy was speedily apparent at Schonburg. Two days later, in the early morning, the custodians at the gate were startled by the shrill Outlaw yell, which had on so many occasions carried terror with it into the hearts of Rhine strongholds.

"Come out, Hangman of Schonburg!" they shouted, "come out, murderer of a defenceless prisoner. Come out, before we drag you forth, for the rope is waiting for your neck and the gallows tree is waiting for the rope."

Count Herbert was first on the battlements, and curtly he commanded his men not to launch bolt at the invaders, knowing the outlaws mistakenly supposed him to be the executioner of their former comrade. A moment later young Wilhelm himself appeared on the wall above the gate, and, lifting his arms above his head raised a great shout of joy at seeing there collected his old companions, calling this one or that by name as he recognised them among the seething, excited throng. There was an instant's cessation of the clamour, then the outlaws sent forth a cheer that echoed from all the hills around. They brandished their weapons aloft, and cheered again and again, the garrison of the castle, now bristling along the battlements, joining in the tumult with strident voices. Gottlieb advanced some distance toward the gate, and holding up his hand for silence addressed Wilhelm.

"Young master," he cried, "we have deposed von Weithoff, and would have hanged him, but that he escaped during the night, fled to Mayence and besought protection of the Archbishop. If you will be our leader we will sack Mayence and hang the Archbishop from his own cathedral tower."

"That can I hardly do, Gottlieb, as a messenger has been sent to the Archbishop asking him to come to Schonburg and marry Elsa to me. He might take our invasion as an unfriendly act and refuse to perform the ceremony."

Gottlieb scratched his head as one in perplexity, seeing before him a question of etiquette that he found difficult to solve. At last he said:

"What need of Archbishop? You and Elsa have been brought up among us, therefore confer honour on our free company by being married by our own Monk who has tied many a knot tight enough to hold the most wayward of our band. The aisles of the mighty oaks are more grand than the cathedral at Mayence or the great hall of Schonburg."

"Indeed I am agreed, if Elsa is willing. We will be married first in the forest and then by the Archbishop in the great hall of Schonburg."

"In such case there will be delay, for now that I bethink me, his Lordship of Mayence has taken himself to Frankfort, where he is to meet the Archbishops of Treves and Cologne who will presently journey to the capital We were thinking of falling upon his reverence of Cologne as he passed up the river, unless he comes with an escort too numerous for us, which, alas! is most likely, so suspicious has the world grown."

"You will be wise not to meddle with the princes of the Church, be their escorts large or small."

"Then, Master Wilhelm, be our leader, for we are likely to get into trouble unless a man of quality is at our head."

Wilhelm breathed a deep sigh and glanced sideways at his father, who stood some distance off, leaning on his two-handed sword, a silent spectator of the meeting.

"The free life of the forest is no more for me, Gottlieb. My duty is here in the castle of my forefathers, much though I grieve to part with you."

This decision seemed to have a depressing effect on the outlaws within hearing. Gottlieb retired, and the band consulted together for a time, then their spokesman again advanced.

"Some while since," he began in dolorous tone, "we appealed to the Emperor to pardon us, promising in such case to quit our life of outlawry and take honest service with those nobles who needed stout blades, but his Majesty sent reply that if we came unarmed to the capital and tendered submission, he would be graciously pleased to hang a round dozen of us to be selected by him, scourge the rest through the streets of Frankfort and so bestow his clemency on such as survived. This imperial tender we did not accept, as there was some uncertainty regarding whose neck should feel the rope and whose back the scourge. While all were willing to admit that more than a dozen of us sorely needed hanging, yet each man seemed loath to claim precedence over his neighbour in wickedness, and desired, in some sort, a voice in the selection of the victims. But if you will accept our following, Master Wilhelm, we will repair at once to Frankfort and make submission to his Majesty the Emperor. The remnant being well scourged, will then return to Schonburg to place themselves under your command."

"Are you willing then to hang for me, Gottlieb?"

"I hanker not after the hanging, but if hang we must, there is no man I would rather hang for than Wilhelm, formerly of the forest, but now, alas! of Schonburg. And so say they all without dissent, therefore the unanimity must needs include the eleven other danglers."

"Then draw nigh, all of you, to the walls and hear my decision."

Gottlieb waving his arms, hailed the outlaws trooping to the walls, and, his upraised hand bringing silence, Wilhelm spoke:

"Such sacrifice as you propose, I cannot accept, yet I dearly wish to lead a band of men like you. Elsa and I shall be married by our ancient woodland father in the forest and then by the Abbot of St. Werner in the hall of Schonburg. We will make our wedding journey to Frankfort, and you shall be our escort and our protectors."

There was for some moments such cheering at this that the young man was compelled to pause in his address, and then as the outcry was again and again renewed, he looked about for the cause and saw that Elsa and his mother had taken places on the balcony which overlooked the animated scene. The beautiful girl had been recognised by the rebels and she waved her hand in response to their shouting.

"We will part company," resumed Wilhelm, "as near Frankfort as it is safe for you to go, and my wife and I, accompanied by a score of men from this castle, will enter the capital. I will beg your complete pardon from his

Majesty and if at first it is refused, I think Elsa will have better success with the Empress, who may incline her imperial husband toward clemency. All this I promise, providing I receive the consent and support of my father, and I am not likely to be refused, for he already knows the persuasive power of my dear betrothed when she pleads for mercy."

"My consent and support I most willingly bestow," said the Count, with a fervour that left no doubt of his sincerity.

The double marriage was duly solemnised, and Wilhelm, with his newly-made wife, completed their journey to Frankfort, escorted until almost within sight of the capital by five hundred and twenty men, but they entered the gates of the city accompanied by only the score of Schonburg men, the remaining five hundred concealing themselves in the rough country, as they well knew how to do.

Neither Wilhelm nor Elsa had ever seen a large city before, and silence fell upon them as they approached the western gate, for they were coming upon a world strange to them, and Wilhelm felt an unaccustomed elation stir within his breast, as if he were on the edge of some adventure that might have an important bearing on his future. Instead of passing peaceably through the gate as he had expected, the cavalcade was halted after the two had ridden under the gloomy stone archway, and the portcullis was dropped with a sudden clang, shutting out the twenty riders who followed. One of several officers who sat on a stone bench that fronted the guard-house within the walls, rose and came forward.

"What is your name and quality?" he demanded, gruffly.

"I am Wilhelm, son of Count von Schonberg."

"What is your business here in Frankfort?"

"My business relates to the emperor, and is not to be delivered to the first underling who has the impudence to make inquiry," replied Wilhelm in a haughty tone, which could scarcely be regarded, in the circumstances, as diplomatic.

Nevertheless, the answer did not seem to be resented, but rather appeared to have a subduing effect on the questioner, who turned, as if for further instruction, to another officer, evidently his superior in rank. The latter now rose, came forward, doffing his cap, and said:

"I understand your answer better than he to whom it was given, my Lord."

"I am glad there is one man of sense at a gate of the capital," said Wilhelm, with no relaxation of his dignity, but nevertheless bewildered at the turn the talk had taken, seeing there was something underneath all this which he did not comprehend, yet resolved to carry matters with a high hand until greater clearness came to the situation.

"Will you order the portcullis raised and permit my men to follow me?"

"They are but temporarily detained until we decide where to quarter them, my Lord. You know," he added, lowering his voice, "the necessity for caution. Are you for the Archbishop of Treves, of Cologne, or of Mayence?"

"I am from the district of Mayence, of course."

"And are you for the archbishop?"

"For the archbishop certainly. He would have honoured me by performing our marriage ceremony had he not been called by important affairs of state to the capital, as you may easily learn by asking him, now that he is within these walls."

The officer bowed low with great obsequiousness and said:

"Your reply is more than sufficient, my Lord, and I trust you will pardon the delay we have caused you. The men of Mayence are quartered in the Leinwandhaus, where room will doubtless be made for your followers.

"It is not necessary for me to draw upon the hospitality of the good Archbishop, as I lodge in my father's town house near the palace, and there is room within for the small escort I bring."

Again the officer bowed to the ground, and the portcullis being by this time raised, the twenty horsemen came clattering under the archway, and thus, without further molestation, they arrived at the house of the Count von Schonburg.

"Elsa," said Wilhelm, when they were alone in their room, "there is something wrong in this city. Men look with fear one upon another, and pass on hurriedly, as if to avoid question. Others stand in groups at the street corners and speak in whispers, glancing furtively over their shoulders."

"Perhaps that is the custom in cities," replied Elsa.

"I doubt it. I have heard that townsmen are eager for traffic, inviting all comers to buy, but here most of the shops are barred, and no customers are solicited. They seem to me like people under a cloud of fear. What can it be?"

"We are more used to the forest path than to city streets, Wilhelm. They will all become familiar to us in a day or two, yet I feel as if I could not get a full breath in these narrow streets and I long for the trees already, but perhaps content will come with waiting."

"'Tis deeper than that. There is something ominous in the air. Noted you not the questioning at the gate and its purport? They asked me if I favoured Treves, or Cologne, or Mayence, but none inquired if I stood loyal to the Emperor, yet I was entering his capital city of Frankfort."

"Perhaps you will learn all from the Emperor when you see him," ventured Elsa.

"Perhaps," said Wilhelm.

The chamberlain of the von Schonburg household, who had supervised the arrangements for the reception of the young couple, waited upon his master in the evening and informed him that the Emperor would not be visible for some days to come.

"He has gone into retreat, in the cloisters attached to the cathedral, and it is the imperial will that none disturb him on worldly affairs. Each day at the hour when the court assembles at the palace, the Emperor hears exhortation from the pious fathers in the Wahlkapelle of the cathedral; the chapel in which emperors are elected; these exhortations pertaining to the ruling of the land, which his majesty desires to govern justly and well.

"An excellent intention," commented the young man, with suspicion of impatience in his tone, "but meanwhile, how are the temporal affairs of the country conducted?"

"The Empress Brunhilda is for the moment the actual head of the state. Whatever act of the ministers receives her approval, is sent by a monk to the Emperor, who signs any document so submitted to him."

"Were her majesty an ambitious woman, such transference of power might prove dangerous."

"She is an ambitious woman, but devoted to her husband, who, it perhaps may be whispered, is more monk than king," replied the chamberlain under his breath. "Her majesty has heard of your lordship's romantic adventures and has been graciously pleased to command that you and her ladyship, your wife, be presented to her to-morrow in presence of the court."

"This is a command which it will be a delight to obey. But tell me, what is wrong in this great town? There is a sinister feeling in the air; uneasiness is abroad, or I am no judge of my fellow-creatures."

"Indeed, my Lord, you have most accurately described the situation. No man knows what is about to happen. The gathering of the Electors is regarded with the gravest apprehension. The Archbishop of Mayence, who but a short time since crowned the Emperor at the great altar of the cathedral, is herewith a thousand men at his back. The Count Palatine of the Rhine is also within these walls with a lesser entourage. It is rumoured that his haughty lordship, the Archbishop of Treves, will reach Frankfort to-morrow, to be speedily followed by that eminent Prince of the Church, the Archbishop of Cologne. Thus there will be gathered in the capital four Electors, a majority of the college, a conjunction that has not occurred for centuries, except on the death of an emperor, necessitating the nomination and election of his successor."

"But as the Emperor lives and there is no need of choosing another, wherein lies the danger?

"The danger lies in the fact that the college has the power to depose as well as to elect."

"Ah! And do the Electors threaten to depose?"

"No. Treves is much too crafty for any straight-forward statement of policy. He is the brains of the combination, and has put forward Mayence and the Count Palatine as the moving spirits, although it is well known that the former is but his tool and the latter is moved by ambition to have his imbecile son selected emperor."

"Even if the worst befall, it seems but the substitution of a weak-minded man for one who neglects the affairs of state, although I should think the princes of the Church would prefer a monarch who is so much under the influence of the monks."

"The trouble is deeper than my imperfect sketch of the situation would lead you to suppose, my Lord. The Emperor periodically emerges from his retirement, promulgates some startling decree, unheeding the counsel of any adviser, then disappears again, no man knowing what is coming next. Of such a nature was his recent edict prohibiting the harrying of merchants going down the Rhine and the Moselle, which, however just in theory, is impracticable, for how are the nobles to reap revenue if such practices are made unlawful? This edict has offended all the magnates of both rivers, and the archbishops, with the Count Palatine, claim that their prerogatives have been infringed, so they come to Frankfort ostensibly to protest, while the Emperor in his cloister refuses to meet them. The other three Electors hold aloof, as the edict touches them not, but they form a minority which is powerless, even if friendly to the Emperor. Meanwhile his majesty cannot be aroused to an appreciation of the crisis, but says calmly that if it is the Lord's will he remain emperor, emperor he will remain."

"Then at its limit, chamberlain, all we have to expect is a peaceful deposition and election?"

"Not so, my lord. The merchants of Frankfort are fervently loyal, to the Emperor, who, they say, is the first monarch to give forth a just law for their protection. At present the subtlety of Treves has nullified all combined action on their part, for he has given out that he comes merely to petition his over-lord, which privilege is well within his right, and many citizens actually believe him, but others see that a majority of the college will be within these walls before many days are past, and that the present Emperor may be legally deposed and another legally chosen. Then if the citizens object, they are rebels, while at this moment if they fight for the Emperor they are patriots, so you see the position is not without its perplexities, for the citizens well know that if they were to man the walls and keep out Treves and Cologne, the Emperor himself would most likely disclaim their interference, trusting as he does so entirely in Providence that a short time since he actually disbanded the imperial troops, much to the delight of the archbishops, who warmly commended his action. And now, my Lord, if I may venture to tender advice unasked, I would strongly counsel you to quit Frankfort as soon as your business here is concluded, for I am certain that a change of government is intended. All will be done promptly, and the transaction will be consummated before the people are aware that such a step is about to be taken. The Electors will meet in the Wahlzimmer or election room of the Romer and depose the Emperor, then they will instantly select his successor, adjourn to the Wahlkapelle and elect him. The Palatine's son is here with his father, and will be crowned at the high altar by the Archbishop of Mayence. The new Emperor will dine with the Electors in the Kaisersaal and immediately after show himself on the balcony to the people assembled in the Romerberg below. Proclamation of his election will then be made, and all this need not occupy more than two hours. The Archbishop of Mayence already controls the city gates, which since the disbanding of the imperial troops have been unguarded, and none can get in or out of the city without that potentate's permission. The men of Mayence are quartered in the centre of the town, the Count Palatine's troops are near the gate. Treves and Cologne will doubtless command other positions, and thus between them they will control the city. Numerous as the merchants and their dependents are, they will have no chance against the disciplined force of the Electors, and the streets of Frankfort are like to run with blood, for the nobles are but too eager to see a sharp check given to the rising pretensions of the mercantile classes, who having heretofore led peaceful lives, will come out badly in combat, despite their numbers; therefore I beg of you, my Lord, to withdraw with her Ladyship before this hell's caldron is uncovered."

"Your advice is good, chamberlain, in so far as it concerns my wife, and I will beg of her to retire to Schonburg, although I doubt if she will obey, but, by the bones of Saint Werner which floated against the current of the Rhine in this direction, if there must be a fray, I will be in the thick of it."

"Remember, my Lord, that your house has always stood by the Archbishop of Mayence."

"It has stood by the Emperor as well, chamberlain."

The Lady Elsa was amazed by the magnificence of the Emperor's court, when, accompanied by her husband, she walked the length of the great room to make obeisance before the throne. At first entrance she shrank timidly, closer to the side of Wilhelm, trembling at the ordeal of passing, simply costumed as she now felt herself to be, between two assemblages of haughty knights and high-born dames, resplendent in dress, with the proud bearing that pertained to their position in the Empire. Her breath came and went quickly, and she feared that all courage would desert her before she traversed the seemingly endless lane, flanked by the nobility of Germany, which led to the royal presence. Wilhelm, unabashed, holding himself the equal of any there, was not to be cowed by patronising glance, or scornful gaze. The thought flashed through his mind:

"How can the throne fall, surrounded as it is by so many supporters?"

But when the approaching two saw the Empress, all remembrance of others faded from their minds. Brunhilda was a woman of superb stature. She stood alone upon the dais which supported the vacant throne, one hand resting upon its carven arm. A cloak of imperial ermine fell gracefully from her shapely shoulders and her slightly-elevated position on the platform added height to her goddess-like tallness, giving her the appearance of towering above every other person in the room, man or woman. The excessive pallor of her complexion was emphasised by the raven blackness of her wealth of hair, and the sombre midnight of her eyes; eyes with slumbering fire in them, qualified by a haunted look which veiled their burning intensity. Her brow was too broad and her chin too firm for a painter's ideal of beauty; her commanding presence giving the effect of majesty rather than of loveliness. Deep lines of care marred the marble of her forehead, and Wilhelm said to himself:

"Here is a woman going to her doom; knowing it; yet determined to show no sign of fear and utter no cry for mercy."

Every other woman there had eyes of varying shades of blue and gray, and hair ranging from brown to golden yellow; thus the Empress stood before them like a creature from another world.

Elsa was about to sink in lowly courtesy before the queenly woman when the Empress came forward impetuously and kissed the girl on either cheek, taking her by the hand.

"Oh, wild bird of the forest," she cried, "why have you left the pure air of the woods, to beat your innocent wings in this atmosphere of deceit! And you, my young Lord, what brings you to Frankfort in these troublous times? Have you an insufficiency of lands or of honours that you come to ask augmentation of either?"

"I come to ask nothing for myself, your Majesty."

"But to ask, nevertheless," said Brunhilda, with a frown.

"Yes, your Majesty."

"I hope I may live to see one man, like a knight of old, approach the foot of the throne without a request on his lips. I thought you might prove an exception, but as it is not so, propound your question?"

"I came to ask if my sword, supplemented by the weapons of five hundred followers, can be of service to your Majesty."

The Empress seemed taken aback by the young man's unexpected reply, and for some moments she gazed at him searchingly in silence.

At last she said:

"Your followers are the men of Schonburg and Gudenfels, doubtless?"

"No, your Majesty. Those you mention, acknowledge my father as their leader. My men were known as the Outlaws of the Hundsrück, who have deposed von Weithoff, chosen me as their chief, and now desire to lead honest lives."

The dark eyes of the Empress blazed again.

"I see, my Lord, that you have quickly learned the courtier's language. Under proffer of service you are really demanding pardon for a band of marauders."

Wilhelm met unflinchingly the angry look of this imperious woman, and was so little a courtier that he allowed a frown to add sternness to his brow.

"Your Majesty puts it harshly," he said, "I merely petition for a stroke of the pen which will add half a thousand loyal men to the ranks of the Emperor's supporters."

Brunhilda pondered on this, then suddenly seemed to arrive at a decision. Calling one of the ministers of state to her side, she said, peremptorily:

"Prepare a pardon for the Outlaws of the Hundsrück. Send the document at once to the Emperor for signature, and then bring it to me in the Red Room."

The minister replied with some hesitation:

"I should have each man's name to inscribe on the roll, otherwise every scoundrel in the Empire will claim protection under the edict."

"I can give you every man's name," put in Wilhelm, eagerly.

"It is not necessary," said the Empress.

"Your Majesty perhaps forgets," persisted the minister, "that pardon has already been proffered by the Emperor under certain conditions that commended themselves to his imperial wisdom, and that the clemency so graciously tendered was contemptuously refused."

At this veiled opposition all the suspicion in Brunhilda's nature turned from Wilhelm to the high official, and she spoke to him in the tones of one accustomed to prompt obedience.

"Prepare an unconditional pardon, and send it immediately to the Emperor without further comment, either to him or to me."

The minister bowed low and retired. The Empress dismissed the court, detaining Elsa, and said to Wilhelm:

"Seek us half an hour later in the Red Room. Your wife I shall take with me, that I may learn from her own lips the adventures which led to your recognition as the heir of Schonburg, something of which I have already heard. And as for your outlaws, send them word if you think they are impatient to lead virtuous lives, which I take leave to doubt, that before another day passes they need fear no penalty for past misdeed, providing their future conduct escapes censure."

"They are one and all eager to retrieve themselves in your Majesty's eyes!"

"Promise not too much, my young Lord, for they may be called upon to perform sooner than they expect," said Brunhilda, with a significant glance at Wilhelm.

The young man left the imperial presence, overjoyed to know that his mission had been successful.

CHAPTER IV. – THE PERIL OF THE EMPEROR

Wilhelm awaited with impatience the passing of the half hour the Empress had fixed as the period of his probation, for he was anxious to have the signed pardon for the outlaws actually in his hand, fearing the intrigues of the court might at the last moment bring about its withdrawal.

When the time had elapsed he presented himself at the door of the Red Room and was admitted by the guard. He found the Empress alone, and she advanced toward him with a smile on her face, which banished the former hardness of expression.

"Forgive me," she said, "my seeming discourtesy in the Great Hall. I am surrounded by spies, and doubtless Mayence already knows that your outlaws have been pardoned, but that will merely make him more easy about the safety of his cathedral town, especially as he holds Baron von Weithoff their former leader. I was anxious that it should also be reported to him that I had received you somewhat ungraciously. Your wife is to take up her abode in the palace, as she refuses to leave Frankfort if you remain here. She tells me the outlaws are brave men."

"The bravest in the world, your Majesty."

"And that they will follow you unquestioningly."

"They would follow me to the gates of—" He paused, and added as if in afterthought—"to the gates of Heaven."

The lady smiled again.

"From what I have heard of them," she said, "I feared their route lay in another direction, but I have need of reckless men, and although I hand you their pardon freely, it is not without a hope that they will see fit to earn it."

"Strong bodies and loyal souls, we belong to your Majesty. Command and we will obey, while life is left us."

"Do you know the present situation of the Imperial Crown, my Lord?"

"I understand it is in jeopardy through the act of the Electors, who, it is thought, will depose the Emperor and elect a tool of their own. I am also aware that the Imperial troops have been disbanded, and that there will be four thousand armed and trained men belonging to the Electors within the walls of Frankfort before many days are past."

"Yes. What can five hundred do against four thousand?"

"We could capture the gates and prevent the entry of Treves and Cologne."

"I doubt that, for there are already two thousand troops obeying Mayence and the Count Palatine now in Frankfort. I fear we must meet strength by craft. The first step is to get your five hundred secretly into this city. The empty barracks stand against the city wall; if you quartered your score of Schonburg men there, they could easily assist your five hundred to scale the wall at night, and thus your force would be at hand concealed in the barracks without knowledge of the archbishops. Treves and his men will be here to-morrow, before it would be possible for you to capture the gates, even if such a design were practicable. I am anxious above all things to avoid bloodshed, and any plan you have to propose must be drafted with that end in view."

"I will ride to the place where my outlaws are encamped on the Rhine, having first quartered the Schonburg men in the barracks with instructions regarding our reception. If the tales which the spies tell the Archbishop of Mayence concerning my arrival and reception at court lead his lordship to distrust me, he will command the guards at the gate not to re-admit me. By to-morrow morning, or the morning after at latest, I expect to occupy the barracks with five hundred and twenty men, making arrangement meanwhile for the quiet provisioning of the place. When I have consulted Gottlieb, who is as crafty as Satan himself, I shall have a plan to lay before your Majesty."

Wilhelm took leave of the Empress, gave the necessary directions to the men he left behind him, and rode through the western gate unmolested and unquestioned. The outlaws hailed him that evening with acclamations that re-echoed from the hills which surrounded them, and their cheers redoubled when Wilhelm presented them with the parchment which made them once more free citizens of the Empire. That night they marched in, five companies, each containing a hundred men, and the cat's task of climbing the walls of Frankfort in the darkness before the dawn, merely gave a pleasant fillip to the long tramp. Daylight, found them sound asleep, sprawling on the floors of the huge barracks.

When Wilhelm explained the situation to Gottlieb the latter made light of the difficulty, as his master expected he would.

"'Tis the easiest thing in the world," he said.

"There are the Mayence men quartered in the Leinwandhaus. The men of Treves are here, let us say, and the men of Cologne there. Very well, we divide our company into four parties, as there is also the Count Palatine to reckon with. We tie ropes round the houses containing these sleeping men, set fire to the buildings all at the same time, and, pouf! burn the vermin where they lie. The hanging of the four Electors after, will be merely a job for a dozen of our men, and need not occupy longer than while one counts five score."

Wilhelm laughed.

"Your plan has the merit of simplicity, Gottlieb, but it does not fall in with the scheme of the Empress, who is anxious that everything be accomplished legally and without bloodshed. But if we can burn them, we can capture them, imprisonment being probably more to the taste of the vermin, as you call them, than cremation, and equally satisfactory to us. Frankfort prison is empty, the Emperor having recently liberated all within it. The place will amply accommodate four thousand men. Treves has arrived to-day with much pomp, and Cologne will be here to-morrow. To-morrow night the Electors hold their first meeting in the election chamber of the Romer. While they are deliberating, do you think you and your five hundred could lay four thousand men by the heels and leave each bound and gagged in the city prison with good strong bolts shot in on them?"

"Look on it as already done, my Lord. It is a task that requires speed, stealth and silence, rather than strength. The main point is to see that no alarm is prematurely given, and that no fugitive from one company escape to give warning to the others. We fall upon sleeping men, and if some haste is used, all are tied and gagged before they are full awake."

"Very well. Make what preparations are necessary, as this venture may be wrecked through lack of a cord or a gag, so see that you have everything at hand, for we cannot afford to lose a single trick. The stake, if we fail, is our heads."

Wilhelm sought the Empress to let her know that he had got his men safely housed in Frankfort, and also to lay before her his plan for depositing the Electors' followers in prison.

Brunhilda listened to his enthusiastic recital in silence, then shook her head slowly.

"How can five hundred men hope to pinion four thousand?" she asked. "It needs but one to make an outcry from an upper window, and, such is the state of tension in Frankfort at the present moment that the whole city will be about your ears instantly, thus bringing forth with the rest the comrades of those you seek to imprison."

"My outlaws are tigers, your Majesty. The Electors' men will welcome prison, once the Hundsrückers are let loose on them."

"Your outlaws may understand the ways of the forest, but not those of a city."

"Well, your Majesty, they have sacked Coblentz, if that is any recommendation for them."

The reply of the Empress seemed irrelevant.

"Have you ever seen the hall in which the Emperors are nominated—or deposed?" she asked.

"No, your Majesty."

"Then follow me."

The lady led him along a passage that seemed interminable, then down a narrow winding stair, through a vaulted tunnel, the dank air of which struck so cold and damp that the young man felt sure it was subterranean; lastly up a second winding stair, at the top of which, pushing aside some hanging tapestry, they stood within the noble chamber known as the Wahlzimmer. The red walls were concealed by hanging tapestry, the rich tunnel groining of the roof was dim in its lofty obscurity. A long table occupied the centre of the room, with three heavily-carved chairs on either side, and one, as ponderous as a throne, at the head.

"There," said the Empress, waving her hand, "sit the seven Electors when a monarch of this realm is to be chosen. There, to-morrow night will sit a majority of the Electoral College. In honour of this assemblage I have caused these embroidered webs to be hung round the walls, so you see, I, too, have a plan. Through this secret door which the Electors know nothing of, I propose to admit a hundred of your men to be concealed behind the tapestry. My plan differs from yours in that I determine to imprison four men, while you would attempt to capture four thousand; I consider therefore that my chances of success, compared with yours, are as a thousand to one. I strike at the head; you strike at the body. If I paralyse the head, the body is powerless."

Wilhelm knit his brows, looked around the room, but made no reply.

"Well," cried the Empress, impatiently, "I have criticised your plan; criticise mine if you find a flaw in it."

"Is it your Majesty's intention to have the men take their places behind the hangings before the archbishops assemble?"

"Assuredly."

"Then you will precipitate a conflict before all the Electors are here, for it is certain that the first prince to arrive will have the place thoroughly searched for spies. So momentous a meeting will never be held until all fear of eavesdroppers is allayed."

"That is true, Wilhelm," said the Empress with a sigh, "then there is nothing left but your project; which I fear will result in a mêlée and frightful slaughter."

"I propose, your Majesty, that we combine the two plans. We will imprison as many as may be of the archbishops' followers and then by means of the secret stairway surround their lordships."

"But they will, in the silence of the room, instantly detect the incoming of your men."

"Not so, if the panel which conceals the stair, work smoothly. My men are like cats, and their entrance and placement will not cause the most timid mouse to cease nibbling."

"The panel is silent enough, and it may be that your men will reach their places without betraying their presence to the archbishops, but it would be well to instruct your leaders that in case of discovery they are to rush forward, without waiting for your arrival or mine, hold the door of the Wahlzimmer at all hazards, and see that no Elector escapes. I am firm in my belief that once the persons of the archbishops are secured, this veiled rebellion ends, whether you imprison your four thousand or not, for I swear by my faith that if their followers raise a hand against me, I will have the archbishops slain before their eyes, even though I go down in disaster the moment after."

The stern determination of the Empress would have inspired a less devoted enthusiast than Wilhelm. He placed his hand on the hilt of his sword.

"There will be no disaster to the Empress," he said, fervently.

They retired into the palace by the way they came, carefully closing the concealed panel behind them.

As Wilhelm passed through the front gates of the Palace to seek Gottlieb at the barracks, he pondered over the situation and could not conceal from himself the fact that the task he had undertaken was almost impossible of accomplishment. It was an unheard of thing that five hundred men should overcome eight times their number and that without raising a disturbance in so closely packed a city as Frankfort, where, as the Empress had said, the state of tension was already extreme. But although he found that the pessimism of the Empress regarding his project was affecting his own belief in it, he set his teeth resolutely and swore that if it failed it would not be through lack of taking any precaution that occurred to him.

At the barracks he found Gottlieb in high feather. The sight of his cheerful, confident face revived the drooping spirits of the young man.

"Well, master," he cried, the freedom of outlawry still in the abruptness of his speech, "I have returned from a close inspection of the city."

"A dangerous excursion," said Wilhelm. "I trust no one else left the barracks."

"Not another man, much as they dislike being housed, but it was necessary some one should know where our enemies are placed. The Archbishop of Treves, with an assurance that might have been expected of him, has stalled his men in the cathedral, no less, but a most excellent place for our purposes. A guard at each door, and there you are.

"Ah, he has selected the cathedral not because of his assurance, but to intercept any communication with the Emperor, who is in the cloisters attached to it, and doubtless his lordship purposes to crown the new emperor before daybreak at the high altar. The design of the archbishop is deeper than appears on the surface, Gottlieb. His men in the cathedral gives him possession of the Wahlkapelle where emperors are elected, after having been nominated in the Wahlzimmer. His lordship has a taste for doing things legally. Where are the men of Cologne?"

"In a church also; the church of St. Leonhard on the banks of the Main. That is as easily surrounded and is as conveniently situated as if I had selected it myself. The Count Palatine's men are in a house near the northern gate, a house which has no back exit, and therefore calls but for the closing of a street. Nothing could be better."

"But the Drapers' Hall which holds the Mayence troops, almost adjoins the cathedral. Is there not a danger in this circumstance that a turmoil in the one may be heard in the other?"

"No, because we have most able allies."

"What? the townsmen? You have surely taken none into your confidence, Gottlieb?"

"Oh, no, my Lord. Our good copartners are none other than the archbishops themselves. It is evident they expect trouble to-morrow, but none to-night. Orders have been given that all their followers are to get a good night's rest, each man to be housed and asleep by sunset. The men of both Treves and Cologne are tired with their long and hurried march and will sleep like the dead. We will first attack the men of Mayence surrounding the Leinwandhaus, and I warrant you that no matter what noise there is, the Treves people will not hear. Then being on the spot, we will, when the Mayence soldiers are well bound, tie up those in the cathedral. I purpose if your lordship agrees to leave our bound captives where they are, guarded by a sufficient number of outlaws, in case one attempts to help the other, until we have pinioned those of Cologne and the Count Palatine. When this is off our minds we can transport all our prisoners to the fortress at our leisure."

Thus it was arranged, and when night fell on the meeting of the Electors, so well did Gottlieb and his men apply themselves to the task that before an hour had passed the minions of the Electors lay packed in heaps in the aisles and the rooms where they lodged, to be transported to the prison at the convenience of their captors.

Many conditions favoured the success of the seemingly impossible feat. Since the arrival of the soldiery there had been so many night brawls in the streets that one more or less attracted little attention, either from the military or from the civilians. The very boldness and magnitude of the scheme was an assistance to it. Then the stern cry of "In the name of the Emperor!" with which the assaulters once inside cathedral, church or house, fell upon their victims, deadened opposition, for the common soldiers, whether enlisted by Treves, Cologne, or Mayence, knew that the Emperor was over all, and they had no inkling of the designs of their immediate masters. Then, as Gottlieb had surmised, the extreme fatigue of the followers of Treves and Cologne, after their toilsome march from their respective cities, so overcame them that many went to sleep when being conveyed from church and cathedral to prison. There was some resistance on the part of officers, speedily quelled by the victorious woodlanders, but aside from this there were few heads broken, and the wish of the Empress for a bloodless conquest was amply fulfilled.

Two hours after darkness set in, Gottlieb, somewhat breathless, saluted his master at the steps of the palace and announced that the followers of the archbishops and the Count Palatine were behind bars in the Frankfort prison, with a strong guard over them to discourage any attempt at jailbreaking. When Wilhelm led his victorious soldiery silently up the narrow secret stair, pushed back, with much circumspection and caution, the sliding panel, listened for a moment to the low murmur of their lordships' voices, waited until each of his men had gone stealthily behind the tapestry, listened again and still heard the drone of speech, he returned as he came, and accompanied by a guard of two score, escorted the Empress to the broad public stairway that led up one flight to the door of the Wahlzimmer. The two sentinels at the foot of the stairs crossed their pikes to bar the entrance of Brunhilda, but they were overpowered and gagged so quickly and silently that their two comrades at the top had no suspicion of what was going forward until they had met a similar fate. The guards at the closed door, more alert, ran forward, only to be carried away with their fellow-sentinels. Wilhelm, his sword drawn, pushed open the door and cried, in a loud voice:

"My Lords, I am commanded to announce to you that her Majesty the Empress honours you with her presence."

It would have been difficult at that moment to find four men in all Germany more astonished than were the Electors. They saw the young man who held open the door, bow low, then the stately lady so sonorously announced come slowly up the hall and stand silently before them. Wilhelm closed the door and set his back against it, his naked sword still in his right hand. Three of the Electors were about to rise to their feet, but a motion of the hand by the old man of Treves, who sat the head of the table, checked them.

"I have come," said the Empress in a low voice, but distinctly heard in the stillness of the room, "to learn why you are gathered here in Frankfort and in the Wahlzimmer, where no meeting has taken place for three hundred years, except on the death of an emperor."

"Madame," said the Elector of Treves, leaning back in his chair and placing the tips of his fingers together before him, "all present have the right to assemble in this hall unquestioned, with the exception of yourself and the young man who erroneously styled you Empress, with such unnecessary flourish, as you entered. You are the wife of our present Emperor, but under the Salic law no woman can occupy the German throne. If flatterers have misled you by bestowing a title to which you have no claim, and if the awe inspired by that spurious appellation has won your admission past ignorant guards who should have prevented your approach, I ask that you will now withdraw, and permit us to resume deliberations that should not have been interrupted."

"What is the nature of those deliberations, my Lord?"

"The question is one improper for you to ask. To answer it would be to surrender our rights as Electors of the Empire. It is enough for you to be assured, madame, that we are lawfully assembled, and that our purposes are strictly legal."

"You rest strongly on the law, my Lord, so strongly indeed that were I a suspicious person I might surmise that your acts deserved strict scrutiny. I will appeal to you, then, in the name of the law. Is it the law of this realm that he who directly or indirectly conspires against the peace and comfort of his emperor is adjudged a traitor, his act being punishable by death?"

"The law stands substantially as you have cited it, madame, but its bearing upon your presence in this room is, I confess, hidden from me."

"I shall endeavour to enlighten you, my Lord. Are you convened here to further the peace and comfort of his Majesty the Emperor?"

"We devoutly trust so, madame. His Majesty is so eminently fitted for a cloister, rather than for domestic bliss or the cares of state, that we hope to pleasure him by removing all barriers in his way to a monastery."

"Then until his Majesty is deposed you are, by your own confession, traitors."

"Pardon me, madame, but the law regarding traitors which you quoted with quite womanly inaccuracy, and therefore pardonable, does not apply to eight persons within this Empire, namely, the seven Electors and the Emperor himself."

"I have been unable to detect the omission you state, my Lord. There are no exceptions, as I read the law."

"The exceptions are implied, madame, if not expressly set down, for it would be absurd to clothe Electors with a power in the exercise of which they would constitute themselves traitors. But this discussion is as painful as it is futile, and therefore it must cease. In the name of the Electoral College here in session assembled, I ask you to withdraw, madame."

"Before obeying your command, my Lord Archbishop, there is another point which I wish to submit to your honourable body, so learned in the law. I see three vacant chairs before me, and I am advised that it is illegal to depose an emperor unless all the members of the college are present and unanimous."

"Again you have been misinformed. A majority of the college elects; a majority can depose, and in retiring to private life, madame, you have the consolation of knowing that your intervention prolonged your husband's term of office by several minutes. For the third time I request you to leave this room, and if you again refuse I shall be reluctantly compelled to place you under arrest. Young man, open the door and allow this woman to pass through."

"I would have you know, my Lord," said Wilhelm, "that I am appointed commander of the imperial forces, and that I obey none but his Majesty the Emperor."

"I understood that the Emperor depended upon the Heavenly Hosts," said the Archbishop, with the suspicion of a smile on his grim lips.

"It does not become a prince of the Church to sneer at Heaven or its power," said the Empress, severely.

"Nothing was further from my intention, madame, but you must excuse me if I did not expect to see the Heavenly Hosts commanded by a young man so palpably German. Still all this is aside from the point. Will you retire, or must I reluctantly use force?"

"I advise your lordship not to appeal to force."

The old man of Treves rose slowly to his feet, an ominous glitter in his eyes. He stood for some minutes regarding angrily the woman before him, as if to give her time to reconsider her stubborn resolve to hold her ground. Then raising his voice the Elector cried:

"Men of Treves! enter!"

While one might count ten, dense silence followed this outcry, the seated Electors for the first time glancing at their leader with looks of apprehension.

"Treves! Treves! Treves!"

That potent name reverberated from the lips of its master, who had never known its magic to fail in calling round him stout defenders, and who could not yet believe that its power should desert him at this juncture. Again there was no response.

"As did the prophet of old, ye call on false gods."

The low vibrant voice of the Empress swelled like the tones of a rich organ as the firm command she had held over herself seemed about to depart.

"Lord Wilhelm, give them a name, that carries authority in its sound."

Wilhelm strode forward from the door, raised his glittering sword high above his head and shouted:

"THE EMPEROR! Cheer, ye woodland wolves!"

With a downward sweep of his sword, he cut the two silken cords which, tied to a ring near the door, held up the tapestry. The hangings fell instantly like the drop curtain of a theatre, its rustle overwhelmed in the vociferous yell that rang to the echoing roof.

"Forward! Close up your ranks!"

With simultaneous movement the men stepped over the folds on the floor and stood shoulder to shoulder, an endless oval line of living warriors, surrounding the startled group in the centre of the great hall.

"Aloft, rope-men."

Four men, with ropes wound round their bodies, detached themselves from the circle, and darting to the four corners of the room, climbed like squirrels until they reached the tunnelled roofing, where, making their way to the centre with a dexterity that was marvellous, they threw their ropes over the timbers and came spinning down to the floor, like gigantic spiders, each suspended on his own line. The four men, looped nooses in hand, took up positions behind the four Electors, all of whom were now on their feet. Wilhelm saluted the Empress, bringing the hilt of his sword to his forehead, and stepped back.

The lady spoke:

"My Lords, learned in the law, you will perhaps claim with truth that there is no precedent for hanging an Electoral College, but neither is there precedent for deposing an Emperor. It is an interesting legal point on which we shall have definite opinion pronounced in the inquiry which will follow the death of men so distinguished as yourselves, and if it should be held that I have exceeded my righteous authority in thus pronouncing sentence upon you as traitors, I shall be nothing loath to make ample apology to the state."

"Such reparation will be small consolation to us, your Majesty," said the Archbishop of Cologne, speaking for the first time. "My preference is for an ante-mortem rather than a post-mortem adjustment of the law. My colleague of Treves, in the interests of a better understanding, I ask you to destroy the document of deposition, which you hold in your hand, and which I beg to assure her Majesty, is still unsigned."

The trembling fingers of the Archbishop of Treves proved powerless to tear the tough parchment, so he held it for a moment until it was consumed in the flame of a taper which stood on the table.

"And now, your Majesty, speaking entirely for myself, I give you my word as a prince of the Church and a gentlemen of the Empire, that my vote as an Elector will always be against the deposition of the Emperor, for I am convinced that imperial power is held in firm and capable hands."

The great prelate of Cologne spoke as one making graceful concession to a lady, entirely uninfluenced by the situation in which he so unexpectedly found himself. A smile lit up the face of the Empress as she returned his deferential bow.

"I accept your word with pleasure, my Lord, fully assured that, once given, it will never be tarnished by any mental reservation."

"I most cordially associate myself with my brother of Cologne and take the same pledge," spoke up his Lordship of Mayence.

The Count Palatine of the Rhine moistened his dry lips and said:

"I was misled by ambition, your Majesty, and thus in addition to giving you my word, I crave your imperial pardon as well."

The Archbishop of Treves sat in his chair like a man collapsed. He had made no movement since the burning of the parchment. All eyes were turned upon him in the painful stillness. With visible effort he enunciated in deep voice the two words: "And I."

The face of the Empress took on a radiance that had long been absent from it.

"It seems, my Lords, that there has been merely a slight misunderstanding, which a few quiet words and some legal instruction has entirely dissipated. To seal our compact, I ask you all to dine with me to-morrow night, when I am sure it will afford intense gratification to prelates so pious as yourselves to send a message to his Majesty the Emperor, informing him that his trust in Providence has not been misplaced."

CHAPTER V. – THE NEEDLE DAGGER

Wilhelm Von Schonburg, Commander of the Imperial Forces at Frankfort, applied himself to the task of building up an army round his nucleus of five hundred with all the energy and enthusiasm of youth. He first put parties of trusty men at the various city gates so that he might control, at least in a measure, the human intake and output of the city. The power which possession of the gates gave him he knew to be more apparent than real, for Frankfort was a commercial city, owing its prosperity to traffic, and any material interference with the ebb or flow of travel had a depressing influence on trade. If the Archbishops meant to keep their words given to the Empress, all would be well, but of their good faith Wilhelm had the gravest doubts. It would be impossible to keep secret the defeat of their Lordships, when several thousands of their men lay immured in the city prison. The whole world would thus learn sooner or later that the great Princes of the Church had come to shear and had departed shorn; and this blow to their pride was one not easily forgiven by men so haughty and so powerful as the prelates of Treves, Mayence and Cologne. Young as he was, Wilhelm's free life in the forest, among those little accustomed to control the raw passions of humanity, had made him somewhat a judge of character, and he had formed the belief that the Archbishop of Cologne, was a gentleman, and would keep his word, that the Archbishop of Treves would have no scruple in breaking his, while the Archbishop of Mayence would follow the lead of Treves. This suspicion he imparted to the Empress Brunhilda, but she did not agree with him, believing that all three, with the Count Palatine, would hereafter save their heads by attending strictly to their ecclesiastical business, leaving the rule of the Empire in the hands which now held it.

"Cologne will not break the pledge he has given me," she said; "of that I am sure. Mayence is too great an opportunist to follow an unsuccessful leader; and the Count Palatine is too great a coward to enter upon such a dangerous business as the deposing of an emperor who is my husband. Besides, I have given the Count Palatine a post at Court which requires his constant presence in Frankfort, and so I have him in some measure a prisoner. The Electors are powerless if even one of their number is a defaulter, so what can Treves do, no matter how deeply his pride is injured, or how bitterly he thirsts for revenge? His only resource is boldly to raise the flag of rebellion and march his troops on Frankfort. He is too crafty a man to take such risk or to do anything so open. For this purpose he must set about the collection of an army secretly, while we may augment the Imperial troops in the light of day. So, unless he strikes speedily, we will have a force that will forever keep him in awe."

This seemed a reasonable view, but it only partly allayed the apprehensions of Wilhelm. He had caught more than one fierce look of hatred directed toward him by the Archbishop of Treves, since the meeting in the Wahlzimmer, and the regard of his Lordship of Mayence had been anything but benign. These two dignitaries had left Frankfort together, their way lying for some distance in the same direction. Wilhelm liberated their officers, and thus the two potentates had scant escort to their respective cities. Their men he refused to release, which refusal both Treves and Mayence accepted with bad grace, saying the withholding cast an aspersion on their honour. This example was not followed by the suave Archbishop of Cologne, who departed some days after his colleagues. He laughed when Wilhelm informed him that his troops would remain in Frankfort, and said he would be at the less expense in his journey down the Rhine, as his men were gross feeders.

Being thus quit of the three Archbishops, the question was what to do with their three thousand men. It was finally resolved to release them by detachments, drafting into the Imperial army such as were willing so to serve and take a special oath of allegiance to the Emperor, allowing those who declined to enlist to depart from the city in whatever direction pleased them, so that they went away in small parties. It was found, however, that the men cared little for whom they fought, providing the pay was good and reasonably well assured. Thus the Imperial army received many recruits and the country round Frankfort few vagrants.

The departed Archbishops made no sign, the Count Palatine seemed engrossed with his duties about the Court, the army increased daily and life went on so smoothly that Wilhelm began to cease all questioning of the future, coming at last to believe that the Empress was right in her estimate of the situation. He was in this pleasing state of mind when an incident occurred which would have caused him greater anxiety than it did had he been better acquainted with the governing forces of his country. On arising one morning he found on the table of his room a parchment, held in place by a long thin dagger of peculiar construction. His first attention was given to the weapon and not to the scroll. The blade was extremely thin and sharp at the point, and seemed at first sight to be so exceedingly frail as to be of little service in actual combat, but a closer examination proved that it was practically unbreakable, and of a temper so fine that nothing made an impression on its keen edge. Held at certain angles, the thin blade seemed to disappear altogether and leave the empty hilt in the hand. The hilt had been treated as if it were a crucifix, and in slightly raised relief there was a figure of Christ, His outstretched arms extending along the transverse guard. On the opposite side of the handle were the sunken letters "S. S. G. G."

Wilhelm fingered this dainty piece of mechanism curiously, wondering where it was made. He guessed Milan as the place of its origin, knowing enough of cutlery to admire the skill and knowledge of metallurgy that had gone to its construction, and convinced as he laid it down that it was foreign. He was well aware that no smith in Germany could fashion a lancet so exquisitely tempered. He then turned his attention to the document which had been fastened to the table by this needle-like stiletto. At the top of the parchment were the same letters that had been cut in the handle of the dagger.

S. S. G. G.

First warning. Wear this dagger thrust into your doublet over the heart, and allow him who accosts you, fearing nothing if your heart be true and loyal. In strict silence safety lies.

Wilhelm laughed.

"It is some lover's nonsense of Elsa's," he said to himself. "'If your heart be true and loyal,' that is a woman's phrase and nothing else."

Calling his wife, he held out the weapon to her and said:

"Where did you get this, Elsa? I would be glad to know who your armourer is, for I should dearly love to provide my men with weapons of such temper."

Elsa looked alternately at the dagger and at her husband, bewildered.

"I never saw it before, nor anything like it," she replied. "Where did you find it? It is so frail it must be for ornament merely."

"Its frailness is deceptive. It is a most wonderful instrument, and I should like to know where it comes from. I thought you had bought it from some armourer and intended me to wear it as a badge of my office. Perhaps it was sent by the Empress. The word 'loyalty' seems to indicate that, though how it got into this room and on this table unknown to me is a mystery."

Elsa shook her head as she studied the weapon and the message critically.

"Her Majesty is more direct than this would indicate. If she had aught to say to you she would say it without ambiguity. Do you intend to wear the dagger as the scroll commands?"

"If I thought it came from the Empress I should, not otherwise."

"You may be assured some one else has sent it. Perhaps it is intended for me," and saying this Elsa thrust the blade of the dagger through the thick coil of her hair and turned coquettishly so that her husband might judge of the effect.

"Are you ambitious to set a new fashion to the Court, Elsa?" asked Wilhelm, smiling.

"No; I shall not wear it in public, but I will keep the dagger if I may."

Thus the incident passed, and Wilhelm gave no more thought to the mysterious warning. His duties left him little time for meditation during the day, but as he returned at night from the barracks his mind reverted once more to the dagger, and he wondered how it came without his knowledge into his private room. His latent suspicion of the Archbishops became aroused again, and he pondered on the possibility of an emissary of theirs placing the document on his table. He had given strict instructions that if any one supposed to be an agent of their lordships presented himself at the gates he was to be permitted to enter the city without hindrance, but instant knowledge of such advent was to be sent to the Commander, which reminded him that he had not seen Gottlieb that day, this able lieutenant having general charge of all the ports. So he resolved to return to the barracks and question his underling regarding the recent admittances. Acting instantly on this determination, he turned quickly and saw before him a man whom he thought he recognised by his outline in the darkness as von Brent, one of the officers of Treves whom he had released, and who had accompanied the Archbishop on his return to that city. The figure, however, gave him no time for a closer inspection, and, although evidently taken by surprise, reversed his direction, making off with speed down the street. Wilhelm, plucking sword from scabbard, pursued no less fleetly. The scanty lighting of the city thoroughfares gave advantage to the fugitive, but Wilhelm's knowledge of the town was now astonishingly intimate, considering the short time he had been a resident, and his woodlore, applied to the maze of tortuous narrow alleys made him a hunter not easily baffled. He saw the flutter of a cloak as its wearer turned down a narrow lane, and a rapid mental picture of the labyrinth illuminating his mind, Wilhelm took a dozen long strides to a corner and there stood waiting. A few moments later a panting man with cloak streaming behind him came near to transfixing himself on the point of the Commander's sword. The runner pulled himself up with a gasp and stood breathless and speechless.

"I tender you good-evening, sir," said Wilhelm, civilly, "and were I not sure of your friendliness, I should take it that you were trying to avoid giving me salutation."

"I did not recognise you, my Lord, in the darkness."

The man breathed heavily, which might have been accounted for by his unaccustomed exertion.

"'Tis strange, then, that I should have recognised you, turning unexpectedly as I did, while you seemingly had me in your eye for some time before."

"Indeed, my Lord, and that I had not. I but just emerged from this crooked lane, and seeing you turn so suddenly, feared molestation, and so took to my heels, which a warrior should be shamed to confess, but I had no wish to be embroiled in a street brawl."

"Your caution does you credit, and should commend you to so peacefully-minded a master as his Lordship of Treves, who, I sincerely trust, arrived safely in his ancient city."

"He did, my Lord."

"I am deeply gratified to hear it, and putting my knowledge of his lordship's methods in conjunction with your evident desire for secrecy, I should be loath to inquire into the nature of the mission that brings you to the capital so soon after your departure from it."

"Well, my Lord," said von Brent, with an attempt at a laugh, "I must admit that it was my purpose to visit Frankfort with as little publicity as possible. You are mistaken, however, in surmising that I am entrusted with any commands from my lord, the Archbishop, who, at this moment, is devoting himself with energy to his ecclesiastical duties and therefore has small need for a soldier. This being the case, I sought and obtained leave of absence, and came to Frankfort on private affairs of my own. To speak truth, as between one young man and another, not to be further gossiped about, while, stationed here some days ago, I became acquainted with a girl whom I dearly wish to meet again, and this traffic, as you know, yearns not for either bray of trumpet or rattle of drum."

"The gentle power of love," said Wilhelm in his most affable tone, "is a force few of us can resist. Indeed, I am myself not unacquainted with its strength, and I must further congratulate you on your celerity of conquest, for you came to Frankfort in the morning, and were my guest in the fortress in the evening, so you certainly made good use of the brief interval. By what gate did you enter Frankfort?"

"By the western gate, my Lord."

"This morning?"

"No, my Lord. I entered but a short time since, just before the gates were closed for the night."

"Ah! that accounts for my hearing no report of your arrival, for it is my wish, when distinguished visitors honour us with their presence, that I may be able to offer them every courtesy."

Von Brent laughed, this time with a more genuine ring to his mirth.

"Seeing that your previous hospitality included lodging in the city prison, my Lord, as you, a moment ago, reminded me, you can scarcely be surprised that I had no desire to invite a repetition of such courtesy, if you will pardon the frank speaking of a soldier."

"Most assuredly. And to meet frankness with its like, I may add that the city prison still stands intact. But I must no longer delay an impatient lover, and so, as I began, I give you a very good evening, sir."

Von Brent returned the salutation, bowing low, and Wilhelm watched him retrace his steps and disappear in the darkness. The Commander, returning his blade to its scabbard, sought Gottlieb at the barracks.

"Do you remember von Brent, of Treves' staff?"

"That hangdog-looking officer? Yes, master. I had the pleasure of knocking him down in the Cathedral before pinioning him."

"He is in Frankfort to-night, and said he entered by the western gate just before it was closed."

"Then he is a liar," commented Gottlieb, with his usual bluntness.

"Such I strongly suspect him to be. Nevertheless, here he is, and the question I wish answered is, how did he get in?"

"He must have come over the wall, which can hardly be prevented if an incomer has a friend who will throw him a rope."

"It may be prevented if the walls are efficiently patrolled. See instantly to that, Gottlieb, and set none but our own woodlanders on watch."

Several days passed, and Wilhelm kept a sharp lookout for von Brent, or any other of the Archbishop's men, but he saw none such, nor could he learn that the lieutenant had left the city. He came almost to believe that the officer had spoken the truth, when distrust again assailed him on finding in the barracks a second document almost identical with the first, except that it contained the words, "Second warning," and the dirk had been driven half its length into the lid of the desk. At first he thought it was the same parchment and dagger, but the different wording showed him that at least the former was not the same. He called Gottlieb, and demanded to know who had been allowed to pass the guards and enter that room. The honest warrior was dismayed to find such a thing could have happened, and although he was unable to read the lettering, he turned the missive over and over in his hand as if he expected close scrutiny to unravel the skein. He then departed and questioned the guards closely, but was assured that no one had entered except the Commander.

"I cannot fathom it," he said on returning to his master, "and, to tell truth, I wish we were well back in the forest again, for I like not this mysterious city and its ways. We have kept this town as close sealed as a wine butt, yet I dare swear that I have caught glimpses of the Archbishop's men, flitting here and there like bats as soon as darkness gathers. I have tried to catch one or two of them to make sure, but I seem to have lost all speed of foot on these slippery stones, and those I follow disappear as if the earth swallowed them."

"Have you seen von Brent since I spoke to you about him?"

"I thought so, Master Wilhelm, but I am like a man dazed in the mazes of an evil dream, who can be certain of nothing. I am afraid of no man who will stand boldly up to me, sword in hand, with a fair light on both of us, but this chasing of shadows with nothing for a pike to pierce makes a coward of me."

"Well, the next shadow that follows me will get my blade in its vitals, for I think my foot is lighter than yours, Gottlieb. There is no shadow in this town that is not cast by a substance, and that substance will feel a sword thrust if one can but get within striking distance. Keep strict watch and we will make a discovery before long, never fear. Do you think the men we have enlisted from the Archbishop's company are trying to play tricks with us? Are they to be trusted?"

"Oh, they are stout rascals with not enough brains among them all to plan this dagger and parchment business, giving little thought to anything beyond eating and drinking, and having no skill of lettering."

"Then we must look elsewhere for the explanation. It may be that your elusive shadows will furnish a clue."

On reaching his own house Wilhelm said carelessly to his wife, whom he did not wish to alarm unnecessarily:

"Have you still in your possession that dagger which I found on my table?"

"Yes, it is here. Have you found an owner for it or learned how it came there?"

"No. I merely wished to look at it again."

She gave it to him, and he saw at once that it was a duplicate of the one he had hidden under his doublet. The mystery was as far from solution as ever, and the closest examination of the weapon gave no hint pertaining to the purport of the message. Yet it is probable that Wilhelm was the only noble in the German Empire who was ignorant of the significance of the four letters, and doubtless the senders were amazed at his temerity in nonchalantly ignoring the repeated warnings, which would have brought pallor to the cheeks of the highest in the land. Wilhelm had been always so dependent on the advice of Gottlieb that it never occurred to him to seek explanation from any one else, yet in this instance Gottlieb, from the same cause of woodland training, was as ignorant as his master.

It is possible that the two warnings might have made a greater impression on the mind of the young man were it not that he was troubled about his own status in the Empire. There had been much envy in the Court at the elevation of a young man practically unknown, to the position of commander-in-chief of the German army, and high officials had gone so far as to protest against what they said was regarded as a piece of unaccountable favouritism. The Empress, however, was firm, and for a time comment seemed to cease, but it was well known that Wilhelm had no real standing, unless his appointment was confirmed by the Emperor, and his commission made legal by the royal signature. It became known, or, at least, was rumoured that twice the Empress had sent this document to her husband and twice it had been returned unsigned. The Emperor went so far as to refuse to see his wife, declining to have any discussion about the matter, and Wilhelm well knew that every step he took in the fulfilment of his office was an illegal step, and if a hint of this got to the ears of the Archbishops they would be more than justified in calling him to account, for every act he performed relating to the army after he knew that his monarch had refused to sanction his nomination was an act of rebellion and usurpation punishable by death. The Empress was well aware of the jeopardy in which her attaché stood, but she implored him not to give up the position, although helpless to make his appointment regular. She hoped her husband's religious fervour would abate and that he would deign to bestow some attention upon earthly things, allowing himself to be persuaded of the necessity of keeping up a standing army, commanded by one entirely faithful to him. Wilhelm himself often doubted the wisdom of his interference, which had allowed the throne to be held by a man who so neglected all its duties that intrigues and unrest were honeycombing the whole fabric of society, beginning at the top and working its way down until now even the merchants were in a state of uncertainty, losing faith in the stability of the government. The determined attitude of Wilhelm, the general knowledge that he came from a family of fighters, and the wholesome fear of the wild outlaws, under his command, did more than anything else to keep down open rebellion in Court and to make the position of the Empress possible. It was believed that Wilhelm would have little hesitation in obliterating half the nobility of the Court, or the whole of it for that matter, if but reasonable excuse were given him for doing so, and every one was certain that his cut-throats, as they were called, would obey any command he liked to give, and would delight in whatever slaughter ensued. The Commander held aloof from the Court, although, because of his position, he had a room in the palace which no one but the monarch and the chief officer of the army might enter, yet he rarely occupied this apartment, using, instead, the suite at the barracks.

Some days after the second episode of the dagger he received a summons from the Empress commanding his instant presence at the palace. On arriving at the Court, he found Brunhilda attended by a group of nobles, who fell back as the young commander approached. The Empress smiled as he bent his knee and kissed her hand, but Wilhelm saw by the anxiety in her eye that something untoward had happened, guessing that his commission was returned for the third time unsigned from the Emperor, and being correct in his surmise.

"Await me in the Administration Room of the Army," said the Empress. "I will see you presently. You have somewhat neglected that room of late, my Lord."

"I found I could more adequately fulfil your Majesty's command and keep in closer touch with the army by occupying my apartments at the barracks."

"I trust, then, that you will have a good report to present to me regarding the progress of my soldiers," replied the Empress, dismissing him with a slight inclination of her head.

Wilhelm left the audience chamber and proceeded along the corridor with which his room was connected. The soldier at the entrance saluted him, and Wilhelm entered the Administration Chamber. It was a large room and in the centre of it stood a large table. After closing the door Wilhelm paused in his advance, for there in the centre of the table, buried to its very hilt through the planks, was a duplicate of the dagger he had concealed inside his doublet. It required some exertion of Wilhelm's great strength before he dislodged the weapon from the timber into which it had been so fiercely driven. The scroll it affixed differed from each of the other two. It began with the words, "Final warning," and ended with "To Wilhelm of Schonburg, so-called Commander of the Imperial forces," as if from a desire on the part of the writer that there should be no mistake regarding the destination of the missive. The young man placed the knife on the parchment and stood looking at them both until the Empress was announced. He strode forward to meet her and conducted her to a chair, where she seated herself, he remaining on his feet.

"I am in deep trouble," she began, "the commission authorising you to command the Imperial troops has been returned for the third time unsigned; not only that, but the act authorising the reconstruction of the army, comes back also without the Emperor's signature."

Wilhelm remained silent, for he well knew that the weakness of their position was the conduct of the Emperor, and this was an evil which he did not know how to remedy.

"When he returned both documents the first time," continued the Empress, "I sent to him a request for an interview that I might explain the urgency and necessity of the matter. This request was refused, and although I know of course that my husband might perhaps be called eccentric, still he had never before forbade my presence. This aroused my suspicion."

"Suspicion of what, your Majesty?" inquired Wilhelm.

"My suspicion that the messages I sent him have been intercepted."

"Who would dare do such a thing, your Majesty?" cried Wilhelm in amazement.

"Where large stakes are played for, large risks must be taken," went on the lady. "I said nothing at the time, but yesterday I sent to him two acts which he himself had previously sanctioned, but never carried out; these were returned to me to-day unsigned, and now I fear one of three things. The Emperor is ill, is a prisoner, or is dead."

"If it is your Majesty's wish," said Wilhelm, "I will put myself at the head of a body of men, surround the cathedral, search the cloisters, and speedily ascertain whether the Emperor is there or no."

"I have thought of such action," declared the Empress, "but I dislike to take it. It would bring me in conflict with the Church, and then there is always the chance that the Emperor is indeed within the cloisters, and that, of his own free will, he refuses to sign the documents I have sent to him. In such case what excuse could we give for our interference? It might precipitate the very crisis we are so anxious to avoid."

The Empress had been sitting by the table with her arm resting upon it, her fingers toying unconsciously with the knife while she spoke, and now as her remarks reached their conclusion her eyes fell upon its hilt and slender blade. With an exclamation almost resembling a scream the Empress sprang to her feet and allowed the dagger to fall clattering on the floor.

"Where did that come from?" she cried. "Is it intended for me?" and she shook her trembling hands as if they had touched a poisonous scorpion.

"Where it comes from I do not know, but it is not intended for your Majesty, as this scroll will inform you."

Brunhilda took the parchment he offered and held it at arm's length from her, reading its few words with dilated eyes, and Wilhelm was amazed to see in them the fear which they failed to show when she faced the three powerful Archbishops. Finally the scroll fluttered from her nerveless fingers to the floor and the Empress sank back in her chair.

"You have received two other warnings then?" she said in a low voice.

"Yes, your Majesty. What is their meaning?"

"They are the death warrants of the Fehmgerichte, a dread and secret tribunal before which even emperors quail. If you obey this mandate you will never be seen on earth again; if you disobey you will be secretly assassinated by one of these daggers, for after ignoring the third warning a hundred thousand such blades are lying in wait for your heart, and ultimately one of them will reach it, no matter in what quarter of Germany you hide yourself."

"And who are the members of this mysterious association, your Majesty?

"That, you can tell as well as I, better perhaps, for you may be a member while I cannot be. Perhaps the soldier outside this door belongs to the Fehmgerichte, or your own Chamberlain, or perhaps your most devoted lieutenant, the lusty Gottlieb."

"That, your Majesty, I'll swear he is not, for he was as amazed as I when he saw the dagger at the barracks."

Brunhilda shook her head.

"You cannot judge from pretended ignorance," she said, "because a member is sworn to keep all secrets of the holy Fehm from wife and child, father and mother, sister and brother, fire and wind; from all that the sun shines on and the rain wets, and from every being between heaven and earth. Those are the words of the oath."

Wilhelm found himself wondering how his informant knew so much about the secret court if all those rules were strictly kept, but he naturally shrank from any inquiry regarding the source of her knowledge. Nevertheless her next reply gave him an inkling of the truth.

"Who is the head of this tribunal?" he asked.

"The Emperor is the nominal head, but my husband never approved of the Fehmgerichte; originally organised to redress the wrongs of tyranny, it has become a gigantic instrument of oppression. The Archbishop of Cologne is the actual president of the order, not in his capacity as an elector, nor as archbishop, but because he is Duke of Westphalia, where this tragic court had its origin."

"Your Majesty imagines then, that this summons comes from the Archbishop of Cologne?"

"Oh, no. I doubt if he has any knowledge of it. Each district has a freigraf, or presiding judge, assisted by seven assessors, or freischoffen, who sit in so called judgment with him, but literally they merely record the sentence, for condemnation is a foregone conclusion."

"Is the sentence always death?"

"Always, at this secret tribunal; a sentence of death immediately carried out. In the open Fehmic court, banishment, prison, or other penalty may be inflicted, but you are summoned to appear before the secret tribunal."

"Does your Majesty know the meaning of these cabalistic letters on the dagger's hilt and on the parchment?"

"The letters 'S. S. G. G.' stand for Strick, Stein, Gras, Grün: Strick meaning, it is said, the rope which hangs you; Stein, the stone at the head of your grave, and Gras, Grün, the green grass covering it."

"Well, your Majesty," said Wilhelm, picking up the parchment from the floor and tearing it in small pieces, "if I have to choose between the rope and the dagger, I freely give my preference to the latter. I shall not attend this secret conclave, and if any of its members think to strike a dagger through my heart, he will have to come within the radius of my sword to do so."

"God watch over you," said the Empress fervently, "for this is a case in which the protection of an earthly throne is of little avail. And remember, Lord Wilhelm, trust not even your most intimate friend within arm's length of you. The only persons who may not become members of this dread order are a Jew, an outlaw, an infidel, a woman, a servant, a priest, or a person excommunicated."

Wilhelm escorted the Empress to the door of the red room, and there took leave of her; he being unable to suggest anything that might assuage her anxiety regarding her husband, she being unable to protect him from the new danger that threatened. Wilhelm was as brave as any man need be, and in a fair fight was content to take whatever odds came, but now he was confronted by a subtle invisible peril, against which ordinary courage was futile. An unaccustomed shiver chilled him as the palace sentinel, in the gathering gloom of the corridor, raised his hand swiftly to his helmet in salute. He passed slowly down the steps of the palace into the almost deserted square in front of it, for the citizens of Frankfort found it expedient to get early indoors when darkness fell. The young man found himself glancing furtively from right to left, starting at every shadow and scrutinising every passerby who was innocently hurrying to his own home. The name "Fehmgerichte" kept repeating itself in his brain like an incantation. He took the middle of the square and hesitated when he came to the narrow street down which his way lay. At the street corner he paused, laid his hand on the hilt of his sword and drew a deep breath.

"Is it possible," he muttered to himself, "that I am afraid? Am I at heart a coward? By the cross which is my protection," he cried, "if they wish to try their poniarding, they shall have an opportunity!"

And drawing his sword he plunged into the dark and narrow street, his footsteps ringing defiantly in the silence on the stone beneath him as he strode resolutely along. He passed rapidly through the city until he came to the northern gate. Here accosting his warders and being assured that all was well, he took the street which, bending like a bow, followed the wall until it came to the river. Once or twice he stopped, thinking himself followed, but the darkness was now so impenetrable that even if a pursuer had been behind him he was safe from detection if he kept step with his victim and paused when he did. The street widened as it approached the river, and Wilhelm became convinced that some one was treading in his footsteps. Clasping his sword hilt more firmly in his hand he wheeled about with unexpectedness that evidently took his follower by surprise, for he dashed across the street and sped fleetly towards the river. The glimpse Wilhelm got of him in the open space between the houses made him sure that he was once more on the track of von Brent, the emissary of Treves. The tables were now turned, the pursuer being the pursued, and Wilhelm set his teeth, resolved to put a sudden end to this continued espionage. Von Brent evidently remembered his former interception, and now kept a straight course. Trusting to the swiftness of his heels, he uttered no cry, but directed all his energies toward flight, and Wilhelm, equally silent, followed as rapidly.

Coming to the river, von Brent turned to the east, keeping in the middle of the thoroughfare. On the left hand side was a row of houses, on the right flowed the rapid Main. Some hundreds of yards further up there were houses on both sides of the street, and as the water of the river flowed against the walls of the houses to the right, Wilhelm knew there could be no escape that way. Surmising that his victim kept the middle of the street in order to baffle the man at his heels, puzzling him as to which direction the fugitive intended to bolt, Wilhelm, not to be deluded by such a device, ran close to the houses on the left, knowing that if von Brent turned to the right he would be speedily stopped by the Main. The race promised to reach a sudden conclusion, for

Wilhelm was perceptibly gaining on his adversary, when coming to the first house by the river the latter swerved suddenly, jumped to a door, pushed it open and was inside in the twinkling of an eye, but only barely in time to miss the sword thrust that followed him. Quick as thought Wilhelm placed his foot in such a position that the door could not be closed. Then setting his shoulder to the panels, he forced it open in spite of the resistance behind it. Opposition thus overborne by superior strength, Wilhelm heard the clatter of von Brent's footsteps down the dark passage, and next instant the door was closed with a bang, and it seemed to the young man that the house had collapsed upon him. He heard his sword snap and felt it break beneath him, and he was gagged and bound before he could raise a hand to help himself. Then when it was too late, he realised that he had allowed the heat and fervour of pursuit to overwhelm his judgment, and had jumped straight into the trap prepared for him. Von Brent returned with a lantern in his hand and a smile on his face, breathing quickly after his exertions. Wilhelm, huddled in a corner, saw a dozen stalwart ruffians grouped around him, most of them masked, but two or three with faces bare, their coverings having come off in the struggle. These slipped quickly out of sight, behind the others, as if not wishing to give clue for future recognition.

"Well, my Lord," said von Brent, smiling, "you see that gagging and binding is a game that two may play at."

There was no reply to this, first, because Wilhelm was temporarily in a speechless condition, and, second, because the proposition was not one to be contradicted.

"Take him to the Commitment Room," commanded von Brent.

Four of the onlookers lifted Wilhelm and carried him down a long stairway, across a landing and to the foot of a second flight of steps, where he was thrown into a dark cell, the dimensions of which he could not estimate. When the door was closed the prisoner lay with his head leaning against it, and for a time the silence was intense. By and by he found that by turning his head so that his ear was placed against the panel of the door, he heard distinctly the footfalls outside, and even a shuffling sound near him, which seemed to indicate that a man was on guard at the other side of the oak. Presently some one approached, and in spite of the low tones used, Wilhelm not only heard what was being said, but recognised the voice of von Brent, who evidently was his jailer.

"You have him safely then?"

"Gagged and bound, my Lord."

"Is he disarmed?"

"His sword was broken under him, my Lord, when we fell upon him."

"Very well. Remove the gag and place him with No. 13. Bar them in and listen to their conversation. I think they have never met, but I want to be sure of it."

"Is there not a chance that No. 13 may make himself known, my Lord?"

"No matter if he does. In fact, it is my object to have No. 13 and No. 14 known to each other, and yet be not aware that we have suspicion of their knowledge."

When the door of the cell was opened four guards came in. It was manifest they were not going to allow Wilhelm any chance to escape, and were prepared to overpower him should he attempt flight or resistance. The gag was taken from his mouth and the thongs which bound his legs were untied, and thus he was permitted to stand on his feet. Once outside his cell he saw that the subterranean region in which he found himself was of vast extent, resembling the crypt of a cathedral, the low roof being supported by pillars of tremendous circumference. From the direction in which he had been carried from the foot of the stairs he surmised, and quite accurately, that this cavern was under the bed of the river. Those who escorted him and those whom he met were masked. No torches illuminated the gloom of this sepulchral hall, but each individual carried, attached in some way to his belt, a small horn lantern, which gave for a little space around a dim uncertain light, casting weird shadows against the pillars of the cavern. Once or twice they met a man clothed in an apparently seamless cloak of black cloth, that covered the head and extended to the feet. Two holes in front of the face allowed a momentary glimpse of a pair of flashing eyes as the yellow light from the lanterns smote them. These grim figures were presumably persons of importance, for the guards stopped, and saluted, as each one approached, not going forward until he had silently passed them. When finally the door of the cell they sought was reached, the guards drew back the bolts, threw it open, and pushed Wilhelm into the apartment that had been designated for him. Before closing the door, however, one of the guards placed a lantern on the floor so that the fellow-prisoners might have a chance of seeing each other. Wilhelm beheld, seated on a pallet of straw, a man well past middle-age, his face smooth-shaven and of serious cast, yet having, nevertheless, a trace of irresolution in his weak chin. His costume was that of a mendicant monk, and his face seemed indicative of the severity of monastic rule. There was, however, a serenity of courage in his eye which seemed to betoken that he was a man ready to die for his opinions, if once his wavering chin allowed him to form them. Wilhelm remembering that priests were not allowed to join the order of the Fehmgerichte reflected that here was a man who probably, from his fearless denunciations of the order, had brought down upon himself the hatred of the secret tribunal, whose only penalty was that of death. The older man was the first to speak.

"So you also are a victim of the Fehmgerichte?"

"I have for some minutes suspected as much," replied von Schonburg.

"Were you arrested and brought here, or did you come here willingly?"

"Oh, I came here willingly enough. I ran half a league in my eagerness to reach this spot and fairly jumped into it," replied Wilhelm, with a bitter laugh.

"You were in such haste to reach this spot?" said the old man, sombrely, "what is your crime?"

"That I do not know, but I shall probably soon learn when I come before the court."

"Are you a member of the order, then?"

"No, I am not."

"In that case, it will require the oaths of twenty-one members to clear you, therefore, if you have not that many friends in the order I look upon you as doomed."

"Thank you. That is as God wills."

"Assuredly, assuredly. We are all in His hands," and the good man devoutedly crossed himself.

"I have answered your questions," said Wilhelm, "answer you some of mine. Who are you?"

"I am a seeker after light."

"Well, there it is," said Wilhelm, touching the lantern with his foot as he paced up and down the limits of the cell.

"Earthly light is but dim at best, it is the light of Heaven I search after."

"Well, I hope you may be successful in finding it. I know of no place where it is needed so much as here."

"You speak like a scoffer. I thought from what you said of God's will, that you were a religious man."

"I am a religious man, I hope, and I regret if my words seem lightly spoken.

"What action of man, think you then, is most pleasing to God?"

"That is a question which you, to judge by your garb, are more able to answer than I."

"Nay, nay, I want your opinion."

"Then in my opinion, the man most pleasing to God is he who does his duty here on earth."

"Ah! right, quite right," cried the older man, eagerly. "But there lies the core of the whole problem. What is duty; that is what I have spent my life trying to learn."

"Then at a venture I should say your life has been a useless one. Duty is as plain as the lighted lantern there before us. If you are a priest, fulfil your priestly office well; comfort the sick, console the dying, bury the dead. Tell your flock not to speculate too much on duty, but to try and accomplish the work in hand."

"But I am not a priest," faltered the other, rising slowly to his feet.

"Then if you are a soldier, strike hard for your King. Kill the man immediately before you, and if, instead, he kills you, be assured that the Lord will look after your soul when it departs through the rent thus made in your body."

"There is a ring of truth in that, but it sounds worldly. How can we tell that such action is pleasing to God? May it not be better to depend entirely on the Lord, and let Him strike your blows for you?"

"Never! What does He give you arms for but to protect your own head, and what does He give you swift limbs for if not to take your body out of reach when you are threatened with being overmatched? God must despise such a man as you speak of, and rightly so. I am myself a commander of soldiers, and if I had a lieutenant who trusted all to me and refused to strike a sturdy blow on his own behalf I should tear his badge from him and have him scourged from out the ranks."

"But may we not, by misdirected efforts, thwart the will of God?"

"Oh! the depths of human vanity! Thwart the will of God? What, a puny worm like you? You amaze me, sir, with your conceit, and I lose the respect for you which at first your garb engendered in my mind. Do your work manfully, and flatter not yourself that your most strenuous efforts are able to cross the design of the Almighty. My own poor belief is that He has patience with any but a coward and a loiterer."

The elder prisoner staggered into the centre of the room and raised his hands above his head.

"Oh, Lord, have mercy upon me," he cried. "Thou who hast brought light to me in this foul dungeon which was refused to me in the radiance of Thy Cathedral. Have mercy on me, oh, Lord, the meanest of Thy servants—a craven Emperor."

"The Emperor!" gasped Wilhelm, the more amazed because he had his Majesty in mind when he spoke so bitterly of neglected duty, unconsciously blaming his sovereign rather than his own rashness for the extreme predicament in which he found himself.

Before either could again speak the door suddenly opened wide, and a deep voice solemnly enunciated the words:

"Wilhelm of Schonburg, pretended Commander of his Majesty's forces, you are summoned to appear instantly before the court of the Holy Fehm, now in session and awaiting you."

CHAPTER VI. – THE HOLY FEHM

When the spokesman of the Fehmgerichte had finished his ominous summons, his attendants crowded round Wilhelm swiftly and silently as if to forestall any attempt at resistance either on his part or on the part of the Emperor. They hurried their victim immediately out of the cell and instantly barred the door on the remaining prisoner. First they crossed the low-roofed, thickly-pillared great hall, passing through a doorway at which two armed men stood guard, masked, as were all the others. The Judgment Hall of the dread Fehmgerichte was a room of about ten times the extent of the cell Wilhelm had just left, but still hardly of a size that would justify the term large. The walls and vaulted roof were of rough stone, and on the side opposite the entrance had been cut deeply the large letters S. S. G. G. A few feet distant from this lettered wall stood a long table, and between the wall and the table sat seven men. The Freigraf, as Wilhelm surmised him to be, occupied in the centre of this line a chair slightly more elevated than those of the three who sat on either hand. Seven staples had been driven into the interstices of the stones above the heads of the Court and from each staple hung a lighted lantern, which with those at the belts of the guard standing round, illuminated the dismal chamber fairly well. To the left of the Court was a block draped in black and beside it stood the executioner with his arms resting on the handle of his axe. In the ceiling above his head was an iron ring and from this ring depended a rope, the noose of which dangled at the shoulder of the headsman, for it was the benevolent custom of the Court to allow its victim a choice in the manner of his death. It was also a habit of the judges of this Court to sit until the sentence they had pronounced was carried out, and thus there could be no chance of mistake or rescue. No feature of any judge was visible except the eyes through the holes pierced for the purposes of vision in the long black cloaks which completely enveloped their persons.

As Wilhelm was brought to a stand before this assemblage, the Freigraf nodded his head and the guards in silence undid the thongs which pinioned together wrists and elbows, leaving the prisoner absolutely unfettered.—This done, the guard retreated backwards to the opposite wall, and Wilhelm stood alone before the seven sinister doomsmen. He expected that his examination, if the Court indulged in any such, would be begun by the Freigraf, but this was not the case. The last man to the left in the row had a small bundle of documents on the table before him. He rose to his feet, bowed low to his brother judges, and then with less deference to the prisoner. He spoke in a voice lacking any trace of loudness, but distinctly heard in every corner of the room because of the intense stillness. There was a sweet persuasiveness in the accents he used, and his sentences resembled those of a lady anxious not to give offence to the person addressed.

"Am I right in supposing you to be Wilhelm, lately of Schonburg, but now of Frankfort?"

"You are right."

"May I ask if you are a member of the Fehmgerichte?"

"I am not. I never heard of it until this afternoon."

"Who was then your informant regarding the order?"

"I refuse to answer."

The examiner inclined his head gracefully as if, while regretting the decision of the witness, he nevertheless bowed to it.

"Do you acknowledge his lordship the Archbishop of Mayence as your over lord?"

"Most assuredly."

"Have you ever been guilty of an act of rebellion or insubordination against his lordship?"

"My over-lord, the Archbishop of Mayence, has never preferred a request to me which I have refused."

"Pardon me, I fear I have not stated my proposition with sufficient clearness, and so you may have misunderstood the question. I had in my mind a specific act, and so will enter into further detail. Is it true that in the Wahlzimmer you entered the presence of your over-lord with a drawn sword in your hand, commanding a body of armed men lately outlaws of the Empire, thus intimidating your over-lord in the just exercise of his privileges and rights as an Elector?"

"My understanding of the Feudal law," said Wilhelm, "is that the commands of an over-lord are to be obeyed only in so far as they do not run counter to orders from a still higher authority."

"Your exposition of the law is admirable, and its interpretation stands exactly as you have stated it. Are we to understand then that you were obeying the orders of some person in authority who is empowered to exercise a jurisdiction over his lordship the Archbishop, similar to that which the latter in his turn claims over you?"

"That is precisely what I was about to state."

"Whose wishes were you therefore carrying out?

"Those of his Majesty the Emperor."

The examiner bowed with the utmost deference when the august name was mentioned.

"I have to thank you in the name of the Court," he went on, "for your prompt and comprehensive replies, which have thus so speedily enabled us to come to a just and honourable verdict, and it gives me pleasure to inform you that the defence you have made is one that cannot be gainsaid, and, therefore, with the exception of one slight formality, there is nothing more for us to do but to set you at liberty and ask pardon for the constraint we regret having put upon you, and further to request that you take oath that neither to wife nor child, father nor mother, sister nor brother, fire nor wind, will you reveal anything that has happened to you; that you will conceal it from all that the sun shines on and from all that the rain wets, and from every being between heaven and earth. And now before our doors are thus opened I have to beg that you will favour the Court with the privilege of examining the commission that his Majesty the Emperor has signed."

"You cannot expect me to carry my commission about on my person, more especially as I had no idea I should be called upon to undergo examination upon it."

"Such an expectation would certainly be doomed to disappointment, but you are doubtless able to tell us where the document lies, and I can assure you that, wherever it is placed, an emissary of this order will speedily fetch it, whether, it is concealed in palace or in hut. Allow me to ask you then, where this commission is?"

"I cannot tell you."

"Do you mean you cannot, or you will not?"

"Take it whichever way you please, it is a matter of indifference to me."

The examiner folded his arms under his black cloak and stood for some moments in silence, looking reproachfully at the prisoner. At last he spoke in a tone which seemed to indicate that he was pained at the young man's attitude:

"I sincerely trust I am mistaken in supposing that you refuse absolutely to assist this Court in the securing of a document which not only stands between you and your liberty, but also between you and your death."

"Oh, a truce to this childish and feigned regret," cried Wilhelm with rude impatience. "I pray you end the farce with less of verbiage and of pretended justice. You have his Majesty here a prisoner. You have, through my own folly, my neck at the mercy of your axe or your rope. There stands the executioner eager for his gruesome work. Finish that which you have already decided upon, and as sure as there is a God in heaven there will be quick retribution for the crimes committed in this loathsome dungeon."

The examiner deplored the introduction of heat into a discussion that required the most temperate judgment.

"But be assured," he said, "that the hurling of unfounded accusations against this honourable body will not in the least prejudice their members in dealing with your case."

"I know it," said Wilhelm with a sneering laugh.

"We have been informed that no such commission exists, that the document empowering you to take instant command of the Imperial troops rests in the hands of the wife of his Majesty the Emperor and is unsigned."

"If you know that, then why do you ask me so many questions about it?"

"In the sincere hope that by the production of the document itself, you may be able to repudiate so serious an accusation. You admit then that you have acted without the shelter of a commission from his Majesty?"

"I admit nothing."

The examiner looked up and down the row of silent figures as much as to say, "I have done my best; shall any further questions be put?" There being no response to this the examiner said, still without raising his voice:

"There is a witness in this case, and I ask him to stand forward."

A hooded and cloaked figure approached the table.

"Are you a member of the Fehmgerichte?"

"I am."

"In good and honourable standing?"

"In good and honourable standing."

"You swear by the order to which you belong that the evidence you give shall be truth without equivocation and without mental reservation?"

"I swear it."

"Has the prisoner a commission signed by the Emperor empowering him to command the Imperial troops?"

"He has not, and never has had such a commission. A document was made out and sent three times to his Majesty for signature; to-day it was returned for the third time unsigned."

"Prisoner, do you deny that statement?"

"I neither deny nor affirm."

Wilhelm was well aware that his fate was decided upon. Even if he had appeared before a regularly constituted court of the Empire instead of at the bar of an underground secret association, the verdict must inevitably have gone against him, so long as the Emperor's signature was not appended to the document which would have legalised his position.

"It would appear then," went on the examiner, "that in the action you took against your immediate over-lord, the Archbishop of Mayence, you were unprotected by the mandate of the Emperor. Freigraf and Freischoffen have heard question and answer. With extreme reluctance I am compelled to announce to this honourable body, that nothing now remains except to pronounce the verdict."

With this the examiner sat down, and for a few moments there was silence, then the Freigraf enunciated in a low voice the single word:

"Condemned."

And beginning at the right hand, each member of the Court pronounced the word "Condemned."

Wilhelm listened eagerly to the word, expecting each moment to hear the voice of one or other of the Archbishops, but in this he was disappointed. The low tone universally used by each speaker gave a certain monotony of sound which made it almost impossible to distinguish one voice from another. This evident desire for concealment raised a suspicion in the young man's mind that probably each member of the Court did not know who his neighbours were. When the examiner at the extreme left had uttered the word "Condemned" the Freigraf again spoke:

"Is there any reason why the sentence just pronounced be not immediately carried out?"

The examiner again rose to his feet and said quietly, but with great respect:

"My Lord, I ask that this young man be not executed immediately, but on the contrary, be taken to his cell, there to be held during the pleasure of the Court."

There seemed to be a murmured dissent to this, but a whispered explanation passed along the line and the few that had at first objected, nodded their heads in assent.

"Our rule cannot be set aside," said the Freigraf, "unless with unanimous consent. Does any member demur?"

No protests being made the Freigraf ordered Wilhelm to be taken to a cell, which was accordingly done.

The young man left alone in the darkness felt a pleasure in being able to stretch his arms once more, and he paced up and down the narrow limits of his cell, wondering what the next move would be in this mysterious drama. In the Judgment Chamber he had abandoned all hope, and had determined that when the order was given to seize him he would pluck the dagger of the order from the inside of his doublet, and springing over the table, kill one or more of these illegal judges before he was overpowered. The sudden change in tactics persuaded him that something else was required of him rather than the death which seemed so imminent. It was palpable that several members of the Court at least were unacquainted with the designs of the master mind which was paramount in his prosecution. They had evinced surprise when the examiner had demanded postponement of the execution. There was something behind all this that betrayed the crafty hand of the Archbishop of Treves. He was not long left in doubt. The door of the cell opened slowly and the pale rays of a lantern illuminated the blackness which surrounded him. The young man stopped in his walk and awaited developments. There entered to him one of the cloak-enveloped figures, who might, or might not, be a member of the Holy Court. Wilhelm thought that perhaps his visitor was the examiner, but the moment the silence was broken, in spite of the fact that the speaker endeavoured to modulate his tones as the others had done, the young man knew the incomer was not the person who had questioned him.

"We are somewhat loth," the intruder began, "to cut short the career of one so young as you are, and one who gives promise of becoming a notable captain."

"What have you seen of me," inquired Wilhelm, "that leads you to suppose I have the qualities of a capable officer in me?"

The other did not reply for a moment or two; then he said slowly:

"I do not say that I have seen anything to justify such a conclusion, but I have heard of your action in the Wahlzimmer, and by the account given, I judge you to be a young man of resource."

"I am indebted to you for the good opinion you express. It is quite in your power to set me free, and then the qualities you are kind enough to commend, may have an opportunity for development."

"Alas!" said the visitor, "it is not in my power to release you; that lies entirely with yourself."

"You bring comforting news. What is the price?"

"You are asked to become a member of the Fehmgerichte."

"I should suppose that to be easily accomplished, as I am now a partaker of its hospitality. What else?"

"The remaining proviso is that you take service, with his lordship, the Archbishop of Treves, and swear entire allegiance to him."

"I am already in the service of the Emperor."

"It has just been proven that you are not."

"How could the Archbishop expect faithful service from me, if I prove traitor to the one I deem my master?"

"The Archbishop will probably be content to take the risk of that."

"Are you commissioned to speak for the Archbishop?"

"I am."

"Are you one of the Archbishop's men?"

"My disposition towards him is friendly; I cannot say that I am one of his men."

"Granting, then, that I took service with the Archbishop to save my life, what would he expect me to do?"

"To obey him in all things."

"Ah, be more explicit, as the examiner said. I am not a man to enter into a bargain blindly. I must know exactly what is required of me."

"It is probable that your first order would be to march your army from Frankfort to Treves. Would the men follow you, do you think?"

"Undoubtedly. The men will follow wherever I choose to lead them. Another question. What becomes of the Emperor in case I make this bargain?"

"That question it is impossible at the present moment, to answer. The Court of the Holy Fehm is now awaiting my return, and when I take my place on the bench the Emperor will be called upon to answer for his neglect of duty."

"Nevertheless you may hazard a guess regarding his fate."

"I hazard this guess then, that his fate will depend largely upon himself, just as your fate depends upon yourself."

"I must see clearly where I am going, therefore I request you to be more explicit. What will the Court demand of the Emperor that he may save his life?"

"You are questioning me touching the action of others; therefore, all I can do is merely to surmise. My supposition is that if the Emperor promises to abdicate he will be permitted to pass unscathed from the halls of the Fehmgerichte."

"And should he refuse?"

"Sir, I am already at the end of my patience through your numerous questions," and as the voice rose in something approaching anger, Wilhelm seemed to recognise its ring. "I came here, not to answer your questions, but to have you answer mine. What is your decision?"

"My decision is that you are a confessed traitor; die the death of such!"

Wilhelm sprang forward and buried the dagger of the Fehmgerichte into the heart of the man before him. His action was so unexpected that the victim could make no motion to defend himself. So truly was the fierce blow dealt that the doomed man, without a cry or even a groan, sank in his death collapse at the young man's feet in a heap on the floor.

Wilhelm, who thought little of taking any man's life in a fair fight, shuddered as he gazed at the helpless bundle at his feet; a moment before, this uncouth heap stood erect, a man like himself, conversing with him, then the swift blow and the resulting huddle of clay.

"Oh, God above me, Over-lord of all, I struck for my King, yet I feel myself an assassin. If I am, indeed, a murderer in Thy sight, wither me where I stand, and crush me to the ground, companion to this dead body."

For a few moments Wilhelm stood rigid, his face uplifted, listening to the pulsations in his own throat and the strident beatings of his own heart. No bolt from heaven came to answer his supplication. Stooping, he, with some difficulty, drew the poniard from its resting-place. The malignant ingenuity of its construction had caused its needle point to penetrate the chain armour, while its keen double edge cut link after link of the hard steel as it sunk into the victim's breast. The severed ends of the links now clutched the blade as if to prevent its removal. Not a drop of blood followed its exit, although it had passed directly through the citadel of life itself. Again concealing the weapon within his doublet, a sudden realisation of the necessity for speed overcame the assaulter. He saw before him a means of escape. He had but to don the all-concealing cloak and walk out of this subterranean charnel house by the way he had entered it, if he could but find the foot of the stairs, down which they had carried him. Straightening out the body he pulled the cloak free from it, thus exposing the face to the yellow light of the lantern. His heart stood still as he saw that the man he had killed was no other than that exalted Prince of the Church, the venerable Archbishop of Treves. He drew the body to the pallet of straw in the corner of the cell, and there, lying on its face, he left it. A moment later he was costumed as a high priest of the order of the Fehmgerichte. Taking the lantern in his hand he paused before the closed door. He could not remember whether or not he had heard the bolts shot after the Archbishop had entered. Conning rapidly in his mind the startling change in the situation, he stood there until he had recovered command of himself, resolved that if possible no mistake on his part should now mar his chances of escape, and in this there was no thought of saving his own life, but merely a determination to get once more into the streets of Frankfort, rally his men, penetrate into these subterranean regions, and rescue the Emperor alive. He pushed with all his might against the door, and to his great relief the heavy barrier swung slowly round on its hinges. Once outside he pushed it shut again, and was startled by two guards springing to his assistance, one of them saying:

"Shall we thrust in the bolts, my Lord?"

"Yes," answered Wilhelm in the low tone which all, costumed as he was, had used. He turned away but was dismayed to find before him two brethren of the order arrayed in like manner to himself, who had evidently been waiting for him.

"What is the result of the conference? Does he consent?"

Rapidly Wilhelm had to readjust events in his own mind to meet this unexpected emergency.

"No," he replied slowly, "he does not consent, at least, not just at the moment. He has some scruples regarding his loyalty to the Emperor."

"Those scruples will be speedily removed then, when we remove his Majesty. The other members of the Court are but now awaiting us in the Judgment Chamber. Let us hasten there, and make a quick disposal of the Emperor."

Wilhelm saw that there was no possibility of retreat. Any attempt at flight would cause instant alarm and the closing of the exits, then both the Emperor and himself would be caught like rats in a trap, yet there was almost equal danger in entering the Council Chamber. He had not the remotest idea which seat at the table he should occupy, and he knew that a mistake in placing himself would probably lead to discovery. He lagged behind, but the others persistently gave him precedence, which seemed to indicate that they knew the real quality of the man they supposed him to be. He surmised that his seat was probably that of the Freigraf in the centre, but on crossing the threshold past the saluting guards, he saw that the Freigraf occupied the elevated seat, having at his left three Freischoffen, while the remaining seats at his right were unoccupied. It was a space of extreme anxiety when his two companions stopped to allow him to go first. He dared not take the risk of placing himself wrongly at the board. There was scant time for consideration, and Wilhelm speedily came to a decision. It was merely one risk to take where several were presented, and he chose that which seemed to be the safest. Leaning towards his companions he said quietly:

"I beg of you, be seated. I have a few words to address to the Holy Court."

The two inclined their heads in return, and one of them in passing him murmured the scriptural words, "The first shall be last," which remark still further assisted in reversing Wilhelm's former opinion and convinced him that the identity of the Archbishop was known to them. When they were seated, the chair at the extreme right was the only one vacant, and Wilhelm breathed easier, having nothing further to fear from that source, if he could but come forth scatheless from his speech.

"I have to acquaint the Court of the Holy Fehm," he said, speaking audibly, but no more, "that my mission to the cell of the prisoner who has just left us, resulted partly in failure and partly in success. The young man has some hesitation in placing himself in open opposition to the Emperor. I therefore suggest that we go on with our deliberations, leaving the final decision of his case until a later period."

To this the Court unanimously murmured the word: "Agreed," and Wilhelm took his place at the table.

"Bring in prisoner No. 13," said the Freigraf, and a few moments later the Emperor of Germany stood before the table.

He regarded the dread tribunal with a glance of haughty scorn while countenance and demeanour exhibited a dignity which Wilhelm had fancied was lacking during their interview in the cell.

The examiner rose to his feet and in the same suave tones he had used in questioning Wilhelm, propounded the usual formal interrogatory regarding name and quality. When he was asked:

"Are you a member of the Holy Order of the Fehmgerichte?" the Emperor's reply seemed to cause some consternation among the judges.

"I am not only a member of the Fehmgerichte, but by its constitution, I am the head of it, and I warn you that any action taken by this Court without my sanction, is, by the statutes of the order, illegal."

The examiner paused in his questioning apparently taken aback by this assertion, and looked towards the Freigraf as if awaiting a decision before proceeding further.

"We acknowledge freely," said the Freigraf, "that you are the figure-head of the order, and that in all matters pertaining to a change of constitution your consent would probably be necessary, but stretching your authority to its utmost limit, it does not reach to the Courts of the Holy Fehm, which have before now sat in judgment on the highest in the land. For more than a century the position of the Emperor as head of the Fehmgerichte has been purely nominal, and I know of no precedent where the ruler of the land has interfered with the proceedings of the secret Court. We avow allegiance to the actual head of the order, who is the Duke of Westphalia."

"Is the Duke of Westphalia here present?"

"That is a question improper for you to ask."

"If the Duke of Westphalia is one of the members of this Court, I command him by the oath which he took at his installation, to descend from his place and render his seat to me, the head of this order."

"The nominal head," corrected the Freigraf.

"The actual head," persisted the prisoner. "The position remained nominal only because the various occupants did not choose to exercise the authority vested in them. It is my pleasure to resume the function which has too long remained in abeyance, thus allowing inferior officers to pretend to a power which is practical usurpation, and which, according to the constitution of our order, is not to be tolerated. Disobey at your peril. I ask the Archbishop of Cologne, Duke of Westphalia, as the one, high vassal of the Empire, as the other, my subordinate in the Fehmgerichte, to stand forth and salute his chief."

Wilhelm's heart beat rapidly underneath his black cloak as he saw this spectacle of helpless prisoner defying a power, which, in its sphere of action, was almost omnipotent. It was manifest that the Emperor's trenchant sentences had disturbed more than one member of the convention, and even the Freigraf glanced in perplexity towards the supposed Archbishop of Treves as if for a hint anent the answer that should be given. As if in response to the silent appeal, Wilhelm rose slowly to his feet, while the examiner seated himself.

"It is my privilege," he began, "on behalf of my fellow members, to inform the prisoner that the Court of the Holy Fehm has ever based its action on the broad principles of eternal justice."

A sarcastic smile wreathed the lips of the Emperor at this. Wilhelm went on unheeding.

"A point of law has been raised by the prisoner, which, I think, at least merits our earnest consideration, having regard for the future welfare of this organisation, and being anxious not to allow any precedent to creep in, which may work to the disadvantage of those who follow us. In order that our deliberations may have that calm impartiality which has ever distinguished them, I ask unanimous consent to my suggestion that the prisoner be taken back to his cell until we come to a decision regarding the matter in dispute."

This proposition being agreed to without a dissenting voice, the prisoner was removed from the room and the eyes of all the judges were turned towards Wilhelm. The Freigraf was the first to break the silence.

"Although I have agreed to the removal of the prisoner," he said, "yet I see not the use of wasting so many words on him. While there is undoubted wisdom in winning to our side the man who controls the army, there seems to me little to gain in prolonging discussion with the Emperor, who is a nonentity at best, and has no following. The path to the throne must be cleared, and there is but one way of doing it."

"Two, I think," murmured Wilhelm.

"What other than by this prisoner's death?"

"His abdication would suffice."

"But, as you know, he has already refused to abdicate."

"Ah, that was before he saw the executioner standing here. I think he is now in a condition to reconsider his determination. Thus we will avoid discussion of the knotty points which he raised, and which I, for one, would prefer to see remain where they are. The moment he consents to abdicate, the commander of the forces is willing to swear allegiance to us. It must not be forgotten that even if we execute these two men we have still the troops who hold the city of Frankfort to reckon with, and although their leader may have disappeared, the young man has some sturdy lieutenants who will give us trouble."

"What do you propose?" asked the Freigraf.

"If the colleague at my left will accompany me, we will visit the prisoner and may have some proposals to submit to you on our return."

This being acceded to, the two left the Judgment Chamber and proceeded slowly to the cell of No. 13. On the way thither Wilhelm said to his companion:

"As the prisoner may be on his guard if we enter together, I prefer to sound him first alone, and at the proper moment, if you stay outside the door of the cell, I shall summon you to enter."

This meeting the sanction of Wilhelm's companion, the young man entered the cell alone, carefully closing the door behind him.

"Your Majesty," he whispered, "the situation is extremely critical, and I entreat you to maintain silence while I make explanation to you. I am Wilhelm, the loyal commander of the Imperial forces, your Majesty's most devoted servant."

"Are you then," said the amazed monarch, "also a member of the Fehmgerichte? I thought you came here as a prisoner, and, like myself, a victim."

Wilhelm drew off over his head the cloak which enveloped him, leaving his limbs free, standing thus in his own proper person before the Emperor.

"I was, indeed, a prisoner, and was visited in my cell by the Archbishop of Treves. It was in his robe that I emerged from my cell undetected, hoping to escape and bring rescue to your Majesty, but other brethren were awaiting me outside, and I found myself compelled to sit in the Court before which you made such an able defence."

"It was you, then, who proposed that I should be taken back to my cell?"

"Yes, your Majesty. And now a colleague remains outside this door, who waits, expecting a summons to enter, but first I came to give warning to your Majesty that you may make no outcry, if you should see what appears to be two brothers of the order struggling together."

"I shall keep strict silence. Is the Archbishop of Treves then a prisoner in your cell?"

"He is, I assure you, a fast prisoner."

"You propose that I should don the cloak of the incomer, and that thus we make our escape together. We must be in haste, then, for if the Archbishop releases himself from his bonds, he may produce such an uproar in his cell that suspicion will be aroused."

"The bonds in which I left the Archbishop of Treves will hold him firm until we are outside this nest of vipers. And now, your Majesty, I beg you to put on this cloak which I have been wearing, which will leave me free speedily to overpower our visitor."

The Emperor arrayed himself and stood, as he was fully entitled to do, a fully costumed member of the Fehmgerichte. Wilhelm opened the door and said softly:

"Enter, brother, that I may learn if the arrangements just made are confirmed by your wisdom."

The light within had been placed at the further end of the cell, and the visitor's own lantern gave but scant illumination. The moment the door was firmly closed Wilhelm sprang upon him and bore him to the ground. If the assaulted man attempted to make any sound, it was muffled by the folds of his own cloak. A moment later, however, Wilhelm got a firm grip on his bare throat, and holding him thus, pulled away his disguise from him, revealing the pallid face of the Archbishop of Mayence. The young man plucked the dagger from the inside of his doublet and placed it at the breast of the prostrate man.

"If you make the slightest sound," he whispered, "I shall bury this dagger in your heart. It is the weapon of the Fehmgerichte and you know it will penetrate chain armour."

It was evident that the stricken Archbishop was much too frightened to do anything to help himself, and Wilhelm unbuckling his own empty sword-belt, proceeded to tie his trembling limbs. The Emperor whispered:

"The cords which bound me are still here, as well as the gag which silenced me."

Wilhelm put those instruments of tyranny to immediate use, and shortly the Archbishop was a helpless silent heap in the further corner of the room. Wilhelm and the Emperor each with a lantern, and each indistinguishable from other members of the secret organisation, pushed open the door and emerged from the cell. Closing the door again, Wilhelm said to the guard:

"Bolt this portal firmly and allow no one to enter who does not give you this password."

The young man stooped and whispered into the ear of the guard the word "Elsa." The two fugitives then walked slowly along the great hall, the young man peering anxiously to his right for any sign of the stairway by which he had descended. They passed numerous doors, all closed, and at last Wilhelm began to wonder if one of these covered the exit which he sought. Finally they came to the end of the large hall without seeing trace of any outlet, and Wilhelm became conscious of the fact that getting free from this labyrinth was like to prove more difficult than the entering had been. Standing puzzled, not knowing where next to turn, aware that precious time was being wasted fruitlessly, Wilhelm saw a man masked and accoutred as a guard approach them.

"Is there anything in which I can pleasure your Lordships?" he asked deferentially.

"Yes," said Wilhelm, "we desire to have a breath of fresh air; where is the exit?"

"If your Lordship has the password, you may go out by the entrance in the city. If you have not the word, then must you use the exit without the wall, which is a long walk from here."

"That does not matter," replied Wilhelm, "it is the country air we wish to breathe."

"I cannot leave my post, but I shall get one who will guide you."

So saying, the man left them for several anxious minutes, going into a room that apparently was used as guard-house, and reappearing with a man who rubbed his eyes sleepily, as if newly awakened. Then the first guard drew bolts from a stout door and pulled it open, revealing a dark chasm like the entrance to a cell. Both Wilhelm and the Emperor viewed this black enigma with deep suspicion, but their guide with his lantern plunged into it and they followed, after which the door was closed and barred behind them.

It was, indeed, as the first man had said, a long walk, as Wilhelm knew it must be if it extended under the western gate and out into the country. The passage was so narrow that two could not walk abreast, and frequently the arched ceiling was so low that the guide ahead warned them to stoop as they came on. At last he reached the foot of a stairway, and was about to mount when Wilhelm said to him:

"Stand here till we return. Allow no one to pass who does not give you this word," and again he whispered the word "Elsa" in the man's ear.

To the dismay of Wilhelm, the Emperor addressed the guard:

"Are there many prisoners within?"

"There are two only," replied the man, "numbers 13 and 14. I helped to carry No. 14 down the stair, and am glad his sword broke beneath him as he fell, for, indeed, we had trouble enough with him as it was."

Here Wilhelm took the liberty of touching the Emperor on the arm as if to warn him that such discourse was untimely and dangerous. With beating heart the young man led the way up the stairs, and at the top of the second flight, came into what seemed to be the vestibule of a house, in which, on benches round the wall, there sat four men seemingly on guard, who immediately sprang to their feet when they saw the ghostly apparitions before them.

"Unbar the door," said Wilhelm, quietly, in the tone of one whose authority is not to be disputed. "Close it after us and allow none to enter or emerge who does not give you the word 'Elsa.'"

This command was so promptly obeyed that Wilhelm could scarcely believe they had won so easily to the outer air. The house stood alone on the bank of the river at the end of a long garden which extended to the road. Facing the thoroughfare and partly concealing the house from any chance straggler was a low building which Wilhelm remembered was used as a wayside drinking-place, in which wine, mostly of a poor quality, was served to thirsty travellers. The gate to the street appeared deserted, but as the two approached by the walk leading from the house, a guard stood out from the shadow of the wall, scrutinised for a moment their appearance, then saluting, held the gate open for them.

Once on the road, the two turned towards the city, whose black wall barred their way some distance ahead, and whose towers and spires stood out dimly against the starlit sky. A great silence, broken only by the soothing murmur of the river, lay on the landscape. Wilhelm cast a glance aloft at the star-sprinkled dome of heaven, and said:

"I judge it to be about an hour after midnight."

"It may be so," answered the Emperor, "I have lost all count of time.

"Has your Majesty been long in prison?"

"That I do not know. I may have lain there two days or a dozen. I had no means of measuring the length of my imprisonment."

"May I ask your Majesty in what manner you were lured into the halls of the Fehmgerichte?"

"It was no lure. While I lay asleep at night in the cloisters by the Cathedral I was bound and gagged, carried through the dark streets helpless on a litter and finally flung into the cell in which you found me."

"May I further inquire what your Majesty's intentions are regarding the fulfilment of the duties imposed upon you by your high office?"

There was a long pause before the Emperor replied, then he said:

"Why do you ask?"

"Because, your Majesty, I have on several occasions imperilled my life for an Emperor who does not rule, who has refused even to sign my commission as officer of his troops."

"Your commission was never sent to me."

"I beg your Majesty's pardon, but it was sent three times to you in the cloisters of the Cathedral, and returned three times unsigned."

"Then it is as I suspected," returned the Emperor, "the monks must have connived at my capture. I have pleasure in confirming your appointment. I am sure that the command could not be in more capable hands. And in further reply to your question, if God permits me to see the light of day, I shall be an emperor who rules."

"It delights my heart to hear you say so. And now I ask, as a favour, that you allow me to deal untrammelled with the Fehmgerichte."

"I grant that most willingly."

By this time they were almost under the shadow of the great wall of the city, and Wilhelm, stopping, said to the Emperor:

"I think it well that we now divest ourselves of these disguises."

They had scarcely thrown their cloaks behind the bushes at the side of the road when they were accosted by the guard at the top of the wall.

"Halt! Who approaches the gate?"

Wilhelm strode forward.

"Is Gottlieb at the guard-house or at the barracks?" he asked.

"He is at the guard-house," replied the sentinel, recognising the questioner.

"Then arouse him immediately, and open the gates."

"Gottlieb," said Wilhelm, when once within the walls, "take a score of men with you and surround the first house on the margin of the river up this street. I shall accompany you so that there may be no mistake. Send another score under a trusty leader to the house which stands alone outside of the gates also on the margin of the stream. Give orders that the men are to seize any person who attempts to enter or to come out; kill if necessary, but let none escape you. Let a dozen men escort me to the Palace."

Having seen the Emperor safely housed in the Palace, Wilhelm returned quickly to the place where Gottlieb and his score held guard over the town entrance of the cellars he had quitted.

"Gottlieb, are you fully awake?" asked Wilhelm.

"Oh, yes, master; awake and ready for any emergency."

"Then send for some of your most stalwart sappers with tools to break through a stone wall, and tell them to bring a piece of timber to batter in this door."

When the men arrived three blows from the oaken log sent the door shattering from its hinges. Wilhelm sprang at once over the prostrate portal, but not in time to prevent the flight of the guard down the stairway. Calling the sappers to the first landing, and pointing to the stone wall on the right:

"Break through that for me," he cried.

"Master," expostulated Gottlieb, "if you break through that wall I warn you that the river will flow in."

"Such is my intention, Gottlieb, and a gold piece to each man who works as he has never wrought before."

For a few moments there was nothing heard but the steady ring of iron on stone as one by one the squares were extracted, the water beginning to ooze in as the energetic sappers reached the outer course. At last the remaining stones gave way, carried in with a rush by the torrent.

"Save yourselves!" cried Wilhelm, standing knee deep in the flood and not stepping out until each man had passed him. There was a straining crash of rending timber, and Gottlieb, dashing down, seized his master by the arm, crying:

"My Lord, my Lord, the house is about to fall!"

With slight loss of time commander and lieutenant stood together in the street and found that the latter's panic was unwarranted, for the house, although it trembled dangerously and leaned perceptibly toward the river, was stoutly built of hewn stone. Grey daylight now began to spread over the city, but still Wilhelm stood there listening to the inrush of the water.

"By the great wine tub of Hundsrück!" exclaimed Gottlieb in amazement, "that cellar is a large one. It seems to thirst for the whole flood of the Main."

"Send a messenger," cried Wilhelm, "to the house you are guarding outside the gates and discover for me whether your men have captured any prisoners."

It was broad daylight when the messenger returned, and the torrent down the stair had become a rippling surface of water at the level of the river, showing that all the cavern beneath was flooded.

"Well, messenger, what is your report?" demanded his commander.

"My Lord, the officer in charge says that a short time ago the door of the house was blown open as if by a strong wind; four men rushed out and another was captured in the garden; all were pinioned and gagged, as you commanded."

"Are the prisoners men of quality or common soldiers?"

"Common soldiers, my Lord."

"Very well; let them be taken to the prison. I will visit them later in the day."

As Wilhelm, thoroughly fatigued after a night so exciting, walked the streets of Frankfort toward his home the bells of the city suddenly began to ring a merry peal, and, as if Frankfort had become awakened by the musical clangor, windows were raised and doors opened, while citizens inquired of each other the meaning of the clangor, a question which no one seemed prepared to answer.

Reaching his own house, Wilhelm found Elsa awaiting him with less of anxiety on her face than he had expected.

"Oh, Wilhelm!" she cried, "what a fright you gave me, and not until I knew where you were, did any peace come to my heart."

"You knew where I was?" said Wilhelm in amazement. "Where was I, then?"

"You were with the Emperor, of course. That is why the bells are ringing; the Emperor has returned, as you know, and is resolved to take his proper place at the head of the state, much to the delight of the Empress, I can assure you. But what an anxious time we spent until shortly after midnight, when the Emperor arrived and told us you had been with him."

"How came you to be at the Palace?"

"It happened in this way. You had hardly left the court last night when his lordship the Archbishop of Cologne came and seemed anxious about the welfare of the Emperor."

"The Archbishop of Cologne! Is he still there or did he go elsewhere?"

"He is still there, and was there when the Emperor came in. Why do you ask so eagerly? Is there anything wrong?"

"Not so far as the Archbishop is concerned, apparently. He has kept his word and so there is one less high office vacant. Well, what did the Archbishop say?"

"He wished to see you, and so the Empress sent for you, but search as we would, you were nowhere to be found. On hearing this I became alarmed and went at once to the Palace. The Archbishop seemed in deep trouble, but he refused to tell the Empress the cause of it, and so increased our anxiety. However, all was right when the Emperor came, and now they are ringing the bells, for he is to appear before the people on the balcony of the Romer, as if he were newly crowned. We must make haste if we are to see him."

Wilhelm escorted his wife to the square before the Romer, but so dense was the cheering crowd that it was impossible for him to force a way through. They were in time to see the Emperor appear on the balcony, and Wilhelm, raising his sword aloft, shouted louder than any in that throng, Elsa herself waving a scarf above her head in the enthusiasm of the moment.

THE COUNT'S APOLOGY

The fifteen nobles, who formed the Council of State for the Moselle Valley, stood in little groups in the Rittersaal of Winneburg's Castle, situated on a hill-top in the Ender Valley, a league or so from the waters of the Moselle. The nobles spoke in low tones together, for a greater than they were present, no other than their over-lord, the Archbishop of Treves, who, in his stately robes of office, paced up and down the long room, glancing now and then through the narrow windows which gave a view down the Ender Valley.

There was a trace of impatience in his Lordship's bearing, and well there might be, for here was the Council of State in assemblage, yet their chairman was absent, and the nobles stood there helplessly, like a flock of sheep whose shepherd is missing. The chairman was the Count of Winneburg, in whose castle they were now collected, and his lack of punctuality was thus a double discourtesy, for he was host as well as president.

Each in turn had tried to soothe the anger of the Archbishop, for all liked the Count of Winneburg, a bluff and generous-hearted giant, who would stand by his friends against all comers, was the quarrel his own or no. In truth little cared the stalwart Count of Winneburg whose quarrel it was so long as his arm got opportunity of wielding a blow in it. His Lordship of Treves had not taken this championship of the absent man with good grace, and now strode apart from the group, holding himself haughtily; muttering, perhaps prayers, perhaps something else.

When one by one the nobles had arrived at Winneburg's Castle, they were informed that its master had gone hunting that morning, saying he would return in time for the mid-day meal, but nothing had been heard of him since, although mounted messengers had been sent forth, and the great bell in the southern tower had been set ringing when the Archbishop arrived. It was the general opinion that Count Winneburg, becoming interested in the chase, had forgotten all about the Council, for it was well known that the Count's body was better suited for athletic sports or warfare than was his mind for the consideration of questions of State, and the nobles, themselves of similar calibre, probably liked him none the less on that account.

Presently the Archbishop stopped in his walk and faced the assemblage. "My Lords," he said, "we have already waited longer than the utmost stretch of courtesy demands. The esteem in which Count Winneburg holds our deliberations is indicated by his inexcusable neglect of a duty conferred upon him by you, and voluntarily accepted by him. I shall therefore take my place in his chair, and I call upon you to seat yourselves at the Council table."

Saying which the Archbishop strode to the vacant chair, and seated himself in it at the head of the board. The nobles looked one at the other with some dismay, for it was never their intention that the Archbishop should preside over their meeting, the object of which was rather to curb that high prelate's ambition, than to confirm still further the power he already held over them.

When, a year before, these Councils of State had been inaugurated, the Archbishop had opposed them, but, finding that the Emperor was inclined to defer to the wishes of his nobles, the Lord of Treves had insisted upon his right to be present during the deliberations, and this right the Emperor had conceded. He further proposed that the meeting should be held at his own castle of Cochem, as being conveniently situated midway between Coblentz and Treves, but to this the nobles had, with fervent unanimity, objected. Cochem Castle, they remembered, possessed strong walls and deep dungeons, and they had no desire to trust themselves within the lion's jaws, having little faith in his Lordship's benevolent intentions towards them.

The Emperor seemed favourable to the selection of Cochem as a convenient place of meeting, and the nobles were nonplussed, because they could not give their real reason for wishing to avoid it, and the Archbishop continued to press the claims of Cochem as being of equal advantage to all.

"It is not as though I asked them to come to Treves," said the Archbishop, "for that would entail a long journey upon those living near the Rhine, and in going to Cochem I shall myself be called upon to travel as far as those who come from Coblentz."

The Emperor said:

"It seems a most reasonable selection, and, unless some strong objection be urged, I shall confirm the choice of Cochem."

The nobles were all struck with apprehension at these words, and knew not what to say, when suddenly, to their great delight, up spoke the stalwart Count of Winneburg.

"Your Majesty," he said, "my Castle stands but a short league from Cochem, and has a Rittersaal as large as that in the pinnacled palace owned by the Archbishop. It is equally convenient for all concerned, and every gentleman is right welcome to its hospitality. My cellars are well filled with good wine, and my larders are stocked with an abundance of food. All that can be urged in favour of Cochem applies with equal truth to the Schloss Winneburg. If, therefore, the members of the Council will accept of my roof, it is theirs."

The nobles with universal enthusiasm cried:

"Yes, yes; Winneburg is the spot."

The Emperor smiled, for he well knew that his Lordship of Treves was somewhat miserly in the dispensing of his hospitality. He preferred to see his guests drink the wine of a poor vintage rather than tap the cask which contained the yield of a good year. His Majesty smiled, because he imagined his nobles thought of the replenishing of their stomachs, whereas they were concerned for the safety of their necks; but seeing them unanimous in their choice, he nominated Schloss Winneburg as the place of meeting, and so it remained.

When, therefore, the Archbishop of Treves set himself down in the ample chair, to which those present had, without a dissenting vote, elected Count Winneburg, distrust at once took hold of them, for they were ever jealous of the encroachments of their over-lord. The Archbishop glared angrily around him, but no man moved from where he stood.

"I ask you to be seated. The Council is called to order."

Baron Beilstein cleared his throat and spoke, seemingly with some hesitation, but nevertheless with a touch of obstinacy in his voice:

"May we beg a little more time for Count Winneburg? He has doubtless gone farther afield than he intended when he set out. I myself know something of the fascination of the chase, and can easily understand that it wipes out all remembrance of lesser things."

"Call you this Council a lesser thing?" demanded the Archbishop. "We have waited an hour already, and I shall not give the laggard a moment more."

"Indeed, my Lord, then I am sorry to hear it. I would not willingly be the man who sits in Winneburg's chair, should he come suddenly upon us."

"Is that a threat?" asked the Archbishop, frowning.

"It is not a threat, but rather a warning. I am a neighbour of the Count, and know him well, and whatever his virtues may be, calm patience is not one of them. If time hangs heavily, may I venture to suggest that your Lordship remove the prohibition you proclaimed when the Count's servants offered us wine, and allow me to act temporarily as host, ordering the flagons to be filled, which I think will please Winneburg better when he comes, than finding another in his chair."

"This is no drunken revel, but a Council of State," said the Archbishop sternly; "and I drink no wine when the host is not here to proffer it.

"Indeed, my Lord," said Beilstein, with a shrug of the shoulders, "some of us are so thirsty that we care not who makes the offer, so long as the wine be sound."

What reply the Archbishop would have made can only be conjectured, for at that moment the door burst open and in came Count Winneburg, a head and shoulders above any man in that room, and huge in proportion.

"My Lords, my Lords," he cried, his loud voice booming to the rafters, "how can I ask you to excuse such a breach of hospitality. What! Not a single flagon of wine in the room? This makes my deep regret almost unbearable. Surely, Beilstein, you might have amended that, if only for the sake of an old and constant comrade. Truth, gentlemen, until I heard the bell of the castle toll, I had no thought that this was the day of our meeting, and then, to my despair, I found myself an hour away, and have ridden hard to be among you."

Then, noticing there was something ominous in the air, and an unaccustomed silence to greet his words, he looked from one to the other, and his eye, travelling up the table, finally rested upon the Archbishop in his chair. Count Winneburg drew himself up, his ruddy face colouring like fire. Then, before any person could reach out hand to check him, or move lip in counsel, the Count, with a fierce oath, strode to the usurper, grasped him by the shoulders, whirled his heels high above his head, and flung him like a sack of corn to the smooth floor, where the unfortunate Archbishop, huddled in a helpless heap, slid along the polished surface as if he were on ice. The fifteen nobles stood stock-still, appalled at this unexpected outrage upon their over-lord. Winneburg seated himself in the chair with an emphasis that made even the solid table rattle, and bringing down his huge fist crashing on the board before him, shouted:

"Let no man occupy my chair, unless he has weight enough to remain there."

Baron Beilstein, and one or two others, hurried to the prostrate Archbishop and assisted him to his feet.

"Count Winneburg," said Beilstein, "you can expect no sympathy from us for such an act of violence in your own hall."

"I want none of your sympathy," roared the angry Count. "Bestow it on the man now in your hands who needs it. If you want the Archbishop of Treves to act as your chairman, elect him to that position and welcome. I shall have no usurpation in my Castle. While I am president I sit in the chair, and none other."

There was a murmur of approval at this, for one and all were deeply suspicious of the Archbishop's continued encroachments.

His Lordship of Treves once more on his feet, his lips pallid, and his face colourless, looked with undisguised hatred at his assailant. "Winneburg," he said slowly, "you shall apologise abjectly for this insult, and that in presence of the nobles of this Empire, or I will see to it that not one stone of this castle remains upon another."

"Indeed," said the Count nonchalantly, "I shall apologise to you, my Lord, when you have apologised to me for taking my place. As to the castle, it is said that the devil assisted in the building of it, and it is quite likely that through friendship for you, he may preside over its destruction."

The Archbishop made no reply, but, bowing haughtily to the rest of the company, who looked glum enough, well knowing that the episode they had witnessed meant, in all probability, red war let loose down the smiling valley of the Moselle, left the Rittersaal.

"Now that the Council is duly convened in regular order," said Count Winneburg, when the others had seated themselves round his table, "what questions of state come up for discussion?"

For a moment there was no answer to this query, the delegates looking at one another speechless. But at last Baron Beilstein shrugging his shoulder, said drily:

"Indeed, my Lord Count, I think the time for talk is past, and I suggest that we all look closely to the strengthening of our walls, which are likely to be tested before long by the Lion of Treves. It was perhaps unwise, Winneburg, to have used the Archbishop so roughly, he being unaccustomed to athletic exercise; but, let the consequences be what they may, I, for one, will stand by you."

"And I; and I; and I; and I," cried the others, with the exception of the Knight of Ehrenburg, who, living as he did near the town of Coblentz, was learned in the law, and not so ready as some of his comrades to speak first and think afterwards.

"My good friends," cried their presiding officer, deeply moved by this token of their fealty, "what I have done I have done, be it wise or the reverse, and the results must fall on my head alone. No words of mine can remove the dust of the floor from the Archbishop's cloak, so if he comes, let him come. I will give him as hearty a welcome as it is in my power to render. All I ask is fair play, and those who stand aside shall see a good fight. It is not right that a hasty act of mine should embroil the peaceful country side, so if Treves comes on I shall meet him alone here in my castle. But, nevertheless, I thank you all for your offers of help; that is all, except the Knight of Ehrenburg, whose tender of assistance, if made, has escaped my ear."

The Knight of Ehrenburg had, up to that moment, been studying the texture of the oaken table on which his flagon sat. Now he looked up and spoke slowly.

"I made no proffer of help," he said, "because none will be needed, I believe, so far as the Archbishop of Treves is concerned. The Count a moment ago said that all he wanted was fair play, but that is just what he has no right to expect from his present antagonist. The Archbishop will make no attempt on this castle; he will act much more subtly than that. The Archbishop will lay the redress of his quarrel upon the shoulders of the Emperor, and it is the oncoming of the Imperial troops you have to fear, and not an invasion from Treves. Against the forces of the Emperor we are powerless, united or divided. Indeed, his Majesty may call upon us to invest this castle, whereupon, if we refuse, we are rebels who have broken our oaths."

"What then is there left for me to do?" asked the Count, dismayed at the coil in which he had involved himself.

"Nothing," advised the Knight of Ehrenburg, "except to apologise abjectly to the Archbishop, and that not too soon, for his Lordship may refuse to accept it. But when he formally demands it, I should render it to him on his own terms, and think myself well out of an awkward position."

The Count of Winneburg rose from his seat, and lifting his clinched fist high above his head, shook it at the timbers of the roof.

"That," he cried, "will I never do, while one stone of Winneburg stands upon another."

At this, those present, always with the exception of the Knight of

Ehrenburg, sprang to their feet, shouting:

"Imperial troops or no, we stand by the Count of Winneburg!"

Some one flashed forth a sword, and instantly a glitter of blades was in the air, while cheer after cheer rang to the rafters. When the uproar had somewhat subsided, the Knight of Ehrenburg said calmly:

"My castle stands nearest to the capital, and will be the first to fall, but, nevertheless, hoping to do my shouting when the war is ended, I join my forces with those of the rest of you."

And amidst this unanimity, and much emptying of flagons, the assemblage dissolved, each man with his escort taking his way to his own stronghold, perhaps to con more soberly, next day, the problem that confronted him. They were fighters all, and would not flinch when the pinch came, whatever the outcome.

Day followed day with no sign from Treves. Winneburg employed the time in setting his house in order to be ready for whatever chanced, and just as the Count was beginning to congratulate himself that his deed was to be without consequences, there rode up to his castle gates a horseman, accompanied by two lancers, and on the newcomer's breast were emblazoned the Imperial arms. Giving voice to his horn, the gates were at once thrown open to him, and, entering, he demanded instant speech with the Count.

"My Lord, Count Winneburg," he said, when that giant had presented himself, "His Majesty the Emperor commands me to summon you to the court at Frankfort."

"Do you take me as prisoner, then?" asked the Count.

"Nothing was said to me of arrest. I was merely commissioned to deliver to you the message of the Emperor."

"What are your orders if I refuse to go?"

A hundred armed men stood behind the Count, a thousand more were within call of the castle bell; two lances only were at the back of the messenger; but the strength of the broadcast empire was betokened by the symbol on his breast.

"My orders are to take back your answer to his Imperial Majesty," replied the messenger calmly.

The Count, though hot-headed, was no fool, and he stood for a moment pondering on the words which the Knight of Ehrenburg had spoken on taking his leave:

"Let not the crafty Archbishop embroil you with the Emperor."

This warning had been the cautious warrior's parting advice to him.

"If you will honour my humble roof," said the Count slowly, "by taking refreshment beneath it, I shall be glad of your company afterwards to Frankfort, in obedience to his Majesty's commands."

The messenger bowed low, accepted the hospitality, and together they made way across the Moselle, and along the Roman road to the capital.

Within the walls of Frankfort the Count was lodged in rooms near the palace, to which his conductor guided him, and, although it was still held that he was not a prisoner, an armed man paced to and fro before his door all night. The day following his arrival, Count Winneburg was summoned to the Court, and in a large ante-room found himself one of a numerous throng, conspicuous among them all by reason of his great height and bulk.

The huge hall was hung with tapestry, and at the further end were heavy curtains, at each edge of which stood half-a-dozen armoured men, the detachments being under command of two gaily-uniformed officers. Occasionally the curtains were parted by menials who stood there to perform that duty, and high nobles entered, or came out, singly and in groups. Down the sides of the hall were packed some hundreds of people, chattering together for the most part, and gazing at those who passed up and down the open space in the centre.

The Count surmised that the Emperor held his Court in whatever apartment was behind the crimson curtains. He felt the eyes of the multitude upon him, and shifted uneasily from one foot to another, cursing his ungainliness, ashamed of the tingling of the blood in his cheeks. He was out of plaice in this laughing, talking crowd, experiencing the sensations of an uncouth rustic suddenly thrust into the turmoil of a metropolis, resenting bitterly the supposed sneers that were flung at him. He suspected that the whispering and the giggling were directed towards himself, and burned to draw his sword and let these popinjays know for once what a man could do. As a matter of fact it was a buzz of admiration at his stature which went up when he entered, but the Count had so little of self-conceit in his soul that he never even guessed the truth.

Two nobles passing near him, he heard one of them say distinctly:

"That is the fellow who threw the Archbishop over his head," while the other, glancing at him, said:

"By the Coat, he seems capable of upsetting the three of them, and I, for one, wish more power to his muscle should he attempt it."

The Count shrank against the tapestried walls, hot with anger, wishing himself a dwarf that he might escape the gaze of so many inquiring eyes. Just as the scrutiny was becoming unbearable, his companion touched him on the elbow, and said in a low voice:

"Count Winneburg, follow me."

He held aside the tapestry at the back of the Count, and that noble, nothing loth, disappeared from view behind it.

Entering a narrow passage-way, they traversed it until they came to a closed door, at each lintel of which stood a pikeman, fronted with a shining breastplate of metal. The Count's conductor knocked gently at the closed door, then opened it, holding it so that the Count could pass in, and when he had done so, the door closed softly behind him. To his amazement, Winneburg saw before him, standing at the further end of the small room, the Emperor Rudolph, entirely alone. The Count was about to kneel awkwardly, when his liege strode forward and prevented him.

"Count Winneburg," he said, "from what I hear of you, your elbow-joints are more supple than those of your knees, therefore let us be thankful that on this occasion there is no need to use either. I see you are under the mistaken impression that the Emperor is present. Put that thought from your mind, and regard me simply as Lord Rudolph—one gentleman wishing to have some little conversation with another."

"Your Majesty—" stammered the Count.

"I have but this moment suggested that you forget that title, my Lord. But, leaving aside all question of salutation, let us get to the heart of the matter, for I think we are both direct men. You are summoned to Frankfort because that high and mighty Prince of the Church, the Archbishop of Treves, has made complaint to the Emperor against you alleging what seems to be an unpardonable indignity suffered by him at your hands."

"Your Majesty—my Lord, I mean," faltered the Count. "The indignity was of his own seeking; he sat down in my chair, where he had no right to place himself, and I—I—persuaded him to relinquish his position."

"So I am informed—that is to say, so his Majesty has been informed," replied Rudolph, a slight smile hovering round his finely chiselled lips. "We are not here to comment upon any of the Archbishop's delinquencies, but, granting, for the sake of argument, that he had encroached upon your rights, nevertheless, he was under your roof, and honestly, I fail to see that you were justified in cracking his heels against the same."

"Well, your Majesty—again I beg your Majesty's pardon—"

"Oh, no matter," said the Emperor, "call me what you like; names signify little."

"If then the Emperor," continued the Count, "found an intruder sitting on his throne, would he like it, think you?"

"His feeling, perhaps, would be one of astonishment, my Lord Count, but speaking for the Emperor, I am certain that he would never lay hands on the usurper, or treat him like a sack of corn in a yeoman's barn."

The Count laughed heartily at this, and was relieved to find that this quitted him of the tension which the great presence had at first inspired.

"Truth to tell, your Majesty, I am sorry I touched him. I should have requested him to withdraw, but my arm has always been more prompt in action than my tongue, as you can readily see since I came into this room."

"Indeed, Count, your tongue does you very good service," continued the Emperor, "and I am glad to have from you an expression of regret. I hope, therefore, that you will have no hesitation in repeating that declaration to the Archbishop of Treves."

"Does your Majesty mean that I am to apologise to him?"

"Yes," answered the Emperor.

There was a moment's pause, then the Count said slowly:

"I will surrender to your Majesty my person, my sword, my castle, and my lands. I will, at your word, prostrate myself at your feet, and humbly beg pardon for any offence I have committed against you, but to tell the Archbishop I am sorry when I am not, and to cringe before him and supplicate his grace, well, your Majesty, as between man and man, I'll see him damned first."

Again the Emperor had some difficulty in preserving that rigidity of expression which he had evidently resolved to maintain.

"Have you ever met a ghost, my Lord Count?" he asked.

Winneburg crossed himself devoutly, a sudden pallor sweeping over his face.

"Indeed, your Majesty, I have seen strange things, and things for which there was no accounting; but it has been usually after a contest with the wine flagon, and at the time my head was none of the clearest, so I could not venture to say whether they were ghosts or no."

"Imagine, then, that in one of the corridors of your castle at midnight you met a white-robed transparent figure, through whose form your sword passed scathlessly. What would you do, my Lord?"

"Indeed, your Majesty, I would take to my heels, and bestow myself elsewhere as speedily as possible."

"Most wisely spoken and you, who are no coward, who fear not to face willingly in combat anything natural, would, in certain circumstances, trust to swift flight for your protection. Very well, my Lord, you are now confronted with something against which your stout arm is as unavailing as it would be if an apparition stood in your path. There is before you the spectre of subtlety. Use arm instead of brain, and you are a lost man.

"The Archbishop expects no apology. He looks for a stalwart, stubborn man, defying himself and the Empire combined. You think, perhaps, that the Imperial troops will surround your castle, and that you may stand a siege. Now the Emperor would rather have you fight with him than against him, but in truth there will be no contest. Hold to your refusal, and you will be arrested before you leave the precincts of this palace. You will be thrown into a dungeon, your castle and your lands sequestered; and I call your attention to the fact that your estate adjoins the possessions of the Archbishop at Cochem, and Heaven fend me for hinting that his Lordship casts covetous eyes over his boundary; yet, nevertheless, he will probably not refuse to accept your possessions in reparation for the insult bestowed upon him. Put it this way if you like. Would you rather pleasure me or pleasure the Archbishop of Treves?"

"There is no question as to that," answered the Count.

"Then it will please me well if you promise to apologise to his Lordship the Archbishop of Treves. That his Lordship will be equally pleased, I very much doubt."

"Will your Majesty command me in open Court to apologise?"

"I shall request you to do so. I must uphold the Feudal law."

"Then I beseech your Majesty to command me, for I am a loyal subject, and will obey."

"God give me many such," said the Emperor fervently, "and bestow upon me the wisdom to deserve them!"

He extended his hand to the Count, then touched a bell on the table beside him. The officer who had conducted Winneburg entered silently, and acted as his guide back to the thronged apartment they had left. The Count saw that the great crimson curtains were now looped up, giving a view of the noble interior of the room beyond, thronged with the notables of the Empire. The hall leading to it was almost deserted, and the Count, under convoy of two lancemen, himself nearly as tall as their weapons, passed in to the Throne Room, and found all eyes turned upon him.

He was brought to a stand before an elevated dais, the centre of which was occupied by a lofty throne, which, at the moment, was empty. Near it, on the elevation, stood the three Archbishops of Treves, Cologne, and Mayence, on the other side the Count Palatine of the Rhine with the remaining three Electors. The nobles of the realm occupied places according to their degree.

As the stalwart Count came in, a buzz of conversation swept over the hall like a breeze among the leaves of a forest. A malignant scowl darkened the countenance of the Archbishop of Treves, but the faces of Cologne and Mayence expressed a certain Christian resignation regarding the contumely which had been endured by their colleague. The Count stood stolidly where he was placed, and gazed at the vacant throne, turning his eyes neither to the right nor the left.

Suddenly there was a fanfare of trumpets, and instant silence smote the assembly. First came officers of the Imperial Guard in shining armour, then the immediate advisers and councillors of his Majesty, and last of all, the Emperor himself, a robe of great richness clasped at his throat, and trailing behind him; the crown of the Empire upon his head. His face was pale and stern, and he looked what he was, a monarch, and a man. The Count rubbed his eyes, and could scarcely believe that he stood now in the presence of one who had chatted amiably with him but a few moments before.

The Emperor sat on his throne and one of his councillors whispered for some moments to him; then the Emperor said, in a low, clear voice, that penetrated to the farthest corner of the vast apartment:

"Is the Count of Winneburg here?"

"Yes, your Majesty."

"Let him stand forward."

The Count strode two long steps to the front, and stood there, red-faced and abashed. The officer at his side whispered:

"Kneel, you fool, kneel."

And the Count got himself somewhat clumsily down upon his knees, like an elephant preparing to receive his burden. The face of the Emperor remained impassive, and he said harshly:

"Stand up."

The Count, once more upon his feet, breathed a deep sigh of satisfaction at finding himself again in an upright posture.

"Count of Winneburg," said the Emperor slowly, "it is alleged that upon the occasion of the last meeting of the Council of State for the Moselle valley, you, in presence of the nobles there assembled, cast a slight upon your over-lord, the Archbishop of Treves. Do you question the statement?"

The Count cleared his throat several times, which in the stillness of that vaulted room sounded like the distant booming of cannon.

"If to cast the Archbishop half the distance of this room is to cast a slight upon him, I did so, your Majesty."

There was a simultaneous ripple of laughter at this, instantly suppressed when the searching eye of the Emperor swept the room.

"Sir Count," said the Emperor severely, "the particulars of your outrage are not required of you; only your admission thereof. Hear, then, my commands. Betake yourself to your castle of Winneburg, and hold yourself there in readiness to proceed to Treves on a day appointed by his Lordship the Archbishop, an Elector of this Empire, there to humble yourself before him, and crave his pardon for the offence you have committed. Disobey at your peril."

Once or twice the Count moistened his dry lips, then he said:

"Your Majesty, I will obey any command you place upon me."

"In that case," continued the Emperor, his severity visibly relaxing, "I can promise that your over-lord will not hold this incident against you. Such, I understand, is your intention, my Lord Archbishop?" and the Emperor turned toward the Prince of Treves.

The Archbishop bowed low, and thus veiled the malignant hatred in his eyes. "Yes, your Majesty," he replied, "providing the apology is given as publicly as was the insult, in presence of those who were witnesses of the Count's foolishness."

"That is but a just condition," said the Emperor. "It is my pleasure that the Council be summoned to Treves to hear the Count's apology. And now, Count of Winneburg, you are at liberty to withdraw."

The Count drew his mammoth hand across his brow, and scattered to the floor the moisture that had collected there. He tried to speak, but apparently could not, then turned and walked resolutely towards the door. There was instant outcry at this, the Chamberlain of the Court standing in stupefied amazement at a breach of etiquette which exhibited any man's back to the Emperor; but a smile relaxed the Emperor's lips, and he held up his hand.

"Do not molest him," he said, as the Count disappeared. "He is unused to the artificial manners of a Court. In truth, I take it as a friendly act, for I am sure the valiant Count never turned his back upon a foe," which Imperial witticism was well received, for the sayings of an Emperor rarely lack applause.

The Count, wending his long way home by the route he had come, spent the first half of the journey in cursing the Archbishop, and the latter half in thinking over the situation. By the time he had reached his castle he had formulated a plan, and this plan he proceeded to put into execution on receiving the summons of the Archbishop to come to Treves on the first day of the following month and make his apology, the Archbishop, with characteristic penuriousness, leaving the inviting of the fifteen nobles, who formed the Council, to Winneburg, and thus his Lordship of Treves was saved the expense of sending special messengers to each. In case Winneburg neglected to summon the whole Council, the Archbishop added to his message, the statement that he would refuse to receive the apology if any of the nobles were absent.

Winneburg sent messengers, first to Beilstein, asking him to attend at Treves on the second day of the month, and bring with him an escort of at least a thousand men. Another he asked for the third, another for the fourth, another for the fifth, and so on, resolved that before a complete quorum was present, half of the month would be gone, and with it most of the Archbishop's provender, for his Lordship, according to the laws of hospitality, was bound to entertain free of all charge to themselves the various nobles and their followings.

On the first day of the month Winneburg entered the northern gate of Treves, accompanied by two hundred horsemen and eight hundred foot soldiers. At first, the officers of the Archbishop thought that an invasion was contemplated, but Winneburg suavely explained that if a thing was worth doing at all, it was worth doing well, and he was not going to make any hole-and-corner affair of his apology. Next day Beilstein came along accompanied by five hundred cavalry, and five hundred foot soldiers.

The Chamberlain of the Archbishop was in despair at having to find quarters for so many, but he did the best he could, while the Archbishop was enraged to observe that the nobles did not assemble in greater haste, but each as he came had a plausible excuse for his delay. Some had to build bridges, sickness had broken out in another camp, while a third expedition had lost its way and wandered in the forest.

The streets of Treves each night resounded with songs of revelry, varied by the clash of swords, when a party of the newcomers fell foul of a squad of the town soldiers, and the officers on either side had much ado to keep the peace among their men. The Archbishop's wine cups were running dry, and the price of provisions had risen, the whole surrounding country being placed under contribution for provender and drink. When a week had elapsed the Archbishop relaxed his dignity and sent for Count Winneburg.

"We will not wait for the others," he said. "I have no desire to humiliate you unnecessarily. Those who are here shall bear witness that you have apologised, and so I shall not insist on the presence of the laggards, but will receive your apology to-morrow at high noon in the great council chamber."

"Ah, there speaks a noble heart, ever thinking generously of those who despitefully use you, my Lord Archbishop," said Count Winneburg. "But no, no, I cannot accept such a sacrifice. The Emperor showed me plainly the enormity of my offence. In the presence of all I insulted you, wretch that I am, and in the presence of all shall I abase myself."

"But I do not seek your abasement," protested the Archbishop, frowning.

"The more honour, then, to your benevolent nature," answered the Count, "and the more shameful would it be of me to take advantage of it. As I stood a short time since on the walls, I saw coming up the river the banners of the Knight of Ehrenburg. His castle is the furthest removed from Treves, and so the others cannot surely delay long. We will wait, my Lord Archbishop, until all are here. But I thank you just as much for your generosity as if I were craven enough to shield myself behind it."

The Knight of Ehrenburg in due time arrived, and behind him his thousand men, many of whom were compelled to sleep in the public buildings, for all the rooms in Treves were occupied. Next day the Archbishop summoned the assembled nobles and said he would hear the apology in their presence. If the others missed it, it was their own fault—they should have been in time.

"I cannot apologise;" said the Count, "until all are here. It was the Emperor's order, and who am I to disobey my Emperor? We must await their coming with patience, and, indeed, Treves is a goodly town, in which all of us find ourselves fully satisfied."

"Then, my blessing on you all," said the Archbishop in a sour tone most unsuited to the benediction he was bestowing. "Return, I beg of you, instantly, to your castles. I forego the apology."

"But I insist on tendering it," cried the Count, his mournful voice giving some indication of the sorrow he felt at his offence if it went unrequited. "It is my duty, not only to you, my Lord Archbishop, but also to his Majesty the Emperor."

"Then, in Heaven's name get on with it and depart. I am willing to accept it on your own terms, as I have said before."

"No, not on my own terms, but on yours. What matters the delay of a week or two? The hunting season does not begin for a fortnight, and we are all as well at Treves as at home. Besides, how could I ever face my Emperor again, knowing I had disobeyed his commands?"

"I will make it right with the Emperor," said the Archbishop.

The Knight of Ehrenburg now spoke up, calmly, as was his custom:

"'Tis a serious matter," he said, "for a man to take another's word touching action of his Majesty the Emperor. You have clerks here with you; perhaps then you will bid them indite a document to be signed by yourself absolving my friend, the Count of Winneburg, from all necessity of apologising, so that should the Emperor take offence at his disobedience, the parchment may hold him scathless."

"I will do anything to be quit of you," muttered the Archbishop more to himself than to the others.

And so the document was written and signed. With this parchment in his saddle-bags the Count and his comrades quitted the town, drinking in half flagons the health of the Archbishop, because there was not left in Treves enough wine to fill the measures to the brim.

CONVERTED

In the ample stone-paved courtyard of the Schloss Grunewald, with its mysterious bubbling spring in the centre, stood the Black Baron beside his restive horse, both equally eager to be away. Round the Baron were grouped his sixteen knights and their saddled chargers, all waiting the word to mount. The warder was slowly opening the huge gates that hung between the two round entrance towers of the castle, for it was the Baron's custom never to ride out at the head of his men until the great leaves of the strong gate fell full apart, and showed the green landscape beyond. The Baron did not propose to ride unthinkingly out, and straightway fall into an ambush.

He and his sixteen knights were the terror of the country-side, and many there were who would have been glad to venture a bow shot at him had they dared. There seemed to be some delay about the opening of the gates, and a great chattering of underlings at the entrance, as if something unusual had occurred, whereupon the rough voice of the Baron roared out to know the cause that kept him waiting, and every one scattered, each to his own affair, leaving only the warder, who approached his master with fear in his face.

"My Lord," he began, when the Baron had shouted what the devil ailed him, "there has been nailed against the outer gate; sometime in the night, a parchment with characters written thereon."

"Then tear it down and bring it to me," cried the Baron. "What's all this to-do about a bit of parchment?"

The warder had been loath to meddle with it, in terror of that witchcraft which he knew pertained to all written characters; but he feared the Black Baron's frown even more than the fiends who had undoubtedly nailed the documents on the gate, for he knew no man in all that well-cowed district would have the daring to approach the castle even in the night, much less meddle with the gate or any other belonging of the Baron von Grunewald; so, breathing a request to his patron saint (his neglect of whom he now remembered with remorse) for protection, he tore the document from its fastening and brought it, trembling, to the Baron. The knights crowded round as von Grunewald held the parchment in his hand, bending his dark brows upon it, for it conveyed no meaning to him. Neither the Baron nor his knights could read.

"What foolery, think you, is this?" he said, turning to the knight nearest him. "A Defiance?"

The knight shook his head. "I am no clerk," he answered.

For a moment the Baron was puzzled; then he quickly bethought himself of the one person in the castle who could read.

"Bring hither old Father Gottlieb," he commanded, and two of those waiting ran in haste towards the scullery of the place, from which they presently emerged dragging after them an old man partly in the habit of a monk and partly in that of a scullion, who wiped his hands on the coarse apron, that was tied around his waist, as he was hurried forward.

"Here, good father, excellent cook and humble servitor, I trust your residence with us has not led you to forget the learning you put to such poor advantage in the Monastery of Monnonstein. Canst thou construe this for us? Is it in good honest German or bastard Latin?"

"It is in Latin," said the captive monk, on glancing at the document in the other's hand.

"Then translate it for us, and quickly."

Father Gottlieb took the parchment handed him by the Baron, and as his eyes scanned it more closely, he bowed his head and made the sign of the cross upon his breast.

"Cease that mummery," roared the Baron, "and read without more waiting or the rod's upon thy back again. Who sends us this?"

"It is from our Holy Father the Pope," said the monk, forgetting his menial position for the moment, and becoming once more the scholar of the monastery. The sense of his captivity faded from him as he realised that the long arm of the Church had extended within the impregnable walls of that tyrannical castle.

"Good. And what has our Holy Father the Pope to say to us? Demands he the release of our excellent scullion, Father Gottlieb?"

The bent shoulders of the old monk straightened, his dim eye brightened, and his voice rang clear within the echoing walls of the castle courtyard.

"It is a ban of excommunication against thee, Lord Baron von Grunewald, and against all within these walls, excepting only those unlawfully withheld from freedom."

"Which means thyself, worthy Father. Read on, good clerk, and let us hear it to the end."

As the monk read out the awful words of the message, piling curse on curse with sonorous voice, the Baron saw his trembling servitors turn pale, and even his sixteen knights, companions in robbery and rapine, fall away from him. Dark red anger mounted to his temples; he raised his mailed hand and smote the reading monk flat across the mouth, felling the old man prone upon the stones of the court.

"That is my answer to our Holy Father the Pope, and when thou swearest to deliver it to him as I have given it to thee, the gates are open and the way clear for thy pilgrimage to Rome."

But the monk lay where he fell and made no reply.

"Take him away," commanded the Baron impatiently, whereupon several of the menials laid hands on the fallen monk and dragged him into the scullery he had left.

Turning to his men-at-arms, the Baron roared: "Well, my gentle wolves, have a few words in Latin on a bit of sheep-skin turned you all to sheep?"

"I have always said," spoke up the knight Segfried, "that no good came of captured monks, or meddling with the Church. Besides, we are noble all, and do not hold with the raising of a mailed hand against an unarmed man."

There was a low murmur of approval among the knights at Segfried's boldness.

"Close the gates," shouted the maddened Baron. Every one flew at the word of command, and the great oaken hinges studded with iron, slowly came together, shutting out the bit of landscape their opening had discovered. The Baron flung the reins on his charger's neck, and smote the animal on the flank, causing it to trot at once to its stable.

"There will be no riding to-day," he said, his voice ominously lowering. The stablemen of the castle came forward and led away the horses. The sixteen knights stood in a group together with Segfried at their head, waiting with some anxiety on their brows for the next move in the game. The Baron, his sword drawn in his hand, strode up and down before them, his brow bent on the ground, evidently struggling to get the master hand over his own anger. If it came to blows the odds were against him and he was too shrewd a man to engage himself single-handed in such a contest.

At length the Baron stopped in his walk and looked at the group. He said, after a pause, in a quiet tone of voice: "Segfried, if you doubt my courage because I strike to the ground a rascally monk, step forth, draw thine own good sword, our comrades will see that all is fair betwixt us, and in this manner you may learn that I fear neither mailed nor unmailed hand."

But the knight made no motion to lay his hand upon his sword, nor did he move from his place. "No one doubts your courage, my Lord," he said, "neither is it any reflection on mine that in answer to your challenge my sword remains in its scabbard. You are our overlord and it is not meet that our weapons should be raised against you."

"I am glad that point is firmly fixed in your minds. I thought a moment since that I would be compelled to uphold the feudal law at the peril of my own body. But if that comes not in question, no more need be said. Touching the unarmed, Segfried, if I remember aright you showed no such squeamishness at our sacking of the Convent of St. Agnes."

"A woman is a different matter, my Lord," said Segfried uneasily.

The Baron laughed and so did some of the knights, openly relieved to find the tension of the situation relaxing.

"Comrades!" cried the Baron, his face aglow with enthusiasm, all traces of his former temper vanishing from his brow. "You are excellent in a mêlée, but useless at the council board. You see no further ahead of you than your good right arms can strike. Look round you at these stout walls; no engine that man has yet devised can batter a breach in them. In our vaults are ten years' supply of stolen grain. Our cellars are full of rich red wine, not of our vintage, but for our drinking. Here in our court bubbles forever this good spring, excellent to drink when wine gives out, and medicinal in the morning when too much wine has been taken in." He waved his hand towards the overflowing well, charged with carbonic acid gas, one of the many that have since made this region of the Rhine famous. "Now I ask you, can this Castle of Grunewald ever be taken—excommunication or no excommunication?"

A simultaneous shout of "No! Never!" arose from the knights.

The Baron stood looking grimly at them for several moments. Then he said in a quiet voice, "Yes, the Castle of Grunewald can be taken. Not from without but from within. If any crafty enemy sows dissension among us; turns the sword of comrade against comrade; then falls the Castle of Grunewald! To-day we have seen how nearly that has been done. We have against us in the monastery of Monnonstein no fat-headed Abbot, but one who was a warrior before he turned a monk. 'Tis but a few years since, that the Abbot Ambrose stood at the right hand of the Emperor as Baron von Stern, and it is known that the Abbot's robes are but a thin veneer over the iron knight within. His hand, grasping the cross, still itches for the sword. The fighting Archbishop of Treves has sent him to Monnonstein for no other purpose than to leave behind him the ruins of Grunewald, and his first bolt was shot straight into our courtyard, and for a moment I stood alone, without a single man-at-arms to second me."

The knights looked at one another in silence, then cast their eyes to the stone-paved court, all too shamed-faced to attempt reply to what all knew was the truth. The Baron, a deep frown on his brow, gazed sternly at the chap-fallen group.... "Such was the effect of the first shaft shot by good Abbot Ambrose, what will be the result of the second?"

"There will be no second," said Segfried stepping forward. "We must sack the Monastery, and hang the Abbot and his craven monks in their own cords."

"Good," cried the Baron, nodding his head in approval, "the worthy Abbot, however, trusts not only in God, but in walls three cloth yards thick. The monastery stands by the river and partly over it. The besieged monks will therefore not suffer from thirst. Their larder is as amply provided as are the vaults of this castle. The militant Abbot understands both defence and sortie. He is a master of siege-craft inside or outside stone walls. How then do you propose to sack and hang, good Segfried?"

The knights were silent. They knew the Monastery was as impregnable as the castle, in fact it was the only spot for miles round that had never owned the sway of Baron von Grunewald, and none of them were well enough provided with brains to venture a plan for its successful reduction. A cynical smile played round the lips of their over-lord, as he saw the problem had overmatched them. At last he spoke.

"We must meet craft with craft. If the Pope's Ban cast such terror among my good knights, steeped to the gauntlets in blood, what effect, think you, will it have over the minds of devout believers in the Church and its power? The trustful monks know that it has been launched against us, therefore are they doubtless waiting for us to come to the monastery, and lay our necks under the feet of their Abbot, begging his clemency. They are ready to believe any story we care to tell touching the influence of such scribbling over us. You Segfried, owe me some reparation for this morning's temporary defection, and to you, therefore, do I trust the carrying out of my plans. There was always something of the monk about you, Segfried, and you will yet end your days sanctimoniously in a monastery, unless you are first hanged at Treves or knocked on the head during an assault.

"Draw, then, your longest face, and think of the time when you will be a monk, as Ambrose is, who, in his day, shed as much blood as ever you have done. Go to the Monastery of Monnonstein in most dejected fashion, and unarmed. Ask in faltering tones, speech of the Abbot, and say to him, as if he knew nought of it, that the Pope's Ban is on us. Say that at first I defied it, and smote down the good father who was reading it, but add that as the pious man fell, a sickness like unto a pestilence came over me and over my men, from which you only are free, caused, you suspect, by your loudly protesting against the felling of the monk. Say that we lie at death's door, grieving for our sins, and groaning for absolution. Say that we are ready to deliver up the castle and all its contents to the care of the holy Church, so that the Abbot but sees our tortured souls safely directed towards the gates of Paradise. Insist that all the monks come, explaining that you fear we have but few moments to live, and that the Abbot alone would be as helpless as one surgeon on a battle-field. Taunt them with fear of the pestilence if they hesitate, and that will bring them."

Segfried accepted the commission, and the knights warmly expressed their admiration of their master's genius. As the great red sun began to sink behind the westward hills that border the Rhine, Segfried departed on horseback through the castle gates, and journeyed toward the monastery with bowed head and dejected mien. The gates remained open, and as darkness fell, a lighted torch was thrust in a wrought iron receptacle near the entrance at the outside, throwing a fitful, flickering glare under the archway and into the deserted court. Within, all was silent as the ruined castle is to-day, save only the tinkling sound of the clear waters of the effervescing spring as it flowed over the stones and trickled down to disappear under the walls at one corner of the courtyard.

The Baron and his sturdy knights sat in the darkness, with growing impatience, in the great Rittersaal listening for any audible token of the return of Segfried and his ghostly company. At last in the still night air there came faintly across the plain a monkish chant growing louder and louder, until finally the steel-shod hoofs of Segfried's charger rang on the stones of the causeway leading to the castle gates. Pressed behind the two heavy open leaves of the gates stood the warder and his assistants, scarcely breathing, ready to close the gates sharply the moment the last monk had entered.

Still chanting, led by the Abbot in his robes of office, the monks slowly marched into the deserted courtyard, while Segfried reined his horse close inside the entrance. "Peace be upon this house and all within," said the deep voice of the Abbot, and in unison the monks murmured "Amen," the word echoing back to them in the stillness from the four grey walls.

Then the silence was rudely broken by the ponderous clang of the closing gates and the ominous rattle of bolts being thrust into their places with the jingle of heavy chains. Down the wide stairs from the Rittersaal came the clank of armour and rude shouts of laughter. Newly lighted torches flared up here and there, illuminating the courtyard, and showing, dangling against the northern wall a score of ropes with nooses at the end of each. Into the courtyard clattered the Baron and his followers. The Abbot stood with arms folded, pressing a gilded cross across his breast. He was a head taller than any of his frightened, cowering brethren, and his noble emaciated face was thin with fasting caused by his never-ending conflict with the world that was within himself. His pale countenance betokened his office and the Church; but the angry eagle flash of his piercing eye spoke of the world alone and the field of conflict.

The Baron bowed low to the Abbot, and said: "Welcome, my Lord Abbot, to my humble domicile! It has long been the wish of my enemies to stand within its walls, and this pleasure is now granted you. There is little to be made of it from without."

"Baron Grunewald," said the Abbot, "I and my brethren are come hither on an errand of mercy, and under the protection of your knightly word."

The Baron raised his eyebrows in surprise at this, and, turning to Segfried, he said in angry tones: "Is it so? Pledged you my word for the safety of these men?"

"The reverend Abbot is mistaken," replied the knight, who had not yet descended from his horse. "There was no word of safe conduct between us."

"Safe conduct is implied when an officer of the Church is summoned to administer its consolations to the dying," said the Abbot.

"All trades," remarked the Baron suavely, "have their dangers—yours among the rest, as well as ours. If my follower had pledged my word regarding your safety, I would now open the gates and let you free. As he has not done so, I shall choose a manner for your exit more in keeping with your lofty aspirations."

Saying this, he gave some rapid orders; his servitors fell upon the unresisting monks and bound them hand and foot. They were then conducted to the northern wall, and the nooses there adjusted round the neck of each. When this was done, the Baron stood back from the pinioned victims and addressed them:

"It is not my intention that you should die without having time to repent of the many wicked deeds you have doubtless done during your lives. Your sentence is that ye be hanged at cockcrow to-morrow, which was the hour when, if your teachings cling to my memory, the first of your craft turned traitor to his master. If, however, you tire of your all-night vigil, you can at once obtain release by crying at the top of your voices 'So die all Christians.' Thus you will hang yourselves, and so remove some responsibility from my perhaps overladen conscience. The hanging is a device of my own, of which I am perhaps pardonably proud, and it pleases me that it is to be first tried on so worthy an assemblage. With much labour we have elevated to the battlements an oaken tree, lopped of its branches, which will not burn the less brightly next winter in that it has helped to commit some of you to hotter flames, if all ye say be true. The ropes are tied to this log, and at the cry 'So die all Christians,' I have some stout knaves in waiting up above with levers, who will straightway fling the log over the battlements on which it is now poised, and the instant after your broken necks will impinge against the inner coping of the northern wall. And now good-night, my Lord Abbot, and a happy release for you all in the morning."

"Baron von Grunewald, I ask of you that you will release one of us who may thus administer the rites of the Church to his brethren and receive in turn the same from me."

"Now, out upon me for a careless knave!" cried the Baron. "I had forgotten that; it is so long since I have been to mass and such like ceremonies myself. Your request is surely most reasonable, and I like you the better that you keep up the farce of your calling to the very end. But think not that I am so inhospitable, as to force one guest to wait upon another, even in matters spiritual. Not so. We keep with us a ghostly father for such occasions, and use him between times to wait on us with wine and other necessaries. As soon as he has filled our flagons, I will ask good Father Gottlieb to wait upon you, and I doubt not he will shrive with any in the land, although he has been this while back somewhat out of practice. His habit is rather tattered and stained with the drippings of his new vocation, but I warrant you, you will know the sheep, even though his fleece be torn. And now, again, good-night, my Lord."

The Baron and his knights returned up the broad stairway that led to the Rittersaal. Most of the torches were carried with them. The defences of the castle were so strong that no particular pains were taken to make all secure, further than the stationing of an armed man at the gate. A solitary torch burnt under the archway, and here a guard paced back and forth. The courtyard was in darkness, but the top of the highest turrets were silvered by the rising moon. The doomed men stood with the halters about their necks, as silent as a row of spectres.

The tall windows of the Rittersaal, being of coloured glass, threw little light into the square, although they glowed with a rainbow splendour from the torches within. Into the silence of the square broke the sound of song and the clash of flagons upon the oaken table.

At last there came down the broad stair and out into the court a figure in the habit of a monk, who hurried shufflingly across the stones to the grim row of brown-robed men. He threw himself sobbing at the feet of the tall Abbot.

"Rise, my son, and embrace me," said his superior. When Father Gottlieb did so, the other whispered in his ear: "There is a time to weep and a time for action. Now is the time for action. Unloosen quickly the bonds around me, and slip this noose from my neck."

Father Gottlieb acquitted himself of his task as well as his agitation and trembling hands would let him.

"Perform a like service for each of the others," whispered the Abbot curtly. "Tell each in a low voice to remain standing just as if he were still bound. Then return to me."

When the monk had done what he was told, he returned to his superior.

"Have you access to the wine cellar?" asked the Abbot.

"Yes, Father."

"What are the strongest wines?"

"Those of the district are strong. Then there is a barrel or two of the red wine of Assmannshausen."

"Decant a half of each in your flagons. Is there brandy?"

"Yes, Father."

"Then mix with the two wines as much brandy as you think their already drunken palates will not detect. Make the potation stronger with brandy as the night wears on. When they drop off into their sodden sleep, bring a flagon to the guard at the gate, and tell him the Baron sends it to him."

"Will you absolve me, Father, for the—"

"It is no falsehood, Gottlieb. I, the Baron, send it. I came hither the Abbot Ambrose: I am now Baron von Stern, and if I have any influence with our mother Church the Abbot's robe shall fall on thy shoulders, if you but do well what I ask of you to-night. It will be some compensation for what, I fear, thou hast already suffered."

Gottlieb hurried away, as the knights were already clamouring for more wine. As the night wore on and the moon rose higher the sounds of revelry increased, and once there was a clash of arms and much uproar, which subsided under the over-mastering voice of the Black Baron. At last the Abbot, standing there with the rope dangling behind him, saw Gottlieb bring a huge beaker of liquor to the sentinel, who at once sat down on the stone bench under the arch to enjoy it.

Finally, all riot died away in the hall except one thin voice singing, waveringly, a drinking song, and when that ceased silence reigned supreme, and the moon shone full upon the bubbling spring.

Gottlieb stole stealthily out and told the Abbot that all the knights were stretched upon the floor, and the Baron had his head on the table, beside his overturned flagon. The sentinel snored upon the stone bench.

"I can now unbar the gate," said Father Gottlieb, "and we may all escape."

"Not so," replied the Abbot. "We came to convert these men to Christianity, and our task is still to do."

The monks all seemed frightened at this, and wished themselves once more within the monastery, able to say all's well that ends so, but none ventured to offer counsel to the gaunt man who led them. He bade each bring with him the cords that had bound him, and without a word they followed him into the Rittersaal, and there tied up the knights and their master as they themselves had been tied.

"Carry them out," commanded the Abbot, "and lay them in a row, their feet towards the spring and their heads under the ropes. And go you, Gottlieb, who know the ways of the castle, and fasten the doors of all the apartments where the servitors are sleeping."

When this was done, and they gathered once more in the moonlit courtyard, the Abbot took off his robes of office and handed them to Father Gottlieb, saying significantly: "The lowest among you that suffers and is true shall be exalted." Turning to his own flock, he commanded them to go in and obtain some rest after such a disquieting night; then to Gottlieb, when the monks had obediently departed: "Bring me, an' ye know where to find such, the apparel of a fighting man and a sword."

Thus arrayed, he dismissed the old man, and alone in the silence, with the row of figures like effigies on a tomb beside him, paced up and down through the night, as the moon dropped lower and lower, in the heavens.

There was a period of dark before the dawn, and at last the upper walls began to whiten with the coming day, and the Black Baron moaned uneasily in his drunken sleep. The Abbot paused in his walk and looked down upon them, and Gottlieb stole out from the shadow of the door and asked if he could be of service. He had evidently not slept, but had watched his chief, until he paused in his march.

"Tell our brothers to come out and see the justice of the Lord."

When the monks trooped out, haggard and wan, in the pure light of the dawn, the Abbot asked Gottlieb to get a flagon and dash water from the spring in the faces of the sleepers.

The Black Baron was the first to come to his senses and realise dimly, at first, but afterwards more acutely, the changed condition of affairs. His eye wandered apprehensively to the empty noose swaying slightly in the morning breeze above him. He then saw that the tall, ascetic man before him had doffed the Abbot's robes and wore a sword by his side, and from this he augured ill. At the command of the Abbot the monks raised each prostrate man and placed him against the north wall.

"Gottlieb," said, the Abbot slowly, "the last office that will be required of you. You took from our necks the nooses last night. Place them, I pray you, on the necks of the Baron and his followers."

The old man, trembling, adjusted the ropes.

"My Lord Abbot——" began the Baron.

"Baron von Grunewald," interrupted the person addressed, "the Abbot Ambrose is dead. He was foully assassinated last night. In his place stands Conrad von Stern, who answers for his deeds to the Emperor, and after him, to God."

"Is it your purpose to hang me, Baron?"

"Was it your purpose to have hanged us, my Lord?"

"I swear to heaven, it was not. 'Twas but an ill-timed pleasantry. Had I wished to hang you I would have done so last night."

"That seems plausible."

The knights all swore, with many rounded oaths, that their over-lord spoke the truth, and nothing was further from their intention than an execution.

"Well, then, whether you hang or no shall depend upon yourselves."

"By God, then," cried the Baron, "an' I have aught to say on that point, I shall hang some other day."

"Will you then, Baron, beg admittance to Mother Church, whose kindly tenets you have so long outraged?"

"We will, we do," cried the Baron fervently, whispering through his clenched teeth to Segfried, who stood next him: "Wait till I have the upper hand again." Fortunately the Abbot did not hear the whisper. The knights all echoed aloud the Baron's pious first remark, and, perhaps, in their hearts said "Amen" to his second.

The Abbot spoke a word or two to the monks, and they advanced to the pinioned men and there performed the rites sacred to their office and to the serious situation of the penitents. As the good brothers stood back, they begged the Abbot for mercy to be extended towards the new converts, but the sphinx-like face of their leader gave no indication as to their fate, and the good men began to fear that it was the Abbot's intention to hang the Baron and his knights.

"Now—brothers," said the Abbot, with a long pause before he spoke the second word, whereupon each of the prisoners heaved a sigh of relief, "I said your fate would depend on yourselves and on your good intent."

They all vociferously proclaimed that their intentions were and had been of the most honourable kind.

"I trust that is true, and that you shall live long enough to show your faith by your works. It is written that a man digged a pit for his enemy and fell himself therein. It is also written that as a man sows, so shall he reap. If you meant us no harm then your signal shouted to the battlements will do you no harm."

"For God's sake, my Lord...." screamed the Baron. The Abbot, unheeding, raised his face towards the northern wall and shouted at the top of his voice:

"So die SUCH Christians!" varying the phrase by one word. A simultaneous scream rose from the doomed men, cut short as by a knife, as the huge log was hurled over the outer parapet, and the seventeen victims were jerked into the air and throttled at the coping around the inner wall.

Thus did the Abbot Ambrose save the souls of Baron von Grunewald and his men, at some expense to their necks.

AN INVITATION

The proud and warlike Archbishop Baldwin of Treves was well mounted, and, although the road by the margin of the river was in places bad, the august horseman nevertheless made good progress along it, for he had a long distance to travel before the sun went down. The way had been rudely constructed by that great maker of roads—the army—and the troops who had built it did not know, when they laboured at it, that they were preparing a path for their own retreat should disaster overtake them. The grim and silent horseman had been the brains, where the troops were the limbs; this thoroughfare had been of his planning, and over it, back into Treves, had returned a victorious, not a defeated, army. The iron hand of the Archbishop had come down on every truculent noble in the land, and every castle gate that had not opened to him through fear, had been battered in by force. Peace now spread her white wings over all the country, and where opposition to his Lordship's stubborn will had been the strongest, there was silence as well, with, perhaps, a thin wreath of blue smoke hovering over the blackened walls. The provinces on each bank of the Moselle from Treves to the Rhine now acknowledged Baldwin their over-lord—a suzerainty technically claimed by his Lordship's predecessors—but the iron Archbishop had changed the nominal into the actual, and it had taken some hard knocks to do it. His present journey was well earned, for he was betaking himself from his more formal and exacting Court at Treves to his summer palace at Cochem, there to rest from the fatigues of a campaign in which he had used not only his brain, but his good right arm as well.

The palace which was to be the end of his journey was in some respects admirably suited to its master, for, standing on an eminence high above Cochem, with its score of pinnacles glittering in the sun, it seemed, to one below, a light and airy structure; but it was in reality a fortress almost impregnable, and three hundred years later it sent into a less turbulent sphere the souls of one thousand six hundred Frenchmen before its flag was lowered to the enemy.

The personal appearance of the Archbishop and the smallness of his escort were practical illustrations of the fact that the land was at peace, and that he was master of it. His attire was neither clerical nor warlike, but rather that of a nobleman riding abroad where no enemy could possibly lurk. He was to all appearance unarmed, and had no protection save a light chain mail jacket of bright steel, which was worn over his vesture, and not concealed as was the custom. This jacket sparkled in the sun as if it were woven of fine threads strung with small and innumerable diamonds. It might ward off a dagger thrust, or turn aside a half-spent arrow, but it was too light to be of much service against sword or pike. The Archbishop was well mounted on a powerful black charger that had carried him through many a hot contest, and it now made little of the difficulties of the ill-constructed road, putting the other horses on their mettle to equal the pace set to them.

The escort consisted of twelve men, all lightly armed, for Gottlieb, the monk, who rode sometimes by the Archbishop's side, but more often behind him, could hardly be counted as a combatant should defence become necessary. When the Archbishop left Treves his oldest general had advised his taking an escort of a thousand men at least, putting it on the ground that such a number was necessary to uphold the dignity of his office; but Baldwin smiled darkly, and said that where he rode the dignity of the Electorship would be safe, even though none rode beside or behind him. Few dared offer advice to the Elector, but the bluff general persisted, and spoke of danger in riding down the Moselle valley with so small a following.

"Who is there left to molest me?" asked the Archbishop; and the general was forced to admit that there was none.

An army builds a road along the line of the least resistance; and often, when a promontory thrust its rocky nose into the river, the way led up the hill through the forest, getting back into the valley again as best it could. During these inland excursions, the monk, evidently unused to equestrianism, fell behind, and sometimes the whole troop was halted by command of its chief, until Gottlieb, clinging to his horse's mane, emerged from the thicket, the Archbishop curbing the impatience of his charger and watching, with a cynical smile curling his stern lips, the reappearance of the good father.

After one of the most laborious ascents and descents they had encountered that day, the Archbishop waited for the monk; and when he came up with his leader, panting and somewhat dishevelled, the latter said, "There appears to be a lesson in your tribulations which hereafter you may retail with profit to your flock, relating how a good man leaving the right and beaten path and following his own devices in the wilderness may bring discomfiture upon himself."

"The lesson it conveys to me, my Lord," said the monk, drily, "is that a man is but a fool to leave the stability of good stout sandals with which he is accustomed, to venture his body on a horse that pays little heed to his wishes."

"This is our last detour," replied the Elector; "there are now many miles of winding but level road before us, and you have thus a chance to retrieve your reputation as a horseman in the eyes of our troop."

"In truth, my Lord, I never boasted of it," returned the monk, "but I am right glad to learn that the way will be less mountainous. To what district have we penetrated?"

"Above us, but unseen from this bank of the river, is the castle of the Widow Starkenburg. Her days of widowhood, however, are nearly passed, for I intend to marry her to one of my victorious knights, who will hold the castle for me."

"The Countess of Starkenburg," said the monk, "must surely now be at an age when the thoughts turn toward Heaven rather than toward matrimony."

"I have yet to meet the woman," replied the Archbishop, gazing upward, "who pleads old age as an excuse for turning away from a suitable lover. It is thy misfortune, Gottlieb, that in choosing a woollen cowl rather than an iron head-piece, thou should'st thus have lost a chance of advancement. The castle, I am told, has well-filled wine vaults, and old age in wine is doubtless more to thy taste than the same quality in woman. 'Tis a pity thou art not a knight, Gottlieb."

"The fault is not beyond the power of our Holy Father to remedy by special dispensation," replied the monk, with a chuckle.

The Elector laughed silently, and looked down on his comrade in kindly fashion, shaking his head.

"The wines of Castle Starkenburg are not for thy appreciative palate, ghostly father. I have already selected a mate for the widow."

"And what if thy selection jumps not with her approval. They tell me the countess has a will of her own."

"It matters little to me, and I give her the choice merely because I am loth to war with a woman. The castle commands the river and holds the district. The widow may give it up peaceably at the altar, or forcibly at the point of the sword, whichever method most commends itself to her ladyship. The castle must be in the command of one whom I can trust."

The conversation here met a startling interruption. The Archbishop and his guard were trotting rapidly round a promontory and following a bend of the river, the nature of the country being such that it was impossible to see many hundred feet ahead of them. Suddenly, they came upon a troop of armed and mounted men, standing like statues before them. The troop numbered an even score, and completely filled the way between the precipice on their left and the stream on their right. Although armed, every sword was in its scabbard, with the exception of the long two-handed weapon of the leader, who stood a few paces in advance of his men, with the point of his sword resting on the ground. The black horse, old in campaigns, recognised danger ahead, and stopped instantly, without waiting for the drawing of the rein, planting his two forefeet firmly in front, with a suddenness of action that would have unhorsed a less alert rider. Before the archbishop could question the silent host that barred his way, their leader raised his long sword until it was poised perpendicularly in the air above his head, and, with a loud voice, in measured tones, as one repeats a lesson he has learned by rote, he cried, "My Lord Archbishop of Treves, the Countess Laurette von Starkenburg invites you to sup with her."

In the silence that followed, the leader's sword still remained uplifted untrembling in the air. Across the narrow gorge, from the wooded sides of the opposite mountains, came, with mocking cadence, the echo of the last words of the invitation, clear and distinct, as if spoken again by some one concealed in the further forest. A deep frown darkened the brow of the fighting archbishop.

"The Countess is most kind," he said, slowly. "Convey to her my respectful admiration, and express my deep regret that I am unable to accept her hospitality, as I ride to-night to my Castle at Cochem."

The leader of the opposing host suddenly lowered his upraised sword, as if in salute, but the motion seemed to be a preconcerted signal, for every man behind him instantly whipped blade from scabbard, and stood there with naked weapon displayed. The leader, raising his sword once more to its former position, repeated in the same loud and monotonous voice, as if the archbishop had not spoken. "My Lord Archbishop of Treves, the Countess Laurette von Starkenburg invites you to sup with her."

The intelligent war-horse, who had regarded the obstructing force with head held high, retreated slowly step by step, until now a considerable distance separated the two companies. The captain of the guard had seen from the first that attack or defence was equally useless, and, with his men, had also given way gradually as the strange colloquy went on. Whether any of the opposing force noticed this or not, they made no attempt to recover the ground thus almost imperceptibly stolen from them, but stood as if each horse were rooted to the spot.

Baldwin the Fighter, whose compressed lips showed how loth he was to turn his back upon any foe, nevertheless saw the futility of resistance, and in a quick, clear whisper, he said, hastily, "Back! Back! If we cannot fight them, we can at least out-race them."

The good monk had taken advantage of his privilege as a non-combatant to retreat well to the rear while the invitation was being given and declined, and in the succeeding flight found himself leading the van. The captain of the guard threw himself between the Starkenburg men and the prince of the Church, but the former made no effort at pursuit, standing motionless as they had done from the first until the rounding promontory hid them from view. Suddenly, the horse on which the monk rode stood stock still, and its worthy rider, with a cry of alarm, clinging to the animal's mane, shot over its head and came heavily to the ground. The whole flying troop came to a sudden halt, for there ahead of them was a band exactly similar in numbers and appearance to that from which they were galloping. It seemed as if the same company had been transported by magic over the promontory and placed across the way. The sun shone on the uplifted blade of the leader, reminding the archbishop of the flaming sword that barred the entrance of our first parents to Paradise.

The leader, with ringing voice, that had a touch of menace in it, cried:

"My Lord Archbishop of Treves, the Countess Laurette von Starkenburg invites you to sup with her."

"Trapped, by God!" muttered the Elector between his clinched teeth. His eyes sparkled with anger, and the sinister light that shot from them had before now made the Emperor quail. He spurred his horse toward the leader, who lowered his sword and bowed to the great dignitary approaching him.

"The Countess of Starkenburg is my vassal," cried the Archbishop. "You are her servant; and in much greater degree, therefore, are you mine. I command you to let us pass unmolested on our way; refuse at your peril."

"A servant," said the man, slowly, "obeys the one directly above him, and leaves that one to account to any superior authority. My men obey me; I take my orders from my lady the countess. If you, my Lord, wish to direct the authority which commands me, my lady the countess awaits your pleasure at her castle of Starkenburg."

"What are your orders, fellow?" asked the Archbishop, in a calmer tone.

"To convey your Lordship without scathe to the gates of Starkenburg."

"And if you meet resistance, what then?"

"The orders stand, my Lord."

"You will, I trust, allow this mendicant monk to pass peaceably on his way to Treves."

"In no castle on the Moselle does even the humblest servant of the

Church receive a warmer welcome than at Starkenburg. My lady would hold me to blame were she prevented from offering her hospitality to the mendicant."

"Does the same generous impulse extend to each of my followers?"

"It includes them all, my Lord."

"Very well. We will do ourselves the honour of waiting upon this most bountiful hostess."

By this time the troop which had first stopped the Archbishop's progress came slowly up, and the little body-guard of the Elector found themselves hemmed in with twenty men in the front and twenty at the rear, while the rocky precipice rose on one hand and the rapid river flowed on the other.

The cortège reformed and trotted gently down the road until it came to a by-way leading up the hill. Into this by-way the leaders turned, reducing their trot to a walk because of the steepness of the ascent. The Archbishop and his men followed, with the second troop of Starkenburg bringing up the rear. His Lordship rode at first in sullen silence, then with a quick glance of his eye he summoned the captain to his side. He slipped the ring of office from his finger and passed it unperceived into the officer's hand.

"There will be some confusion at the gate," he said, in a low voice. "Escape then if you can. Ride for Treves as you never rode before. Stop not to fight with any; everything depends on outstripping pursuit. Take what horses you need wherever you find them, and kill them all if necessary, but stop for nothing. This ring will be warrant for whatever you do. Tell my general to invest this castle instantly with ten thousand men and press forward the siege regardless of my fate. Tell him to leave not one stone standing upon another, and to hang the widow of Starkenburg from her own blazing timbers. Succeed, and a knighthood and the command of a thousand men awaits you."

"I will succeed or die, my Lord."

"Succeed and live," said the Archbishop, shortly.

As the horses slowly laboured up the zigzagging road, the view along the silvery Moselle widened and extended, and at last the strong grey walls of the castle came into sight, with the ample gates wide open. The horsemen in front drew up in two lines on each side of the gates without entering, and thus the Archbishop, at the head of his little band, slowly rode first under the archway into the courtyard of the castle.

On the stone steps that led to the principal entrance of the castle stood a tall, graceful lady, with her women behind her. She was robed in black, and the headdress of her snow-white hair gave her the appearance of a dignified abbess at her convent door. Her serene and placid face had undoubtedly once been beautiful; and age, which had left her form as straight and slender as one of her own forest pines, forgetting to place its customary burden upon her graceful shoulders, had touched her countenance with a loving hand. With all her womanliness, there was, nevertheless, a certain firmness in the finely-moulded chin that gave evidence of a line of ancestry that had never been too deferential to those in authority.

The stern Archbishop reined in his black charger when he reached the middle of the courtyard, but made no motion to dismount. The lady came slowly down the broad stone steps, followed by her feminine train, and, approaching the Elector, placed her white hand upon his stirrup, in mute acknowledgment of her vassalage.

"Welcome, prince of the Church and protector of our Faith," she said. "It is a hundred years since my poor house has sheltered so august a guest."

The tones were smooth and soothing as the scarcely audible plash of a distant fountain; but the incident she cited struck ominously on the Archbishop's recollection, rousing memory and causing him to dart a quick glance at the countess, in which was blended sharp enquiry and awakened foreboding; but the lady, unconscious of his scrutiny, stood with drooping head and downcast eyes, her shapely hand still on his stirrup-iron.

"If I remember rightly, madame, my august predecessor slept well beneath this roof."

"Alas, yes!" murmured the lady, sadly. "We have ever accounted it the greatest misfortune of our line, that he should have died mysteriously here. Peace be to his soul!"

"Not so mysteriously, madame, but that there were some shrewd guesses concerning his malady."

"That is true, my Lord," replied the countess, simply. "It was supposed that in his camp upon the lowlands by the river he contracted a fever from which he died."

"My journey by the Moselle has been of the briefest. I trust, therefore, I have not within me the seeds of his fatal distemper."

"I most devoutly echo that trust, my Lord, and pray that God, who watches over us all, may guard your health while sojourning here."

"Forgive me, madame, if, within the shadow of these walls, I say 'Amen' to your prayer with some emphasis."

The Countess Laurette contented herself with bowing low and humbly crossing herself, making no verbal reply to his Lordship's remark. She then beseeched the Archbishop to dismount, saying something of his need of rest and refreshment, begging him to allow her to be his guide to the Rittersaal.

When the Archbishop reached the topmost step that led to the castle door, he cast an eye, not devoid of anxiety, over the court-yard, to see how his following had fared. The gates were now fast closed, and forty horses were ranged with their tails to the wall, the silent riders in their saddles. Rapid as was his glance, it showed him his guard huddled together in the centre of the court, his own black charger, with empty saddle, the only living thing among them that showed no sign of dismay. Between two of the hostile horsemen stood his captain, with doublet torn and headgear awry, evidently a discomfited prisoner.

The Archbishop entered the gloomy castle with a sense of defeat tugging down his heart to a lower level than he had ever known it to reach before; for in days gone by, when fate had seemed to press against him, he had been in the thick of battle, and had felt an exultation in rallying his half-discouraged followers, who had never failed to respond to the call of a born leader of men. But here he had to encounter silence, with semi-darkness over his head, cold stone under foot, and round him the unaccustomed hiss of women's skirts.

The Countess conducted her guest through the lofty Knight's Hall, in which his Lordship saw preparations for a banquet going forward. An arched passage led them to a small room that seemed to be within a turret hanging over a precipice, as if it were an eagle's nest. This room gave an admirable and extended view over the winding Moselle and much of the surrounding country. On a table were flagons of wine and empty cups, together with some light refection, upon all of which the Archbishop looked with suspicious eye. He did not forget the rumoured poisoning of his predecessor in office. The countess asked him, with deference, to seat himself; then pouring out a cup of wine, she bowed to him and drank it. Turning to rinse the cup in a basin of water which a serving-woman held, she was interrupted by her guest, who now, for the first time, showed a trace of gallantry.

"I beg of you, madame," said the Archbishop, rising; and, taking the unwashed cup from her hand, he filled it with wine, drinking prosperity to herself and her home. Then, motioning her to a chair, he said seating himself: "Countess von Starkenburg, I am a man more used to the uncouth rigour of a camp than the dainty etiquette of a lady's boudoir. Forgive me, then, if I ask you plainly, as a plain man may, why you hold me prisoner in your castle."

"Prisoner, my lord?" echoed the lady, with eyebrows raised in amazement. "How poorly are we served by our underlings, if such a thought has been conveyed to your lordship's mind. I asked them to invite you hither with such deference as a vassal should hold toward an over-lord. I am grievously distressed to learn that my commands have been so ill obeyed."

"Your commands were faithfully followed, madame, and I have made no complaint regarding lack of deference, but when two-score armed men carry a respectful invitation to one having a bare dozen at his back, then all option vanishes, and compulsion takes its place."

"My lord, a handful of men were fit enough escort for a neighbouring baron should he visit us, but, for a prince of the Church, all my retainers are but scanty acknowledgment of a vassal's regard. I would they had been twenty thousand, to do you seemly honour."

"I am easily satisfied, madame, and had they been fewer I might have missed this charming outlook. I am to understand, then, that you have no demands to make of me; and that I am free to depart, accompanied by your good wishes."

"With my good wishes now and always, surely, my Lord. I have no demands to make—the word ill befits the lips of a humble vassal; but, being here——"

"Ah! But, being here——" interrupted the Archbishop, glancing keenly at her.

"I have a favour to beg of you. I wish to ask permission to build a castle on the heights above Trarbach, for my son."

"The Count Johann, third of the name?"

"The same, my Lord, who is honoured by your Lordship's remembrance of him."

"And you wish to place this stronghold between your castle of Starkenburg and my town of Treves? Were I a suspicious man, I might imagine you had some distrust of me."

"Not so, my lord. The Count Johann will hold the castle in your defence."

"I have ever been accustomed to look to my own defence," said the Archbishop, drily; adding, as if it were an afterthought, "with the blessing of God upon my poor efforts."

The faintest suspicion of a smile hovered for an instant on the lips of the countess, that might have been likened to the momentary passing of a gleam of sunshine over the placid waters of the river far below; for she well knew, as did all others, that it was the habit of the fighting Archbishop to smite sturdily first, and ask whatever blessing might be needed on the blow afterwards.

“The permission being given, what follows?”

“That you will promise not to molest me during the building.”

“A natural corollary. ‘Twould be little worth to give permission and then bring up ten thousand men to disturb the builders. That granted, remains there anything more?”

“I fear I trespass on your Lordship’s patience but this is now the end. A strong house is never built with a weak purse. I do entreat your lordship to cause to be sent to me from your treasury in Treves thousand pieces of gold, that the castle may be a worthy addition to your province.”

The Archbishop arose with a scowl on his face, and paced the narrow limits of the room like a caged lion. The hot anger mounted to his brow and reddened it, but he strode up and down until he regained control of himself, then spoke with a touch of hardness in his voice:

“A good fighter, madame, holds his strongest reserves to the last. You have called me a prince of the Church, and such I am. But you flatter me, madame; you rate me too high. The founder of our Church, when betrayed, was sold for silver, and for a lesser number of pieces than you ask in gold.”

The lady, now standing, answered nothing to this taunt, but the colour flushed her pale cheeks.

“I am, then, a prisoner, and you hold me for ransom, but it will avail you little. You may close your gates and prevent my poor dozen of followers from escaping, but news of this outrage will reach Treves, and then, by God, your walls shall smoke for it. There will be none of the Starkenburgs left, either to kidnap or to murder future archbishops.”

Still the lady stood silent and motionless as a marble statue. The Elector paced up and down for a time, muttering to himself, then smote his open palm against a pillar of the balcony, and stood gazing on the fair landscape of river and rounded hill spread below and around him. Suddenly he turned and looked at the Countess, meeting her clear, fearless grey eyes, noticing, for the first time, the resolute contour of her finely-moulded chin.

"Madame," he said, with admiration in his tone, "you are a brave woman."

"I am not so brave as you think me, my Lord," she answered, coldly. "There is one thing I dare not do. I am not brave enough to allow your Lordship to go free, if you refuse what I ask."

"And should I not relent at first, there are dungeons in Starkenburg where this proud spirit, with which my enemies say I am cursed, will doubtless be humbled."

"Not so, my Lord. You will be treated with that consideration which should be shown to one of your exalted station."

"Indeed! And melted thus by kindness, how long, think you, will the process take?"

"It will be of the shortest, my Lord, for if, as you surmise rumour should get abroad and falsely proclaim that the Archbishop lodges here against his will, there's not a flying baron or beggared knight in all the land but would turn in his tracks and cry to Starkenburg, 'In God's name, hold him, widow, till we get our own again!' Willingly would they make the sum I beg of you an annual tribute, so they might be certain your Lordship were well housed in this castle."

"Widow, there is truth in what you say, even if a woman hath spoken it," replied the Archbishop, with a grim smile on his lips and undisguised admiration gleaming from his dark eye. "This cowardly world is given to taking advantage of a man when opportunity offers. But there is one point you have not reckoned upon: What of my stout army lying at Treves?"

"What of the arch when the keystone is withdrawn? What of the sheep when the shepherd disappears? My Lord, you do yourself and your great military gifts a wrong. Through my deep regard for you I gave strict command that not even the meanest of your train should be allowed to wander till all were safe within these gates, for I well knew that, did but a whisper of my humble invitation and your gracious acceptance of the same reach Treves, it might be misconstrued; and although some sturdy fellows would be true, and beat their stupid heads against these walls, the rest would scatter like a sheaf of arrows suddenly unloosed, and seek the strongest arm upraised in the mêlée sure to follow. Against your army, leaderless, I would myself march out at the head of my two-score men without a tremor at my heart; before that leader, alone and armyless, I bow my head with something more akin to fear than I have ever known before, and crave his generous pardon for my bold request."

The Archbishop took her unresisting hand, and, bending, raised it to his lips with that dignified courtesy which, despite his disclaimer, he knew well how, upon occasion, to display.

"Madame," he said, "I ask you to believe that your request was granted even before you marshalled such unanswerable arguments to stand, like armoured men, around it. There is a tern and stringent law of our great Church which forbids its servants suing for a lady's hand. Countess, I never felt the grasp of that iron fetter until now."

Thus came the strong castle above Trarbach to be builded, and that not at the expense of its owners.

THE ARCHBISHOP'S GIFT

Arras, blacksmith and armourer, stood at the door of his hut in the valley of the Alf, a league or so from the Moselle, one summer evening. He was the most powerful man in all the Alf-thal, and few could lift the iron sledge-hammer he wielded as though it were a toy. Arras had twelve sons scarce less stalwart than himself, some of whom helped him in his occupation of blacksmith and armourer, while the others tilled the ground near by, earning from the rich soil of the valley such sustenance as the whole family required.

The blacksmith thus standing at his door, heard, coming up the valley of the Alf, the hoof-beats of a horse, and his quick, experienced ear told him, though the animal was yet afar, that one of its shoes was loose. As the hurrying rider came within call, the blacksmith shouted to him in stentorian tones:

"Friend, pause a moment, until I fasten again the shoe on your horse's foot."

"I cannot stop," was the brief answer.

"Then your animal will go lame," rejoined the blacksmith.

"Better lose a horse than an empire," replied the rider, hurrying by.

"Now what does that mean?" said the blacksmith to himself as he watched the disappearing rider, while the click-clack of the loosened shoe became fainter and fainter in the distance.

Could the blacksmith have followed the rider into Castle Bertrich, a short distance further up the valley, he would speedily have learned the meaning of the hasty phrase the horseman had flung behind him as he rode past. Ascending the winding road that led to the gates of the castle as hurriedly as the jaded condition of his beast would permit, the horseman paused, unloosed the horn from his belt, and blew a blast that echoed from the wooded hills around. Presently an officer appeared above the gateway, accompanied by two or three armed men, and demanded who the stranger was and why he asked admission. The horseman, amazed at the officer's ignorance of heraldry that caused him to inquire as to his quality, answered with some haughtiness:

"Messenger of the Archbishop of Treves, I demand instant audience with Count Bertrich."

The officer, without reply, disappeared from the castle wall, and presently the great leaves of the gate were thrown open, whereupon the horseman rode his tired animal into the courtyard and flung himself off.

"My horse's shoe is loose," he said to the Captain. "I ask you to have your armourer immediately attend to it."

"In truth," replied the officer, shrugging his shoulders, "there is more drinking than fighting in Castle Bertrich; consequently we do not possess an armourer. If you want blacksmithing done you must betake yourself to armourer Arras in the valley, who will put either horse or armour right for you."

With this the messenger was forced to be content; and, begging the attendants who took charge of his horse to remember that it had travelled far and had still, when rested, a long journey before it, he followed the Captain into the great Rittersaal of the castle, where, on entering, after having been announced, he found the Count of Bertrich sitting at the head of a long table, holding in his hand a gigantic wine flagon which he was industriously emptying. Extending down each side of the table were many nobles, knights, and warriors, who, to judge by the hasty glance bestowed upon them by the Archbishop's messenger, seemed to be energetically following the example set them by their over-lord at the head. Count Bertrich's hair was unkempt, his face a purplish red, his eye bloodshot; and his corselet, open at the throat, showed the great bull-neck of the man, on whose gigantic frame constant dissipation seemed to have merely temporary effect.

"Well!" roared the nobleman, in a voice that made the rafters ring. "What would you with Count Bertrich?"

"I bear an urgent despatch to you from my Lord the Archbishop of Treves," replied the messenger.

"Then down on your knees and present it," cried the Count, beating the table with his flagon.

"I am Envoy of his Lordship of Treves," said the messenger, sternly.

"You told us that before," shouted the Count; "and now you stand in the hall of Bertrich. Kneel, therefore, to its master."

"I represent the Archbishop," reiterated the messenger, "and I kneel to none but God and the Emperor."

Count Bertrich rose somewhat uncertainly to his feet, his whole frame trembling with anger, and volleyed forth oaths upon threats. The tall nobleman at his right hand also rose, as did many of the others who sat at the table, and, placing his hand on the arm of his furious host, said warningly:

"My Lord Count, the man is right. It is against the feudal law that he should kneel, or that you should demand it. The Archbishop of Treves is your overlord, as well as ours, and it is not fitting that his messenger should kneel before us."

"That is truth—the feudal law," muttered others down each side of the table.

The enraged Count glared upon them one after another, partially subdued by their breaking away from him.

The Envoy stood calm and collected, awaiting the outcome of the tumult. The Count, cursing the absent Archbishop and his present guests with equal impartiality, sat slowly down again, and flinging his empty flagon at an attendant, demanded that it should be refilled. The others likewise resumed their seats; and the Count cried out, but with less of truculence in his tone:

"What message sent the Archbishop to Castle Bertrich?"

"My Lord, the Archbishop of Treves requires me to inform Count

Bertrich and the assembled nobles that the Hungarians have forced passage across the Rhine, and are now about to make their way through the defiles of the Eifel into this valley, intending to march thence upon Treves, laying that ancient city in ruin and carrying havoc over the surrounding country. His Lordship commands you, Count Bertrich, to rally your men about you and to hold the infidels in check in the defiles of the Eifel until the Archbishop comes, at the bead of his army, to your relief from Treves."

There was deep silence in the vast hall after this startling announcement. Then the Count replied:

"Tell the Archbishop of Treves that if the Lords of the Rhine cannot keep back the Hungarians, it is hardly likely that we, less powerful, near the Moselle, can do it."

"His Lordship urges instant compliance with his request, and I am to say that you refuse at your peril. A few hundred men can hold the Hungarians in check while they are passing through the narrow ravines of the Eifel, while as many thousands might not be successful against them should they once reach the open valleys of the Alf and the Moselle. His Lordship would also have you know that this campaign is as much in your own interest as in his, for the Hungarians, in their devastating march, spare neither high nor low."

"Tell his Lordship," hiccoughed the Count, "that I sit safely in my Castle of Bertrich, and that I defy all the Hungarians who were ever let loose to disturb me therein. If the Archbishop keeps Treves as tightly as I shall hold Castle Bertrich, there is little to fear from the invaders."

"Am I to return to Treves then with your refusal?" asked the Envoy.

"You may return to Treves as best pleases you, so that you rid us of your presence here, where you mar good company."

The Envoy, without further speech, bowed to Count Bertrich and also to the assembled nobles, passed silently out of the hall, once more reaching the courtyard of the castle, where he demanded that his horse be brought to him.

"The animal has had but scant time for feeding and rest," said the

Captain.

"'Twill be sufficient to carry us to the blacksmith's hut," answered the Envoy, as he put his foot in stirrup.

The blacksmith, still standing at the door of his smithy, heard, coming from the castle, the click of the broken shoe, but this time the rider drew up before him and said:

"The offer of help which you tendered me a little ago I shall now be glad to accept. Do your work well, smith, and know that in performing it, you are obliging an envoy of the Archbishop of Treves."

The armourer raised his cap at the mention of the august name, and invoked a blessing upon the head of that renowned and warlike prelate.

"You said something," spoke up the smith, "of loss of empire, as you rode by. I trust there is no disquieting news from Treves?"

"Disquieting enough," replied the messenger. "The Hungarians have crossed the Rhine, and are now making their way towards the defiles of the Eifel. There a hundred men could hold the infidels in check; but you breed a scurvy set of nobles in the Alf-thal, for Count Bertrich disdains the command of his over-lord to rise at the head of his men and stay the progress of the invader until the Archbishop can come to his assistance."

"Now, out upon the drunken Count for a base coward!" cried the armourer in anger. "May his castle be sacked and himself hanged on the highest turret, for refusing aid to his over-lord in time of need. I and my twelve sons know every rock and cave in the Eifel. Would the Archbishop, think you, accept the aid of such underlings as we, whose only commendation is that our hearts are stout as our sinews?"

"What better warranty could the Archbishop ask than that?" replied the Envoy. "If you can hold back the Hungarians for four or five days, then I doubt not that whatever you ask of the Archbishop will speedily be granted."

"We shall ask nothing," cried the blacksmith, "but his blessing, and be deeply honoured in receiving it."

Whereupon the blacksmith, seizing his hammer, went to the door of his hut, where hung part of a suit of armour, that served at the same time as a sign of his profession and as a tocsin. He smote the hanging iron with his sledge until the clangorous reverberation sounded through the valley, and presently there came hurrying to him eight of his stalwart sons, who had been occupied in tilling the fields.

"Scatter ye," cried the blacksmith, "over the land. Rouse the people, and tell them the Hungarians are upon us. Urge all to collect here at midnight, with whatever of arms or weapons they may possess. Those who have no arms, let them bring poles, and meanwhile your brothers and myself will make pike-heads for them. Tell them they are called to, action by a Lord from the Archbishop of Treves himself, and that I shall lead them. Tell them they fight for their homes, their wives, and their children. And now away."

The eight young men at once dispersed in various directions. The smith himself shod the Envoy's horse, and begged him to inform the Archbishop that they would defend the passes of the Eifel while a man of them remained alive.

Long before midnight the peasants came straggling to the smithy from all quarters, and by daylight the blacksmith had led them over the volcanic hills to the lip of the tremendous pass through which the Hungarians must come. The sides of this chasm were precipitous and hundreds of feet in height. Even the peasants themselves, knowing the rocks as they did, could not have climbed from the bottom of the pass to the height they now occupied. They had, therefore, no fear that the Hungarians could scale the walls and decimate their scanty band.

When the invaders appeared the blacksmith and his men rolled great stones and rocks down upon them, practically annihilating the advance guard and throwing the whole army into confusion. The week's struggle that followed forms one of the most exciting episodes in German history. Again and again the Hungarians attempted the pass, but nothing could withstand the avalanche of stones and rocks wherewith they were overwhelmed. Still, the devoted little band did not have everything its own way. They were so few—and they had to keep watch night and day—that ere the week was out many turned longing eyes towards the direction whence the Archbishop's army was expected to appear. It was not until the seventh day that help arrived, and then the Archbishop's forces speedily put to flight the now demoralised Hungarians, and chased them once more across the Rhine.

"There is nothing now left for us to do," said the tired blacksmith to his little following; "so I will get back to my forge and you to your farms."

And this without more ado they did, the cheering and inspiring ring of iron on anvil awakening the echoes of the Alf-thal once again.

The blacksmith and his twelve sons were at their noon-day meal when an imposing cavalcade rode up to the smithy. At the head was no other than the Archbishop himself, and the blacksmith and his dozen sons were covered with confusion to think that they had such a distinguished visitor without the means of receiving him in accordance with his station. But the Archbishop said:

"Blacksmith Arras, you and your sons would not wait for me to thank you; so I am now come to you that in presence of all these followers of mine I may pay fitting tribute to your loyalty and your bravery."

Then, indeed, did the modest blacksmith consider he had received more than ample compensation for what he had done, which, after all, as he told his neighbours, was merely his duty. So why should a man be thanked for it?

"Blacksmith," said the Archbishop, as he mounted his horse to return to Treves, "thanks cost little and are easily bestowed. I hope, however, to have a present for you that will show the whole country round how much I esteem true valour."

At the mouth of the Alf-thal, somewhat back from the small village of Alf and overlooking the Moselle, stands a conical hill that completely commands the valley. The Archbishop of Treves, having had a lesson regarding the dangers of an incursion through the volcanic region of the Eifel, put some hundreds of men at work on this conical hill, and erected on the top a strong castle, which was the wonder of the country. The year was nearing its end when this great stronghold was completed, and it began to be known throughout the land that the Archbishop intended to hold high revel there, and had invited to the castle all the nobles in the country, while the chief guest was no other than the Emperor himself. Then the neighbours of the blacksmith learned that a gift was about to be bestowed upon that stalwart man. He and his twelve sons received notification to attend at the castle, and to enjoy the whole week's festivity. He was commanded to come in his leathern apron, and to bring with him his huge sledge-hammer, which, the Archbishop said, had now become a weapon as honourable as the two-handed sword itself.

Never before had such an honour been bestowed upon a common man, and though the peasants were jubilant that one of their caste should be thus singled out to receive the favour of the famous Archbishop, and meet not only great nobles, but even the Emperor himself, still, it was gossiped that the Barons grumbled at this distinction being placed upon a serf like the blacksmith Arras, and none were so loud in their complaints as Count Bertrich, who had remained drinking in the castle while the blacksmith fought for the land. Nevertheless, all the nobility accepted the invitation of the powerful Archbishop of Treves, and assembled in the great room of the new castle, each equipped in all the gorgeous panoply of full armour. It had been rumoured among the nobles that the Emperor would not permit the Archbishop to sully the caste of knighthood by asking the Barons to recognise or hold converse with one in humble station of life. Indeed, had it been otherwise, Count Bertrich, with the Barons to back him, were resolved to speak out boldly to the Emperor, upholding the privileges of their class, and protesting against insult to it in presence of the blacksmith and his sons.

When all assembled in the great hall they found at the centre of the long side wall a magnificent throne erected, with a daïs in front of it, and on this throne sat, the Emperor in state, while at his right hand stood the lordly Archbishop of Treves. But what was more disquieting, they beheld also the blacksmith standing before the daïs, some distance in front of the Emperor, clad in his leathern apron, with his big brawny hands folded over the top of the handle of his huge sledge-hammer. Behind him were ranged his twelve sons. There were deep frowns on the brows of the nobles when they saw this, and, after kneeling and protesting their loyalty to the Emperor, they stood aloof and apart, leaving a clear space between themselves and the plebeian blacksmith on whom they cast lowering looks. When the salutations of the Emperor had been given, the Archbishop took a step forward on the daïs and spoke in a clear voice that could be heard to the furthermost corner of the room.

"My Lords," he said, "I have invited you hither that you may have the privilege of doing honour to a brave man. I ask you to salute the blacksmith Arras, who, when his country was in danger, crushed the invaders as effectually as ever his right arm, wielding sledge, crushed hot iron."

A red flush of confusion overspread the face of the blacksmith, but loud murmurs broke out among the nobility, and none stepped forward to salute him. One, indeed, stepped forward, but it was to appeal to the Emperor.

"Your Majesty," exclaimed Count Bertrich, "this is an unwarranted breach of our privileges. It is not meet that we, holding noble names, should be asked to consort with an untitled blacksmith. I appeal to your Majesty against the Archbishop under the feudal law."

All eyes turned upon the Emperor, who, after a pause, said:

"Count Bertrich is right, and I sustain his appeal."

An expression of triumph came into the red bibulous face of Count Bertrich, and the nobles shouted joyously:

"The Emperor, the Emperor!"

The Archbishop, however, seemed in no way non-plussed by his defeat, but, addressing the armourer, said:

"Advance, blacksmith, and do homage to your Emperor and mine."

When the blacksmith knelt before the throne, the Emperor, taking his jewelled sword from his side, smote the kneeling man lightly on his broad shoulders, saying:

"Arise, Count Arras, noble of the German Empire, and first Lord of the

Alf-thal."

The blacksmith rose slowly to his feet, bowed lowly to the Emperor, and backed to the place where he had formerly stood, again resting his hands on the handle of his sledge-hammer. The look of exultation faded from the face of Count Bertrich, and was replaced by an expression of dismay, for he had been until that moment, himself first Lord of the Alf-thal, with none second.

"My Lords," once more spoke up the Archbishop, "I ask you to salute Count Arras, first Lord of the Alf-thal."

No noble moved, and again Count Bertrich appealed to the Emperor.

"Are we to receive on terms of equality," he said, "a landless man; the count of a blacksmith's hut; a first lord of a forge? For the second time I appeal to your Majesty against such an outrage."

The Emperor replied calmly:

"Again I support the appeal of Count Bertrich."

There was this time no applause from the surrounding nobles, for many of them had some smattering idea of what was next to happen, though the muddled brain of Count Bertrich gave him no intimation of it.

"Count Arras," said the Archbishop, "I promised you a gift when last I left you at your smithy door. I now bestow upon you and your heirs forever this castle of Burg Arras, and the lands adjoining it. I ask you to hold it for me well and faithfully, as you held the pass of the Eifel. My Lords," continued the Archbishop, turning to the nobles, with a ring of menace in his voice, "I ask you to salute Count Arras, your equal in title, your equal in possessions, and the superior of any one of you in patriotism and bravery. If any noble question his courage, let him neglect to give Count of Burg Arras his title and salutation as he passes before him."

"Indeed, and that will not I," said the tall noble who had sat at Bertrich's right hand in his castle, "for, my Lords, if we hesitate longer, this doughty blacksmith will be Emperor before we know it." Then, advancing towards the ex-armourer, he said: "My Lord, Count of Burg Arras, it gives me pleasure to salute you, and to hope that when Emperor or Archbishop are to be fought for, your arm will be no less powerful in a coat of mail than it was when you wore a leathern apron."

One by one the nobles passed and saluted as their leader had done. Count Bertrich hung back until the last, and then, as he passed the new Count of Burg Arras, he hissed at him, with a look of rage, the single word, "Blacksmith!"

The Count of Burg Arras, stirred to sudden anger, and forgetting in whose presence he stood, swung his huge sledge-hammer round his head, and brought it down on the armoured back of Count Bertrich, roaring the word "ANVIL!"

The armour splintered like crushed ice, and Count Bertrich fell prone on his face and lay there. There was instant cry of "Treason! Treason!" and shouts of "No man may draw arms in the Emperor's presence."

"My Lord Emperor," cried the Count of Burg Arras, "I crave pardon if I have done amiss. A man does not forget the tricks of his old calling when he takes on new honours. Your Majesty has said that I am a Count. This man, having heard your Majesty's word, proclaims me blacksmith, and so gave the lie to his Emperor. For this I struck him, and would again, even though he stood before the throne in a palace, or the altar in a cathedral. If that be treason, take from me your honours, and let me back to my forge, where this same hammer will mend the armour it has broken, or beat him out a new back-piece."

"You have broken no tenet of the feudal law," said the Emperor. "You have broken nothing, I trust, but the Count's armour, for, as I see, he is arousing himself, doubtless no bones are broken as well. The feudal law does not regard a blacksmith's hammer as a weapon. And as for treason, Count of Burg Arras, may my throne always be surrounded by such treason as yours."

And for centuries after, the descendants of the blacksmith were Counts of Burg Arras, and held the castle of that name, whose ruins to-day attest the excellence of the Archbishop's building.

COUNT KONRAD'S COURTSHIP

It was nearly midnight when Count Konrad von Hochstaden reached his castle on the Rhine, with a score of very tired and hungry men behind him. The warder at the gate of Schloss Hochstaden, after some cautious parley with the newcomers, joyously threw apart the two great iron-studded oaken leaves of the portal when he was convinced that it was indeed his young master who had arrived after some tumultuous years at the crusades, and Count Konrad with his followers rode clattering under the stone arch, into the ample courtyard. It is recorded that, in the great hall of the castle, the Count and his twenty bronzed and scarred knights ate such a meal as had never before been seen to disappear in Hochstaden, and that after drinking with great cheer to the downfall of the Saracene and the triumph of the true cross, they all lay on the floor of the Rittersaal and slept the remainder of the night, the whole of next day, and did not awaken until the dawn of the second morning. They had had years of hard fighting in the east, and on the way home they had been compelled to work their passage through the domains of turbulent nobles by good stout broadsword play, the only argument their opposers could understand, and thus they had come through to the Rhine without contributing aught to their opponents except fierce blows, which were not commodities as marketable as yellow gold, yet with this sole exchange did the twenty-one win their way from Palestine to the Palatinate, and thus were they so long on the road that those in Schloss Hochstaden had given up all expectation of their coming.

Count Konrad found that his father, whose serious illness was the cause of his return, had been dead for months past, and the young man wandered about the castle which, during the past few years, he had beheld only in dreams by night and in the desert mirages by day, saddened because of his loss. He would return to the Holy Land, he said to himself, and let the castle be looked after by its custodian until the war with the heathen was ended.

The young Count walked back and forth on the stone paved terrace which commanded from its height such a splendid view of the winding river, but he paid small attention to the landscape, striding along with his hands clasped behind him; his head bent, deep in thought. He was awakened from his reverie by the coming of the ancient custodian of the castle, who shuffled up to him and saluted him with reverential respect, for the Count was now the last of his race; a fighting line, whose members rarely came to die peaceably in their beds as Konrad's father had done.

The Count, looking up, swept his eye around the horizon and then to his astonishment saw the red battle flag flying grimly from the high northern tower of Castle Bernstein perched on the summit of the next hill to the south. In the valley were the white tents of an encampment, and fluttering over it was a flag whose device, at that distance, the Count could not discern.

"Why is the battle flag flying on Bernstein, Gottlieb, and what means those tents in the valley?" asked Konrad.

The old man looked in the direction of the encampment, as if the sight were new to him, but Konrad speedily saw that the opposite was the case. The tents had been there so long that they now seemed a permanent part of the scenery.

"The Archbishop of Cologne, my Lord, is engaged in the besiegement of Schloss Bernstein, and seems like to have a long job of it. He has been there for nearly a year now."

"Then the stout Baron is making a brave defence; good luck to him!"

"Alas, my Lord, I am grieved to state that the Baron went to his rest on the first day of the assault. He foolishly sallied out at the head of his men and fell hotly on the Archbishop's troops, who were surrounding the castle. There was some matter in dispute between the Baron and the Archbishop, and to aid the settlement thereof, his mighty Lordship of Cologne sent a thousand armed men up the river, and it is said that all he wished was to have parley with Baron Bernstein, and to overawe him in the discussion, but the Baron came out at the head of his men and fell upon the Cologne troops so mightily that he nearly put the whole battalion to flight, but the officers rallied their panic-stricken host, seeing how few were opposed to them, and the order was given that the Baron should be taken prisoner, but the old man would not have it so, and fought so sturdily with his long sword, that he nearly entrenched himself with a wall of dead. At last the old man was cut down and died gloriously, with scarcely a square inch unwounded on his whole body. The officers of the Archbishop then tried to carry the castle by assault, but the Lady of Bernstein closed and barred the gate, ran, up the battle flag on the northern tower and bid defiance to the Archbishop and all his men."

"The Lady of Bernstein? I thought the Baron was a widower. Whom, then, did he again marry?"

"'Twas not his wife, but his daughter."

"His daughter? Not Brunhilda? She's but a child of ten."

"She was when you went away, my Lord, but now she is a woman of eighteen, with all the beauty of her mother and all the bravery of her father."

"Burning Cross of the East, Gottlieb! Do you mean to say that for a year a prince of the Church has been warring with a girl, and her brother, knowing nothing of this cowardly assault, fighting the battles for his faith on the sands of the desert? Let the bugle sound! Call up my men and arouse those who are still sleeping."

"My Lord, my Lord, I beg of you to have caution in this matter."

"Caution? God's patience! Has caution rotted the honour out of the bones of all Rhine men, that this outrage should pass unmolested before their eyes! The father murdered; the daughter beleaguered; while those who call themselves men sleep sound in their safe castles! Out of my way, old man! Throw open the gates!"

But the ancient custodian stood firmly before his over-lord, whose red angry face seemed like that of the sun rising so ruddily behind him.

"My Lord, if you insist on engaging in this enterprise it must be gone about sanely. You need the old head as well as the young arm. You have a score of well-seasoned warriors, and we can gather into the castle another hundred. But the Archbishop has a thousand men around Bernstein. Your score would but meet the fate of the old Baron and would not better the case of those within the castle. The Archbishop has not assaulted Bernstein since the Baron's death, but has drawn a tight line around it and so has cut off all supplies, daily summoning the maiden to surrender. What they now need in Bernstein is not iron, but food. Through long waiting they keep slack watch about the castle, and it is possible that, with care taken at midnight, you might reprovision Bernstein so that she could hold out until her brother comes, whom it is said she has summoned from the Holy Land."

"Thou art wise, old Gottlieb," said the Count slowly, pausing in his wrath as the difficulties of the situation were thus placed in array before him; "wise and cautious, as all men seem to be who now keep ward on the Rhine. What said my father regarding this contest?"

"My Lord, your honoured father was in his bed stricken with the long illness that came to be his undoing at the last, and we never let him know that the Baron was dead or the siege in progress."

"Again wise and cautious, Gottlieb, for had he known it, he would have risen from his deathbed, taken down his two-handed sword from the wall, and struck his last blow in defence of the right against tyranny."

"Indeed, my Lord, under danger of your censure, I venture to say that you do not yet know the cause of the quarrel into which you design to precipitate yourself. It may not be tyranny on the part of the overlord, but disobedience on the part of the vassal, which causes the environment of Bernstein. And the Archbishop is a prince of our holy Church."

"I leave those nice distinctions to philosophers like thee, Gottlieb. It is enough for me to know that a thousand men are trying to starve one woman, and as for being a prince of the Church, I shall give his devout Lordship a taste of religion hot from its birthplace, and show him how we uphold the cause in the East, for in this matter the Archbishop grasps not the cross but the sword, and by the sword shall he be met. And now go, Gottlieb, set ablaze the fires on all our ovens and put the bakers at work. Call in your hundred men as speedily as possible, and bid each man bring with him a sack of wheat.

Spend the day at the baking and fill the cellars with grain and wine. It will be reason enough, if any make inquiry, to say that the young Lord has returned and intends to hold feasts in his castle. Send hither my Captain to me."

Old Gottlieb hobbled away, and there presently came upon the terrace a stalwart, grizzled man, somewhat past middle age, whose brown face showed more seams of scars than remnants of beauty. He saluted his chief and stood erect in silence.

The Count waved his hand toward the broad valley and said grimly:

"There sits the Archbishop of Cologne, besieging the Castle of Bernstein."

The Captain bowed low and crossed himself.

"God prosper his Lordship," he said piously.

"You may think that scarcely the phrase to use, Captain, when I tell you that you will lead an assault on his Lordship to-night."

"Then God prosper us, my Lord," replied the Captain cheerfully, for he was ever a man who delighted more in fighting than in inquiring keenly into the cause thereof.

"You may see from here that a ridge runs round from this castle, bending back from the river, which it again approaches, touching thus Schloss Bernstein. There is a path along the summit of the ridge which I have often trodden as a boy, so I shall be your guide. It is scarce likely that this path is guarded, but if it is we will have to throw its keepers over the precipice; those that we do not slay outright, when we come upon them."

"Excellent, my Lord, most excellent," replied the Captain, gleefully rubbing his huge hands one over the other.

"But it is not entirely to fight that we go. You are to act as convoy to those who carry bread to Castle Bernstein. We shall leave here at the darkest hour after midnight and you must return before daybreak so that the Archbishop cannot estimate our numbers. Then get out all the old armour there is in the castle and masquerade the peasants in it. Arrange them along the battlements so that they will appear as numerous as possible while I stay in Castle Bernstein and make terms with the Archbishop, for it seems he out-mans us, so we must resort, in some measure, to strategy. On the night assault let each man yell as if he were ten and lay about him mightily. Are the knaves astir yet?"

"Most of them, my Lord, and drinking steadily the better to endure the dryness of the desert when we go eastward again."

"Well, see to it that they do not drink so much as to interfere with clean sword-play against to-night's business."

"Indeed, my Lord, I have a doubt if there is Rhine wine enough in the castle's vaults to do that, and the men yell better when they have a few gallons within them."

At the appointed hour Count Konrad and his company went silently forth, escorting a score more who carried sacks of the newly baked bread on their backs, or leathern receptacles filled with wine, as well as a stout cask of the same seductive fluid. Near the Schloss Bernstein the rescuing party came upon the Archbishop's outpost, who raised the alarm before the good sword of the Captain cut through the cry. There were bugle calls throughout the camp and the sound of men hurrying to their weapons, but all the noise of preparation among the besiegers was as nothing to the demoniac din sent up by the Crusaders, who rushed to the onslaught with a zest sharpened by their previous rest and inactivity. The wild barbaric nature of their yells, such as never before were heard on the borders of the placid Rhine, struck consternation into the opposition camp, because some of the Archbishop's troops had fought against the heathen in the East, and they now recognised the clamour which had before, on many an occasion, routed them, and they thought that the Saracenes had turned the tables and invaded Germany; indeed from the deafening clamour it seemed likely that all Asia was let loose upon them. The alarm spread quickly to Castle Bernstein itself, and torches began to glimmer on its battlements. With a roar the Crusaders rushed up to the foot of the wall, as a wave dashes against a rock, sweeping the frightened bread-carriers with them. By the light of the torches Konrad saw standing on the wall a fair young girl clad in chain armour whose sparkling links glistened like countless diamonds in the rays of the burning pitch. She leaned on the cross-bar of her father's sword and, with wide-open, eager eyes peered into the darkness beyond, questioning the gloom for reason of the terrifying tumult. When Konrad strode within the radius of the torches, the girl drew back slightly and cried:

"So the Archbishop has at last summoned courage to attack, after all this patient waiting."

"My Lady," shouted the Count, "these are my forces and not the Archbishop's. I am Konrad, Count of Hochstaden."

"The more shame, then, that you, who have fought bravely with men, should now turn your weapons against a woman, and she your neighbour and the sister of your friend."

"Indeed, Lady Brunhilda, you misjudge me. I am come to your rescue and not to your disadvantage.. The Archbishop's men were put to some inconvenience by our unexpected arrival, and to gather from the sounds far down the valley they have not ceased running yet. We come with bread, and use the sword but as a spit to deliver it."

"Your words are welcome were I but sure of their truth," said the lady with deep distrust in her tone, for she had had experience of the Archbishop's craft on many occasions, and the untimely hour of the succour led her to fear a ruse. "I open my gates neither to friend nor to foe in the darkness," she added.

"Tis a rule that may well be commended to others of your bewitching sex," replied the Count, "but we ask not the opening of the gates, although you might warn those within your courtyard to beware what comes upon them presently."

So saying, he gave the word, and each two of his servitors seized a sack of bread by the ends and, heaving it, flung it over the wall. Some of the sacks fell short, but the second effort sent them into the courtyard, where many of them burst, scattering the round loaves along the cobble-stoned pavement, to be eagerly pounced upon by the starving servitors and such men-at-arms as had escaped from the encounter with the Archbishop's troops when the Baron was slain. The cries of joy that rang up from within the castle delighted the ear of the Count and softened the suspicion of the lady on the wall.

"Now," cried Konrad to his Captain, "back to Schloss Hochstaden before the dawn approaches too closely, and let there be no mistake in the Archbishop's camp that you are on the way."

They all departed in a series of earsplitting, heart-appalling whoops that shattered the still night air and made a vocal pandemonium of that portion of the fair Rhine valley. The colour left the cheeks of the Lady of Bernstein as she listened in palpable terror to the fiendish outcry which seemed to scream for blood and that instantly, looking down she saw the Knight of Hochstaden still there at the foot of her wall gazing up at her.

"My Lord," she said with concern, "if you stay thus behind your noisy troop you will certainly be captured when it comes day."

"My Lady of Bernstein, I am already a captive, and all the Archbishop's men could not hold me more in thrall did they surround me at this moment."

"I do not understand you, sir," said Brunhilda coldly, drawing herself up with a dignity that well became her, "your language seems to partake of an exaggeration that doubtless you have learned in the tropical East, and which we have small patience with on the more temperate banks of the Rhine."

"The language that I use, fair Brunhilda, knows neither east nor west; north nor south, but is common to every land, and if it be a stranger to the Rhine, the Saints be witness 'tis full time 'twere introduced here, and I hold myself as competent to be its spokesman, as those screeching scoundrels of mine hold themselves the equal in battle to all the archbishops who ever wore the robes of that high office."

"My Lord," cried Brunhilda, a note of serious warning in her voice, "my gates are closed and they remain so. I hold myself your debtor for unasked aid, and would fain see you in a place of safety."

"My reverenced Lady, that friendly wish shall presently be gratified," and saying this, the Count unwound from his waist a thin rope woven of horse-hair, having a long loop at the end of it. This he whirled round his head and with an art learned in the scaling of eastern walls flung the loop so that it surrounded one of the machicolations of the bastion, and, with his feet travelling against the stone work, he walked up the wall by aid of this cord and was over the parapet before any could hinder his ascent. The Maid of the Schloss, her brows drawn down in anger, stood with sword ready to strike, but whether it was the unwieldiness of the clumsy weapon, or whether it was the great celerity with which the young man put his nimbleness to the test, or whether it was that she recognised him as perhaps her one friend on earth, who can tell; be that as it may, she did not strike in time, and a moment, later the Count dropped on one knee and before she knew it raised one of her hands to his bending lips.

"Lovely Warder of Bernstein," cried Count Konrad, with a tremor of emotion in his voice that thrilled the girl in spite of herself, "I lay my devotion and my life at your feet, to use them as you will."

"My Lord," she said quaveringly, with tears nearer the surface than she would have cared to admit, "I like not this scaling of the walls; my permission unasked."

"God's truth, my Lady, and you are not the first to so object, but the others were men, and I may say, without boasting, that I bent not the knee to them when I reached their level, but I have been told that custom will enable a maid to look more forgivingly on such escapades if her feeling is friendly toward the invader, and I am bold enough to hope that the friendship with which your brother has ever regarded me in the distant wars, may be extended to my unworthy self by his sister at home."

Count Konrad rose to his feet and the girl gazed at him in silence, seeing how bronzed and manly he looked in his light well-polished eastern armour, which had not the cumbrous massiveness of western mail, but, while amply protecting the body, bestowed upon it lithe freedom for quick action; and unconsciously she compared him, not to his disadvantage, with the cravens on the Rhine, who, while sympathising with her, dared not raise weapon on her behalf against so powerful an over-lord as the warlike Archbishop. The scarlet cross of the Crusader on his broad breast seemed to her swimming eyes to blaze with lambent flame in the yellow torchlight. She dared not trust her voice to answer him, fearing its faintness might disown the courage with which she had held her castle for so long, and he, seeing that she struggled to hold control of herself, standing there like a superb Goddess of the Rhine, pretended to notice nothing and spoke jauntily with a wave of his hand: "My villains have brought to the foot of the walls a cask of our best wine which we dared not adventure to cast into the courtyard with that freedom which forwarded the loaves; there is also a packet of dainties more suited to your Ladyship's consideration than the coarse bread from our ovens. Give command, I beg of you, that the gates be opened and that your men bring the wine and food to safety within the courtyard, and bestow on me the privilege of guarding the open gate while this is being done."

Then gently, with insistent deference, the young man took from her the sword of her father which she yielded to him with visible reluctance, but nevertheless yielded, standing there disarmed before him. Together in silence they went down the stone steps that led from the battlements to the courtyard, followed by the torch-bearers, whom the lightening east threatened soon to render unnecessary. A cheer went up, the first heard for many days within those walls, and the feasters, flinging their caps in the air, cried "Hochstaden! Hochstaden!" The Count turned to his fair companion and said, with a smile:

"The garrison is with me, my Lady."

She smiled also, and sighed, but made no other reply, keeping her eyes steadfast on the stone steps beneath her. Once descended, she gave the order in a low voice, and quickly the gates were thrown wide, creaking grumblingly on their hinges, long unused. Konrad stood before the opening with the sword of Bernstein in his hands, swinging it this way and that to get the hang of it, and looking on it with the admiration which a warrior ever feels for a well hung, trusty blade, while the men-at-arms nodded to one another and said: "There stands a man who knows the use of a weapon. I would that he had the crafty Archbishop before him to practise on."

When the barrel was trundled in, the Lady of Bernstein had it broached at once, and with her own hand served to each of her men a flagon of the golden wine. Each took his portion, bowing low to the lady, then doffing cap, drank first to the Emperor, and after with an enthusiasm absent from the Imperial toast, to the young war lord whom the night had flung thus unexpectedly among them. When the last man had refreshed himself, the Count stepped forward and begged a flagon full that he might drink in such good company, and it seemed that Brunhilda had anticipated such a request, for she turned to one of her women and held out her hand, receiving a huge silver goblet marvellously engraved that had belonged to her forefathers, and plenishing it, she gave it to the Count, who, holding it aloft, cried, "The Lady of Bernstein," whereupon there arose such a shout that the troubled Archbishop heard it in his distant tent.

"And yet further of your hospitality must I crave," said Konrad, "for the morning air is keen, and gives me an appetite for food of which I am deeply ashamed, but which nevertheless clamours for an early breakfast."

The lady, after giving instruction to the maids who waited upon her, led the way into the castle, where Konrad following, they arrived in the long Rittersaal, at the end of which, facing the brightening east, was placed a huge window of stained glass, whose great breadth was gradually lightening as if an unseen painter with magic brush was tinting the glass with transparent colour, from the lofty timbered ceiling to the smoothly polished floor. At the end of the table, with her back to the window, Brunhilda sat, while the Count took a place near her, by the side, turning so that he faced her, the ever-increasing radiance illumining his scintillating armour. The girl ate sparingly, saying little and glancing often at her guest. He fell to like the good trencherman he was, and talked unceasingly of the wars in the East, and the brave deeds done there, and as he talked the girl forgot all else, rested her elbows on the table and her chin in her hands, regarding him intently, for he spoke not of himself but of her brother, and of how, when grievously pressed, he had borne himself so nobly that more than once, seemingly certain defeat was changed into glorious victory. Now and then when Konrad gazed upon Brunhilda, his eloquent tongue faltered for a moment and he lost the thread of his narrative, for all trace of the warrior maid had departed, and there, outlined against the glowing window of dazzling colours, she seemed indeed a saint with her halo of golden hair, a fit companion to the angels that the marvellous skill of the artificer had placed in that gorgeous collection of pictured panes, lead-lined and cut in various shapes, answering the needs of their gifted designer, as a paint-brush follows the will of the artist. From where the young man sat, the girl against the window seemed a member of that radiant company, and thus he paused stricken speechless by her beauty.

She spoke at last, the smile on her lips saddened by the down turning of their corners, her voice the voice of one hovering uncertain between laughter and tears.

"And you," she said, "you seem to have had no part in all this stirring recital. It was my brother and my brother and my brother, and to hear you one would think you were all the while hunting peacefully in your Rhine forests. Yet still I do believe the Count of Hochstaden gave the heathen to know he was somewhat further to the east of Germany."

"Oh, of me," stammered the Count. "Yes, I was there, it is true, and sometimes—well, I have a fool of a captain, headstrong and reckless, who swept me now and then into a melee, before I could bring cool investigation to bear upon his mad projects, and once in the fray of course I had to plead with my sword to protect my head, otherwise my bones would now be on the desert sands, so I selfishly lay about me and did what I could to get once more out of the turmoil."

The rising sun now struck living colour into the great window of stained glass, splashing the floor and the further wall with crimson and blue and gold. Count Konrad sprang to his feet. "The day is here," he cried, standing in the glory of it, while the girl rose more slowly. "Let us have in your bugler and see if he has forgotten the battle call of the Bernsteins. Often have I heard it in the desert. 'Give us the battle call,' young Heinrich would cry and then to its music all his followers would shout 'Bernstein! Bernstein!' until it seemed the far-off horizon must have heard."

The trumpeter came, and being now well fed, blew valiantly, giving to the echoing roof the war cry of the generations of fighting men it had sheltered.

"That is it," cried the Count, "and it has a double significance. A challenge on the field, and a summons to parley when heard from the walls. We shall now learn whether or no the Archbishop has forgotten it, and I crave your permission to act as spokesman with his Lordship."

"That I most gratefully grant," said the Lady of the Castle.

Once more on the battlements, the Lord of Hochstaden commanded the trumpeter to sound the call The martial music rang out in the still morning air and was echoed mockingly by the hills on the other side of the river. After that, all was deep silence.

"Once again," said Konrad.

For a second time the battle blast filled the valley, and for a second time returned faintly back from the hills. Then from near the great tent of the Archbishop, by the margin of the stream, came the answering call, accepting the demand for a parley.

When at last the Archbishop, mounted on a black charger, came slowly up the winding path which led to the castle, attended by only two of his officers, he found the Count of Hochstaden awaiting him on the battlements above the gate. The latter's hopes arose when he saw that Cologne himself had come, and had not entrusted the business to an envoy, and it was also encouraging to note that he came so poorly attended, for when a man has made up his mind to succumb he wishes as few witnesses as possible, while if he intends further hostilities, he comes in all the pomp of his station.

"With whom am I to hold converse?" began the Archbishop, "I am here at the behest of the Bernstein call to parley, but I see none, of that name on the wall to greet me."

"Heinrich, Baron Bernstein, is now on his way to his castle from the Holy Land, and were he here it were useless for me to summon a parley, for he would answer you with the sword and not with the tongue when he learned his father was dead at your hand."

"That is no reply to my question. With whom do I hold converse?"

"I am Konrad, Count of Hochstaden, and your Lordship's vassal."

"I am glad to learn of your humility and pleased to know that I need not call your vassalage to your memory, but I fear that in the darkness you have less regard for either than you now pretend in the light of day."

"In truth, my Lord, you grievously mistake me, for in the darkness I stood your friend. I assure you I had less than a thousand rascals at my back last night, and yet nothing would appease them but that they must fling themselves upon your whole force, had I not held them in check. I told them you probably outnumbered us ten to one, but they held that one man who had gone through an eastern campaign was worth ten honest burghers from Cologne, which indeed I verily believe, and for the fact that you were not swept into the Rhine early this morning you have me and my peaceful nature to thank, my Lord. Perhaps you heard the rogues discussing the matter with me before dawn, and going angrily home when I so ordered them."

"A man had need to be dead and exceedingly deep in his grave not to have heard them," growled the Archbishop.

"And there they stand at this moment, my Lord, doubtless grumbling among themselves that I am so long giving the signal they expect, which will permit them to finish this morning's work. The men I can generally control, but my captains are a set of impious cut-throats who would sooner sack an Archbishop's palace than listen to the niceties of the feudal law which protects over-lords from such pleasantries."

The Archbishop turned on his horse and gazed on the huge bulk of Schloss Hochstaden, and there a wonderful sight met his eye. The walls bristled with armed men, the sun glistening on their polished breastplates like the shimmer of summer lightning. The Archbishop turned toward the gate again, as though the sight he beheld brought small comfort to him.

"What is your desire?" he said with less of truculence in his tone than there had been at the beginning.

"I hold it a scandal," said the Count gravely, "that a prince of the Church should assault Christian walls while their owner is absent in the East venturing his life in the uplifting of the true faith. You can now retreat without loss of prestige; six hours hence that may be impossible. I ask you then to give your assurance to the Lady of Bernstein, pledging your knightly word that she will be no longer threatened by you, and I ask you to withdraw your forces immediately to Cologne where it is likely they will find something to do if Baron Heinrich, as I strongly suspect, marches directly on that city."

"I shall follow the advice of my humble vassal, for the strength of a prince is in the sage counsel of his war lords. Will you escort the lady to the battlements?"

Then did Count Konrad von Hochstaden see that his cause was won, and descending he came up again, leading the Lady Brunhilda by the hand.

"I have to acquaint you, madame," said the Archbishop, "that the siege is ended, and I give you my assurance that you will not again be beleaguered by my forces."

The Lady of Bernstein bowed, but made no answer. She blushed deeply that the Count still held her hand, but she did not withdraw it.

"And now, my Lord Archbishop, that this long-held contention is amicably adjusted," began Von Hochstaden, "I crave that you bestow on us two your gracious blessing, potentate of the Church, for this lady is to be my wife."

"What!" cried Brunhilda in sudden anger, snatching her hand from his, "do you think you can carry me by storm as you did my castle, without even asking my consent?"

"Lady of my heart," said Konrad tenderly, "I did ask your consent. My eyes questioned in the Rittersaal and yours gave kindly answer. Is there then no language but that which is spoken? I offer you here before the world my open hand; is it to remain empty?"

He stood before her with outstretched palm, and she gazed steadfastly at him, breathing quickly. At length a smile dissolved the sternness of her charming lips, she glanced at his extended hand and said:

"'Twere a pity so firm and generous a hand should remain tenantless," and with that she placed her palm in his.

The Archbishop smiled grimly at this lovers' by-play, then solemnly, with upraised hands, invoked God's blessing upon them.

THE LONG LADDER

Every fortress has one traitor within its walls; the Schloss Eltz had two. In this, curiously enough, lay its salvation; for as some Eastern poisons when mixed neutralise each other and form combined a harmless fluid, so did the two traitors unwittingly react, the one upon the other, to the lasting glory of Schloss Eltz, which has never been captured to this day.

It would be difficult to picture the amazement of Heinrich von Richenbach when he sat mute upon his horse at the brow of the wooded heights and, for the first time, beheld the imposing pile which had been erected by the Count von Eltz. It is startling enough to come suddenly upon a castle where no castle should be; but to find across one's path an erection that could hardly have been the product of other agency than the lamp of Aladdin was stupefying, and Heinrich drew the sunburned back of his hand across his eyes, fearing that they were playing him a trick; then seeing the wondrous vision still before him, he hastily crossed himself, an action performed somewhat clumsily through lack of practice, so that he might ward off enchantment, if, as seemed likely, that mountain of pinnacles was the work of the devil, and not placed there, stone on stone, by the hand of man. But in spite of crossing and the clearing of his eyes, Eltz Castle remained firmly seated on its stool of rock, and, when his first astonishment had somewhat abated, Von Richenbach, who was a most practical man, began to realise that here, purely by a piece of unbelievable good luck, the very secret he had been sent to unravel had been stumbled upon, the solving of which he had given up in despair, returning empty-handed to his grim master, the redoubtable Archbishop Baldwin of Treves.

It was now almost two months since the Archbishop had sent him on the mission to the Rhine from which he was returning as wise as he went, well knowing that a void budget would procure him scant welcome from his imperious ruler. Here, at least, was important matter for the warlike Elector's stern consideration—an apparently impregnable fortress secretly built in the very centre of the Archbishop's domain; and knowing that the Count von Eltz claimed at least partial jurisdiction over this district, more especially that portion known as the Eltz-thal, in the middle of which this mysterious citadel had been erected. Heinrich rightly surmised that its construction had been the work of this ancient enemy of the Archbishop.

Two months before, or nearly so, Heinrich von Richenbach had been summoned into the presence of the Lion of Treves at his palace in that venerable city. When Baldwin had dismissed all within the room save only Von Richenbach, the august prelate said:

"It is my pleasure that you take horse at once and proceed to my city of Mayence on the Rhine, where I am governor. You will inspect the garrison there and report to me."

Heinrich bowed, but said nothing.

"You will then go down the Rhine to Elfield, where my new castle is built, and I shall be pleased to have an opinion regarding it."

The Archbishop paused, and again his vassal bowed and remained silent.

"It is my wish that you go without escort, attracting as little attention as possible, and perhaps it may be advisable to return by the northern side of the Moselle, but some distance back from the river, as there are barons on the banks who might inquire your business, and regret their curiosity when they found they questioned a messenger of mine. We should strive, during our brief sojourn on this inquisitive earth, to put our fellow creatures to as little discomfort as possible."

Von Richenbach saw that he was being sent on a secret and possibly dangerous mission, and he had been long enough in the service of the crafty Archbishop to know that the reasons ostensibly given for his journey were probably not those which were the cause of it, so he contented himself with inclining his head for the third time and holding his peace. The Archbishop regarded him keenly for a few moments, a derisive smile parting his firm lips; then said, as if his words were an afterthought:

"Our faithful vassal, the Count von Eltz, is, if I mistake not, a neighbor of ours at Elfield?"

The sentence took, through its inflection, the nature of a query, and for the first time Heinrich von Richenbach ventured reply.

"He is, my Lord."

The Archbishop raised his eyes to the vaulted ceiling, and seemed for a time lost in thought, saying, at last, apparently in soliloquy, rather than by direct address:

"Count von Eltz has been suspiciously quiet of late for a man so impetuous by nature. It might be profitable to know what interests him during this unwonted seclusion. It behooves us to acquaint ourselves with the motives that actuate a neighbour, so that, opportunity arising, we may aid him with counsel or encouragement. If, therefore, it should so chance that, in the intervals of your inspection of governorship or castle, aught regarding the present occupation of the noble count comes to your ears, the information thus received may perhaps remain in your memory until you return to Treves."

The Archbishop withdrew his eyes from the ceiling, the lids lowering over them, and flashed a keen, rapier-like glance at the man who stood before him.

Heinrich von Richenbach made low obeisance and replied:

"Whatever else fades from my memory, my Lord, news of Count von Eltz shall remain there."

"See that you carry nothing upon you, save your commission as inspector, which my secretary will presently give to you. If you are captured it will be enough to proclaim yourself my emissary and exhibit your commission in proof of the peaceful nature of your embassy. And now to horse and away."

Thus Von Richenbach, well mounted, with his commission legibly engrossed in clerkly hand on parchment, departed on the Roman road for Mayence, but neither there nor at Elfield could he learn more of Count von Eltz than was already known at Treves, which was to the effect that this nobleman, repenting him, it was said, of his stubborn opposition to the

Archbishop, had betaken himself to the Crusades in expiation of his wrong in shouldering arms against one who was both his temporal and spiritual over-lord; and this rumour coming to the ears of Baldwin, had the immediate effect of causing that prince of the Church to despatch Von Richenbach with the purpose of learning accurately what his old enemy was actually about; for Baldwin, being an astute man, placed little faith in sudden conversion.

When Heinrich von Richenbach returned to Treves he was immediately ushered into the presence of his master.

"You have been long away," said the Archbishop, a frown on his brow. "I trust the tidings you bring offer some slight compensation for the delay." Then was Heinrich indeed glad that fate, rather than his own perspicacity, had led his horse to the heights above Schloss Eltz.

"The tidings I bring, my Lord, are so astounding that I could not return to Treves without verifying them. This led me far afield, for my information was of the scantiest; but I am now enabled to vouch for the truth of my well-nigh incredible intelligence."

"Have the good deeds of the Count then translated him bodily to heaven, as was the case with Elijah? Unloose your packet, man, and waste not so much time in the vaunting of your wares."

"The Count von Eltz, my Lord, has built a castle that is part palace, part fortress, and in its latter office well-nigh impregnable."

"Yes? And where?"

"In the Eltz-thal, my Lord, a league and a quarter from the Moselle."

"Impossible!" cried Baldwin, bringing his clenched fist down on the table before him. "Impossible! You have been misled, Von Richenbach."

"Indeed, my Lord, I had every reason to believe so until I viewed the structure with my own eyes."

"This, then, is the fruit of Von Eltz's contrition! To build a castle without permission within my jurisdiction, and defy me in my own domain. By the

Coat, he shall repent his temerity and wish himself twice over a captive of the Saracen ere I have done with him. I will despatch at once an army to the Eltz-thal, and there shall not be left one stone upon another when it returns."

"My Lord, I beseech you not to move with haste in this matter. If twenty thousand men marched up to the Eltz-thal they could not take the castle. No such schloss was ever built before, and none to equal it will ever be built again, unless, as I suspect to be the case in this instance, the devil lends his aid."

"Oh, I doubt not that Satan built it, but he took the form and name of Count von Eltz while doing so," replied the Archbishop, his natural anger at this bold defiance of his power giving way to his habitual caution, which, united with his resources and intrepidity, had much to do with his success. "You hold the castle, then, to be unassailable. Is its garrison so powerful, or its position so strong?"

"The strength of its garrison, my Lord, is in its weakness; I doubt if there are a score of men in the castle, but that is all the better, as there are fewer mouths to feed in case of siege, and the Count has some four years' supplies in his vaults. The schloss is situated on a lofty, unscalable rock that stands in the centre of a valley, as if it were a fortress itself. Then the walls of the building are of unbelievable height, with none of the round or square towers which castles usually possess, but having in plenty conical turrets, steep roofs, and the like, which give it the appearance of a fairy palace in a wide, enchanted amphitheatre of green wooded hills, making the Schloss Eltz, all in all, a most miraculous sight, such as a man may not behold in many years' travel."

"In truth, Von Richenbach," said the Archbishop, with a twinkle in his eye, "we should have made you one of our scrivening monks rather than a warrior, so marvellously do you describe the entrancing handiwork of our beloved vassal, the Count von Eltz. Perhaps you think it pity to destroy so fascinating a creation."

"Not so, my Lord. I have examined the castle well, and I think were I entrusted with the commission I could reduce it."

"Ah, now we have modesty indeed! You can take the stronghold where

I should fail."

"I did not say that you would fail, my Lord. I said that twenty thousand men marching up the valley would fail, unless they were content to sit around the castle for four years or more."

"Answered like a courtier, Heinrich. What, then, is your method of attack?"

"On the height to the east, which is the nearest elevation to the castle, a strong fortress might be built, that would in a measure command the Schloss Eltz, although I fear the distance would be too great for any catapult to fling stones within its courtyard. Still, we might thus have complete power over the entrance to the schloss, and no more provender could be taken in."

"You mean, then, to wear Von Eltz out? That would be as slow a method as besiegement."

"To besiege would require an army, my Lord, and would have this disadvantage, that, besides withdrawing from other use so many of your men, rumour would spread abroad that the Count held you in check. The building of a fortress on the height would merely be doing what the Count has already done, and it could be well garrisoned by twoscore men at the most, vigilant night and day to take advantage of any movement of fancied security to force way into the castle. There need be no formal declaration of hostilities, but a fortress built in all amicableness, to which the Count could hardly object, as you would be but following his own example."

"I understand. We build a house near his for neighbourliness. There is indeed much in your plan that commends itself to me, but I confess a liking for the underlying part of a scheme. Remains there anything else which you have not unfolded to me?"

"Placing in command of the new fortress a stout warrior who was at the same time a subtle man——"

"In other words, thyself, Heinrich—well, what then?"

"There is every chance that such a general may learn much of the castle from one or other of its inmates. It might be possible that, through neglect or inadvertence, the drawbridge would be left down some night and the portcullis raised. In other words, the castle, impervious to direct assault, may fall by strategy."

"Excellent, excellent, my worthy warrior! I should dearly love to have captain of mine pay such an informal visit to his estimable Countship. We shall build the fortress you suggest, and call it Baldwineltz. You shall be its commander, and I now bestow upon you Schloss Eltz, the only proviso being that you are to enter into possession of it by whatever means you choose to use."

Thus the square, long castle of Baldwineltz came to be builded, and thus Heinrich von Richenbach, brave, ingenious, and unscrupulous, was installed captain of it, with twoscore men to keep him company, together with a plentiful supply of gold to bribe whomsoever he thought worth suborning.

Time went on without much to show for its passing, and Heinrich began to grow impatient, for his attempt at corrupting the garrison showed that negotiations were not without their dangers. Stout Baumstein, captain of the gate, was the man whom Heinrich most desired to purchase, for Baumstein could lessen the discipline at the portal of Schloss Eltz without attracting undue attention. But he was an irascible German, whose strong right arm was readier than his tongue; and when Heinrich's emissary got speech with him, under a flag of truce, whispering that much gold might be had for a casual raising of the portcullis and lowering of the drawbridge, Baumstein at first could not understand his purport, for he was somewhat thick in the skull; but when the meaning of the message at last broke in upon him, he wasted no time in talk, but, raising his ever-ready battle-axe, clove the Envoy to the midriff. The Count von Eltz himself, coming on the scene at this moment, was amazed at the deed, and sternly demanded of his gate-captain why he had violated the terms of a parley. Baumstein's slowness of speech came near to being the undoing of him, for at first he merely said that such creatures as the messenger should not be allowed to live and that an honest soldier was insulted by holding converse with him; whereupon the Count, having nice notions, picked up in polite countries, regarding the sacredness of a flag of truce, was about to hang Baumstein, scant though the garrison was, and even then it was but by chance that the true state of affairs became known to the Count. He was on the point of sending back the body of the Envoy to Von Richenbach with suitable apology for his destruction and offer of recompense, stating that the assailant would be seen hanging outside the gate, when Baumstein said that while he had no objection to being hanged if it so pleased the Count, he begged to suggest that the gold which the Envoy brought with him to bribe the garrison should be taken from the body before it was returned, and divided equally among the guard at the gate. As Baumstein said this, he was taking off his helmet and unbuckling his corselet, thus freeing his neck for the greater convenience of the castle hangman. When the Count learned that the stout stroke of the battle-axe was caused by the proffer of a bribe for the betraying of the castle, he, to the amazement of all present, begged the pardon of Baumstein; for such a thing was never before known under the feudal law that a noble should apologise to a common man, and Baumstein himself muttered that he wot not what the world was coming to if a mighty Lord might not hang an underling if it so pleased him, cause or no cause.

The Count commanded the body to be searched, and finding thereon some five bags of gold, distributed the coin among his men, as a good commander should, sending back the body to Von Richenbach, with a most polite message to the effect that as the Archbishop evidently intended the money to be given to the garrison, the Count had endeavoured to carry out his Lordship's wishes, as was the duty of an obedient vassal. But Heinrich, instead of being pleased with the courtesy of the message, broke into violent oaths, and spread abroad in the land the false saying that Count von Eltz had violated a flag of truce.

But there was one man in the castle who did not enjoy a share of the gold, because he was not a warrior, but a servant of the Countess. This was a Spaniard named Rego, marvellously skilled in the concocting of various dishes of pastry and other niceties such as high-born ladies have a fondness for. Rego was disliked by the Count, and, in fact, by all the stout Germans who formed the garrison, not only because it is the fashion for men of one country justly to abhor those of another, foreigners being in all lands regarded as benighted creatures whom we marvel that the Lord allows to live when he might so easily have peopled the whole world with men like unto ourselves; but, aside from this, Rego had a cat-like tread, and a furtive eye that never met another honestly as an eye should. The count, however, endured the presence of this Spaniard, because the Countess admired his skill in confections, then unknown in Germany, and thus Rego remained under her orders.

The Spaniard's eye glittered when he saw the yellow lustre of the gold, and his heart was bitter that he did not have a share of it. He soon learned where it came from, and rightly surmised that there was more in the same treasury, ready to be bestowed for similar service to that which the unready Baumstein had so emphatically rejected; so Rego, watching his opportunity, stole away secretly to Von Richenbach and offered his aid in the capture of the castle, should suitable compensation be tendered him. Heinrich questioned him closely regarding the interior arrangements of the castle, and asked him if he could find any means of letting down the drawbridge and raising the portcullis in the night. This, Rego said quite truly, was impossible, as the guard at the gate, vigilant enough before, had become much more so since the attempted bribery of the Captain. There was, however, one way by which the castle might be entered, and that entailed a most perilous adventure. There was a platform between two of the lofty, steep roofs, so elevated that it gave a view over all the valley. On this platform a sentinel was stationed night and day, whose duty was that of outlook, like a man on the cross-trees of a ship. From this platform a stair, narrow at the top, but widening as it descended to the lower stories, gave access to the whole castle. If, then, a besieger constructed a ladder of enormous length, it might be placed at night on the narrow ledge of rock far below this platform, standing almost perpendicular, and by this means man after man would be enabled to reach the roof of the castle, and, under the guidance of Rego, gain admittance to the lower rooms unsuspected.

"But the sentinel?" objected Von Richenbach.

"The sentinel I will myself slay. I will steal up behind him in the night when you make your assault, and running my knife into his neck, fling him over the castle wall; then I shall be ready to guide you down into the courtyard."

Von Richenbach, remembering the sheer precipice of rock at the foot of the castle walls and the dizzy height of the castle roof above the rock, could scarcely forbear a shudder at the thought of climbing so high on a shaky ladder, even if such a ladder could be made, of which he had some doubts. The scheme did not seem so feasible as the Spaniard appeared to imagine.

"Could you not let down a rope ladder from the platform when you had slain the sentinel, and thus allow us to climb by that?"

"It would be impossible for me to construct and conceal a contrivance strong enough to carry more than one man at a time, even if I had the materials," said the wily Spaniard, whose thoughtfulness and ingenuity Heinrich could not but admire, while despising him as an oily foreigner. "If you made the rope ladder there would be no method of getting it into Schloss Eltz; besides, it would need to be double the length of a wooden ladder, for you can place your ladder at the foot of the ledge, then climb to the top of the rock, and, standing there, pull the ladder up, letting the higher end scrape against the castle wall until the lower end stands firm on the ledge of rock. Your whole troop could then climb, one following another, so that there would be no delay."

Thus it was arranged, and then began and was completed the construction of the longest and most wonderful ladder ever made in Germany or anywhere else, so far as history records. It was composed of numerous small ladders, spliced and hooped with iron bands by the castle armourer. At a second visit, which Rego paid to Baldwineltz when the ladder was completed, all arrangements were made and the necessary signals agreed upon.

It was the pious custom of those in the fortress of Baldwineltz to ring the great bell on Saints' days and other festivals that called for special observance, because Von Richenbach conducted war on the strictest principles, as a man knowing his duty both spiritual and temporal. It was agreed that on the night of the assault, when it was necessary that Rego should assassinate the sentinel, the great bell of the fortress should be rung, whereupon the Spaniard was to hie himself up the stair and send the watchman into another sphere of duty by means of his dagger. The bell-ringing seems a perfectly justifiable device, and one that will be approved by all conspirators, for the sounding of the bell, plainly heard in Schloss Eltz, would cause no alarm, as it was wont to sound at uncertain intervals, night and day, and was known to give tongue only during moments allotted by the Church to devout thoughts. But the good monk Ambrose, in setting down on parchment the chronicles of this time, gives it as his opinion that no prosperity could have been expected in thus suddenly changing the functions of the bell from sacred duty to the furtherance of a secular object. Still, Ambrose was known to be a sympathiser with the house of Eltz, and, aside from this, a monk in his cell cannot be expected to take the same view of military necessity that would commend itself to a warrior on a bastion; therefore, much as we may admire Ambrose as an historian, we are not compelled to accept his opinions on military ethics.

On the important night, which was of great darkness, made the more intense by the black environment of densely-wooded hills which surrounded Schloss Eltz, the swarthy Spaniard became almost pale with anxiety as he listened for the solemn peal that was to be his signal. At last it tolled forth, and he, with knife to hand in his girdle, crept softly along the narrow halls to his fatal task. The interior of Schloss Eltz is full of intricate passages, unexpected turnings, here a few steps up, there a few steps down, for all the world like a maze, in which even one knowing the castle might well go astray. At one of the turnings Rego came suddenly upon the Countess, who screamed at sight of him, and then recognising him said, half laughing, half crying, being a nervous woman:

"Ah, Rego, thank heaven it is you! I am so distraught with the doleful ringing of that bell that I am frightened at the sound of my own footsteps. Why rings it so, Rego?"

"'Tis some Church festival, my Lady, which they, fighting for the Archbishop, are more familiar with than I," answered the trembling Spaniard, as frightened as the lady herself at the unexpected meeting. But the Countess was a most religious woman, well skilled in the observances of her Church, and she replied:

"No, Rego. There is no cause for its dolorous music, and to-night there seems to me something ominous and menacing in its tone, as if disaster impended."

"It may be the birthday of the Archbishop, my Lady, or of the Pope himself."

"Our Holy Father was born in May, and the Archbishop in November. Ah, I would that this horrid strife were done with! But our safety lies in Heaven, and if our duty be accomplished here on earth, we should have naught to fear; yet I tremble as if great danger lay before me. Come, Rego, to the chapel, and light the candles at the altar."

The Countess passed him, and for one fateful moment Rego's hand hovered over his dagger, thinking to strike the lady dead at his feet; but the risk was too great, for there might at any time pass along the corridor one of the servants, who would instantly raise the alarm and bring disaster upon him. He dare not disobey. So grinding his teeth in impotent rage and fear, he followed his mistress to the chapel, and, as quickly as he could, lit one candle after another, until the usual number burned before the sacred image. The Countess was upon her knees as he tried to steal softly from the room. "Nay, Rego," she said, raising her bended head, "light them all to-night. Hearken! That raven bell has ceased even as you lighted the last candle."

The Countess, as has been said was a devout lady, and there stood an unusual number of candles before the altar, several of which burned constantly, but only on notable occasions were all the candles lighted. As Rego hesitated, not knowing what to do in this crisis, the lady repeated: "Light all the candles to-night, Rego."

"You said yourself, my Lady," murmured the agonised man, cold sweat breaking out on his forehead, "that this was not a Saint's day."

"Nevertheless, Rego," persisted the Countess, surprised that even a favourite servant should thus attempt to thwart her will, "I ask you to light each candle. Do so at once."

She bowed her head as one who had spoken the final word, and again her fate trembled in the balance; but Rego heard the footsteps of the Count entering the gallery above him, that ran across the end of the chapel, and he at once resumed the lighting of the candles, making less speed in his eagerness than if he had gone about his task with more care.

The monk Ambrose draws a moral from this episode, which is sufficiently obvious when after-events have confirmed it, but which we need not here pause to consider, when an episode of the most thrilling nature is going forward on the lofty platform on the roof of Eltz Castle.

The sentinel paced back and forward within his narrow limit, listening to the depressing and monotonous tolling of the bell and cursing it, for the platform was a lonely place and the night of inky darkness. At last the bell ceased, and he stood resting on his long pike, enjoying the stillness, and peering into the blackness surrounding him, when suddenly he became aware of a grating, rasping sound below, as if some one were attempting to climb the precipitous beetling cliff of castle wall and slipping against the stones. His heart stood still with fear, for he knew it could be nothing human. An instant later something appeared over the parapet that could be seen only because it was blacker than the distant dark sky against which it was outlined. It rose and rose until the sentinel saw it was the top of a ladder, which was even more amazing than if the fiend himself had scrambled over the stone coping, for we know the devil can go anywhere, while a ladder cannot. But the soldier was a common-sense man, and, dark as was the night, he knew that, tall as such a ladder must be, there seemed a likelihood that human power was pushing it upward. He touched it with his hands and convinced himself that there was nothing supernatural about it. The ladder rose inch by inch, slowly, for it must have been no easy task for even twoscore men to raise it thus with ropes or other devices, especially when the bottom of it neared the top of the ledge. The soldier knew he should at once give the alarm: but he was the second traitor in the stronghold, corrupted by the sight of the glittering gold he had shared, and only prevented from selling himself because the rigours of military rule did not give him opportunity of going to Baldwineltz as the less exacting civilian duties had allowed the Spaniard to do and thus market his ware. So the sentry made no outcry, but silently prepared a method by which he could negotiate with advantage to himself when the first head appeared above the parapet. He fixed the point of his lance against a round of the ladder, and when the leading warrior, who was none other than Heinrich von Richenbach, himself came slowly and cautiously to the top of the wall, the sentinel, exerting all his strength, pushed the lance outward, and the top of the ladder with it, until it stood nearly perpendicular some two yards back from the wall.

"In God's name, what are you about? Is that you, Rego?"

The soldier replied, calmly:

"Order your men not to move, and do not move yourself, until I have some converse with you. Have no fear if you are prepared to accept my terms; otherwise you will have ample time to say your prayers before you reach the ground, for the distance is great."

Von Richenbach, who now leaned over the top round, suspended thus between heaven and earth, grasped the lance with both hands, so that the ladder might not be thrust beyond the perpendicular. In quivering voice he passed down the word that no man was to shift foot or hand until he had made bargain with the sentinel who held them in such extreme peril.

"What terms do you propose to me, soldier?" he asked, breathlessly.

"I will conduct you down to the courtyard, and when you have surprised and taken the castle you will grant me safe conduct and give me five bags of gold equal in weight to those offered to our captain."

"All that will I do and double the treasure. Faithfully and truly do I promise it."

"You pledge me your knightly word, and swear also by the holy coat of Treves?"

"I pledge and swear. And pray you be careful; incline the ladder yet a little more toward the wall."

"I trust to your honour," said the traitor, for traitors love to prate of honour, "and will now admit you to the castle; but until we are in the courtyard there must be silence."

"Incline the ladder gently, for it is so weighted that if it come suddenly against the wall, it may break in the middle."

At this supreme moment, as the sentinel was preparing to bring them cautiously to the wall, when all was deep silence, there crept swiftly and noiselessly through the trap-door the belated Spaniard. His catlike eyes beheld the shadowy form of the sentinel bending apparently over the parapet, but they showed him nothing beyond. With the speed and precipitation of a springing panther, the Spaniard leaped forward and drove his dagger deep into the neck of his comrade, who, with a gurgling cry, plunged headlong forward, and down the precipice, thrusting his lance as he fell. The Spaniard's dagger went with the doomed sentinel, sticking fast in his throat, and its presence there passed a fatal noose around the neck of Rego later, for they wrongly thought the false sentinel had saved the castle and that the Spaniard had murdered a faithful watchman.

Rego leaned panting over the stone coping, listening for the thud of the body. Then was he frozen with horror when the still night air was split with the most appalling shriek of combined human voice in an agony of fear that ever tortured the ear of man. The shriek ended in a terrorising crash far below, and silence again filled the valley.

"GENTLEMEN: THE KING!"

The room was large, but with a low ceiling, and at one end of the lengthy, broad apartment stood a gigantic fireplace, in which was heaped a pile of blazing logs, whose light, rather than that of several lanterns hanging from nails along the timbered walls, illuminated the faces of the twenty men who sat within. Heavy timbers, blackened with age and smoke, formed the ceiling. The long, low, diamond-paned window in the middle of the wall opposite the door, had been shuttered as completely as possible, but less care than usual was taken to prevent the light from penetrating into the darkness beyond, for the night was a stormy and tempestuous one, the rain lashing wildly against the hunting châlet, which, in its time, had seen many a merry hunting party gathered under its ample roof.

Every now and then a blast of wind shook the wooden edifice from garret to foundation, causing a puff of smoke to come down the chimney, and the white ashes to scatter in little whirlwinds over the hearth. On the opposite side from the shuttered window was the door, heavily barred. A long, oaken table occupied the centre of the room, and round this in groups, seated and standing, were a score of men, all with swords at their sides; bearing, many of them, that air of careless hauteur which is supposed to be a characteristic of noble birth.

Flagons were scattered upon the table, and a barrel of wine stood in a corner of the room farthest from the fireplace, but it was evident that this was no ordinary drinking party, and that the assemblage was brought about by some high purport, of a nature so serious that it stamped anxiety on every brow. No servants were present, and each man who wished a fresh flagon of wine had to take his measure to the barrel in the corner and fill for himself.

The hunting châlet stood in a wilderness, near the confines of the kingdom of Alluria, twelve leagues from the capital, and was the property of Count Staumn, whose tall, gaunt form stood erect at the head of the table as he silently listened to the discussion which every moment was becoming more and more heated, the principal speaking parts being taken by the obstinate, rough-spoken Baron Brunfels, on the one hand, and the crafty, fox-like ex-Chancellor Steinmetz on the other.

"I tell you," thundered Baron Brunfels, bringing his fist down on the table, "I will not have the King killed. Such a proposal goes beyond what was intended when we banded ourselves together. The King is a fool, so let him escape like a fool. I am a conspirator, but not an assassin."

"It is justice rather than assassination," said the ex-Chancellor suavely, as if his tones were oil and the Baron's boisterous talk were troubled waters.

"Justice!" cried the Baron, with great contempt. "You have learned that cant word in the Cabinet of the King himself, before he thrust you out. He eternally prates of justice, yet, much as I loathe him, I have no wish to compass his death, either directly or through gabbling of justice."

"Will you permit me to point out the reason that induces me to believe his continued exemption, and State policy, will not run together?" replied the advocate of the King's death. "If Rudolph escape, he will take up his abode in a neighbouring territory, and there will inevitably follow plots and counter-plots for his restoration—thus Alluria will be kept in a state of constant turmoil. There will doubtless grow up within the kingdom itself a party sworn to his restoration. We shall thus be involved in difficulties at home and abroad, and all for what? Merely to save the life of a man who is an enemy to each of us. We place thousands of lives in jeopardy, render our own positions insecure, bring continual disquiet upon the State, when all might be avoided by the slitting of one throat, even though that throat belong to the King."

It was evident that the lawyer's persuasive tone brought many to his side, and the conspirators seemed about evenly divided upon the question of life or death to the King. The Baron was about to break out again with some strenuousness in favour of his own view of the matter, when Count Staumn made a proposition that was eagerly accepted by all save Brunfels himself.

"Argument," said Count Staumn, "is ever the enemy of good comradeship. Let us settle the point at once and finally, with the dice-box. Baron Brunfels, you are too seasoned a gambler to object to such a mode of terminating a discussion. Steinmetz, the law, of which you are so distinguished a representative, is often compared to a lottery, so you cannot look with disfavour upon a method that is conclusive, and as reasonably fair as the average decision of a judge. Let us throw, therefore, for the life of the King. I, as chairman of this meeting, will be umpire. Single throws, and the highest number wins. Baron Brunfels, you will act for the King, and, if you win, may bestow upon the monarch his life. Chancellor Steinmetz stands for the State. If he wins, then is the King's life forfeit. Gentlemen, are you agreed?"

"Agreed, agreed," cried the conspirators, with practically unanimous voice.

Baron Brunfels grumbled somewhat, but when the dice-horn was brought, and he heard the rattle of the bones within the leathern cylinder, the light of a gambler's love shone in his eyes, and he made no further protest.

The ex-Chancellor took the dice-box in his hand, and was about to shake, when there came suddenly upon them three stout raps against the door, given apparently with the hilt of a sword. Many not already standing, started to their feet, and nearly all looked one upon another with deep dismay in their glances. The full company of conspirators was present; exactly a score of men knew of the rendezvous, and now the twenty-first man outside was beating the oaken panels. The knocking was repeated, but now accompanied by the words:

"Open, I beg of you."

Count Staumn left the table and, stealthily as a cat, approached the door.

"Who is there?" he asked.

"A wayfarer, weary and wet, who seeks shelter from the storm."

"My house is already filled," spoke up the Count. "I have no room for another."

"Open the door peacefully," cried the outlander, "and do not put me to the necessity of forcing it."

There was a ring of decision in the voice which sent quick pallor to more than one cheek. Ex-Chancellor Steinmetz rose to his feet with chattering teeth, and terror in his eyes; he seemed to recognise the tones of the invisible speaker. Count Staumn looked over his shoulder at the assemblage with an expression that plainly said: "What am I to do?"

"In the fiend's name," hissed Baron Brunfels, taking the precaution, however, to speak scarce above his breath, "if you are so frightened when it comes to a knock at the door, what will it be when the real knocks are upon you. Open, Count, and let the insistent stranger in. Whether he leave the place alive or no, there are twenty men here to answer."

The Count undid the fastenings and threw back the door. There entered a tall man completely enveloped in a dark cloak that was dripping wet. Drawn over his eyes was a hunter's hat of felt, with a drooping bedraggled feather on it.

The door was immediately closed and barred behind him, and the stranger, pausing a moment when confronted by so many inquiring eyes, flung off his cloak, throwing it over the back of a chair; then he removed his hat with a sweep, sending the raindrops flying. The intriguants gazed at him, speechless, with varying emotions. They saw before them His Majesty, Rudolph, King of Alluria.

If the King had any suspicion of his danger, he gave no token of it. On his smooth, lofty forehead there was no trace of frown, and no sign of fear. His was a manly figure, rather over, than under, six feet in height; not slim and gaunt, like Count Staumn, nor yet stout to excess, like Baron Brunfels. The finger of Time had touched with frost the hair at his temples, and there were threads of white in his pointed beard, but his sweeping moustache was still as black as the night from which he came.

His frank, clear, honest eyes swept the company, resting momentarily on each, then he said in a firm voice, without the suspicion of a tremor in it:

"Gentlemen, I give you good evening, and although the hospitality of Count Staumn has needed spurring, I lay that not up against him, because I am well aware his apparent reluctance arose through the unexpectedness of my visit; and, if the Count will act as cup-bearer, we will drown all remembrance of a barred door in a flagon of wine, for, to tell truth, gentlemen, I have ridden hard in order to have the pleasure of drinking with you."

As the King spoke these ominous words, he cast a glance of piercing intensity upon the company, and more than one quailed under it. He strode to the fireplace, spurs jingling as he went, and stood with his back to the fire, spreading out his hands to the blaze. Count Staumn left the bolted door, took an empty flagon from the shelf, filled it at the barrel in the corner, and, with a low bow, presented the brimming measure to the King.

Rudolph held aloft his beaker of Burgundy, and, as he did so, spoke in a loud voice that rang to the beams of the ceiling:

"Gentlemen, I give you a suitable toast. May none here gathered encounter a more pitiless storm than that which is raging without!"

With this he drank off the wine, and, inclining his head slightly to the Count, returned the flagon. No one, save the King, had spoken since he entered. Every word he had uttered seemed charged with double meaning and brought to the suspicious minds of his hearers visions of a trysting place surrounded by troops, and the King standing there, playing with them, as a tiger plays with its victims. His easy confidence appalled them.

When first he came in, several who were seated remained so, but one by one they rose to their feet, with the exception of Baron Brunfels, although he, when the King gave the toast, also stood. It was clear enough their glances of fear were not directed towards the King, but towards Baron Brunfels. Several pairs of eyes beseeched him in silent supplication, but the Baron met none of these glances, for his gaze was fixed upon the King.

Every man present knew the Baron to be reckless of consequences; frankly outspoken, thoroughly a man of the sword, and a despiser of diplomacy. They feared that at any moment he might blurt out the purport of the meeting, and more than one was thankful for the crafty ex-Chancellor's planning, who throughout had insisted there should be no documentary evidence of their designs, either in their houses or on their persons. Some startling rumour must have reached the King's ear to bring him thus unexpectedly upon them.

The anxiety of all was that some one should persuade the King they were merely a storm-besieged hunting party. They trembled in anticipation of Brunfels' open candor, and dreaded the revealing of the real cause of their conference. There was now no chance to warn the Baron; a man who spoke his mind; who never looked an inch beyond his nose, even though his head should roll off in consequence, and if a man does not value his own head, how can he be expected to care for the heads of his neighbours?

"I ask you to be seated," said the King, with a wave of the hand.

Now, what should that stubborn fool of a Baron do but remain standing, when all but Rudolph and himself had seated themselves, thus drawing His Majesty's attention directly towards him, and making a colloquy between them well-nigh inevitable. Those next the ex-Chancellor were nudging him, in God's name, to stand also, and open whatever discussion there must ensue between themselves and His Majesty, so that it might be smoothly carried on, but the Chancellor was ashen grey with fear, and his hand trembled on the table.

"My Lord of Brunfels," said the King, a smile hovering about his lips, "I see that I have interrupted you at your old pleasure of dicing; while requesting you to continue your game as though I had not joined you, may I venture to hope the stakes you play for are not high?"

Every one held his breath, awaiting with deepest concern the reply of the frowning Baron, and when it came growling forth, there was little in it to ease their disquiet.

"Your Majesty," said Baron Brunfels, "the stakes are the highest that a gambler may play for."

"You tempt me, Baron, to guess that the hazard is a man's soul, but I see that your adversary is my worthy ex-Chancellor, and as I should hesitate to impute to him the character of the devil, I am led, therefore, to the conclusion that you play for a human life. Whose life is in the cast, my Lord of Brunfels?"

Before the Baron could reply, ex-Chancellor Steinmetz arose, with some indecision, to his feet. He began in a trembling voice:

"I beg your gracious permission to explain the reason of our gathering—"

"Herr Steinmetz," cried the King sternly, "when I desire your interference I shall call for it; and remember this, Herr Steinmetz; the man who begins a game must play it to the end, even though he finds luck running against him."

The ex-Chancellor sat down again, and drew his hand across his damp forehead.

"Your Majesty," spoke up the Baron, a ring of defiance in his voice, "I speak not for my comrades, but for myself. I begin no game that I fear to finish. We were about dice in order to discover whether Your Majesty should live or die."

A simultaneous moan seemed to rise from the assembled traitors. The smile returned to the King's lips.

"Baron," he said, "I have ever chided myself for loving you, for you were always a bad example to weak and impressionable natures. Even when your overbearing, obstinate intolerance compelled me to dismiss you from the command of my army, I could not but admire your sturdy honesty. Had I been able to graft your love of truth upon some of my councillors, what a valuable group of advisers might I have gathered round me. But we have had enough of comedy and now tragedy sets in. Those who are traitors to their ruler must not be surprised if a double traitor is one of their number. Why am I here? Why do two hundred mounted and armed men surround this doomed châlet? Miserable wretches, what have you to say that judgment be not instantly passed upon you?"

"I have this to say," roared Baron Brunfels, drawing his sword, "that whatever may befall this assemblage, you, at least, shall not live to boast of it."

The King stood unmoved as Baron Brunfels was about to rush upon him, but Count Staumn and others threw themselves between the Baron and his victim, seeing in the King's words some intimation of mercy to be held out to them, could but actual assault upon his person be prevented.

"My Lord of Brunfels," said the King, calmly, "sheath your sword. Your ancestors have often drawn it, but always for, and never against the occupant of the Throne. Now, gentlemen, hear my decision, and abide faithfully by it. Seat yourselves at the table, ten on each side, the dice-box between you. You shall not be disappointed, but shall play out the game of life and death. Each dices with his opposite. He who throws the higher number escapes. He who throws the lower places his weapons on the empty chair, and stands against yonder wall to be executed for the traitor that he is. Thus half of your company shall live, and the other half seek death with such courage as may be granted them. Do you agree, or shall I give the signal?"

With unanimous voice they agreed, all excepting Baron Brunfels, who spoke not.

"Come, Baron, you and my devoted ex-Chancellor were about to play when I came in. Begin the game."

"Very well," replied the Baron nonchalantly. "Steinmetz, the dice-box is near your hand: throw."

Some one placed the cubes in the leathern cup and handed it to the ex-Chancellor, whose shivering fingers relieved him of the necessity of shaking the box. The dice rolled out on the table; a three, a four, and a one. Those nearest reported the total.

"Eight!" cried the King. "Now, Baron."

Baron Brunfels carelessly threw the dice into their receptacle, and a moment after the spotted bones clattered on the table.

"Three sixes!" cried the Baron. "Lord, if I only had such luck when I played for money!"

The ex-Chancellor's eyes were starting from his head, wild with fear.

"We have three throws," he screamed.

"Not so," said the King.

"I swear I understood that we were to have three chances," shrieked Steinmetz, springing from his chair. "But it is all illegal, and not to be borne. I will not have my life diced away to please either King or commons."

He drew his sword and placed himself in an attitude of defence.

"Seize him; disarm him, and bind him," commanded the King. "There are enough gentlemen in this company to see that the rules of the game are adhered to."

Steinmetz, struggling and pleading for mercy, was speedily overpowered and bound; then his captors placed him against the wall, and resumed their seats at the table. The next man to be doomed was Count Staumn. The Count arose from his chair, bowed first to the King and then to the assembled company; drew forth his sword, broke it over his knee, and walked to the wall of the condemned.

The remainder of the fearful contest was carried on in silence, but with great celerity, and before a quarter of an hour was past, ten men had their backs to the wall, while the remaining ten were seated at the table, some on one side, and some on the other.

The men ranged against the wall were downcast, for however bravely a soldier may meet death in hostile encounter, it is a different matter to face it bound and helpless at the hands of an executioner.

A shade of sadness seemed to overspread the countenance of the King, who still occupied the position he had taken at the first, with his back towards the fire.

Baron Brunfels shifted uneasily in his seat, and glanced now and then with compassion at his sentenced comrades. He was first to break the silence.

"Your Majesty," he said, "I am always loath to see a coward die. The whimpering of your former Chancellor annoys me; therefore, will I gladly take his place, and give to him the life and liberty you perhaps design for me, if, in exchange, I have the privilege of speaking my mind regarding you and your precious Kingship."

"Unbind the valiant Steinmetz," said the King. "Speak your mind freely, Baron Brunfels."

The Baron rose, drew sword from scabbard, and placed it on the table.

"Your Majesty, backed by brute force," he began, "has condemned to death ten of your subjects. You have branded us as traitors, and such we are, and so find no fault with your sentence; merely recognising that you represent, for the time being, the upper hand. You have reminded me that my ancestors fought for yours, and that they never turned their swords against their sovereign. Why, then, have our blades been pointed towards your breast? Because, King Rudolph, you are yourself a traitor. You belong to the ruling class and have turned your back upon your order. You, a King, have made yourself a brother to the demagogue at the street corner; yearning for the cheap applause of the serf. You have shorn nobility of its privileges, and for what?"

"And for what?" echoed the King with rising voice. "For this; that the ploughman on the plain may reap what he has sown; that the shepherd on the hillside may enjoy the increase which comes to his flock; that taxation may be light; that my nobles shall deal honestly with the people, and not use their position for thievery and depredation; that those whom the State honours by appointing to positions of trust shall content themselves with the recompense lawfully given, and refrain from peculation; that peace and security shall rest on the land; and that bloodthirsty swashbucklers shall not go up and down inciting the people to carnage and rapine under the name of patriotism. This is the task I set myself when I came to the Throne. What fault have you to find with the programme, my Lord Baron?"

"The simple fault that it is the programme of a fool," replied the Baron calmly. "In following it you have gained the resentment of your nobles, and have not even received the thanks of those pitiable hinds, the ploughman in the valley or the shepherd on the hills. You have impoverished us so that the clowns may have a few more coins with which to muddle in drink their already stupid brains. You are hated in cot and castle alike. You would not stand in your place for a moment, were not an army behind you. Being a fool, you think the common people love honesty, whereas, they only curse that they have not a share in the thieving."

"The people," said the King soberly, "have been misled. Their ear has been abused by calumny and falsehood. Had it been possible for me personally to explain to them the good that must ultimately accrue to a land where honesty rules, I am confident I would have had their undivided support, even though my nobles deserted me."

"Not so, Your Majesty; they would listen to you and cheer you, but when the next orator came among them, promising to divide the moon, and give a share to each, they would gather round his banner and hoot you from the kingdom. What care they for rectitude of government? They see no farther than the shining florin that glitters on their palm. When your nobles were rich, they came to their castles among the people, and scattered their gold with a lavish hand. Little recked the peasants how it was got, so long as they shared it. 'There,' they said, 'the coin comes to us that we have not worked for.'

"But now, with castles deserted, and retainers dismissed, the people have to sweat to wring from traders the reluctant silver, and they cry: 'Thus it was not in times of old, and this King is the cause of it,' and so they spit upon your name, and shrug their shoulders, when your honesty is mentioned. And now, Rudolph of Alluria, I have done, and I go the more jauntily to my death that I have had fair speech with you before the end."

The King looked at the company, his eyes veiled with moisture. "I thought," he said slowly, "until to-night, that I had possessed some qualities at least of a ruler of men. I came here alone among you, and although there are brave men in this assembly, yet I had the ordering of events as I chose to order them, notwithstanding that odds stood a score to one against me. I still venture to think that whatever failures have attended my eight years' rule in Alluria arose from faults of my own, and not through imperfections in the plan, or want of appreciation in the people.

"I have now to inform you that if it is disastrous for a King to act without the co-operation of his nobles, it is equally disastrous for them to plot against their leader. I beg to acquaint you with the fact that the insurrection so carefully prepared has broken out prematurely. My capital is in possession of the factions, who are industriously cutting each other's throats to settle which one of two smooth-tongued rascals shall be their President. While you were dicing to settle the fate of an already deposed King, and I was sentencing you to a mythical death, we were all alike being involved in common ruin.

"I have seen to-night more property in flames than all my savings during the last eight years would pay for. I have no horsemen at my back, and have stumbled here blindly, a much bedraggled fugitive, having lost my way in every sense of the phrase. And so I beg of the hospitality of Count Staumn another flagon of wine, and either a place of shelter for my patient horse, who has been left too long in the storm without, or else direction towards the frontier, whereupon my horse and I will set out to find it."

"Not towards the frontier!" cried Baron Brunfels, grasping again his sword and holding it aloft, "but towards the capital. We will surround you, and hew for you a way through that fickle mob back to the throne of your ancestors."

Each man sprang to his weapon and brandished it above his head, while a ringing cheer echoed to the timbered ceiling.

"The King! The King!" they cried.

Rudolph smiled and shook his head.

"Not so," he said. "I leave a thankless throne with a joy I find it impossible to express. As I sat on horseback, half-way up the hill above the burning city, and heard the clash of arms, I was filled with amazement to think that men would actually fight for the position of ruler of the people. Whether the insurrection has brought freedom to themselves or not, the future alone can tell, but it has at least brought freedom to me. I now belong to myself. No man may question either my motives or my acts. Gentlemen, drink with me to the new President of Alluria, whoever he may be."

But the King drank alone, none other raising flagon to lip. Then Baron Brunfels cried aloud:

"Gentlemen: the King!"

And never in the history of Alluria was a toast so heartily honoured.

THE HOUR-GLASS

Bertram Eastford had intended to pass the shop of his old friend, the curiosity dealer, into whose pockets so much of his money had gone for trinkets gathered from all quarters of the globe. He knew it was weakness on his part, to select that street when he might have taken another, but he thought it would do no harm to treat himself to one glance at the seductive window of the old curiosity shop, where the dealer was in the habit of displaying his latest acquisitions. The window was never quite the same, and it had a continued fascination for Bertram Eastford; but this time, he said to himself resolutely, he would not enter, having, as he assured himself, the strength of mind to forego this temptation. However, he reckoned without his window, for in it there was an old object newly displayed which caught his attention as effectually as a half-driven nail arrests the hem of a cloak. On the central shelf of the window stood an hour-glass, its framework of some wood as black as ebony. He stood gazing at it for a moment, then turned to the door and went inside, greeting the ancient shopman, whom he knew so well.

"I want to look at the hour-glass you have in the window," he said.

"Ah, yes," replied the curiosity dealer; "the cheap watch has driven the hour-glass out of the commercial market, and we rarely pick up a thing like that nowadays." He took the hour-glass from the shelf in the window, reversed it, and placed it on a table. The ruddy sand began to pour through into the lower receptacle in a thin, constant stream, as if it were blood that had been dried and powdered. Eastford watched the ever-increasing heap at the bottom, rising conically, changing its shape every moment, as little avalanches of the sand fell away from its heightening sides.

"There is no need for you to extol its antiquity," said Eastford, with a smile. "I knew the moment I looked at it that such glasses are rare, and you are not going to find me a cheapening customer."

"So far from over-praising it," protested the shopman, "I was about to call your attention to a defect. It is useless as a measurer of time."

"It doesn't record the exact hour, then?" asked Eastford.

"Well, I suppose the truth is, they were not very particular in the old days, and time was not money, as it is now. It measures the hour with great accuracy," the curio dealer went on—"that is, if you watch it; but, strangely enough, after it has run for half an hour, or thereabouts, it stops, because of some defect in the neck of the glass, or in the pulverising of the sand, and will not go again until the glass is shaken."

The hour-glass at that moment verified what the old man said. The tiny stream of sand suddenly ceased, but resumed its flow the moment its owner jarred the frame, and continued pouring without further interruption.

"That is very singular," said Eastford. "How do you account for it?"

"I imagine it is caused by some inequality in the grains of sand; probably a few atoms larger than the others come together at the neck, and so stop the percolation. It always does this, and, of course, I cannot remedy the matter because the glass is hermetically sealed."

"Well, I don't want it as a timekeeper, so we will not allow that defect to interfere with the sale. How much do you ask for it?"

The dealer named his price, and Eastford paid the amount.

"I shall send it to you this afternoon."

"Thank you," said the customer, taking his leave.

That night in his room Bertram Eastford wrote busily until a late hour. When his work was concluded, he pushed away his manuscript with a sigh of that deep contentment which comes to a man who has not wasted his day. He replenished the open fire, drew his most comfortable arm-chair in front of it, took the green shade from his lamp, thus filling the luxurious apartment with a light that was reflected from armour and from ancient weapons standing in corners and hung along the walls. He lifted the paper-covered package, cut the string that bound it, and placed the ancient hour-glass on his table, watching the thin stream of sand which his action had set running. The constant, unceasing, steady downfall seemed to hypnotise him. Its descent was as silent as the footsteps of time itself. Suddenly it stopped, as it had done in the shop, and its abrupt ceasing jarred on his tingling nerves like an unexpected break in the stillness. He could almost imagine an unseen hand clasping the thin cylinder of the glass and throttling it. He shook the bygone time-measurer and breathed again more steadily when the sand resumed its motion. Presently he took the glass from the table and examined it with some attention.

He thought at first its frame was ebony, but further inspection convinced him it was oak, blackened with age. On one round end was carved rudely two hearts overlapping, and twined about them a pair of serpents.

"Now, I wonder what that's for?" murmured Eastford to himself. "An attempt at a coat of arms, perhaps."

There was no clue to the meaning of the hieroglyphics, and Eastford, with the glass balanced on his knee, watched the sand still running, the crimson thread sparkling in the lamplight. He fancied he saw distorted reflections of faces in the convex glass, although his reason told him they were but caricatures of his own. The great bell in the tower near by, with slow solemnity, tolled twelve. He counted its measured strokes one by one, and then was startled by a decisive knock at his door. One section of his brain considered this visit untimely, another looked on it as perfectly usual, and while the two were arguing the matter out, he heard his own voice cry: "Come in."

The door opened, and the discussion between the government and the opposition in his mind ceased to consider the untimeliness of the visit, for here, in the visitor himself, stood another problem. He was a young man in military costume, his uniform being that of an officer. Eastford remembered seeing something like it on the stage, and knowing little of military affairs, thought perhaps the costume of the visitor before him indicated an officer in the Napoleonic war.

"Good evening!" said the incomer. "May I introduce myself? I am

Lieutenant Sentore, of the regular army."

"You are very welcome," returned his host. "Will you be seated?"

"Thank you, no. I have but a few moments to stay. I have come for my hour-glass, if you will be good enough to let me have it."

"Your hour-glass?" ejaculated Eastford, in surprise. "I think you labour under a misapprehension. The glass belongs to me; I bought it to-day at the old curiosity shop in Finchmore Street."

"Rightful possession of the glass would appear to rest with you, technically; but taking you to be a gentleman, I venture to believe that a mere statement of my priority of claim will appeal to you, even though it might have no effect on the minds of a jury of our countrymen."

"You mean to say that the glass has been stolen from you and has been sold?"

"It has been sold undoubtedly over and over again, but never stolen, so far as I have been able to trace its history."

"If, then, the glass has been honestly purchased by its different owners, I fail to see how you can possibly establish any claim to it."

"I have already admitted that my claim is moral rather than legal," continued the visitor. "It is a long story; have I your permission to tell it?"

"I shall be delighted to listen," replied Eastford, "but before doing so I beg to renew my invitation, and ask you to occupy this easy-chair before the fire."

The officer bowed in silence, crossed the room behind Eastford, and sat down in the arm-chair, placing his sword across his knees. The stranger spread his hands before the fire, and seemed to enjoy the comforting warmth. He remained for a few moments buried in deep reflection, quite ignoring the presence of his host, who, glancing upon the hour-glass in dispute upon his knees, seeing that the sands had all run out silently reversed it and set them flowing again. This action caught the corner of the stranger's eye, and brought him to a realisation of why he was there. Drawing a heavy sigh, he began his story.

"In the year 1706 I held the post of lieutenant in that part of the British Army commanded by General Trelawny, the supreme command, of course, being in the hands of the great Marlborough."

Eastford listened to this announcement with a feeling that there was something wrong about the statement. The man sitting there was calmly talking of a time one hundred and ninety-two years past, and yet he himself could not be a day more than twenty-five years old. Somewhere entangled in this were the elements of absurdity. Eastford found himself unable to unravel them, but the more he thought of the matter, the more reasonable it began to appear, and so, hoping his visitor had not noted the look of surprise on his face, he said, quietly, casting his mind back over the history of England, and remembering what he had learned at school:—

"That was during the war of the Spanish Succession?"

"Yes: the war had then been in progress four years, and many brilliant victories had been won, the greatest of which was probably the Battle of Blenheim."

"Quite so," murmured Eastford.

"It was the English," Casper cried,

"That put the French to rout;

"But what they killed each other for,

"I never could make out."

The officer looked up in astonishment.

"I never heard anything like that said about the war. The reason for it was perfectly plain. We had to fight or acknowledge France to be the dictator of Europe. Still, politics have nothing to do with my story. General Trelawny and his forces were in Brabant, and were under orders to join the Duke of Marlborough's army. We were to go through the country as speedily as possible, for a great battle was expected. Trelawny's instructions were to capture certain towns and cities that lay in our way, to dismantle the fortresses, and to parole their garrisons. We could not encumber ourselves with prisoners, and so marched the garrisons out, paroled them, destroyed their arms, and bade them disperse. But, great as was our hurry, strict orders had been given to leave no strongholds in our rear untaken.

"Everything went well until we came to the town of Elsengore, which we captured without the loss of a man. The capture of the town, however, was of little avail, for in the centre of it stood a strong citadel, which we tried to take by assault, but could not. General Trelawny, a very irascible, hotheaded man, but, on the whole, a just and capable officer, impatient at this unexpected delay, offered the garrison almost any terms they desired to evacuate the castle. But, having had warning of our coming, they had provisioned the place, were well supplied with ammunition, and their commander refused to make terms with General Trelawny.

"'If you want the place,' said the Frenchman, 'come and take it.'

"General Trelawny, angered at this contemptuous treatment, flung his men again and again at the citadel, but without making the slightest impression on it.

"We were in no wise prepared for a long siege, nor had we expected stubborn resistance. Marching quickly, as was our custom heretofore, we possessed no heavy artillery, and so were at a disadvantage when attacking a fortress as strong as that of Elsengore. Meanwhile, General Trelawny sent mounted messengers by different roads to his chief giving an account of what had happened, explaining his delay in joining the main army, and asking for definite instructions. He expected that one or two, at least, of the mounted messengers sent away would reach his chief and be enabled to return. And that is exactly what happened, for one day a dusty horseman came to General Trelawny's headquarters with a brief note from Marlborough. The Commander-in-Chief said:—

"'I think the Frenchman's advice is good. We want the place; therefore, take it.'

"But he sent no heavy artillery to aid us in this task, for he could not spare his big guns, expecting, as he did, an important battle. General Trelawny having his work thus cut out for him, settled down to accomplish it as best he might. He quartered officers and men in various parts of the town, the more thoroughly to keep watch on the citizens, of whose good intentions, if the siege were prolonged, we were by no means sure.

"It fell to my lot to be lodged in the house of Burgomaster Seidelmier, of whose conduct I have no reason to complain, for he treated me well. I was given two rooms, one a large, low apartment on the first floor, and communicating directly with the outside, by means of a hall and a separate stairway. The room was lighted by a long, many-paned window, leaded and filled with diamond-shaped glass. Beyond this large drawing-room was my bedroom. I must say that I enjoyed my stay in Burgomaster Seidelmier's house none the less because he had an only daughter, a most charming girl. Our acquaintance ripened into deep friendship, and afterwards into——but that has nothing to do with what I have to tell you. My story is of war, and not of love. Gretlich Seidelmier presented me with the hour-glass you have in your hand, and on it I carved the joined hearts entwined with our similar initials."

"So they are initials, are they?" said Eastford, glancing down at what he had mistaken for twining serpents.

"Yes," said the officer; "I was more accustomed to a sword than to an etching tool, and the letters are but rudely drawn. One evening, after dark, Gretlich and I were whispering together in the hall, when we heard the heavy tread of the general coming up the stair. The girl fled precipitately, and I, holding open the door, waited the approach of my chief. He entered and curtly asked me to close the door.

"'Lieutenant,' he said, 'it is my intention to capture the citadel to-night. Get together twenty-five of your men, and have them ready under the shadow of this house, but give no one a hint of what you intend to do with them. In one hour's time leave this place with your men as quietly as possible, and make an attack on the western entrance of the citadel. Your attack is to be but a feint and to draw off their forces to that point. Still, if any of your men succeed in gaining entrance to the fort they shall not lack reward and promotion. Have you a watch?'

"'Not one that will go, general; but I have an hourglass here.'

"'Very well, set it running. Collect your men, and exactly at the hour lead them to the west front; it is but five minutes' quick march from here. An hour and five minutes from this moment I expect you to begin the attack, and the instant you are before the western gate make as much noise as your twenty-five men are capable of, so as to lead the enemy to believe that the attack is a serious one.'

"Saying this, the general turned and made his way, heavy-footed, through the hall and down the stairway.

"I set the hour-glass running, and went at once to call my men, stationing them where I had been ordered to place them. I returned to have a word with Gretlich before I departed on what I knew was a dangerous mission. Glancing at the hour-glass, I saw that not more than a quarter of the sand had run down during my absence. I remained in the doorway, where I could keep an eye on the hour-glass, while the girl stood leaning her arm against the angle of the dark passageway, supporting her fair cheek on her open palm; and, standing thus in the darkness, she talked to me in whispers. We talked and talked, engaged in that sweet, endless conversation that murmurs in subdued tone round the world, being duplicated that moment at who knows how many places. Absorbed as I was in listening, at last there crept into my consciousness the fact that the sand in the upper bulb was not diminishing as fast as it should. This knowledge was fully in my mind for some time before I realised its fearful significance. Suddenly the dim knowledge took on actuality. I sprang from the door-lintel, saying:—

"'Good heavens, the sand in the hour-glass has stopped running!'

"I remained there motionless, all action struck from my rigid limbs, gazing at the hour-glass on the table.

"Gretlich, peering in at the doorway, looking at the hour-glass and not at me, having no suspicion of the ruin involved in the stoppage of that miniature sandstorm, said, presently:—

"'Oh, yes, I forgot to tell you it does that now and then, and so you must shake the glass.'

"She bent forward as if to do this when the leaden windows shuddered, and the house itself trembled with the sharp crash of our light cannon, followed almost immediately by the deeper detonation of the heavier guns from the citadel. The red sand in the glass began to fall again, and its liberation seemed to unfetter my paralysed limbs. Bareheaded as I was, I rushed like one frantic along the passage and down the stairs. The air was resonant with the quick-following reports of the cannon, and the long, narrow street was fitfully lit up as if by sudden flashes of summer lightning. My men were still standing where I had placed them. Giving a sharp word of command, I marched them down the street and out into the square, where I met General Trelawny coming back from his futile assault. Like myself, he was bareheaded. His military countenance was begrimed with powder-smoke, but he spoke to me with no trace of anger in his voice.

"'Lieutenant Sentore,' he said, 'disperse your men.'

"I gave the word to disband my men, and then stood at attention before him.

"'Lieutenant Sentore,' he said, in the same level voice, 'return to your quarters and consider yourself under arrest. Await my coming there.'

"I turned and obeyed his orders. It seemed incredible that the sand should still be running in the hour-glass, for ages appeared to have passed over my head since last I was in that room. I paced up and down, awaiting the coming of my chief, feeling neither fear nor regret, but rather dumb despair. In a few minutes his heavy tread was on the stair, followed by the measured tramp of a file of men. He came into the room, and with him were a sergeant and four soldiers, fully armed. The general was trembling with rage, but held strong control over himself, as was his habit on serious occasions.

"'Lieutenant Sentore,' he said, 'why were you not at your post?"

"'The running sand in the hour-glass' (I hardly recognised my own voice on hearing it) 'stopped when but half exhausted. I did not notice its interruption until it was too late.'

"The general glanced grimly at the hour-glass. The last sands were falling through to the lower bulb. I saw that he did not believe my explanation.

"'It seems now to be in perfect working order,' he said, at last.

"He strode up to it and reversed it, watching the sand pour for a few moments, then he spoke abruptly:—

"'Lieutenant Sentore, your sword.'

"I handed my weapon to him without a word. Turning to the sergeant, he said: 'Lieutenant Sentore is sentenced to death. He has an hour for whatever preparations he cares to make. Allow him to dispose of that hour as he chooses, so long as he remains within this room and holds converse with no one whatever. When the last sands of this hour-glass are run, Lieutenant Sentore will stand at the other end of this room and meet the death merited by traitors, laggards, or cowards. Do you understand your duty, sergeant?'

"'Yes, general.'

"General Trelawny abruptly left the room, and we heard his heavy steps echoing throughout the silent house, and later, more faintly on the cobble-stones of the street. When they had died away a deep stillness set in, I standing alone at one end of the room, my eyes fixed on the hour-glass, and the sergeant with his four men, like statues at the other, also gazing at the same sinister object. The sergeant was the first to break the silence.

"'Lieutenant,' he said, 'do you wish to write anything——?'

"He stopped short, being an unready man, rarely venturing far beyond 'Yes' and 'No.'

"'I should like to communicate with one in this household,' I said, 'but the general has forbidden it, so all I ask is that you shall have my body conveyed from this room as speedily as possible after the execution.'

"'Very good, lieutenant,' answered the sergeant.

"After that, for a long time no word was spoken. I watched my life run redly through the wasp waist of the transparent glass, then suddenly the sand ceased to flow, half in the upper bulb, half in the lower.

"'It has stopped,' said the sergeant; 'I must shake the glass.'

"'Stand where you are!' I commanded, sharply. 'Your orders do not run to that.'

"The habit of obedience rooted the sergeant to the spot.

"'Send one of your men to General Trelawny,' I said, as if I had still the right to be obeyed. 'Tell him what has happened, and ask for instructions. Let your man tread lightly as he leaves the room.'

"The sergeant did not hesitate a moment, but gave the order I required of him. The soldier nearest the door tip-toed out of the house. As we all stood there the silence seeming the deeper because of the stopping of the sand, we heard the hour toll in the nearest steeple. The sergeant was visibly perturbed, and finally he said:—

"'Lieutenant, I must obey the general's orders. An hour has passed since he left here, for that clock struck as he was going down the stair. Soldiers, make ready. Present.'

"The men, like impassive machines levelled their muskets at my breast. I held up my hand.

"'Sergeant,' I said as calmly as I could, 'you are now about to exceed your instructions. Give another command at your peril. The exact words of the general were, 'When the last sands of this hour-glass are run.' I call your attention to the fact that the conditions are not fulfilled. Half of the sand remains in the upper bulb.'

"The sergeant scratched his head in perplexity, but he had no desire to kill me, and was only actuated by a soldier's wish to adhere strictly to the letter of his instructions, be the victim friend or foe. After a few moments he muttered, 'It is true,' then gave a command that put his men into their former position.

"Probably more than half an hour passed, during which time no man moved; the sergeant and his three remaining soldiers seemed afraid to breathe; then we heard the step of the general himself on the stair. I feared that this would give the needed impetus to the sand in the glass, but, when Trelawny entered, the status quo remained. The general stood looking at the suspended sand, without speaking.

"' That is what happened before, general, and that is why I was not at my place. I have committed the crime of neglect, and have thus deservedly earned my death; but I shall die the happier if my general believes I am neither a traitor nor a coward.'

"The general, still without a word, advanced to the table, slightly shook the hour-glass, and the sand began to pour again. Then he picked the glass up in his hand, examining it minutely, as if it were some strange kind of toy, turning it over and over. He glanced up at me and said, quite in his usual tone, as if nothing in particular had come between us:—

"'Remarkable thing that, Sentore, isn't it?'

"'Very,' I answered, grimly.

"He put the glass down.

"'Sergeant, take your men to quarters. Lieutenant Sentore, I return to you your sword; you can perhaps make better use of it alive than dead; I am not a man to be disobeyed, reason or no reason. Remember that, and now go to bed.'

"He left me without further word, and buckling on my sword, I proceeded straightway to disobey again.

"I had a great liking for General Trelawny. Knowing how he fumed and raged at being thus held helpless by an apparently impregnable fortress in the unimportant town of Elsengore, I had myself studied the citadel from all points, and had come to the conclusion that it might be successfully attempted, not by the great gates that opened on the square of the town, nor by the inferior west gates, but by scaling the seemingly unclimbable cliffs at the north side. The wall at the top of this precipice was low, and owing to the height of the beetling cliff, was inefficiently watched by one lone sentinel, who paced the battlements from corner tower to corner tower. I had made my plans, intending to ask the general's permission to risk this venture, but now I resolved to try it without his knowledge or consent, and thus retrieve, if I could, my failure of the foregoing part of the night.

"Taking with me a long, thin rope which I had in my room, anticipating such a trial for it, I roused five of my picked men, and silently we made our way to the foot of the northern cliff. Here, with the rope around my waist, I worked my way diagonally up along a cleft in the rock, which, like others parallel to it, marked the face of the precipice. A slip would be fatal. The loosening of a stone would give warning to the sentinel, whose slow steps I heard on the wall above me, but at last I reached a narrow ledge without accident, and standing up in the darkness, my chin was level with the top of the wall on which the sentry paced. The shelf between the bottom of the wall and the top of the cliff was perhaps three feet in width, and gave ample room for a man careful of his footing. Aided by the rope, the others, less expert climbers than myself, made their way to my side one by one, and the six of us stood on the ledge under the low wall. We were all in our stockinged feet, some of the men, in fact, not even having stockings on. As the sentinel passed, we crouching in the darkness under the wall, the most agile of our party sprang up behind him. The soldier had taken off his jacket, and tip-toeing behind the sentinel, he threw the garment over his head, tightening it with a twist that almost strangled the man. Then seizing his gun so that it would not clatter on the stones, held him thus helpless while we five climbed up beside him. Feeling under the jacket, I put my right hand firmly on the sentinel's throat, and nearly choking the breath out of him, said:—

"'Your life depends on your actions now. Will you utter a sound if I let go your throat?'

"The man shook his head vehemently, and I released my clutch.

"'Now,' I said to him, 'where is the powder stored? Answer in a whisper, and speak truly.'

"'The bulk of the powder,' he answered, 'is in the vault below the citadel.'

"'Where is the rest of it?' I whispered.

"'In the lower room of the round tower by the gate.'

"'Nonsense,' I said: 'they would never store it in a place so liable to attack.'

"'There was nowhere else to put it,' replied the sentinel, 'unless they left it in the open courtyard, which would be quite as unsafe.'

"'Is the door to the lower room in the tower bolted?'

"'There is no door,' replied the sentry, 'but a low archway. This archway has not been closed, because no cannon-balls ever come from the northern side.'

"'How much powder is there in this room?'

"'I do not know; nine or ten barrels, I think.'

"It was evident to me that the fellow, in his fear, spoke the truth. Now, the question was, how to get down from the wall into the courtyard and across that to the archway at the southern side? Cautioning the sentinel again, that if he made the slightest attempt to escape or give the alarm, instant death would be meted to him, I told him to guide us to the archway, which he did, down the stone steps that led from the northern wall into the courtyard. They seemed to keep loose watch inside, the only sentinels in the place being those on the upper walls. But the man we had captured not appearing at his corner in time, his comrade on the western side became alarmed, spoke to him, and obtaining no answer, shouted for him, then discharged his gun. Instantly the place was in an uproar. Lights flashed, and from different guard-rooms soldiers poured out. I saw across the courtyard the archway the sentinel had spoken of, and calling my men made a dash for it. The besieged garrison, not expecting an enemy within, had been rushing up the stone steps at each side to the outer wall to man the cannon they had so recently quitted, and it was some minutes before a knowledge of the real state of things came to them. These few minutes were all we needed, but I saw there was no chance for a slow match, while if we fired the mine we probably would die under the tottering tower.

"By the time we reached the archway and discovered the powder barrels, the besieged, finding everything silent outside, came to a realisation of the true condition of affairs. We faced them with bayonets fixed, while Sept, the man who had captured the sentinel, took the hatchet he had brought with him at his girdle, flung over one of the barrels on its side, knocked in the head of it, allowing the dull black powder to pour on the cobblestones. Then filling his hat with the explosive, he came out towards us, leaving a thick trail behind him. By this time we were sorely beset, and one of our men had gone down under the fire of the enemy, who shot wildly, being baffled by the darkness, otherwise all of us had been slaughtered. I seized a musket from a comrade and shouted to the rest:—

"'Save yourselves', and to the garrison, in French, I gave the same warning; then I fired the musket into the train of powder, and the next instant found myself half stunned and bleeding at the farther end of the courtyard. The roar of the explosion and the crash of the falling tower were deafening. All Elsengore was groused by the earthquake shock, I called to my men when I could find my voice, and Sept answered from one side, and two more from another. Together we tottered across the débris-strewn courtyard. Some woodwork inside the citadel had taken fire and was burning fiercely, and this lit up the ruins and made visible the great gap in the wall at the fallen gate. Into the square below we saw the whole town pouring, soldiers and civilians alike coming from the narrow streets into the open quadrangle. I made my way, leaning on Sept, over the broken gate and down the causeway into the square, and there, foremost of all, met my general, with a cloak thrown round him, to make up for his want of coat.

"'There, general,' I gasped, 'there is your citadel, and through this gap can we march to meet Marlborough.'

"'Pray, sir, who the deuce are you?' cried the general, for my face was like that of a blackamoor.

"'I am the lieutenant who has once more disobeyed your orders, general, in the hope of retrieving a former mistake.'

"'Sentore!' he cried, rapping out an oath. 'I shall have you court-martialled, sir.'

"'I think, general,' I said, 'that I am court-martialled already,' for I thought then that the hand of death was upon me, which shows the effect of imagination, for my wounds were not serious, yet I sank down unconscious at the general's feet. He raised me in his arms as if I had been his own son, and thus carried me to my rooms. Seven years later, when the war ended, I got leave of absence and came back to Elsengore for Gretlich Seidelmier and the hour-glass."

As the lieutenant ceased speaking, Eastford thought he heard again the explosion under the tower, and started to his feet in nervous alarm, then looked at the lieutenant and laughed, while he said:—

"Lieutenant, I was startled by that noise just now, and imagined for the moment that I was in Brabant. You have made good your claim to the hour-glass, and you are welcome to it."

But as Eastford spoke, he turned his eyes towards the chair in which the lieutenant had been seated, and found it vacant. Gazing round the room, in half somnolent dismay, he saw that he was indeed alone. At his feet was the shattered hour-glass, which had fallen from his knee, its blood-red sand mingling with the colours on the carpet. Eastford said, with an air of surprise:—

"By Jove!"

THE WARRIOR MAID OF SAN CARLOS

The young naval officer came into this world with two eyes and two arms; he left it with but one of each—nevertheless the remaining eye was ever quick to see, and the remaining arm ever strong to seize. Even his blind eye became useful on one historic occasion. But the loss of eye or arm was as nothing to the continual loss of his heart, which often led him far afield in the finding of it. Vanquished when he met the women; invincible when he met the men; in truth, a most human hero, and so we all love Jack—the we, in this instant, as the old joke has it, embracing the women.

In the year 1780 Britain ordered Colonel Polson to invade Nicaragua. The task imposed on the gallant Colonel was not an onerous one, for the Nicaraguans never cared to secure for themselves the military reputation of Sparta. In fact, some years after this, a single American, Walker, with a few Californian rifles under his command, conquered the whole nation and made himself President of it, and perhaps would have been Dictator of Nicaragua to-day if his own country had not laid him by the heels. It is no violation of history to state that the entire British fleet was not engaged in subduing Nicaragua, and that Colonel Polson felt himself amply provided for the necessities of the crisis by sailing into the harbour of San Juan del Norte with one small ship. There were numerous fortifications at the mouth of the river, and in about an hour after landing, the Colonel was in possession of them all.

The flight of time, brief as it was, could not be compared in celerity with the flight of the Nicaraguans, who betook themselves to the backwoods with an impetuosity seldom seen outside of a race-course. There was no loss of life so far as the British were concerned, and the only casualties resulting to the Nicaraguans were colds caught through the overheating of themselves in their feverish desire to explore immediately the interior of their beloved country. "He who bolts and runs away will live to bolt another day," was the motto of the Nicaraguans. So far, so good, or so bad, as the case may be.

The victorious Colonel now got together a flotilla of some half a score of boats, and the flotilla was placed under the command of the young naval officer, the hero of this story. The expedition proceeded cautiously up the river San Juan, which runs for eighty miles, or thereabouts, from Lake Nicaragua to the salt water. The voyage was a sort of marine picnic. Luxurious vegetation on either side, and no opposition to speak of, even from the current of the river; for Lake Nicaragua itself is but a hundred and twenty feet above the sea level, and a hundred and twenty feet gives little rapidity to a river eighty miles long.

As the flotilla approached the entrance to the lake caution increased, for it was not known how strong Fort San Carlos might prove. This fort, perhaps the only one in the country strongly built, stood at once on the shore of the lake and bank of the stream. There was one chance in a thousand that the speedy retreat of the Nicaraguans had been merely a device to lure the British into the centre of the country, where the little expedition of two hundred sailors and marines might be annihilated. In these circumstances Colonel Poison thought it well, before coming in sight of the fort, to draw up his boats along the northern bank of the San Juan River, sending out scouts to bring in necessary information regarding the stronghold.

The young naval officer all through his life was noted for his energetic and reckless courage, so it was not to be wondered at that the age of twenty-two found him impatient with the delay, loth to lie inactive in his boat until the scouts returned; so he resolved upon an action that would have justly brought a court-martial upon his head had a knowledge of it come to his superior officer. He plunged alone into the tropical thicket, armed only with two pistols and a cutlass, determined to force his way through the rank vegetation along the bank of the river, and reconnoitre Fort San Carlos for himself. If he had given any thought to the matter, which it is more than likely he did not, he must have known that he ran every risk of capture and death, for the native of South America, then as now, has rarely shown any hesitation about shooting prisoners of war. Our young friend, therefore, had slight chance for his life if cut off from his comrades, and, in the circumstances, even a civilised nation would have been perfectly within its right in executing him as a spy.

After leaving the lake the river San Juan bends south, and then north again. The scouts had taken the direct route to the fort across the land, but the young officer's theory was that, if the Nicaraguans meant to fight, they would place an ambush in the dense jungle along the river, and from this place of concealment harass the flotilla before it got within gunshot of the fort. This ambuscade could easily fall back upon the fort if directly attacked and defeated. This, the young man argued was what he himself would have done had he been in command of the Nicaraguan forces, so it naturally occurred to him to discover whether the same idea had suggested itself to the commandant at San Carlos.

Expecting every moment to come upon this ambuscade, the boy proceeded, pistol in hand, with the utmost care, crouching under the luxuriant tropical foliage, tunnelling his way, as one might say, along the dark alleys of vegetation, roofed in by the broad leaves overhead. Through cross-alleys he caught glimpses now and then of the broad river, of which he was desirous to keep within touch. Stealthily crossing one of these riverward alleys the young fellow came upon his ambuscade, and was struck motionless with amazement at the form it took. Silhouetted against the shining water beyond was a young girl. She knelt at the very verge of the low, crumbling cliff above the water; her left hand, outspread, was on the ground, her right rested against the rough trunk of a palm-tree, and counter-balanced the weight of her body, which leaned far forward over the brink. Her face was turned sideways towards him, and her lustrous eyes peered intently down the river at the British flotilla stranded along the river's bank. So intent was her gaze, so confident was she that she was alone, that the leopard-like approach of her enemy gave her no hint of attack. Her perfect profile being towards him, he saw her cherry-red lips move silently as if she were counting the boats and impressing their number upon her memory.

A woman in appearance, she was at this date but sixteen years old, and the breathless young man who stood like a statue regarding her thought he had never seen a vision of such entrancing beauty, and, as I have before intimated, he was a judge of feminine loveliness. Pulling himself together, and drawing a deep but silent breath, he went forward with soft tread, and the next instant there was a grip of steel on the wrist of the young girl that rested on the earth. With a cry of dismay she sprang to her feet and confronted her assailant, nearly toppling over the brink as she did so; but he grasped her firmly, and drew her a step or two up the arcade. As he held her left wrist there was in the air the flash of a stiletto, and the naval officer's distinguished career would have ended on that spot had he not been a little quicker than his fair opponent. His disengaged hand gripped the descending wrist and held her powerless.

"Ruffian!" she hissed, in Spanish.

The young man had a workable knowledge of the language, and he thanked his stars now that it was so. He smiled at her futile struggles to free herself, then said:—

"When they gave me my commission, I had no hope that I should meet so charming an enemy. Drop the knife, señorita, and I will release your hand."

The girl did not comply at first. She tried to wrench herself free, pulling this way and that with more strength than might have been expected from one so slight. But finding herself helpless in those rigid bonds, she slowly relaxed the fingers of her right hand, and let the dagger drop point downward into the loose soil, where it stood and quivered.

"Now let me go," she said, panting. "You promised."

The young man relinquished his hold, and the girl, with the quick movement of a humming-bird, dived into the foliage, and would have disappeared, had he not with equal celerity intercepted her, again imprisoning her wrist.

"You liar!" she cried, her magnificent eyes ablaze with anger. "Faithless minion of a faithless race, you promised to let me go."

"And I kept my promise," said the young man, still with a smile. "I said I would release your hand, and I did so; but as for yourself, that is a different matter. You see, señorita, to speak plainly, you are a spy. I have caught you almost within our lines, counting our boats, and, perhaps, our men. There is war between our countries, and I arrest you as a spy."

"A brave country, yours," she cried, "to war upon women!"

"Well," said the young man, with a laugh, "what are we to do? The men won't stay and fight us."

She gave him a dark, indignant glance at this, which but heightened her swarthy beauty.

"And what are you," she said, "but a spy?"

"Not yet," he replied. "If you had found me peering at the fort, then, perhaps, I should be compelled to plead guilty. But as it is, you are the only spy here at present, señorita. Do you know what the fate of a spy is?"

The girl stood there for a few moments, her face downcast, the living gyves still encircling her wrists. When she looked up it was with a smile so radiant that the young man gasped for breath, and his heart beat faster than ever it had done in warfare.

"But you will not give me up?" she murmured, softly.

"Then would I be in truth a faithless minion," cried the young man, fervently; "not, indeed, to my country, but to your fascinating sex, which I never adored so much as now."

"You mean that you would be faithless to your country, but not to me?"

"Well," said the young man, with some natural hesitation, "I shouldn't care to have to choose between my allegiance to one or the other. England can survive without warring upon women, as you have said; so I hope that if we talk the matter amicably over, we may find that my duty need not clash with my inclination."

"I am afraid that is impossible," she answered, quickly. "I hate your country."

"But not the individual members of it, I hope."

"I know nothing of its individual members, nor do I wish to, as you shall soon see, if you will but let go my wrist."

"Ah, señorita," exclaimed the young man, "you are using an argument now that will make me hold you forever."

"In that case," said the girl, "I shall change my argument, and give instead a promise. If you release me I shall not endeavour to escape—I may even be so bold as to expect your escort to the fort, where, if I understand you aright, you were but just now going."

"I accept your promise, and shall be delighted if you will accept my escort. Meanwhile, in the interest of our better acquaintance, can I persuade you to sit down, and allow me to cast myself at your feet?"

The girl, with a clear, mellow laugh, sat down, and the young man reclined in the position he had indicated, gazing up at her with intense admiration in his eyes.

"If this be war," he said to himself, "long may I remain a soldier." Infatuated as he certainly was, his natural alertness could not but notice that her glance wandered to the stiletto, the perpendicular shining blade of which looked like the crest of a glittering, dangerous serpent, whose body was hidden in the leaves. She had seated herself as close to the weapon as possible, and now, on one pretext or another, edged nearer and nearer to it. At last the young man laughed aloud, and, sweeping his foot round, knocked down the weapon, then indolently stretching out his arm, he took it.

"Señorita," he said, examining its keen edge, "will you give me this dagger as a memento of our meeting?"

"It is unlucky," she murmured, "to make presents of stilettos."

"I think," said the young man, glancing up at her with a smile on his lips, "it will be more lucky for me if I place it here in my belt than if I allow it to reach the possession of another."

"Do you intend to steal it, señor?"

"Oh, no. If you refuse to let me have it, I will give it back to you when our interview ends; but I should be glad to possess it, if you allow me to keep it."

"It is unlucky, as I have said; to make a present of it, but I will exchange. If you will give me one of your loaded pistols, you may have the stiletto."

"A fair exchange," he laughed, but he made no motion to fulfil his part to the barter. "May I have the happiness of knowing your name, señorita?" he asked.

"I am called Donna Rafaela Mora," answered the girl, simply. "I am daughter of the Commandant of Fort San Carlos. I am no Nicaraguan, but a Spaniard And, señor, what is your name?"

"Horatio Nelson, an humble captain in His Majesty's naval forces, to be heard from later, I hope, unless Donna Rafaela cuts short my thread of life with her stiletto."

"And does a captain in His Majesty's forces condescend to play the part of a spy?" asked the girl, proudly.

"He is delighted to do so when it brings him the acquaintance of another spy so charming as Donna Rafaela. My spying, and I imagine yours also, is but amateurish, and will probably be of little value to our respective forces. Our real spies are now gathered round your fort, and will bring to us all the information we need. Thus, I can recline at your feet, Donna Rafaela, with an easy conscience, well aware that my failure as a spy will in no way retard our expedition."

"How many men do you command, Señor Captain?" asked the girl, with ill-concealed eagerness.

"Oh, sometimes twenty-five, sometimes fifty, or a hundred or two hundred, or more, as the case may be," answered the young man, carelessly.

"But how many are there in your expedition now?"

"Didn't you count them, Donna? To answer truly, I must not, to answer falsely, I will not, Donna."

"Why?" asked the girl, impetuously. "There is no such secrecy about our forces; we do not care who knows the number in our garrison."

"No? Then how many are there, Donna?"

"Three hundred and forty," answered the girl.

"Men, or young ladies like yourself, Donna? Be careful how you answer, for if the latter, I warn you that nothing will keep the British out of Fort San Carlos. We shall be with you, even if we have to go as prisoners. In saying this, I feel that I am speaking for our entire company."

The girl tossed her head scornfully.

"There are three hundred and forty men," she said, "as you shall find to your cost, if you dare attack the fort."

"In that case," replied Nelson, "you are nearly two to one, and I venture to think that we have not come up the river for nothing."

"What braggarts you English are!"

"Is it bragging to welcome a stirring fight? Are you well provided with cannon?"

"You will learn that for yourself when you come within sight of the fort. Have you any more questions to ask, Señor Sailor?"

"Yes; one. The number in the fort, which you give, corresponds with what I have already heard. I have heard also that you were well supplied with cannon, but I have been told that you have no cannonballs in Fort San Carlos."

"That is not true; we have plenty.

"Incredible as it may seem, I was told that the cannon-balls were made of clay. When I said you had none, I meant that you had none of iron."

"That also is quite true," answered the girl. "Do you mean to say that you are going to shoot baked clay at us? It will be like heaving bricks," and the young man threw back his head and laughed.

"Oh, you may laugh," cried the girl, "but I doubt if you will be so merry when you come to attack the fort. The clay cannon-balls were made under the superintendence of my father, and they are filled with links of chain, spikes, and other scraps of iron."

"By Jove!" cried young Nelson, "that's an original idea. I wonder how it will work?"

"You will have every opportunity of finding out, if you are foolish enough to attack the fort."

"You advise us then to retreat?"

"I most certainly do."

"And why, Donna, if you hate our country, are you so anxious that we shall not be cut to pieces by your scrap-iron?"

The girl shrugged her pretty shoulders.

"It doesn't matter in the least to me what you do," she said, rising to her feet. "Am I your prisoner, Señor Nelson?"

"No," cried the young man, also springing up; "I am yours, and have been ever since you looked at me."

Again the girl shrugged her shoulders. She seemed to be in no humour for light compliments, and betrayed an eagerness to be gone.

"I have your permission, then, to depart? Do you intend to keep your word?"

"If you will keep yours, Donna."

"I gave you no promise, except that I would not run away, and I have not done so. I now ask your permission to depart."

"You said that I might accompany you to the fort."

"Oh, if you have the courage, yes," replied the girl, carelessly.

They walked on together through the dense alleys of vegetation, and finally came to an opening which showed them a sandy plain, and across it the strong white stone walls of the fort, facing the wide river, and behind it the blue background of Lake Nicaragua.

Not a human form was visible either on the walls or on the plain. Fort San Carlos, in spite of the fact that it bristled with cannon, seemed like an abandoned castle. The two stood silent for a moment at the margin of the jungle, the young officer running his eye rapidly over the landscape, always bringing back his gaze to the seemingly deserted stronghold.

"Your three hundred and forty men keep themselves well hidden," he said at last.

"Yes," replied the girl, nonchalantly, "they fear that if they show themselves you may hesitate to attack a fortress that is impregnable."

"Well, you may disabuse their minds of that error when you return."

"Are you going to keep my stiletto?" asked the girl, suddenly changing the subject.

"Yes, with your permission."

"Then keep your word, and give me your pistol in return."

"Did I actually promise it?"

"You promised, Señor."

"Then in that case, the pistol is yours."

"Please hand it to me."

Her eagerness to obtain the weapon was but partially hidden, and the young man laughed as he weighed the fire-arm in his hand, holding it by the muzzle.

"It is too heavy for a slim girl like you to handle," he said, at last. "It can hardly be called a lady's toy."

"You intend, then, to break your word," said the girl, with quick intuition, guessing with unerring instinct his vulnerable point.

"Oh, no," he cried, "but I am going to send the pistol half-way home for you," and with that, holding it still by the barrel, he flung it far out on the sandy plain, where it fell, raising a little cloud of dust. The girl was about to speed to the fort, when, for the third time, the young man grasped her wrist. She looked at him with indignant surprise.

"Pardon me," he said, "but in case you should wish to fire the weapon, you must have some priming. Let me pour a quantity of this gunpowder into your hand."

"Thank you," she said, veiling her eyes, to hide their hatred.

He raised the tiny hand to his lips, without opposition, and then into her satin palm, from his powderhorn, he poured a little heap of the black grains.

"Good-bye, señor," she said, hurrying away. She went directly to where the pistol had fallen, stooped and picked it up. He saw her pour the powder from her hand on its broad, unshapely pan. She knelt on the sand, studied the clumsy implement, resting her elbow on her knee. The young man stood there motionless, bareheaded, his cap in his hand. There was a flash and a loud report; and the bullet cut the foliage behind him, a little nearer than he expected. He bowed low to her, and she, rising with an angry gesture, flung the weapon from her.

"Donna Rafaela," he shouted, "thank you for firing the pistol. Its report brings no one to the walls of San Carlos. Your fortress is deserted, Donna. Tomorrow may I have the pleasure of showing you how to shoot?"

The girl made no answer, but turning, ran as fast as she could towards the fort.

The young man walked toward the fort, picked up his despised weapon, thrust it in his belt, and went back to the camp. The scouts were returning, and reported that, as far as they could learn, the three hundred and forty Nicaraguans had, in a body, abandoned Fort San Carlos.

"It is some trick," said the Colonel. "We must approach the fortress cautiously, as if the three hundred and forty were there."

The flotilla neared the fort in a long line. Each boat was filled with men, and in each prow was levelled a small cannon—a man with a lighted match beside it—ready to fire the moment word was given. Nelson himself stood up in his boat, and watched the silent fort. Suddenly the silence was broken by a crash of thunder, and Nelson's boat (and the one nearest to it) was wrecked, many of the men being killed, and himself severely wounded.

"Back, back!" cried the commander. "Row out of range, for your lives!" The second cannon spoke, and the whole line of boats was thrown into inextricable confusion. Cannon after cannon rang out, and of the two hundred men who sailed up the river San Juan only ten reached the ship alive.

The Commandant of the fort lay ill in his bed, unable to move, but his brave daughter fired the cannon that destroyed the flotilla. Here Nelson lost his eye, and so on a celebrated occasion was unable to see the signals that called upon him to retreat. Thus victory ultimately rose out of disaster.

The King of Spain decorated Donna Rafaela Mora, made her a colonel, and gave her a pension for life. So recently as 1857, her grandson, General Martinez, was appointed President of Nicaragua solely because he was a descendant of the girl who defeated Horatio Nelson.

THE AMBASSADOR'S PIGEONS

Haziddin, the ambassador, stood at the door of his tent and gazed down upon the famous city of Baalbek, seeing it now for the first time. The night before, he had encamped on the heights to the south of Baalbek, and had sent forward to that city, messengers to the Prince, carrying greetings and acquainting him with the fact that an embassy from the Governor of Damascus awaited permission to enter the gates. The sun had not yet risen, but the splendour in the East, lighting the sky with wondrous colourings of gold and crimson and green, announced the speedy coming of that god which many of the inhabitants of Baalbek still worshipped. The temples and palaces of the city took their tints from the flaming sky, and Haziddin, the ambassador, thought he had never seen anything so beautiful, notwithstanding the eulogy Mahomet himself had pronounced upon his own metropolis of Damascus.

The great city lay in silence, but the moment the rim of the sun appeared above the horizon the silence was broken by a faint sound of chanting from that ornate temple, seemingly of carven ivory, which had bestowed upon the city its Greek name of Heliopolis. The Temple of the Sun towered overall other buildings in the place, and, as if the day-god claimed his own, the rising sun shot his first rays upon this edifice, striking from it instantly all colour, leaving its rows of pillars a dazzling white as if they were fashioned from the pure snows of distant Lebanon. The sun seemed a mainspring of activity, as well as an object of adoration, for before it had been many minutes above the horizon the ambassador saw emerging from the newly opened gate the mounted convoy that was to act as his escort into the city; so, turning, he gave a quick command which speedily levelled the tents, and brought his retinue; into line to receive their hosts.

The officer, sent by the Prince of Baalbek to welcome the ambassador and conduct him into the city, greeted the visitor with that deferential ceremony so beloved of the Eastern people, and together they journeyed down the hill to the gates, the followers of the one mingling fraternally with the followers of the other. As if the deities of the wonderful temples they were approaching wished to show the futility of man's foresight, a thoughtless remark made by one of the least in the ambassador's retinue to one of the least who followed the Baalbek general, wrought ruin to one empire, and saved another from disaster.

A mule-driver from Baalbek said to one of his lowly a profession from Damascus that the animals of the northern city seemed of superior breed to those of the southern. Then the Damascus man, his civic pride disturbed by the slighting remark, replied haughtily that if the mules of Baalbek had endured such hardships as those of Damascus, journeying for a month without rest through a rugged mountain country, they would perhaps look in no better condition than those the speaker then drove.

"Our mules were as sleek as yours a month ago, when we left Damascus."

As Baalbek is but thirty-one miles north of Damascus, the muleteer of the former place marvelled that so long a time had been spent on the journey, and he asked his fellow why they had wandered among the mountains. The other could but answer that so it was, and he knew no reason for it, and with this the man of Baalbek had to content himself. And so the tale went from mouth to ear of the Baalbek men until it reached the general himself. He thought little of it for the moment, but, turning to the ambassador, said, having nothing else to say:

"How long has it taken you from Damascus to Baalbek?"

Then the ambassador answered:

"We have done the journey in three days; it might have taken us but two, or perhaps it could have been accomplished in one, but there being no necessity for speed we travelled leisurely."

Then the general, remaining silent, said to himself:

"Which has lied, rumour or the ambassador?"

He cast his eyes over the animals the ambassador had brought with him, and saw that they indeed showed signs of fatigue, and perhaps of irregular and improper food.

Prince Ismael himself received Haziddin, ambassador of Omar, Governor of Damascus, at the gates of Baalbek, and the pomp and splendour of that reception was worthy of him who gave it, but the general found opportunity to whisper in the ear of the Prince:

"The ambassador says he was but three days coming, while a follower of his told a follower of mine that they have been a month on the road, wandering among the mountains."

Suspicion is ever latent in the Eastern mind, and the Prince was quick to see a possible meaning for this sojourn among the mountains. It might well be that the party were seeking a route at once easy and unknown by which warriors from Damascus might fall upon Baalbek; yet, if this were the case, why did not the explorers return directly to Damascus rather than venture within the walls of Baalbek? It seemed to Prince Ismael that this would have been the more crafty method to pursue, for, as it was, unless messengers had returned to Damascus to report the result of their mountain excursion, he had the whole party practically prisoners within the walls of his city, and he could easily waylay any envoy sent by the ambassador to his chief in Damascus. The Prince, however, showed nothing in his manner of what was passing through his mind, but at the last moment he changed the programme he had laid out for the reception of the ambassador. Preparation had been made for a great public breakfast, for Haziddin was famed throughout the East, not only as a diplomatist, but also as physician and a man of science. The Prince now gave orders that his officers were to entertain the retinue of the ambassador at the public breakfast, while he bestowed upon the ambassador the exceptional honour of asking him to his private table, thus giving Haziddin of Damascus no opportunity to confer with his followers after they had entered the gates of Baalbek.

It was impossible for Haziddin to demur, so he could but bow low and accept the hospitality which might at that moment be most unwelcome, as indeed it was. The Prince's manner was so genial and friendly that, the physician, Haziddin, soon saw he had an easy man to deal with, and he suspected no sinister motive beneath the cordiality of the Prince.

The red wine of Lebanon is strong, and his Highness, Ismael, pressed it upon his guest, urging that his three days' journey had been fatiguing. The ambassador had asked that his own servant might wait upon him, but the Prince would not hear of it, and said that none should serve him who were not themselves among the first nobles in Baalbek.

"You represent Omar, Governor of Damascus, son of King Ayoub, and as such I receive you on terms of equality with myself."

The ambassador, at first nonplussed with a lavishness that was most unusual, gradually overcame his diffidence, became warm with the wine, and so failed to notice that the Prince himself remained cool, and drank sparingly. At last the head of Haziddin sank on his breast, and he reclined at full length on the couch he occupied, falling into a drunken stupor, for indeed he was deeply fatigued, and had spent the night before sleepless. As his cloak fell away from him it left exposed a small wicker cage attached to his girdle containing four pigeons closely huddled, for the cage was barely large enough to hold them, and here the Prince saw the ambassador's swift messengers to Damascus. Let loose from the walls of Baalbek, and flying direct, the tidings would, in a few hours, be in the hands of the Governor of Damascus. Haziddin then was spy as well as ambassador. The Prince also possessed carrier pigeons, and used them as a means of communication between his armies at Tripoli and at Antioch, so he was not ignorant of their consequence. The fact that the ambassador himself carried this small cage under his cloak attached to his girdle showed the great importance that was attached to these winged messengers, otherwise Haziddin would have entrusted them to one of his subordinates.

"Bring me," whispered the Prince to his general, "four of my own pigeons. Do not disturb the thongs attached to the girdle when you open the cage, but take the ambassador's pigeons out and substitute four of my own. Keep these pigeons of Damascus separate from ours; we may yet have use for them in communicating with the Governor."

The general, quick to see the scheme which was in the Prince's mind, brought four Baalbek pigeons, identical with the others in size and colour. He brought with him also a cage into which the Damascus pigeons were put, and thus the transfer was made without the knowledge of the slumbering ambassador. His cloak was arranged about him so that it concealed the cage attached to the girdle, then the ambassador's own servants were sent for, and he was confided to their care.

When Haziddin awoke he found himself in a sumptuous room of the palace. He had but a hazy remembrance of the latter part of the meal with the Prince, and his first thought went with a thrill of fear towards the cage under his cloak; finding, however, that this was intact, he was much relieved in his mind, and could but hope that in his cups he had not babbled anything of his mission which might arouse suspicion in the mind of the Prince. His first meeting with the ruler of Baalbek after the breakfast they had had together, set all doubts finally at rest, because the Prince received him with a friendship which was unmistakable. The physician apologised for being overcome by the potency of the wine, and pleaded that he had hitherto been unused to liquor of such strength. The Prince waved away all reference to the subject, saying that he himself had succumbed on the same occasion, and had but slight recollection of what had passed between them.

Ismael assigned to the ambassador one of the palaces near the Pantheon, and Haziddin found himself free to come and go as he pleased without espionage or restriction. He speedily learned that one of the armies of Baalbek was at the north, near Antioch, the other to the west at Tripoli, leaving the great city practically unprotected, and this unprecedented state of affairs jumped so coincident with the designs of his master, that he hastened to communicate the intelligence. He wrote:

"If Baalbek is immediately attacked, it cannot be protected. Half of the army is on the shore of the Mediterranean, near Tripoli, the other half is north, at Antioch. The Prince has no suspicion. If you conceal the main body of your army behind the hills to the south of Baalbek, and come on yourself with a small: retinue, sending notice to the Prince of your arrival, he will likely himself come out to the gates to meet you, and having secured his person, while I, with my followers, hold the open gates, you can march into Baalbek unmolested. Once with a force inside the walls of Baalbek, the city is as nearly as possible impregnable, and holding the Prince prisoner, you may make with him your own terms. The city is indescribably rich, and probably never before in the history of the world has there been opportunity of accumulating so much treasure with so little risk."

This writing Haziddin attached to the leg of a pigeon, and throwing the bird aloft from the walls, it promptly disappeared over the housetops, and a few moments later was in the hands of its master, the Prince of Baalbek, who read the treacherous message with amazement. Then, imitating the ambassador's writing, he penned a note, saying that this was not the time to invade Baalbek, but as there were rumours that the armies were about to leave the city, one going to the north and the other to the west, the ambassador would send by another pigeon news of the proper moment to strike.

This communication the Prince attached to the leg of one of the Damascus pigeons, and throwing it into the air, saw with satisfaction that the bird flew straight across the hills towards the south.

Ismael that night sent messengers mounted on swift Arabian horses to Tripoli and to Antioch recalling his armies, directing his generals to avoid Baalbek and to join forces in the mountains to the south of that city and out of sight of it. This done, the Prince attended in state a banquet tendered to him by the ambassador from Damascus, where he charmed all present by his genial urbanity, speaking touchingly on the blessings of peace, and drinking to a thorough understanding between the two great cities of the East, Damascus and Baalbek, sentiments which, were cordially reciprocated by the ambassador.

Next morning the second pigeon came to the palace of the Prince.

"Ismael is still unsuspicious," the document ran. "He will fall an easy prey if action be prompt. In case of a failure to surprise, it would be well to impress upon your generals the necessity of surrounding the city instantly so that messengers cannot be sent to the two armies. It will then be advisable to cut off the water-supply by diverting the course of the small river which flows into Baalbek. The walls of the city are incredibly strong, and a few men can defend them successfully against a host, once the gates are shut. Thirst, however, will soon compel them, to surrender. Strike quickly, and Baalbek is yours."

The Prince sent a note of another tenor to Damascus, and the calm days passed serenely on, the ambassador watching anxiously from his house-top, his eyes turned to the south, while the Prince watched as anxiously from the roof of his palace, his gaze turning now westward now northward.

The third night after the second message had been sent, the ambassador paced the long level promenade of his roof, ever questioning the south. A full moon shone down on the silent city, and in that clear air the plain outside the walls and the nearer hills were as distinctly visible as if it were daylight. There was no sign of an approaching army. Baalbek lay like a city of the dead, the splendid architecture of its countless temples gleaming ghostlike, cold, white and unreal in the pure refulgence of the moon. Occasionally the ambassador paused in his walk and leaned on the parapet. He had become vaguely uneasy, wondering why Damascus delayed, and there crept over him that sensation of dumb fear which comes to a man in the middle of the night and leaves him with the breaking of day. He realised keenly the extreme peril of his own position—imprisoned and at the mercy of his enemy should his treachery be discovered. And now as he leaned over the parapet in the breathless stillness, his alert ear missed an accustomed murmur of the night. Baalbek was lulled to sleep by the ever-present tinkle of running water, the most delicious sound that can soothe an Eastern ear, accustomed as it is to the echoless silence of the arid rainless desert.

The little river which entered Baalbek first flowed past the palace of the Prince, then to the homes of the nobles and the priests, meandering through every street and lane until it came to the baths left by the Romans, whence it flowed through the poorer quarters, and at last disappeared under the outer wall. It might be termed a liquid guide to Baalbek, for the stranger, leaving the palace and following its current, would be led past every temple and residence in the city. It was the limpid thread of life running through the veins of the town, and without it Baalbek could not have existed. As the ambassador leaned over the parapet wondering whether it was his imagination which made this night seem more still than all that had gone before since he came to the city, he suddenly became aware that what he missed was the purling trickle of the water. Peering over the wall of his house, and gazing downward on the moonlit street, he saw no reflecting glitter of the current, and realised, with a leap of the heart, that the stream had run dry.

The ambassador was quick to understand the meaning of this sudden drying of the stream. Notwithstanding his vigilance, the soldiers of Damascus had stolen upon the city unperceived by him, and had already diverted the water-course. Instantly his thoughts turned toward his own escape. In the morning the fact of the invasion would be revealed, and his life would lie at the mercy of an exasperated ruler. To flee from Baalbek in the night he knew to be no easy task; all the gates were closed, and not one of them would be opened before daybreak, except through the intervention of the Prince himself. To spring from even the lowest part of the wall would mean instant death. In this extremity the natural ingenuity of the man came to his rescue. That which gave him warning would also provide an avenue of safety.

The stream, conveyed to the city by a lofty aqueduct, penetrated the thick walls through a tunnel cut in the solid stone, just large enough to receive its volume. The tunnel being thus left dry, a man could crawl on his hands and knees through it, and once outside, walk upright on the top of the viaduct, along the empty bed of the river, until he reached the spot where the water had been diverted, and there find his comrades. Wasting not a thought on the jeopardy in which he left his own followers, thus helplessly imprisoned in Baalbek, but bent only on his own safety, he left his house silently, and hurried, deep in the shadow, along the obscure side of the street. He knew he must avoid the guards of the palace, and that done, his path to the invading army was clear. But before he reached the palace of the Prince there remained for him another stupefying surprise.

Coming to a broad thoroughfare leading to the square in which stood the Temple of Life, he was amazed to see at his feet, flowing rapidly, the full tide of the stream, shattering into dancing discs of light the reflection of the full moon on its surface, gurgling swiftly towards the square. The fugitive stood motionless and panic-stricken at the margin of this transparent flood.

He knew that his retreat had been cut off. What had happened? Perhaps the strong current had swept away the impediment placed against it by the invaders, and thus had resumed its course into the city. Perhaps—but there was little use in surmising, and the ambassador, recovering in a measure his self-possession, resolved to see whether or not it would lead him to his own palace.

Crossing the wide thoroughfare into the shadow beyond, he followed it towards the square, keeping his eye on the stream that rippled in the moonlight. The rivulet flowed directly across the square to the Temple of Life; there, sweeping a semicircle half round the huge building, it resumed its straight course. The ambassador hesitated before crossing the moonlit square, but a moment's reflection showed him that no suspicion could possibly attach to his movements in this direction, for the Temple of Life was the only sacred edifice in the city for ever open.

The Temple of Life consisted of a huge dome, which was supported by a double circle of pillars, and beneath this dome had been erected a gigantic marble statue, representing the God of Life, who stood motionless with outstretched arms, as if invoking a blessing upon the city. A circular opening at the top of the dome allowed the rays of the moon to penetrate and illuminate the head of the statue. Against the white polished surface of the broad marble slab, which lay at the foot of the statue, the ambassador saw the dark forms of several prostrate figures, and knew that each was there to beg of the sightless statue, life for some friend, lying at that moment somewhere on a bed of illness. For this reason the Temple of Life was always open, and supplicants prostrated themselves within it at any hour of the night or day. Remembering this, and knowing that it was the resort of high and low alike, for Death respects not rank, Haziddin, with gathering confidence, entered the moonlit square. At the edge of the great circular temple he paused, meeting there his third surprise. He saw that the stream was not deflected round the lower rim of the edifice, but that a stone had been swung at right angles with the lower step, cutting off the flow of the stream to the left, and allowing its waters to pour underneath the temple. Listening, the ambassador heard the low muffled roar of pouring water, and instantly his quick mind jumped at an accurate conclusion. Underneath the Temple was a gigantic tank for the storage of water, and it was being filled during the night. Did the authorities of Baalbek expect a siege, and were they thus preparing for it? Or was the filling of the tank an ordinary function performed periodically to keep the water sweet? The ambassador would have given much for an accurate answer to these questions, but he knew not whom to ask.

Entering the Temple he prostrated himself on the marble slab, and remained there for a few moments, hoping that, if his presence had been observed, this action would provide excuse for his nocturnal wanderings. Rising, he crossed again the broad square, and hurried up the street by which he had entered it. This street led to the northern gate, whose dark arch he saw at the end of it, and just as he was about to turn down a lane which led to his palace, he found himself confronted with a fourth problem. One leaf of the ponderous gate swung inward, and through the opening he caught a glimpse of the moonlit country beyond. Knowing that the gates were never opened at night, except through the direct order of the Prince, he paused for a moment, and then saw a man on horseback enter, fling himself hurriedly from his steed, leaving it in care of those in charge of the gates, and disappear down the street that led directly to the Prince's palace. In a most perturbed state of mind the ambassador sought his own house, and there wrote his final despatch to Damascus. He told of his discovery of the water-tank, and said that his former advice regarding the diverting of the stream was no longer of practical value. He said he would investigate further the reservoir under the Temple of Life, and discover, if possible, how the water was discharged. If he succeeded in his quest he would endeavour, in case of a long siege, to set free Baalbek's store of water; but he reiterated his belief that it was better to attempt the capture of the city by surprise and fierce assault. The message that actually went to Damascus, carried by the third pigeon, was again different in tenor.

"Come at once," it said. "Baalbek is unprotected, and the Prince has gone on a hunting expedition. March through the Pass of El-Zaid, which is unprotected, because it is the longer route. The armies of Baalbek are at Tripoli and at Antioch, and the city is without even a garrison. The southern gate will be open awaiting your coming."

Days passed, and the ambassador paced the roof of his house, looking in vain towards the south. The streamed flowed as usual through the city. Anxiety at the lack of all tidings from Damascus began to plough furrows in his brow. He looked careworn and haggard. To the kindly inquiries of the Prince regarding his health, he replied that there was nothing amiss.

One evening, an urgent message came from the palace requesting his attendance there. The Prince met him with concern on his brow.

"Have you had word from your master, Omar, Governor of Damascus, since you parted with him?" asked Ismael.

"I have had no tidings," replied the ambassador.

"A messenger has just come in from Damascus, who says that Omar is in deadly peril. I thought you should know this speedily, and so I sent for you."

"Of what nature is this peril?" asked the ambassador, turning pale.

"The messenger said something of his falling a prisoner, sorely wounded, in the hands of his enemies."

"Of his enemies," echoed the ambassador. "He has many. Which one has been victorious?"

"I have had no particulars and perhaps the news may not be true," answered the Prince, soothingly.

"May I question your messenger?"

"Assuredly. He has gone to the Temple of Life, to pray for some of his own kin, who are in danger. Let us go there together and find him."

But the messenger had already left the Temple before the arrival of his master, and the two found the great place entirely empty. Standing near the edge of the slab before the mammoth statue, the Prince said:

"Stand upon that slab facing the statue, and it will tell you more faithfully than any messenger whether your master shall live or die, and when."

"I am a Moslem," answered Haziddin, "and pray to none but Allah."

"In Baalbek," said the Prince, carelessly, "all religions are tolerated. Here we have temples for the worship of the Roman and the Greek gods and mosques for the Moslems. Here Christian, or Jew, Sun-worshipper or Pagan implore their several gods unmolested, and thus is Baalbek prosperous. I confess a liking for this Temple of Life, and come here often. I should, however, warn you that it is the general belief of those who frequent this place that he who steps upon the marble slab facing the god courts disaster, unless his heart is as free, from treachery and guile as this stone beneath him is free from flaw. Perhaps you have heard the rumour, and therefore hesitate."

"I have not heard it heretofore, but having heard it, do not hesitate." Saying which, the ambassador stepped upon the stone. Instantly, the marble turned under him, and falling, he clutched its polished surface in vain, dropping helplessly into the reservoir beneath. The air under his cloak bore him up and kept him from sinking. The reservoir into which he had fallen proved to be as large as the Temple itself, circular in form, as was the edifice above it. Steps rose from the water in unbroken rings around it, but even if he could have reached the edge of the huge tank in which he found himself, ascent by the steps was impossible, for upon the first three burned vigorously some chemical substance, which luridly illuminated the surface of this subterranean lake. He was surrounded immediately by water, and beyond that by rising rings of flame, and he rightly surmised that this substance was Greek fire, for where it dripped into the water it still burned, floating on the surface. A moment later the Prince appeared on the upper steps, outside the flaming circumference.

"Ambassador," he cried, "I told you that if you stepped on the marble slab, you would be informed truly of the fate of your master. I now announce to you that he dies to-night, being a prisoner in my hands. His army was annihilated in the Pass of El-Zaid, while he was on his way to capture this city through your treachery. In your last communication to him you said that you would investigate our water storage, and learn how it was discharged. This secret I shall proceed to put you in possession of, but before doing so, I beg to tell you that Damascus has fallen and is in my possession. The reservoir, you will observe, is emptied by pulling this lever, which releases a trap-door at the centre of the bottom of the tank."

The Prince, with both hands on the lever, exerted his strength and depressed it. Instantly the ambassador felt the result. First, a small whirlpool became indented in the placid surface of the water, exactly in the centre of the disc: enlarging its influence, it grew and grew until it reached the outer edges of the reservoir, bringing lines of fire round with it. The ambassador found himself floating with increased rapidity, dizzily round and round. He cried out in a voice that rang against the stone ceiling:

"An ambassador's life is sacred, Prince of Baalbek. It is contrary to the law of nations to do me injury, much less to encompass my death."

"An ambassador is sacred," replied the Prince, "but not a spy. Aside from that, it is the duty of an ambassador to precede his master, and that you are about to do. Tell him, when you meet him, the secret of the reservoir of Baalbek."

This reservoir, now a whirling maelstrom, hurled its shrieking victim into its vortex, and then drowned shriek and man together.

JENNIE BAXTER, JOURNALIST

CHAPTER I. JENNIE MAKES HER TOILETTE AND THE ACQUAINTANCE OF A PORTER.

Miss Jennie Baxter, with several final and dainty touches that put to rights her hat and dress—a little pull here and a pat there—regarded herself with some complacency in the large mirror that was set before her, as indeed she had every right to do, for she was an exceedingly pretty girl. It is natural that handsome young women should attire themselves with extra care, and although Jennie would have been beautiful under any conceivable condition of dress, she nevertheless did not neglect the arraying of herself becomingly on that account. All that was remarkable on this occasion consisted in the fact that she took more than usual pains to make herself presentable, and it must be admitted that the effect was as attractive as anyone could wish to have it. Her appearance was enough to send a friend into ecstasies, or drive an enemy to despair.

Jennie's voluminous hair, without being exactly golden, was—as the poets might term it—the colour of ripe corn, and was distractingly fluffy at the temples. Her eyes were liquidly, bewitchingly black, of melting tenderness, and yet, upon occasion, they would harden into piercing orbs that could look right through a man, and seem to fathom his innermost thoughts. A smooth, creamy complexion, with a touch of red in the cheeks, helped to give this combination of blonde and brunette an appearance so charmingly striking that it may be easily understood she was not a girl to be passed by with a single glance. Being so favoured by nature, Jennie did not neglect the aid of art, and it must be admitted that most of her income was expended in seeing that her wardrobe contained the best that Paris could supply; and the best in this instance was not necessarily the most expensive—at least not as expensive as such supplementing might have been to an ordinary woman, for Jennie wrote those very readable articles on the latest fashionable gowns which have appeared in some of the ladies' weeklies, and it was generally supposed that this fact did not cause her own replenishing from the modistes she so casually mentioned in her writings to be more expensive than her purse could afford.

Be that as it may, Miss Baxter was always most becomingly attired, and her whole effect was so entrancing that men have been known to turn in the street as she passed, and murmur, "By Jove!" a phrase that, when you take into account the tone in which it is said, represents the furthermost point of admiration which the limited vocabulary of a man about town permits him to utter; and it says something for the honesty of Jennie's black eyes, and the straightforwardness of her energetic walk, that none of these momentary admirers ever turned and followed her.

On this occasion Miss Jennie had paid more than usual attention to her toilette, for she was about to set out to capture a man, and the man was no other than Radnor Hardwick, the capable editor of the Daily Bugle, which was considered at that moment to be the most enterprising morning journal in the great metropolis. Miss Baxter had done work for some of the evening papers, several of the weeklies, and a number of the monthlies, and the income she made was reasonably good, but hazardously fitful. There was an uncertainty about her mode of life which was displeasing to her, and she resolved, if possible, to capture an editor on one of the morning papers, and get a salary that was fixed and secure. That it should be large was a matter of course, and pretty Miss Jennie had quite enough confidence in herself to believe she would earn every penny of it. Quite sensibly, she depended upon her skill and her industry as her ultimate recommendation to a large salary, but she was woman enough to know that an attractive appearance might be of some assistance to her in getting a hearing from the editor, even though he should prove on acquaintance to be a man of iron, which was tolerably unlikely. She glanced at the dainty little watch attached to her wristlet, and saw that it lacked a few minutes of five. She knew the editor came to his office shortly after three, and remained there until six or half-past, when he went out to dine, returning at ten o'clock, or earlier, when the serious work of arranging next day's issue began. She had not sent a note to him, for she knew if she got a reply it would be merely a request for particulars as to the proposed interview, and she had a strong faith in the spoken word, as against that which is written. At five o'clock the editor would have read his letters, and would probably have seen most of those who were waiting for him, and Miss Baxter quite rightly conjectured that this hour would be more appropriate for a short conversation than when he was busy with his correspondence, or immersed in the hard work of the day, as he would be after ten o'clock at night. She had enough experience of the world to know that great matters often depend for their success on apparent trivialities, and the young woman had set her mind on becoming a member of the Daily Bugle staff.

She stepped lightly into the hansom that was waiting for her, and said to the cabman, "Office of the Daily Bugle, please; side entrance."

The careful toilette made its first impression upon the surly-looking Irish porter, who, like a gruff and faithful watch-dog, guarded the entrance to the editorial rooms of the Bugle. He was enclosed in a kind of glass-framed sentry-box, with a door at the side, and a small arched aperture that was on a level with his face as he sat on a high stool. He saw to it, not too politely, that no one went up those stairs unless he had undoubted right to do so. When he caught a glimpse of Miss Baxter, he slid off the stool and came out of the door to her, which was an extraordinary concession to a visitor, for Pat Ryan contented himself, as a usual thing, by saying curtly that the editor was busy, and could see no one.

"What did you wish, miss? To see the editor? That's Mr. Hardwick. Have ye an appointment with him? Ye haven't; then I very much doubt if ye'll see him this day, mum. It's far better to write to him, thin ye can state what ye want, an' if he makes an appointment there'll be no throuble at all, at all."

"But why should there be any trouble now?" asked Miss Baxter. "The editor is here to transact business, just as you are at the door to do the same. I have come on business, and I want to see him. Couldn't you send up my name to Mr. Hardwick, and tell him I will keep him but a few moments?"

"Ah, miss, that's what they all say; they ask for a few moments an' they shtay an hour. Not that there'd be any blame to an editor if he kept you as long as he could. An' it's willing I'd be to take up your name, but I'm afraid that it's little good it 'ud be after doin' ye. There's more than a dozen men in the waitin'-room now, an' they've been there for the last half-hour. Not a single one I've sent up has come down again."

"But surely," said Miss Jennie, in her most coaxing tone, "there must be some way to see even such a great man as the editor, and if there is, you know the way."

"Indade, miss, an' I'm not so sure there is a way, unless you met him in the strate, which is unlikely. As I've told ye, there's twelve men now waitin' for him in the big room. Beyont that room there's another one, an' beyont that again is Mr. Hardwick's office. Now, it's as much as my place is worth, mum, to put ye in that room beyont the one where the men are waitin'; but, to tell you the truth, miss," said the Irishman, lowering his voice, as if he were divulging office secrets, "Mr. Hardwick, who is a difficult man to deal with, sometimes comes through the shmall room, and out into the passage whin he doesn't want to see anyone at all, at all, and goes out into the strate, leavin' everybody waitin' for him. Now I'll put ye into this room, and if the editor tries to slip out, then ye can speak with him; but if he asks ye how ye got there, for the sake of hiven don't tell him I sint ye, because that's not my duty at all, at all."

"Indeed, I won't tell him how I got there; or, rather, I'll say I came there by myself; so all you need to do is to show me the door, and there won't need to be any lies told.

"True for ye, an' a very good idea. Well, miss, then will ye just come up the stairs with me? It's the fourth door down the passage."

Miss Jennie beamed upon the susceptible Irishman a look of such melting gratitude that the man, whom bribery had often attempted to corrupt in vain, was her slave for ever after. They went up the stairs together, at the head of which the porter stood while Miss Baxter went down the long passage and stopped at the right door; Ryan nodded and disappeared.

Miss Baxter opened the door softly and entered. She found the room not too brilliantly lighted, containing a table and several chairs. The door to the right hand, which doubtless led into the waiting-room, where the dozen men were patiently sitting, was closed. The opposite door, which led into Mr. Hardwick's office, was partly open. Miss Baxter sat down near the third door, the one by which she had entered from the passage, ready to intercept the flying editor, should he attempt to escape.

In the editor's room someone was walking up and down with heavy footfall, and growling in a deep voice that was plainly audible where Miss Jennie sat. "You see, Alder, it's like this," said the voice. "Any paper may have a sensation every day, if it wishes; but what I want is accuracy, otherwise our sheet has no real influence. When an article appears in the Bugle, I want our readers to understand that that article is true from beginning to end. I want not only sensation, but definiteness and not only definiteness, but absolute truth."

"Well, Mr. Hardwick," interrupted another voice—the owner of which was either standing still or sitting in a chair, so far as Miss Baxter could judge by the tone, while the editor uneasily paced to and fro—"what Hazel is afraid of is that when this blows over he will lose his situation—"

"But," interjected the editor, "no one can be sure that he gave the information. No one knows anything about this but you and I, and we will certainly keep our mouths shut."

"What Hazel fears is that the moment we print the account, the Board of Public Construction will know he gave away the figures, because of their accuracy. He says that if we permit him to make one or two blunders, which will not matter in the least in so far as the general account goes, it will turn suspicion from him. It will be supposed that someone had access to the books, and in the hurry of transcribing figures had made the blunders, which they know he would not do, for he has a reputation for accuracy."

"Quite so," said the editor; "and it is just that reputation—for accuracy—that I want to gain for the Daily Bugle. Don't you think the truth of it is that the man wants more money?"

"Who? Hazel?"

"Certainly. Does he imagine that he could get more than fifty pounds elsewhere?"

"Oh, no; I'm sure the money doesn't come into the matter at all. Of course he wants the fifty pounds, but he doesn't want to lose his situation on the Board of Public Construction in the getting of it."

"Where do you meet this man, at his own house, or in his office at the Board?"

"Oh, in his own house, of course."

"You haven't seen the books, then?"

"No; but he has the accounts all made out, tabulated beautifully, and has written a very clear statement of the whole transaction. You understand, of course, that there has been no defalcation, no embezzlement, or anything of that sort. The accounts as a whole balance perfectly, and there isn't a penny of the public funds wrongly appropriated. All the Board has done is to juggle with figures so that each department seems to have come out all right, whereas the truth is that some departments have been carried on at a great profit, while with others there has been a loss. The object obviously has been to deceive the public and make it think that all the departments are economically conducted."

"I am sorry money hasn't been stolen," said the editor generously, "then we would have had them on the hip; but, even as it is, the Bugle will make a great sensation. What I fear is that the opposition press will seize on those very inaccuracies, and thus try to throw doubt on the whole affair. Don't you think that you can persuade this person to let us have the information intact, without the inclusion of those blunders he seems to insist on? I wouldn't mind paying him a little more money, if that is what he is after."

"I don't think that is his object. The truth is, the man is frightened, and grows more and more so as the day for publication approaches. He is so anxious about his position that he insisted he was not to be paid by cheque, but that I should collect the money and hand it over to him in sovereigns."

"Well, I'll tell you what to do, Alder. We mustn't seem too eager. Let the matter rest where it is until Monday. I suppose he expects you to call upon him again to-day?"

"Yes; I told him I should be there at seven."

"Don't go, and don't write any explanation. Let him transfer a little of his anxiety to the fear of losing his fifty pounds. I want, if possible, to publish this information with absolute accuracy."

"Is there any danger, Mr. Hardwick, that some of the other papers may get on the track of this?"

"No, I don't think so; not for three days, anyway. If we appear too eager, this man Hazel may refuse us altogether."

"Very good, sir."

Miss Baxter heard the editor stop in his walk, and she heard the rustling of paper, as if the subordinate were gathering up some documents on which he had been consulting his chief. She was panic-stricken to think that either of the men might come out and find her in the position of an eavesdropper, so with great quietness she opened the door and slipped out into the hall, going from there to the entrance of the ordinary waiting-room, in which she found, not the twelve men that the porter had expatiated upon, but five. Evidently the other seven had existed only in the porter's imagination, or had become tired of waiting and had withdrawn. The five looked up at her as she entered and sat down on a chair near the door. A moment later the door communicating with the room she had quitted opened, and a clerk came in. He held two or three slips of paper in his hand, and calling out a name, one of the men rose.

"Mr. Hardwick says," spoke up the clerk, "that this matter is in Mr. Alder's department; would you mind seeing him? Room number five."

So that man was thus got rid of. The clerk mentioned another name, and again a man rose.

"Mr. Hardwick," the clerk said, "has the matter under consideration. Call again to-morrow at this hour, then he will give you his decision."

That got rid of number two. The third man was asked to leave his name and address; the editor would write to him. Number four was told that if he would set down his proposition in writing, and send it in to Mr. Hardwick, it would have that gentleman's serious consideration. The fifth man was not so easily disposed of. He insisted upon seeing the editor, and presently disappeared inside with the clerk. Miss Baxter smiled at the rapid dispersion of the group, for it reminded her of the rhyme about the one little, two little, three little nigger-boys. But all the time there kept running through her mind the phrase, "Board of Public Construction," and the name, "Hazel."

After a few minutes, the persistent man who had insisted upon seeing the editor came through the general waiting-room, the secretary, or clerk, or whoever he was, following him.

"Has your name been sent in, madam?" the young man asked Miss Baxter, as she rose. "I think not," answered the girl. "Would you take my card to Mr. Hardwick, and tell him I will detain him but a few moments?"

In a short time the secretary reappeared, and held the door open for her.

CHAPTER II. JENNIE HAS IMPORTANT CONFERENCES WITH TWO IMPORTANT EDITORS.

Mr. Hardwick was a determined-looking young man of about thirty-five, with a bullet head and closely-cropped black hair. He looked like a stubborn, strong-willed person, and Miss Baxter's summing up of him was that he had not the appearance of one who could be coaxed or driven into doing anything he did not wish to do. He held her card between his fingers, and glanced from it to her, then down to the card again.

"Good afternoon, Mr. Hardwick," began Miss Baxter. "I don't know that you have seen any of my work, but I have written a good deal for some of the evening papers and for several of the magazines."

"Yes," said Hardwick, who was standing up preparatory to leaving his office, and who had not asked the young woman to sit down; "your name is familiar to me. You wrote, some months since, an account of a personal visit to the German Emperor; I forget now where it appeared."

"Oh, yes," said Miss Baxter; "that was written for the Summer Magazine, and was illustrated by photographs."

"It struck me," continued Hardwick, without looking at her, "that it was an article written by a person who had never seen the German Emperor, but who had collected and assimilated material from whatever source presented itself."

The young woman, in nowise abashed, laughed; but still the editor did not look up.

"Yes," she admitted, "that is precisely how it was written. I never have had the pleasure of meeting William II. myself."

"What I have always insisted upon in work submitted to me," growled the editor in a deep voice, "is absolute accuracy. I take it that you have called to see me because you wish to do some work for this paper."

"You are quite right in that surmise also," answered Miss Jennie. "Still, if I may say so, there was nothing inaccurate in my article about the German Emperor. My compilation was from thoroughly authentic sources, so I maintain it was as truthfully exact as anything that has ever appeared in the Bugle."

"Perhaps our definitions of truth might not quite coincide. However, if you will write your address on this card I will wire you if I have any work—that is, any outside work—which I think a woman can do. The woman's column of the Bugle, as you are probably aware, is already in good hands."

Miss Jennie seemed annoyed that all her elaborate preparations were thrown away on this man, who never raised his eyes nor glanced at her, except once, during their conversation.

"I do not aspire," she said, rather shortly, "to the position of editor of a woman's column. I never read a woman's column myself, and, unlike Mr. Grant Allen, I never met a woman who did."

She succeeded in making the editor lift his eyes towards her for the second time.

"Neither do I intend to leave you my address so that you may send a wire to me if you have anything that you think I can do. What I wish is a salaried position on your staff."

"My good woman," said the editor brusquely, "that is utterly impossible. I may tell you frankly that I don't believe in women journalists. The articles we publish by women are sent to this office from their own homes. Anything that a woman can do for a newspaper I have men who will do quite as well, if not better; and there are many things that women can't do at all which men must do. I am perfectly satisfied with my staff as it stands, Miss Baxter."

"I think it is generally admitted," said the young woman, "that your staff is an exceptionally good one, and is most capably led. Still, I should imagine that there are many things happening in London, society functions, for instance, where a woman would describe more accurately what she saw than any man you could send. You have no idea how full of blunders a man's account of women's dress is as a general rule, and if you admire accuracy as much as you say, I should think you would not care to have your paper made a laughing-stock among society ladies, who never take the trouble to write you a letter and show you where you are wrong, as men usually do when some mistake regarding their affairs is made."

"There is probably something in what you say," replied the editor, with an air of bringing the discussion to a close. "I don't insist that I am right, but these are my ideas, and while I am editor of this paper I shall stand by them, so it is useless for us to discuss the matter any further, Miss Baxter. I will not have a woman as a member of the permanent staff of the Bugle."

For the third time he looked up at her, and there was dismissal in his glance.

Miss Baxter said indignantly to herself, "This brute of a man hasn't the slightest idea that I am one of the best dressed women he has ever met."

But there was no trace of indignation in her voice when she said to him sweetly, "We will take that as settled. But if upon some other paper, Mr. Hardwick, I should show evidence of being as good a newspaper reporter as any member of your staff, may I come up here, and, without being kept waiting too long, tell you of my triumph?"

"You would not shake my decision," he said.

"Oh, don't say that," she murmured, with a smile. "I am sure you wouldn't like it if anyone called you a fool."

"Called me a fool?" said the editor sharply, drawing down his dark brows. "I shouldn't mind it in the least."

"What, not if it were true? You know it would be true, if I could do something that all your clever men hadn't accomplished. An editor may be a very talented man, but, after all, his mission is to see that his paper is an interesting one, and that it contains, as often as possible, something which no other sheet does."

"Oh, I'll see to that," Mr. Hardwick assured her with resolute confidence.

"I am certain you will," said Miss Baxter very sweetly; "but now you won't refuse to let me in whenever I send up my card? I promise you that I shall not send it until I have done something which will make the whole staff of the Daily Bugle feel very doleful indeed."

For the first time Mr. Hardwick gave utterance to a somewhat harsh and mirthless laugh.

"Oh, very well," he said, "I'll promise that."

"Thank you! And good afternoon, Mr. Hardwick. I am so much obliged to you for consenting to see me. I shall call upon you at this hour to-morrow afternoon."

There was something of triumph in her smiling bow to him, and as she left she heard a long whistle of astonishment in Mr. Hardwick's room. She hurried down the stairs, threw a bewitching glance at the Irish porter, who came out of his den and whispered to her,—

"It's all right, is it, mum?"

"More than all right," she answered. "Thank you very much indeed for your kindness."

The porter preceded her out to the waiting hansom and held his arm so that her skirt would not touch the wheel.

"Drive quickly to the Cafe Royal," she said to the cabman.

When the hansom drew up in front of the Cafe Royal, Miss Jennie Baxter did not step put of it, but waited until the stalwart servitor in gold lace, who ornamented the entrance, hurried from the door to the vehicle. "Do you know Mr. Stoneham?" she asked with suppressed excitement, "the editor of the Evening Graphite? He is usually here playing dominoes with somebody about this hour."

"Oh yes, I know him," was the reply. "I think he is inside at this moment, but I will make certain."

In a short time Mr. Stoneham himself appeared, looking perhaps a trifle disconcerted at having his whereabouts so accurately ascertained.

"What a blessing it is," said Miss Jennie, with a laugh, "that we poor reporters know where to find our editors in a case of emergency."

"This is no case of emergency, Miss Baxter," grumbled Stoneham. "If it's news, you ought to know that it is too late to be of any use for us to-day."

"Ah, yes," was the quick reply, "but what excellent time I am in with news for to-morrow!"

"If a man is to live a long life," growled the disturbed editor, "he must allow to-morrow's news to look after itself. Sufficient for the day are the worries thereof."

"As a general rule that is true," assented the girl, "but I have a most important piece of information for you that wouldn't wait, and in half an hour from now you will be writing your to-morrow's leader, showing forth in terse and forcible language the many iniquities of the Board of Public Construction."

"Oh," cried the editor, brightening, "if it is anything to the discredit of the Board of Public Construction, I am glad you came."

"Well, that's not a bit complimentary to me. You should be glad in any case; but I'll forgive your bad manners, as I wish you to help me. Please step into this hansom, because I have most startling intelligence to impart—news that must not be overheard; and there is no place so safe for a confidential conference as in a hansom driving through the streets of London. Drive slowly towards the Evening Graphite office," she said to the cabman, pushing up the trap-door in the roof of the vehicle. Mr. Stoneham took his place beside her, and the cabman turned his horse in the direction indicated.

"There is little use in going to the office of the paper," said Stoneham; "there won't be anybody there but the watchman."

"I know, but we must go in some direction. We can't talk in front of the Café Royal, you know. Now, Mr. Stoneham, in the first place, I want fifty golden sovereigns. How am I to get them within half an hour?"

"Good gracious! I don't know; the banks are all closed, but there is a man at Charing Cross who would perhaps change a cheque for me; there is a cheque-book at the office."

"Then that's all right and settled. Mr. Stoneham, there's been some juggling with the accounts in the office of the Board of Public Construction."

"What! a defalcation?" cried Stoneham eagerly.

"No; merely a shifting round."

"Ah," said the editor, in a disappointed tone.

"Oh, you needn't say 'Ah.' It's very serious; it is indeed. The accounts are calculated to deceive the dear and confiding public, to whose interests all the daily papers, morning and evening, pretend to be devoted. The very fact of such deception being attempted, Mr. Stoneham, ought to call forth the anger of any virtuous editor."

"Oh, it does, it does; but then it would be a difficult matter to prove. If some money were gone, now——"

"My dear sir, the matter is already proved, and quite ripe for your energetic handling of it; that's what the fifty pounds are for. This sum will secure for you—to-night, mind, not to-morrow—a statement bristling with figures which the Board of Construction cannot deny. You will be able, in a stirring leading article, to express the horror you undoubtedly feel at the falsification of the figures, and your stern delight in doing so will probably not be mitigated by the fact that no other paper in London will have the news, while the matter will be so important that next day all your beloved contemporaries will be compelled to allude to it in some shape or other."

"I see," said the editor, his eyes glistening as the magnitude of the idea began to appeal more strongly to his imagination. "Who makes this statement, and how are we to know that it is absolutely correct?"

"Well, there is a point on which I wish to inform you before going any further. The statement is not to be absolutely correct; two or three errors have been purposely put in, the object being to throw investigators off the track if they try to discover who gave the news to the Press; for the man who will sell me this document is a clerk in the office of the Board of Public Construction. So, you see, you are getting the facts from the inside."

"Is he so accustomed to falsifying accounts that he cannot get over the habit even when preparing an article for the truthful Press?"

"He wants to save his own situation, and quite rightly too, so he has put a number of errors in the figures of the department over which he has direct control. He has a reputation for such accuracy that he imagines the Board will never think he did it, if the figures pertaining to his department are wrong even in the slightest degree."

"Quite so. Then we cannot have the pleasure of mentioning his name, and saying that this honest man has been corrupted by his association with the scoundrels who form the Board of Public Construction?"

"Oh, dear, no; his name must not be mentioned in any circumstances, and that is why payment is to be made in sovereigns rather than by bank cheque or notes."

"Well, the traitor seems to be covering up his tracks rather effectually. How did you come to know him?"

"I don't know him. I've never met him in my life; but it came to my knowledge that one of the morning papers had already made all its plans for getting this information. The clerk was to receive fifty pounds for the document, but the editor and he are at present negotiating, because the editor insists upon absolute accuracy, while, as I said, the man wishes to protect himself, to cover his tracks, as you remarked."

"Good gracious!" cried Stoneham, "I didn't think the editor of any morning paper in London was so particular about the accuracy of what he printed. The pages of the morning sheets do not seem to reflect that anxiety."

"So, you see," continued Miss Jennie, unheeding his satirical comment, "there is no time to be lost; in fact, I should be on my way now to where this man lives."

"Here we are at the office, and I shall just run in and write a cheque for fifty pounds, which we can perhaps get cashed somewhere," cried the editor, calling the hansom to a halt and stepping out.

"Tell the watchman to bring me a London Directory," said the girl, and presently that useful guardian came out with the huge red volume, which Miss Baxter placed on her knees, and, with a celerity that comes of long practice, turned over the leaves rapidly, running her finger quickly down the H column, in which the name "Hazel" was to be found. At last she came to one designated as being a clerk in the office of the Board of Public Construction, and his residence was 17, Rupert Square, Brixton. She put this address down in her notebook and handed back the volume to the waiting watchman, as the editor came out with the cheque in his hand.

The shrewd and energetic dealer in coins, whose little office stands at the exit from Charing Cross Station, proved quite willing to oblige the editor of the Evening Graphite with fifty sovereigns in exchange for the bit of paper, and the editor, handing to Miss Jennie the envelope containing the gold, saw her drive off for Brixton, while he turned, not to resume his game of dominoes at the café, but to his office, to write the leader which would express in good set terms the horror he felt at the action of the Board of Public Construction.

CHAPTER III. JENNIE INTERVIEWS A FRIGHTENED OFFICIAL.

It was a little past seven o'clock when Miss Baxter's hansom drove up to the two-storeyed house in Rupert Square numbered 17. She knocked at the door, and it was speedily opened by a man with some trace of anxiety on his clouded face, who proved to be Hazel himself, the clerk at the Board of Public Construction. "You are Mr. Hazel?" she ventured, on entering.

"Yes," replied the man, quite evidently surprised at seeing a lady instead of the man he was expecting at that hour; "but I am afraid I shall have to ask you to excuse me; I am waiting for a visitor who is a few minutes late, and who may be here at any moment."

"You are waiting for Mr. Alder, are you not?"

"Yes," stammered the man, his expression of surprise giving place to one of consternation.

"Oh, well, that is all right," said Miss Jennie, reassuringly. "I have just driven from the office of the Daily Bugle. Mr. Alder cannot come to-night."

"Ah," said Hazel, closing the door. "Then are you here in his place?"

"I am here instead of him. Mr. Alder is on other business that he had to attend to at the editor's request. Now, Mr. Hardwick—that's the editor, you know——"

"Yes, I know," answered Hazel.

They were by this time seated in the front parlour.

"Well, Mr. Hardwick is very anxious that the figures should be given with absolute accuracy."

"Of course, that would be much better," cried the man; "but, you see, I have gone thoroughly into the question with Mr. Alder already. He said he would mention what I told him to the editor—put my position before him, in fact."

"Oh, he has done so," said Miss Baxter, "and did it very effectively indeed; in fact, your reasons are quite unanswerable. You fear, of course, that you will lose your situation, and that is very important, and no one in the Bugle office wishes you to suffer for what you have done. Of course, it is all in the public interest."

"Of course, of course," murmured Hazel, looking down on the table.

"Well, have you all the documents ready, so that they can be published at any time?"

"Quite ready," answered the man.

"Very well," said the girl, with decision; "here are your fifty pounds. Just count the money, and see that it is correct. I took the envelope as it was handed to me, and have not examined the amount myself."

She poured the sovereigns out on the table, and Hazel, with trembling fingers, counted them out two by two.

"That is quite right," he said, rising. He went to a drawer, unlocked it, and took out a long blue envelope.

"There," he said, with a sigh that was almost a gasp. "There are the figures, and a full explanation of them. You will be very careful that my name does not slip out in any way."

"Certainly," said Miss Jennie, coolly drawing forth the papers from their covering. "No one knows your name except Mr. Alder, Mr. Hardwick, and myself; and I can assure you that I shall not mention it to anyone."

She glanced rapidly over the documents.

"I shall just read what you have written," she said, looking up at him; "and if there is anything here I do not understand you will, perhaps, be good enough to explain it now,—and then I won't need to come here again."

"Very well," said Hazel. The man had no suspicion that his visitor was not a member of the staff of the paper he had been negotiating with. She was so thoroughly self-possessed, and showed herself so familiar with all details which had been discussed by Alder and himself that not the slightest doubt had entered the clerk's mind.

Jennie read the documents with great haste, for she knew she was running a risk in remaining there after seven o'clock. It might be that Alder would come to Brixton to let the man know the result of his talk with the editor, or Mr. Hardwick himself might have changed his mind, and instructed his subordinate to secure the papers. Nevertheless, there was no sign of hurry in Miss Jennie's demeanour as she placed the papers back in their blue envelope and bade the anxious Hazel good-bye.

Once more in the hansom, she ordered the man to drive her to Charing Cross, and when she was ten minutes away from Rupert Square she changed her direction and desired him to take her to the office of the Evening Graphite, where she knew Mr. Stoneham would be busy with his leading article, and probably impatiently awaiting further details of the conspiracy he was to lay open before the public. A light was burning in the editorial rooms of the office of the Evening Graphite, always a suspicious thing in such an establishment, and well calculated to cause the editor of any rival evening paper to tremble, should he catch a glimpse of burning gas in a spot where the work of the day should be finished at latest by five o'clock. Light in the room of the evening journalist usually indicates that something important is on hand.

A glance at the papers Miss Baxter brought to him showed Mr. Stoneham that he had at least got the worth of his fifty pounds. There would be a fluttering in high places next day. He made arrangements before he left to have the paper issued a little earlier than was customary, calculating his time with exactitude, so that rival sheets could not have the news in their first edition, cribbed from the Graphite, and yet the paper would be on the street, with the newsboys shouting, "'Orrible scandal," before any other evening journal was visible. And this was accomplished the following day with a precision truly admirable.

Mr. Stoneham, with a craft worthy of all commendation, kept back from the early issue a small fraction of the figures that were in his possession, so that he might print them in the so-called fourth edition, and thus put upon the second lot of contents—bills sent out, in huge, startling black type, "Further Revelations of the Board of Construction Scandal;" and his scathing leading article, in which he indignantly demanded a Parliamentary inquiry into the conduct of the Board, was recognized, even by the friends of that public body, as having seriously shaken confidence in it. The reception of the news by the other evening papers was most flattering. One or two ignored it altogether, others alluded to it as a rumour, that it "alleged" so and so, and threw doubt on its truth, which was precisely what Mr. Stoneham wished them to do, as he was in a position to prove the accuracy of his statement.

Promptly, at five o'clock that afternoon a hansom containing Miss Jennie Baxter drove up to the side entrance of the Daily Bugle office, and the young woman once more accosted the Irish porter, who again came out of his den to receive her.

"Miss Baxter?" said the Irishman, half by way of salutation, and half by way of inquiry. "Yes," said the girl.

"Well, Mr. Hardwick left strict orders with me that if ye came, or, rather, that whin ye came, I was to conduct ye right up to his room at once."

"Oh, that is very satisfactory," cried Miss Jennie, "and somewhat different from the state of things yesterday."

"Indeed, and that's very true," said the porter, his voice sinking. "To-day is not like yesterday at all, at all. There's been great ructions in this office, mum; although what it's about, fly away with me if I know. There's been ruunin' back and forrad, an' a plentiful deal of language used. The proprietor himself has been here, an' he's here now, an' Mr. Alder came out a minute ago with his face as white as a sheet of paper. They do be sayin'," added the porter, still further lowering his voice, and pausing on the stairway, "that Mr. Hardwick is not goin' to be the editor any more, but that Mr. Alder is to take his place. Anyway, as far as I can tell, Mr. Hardwick an' Mr. Alder have had a fine fall out, an' one or other of them is likely to leave the paper."

"Oh, dear, oh, dear!" said Miss Jennie, also pausing on the stairs. "Is it so serious as all that?"

"Indeed it is, mum, an' we none of us know where we're standin', at all, at all."

The porter led the way to Mr. Hardwick's room, and announced the visitor.

"Ask her to come in," she heard the editor say, and the next instant the porter left them alone together.

"Won't you sit down, Miss Baxter?" said Mr. Hardwick, with no trace of that anger in his voice which she had expected. "I have been waiting for you. You said you would be here at five, and I like punctuality. Without beating round the bush, I suppose I may take it for granted that the Evening Graphite is indebted to you for what it is pleased to call the Board of Public Construction scandal?"

"Yes," said the young woman, seating herself; "I came up to tell you that I procured for the Graphite that interesting bit of information."

"So I supposed. My colleague, Henry Alder, saw Hazel this afternoon at the offices of the Board. The good man Hazel is panic-stricken at the explosion he has caused, and is in a very nervous state of mind, more especially when he learned that his documents had gone to an unexpected quarter. Fortunately for him, the offices of the Board are thronged with journalists who want to get statements from this man or the other regarding the exposure, and so the visit of Alder to Hazel was not likely to be noticed or commented upon. Hazel gave a graphic description of the handsome young woman who had so cleverly wheedled the documents from him, and who paid him the exact sum agreed upon in the exact way that it was to have been paid. Alder had not seen you, and has not the slightest idea how the important news slipped through his fingers; but when he told me what had happened, I knew at once you were the goddess of the machine, therefore I have been waiting for you. May I be permitted to express the opinion that you didn't play your cards at all well, Miss Baxter?"

"No? I think I played my cards very much better than you played yours, you know."

"Oh, I am not instituting any comparison, and am not at all setting myself up as a model of strategy. I admit that, having the right cards in my hands, I played them exceedingly badly; but then, you understand, I thought I was sure of an exclusive bit of news."

"No news is exclusive, Mr. Hardwick, until it is printed, and out in the streets, and the other papers haven't got it."

"That is very true, and has all the conciseness of an adage. I would like to ask, Miss Baxter, how much the Graphite paid you for that article over and above the fifty pounds you gave to Hazel?"

"Oh! it wasn't a question of money with me; the subject hasn't even been discussed. Mr. Stoneham is not a generous paymaster, and that is why I desire to get on a paper which does not count the cost too closely. What I wished to do was to convince you that I would be a valuable addition to the Bugle staff; for you seemed to be of opinion that the staff was already sufficient and complete."

"Oh, my staff is not to blame in this matter; I alone am to blame in being too sure of my ground, and not realizing the danger of delay in such a case. But if you had brought the document to me, you would have found me by far your best customer. You would have convinced me quite as effectually as you have done now that you are a very alert young woman, and I certainly would have been willing to give you four or five times as much as the Graphite will be able to pay."

"To tell the truth, I thought of that as I stood here yesterday, but I saw you were a very difficult man to deal with or to convince, and I dared not take the risk of letting you know I had the news. You might very easily have called in Mr. Alder, told him that Hazel had given up the documents, and sent him flying to Brixton, where very likely the clerk has a duplicate set. It would have been too late to get the sensation into any other morning paper, and, even if it were not too late, you would have had something about the sensation in the Bugle, and so the victory would not have been as complete as it is now. No, I could not take such a risk. I thought it all out very carefully."

"You credit us with more energy, Miss Baxter, than we possess. I can assure you that if you had come here at ten or eleven o'clock with the documents, I should have been compelled to purchase them from you. However, that is all past and done with, and there is no use in our saying anything more about it. I am willing to take all the blame for our defeat on my shoulders, but there are some other things I am not willing to do, and perhaps you are in a position to clear up a little misunderstanding that has arisen in this office. I suppose I may take it for granted that you overheard the conversation which took place between Mr. Alder and myself in this room yesterday afternoon?"

"Well," said Miss Baxter, for the first time in some confusion, "I can assure you that I did not come here with the intention of listening to anything. I came into the next room by myself for the purpose of getting to see you as soon as possible. While not exactly a member of the staff of the Evening Graphite, that paper nevertheless takes about all the work I am able to do, and so I consider myself bound to keep my eyes and ears open on its behalf wherever I am."

"Oh, I don't want to censure you at all," said Hardwick; "I merely wish to be certain how the thing was done. As I said, I am willing to take the blame entirely on my own shoulders. I don't think I should have made use of information obtained in that way myself; still, I am not venturing to find fault with you for doing so."

"To find fault with me!" cried Miss Jennie somewhat warmly, "that would be the pot calling the kettle black indeed. Why, what better were you? You were bribing a poor man to furnish you with statistics, which he was very reluctant to let you have; yet you overcame his scruples with money, quite willing that he should risk his livelihood, so long as you got the news. If you ask me, I don't see very much difference in our positions, and I must say that if two men take the risk of talking aloud about a secret, with a door open leading to another room, which may be empty or may be not, then they are two very foolish persons."

"Oh, quite so, quite so," answered Hardwick soothingly. "I have already disclaimed the critical attitude. The point I wish to be sure of is this—you overheard the conversation between Alder and myself?"

"Yes, I did."

"Would you be able to repeat it?"

"I don't know that I could repeat it word for word, but I could certainly give the gist of it."

"Would you have any objection to telling a gentleman whom I shall call in a moment, as nearly as possible what Alder said and what I said? I may add that the gentleman I speak of is Mr. Hempstead, and he is practically the proprietor of this paper. There has arisen between Mr. Alder and myself a slight divergence of memory, if I may call it so, and it seems that you are the only person who can settle the dispute."

"I am perfectly willing to tell what I heard to anybody."

"Thank you."

Mr. Hardwick pressed an electric button, and his secretary came in from another room.

"Would you ask Mr. Hempstead to step this way, if he is in his room?"

In a few minutes Mr. Hempstead entered, bowed somewhat stiffly towards the lady, but froze up instantly when he heard that she was the person who had given the Board of Public Construction scandal to the Evening Graphite.

"I have just this moment learned, Mr. Hempstead, that Miss Baxter was in the adjoining room when Alder and I were talking over this matter. She heard the conversation. I have not asked her to repeat it, but sent for you at once, and she says she is willing to answer any questions you may ask."

"In that case, Mr. Hardwick, wouldn't it be well to have Henry Alder here?"

"Certainly, if he is on the premises." Then, turning to his secretary, he said, "Would you find out if Mr. Alder is in his room? Tell him Mr. Hempstead wishes to see him here."

When Henry Alder came in, and the secretary had disappeared, Miss

Baxter saw at once that she was in an unenviable situation, for it was quite evident the three men were scarcely on speaking terms with each other. Nothing causes such a state of tension in a newspaper office as the missing of a piece of news that is important.

"Perhaps it would be better," suggested Hardwick, "if Miss Baxter would repeat the conversation as she heard it."

"I don't see the use of that," said Mr. Hempstead. "There is only one point at issue. Did Mr. Alder warn Mr. Hardwick that by delay he would lose the publication of this report?"

"Hardly that," answered the girl. "As I remember it, he said, 'Isn't there a danger that some other paper may get this?' Mr. Hardwick replied, 'I don't think so. Not for three days, at least'; and then Mr. Alder said, 'Very good,' or 'Very well,' or something like that."

"That quite tallies with my own remembrance," assented Hardwick. "I admit I am to blame, but I decidedly say that I was not definitely warned by Mr. Alder that the matter would be lost to us."

"I told you it would be lost if you delayed," cried Alder, with the emphasis of an angry man, "and it has been lost. I have been on the track of this for two weeks, and it is very galling to have missed it at the last moment through no fault of my own."

"Still," said Mr. Hempstead coldly, "your version of the conversation does not quite agree with what Miss Baxter says."

"Oh, well," said Alder, "I never pretended to give the exact words. I warned him, and he did not heed the warning."

"You admit, then, that Miss Baxter's remembrance of the conversation is correct?"

"It is practically correct. I do not 'stickle' about words."

"But you did stickle about words an hour ago," said Mr. Hempstead, with some severity. "There is a difference in positively stating that the item would be lost and in merely suggesting that it might be lost."

"Oh, have it as you wish," said Alder truculently. "It doesn't matter in the least to me. It is very provoking to work hard for two weeks, and then have everything nullified by a foolish decision from the editor. However, as I have said, it doesn't matter to me. I have taken service on the Daily Trumpet, and you may consider my place on the Bugle vacant"—saying which, the irate Mr. Alder put his hat on his head and left the room.

Mr. Hempstead seemed distressed by the discussion, but, for the first time, Mr. Hardwick smiled grimly.

"I always insist on accuracy," he said, "and lack of it is one of Alder's failings."

"Nevertheless, Mr. Hardwick, you have lost one of your best men. How are you going to replace him?" inquired the proprietor anxiously.

"There is little difficulty in replacing even the best man on any staff in London," replied Hardwick, with a glance at Miss Baxter. "As this young lady seems to keep her wits about her when the welfare of her paper is concerned, I shall, if you have no objection, fill Henry Alder's place with Miss Baxter?"

Mr. Hempstead arched his eyebrows a trifle, and looked at the girl in some doubt.

"I thought you didn't believe in women journalists, Mr. Hardwick," he murmured at last.

"I didn't up till to-day, but since the evening papers came out I have had reason to change my mind. I should much rather have Miss Baxter for me than against me."

"Do you think you can fill the position, Miss Baxter?" asked the proprietor, doubtingly.

"Oh, I, am sure of it," answered the girl. "I have long wanted a place on a well-edited paper like the Bugle." Again Mr. Hardwick smiled grimly. The proprietor turned to him, and said, "I don't quite see, Mr. Hardwick, what a lady can do on this paper outside of the regular departments."

"I hardly think there will be any trouble about that, Mr. Hempstead. For example, who could be better equipped to attempt the solution of that knotty question about the Princess von Steinheimer's diamonds?"

"By Jove!" cried Hempstead, his eyes glittering with excitement. "That is an inspiration. I imagine that if anyone can unravel the mystery, it is Miss Baxter."

CHAPTER IV. JENNIE LEARNS ABOUT THE DIAMONDS OF THE PRINCESS.

"What about the diamonds of the Princess?" asked Miss Baxter, her curiosity piqued by the remark of the editor.

"That is rather a long story," replied Mr. Hardwick, "and before I begin it, I would like to ask you one or two questions. Can you manipulate a typewriter?"

"That depends on what make it is. The ordinary typewriter I understand very thoroughly."

"Good. Have you any knowledge of shorthand?"

"A workable knowledge; I can write about one hundred words a minute."

"Admirable! admirable! Your coming to this office was indeed an inspiration, as Mr. Hempstead remarked. You are just the person I have been looking for."

"You didn't seem to think so yesterday, Mr. Hardwick," said the girl with a sly glance at him.

"Well, many things have happened since yesterday. We are now dealing with to-day, and with the Princess von Steinheimer."

"She is a German princess, of course?"

"An Austrian princess, but an American woman. She was a Miss Briggs of Chicago; a daughter of Briggs, the railway millionaire, worth somewhere between twenty and twenty-five millions—dollars, of course. A year or two ago she married Prince Konrad von Steinheimer; you may remember having read about it in the papers?"

"Oh, yes; the usual international match—the girl after the title, he after the money."

"I suppose so; but be that as it may, she is the only daughter of old Briggs, and had spent a good deal of her time in Europe, but she spent more than time; she spent the old man's money as well, so during her stay in Europe she accumulated a vast stock of diamonds, some of them very notable stones. I don't know what the whole collection is worth, some say a million dollars, while others say double that amount. However that may be, Miss Briggs became the Princess von Steinheimer, and brought to Austria with her a million dollars in gold and the diamonds, which her father gave as dowry; but, of course, being an only child, she will come in for the rest of his money when the railway magnate dies."

"Is he likely to die soon? I don't suppose the Prince gave himself away for a mere million."

"Oh, you forget the diamonds. As to the likelihood of old Briggs's death, it didn't strike me as imminent when I had a conversation with him yesterday."

"Yesterday? Is he here in London, then?"

"Yes; he has come over to disentangle the mystery about the diamonds."

"And what is the mystery? You take a dreadful long time to tell a story, Mr. Hardwick."

"The story is important, and it must be told in detail, otherwise you may go on a long journey for nothing. Are you taking down what I say in shorthand? That is right, and if you are wise you will not transcribe your notes so that anyone can read them; they are safer in that form. The von Steinheimer family have two residences, a house in Vienna and an ancient castle in the Tyrol, situated on the heights above Meran, a most picturesque place, I understand; but very shortly you will know more about it than I do, because the Bugle expects you to go there as its special correspondent. Here the diamond robbery took place something like two months ago, and the affair is still as great a mystery as ever. The Princess was to open the season at Meran, which is a fashionable resort, by giving a fancy dress ball in Schloss Steinheimer, to which all the Austrian and foreign notables were invited. It was just before the ball began that the diamonds were first missed—in fact, the Princess was about to put them on, she representing some gorgeously decorated character from the Arabian Nights, when the discovery was made that the diamonds were gone. She was naturally very much upset over her loss, and sent at once for the Prince, her husband, insisting that the police should be notified immediately and detectives called in, as was perfectly natural. Now here comes a strange feature of the affair, and this is that the Prince positively forbade any publicity, refusing his sanction when she demanded that the police should be informed, and yet the Prince knew better than anyone else the very considerable value of the stones."

"What reason did he give for his refusal?" asked Miss Baxter, looking up from her notes.

"I am not quite certain about that; but I think he said it was infra dig. for the Steinheimers to call in the police. Anyhow, it was an excuse which did not satisfy the Princess; but as guests were arriving, and as it was desirable that there should be no commotion to mar the occasion, the Princess temporarily yielded to the wish of her husband, and nothing was said publicly about the robbery. The great ball was the talk of Meran for several days, and no one suspected the private trouble that was going on underneath this notable event. During these several days the Princess insisted that the aid of the police should be invoked, and the Prince was equally strenuous that nothing should be said or done about the matter. Then, quite unexpectedly, the Prince veered completely round, and proclaimed that he would engage the best detectives in Europe. Strange to say, when he announced this decision to his wife, she had veered round also, and opposed the calling in of the detectives as strenuously as he had done heretofore."

"What reason did she give for her change of front?" asked Miss Jennie.

"She said, I believe, that it was now too late; that the thieves, whoever they were, had had time to make away with their plunder, and there would merely be a fuss and worry for nothing."

"Do you know, I am inclined to agree with her," asserted the girl.

"Are you? Then tell me what you think of the case as far as you have got."

"What do you think?"

"I sha'n't tell you at this stage, because I know of further particulars which I will give you later on. I merely want your opinion now, so that I may see whether what I have to tell you afterwards modifies it in any way."

"Well, to me the case looks decidedly dark against the Prince."

"That is what Mr. Briggs thinks. He imagines his Highness has the jewels."

"Where did you get all these particulars?"

"From Mr. Briggs, who, of course, got them by letter from his daughter."

"Then we have, as it were, a one-sided statement."

"Oh, quite so; but still you must remember the Princess does not in the least suspect her husband of the theft."

"Well, please go on. What are the further particulars?"

"The further particulars are that the Prince made some quiet investigations among the servants, and he found that there was a man who, although he was a friend of his own, was much more the friend of the Princess, and this man had, on the day the ball was given, the entire freedom of the castle. He is a young officer and nobleman. Lieutenant von Schaumberg, and the Prince knew that this young man was being hard pressed for some debts of honour which he did not appear to be in a position to liquidate. The young man went unexpectedly to Vienna the day after the ball, and on his return settled his obligations. The Princess, from one of her women, got word of her husband's suspicion. She went to the Prince at once, and told him she had come to his own opinion with regard to the lost diamonds. She would, in no circumstances, have detectives about the place. Then he told her that he had also changed his mind, and resolved to engage detectives. So here they were at a deadlock again. She wrote to her father with great indignation about the Prince's unjust suspicions, saying von Schaumberg was a gentleman in every sense of the word. I gather that relations between herself and her husband are somewhat strained, so I imagine there is much more in this matter than the lost diamonds."

"You imagine, then, that she is shielding the Lieutenant?"

"Candidly, I do."

"And you are of opinion he stole the diamonds?"

"Yes, I am."

"I don't agree with you. I still think it was the Prince, and I think besides this, that he dexterously managed to throw suspicion on the Lieutenant. Have they called in the detectives yet?"

"No, they are at a deadlock, as I remarked before."

"Well, what am I expected to do?"

"Mr. Briggs cabled to his daughter—he never writes a letter—that he would come over and straighten out the tangle in fifteen minutes. He is certain the Prince stole the diamonds, but he did not tell his daughter so. He informed her he was bringing her a present of a new typewriting machine, and also a young woman from Chicago who could write shorthand and would look after the Princess's correspondence—act as secretary, in fact; for it seems the Princess has a larger correspondence than she can reasonably attend to, and she appears therefore to yearn for a typewriter. The old man tells me she is very careless about her letters, never being able to find anything she wants, and leaving them about a good deal, so he thinks she needs someone to look after her affairs; and I have a suspicion that her father fears she may leave some compromising letter about, so he wishes to ward off a divorce case."

"No, I fancy you are mistaken there. The father hasn't the slightest idea that there can be anything wrong with his daughter. It is probable the Princess has written some libellous statements about her husband, and it is quite likely the Prince is a brute and that young von Schaumberg is a most charming person."

"Well, as I was saying," continued Hardwick, "the old man cabled his daughter that he is bringing her a secretary and a typewriter. He engaged a female Pinkerton detective to enter the castle as secretary to the Princess and, if possible, to solve the diamond mystery. She is a young woman who, when she left Chicago, was very anti-English, but she became acquainted on the steamer with a young Englishman who was tremendously taken with her, and so at Liverpool she quite calmly broke her engagement with the old man and fulfilled a new engagement she had made with the young man by promptly marrying him—special license, I am told. Old Briggs has therefore a new typewriting machine on his hands, and so I was going to propose to you that you take the place of the Chicago Pinkerton person. Briggs has become so disgusted with all these detective women that he abandoned the idea of sending a female detective with the machine, and doesn't imagine that whoever is sent will be either a detective or a newspaper woman. I was introduced to him the other day by one of those lucky chances which sometimes put interesting items of news in our way, and he told me the whole story, requesting me to recommend someone who wrote shorthand and understood the typewriter. I am to dine with him this evening, and I shall cordially recommend you. I may say that Briggs has gone to that celebrated London detective Mr. Cadbury Taylor, and has engaged him to solve the diamond mystery. So you see you will have a clear field. If you can leave for the castle to-morrow night, you may have the pleasure of Mr. Cadbury Taylor's company. He isn't visiting the castle, but goes straight to Vienna; so if you work your cards rightly, you can be in the same carriage with him as far as Munich, and during that time you may find out perhaps what he thinks about the case. I know only this much about his theory, and that is he thinks the right place to begin is in Vienna, where some, at least, of the stones are supposed to have been pawned."

"Oh, this is a delightful case, and I shall enjoy it. Has there been anything published yet with reference to the robbery?"

"Not a word; nobody knows anything about it, except the Prince and Princess, Briggs, myself and yourself, and perhaps one or two of the servants in the castle—oh, yes, and Cadbury Taylor."

CHAPTER V. JENNIE MEETS A GREAT DETECTIVE.

Miss Baxter was early at the station before the Continental train left. She walked up and down the platform, hoping to see Mr. Cadbury Taylor, with whose face and form she was familiar. She secured a porter who spoke French, and pretended to him that she knew no English.

"I desire," she said, "to get into a first-class compartment with a gentleman whom I shall point out to you. I shall give you five shillings, so you must let me have your whole attention. My luggage has been labelled and registered, therefore you will not need to bother about it, but keep your eye on me and follow me into whatever carriage I enter, bringing with you the hand-bag and this heavy package."

The heavy package was a typewriter in its case. Shortly before the train departed, there sauntered into the station the tall, thin, well-known form of the celebrated detective. He wore a light ulster that reached almost to his heels, and his keen, alert face was entirely without beard or moustache. As he came up the platform, a short, stout man accosted him.

"I was afraid you were going to be late," said the detective's friend, "but I see you are just in time as usual."

"A railway station," said Mr. Cadbury Taylor, "is not the most inspiring place in London for the spending of a spare half hour; besides, I had some facts to get together, which are now tabulated in my note-book, and I'm quite ready to go, if the train is."

"I have secured a smoking compartment here where we shall be alone."

"That's right, Smith," said Cadbury Taylor. "You are always so thoughtful," and the two men entered the compartment together.

Just as the guards were shouting, "Take your seats, please," Miss Baxter made a bolt for the compartment in which the detective and his friend sat together in opposite corners.

"I beg your pardon," said Smith, "this is a smoking compartment." The lady replied to him volubly in French, and next instant the porter heaved the typewriter and hand-bag on the seat beside her. Smith seemed to resent the intrusion, and appeared about to blame the porter, but the man answered rapidly as he banged the door shut, "The lady doesn't speak any English," and the next moment the train moved out of the station.

"There was no need," said the detective, "my dear Smith, to depend upon the porter for the information that the lady could not speak English. She is the secretary to a very rich employer in Chicago, and came from that city to New York, where she sailed on the Servia alone, coming to England to transact some special business, of which I could here give you full particulars, if it were worth while. She came from Liverpool to London over the Great Western Railway, and is now on her way to Paris. All this, of course, is obvious to the most casual observer, and so, my dear Smith, we may discuss our case with as much security as though we were entirely alone."

"But, good heavens, Cadbury!" cried Smith in amazement, "how can you tell all that?"

"My dear fellow," said the detective wearily, "no one travels with a typewriting machine unless that person is a typewriter. The girl, if you will notice, is now engaged in filling the leaves of her book with shorthand, therefore that proves her occupation. That she is secretary to a rich man is evidenced by the fact that she crossed in the Servia first cabin, as you may see by glancing at the label on the case; that she came alone, which is to say her employer was not with her, is indicated by the typewriter being marked 'Not Wanted,' so it was put down into the hold. If a Chicago business man had been travelling with his secretary, the typewriter case would have been labelled instead, 'Cabin, wanted,' for a Chicago man of business would have to write some hundreds of letters, even on the ocean, to be ready for posting the moment he came ashore. The typewriter case is evidently new, and is stamped with the name and address of its sellers in Chicago. That she came by the Great Western is shown by the fact that 'Chester' appears on still another label. That she has special business in England we may well believe, otherwise she would have crossed on the French line direct from New York to Havre. So you see, my dear boy, these are all matters of observation, and quite patent to anyone who cares to use his eyes."

"Yes, it all seems very simple now that you have explained it," growled Smith.

"I should be a much more mysterious person than I am," remarked the detective complacently, "if I did not explain so much. This explanation habit is becoming a vice with me, and I fear I must abandon it."

"I hope for my sake you won't," said Smith more good-naturedly, "for if left to myself I never could find out how you arrive at your wonderful conclusions. Do you expect the Austrian diamond mystery to prove difficult?"

"Difficult? Oh, dear no! To tell the truth, I have solved it already, but in order to give the American a run for his money—and surely he ought not to object to that, because he is a millionaire who has made his fortune by giving other people runs for their money, being a railway man—I am now on my way to Vienna. If I solved the problem off-hand for him in London, he would have no more appreciation of my talent than you had a moment ago when I explained why I knew this French girl came from Chicago."

"You mustn't mind that, Cadbury," said Smith contritely. "I confess I was irritated for a moment because it all seemed so simple."

"My dear fellow, every puzzle in this world is simple except one, and that is to find any problem which is difficult."

"Then who stole the diamonds? The lieutenant?"

The detective smiled and gazed upwards for a few tantalizing moments at the roof of the carriage.

"Here we have," he said at last, "an impecunious prince who marries an American heiress, as so many of them do. The girl begins life in Austria on one million dollars, say two hundred thousand pounds, and a case of diamonds said to be worth another two hundred thousand at least—probably more. Not much danger of running through that very speedily, is there, Smith?"

"No, I should think not."

"So the average man would think," continued the detective. "However, I have long since got out of the habit of thinking; therefore I make sure. The first problem I set to myself is this: How much money have the Prince and Princess spent since they were married? I find that the repairs on the Schloss Steinheimer, situated in the Tyrol, cost something like forty thousand pounds. It is a huge place, and the Steinheimers have not had an heiress in the family for many centuries. The Prince owed a good deal of money when he was married, and it took something like sixty thousand pounds to settle those debts; rather expensive as Continental princes go, but if one must have luxuries, one cannot save money. Not to weary you with details, I found that the two hundred thousand pounds were exhausted somewhat more than two months ago; in fact, just before the alleged robbery. The Prince is, of course, without money, otherwise he would not have married a Chicago heiress, and the Princess being without money, what does she naturally do?"

"Pawns her own diamonds!" cried Smith enthusiastically.

The detective smiled.

"I thought it much more probable she would apply to her father for money. I asked him if this was the case, giving him the date, roughly speaking, when such a letter had been sent. The old man opened his eyes at this, and told me he had received such a letter. 'But you did not send the money?' I ventured, 'No,' he said, 'I did not. The fact is, money is very tight in Chicago just now, and so I cabled her to run on her debts for a while.' This exactly bore out the conclusion at which I had already arrived. So now, having failed to get money from her father, the lady turns to her diamonds, the only security she possesses. The chances are that she did so before her father's cable message came, and that was the reason she so confidently wished information to be given to the police. She expected to have money to redeem her jewels, and being a bright woman, she knew the traditional stupidity of the official police, and so thought there was no danger of her little ruse being discovered. But when the cable message came saying no money would be sent her, a different complexion was put upon the whole affair, for she did not know but if the police were given plenty of time they might stumble on the diamonds."

"But, my dear Cadbury, why should she not have taken the diamonds openly and raised money on them?"

"My dear fellow, there are a dozen reasons, any one of which will suffice where a woman is in the case. In the first place, she might fear to offend the family pride of the von Steinheimers; in the second place, we cannot tell what her relations with her husband were. She may not have wished him to know that she was short of money. But that she has stolen her own diamonds there is not the slightest question in my mind. All that is necessary for me to do now is to find out how many persons there are in Vienna who would lend large sums of money on valuable jewels. The second is to find with which one of those the Princess pawned her diamonds."

"But, my dear Cadbury, the lady is in Meran, and Vienna is some hundreds of miles away. How could a lady in the Tyrol pawn diamonds in Vienna without her absence being commented on? or do you think she had an agent to do it for her?" Again the detective smiled indulgently.

"No, she had no agent. The diamonds never left Vienna. You see, the ball had been announced, and immediate money was urgently needed. She pawned the diamonds before she left the capital of Austria, and the chances are she did not intend anyone to know they were missing; but on the eve of the ball her husband insisted that she should wear her diamonds, and therefore, being a quick-witted woman, she announced they had been stolen. After having made such a statement, she, of course, had to stick to it; and now, failing to get the money from America, she is exceedingly anxious that no real detective shall be employed in investigation."

At Dover Miss Baxter, having notes of this interesting conversation in shorthand, witnessed the detective bid good-bye to his friend Smith, who returned to London by a later train. After that she saw no more of Mr. Cadbury Taylor, and reached the Schloss Steinheimer at Meran without further adventure.

CHAPTER VI. JENNIE SOLVES THE DIAMOND MYSTERY.

Miss Baxter found life at the Schloss much different from what she had expected. The Princess was a young and charming lady, very handsome, but in a state of constant depression. Once or twice Miss Baxter came upon her with apparent traces of weeping on her face. The Prince was not an old man, as she had imagined, but young and of a manly, stalwart appearance. He evidently possessed a fiendish temper, and moped about the castle with a constant frown upon his brow.

The correspondence of the Princess was in the utmost disorder. There were hundreds upon hundreds of letters, and Miss Baxter set to work tabulating and arranging them. Meanwhile the young newspaper woman kept her eyes open. She wandered about the castle unmolested, poked into odd corners, talked with the servants, and, in fact, with everyone, but never did she come upon a clue which promised to lead to a solution of the diamond difficulty. Once she penetrated into a turret room, and came unexpectedly upon the Prince, who was sitting on the window-ledge, looking absently out on the broad and smiling valley that lay for miles below the castle. He sprang to his feet and stared so fiercely at the intruder that the girl's heart failed her, and she had not even the presence of mind to turn and run.

"What do you want?" he said to her shortly, for he spoke English perfectly. "You are the young woman from Chicago, I suppose?"

"No," answered Miss Baxter, forgetting for the moment the role she was playing; "I am from London."

"Well, it doesn't matter; you are the young woman who is arranging my wife's correspondence?"

"Yes." The Prince strode rapidly forward and grasped her by the wrist, his brow dark with a forbidding frown. He spoke in a hoarse whisper:

"Listen, my good girl! Do you want to get more money from me than you will get from the Princess in ten years' service? Hearken, then, to what I tell you. If there are any letters from—from—men, will you bring them to me?"

Miss Baxter was thoroughly frightened, but she said to the Prince sharply,—

"If you do not let go my wrist, I'll scream. How dare you lay your hand on me?"

The Prince released her wrist and stepped back.

"Forgive me," he said; "I'm a very miserable man. Forget what I have said."

"How can I forget it?" cried the girl, gathering courage as she saw him quail before her blazing eyes. "What do you want me to do?"

"I want you to bring to me any letters written by—by——"

"Written by von Schaumberg," cried the girl, noticing his hesitation and filling in the blank.

A red wave of anger surged up in the Prince's face.

"Yes," he cried; "bring me a letter to her from von Schaumberg, and I'll pay you what you ask."

The girl laughed.

"Prince," she said, "you will excuse me if I call you a fool. There are no letters from von Schaumberg, and I have gone through the whole of the correspondence."

"What, then, suggested the name von Schaumberg to you? Where did you ever hear it before?"

"I heard that you suspected him of stealing the diamonds."

"And so he did, the cowardly thief. If it were not for mixing the Princess's name with such carrion as he, I would—"

But the Prince in his rage stamped up and down the room without saying what he would do. Miss Baxter quickly brought him to a standstill.

"It is contrary to my duty to the Princess," she began, hesitatingly, when he stopped and turned fiercely upon her.

"What is contrary to your duty?"

"There are letters, tied very daintily with a blue ribbon, and they are from a man. The Princess did not allow me to read them, but locked them away in a secret drawer in her dressing-room, but she is so careless with her keys and everything else, that I am sure I can get them for you, if you want them."

"Yes, yes, I want them," said the Prince, "and will pay you handsomely for them."

"Very well," replied Miss Baxter, "you shall have them. If you will wait here ten minutes, I shall return with them."

"But," hesitated the Prince, "say nothing to the Princess."

"Oh, no, I shall not need to; the keys are sure to be on her dressing-table."

Miss Baxter ran down to the room of the Princess, and had little difficulty in obtaining the keys. She unlocked the secret drawer into which she had seen the Princess place the packet of letters, and taking them out, she drew another sheet of paper along with them, which she read with wide-opening eyes, then with her pretty lips pursed, she actually whistled, which unmaidenly performance merely gave sibilant expression to her astonishment. Taking both the packet of letters and the sheet of paper with her, she ran swiftly up the stair and along the corridor to the room where the Prince was impatiently awaiting her.

"Give them to me," he snapped, rudely snatching the bundle of documents from her hand. She still clung to the separate piece of paper and said nothing. The Prince stood by the window and undid the packet with trembling hands. He examined one and then another of the letters, turning at last towards the girl with renewed anger in his face.

"You are trifling with me, my girl," he cried.

"No, I am not," she said stoutly.

"These are my own letters, written by me to my wife before we were married!"

"Of course they are. What others did you expect? These are the only letters, so far as I have learned, that any man has written to her, and the only letters she cares for of all the thousands she has ever received. Why, you foolish, blind man, I had not been in this castle a day before I saw how matters stood. The Princess is breaking her poor heart because you are unkind to her, and she cares for nobody on earth but you, great stupid dunce that you are."

"Is it true? Will you swear it's true?" cried the Prince, dropping the packet and going hastily toward the girl. Miss Jennie stood with her back to the wall, and putting her hands behind her, she said,—

"No, no; you are not going to touch me again. Of course it's true, and if you had the sense of a six-year-old child, you would have seen it long ago; and she paid sixty thousand pounds of your gambling debts, too."

"What are you talking about? The Princess has never given me a penny of her money; I don't need it. Goodness knows, I have money enough of my own."

"Well, Cadbury Taylor said that you—Oh, I'll warrant you, it is like all the rest of his statements, pure moonshine."

"Of whom are you speaking? And why did my wife protect that wretch whom she knows has stolen her diamonds?"

"You mean von Schaumberg?"

"Yes."

"I believe the Princess does think he stole them, and the reason the Princess protects him is to prevent you from challenging him, for she fears that he, being a military man, will kill you, although I fancy she would be well rid of you."

"But he stole the diamonds—there was nobody else."

"He did nothing of the kind. Read that!"

The Prince, bewildered, took the sheet that she handed to him and read it, a wrinkle of bewilderment corrugating his brow.

"I don't understand what this has to do with the case," he said at last. "It seems to be an order on the bank at Vienna for the diamonds, written by the Princess herself."

"Of course it is. Well, if the diamonds had been delivered, that paper would now be in the possession of the bank instead of in your hands."

"Perhaps she mislaid this order and wrote another."

"Perhaps. Still it might be worth while finding out."

"Take this, then, to the Princess and ask her."

"It is not likely she would remember. The better plan is to telegraph at once to the Vienna bank, asking them to send the diamonds to Meran by special messenger. No one there knows that the diamonds are missing."

"I will do so at once," cried the Prince, with more animation in his voice than Miss Baxter had previously noticed. His Highness was becoming interested in the game.

After luncheon the Princess came to Miss Baxter, who was seated at her desk, and handed her a letter.

"There is an invitation from the Duchess of Chiselhurst for a grand ball she is shortly to give in her London house. It is to be a very swell affair, but I don't care enough for such things to go all the way to England to enjoy them. Would you therefore send her Grace my regrets?"

"I will do so at once."

At that moment there came a messenger from the Prince asking Miss

Baxter to meet him in the library. The girl glanced up at the Princess.

"Have I your permission to go?" she said.

The Princess looked at her steadily for a moment, just the faintest suspicion of a frown on her fair brow.

"I do not suppose you need my permission." Her Highness spoke with slow deliberation. "My husband condescends to take considerable interest in you. Passing along the corridor this morning, I heard your voices in most animated conversation."

"Had you sufficient interest in our discussion to stop and listen to what we said, Princess von Steinheimer?"

"Ah, now you are becoming insolent, and I must ask you to consider your engagement with me at an end."

"Surely you will not dismiss me in this heartless way, Princess. I think I am entitled to a month's notice, or is it only a week's?"

"I will pay you a year's salary, or two years' if that will content you. I have no wish to deal harshly with you, but I desire you to leave at once," said the Princess, who had little sense of humour, and thus thought the girl was in earnest when she asked for notice.

Miss Baxter laughed merrily, and replied when she was able to control her mirth, "I do hate to leave the castle just when things are becoming interesting. Still, I don't suppose I shall really need to go away in spite of your dismissal, for the Prince this morning offered me ten times the amount of money you are paying."

"Did he?"

"Be assured he did; if you don't believe me, ask him. I told him he was a fool, but, alas, we live in a cynical age, and few men believe all they hear, so I fear my expression of opinion made little impression on him."

"I shall not keep you longer from his Highness," said the Princess with freezing dignity.

"Thank you so much. I am just dying to meet him, for I know he has something most interesting to tell me. Don't you think yourself, Princess, that a man acts rather like a fool when he is deeply in love?"

To this there was no reply, and the Princess left the room.

Miss Jennie jumped to her feet and almost ran to the library. She found the Prince walking up and down the long room with a telegraph message in his hand. "You are a most wonderful young woman," he said; "read that."

"I have been told so by more observing men than you, Prince von Steinheimer," said the girl, taking the telegram. It was from the manager of the bank in Vienna, and it ran: "Special messenger leaves with package by the Meran express to-night."

"Just as I thought," said Miss Jennie; "the diamonds never left the bank. I suppose those idiots of servants which the Princess has round her didn't know what they took away from Vienna and what they left. Then, when the diamonds were missing, they completely lost their heads—not that anyone in the castle has much wit to spare. I never saw such an incompetent lot."

The Prince laughed.

"You think, perhaps, I have not wit enough to see that my wife cares for me, is that it? Is that why you gave me my own letters?"

"Oh, you are well mated! The Princess now does me the honour of being jealous. Think of that! As if it were possible that I should take any interest in you, for I have seen real men in my time."

The Prince regarded her with his most severe expression.

"Are you not flattering yourself somewhat, young lady?"

"Oh, dear no! I take it as the reverse of flattering to be supposed that I have any liking for such a ninny as you are. Flattering, indeed! And she has haughtily dismissed me, if you please."

"The Princess has? What have you been saying to her?"

"Oh, I made the most innocent remark, and it was the truth too, which shows that honesty is not always the best policy. I merely told her that you had offered me ten times the amount of money she is paying me. You needn't jump as if somebody had shot off a gun at your ear. You know you did make such an offer."

"You confounded little mischief-maker," cried the Prince in anger. "Did you tell her what it was for?"

"No. She did not ask."

"I will thank you to apply the cleverness you seem to possess to the undoing of the harm you have so light-heartedly caused."

"How can I? I am ordered to leave to-night, when I did so wish to stay and see the diamond dénouement."

"You are not going to-night. I shall speak to the Princess about it if that should be necessary. Your mention of the diamonds reminds me that my respected father-in-law, Mr. Briggs, informs me that a celebrated detective, whom it seems he has engaged—Taylor, I think the name is—will be here to-morrow to explain the diamond mystery, so you see you have a competitor."

"Oh, is Cadbury coming? That is too jolly for anything. I simply must stay and hear his explanation, for he is a very famous detective, and the conclusions he has arrived at must be most interesting."

"I think some explanations are due to me as well. My worthy father-in-law seems to have commissioned this person without thinking it necessary to consult me in the least; in fact, Mr. Briggs goes about the castle looking so dark and lowering when he meets me, that I sometimes doubt whether this is my own house or not."

"And is it?"

"Is it what?"

"Is it your own house? I was told it was mortgaged up to the tallest turret. Still, you can't blame Mr. Briggs for being anxious about the diamonds; they belong to his daughter."

"They belong to my wife."

"True. That complicates matters a bit, and gives both Chicago and Vienna a right to look black. And now, your Highness, I must take my leave of you; and if the diamonds come safely in the morning, remember I intend to claim salvage on them. Meanwhile, I am going to write a nice little story about them."

In the morning the diamonds arrived by special messenger, who first took a formal receipt for them, and then most obsequiously took his departure. By the same train came Mr. Cadbury Taylor, as modest as ever, but giving some indication in his bearing of the importance of the discovery his wonderful system had aided him in making. He blandly evaded the curiosity of Mr. Briggs, and said it would perhaps be better to reveal the secret in the presence of the Prince and Princess, as his investigations had led him to conclusions that might be unpleasant for one of them to hear, yet were not to be divulged in their absence.

"Just what I suspected," muttered Mr. Briggs, who had long been convinced that the Prince was the actual culprit.

The important gathering took place in the library, the Prince, with the diamonds in his coat pocket, seated at the head of the long table, while the Princess sat at the foot, as far from her husband as she could conveniently get without attracting notice. Miss Baxter stood near a window, reading an important letter from London which had reached her that morning. The tall, thin detective and the portly Mr. Briggs came in together, the London man bowing gravely to the Prince and Princess. Mr. Briggs took a seat at the side of the table, but the detective remained standing, looking questioningly at Miss Baxter, but evidently not recognizing her as the lady who had come in upon him and his friend when they had entered the train.

"I beg the pardon of your Highness, but what I have to say had better be said with as few hearers as possible. I should be much obliged if this young person would read her correspondence in another room."

"The young woman," said the Prince coldly, "is secretary to her Highness, and is entirely in her confidence."

The Princess said nothing, but sat with her eyes upon the table, apparently taking no note of what was going on. Rich colour came into her face, and, as the keen detective cast a swift glance at her, he saw before him a woman conscious of her guilt, fearing exposure, yet not knowing how to avert it.

"If your Highness will excuse my persistence," began Mr. Taylor blandly.

"But I will not," interrupted the Prince gruffly. "Go on with your story without so much circumlocution."

The detective, apparently unruffled by the discourtesy he met, bowed profoundly towards the Prince, cleared his throat, and began.

"May I ask your Highness," he said, addressing himself to the Princess, "how much money you possessed just before you left Vienna?"

The lady looked up at him in surprise, but did not answer.

"In Heaven's name, what has that to do with the loss of the diamonds?" rapped out the Prince, his hot temper getting once more the better of him. Cadbury Taylor spread out his hands and shrugged his shoulders in protest at the interruption. He spoke with deference, but nevertheless there was a touch of reproach in his tone.

"I am accustomed to being listened to with patience, and am generally allowed to tell my story my own way, your Highness."

"What I complain of is that you are not telling any story at all, but are asking instead a very impertinent question."

"Questions which seem to you irrelevant may be to a trained mind most—"

"Bosh! Trained donkeys! Do you know where the diamonds are?"

"Yes, I do," answered Cadbury Taylor, still imperturbable, in spite of the provocation he was receiving.

"Well, where are they?"

"They are in the vaults of your bank in Vienna."

"I don't believe it. Who stole them then?"

"They were put there by her Highness the Princess von Steinheimer, doubtless in security for money—"

"What!" roared the Prince, springing to his feet, his stentorian voice ringing to the ceiling. "Do you mean to insinuate, you villain, that my wife stole her own diamonds?"

"If your Highness would allow me to proceed in my own—"

"Enough of this fooling. There are the diamonds," cried the Prince, jerking the box from his pocket and flinging it on the table.

"There!" shouted old man Briggs, bringing his clenched fist down on the oak. "What did I tell you? I knew it all along. The Prince stole the diamonds, and in his excitement yanks them out of his pocket and proves it. That was my opinion all along!"

"Oh, father, father!" moaned the Princess, speaking for the first time. "How can you say such a thing? My husband couldn't do a mean action if he tried. The idea of him stealing the diamonds! Not if they were worth a thousand millions and detection impossible."

The Prince, who had been glaring at Mr. Briggs, and who seemed on the point of giving that red-faced gentleman a bit of his mind, turned a softened gaze upon his wife, who rested her arms on the table and buried her face in them.

"Come, come," cried Miss Jennie Baxter, stepping energetically forward; "I imagine everybody has had enough of this. Clear out, Mr. Briggs, and take Mr. Taylor with you; I am sure he has not had any breakfast yet, and he certainly looks hungry. If you hire detectives, Mr. Briggs, you must take care of them. Out you go. The dining-room is ever so much more inviting just now than the library; and if you don't see what you want, ring for it."

She drove the two speechless men out before her, and, closing the door, said to the Prince, who was still standing bewildered at having his hand forced in this manner,—

"There! Two fools from four leaves two. Now, my dears—I'm not going to Highness either of you—you are simply two lone people who like each other immensely, yet who are drifting apart through foolish misunderstandings that a few words would put right if either of you had sense enough to speak them, which you haven't, and that's why I'm here to speak them for you. Now, madame, I am ready to swear that the Prince has never said anything to me that did not show his deep love for you, and if you had overheard us, you would not need me to tell you so. He thinks that you have a fancy for that idiot von Schaumberg—not that I ever saw the poor man; but he is bound to be an idiot, or the Prince wouldn't be jealous of him. As nobody has stolen the diamonds after all this fuss, so no one has stolen the affection of either of you from the other. I can see by the way you look at each other that I won't need to apologize for leaving you alone together while I run upstairs to pack."

"Oh, but you are not going to leave us?" cried the Princess.

"I should be delighted to stay; but there is no rest for the wicked, and I must get back to London."

With that the girl ran to her room and there re-read the letter she had received.

"Dear Miss Baxter (it ran),—We are in a very considerable dilemma here, so I write asking you to see me in London without delay, going back to the Tyrol later on if the investigation of the diamond mystery renders your return necessary. The Duchess of Chiselhurst is giving a great ball on the 29th. It is to be a very swagger affair, with notables from every part of Europe, and they seem determined that no one connected with a newspaper shall be admitted. We have set at work every influence to obtain an invitation for a reporter, but without success, the reply invariably given being that an official account will be sent to the press. Now, I want you to set your ingenuity at work, and gain admittance if possible, for I am determined to have an account of this ball written in such a way that everyone who reads it will know that the writer was present. If you can manage this, I can hardly tell you how grateful the proprietor and myself will be.—Yours very truly,

"RADNOR HARDWICK."

Miss Jennie Baxter sat for some moments musing, with the letter in her hand. She conned over in her mind the names of those who might be able to assist her in this task, but she dismissed them one by one, well knowing that if Mr. Hardwick and the proprietor of the Bugle had petitioned all their influential friends without avail, she could not hope to succeed with the help of the very few important personages she was acquainted with. She wondered if the Princess could get her an invitation; then suddenly her eyes lit up, and she sprang eagerly to her feet.

"What a fortunate thing it is," she cried aloud, "that I did not send on the refusal of the Princess to the Duchess of Chiselhurst. I had forgotten all about it until this moment."

CHAPTER VII. JENNIE ARRANGES A CINDERELLA VISIT.

The room which had been allotted to Jennie Baxter in the Schloss Steinheimer enjoyed a most extended outlook. A door-window gave access to a stone balcony, which hung against the castle wall like a swallow's nest at the eaves of a house. This balcony was just wide enough to give ample space for one of the easy rocking-chairs which the Princess had imported from America, and which Jennie thought were the only really comfortable pieces of furniture the old stronghold possessed, much as she admired the artistic excellence of the mediæval chairs, tables, and cabinets which for centuries had served the needs of the ancient line that had lived in the Schloss. The rocking-chair was as modern as this morning's daily paper; its woodwork painted a bright scarlet, its arms like broad shelves, its rockers as sensitively balanced as a marine compass; in fact, just such a chair as one would find dotted round the vast verandah of an American summer hotel. In this chair sat Miss Jennie, two open letters on her lap, and perplexity in the dainty little frown that faintly ruffled the smoothness of her fair brow. The scene from the high balcony was one to be remembered; but, although this was her last day at the Castle, the girl saw nothing of the pretty town of Meran so far below; the distant chalk-line down the slope beyond which marked the turbulent course of the foaming Adege; the lofty mountains all around, or the further snow-peaks, dazzling white against the deep blue of the sky.

One of the epistles which lay on her lap was the letter she had received from the editor recounting the difficulties he had met with while endeavouring to make arrangements for reporting adequately the Duchess of Chiselhurst's ball; the other was the still unanswered invitation from the Duchess to the Princess. Jennie was flattered to know that already the editor, who had engaged her with unconcealed reluctance, expected her to accomplish what the entire staff were powerless to effect. She knew that, had she but the courage, it was only necessary to accept the invitation in the name of her present hostess, and attend the great society function as Princess von Steinheimer. Yet she hesitated, not so much on account of the manifest danger of discovery, but because she had grown to like the Princess, and this impersonation, if it came to the knowledge of the one most intimately concerned, as it was almost sure to do, would doubtless be regarded as an unpardonable liberty. As she swayed gently back and forth in the gaudy rocking-chair, she thought of confessing everything to the Princess and asking her assistance; but pondering on this, she saw that it was staking everything on one throw of the dice. If the Princess refused, then the scheme became impossible, as that lady herself would answer the letter of the Duchess and decline the invitation. Jennie soothed her accusing conscience by telling herself that this impersonation would do no harm to Princess von Steinheimer, or to anyone else for that matter, while it would be of inestimable assistance to her own journalistic career. From that she drifted to meditation on the inequalities of this life—the superabundance which some possess, while others, no less deserving, have difficulty in obtaining the scant necessities. And this consoling train of thought having fixed her resolve to take the goods the gods scattered at her feet, or rather threw into her lap, she drew a long sigh of determination as there came a gentle tap at the door of her room, and the voice of the Princess herself said, "May I come in?"

Jennie, a rapid blush flaming her cheeks, sprang to her feet, flung the letters on a table, and opened the door.

The visitor entered, looking attractive enough to be a princess of fairyland, and greeted Miss Baxter most cordially.

"I am so sorry you are leaving," she said. "Cannot you be persuaded to change your mind and stay with me? Where could you find a more lovely view than this from your balcony here?"

"Or a more lovely hostess?" said the girl, looking at her visitor with undisguised admiration and quite ignoring the landscape.

The Princess laughed, and as they now stood together on the balcony she put out her hands, pushed Jennie gently into the rocking-chair again, seating herself jauntily on its broad arm, and thus the two looked like a pair of mischievous schoolgirls, home at vacation time, thoroughly enjoying their liberty.

"There! You are now my prisoner, about to be punished for flattery," cried the Princess. "I saw by the motion of the chair that you had just jumped up from it when I disturbed you, so there you are, back in it again. What were you thinking about? A rocking-chair lends itself deliciously to meditation, and we always dream of someone very particular as we rock."

"I am no exception to the rule," sighed Jennie; "I was thinking of you, Princess."

"How nice of you to say that; and as one good turn deserves another, here is proof that a certain young lady has been in my thoughts."

As she spoke, the Princess took from her pocket an embossed case of Russian leather, opened it and displayed a string of diamonds, lustrous as drops of liquid light.

"I want you to wear these stones in remembrance of our diamond mystery—that is why I chose diamonds—and also, I confess, because I want you to think of me every time you put them on. See how conceited I am! One does not like to be forgotten."

Jennie took the string, her own eyes for a moment rivalling in brilliancy the sparkle of the gems; then the moisture obscured her vision and she automatically poured the stones from one hand to the other, as if their scintillating glitter hypnotized her. She tried once or twice to speak, but could not be sure of her voice, so remained silent. The Princess, noticing her agitation, gently lifted the necklace and clasped it round the girl's white throat, chattering all the while with nervous haste.

"There! you can wear diamonds, and there are so many to whom they are unbecoming. I also look well in diamonds—at least, so I've been told over and over again, and I've come to believe it at last. I suppose the young men have not concealed from you the fact that you are a strikingly good-looking girl, Jennie. Indeed, and this is brag if you like, we two resemble one another enough to be sisters, nearly the same height, the same colour of eyes and hair. Come to the mirror, Miss Handsomeness, and admire yourself."

She dragged Jennie to her feet and drew her into the room, placing her triumphantly before the great looking-glass that reflected back a full-length portrait.

"Now confess that you never saw a prettier girl," cried the Princess gleefully.

"I don't think I ever did," admitted Jennie, but she was looking at the image of the Princess and not at her own. The Princess laughed, but Miss Baxter seemed too much affected by the unexpected present to join in the merriment. She regarded herself solemnly in the glass for a few moments, then slowly undid the clasp, and, slipping the string of brilliants from her neck, handed them back to the Princess. "You are very, very kind, but I cannot accept so costly a present."

"Cannot? Why? Have I offended you by anything I have said since you came?"

"Oh, no, no. It isn't that."

"What, then? Don't you like me, after all?"

"Like you? I love you, Princess!" cried the girl impulsively, throwing her arms round the other's neck.

The Princess tried to laugh as she pressed Jennie closely to her, but there was a tremour of tears in the laughter.

"You must take this little gift as a souvenir of your visit with me. I was really—very unhappy when you came, and now—well, you smoothed away some misunderstandings—I'm more than grateful. And it isn't natural for a woman to refuse diamonds, Jennie."

"I know it isn't; and I won't quite refuse them. I'll postpone. It is possible that something I shall do before long may seriously offend you. If it does—then good-bye to the necklace! If it doesn't, when I have told you all about my misdeed—I shall confess courageously—you will give me the diamonds."

"Dear me, Jennie, what terrible crime are you about to commit? Why not tell me now? You have no idea how you have aroused my curiosity."

"I dare not tell you, Princess; not until my project proves a success or a failure. We women—some have our way made for us—others have our own way to make. I am among the others, and I hope you will remember that, if you are ever angry with me."

"Is it a new kind of speculation? A fortune made in a day? Gambling?"

"Something of that sort. I am going to stake a good deal on the turn of a card; so please pray that luck will not be against me."

"If pluck will make you win, I am sure you will carry it through, but if at first you don't succeed, try, try again; and if you haven't the money, I'll supply the capital. I know I should like to gamble. Anyhow, you have my best wishes for your success."

"Thank you, Princess. I can hardly fail after that."

The time had come when the two friends must part. The carriage was waiting to take Miss Baxter to the station, and the girl bade good-bye to her hostess with an uneasy feeling that she was acting disloyally to one who had befriended her. In her handbag was the invitation to the ball, and also the letter she had written in the Princess's name accepting it, which latter she posted in Meran. In due course she reached London, and presented herself to the editor of the Daily Bugle.

"Well, Miss Baxter," he said, "you have been extraordinarily successful in solving the diamond mystery, and I congratulate you. My letter reached you, I suppose. Have you given any thought to the problem that now confronts us? Can you get us a full report of the Duchess of Chiselhurst's ball, written so convincingly that all the guests who read it will know that the writer was present?"

"It is entirely a question of money, Mr. Hardwick."

"Most things are. Well, we are prepared to spend money to get just what we want."

"How much?"

"Whatever is necessary."

“That’s vague. Put it into figures.”

“Five hundred pounds; seven hundred; a thousand if need be.”

“It will not cost you a thousand, and it may come to more than five hundred. Place the thousand to my credit, and I shall return what is left. I must go at once to Paris and carry out my plans from that city.”

“Then you have thought out a scheme. What is it?”

“I have not only thought it out, but most of the arrangements are already made. I cannot say more about it. You will have to trust wholly to me.”

“There is a good deal of money at stake, Miss Baxter, and our reputation as a newspaper as well. I think I should know what you propose to do.”

“Certainly. I propose to obtain for you an accurate description of the ball, written by one who was present.”

The editor gave utterance to a sort of interjection that always served him in place of a laugh.

“In other words, you want neither interference nor advice.”

“Exactly, Mr. Hardwick. You know from experience that little good comes of talking too much of a secret project not yet completed.”

The editor drummed with his fingers on the table for a few moments thoughtfully.

“Very well, then, it shall be as you say. I should have been very glad to share the responsibility of failure with you; but if you prefer to take the whole risk yourself, there is nothing more to be said. The thousand pounds shall be placed to your credit at once. What next?”

“On the night of the ball I should like you to have three or four expert shorthand writers here; I don’t know how many will be necessary—you understand more about that than I do; but it is my intention to dictate the report right along as fast as I can talk until it is finished, and I don’t wish to be stopped or interrupted, so I want the best stenographers you have; they are to relieve one another just as if they were taking down a parliamentary speech. The men had better be in readiness at midnight; I shall be here as soon after that as possible. If you will kindly run over their type-written MS. before it goes to the compositors, I will glance at the proofs when I have finished dictating."

"Then you hope to attend the ball yourself."

"Perhaps."

"You have just returned from the Tyrol, and I fear you don't quite appreciate the difficulties that are in the way. This is no ordinary society function, and if you think even a thousand pounds will gain admittance to an uninvited guest, you will find yourself mistaken."

"So I understood from your letter."

Again the editorial interjection did duty for a laugh.

"You are very sanguine, Miss Baxter. I wish I felt as confident; however, we will hope for the best, and if we cannot command success, we will at least endeavour to deserve it."

Jennie, with the thousand pounds at her disposal, went to Paris, took rooms at the most aristocratic hotel, engaged a maid, and set about the construction of a ball dress that would be a dream of beauty. Luckily, she knew exactly the gown-making resources of Paris, and the craftsmen to whom she gave her orders were not the less anxious to please her when they knew that the question of cost was not to be considered. From Paris she telegraphed in the name of the Princess von Steinheimer to Claridge's Hotel for an apartment on the night of the ball, and asked that a suitable equipage be provided to convey her to and from that festival.

Arriving at Claridge's, she was well aware her first danger was that someone who knew the Princess von Steinheimer would call upon her; but on the valid plea of fatigue from her journey she proclaimed that in no circumstances could she see any visitor, and thus shipwreck was avoided at the outset. It was unlikely that the Princess von Steinheimer was personally known to many who would attend the ball; in fact, the Princess had given to Jennie as her main reason for refusing the invitation the excuse that she knew no one in London. She had been invited merely because of the social position of the Prince in Vienna, and was unknown by sight even to her hostess, the Duchess of Chiselhurst. Critically, she compared the chances of success with the chances of failure, and often it seemed that disaster was inevitable, unversed as she knew herself to be in the customs of grand society at one of its high functions, but nevertheless she was undaunted by the odds against her, and resolved to stake a career on the fortunes of a night.

CHAPTER VIII. JENNIE MIXES WITH THE ELITE OF EARTH.

It is said that a woman magnificently robed is superior to all earthly tribulations. Such was the case with Jennie as she left her carriage, walked along the strip of carpet which lay across the pavement under a canopy, and entered the great hall of the Duke of Chiselhurst's town house, one of the huge palaces of Western London. Nothing so resplendent had she ever witnessed, or even imagined, as the scene which met her eye when she found herself about to ascend the broad stairway at the top of which the hostess stood to receive her distinguished guests. Early as she was, the stairway and the rooms beyond seemed already thronged. Splendid menials in gorgeous livery, crimson the predominant colour, stood on each step at either side of the stair. Uniforms of every pattern, from the dazzling oriental raiment of Indian princes and eastern potentates, to the more sober, but scarcely less rich apparel of the diplomatic corps, ministers of the Empire, and officers, naval and military, gave the final note of magnificence and picturesque decoration. Like tropical flowers in this garden of colour were the ladies, who, with easy grace, moved to and fro, bestowing a smile here and a whisper there; and yet, despite her agitation, a hurried, furtive glance around brought to Jennie the conviction that she was, perhaps, the best-gowned woman in that assemblage of well-dressed people, which recognition somewhat calmed her palpitating heart. The whole environment seemed unreal to her, and she walked forward as if in a dream. She heard someone cry, "The Princess von Steinheimer," and at first had a difficulty in realizing that the title, for the moment, pertained to herself. The next instant her hand was in that of the Duchess of Chiselhurst, and Jennie heard the lady murmur that it was good of her to come so far to grace the occasion. The girl made some sort of reply which she found herself unable afterwards to recall, but the rapid incoming of other guests led her to hope that, if she had used any unsuitable phrase, it was either unheard or forgotten in the tension of the time. She stood aside and formed one of the brilliant group at the head of the stairs, thankful that this first ordeal was well done with. Her rapidly beating heart had now opportunity to lessen its pulsations, and as she soon realized that she was practically unnoticed, her natural calmness began to return to her. She remembered why she was there, and her discerning eye enabled her to stamp on a retentive memory the various particulars of so unaccustomed a spectacle whose very unfamiliarity made the greater impression upon the girl's mind. She moved away from the group, determined to saunter through the numerous rooms thrown open for the occasion, and thus, as it were, get her bearings. In a short time all fear of discovery left her, and she began to feel very much at home in the lofty, crowded salons, pausing even to enjoy a selection which a military band, partly concealed in the foliage, was rendering in masterly manner, led by the most famous impressario of the day. The remote probability of meeting anyone here who knew the Princess reassured her, and there speedily came over her a sense of delight in all the kaleidoscopic bewilderment of this great entertainment. She saw that each one there had interest in someone else, and, to her great relief, found herself left entirely alone with reasonable assurance that this remoteness would continue to befriend her until the final gauntlet of leave-taking had to be run; a trial still to be encountered, the thought of which she resolutely put away from her, trusting to the luck that had hitherto not deserted her.

Jennie was in this complaisant frame of mind when she was suddenly startled by a voice at her side.

"Ah, Princess, I have been searching everywhere for you, catching glimpses of you now and then, only to lose you, as, alas, has been my fate on more serious occasion. May I flatter myself with the belief that you also remember?"

There was no recognition in the large frightened eyes that were turned upon him. They saw a young man bowing low over the unresisting hand he had taken. His face was clear-cut and unmistakably English. Jennie saw his closely-cropped auburn head, and, as it raised until it overtopped her own, the girl, terrified as she was, could not but admire the sweeping blonde moustache that overshadowed a smile, half-wistful, half-humorous, which lighted up his handsome face. The ribbon of some order was worn athwart his breast; otherwise he wore court dress, which well became his stalwart frame.

"I am disconsolate to see that I am indeed forgotten, Princess, and so another cherished delusion fades away from me."

Her fan concealed the lower part of the girl's face, and she looked at him over its fleecy semicircle.

"Put not your trust in princesses," she murmured, a sparkle of latent mischief lighting up her eyes.

The young man laughed. "Indeed," he said, "had I served my country as faithfully as I have been true to my remembrance of you, Princess, I would have been an ambassador long ere this, covered with decorations. Have you then lost all recollection of that winter in Washington five years ago; that whirlwind of gaiety which ended by wafting you away to a foreign country, and thus the eventful season clings to my memory as if it were a disastrous western cyclone? Is it possible that I must re-introduce myself as Donal Stirling?"

"Not Lord Donal Stirling?" asked Jennie, dimly remembering that she had heard this name in connection with something diplomatic, and her guess that he was in that service was strengthened by his previous remark about being an ambassador.

"Yes, Lord Donal, if you will cruelly insist on calling me so; but this cannot take from me the consolation that once, in the conservatory of the White House, under the very shadow of the President, you condescended to call me Don."

"You cannot expect one to remember what happened in Washington five years ago. You know the administration itself changes every four years, and memories seldom carry back even so far as that."

"I had hoped that my most outspoken adoration would have left reminiscence which might outlast an administration. I have not found forgetting so easy."

"Are you quite sure of that, Lord Donal?" asked the girl archly, closing her fan and giving him for the first time a full view of her face.

The young man seemed for a moment perplexed, but she went on, giving him little time for reflection. "Have your diplomatic duties taken you away from Washington?"

"Yes, to the other end of the earth. I am now in St. Petersburg, with ultimate hopes of Vienna, Princess. I happened to be in London this week, and hearing you were to be here, I moved heaven and earth for an invitation."

"Which you obtained, only to find yourself forgotten. How hollow this world is, isn't it?"

"Alas, yes. A man in my profession sees a good deal of the seamy side of life, and I fully believe that my rapidly lessening dependence on human veracity will be shattered by my superiors sending me to Constantinople. But let me find you a seat out of this crowd where we may talk of old times."

"I don't care so much about the past as I do about the present. Let us go up into that gallery, where you shall point out to me the celebrities. I suppose you know them all, while I am an entire stranger to London Society."

"That is a capital idea," cried the young man enthusiastically. "Yes, I think I know most of the people here, at least by name. Ah, here comes the Royal party; we shall just be in time to have a good look at them."

The band played the National Anthem, and Lord Donal got two chairs, which he placed at the edge of the gallery, well hidden from the promenaders by spreading tropical plants.

"Oh, this is jolly," cried Jennie, quite forgetting the dignity of a Princess. "You told me why you came to the ball. Do you know why I am here?"

"On the remote chance of meeting me whom you pretended to have forgotten," replied the young man audaciously.

"Of course," laughed Jennie; "but aside from that, I came to see the costumes. You know, we women are libellously said to dress for each other. Away from the world, in the Tyrol, I have little opportunity of seeing anything fine in the way of dress, and so I accepted the invitation of the Duchess."

"Have you the invitation of the Duchess with you?"

"Yes, I am going to make some notes on the back of it. Would you like to see it?" She handed him the letter and then leaned back in her chair, regarding him closely. The puzzled expression on his face deepened as he glanced over the invitation, and saw that it was exactly what it purported to be. He gave the letter back to her, saying,—

"So you are here to see the fashions. It is a subject I know little about; but, judging by effect, I should say that the Princess von Steinheimer has nothing to learn from anyone present. If I may touch on a topic so personal, your costume is what they call a creation, is it not, Princess?"

"It isn't bad," said the girl, looking down at her gown and then glancing up at him with merriment dancing in her eyes. The diplomat had his elbow resting on the balustrade, his head leaning on his hand, and, quite oblivious to everything else, was gazing at her with such absorbed intentness that the girl blushed and cast down her eyes. The intense admiration in his look was undisguised. "Still," she rattled on somewhat breathlessly, "one gets many hints from others, and the creation of to-day is merely the old clothes of to-morrow. Invention has no vacation so far as ladies' apparel is concerned. 'Take no thought of the morrow, wherewithal ye shall be clothed,' may have been a good motto for the court of Solomon, but it has little relation with that of Victoria."

"Solomon—if the saying is his—was hedging. He had many wives, you know."

"Well, as I was about to say, you must now turn your attention to the other guests, and tell me who's who. I have already confessed my ignorance, and you promised to enlighten me."

The young man, with visible reluctance, directed his thoughts from the one to the many, and named this person and that, while Jennie, with the pencil attached to her card, made cabalistic notes in shorthand, economizing thus both space and time. When at last she had all the information that could be desired, she leaned back in her chair with a little sigh of supreme content. Whatever might now betide, her mission was fulfilled, if she once got quietly away. The complete details of the most important society event of the season were at her fingers' ends. She closed her eyes for a moment to enjoy the satisfaction which success leaves in its train, and when she opened them again found Lord Donal in his old posture, absorbed in the contemplation of her undeniable beauty.

"I see you are determined I shall have no difficulty in remembering you next time we meet," she said with a smile, at the same time flushing slightly under his ardent gaze.

"I was just thinking," he replied, shifting his position a little, "that the five years which have dealt so hardly with me, have left you five years younger."

"Age has many privileges, Lord Donal," she said to him, laughing outright; "but I don't think you can yet lay claim to any of them. The pose of the prematurely old is not in the least borne out by your appearance, however hardly the girl you met in Washington dealt with you."

"Ah, Princess, it is very easy for you to treat these serious matters lightly. He laughs at scars who never felt a wound. Time, being above all things treacherous, often leaves the face untouched the more effectually to scar the heart. The hurt concealed is ever the more dangerous."

"I fancy it has been concealed so effectually that it is not as deep as you imagined."

"Princess, I will confess to you that the wound at Washington was as nothing to the one received at London."

"Yes; you told me you had been here for a week."

"The week has nothing to do with it. I have been here for a night—for two hours—or three; I have lost count of time since I met you."

What reply the girl might have made to this speech, delivered with all the fervency of a man in thorough earnest, will never be known, for at that moment their tête-à-tête was interrupted by a messenger, who said,—

"His Excellency the Austrian Ambassador begs to be permitted to pay his regards to the Princess von Steinheimer."

Lord Donal Stirling never took his eyes from the face of his companion, and he saw a quick pallor overspread it. He leaned forward and whispered,—

"I know the Ambassador; if you do not wish to meet him, I will intercept him."

Jennie rose slowly to her feet, and, looking at the young man with a calmness she was far from feeling, said coldly,—

"Why should I not wish to meet the Ambassador of my adopted country?"

"I know of no reason. Quite the contrary, for he must be an old friend of yours, having been your guest at the Schloss Steinheimer a year ago."

He stepped back as he said this, and Jennie had difficulty in suppressing the gasp of dismay with which she received his disquieting disclosure, but she stood her ground without wincing. She was face to face with the crisis she had foreseen—the coming of one who knew the Princess. Next instant the aged diplomat was bending over her outstretched hand, which in courtly fashion the old man raised to his lips.

"I am delighted to have the privilege of welcoming you to this gloomy old city, Princess von Steinheimer, which you illumine with your presence. Do you stay long in London?"

"The period of illumination is short, your Excellency. I leave for Paris to-morrow."

"So soon? Without even visiting the Embassy? I am distressed to hear of so speedy a desertion, and yet, knowing the charms of the Schloss Steinheimer, I can hardly wonder at your wish to return there. The Prince, I suppose, is as devoted as ever to the chase. I must censure his Highness, next time we meet, for not coming with you to London; then I am sure you would have stayed longer with us."

"The Prince is a model husband, your Excellency," said Jennie, with a sly glance at Lord Donal, whose expression of uncertainty increased as this colloquy went on, "and he would have come to London without a murmur had his wife been selfish enough to tear him away from his beloved Meran."

"A model husband!" said the ancient count, with an unctuous chuckle. "So few of us excel in that respect; but there is this to be said in our exculpation, few have been matrimonially so fortunate as the Prince von Steinheimer. I have never ceased to long for a repetition of the charming visit I paid to your delightful home."

"If your Excellency but knew how welcome you are, your visits would not have such long intervals between."

"It is most kind of you, Princess, to cheer an old man's heart by such gracious words. It is our misfortune that affairs of State chain us to our pillar, and, indeed, diplomacy seems to become more difficult as the years go on, because we have to contend with the genius of rising young men like Lord Donal Stirling here, who are more than a match for old dogs that find it impossible to learn new tricks."

"Indeed, your Excellency," said his lordship, speaking for the first time since the Ambassador began, "the very reverse of that is the case. We sit humbly at your feet, ambitious to emulate, but without hope of excelling."

The old man chuckled again, and, turning to the girl, began to make his adieux.

"Then my former rooms are waiting for me at the Castle?" he concluded.

"Yes, your Excellency, with the addition of two red rocking-chairs imported from America, which you will find most comfortable resting-places when you are free from the cares of State."

"Ah! The rocking-chairs! I remember now that you were expecting them when I was there. So they have arrived, safely, I hope; but I think you had ordered an incredible number, to be certain of having at least one or two serviceable."

"No; only a dozen, and they all came through without damage."

"You young people, you young people!" murmured the Ambassador, bending again over the hand presented to him, "what unheard-of things you do."

And so the old man shuffled away, leaving many compliments behind him, evidently not having the slightest suspicion that he had met anyone but the person he supposed himself addressing, for his eyesight was not of the best, and an Ambassador meets many fair and distinguished women.

The girl sat down with calm dignity, while Lord Donal dropped into his chair, an expression of complete mystification on his clear-cut, honest face. Jennie slowly fanned herself, for the heat made itself felt at that elevated situation, and for a few moments nothing was said by either. The young man was the first to break silence.

"Should I be so fortunate as to get an invitation to the Schloss Steinheimer, may I hope that a red rocking-chair will be allotted to me? I have not sat in one since I was in the States."

"Yes, one for you; two for the Ambassador," said Jennie, with a laugh.

"I should like further to flatter myself that your double generosity to the Ambassador arises solely from the dignity of his office, and is not in any way personal."

"I am very fond of ambassadors; they are courteous gentlemen who seem to have less distrust than is exhibited by some not so exalted."

"Distrust! You surely cannot mean that I have distrusted you, Princess?"

"Oh, I was speaking generally," replied Jennie airily. "You seem to seek a personal application in what I say."

"I admit, Princess, that several times this evening I have been completely at sea."

"And what is worse, Lord Donal, you have shown it, which is the one unforgivable fault in diplomacy."

"You are quite right. If I had you to teach me, I would be an ambassador within the next five years, or at least a minister."

The girl looked at him over the top of her fan, covert merriment lurking in her eyes.

"When you visit Schloss Steinheimer you might ask the Prince if he objects to my giving you lessons."

Here there was another interruption, and the announcement was made that the United States Ambassador desired to renew his acquaintance with the Princess von Steinheimer. Lord Donal made use of an impatient exclamation more emphatic than he intended to give utterance to, but on looking at his companion in alarm, he saw in her glance a quick flash of gratitude as unmistakable as if she had spoken her thanks. It was quite evident that the girl had no desire to meet his Excellency, which is not to be wondered at, as she had already encountered him three times in her capacity of journalist. He not only knew the Princess von Steinheimer, but he knew Jennie Baxter as well.

She leaned back in her chair and said wearily,—

"I seem to be having rather an abundance of diplomatic society this evening. Are you acquainted with the American Ambassador also, Lord Donal?"

"Yes," cried the young man, eagerly springing to his feet. "He was a prominent politician in Washington while I was there. He is an excellent man, and I shall have no difficulty in making your excuses to him if you don't wish to meet him."

"Thank you so much. You have now an opportunity of retrieving your diplomatic reputation, if you can postpone the interview without offending him."

Lord Donal departed with alacrity, and the moment he was gone all appearance of languor vanished from Miss Jennie Baxter.

"Now is my chance," she whispered to herself. "I must be in my carriage before he returns."

Eager as she was to be gone, she knew that she should betray no haste.

Expecting to find a stair at the other end of the gallery, she sought for it, but there was none. Filled with apprehension that she would meet Lord Donal coming up, she had difficulty in timing her footsteps to the slow measure that was necessary. She reached the bottom of the stair in safety and unimpeded, but once on the main floor a new problem presented itself. Nothing would attract more attention than a young and beautiful lady walking the long distance between the gallery end of the room and the entrance stairway entirely alone and unattended. She stood there hesitating, wondering whether she could venture on finding a quiet side-exit, which she was sure must exist in this large house, when, to her dismay, she found Lord Donal again at her side, rather breathless, as if he had been hurrying in search of her. His brows were knit and there was an anxious expression on his face.

"I must have a word with you alone," he whispered. "Let me conduct you to this alcove under the gallery."

"No; I am tired. I am going home."

"I quite understand that, but you must come with me for a moment."

"Must?" she said, with a suggestion of defiance in her tone.

"Yes," he answered gravely. "I wish to be of assistance to you. I think you will need it."

For a moment she met his unflinching gaze steadily, then her glance fell, and she said in a low voice, "Very well."

When they reached the alcove, she inquired rather quaveringly—for she saw something had happened which had finally settled all the young man's doubts—"Is it the American Ambassador?"

"No; there was little trouble there. He expects to meet you later in the evening. But a telegraphic message has come from Meran, signed by the Princess von Steinheimer, which expresses a hope that the ball will be a success, and reiterates the regret of her Highness that she could not be present. Luckily this communication has not been shown to the Duchess. I told the Duke, who read it to me, knowing I had been with you all the evening, that it was likely a practical joke on the part of the Prince; but the Duke, who is rather a serious person, does not take kindly to that theory, and if he knew the Prince he would dismiss it as absurd—which it is. I have asked him not to show the telegram to anyone, so there is a little time for considering what had best be done."

"There is nothing for me to do but to take my leave as quickly and as quietly as possible," said the girl, with a nervous little laugh bordering closely on the hysterical. "I was about to make my way out by some private exit if I could find one."

"That would be impossible, and the attempt might lead to unexpected complications. I suggest that you take my arm, and that you bid farewell to her Grace, pleading fatigue as the reason for your early departure. Then I will see you to your carriage, and when I return I shall endeavour to get that unlucky telegram from the Duke by telling him I should like to find out whether it is a hoax or not. He will have forgotten about it most likely in the morning. Therefore, all you have to do is to keep up your courage for a few moments longer until you are safe in your carriage."

"You are very kind," she murmured, with downcast eyes.

"You are very clever, my Princess, but the odds against you were tremendous. Some time you must tell me why you risked it."

She made no reply, but took his arm, and together they sauntered through the rooms until they found the Duchess, when Jennie took her leave of the hostess with a demure dignity that left nothing to be desired. All went well until they reached the head of the stair, when the Duke, an ominous frown on his brow, hurried after them and said,—

"My lord, excuse me."

Lord Donal turned with an ill-concealed expression of impatience, but he was helpless, for he feared his host might not have the good sense to avoid a scene even in his own hall. Had it been the Duchess, all would have been well, for she was a lady of infinite tact, but the Duke, as he had said, was a stupid man, who needed the constant eye of his wife upon him to restrain him from blundering. The young man whispered, "Keep right on until you are in your carriage. I shall ask my man here to call it for you, but please don't drive away until I come."

A sign brought a serving man up the stairs.

"Call the carriage of the Princess von Steinheimer," said his master; then, as the lady descended the stair, Lord Donal turned, with no very thankful feeling in his heart, to hear what his host had to say.

"Lord Donal, the American Ambassador says that woman is not the Princess von Steinheimer, but is someone of no importance whom he has met several times in London. He cannot remember her name. Now, who is she, and how did you come to meet her?"

"My Lord Duke, it never occurred to me to question the identity of guests I met under your hospitable roof. I knew the Princess five years ago in Washington, before she was married. I have not seen her in the interval, but until you showed me the telegraphic message there was no question in my mind regarding her."

"But the American Ambassador is positive."

"Then he has more confidence in his eyesight than I have. If such a question, like international difficulties, is to be settled by the Embassies, let us refer it to Austria, who held a long conversation with the lady in my presence. Your Excellency," he continued to the Austrian Ambassador, who was hovering near, waiting to speak to his host, "The Duke of Chiselhurst has some doubt that the lady who has just departed is the Princess von Steinheimer. You spoke with her, and can therefore decide with authority, for his Grace seems disinclined to accept my testimony."

"Not the Princess? Nonsense. I know her very well indeed, and a most charming lady she is. I hope to be her guest again before many months are past."

"There, my Lord Duke, you see everything is as it should be. If you will give me that stupid telegram, I will make some quiet inquiries about it.

Meanwhile, the less said the better. I will see the American Ambassador and convince him of his error. And now I must make what excuses I can to the Princess for my desertion of her."

Placing the telegram in his pocket, he hurried down the stair and out to the street. There had been some delay about the coming of the carriage, and he saw the lady he sought, at that moment entering it.

"Home at once as fast as you can," he heard her say to the coachman. She had evidently no intention of waiting for him. He sprang forward, thrust his arm through the carriage window, and grasped her hand.

"Princess," he cried, "you will not leave me like this. I must see you to-morrow."

"No, no," she gasped, shrinking into the corner of the carriage.

"You cannot be so cruel. Tell me at least where a letter will reach you. I shall not release your hand until you promise."

With a quick movement the girl turned back the gauntlet of her long glove; the next instant the carriage was rattling down the street, while a chagrined young man stood alone on the kerb with a long, slender white glove in his hand.

"By Jove!" he said at last, as he folded it carefully and placed it in the pocket of his coat. "It is the glove this time, instead of the slipper!"

CHAPTER IX. JENNIE REALIZES THAT GREAT EVENTS CAST THEIR SHADOWS BEHIND.

Jennie Baxter reached her hotel as quickly as a fast pair of horses could take her. She had succeeded; yet a few rebellious tears of disappointment trickled down her cheeks now that she was alone in the semi-darkness of the carriage. She thought of the eager young man left standing disconsolately on the kerb, with her glove dangling in his hand, and she bitterly regretted that unkind fortune had made it possible for her to meet him only under false pretences. One consolation was that he had no clue to her identity, and she was resolved never, never to see him again; yet, such is the contrariness of human nature, no sooner was she refreshed by this determination than her tears flowed more freely than ever.

She knew that she was as capable of enjoying scenes like the function she had just left as any who were there; as fitted for them by education, by personal appearance, or by natural gifts of the mind, as the most welcome of the Duchess's guests; yet she was barred out from them as effectually as was the lost Peri at the closed gate. Why had capricious fate selected two girls of probably equal merit, and made one a princess, while the other had to work hard night and day for the mere right to live? Nothing is so ineffectual as the little word "why"; it asks, but never answers.

With a deep sigh Jennie dried her tears as the carriage pulled up at the portal of the hotel. The sigh dismissed all frivolities, all futile "whys"; the girl was now face to face with the realities of life, and the events she had so recently taken part in would soon blend themselves into a dream.

Dismissing the carriage, and walking briskly through the hall, she said to the night porter,—

"Have a hansom at the door for me in fifteen minutes."

"A hansom, my lady?" gasped the astonished man.

"Yes." She slipped a sovereign into his hand and ran lightly up the stairs.

The porter was well accustomed to the vagaries of great ladies, although a hansom at midnight was rather beyond his experience. But if all womankind tipped so generously, they might order an omnibus, and welcome; so the hansom was speedily at the door.

Jennie roused the drowsy maid who was sitting up for her.

"Come," she said, "you must get everything packed at once. Lay out my ordinary dress and help me off with this."

"Where is your other glove, my lady?" asked the maid, busily unhooking, and untying.

"Lost. Don't trouble about it. When everything is packed, get some sleep, and leave word to be called in time for the eight o'clock express for Paris. Here is money to pay the bill and your fare. It is likely I shall join you at the station; but if I do not, go to our hotel in Paris and wait for me there. Say nothing of our destination to anyone, and answer no questions regarding me, should inquiries be made. Are you sure you understand?"

"Yes, my lady." A few moments later Jennie was in the cab, driving through the nearly deserted streets. She dismissed her vehicle at Charing Cross, walked down the Strand until she got another, then proceeded direct to the office of the Daily Bugle, whose upper windows formed a row of lights, all the more brilliant because of the intense darkness below.

She found the shorthand writers waiting for her. The editor met her at the door of the room reserved for her, and said, with visible anxiety on his brow, "Well, what success?"

"Complete success," she answered shortly.

"Good!" he replied emphatically. "Now I propose to read the typewritten sheets as they come from the machine, correct them for obvious clerical errors, and send them right away to the compositors. You can, perhaps, glance over the final proofs, which will be ready almost as soon as you have finished."

"Very well. Look closely to the spelling of proper names and verify titles. There won't be much time for me to go carefully over the last proofs."

"All right. You furnish the material, and I'll see that it's used to the best advantage."

Jennie entered the room, and there at a desk sat the waiting stenographer; over his head hung the bulb of an electric light, its green circular shade throwing the white rays directly down on his open notebook. The girl was once more in the working world, and its bracing air acted as a tonic to her overwrought nerves. All longings and regrets had been put off with the Paris-made gown which the maid at that moment was carefully packing away. The order of nature seemed reversed; the butterfly had abandoned its gorgeous wings of gauze, and was habited in the sombre working garb of the grub. With her hands clasped behind her, the girl paced up and down the room, pouring forth words, two hundred to the minute, and sometimes more. Silently one stenographer, tiptoeing in, replaced another, who as silently departed; and from the adjoining room, the subdued, nervous, rapid click, click, click of the typewriting machine invaded, without disturbing, her consciousness. Towards three o'clock the low drone of the rotaries in the cellar made itself felt rather than heard; the early edition for the country was being run off. Time was flying—danced away by nimble feet in the West End, worked away by nimble fingers in Fleet Street (well-named thoroughfare); play and work, work and play, each supplementing the other; the acts of the frivolous recorded by the industrious.

When a little more than three hours' dictating was finished, the voice of the girl, now as hoarse as formerly it had been musical, ceased; she dropped into a chair and rested her tired head on the deserted desk, closing her wearied eyes. She knew she had spoken between 15,000 and 20,000 words, a number almost equal in quantity to that contained in many a book which had made an author's fame and fortune. And all for the ephemeral reading of a day—of a forenoon, more likely—to be forgotten when the evening journals came out!

Shortly after the typewriter gave its final click the editor came in.

"I didn't like to disturb you while you were at work, and so I kept at my own task, which was no light one, and thus I appreciate the enormous strain that has rested on you. Your account is magnificent, Miss Baxter; just what I wanted, and never hoped to get."

"I am glad you liked it," said the girl, laughing somewhat dismally at the croaking sound of her own voice.

"I need not ask you if you were there, for no person but one who was present, and one who knew how to describe, could have produced such a vivid account of it all. How did you get in?"

"In where?" murmured Jennie drowsily. She found difficulty in keeping her mind on what he was saying.

"To the Duchess of Chiselhurst's ball."

"Oh, getting in was easy enough; it was the getting out that was the trouble."

"Like prison, eh?" suggested the editor. "Now, will you have a little wine, or something stronger?"

"No, no. All I need is rest."

"Then let me call a cab; I will see you home, if you will permit me."

"I am too tired to go home; I shall remain here until morning."

"Nonsense. You must go home and sleep for a week if you want to. Rouse up; I believe you are talking in your sleep now."

"I understand perfectly what you are saying and what I am doing. I have work that must be attended to at eight. Please leave orders that someone is to call me at seven and bring a cup of coffee and biscuits, or rolls, or anything that is to be had at that hour. And please don't trouble further. I am very thankful to you, but will express myself better later on."

With this the editor had to be content, and was shortly on his way to his own well-earned rest. To Jennie it seemed but a moment after he had gone, that the porter placed coffee and rolls on the desk beside her saying, "Seven o'clock, miss!"

The coffee refreshed the girl, and as she passed through the editorial rooms she noted their forlorn, dishevelled appearance, which all places show when seen at an unaccustomed hour, their time of activity and bustle past. The rooms were littered with torn papers; waste-baskets overflowing; looking silent, scrappy, and abandoned in the grey morning light which seemed intrusive, usurping the place of the usual artificial illumination, and betraying a bareness which the other concealed. Jennie recognized a relationship between her own up-all-night feeling and the spirit of the deserted rooms.

At the railway station she found her maid waiting for her, surrounded by luggage.

"Have you got your ticket?"

"Yes, my lady."

"I have changed my mind, and will not go to Paris just now. Ask a porter to put those trunks in the left-luggage office, and bring me the keys and the receipt."

When this was done and money matters had been adjusted between them, Jennie gave the girl five pounds more than was due to her, and saw her into the railway carriage, well pleased with the reward. A hansom brought Jennie to her flat, and so ended the exhausting episode of the Duchess of Chiselhurst's ball.

Yet an event, like a malady, leaves numerous consequences in its train, extending, who shall say, how far into the future? The first symptom of these consequences was a correspondence, and, as there is no reading more dreary than a series of letters, merely their substance is given here. When Jennie was herself again, she wrote a long letter to the Princess von Steinheimer, detailing the particulars of her impersonation, and begging pardon for what she had done, while giving her reasons for doing it; but, perhaps because it did not occur to her, she made not the slightest reference to Lord Donal Stirling. Two answers came to this—one a registered packet containing the diamonds which the Princess had previously offered to her; the other a letter from the Princess's own hand. The glitter of the diamonds showed Jennie that she had been speedily forgiven, and the letter corroborated this. In fact, the Princess upbraided her for not letting her into the secret earlier. "It is just the jolly kind of thing I should have delighted in," wrote her Highness. "And then, if I had known, I should not have sent that unlucky telegram. It serves you right for not taking me into your confidence, and I am glad you had a fright. Think of it coming in at that inopportune moment, just as telegrams do at a play! But, Jennie, are you sure you told me everything? A letter came from London the day before yours arrived, and it bewildered me dreadfully at first. Don Stirling, whom I used to know at Washington (a conceited young fellow he was then—I hope he has improved since), wrote to say that he had met a girl at the Duchess of Chiselhurst's ball who had a letter inviting the Princess von Steinheimer to the festivity. He thought at first she was the Princess (which is very complimentary to each of us), but found later that she wasn't. Now he wants to know, you know, and thinks, quite reasonably, that I must have some inkling who that girl was, and he begs me, by our old friendship, etc., etc., etc. He is a nice young man, if a trifle confident (these young diplomatists think they hold the reins of the universe in their hands), and I should like to oblige him, but I thought first I would hear what you had to say about it. I am to address him care of the Embassy at St. Petersburg; so I suppose he's stationed there now. By the way, how did he get your glove, or is that merely brag on his part? He says that it is the only clue he has, and he is going to trace you from that, it seems, if I do not tell him who you are and send him your address. Now, what am I to say when I write to St. Petersburg?"

In reply to this, Jennie sent a somewhat incoherent letter, very different from her usual style of writing. She had not mentioned the young man in her former communication, she said, because she had been trying to forget the incident in which he was the central figure. In no circumstances could she meet him again, and she implored the Princess not to disclose her identity to him even by a hint. She explained the glove episode exactly as it happened; she was compelled to sacrifice the glove to release her hand. He had been very kind in helping her to escape from a false position, but it would be too humiliating for her ever to see him or speak with him again.

When this letter reached the Schloss at Meran, the Princess telegraphed to London, "Send me the other glove," and Jennie sent it. A few days later came a further communication from the Princess.

"I have puzzled our young man quite effectually, I think, clever as he imagines himself to be. I wrote him a semi-indignant letter to St. Petersburg, and said I thought all along he had not really recognized me at the ball, in spite of his protestations at first. Then I saw how easily he was deluded into the belief that I was some other woman, and so the temptation to cozen him further was irresistible. Am I not a good actress? I asked him. I went on to say, with some show of anger, that a quiet flirtation in the gallery was all very well in its way, but when it came to a young man rushing in a frenzy bare-headed into the street after a respectable married woman who had just got into her carriage and was about to drive away, it was too much altogether, and thus he came into possession of the glove. As the remaining glove was of no use to me, I had great pleasure in sending it to him, but warned him that if the story of the gloves ever came to the ears of my husband, I should deny having either owned or worn them. I should like to see Don's amazed look when the other glove drops out of my letter, which was a bulky package and cost ever so much in postage. I think the sending of the glove was an inspiration. I fancy his lordship will be now completely deluded, and that you need have no further fear of his finding you."

Jennie read this letter over once or twice, and in spite of her friendly feeling for the Princess, there was something in the epistle that jarred on her. Nevertheless she wrote and thanked the Princess for what she had done, and then she tried to forget all about everything pertaining to the ball. However, she was not allowed to erase all thought of Lord Donal from her mind, even if she could have accomplished this task unimpeded. There shortly arrived a brief note from the Princess enclosing a letter the young diplomatist at St. Petersburg had written.

"DEAR PRINCESS" (it ran),—"I am very much obliged to you for the companion glove, as I am thus enabled to keep one and use the other as a clue. I see you not only know who the mysterious young lady is, but that you have since met her, or at least have been in correspondence with her. If the glove does not lead me to the hand, I shall pay a visit to you in the hope that you will atone for your present cruelty by telling me where to find the owner of both glove and hand."

With regard to this note the Princess had written, "Don is not such a fool as I took him to be. He must have improved during the last few years. I wish you would write and tell me exactly what he said to you that evening."

But with this wish Jennie did not comply. She merely again urged the Princess never to divulge the secret.

For many days Jennie heard nothing more from any of the actors in the little comedy, and the episode began to take on in her thoughts that air of unreality which remote events seem to gather round them. She went on with her daily work to the satisfaction of her employers and the augmentation of her own banking account, although no experience worthy of record occurred in her routine for several weeks. But a lull in a newspaper office is seldom of long duration.

One afternoon Mr. Hardwick came to the desk at which Jennie was at work, and said to her,—

"Cadbury Taylor called here yesterday, and was very anxious to see you. Has he been in again this afternoon?"

"You mean the detective? No, I haven't seen him since that day at the Schloss Steinheimer. What did he want with me?"

"As far as I was able to understand, he has a very important case on hand—a sort of romance in high life; and I think he wants your assistance to unravel it; it seems to be baffling him."

"It is not very difficult to baffle Mr. Cadbury Taylor," said the girl, looking up at her employer with a merry twinkle in her eye.

"Well, he appears to be in a fog now, and he expressed himself to me as being very much taken with the neat way in which you unravelled the diamond mystery at Meran, so he thinks you may be of great assistance to him in his present difficulty, and is willing to pay in cash or in kind."

"Cash payment I understand," said the girl, "but what does he mean by payment in kind?"

"Oh, he is willing that you should make a sensational article out of the episode. It deals entirely, he says, with persons in high life—titled persons—and so it might make an interesting column or two for the paper."

"I see—providing, of course, that the tangled skein was unravelled by the transcendent genius of Mr. Cadbury Taylor," said the girl cynically.

"I don't think he wants his name mentioned," continued the editor; "in fact, he said that it wouldn't do to refer to him at all, for if people discovered that he made public any of the cases intrusted to him, he would lose his business. He has been working on this problem for several weeks, and I believe has made little progress towards its solution. His client is growing impatient, so it occurred to the detective that you might consent to help him. He said, with a good deal of complacency, that he did not know you were connected with the Bugle, but he put his wits at work and has traced you to this office."

"How clever he is!" said Jennie, laughing; "I am sure I made no secret of the fact that I work for the Daily Bugle."

"I think Mr. Taylor will have no hesitation in agreeing with you that he is clever; nevertheless, it might be worth while to see him and to assist him if you can, because nothing so takes the public as a romance in high life. Here is his address; would you mind calling on him?"

"Not at all," replied the young woman, copying the street and number in her note-book.

CHAPTER X. JENNIE ASSISTS IN SEARCHING FOR HERSELF.

Next day Jennie Baxter drove to the address the editor had given her, and she found Mr. Cadbury Taylor at home, in somewhat sumptuous offices on the first floor. Fastened to his door was a brass plate, which exposed to public view the carven words—

CADBURY TAYLOR,

Private Enquiry Agent.

The detective was quite evidently very glad to see her.

"I intended calling to-day at the office of the Bugle on the chance of finding you," he said; "but I am delighted to meet you here, because we can talk without fear of interruption. Has the editor told you anything of this case?"

"Very little; he didn't seem to know much about it himself."

"It was impossible for me to go into full particulars with him. I could only give him a hint or two in order to convey to him some idea of the interest which the mystery, when solved, might have from a newspaper standpoint. Of course I wished to gain his assistance so that he might, perhaps, persuade you to help me in this matter."

"He seems to be quite willing that I should lend what aid I can," said Jennie; "but I must have full details before I promise. I have a good deal of work on hand, and, unless this case is interesting from a newspaper point of view, as you have just said, I don't think that I should care to touch it."

"Oh, you will find it of great interest," the detective assured her with much eagerness. "It relates to the sudden and hitherto unexplained disappearance of a woman. That of itself is absorbing, for I may tell you, as one having a large experience, that there is nothing more difficult in this world than for any person, and more especially for a woman, to disappear entirely and leave no trace behind."

"I should have thought it quite easy," said Jennie, "especially in a large city like London."

"You have given expression to the universal opinion, but I pledge you my word that a completely successful disappearance is one of the most rare events that we detectives have to meet with in our line of investigation."

"Please tell me the story," said the girl; "then we can speak more understandingly about it."

The detective selected a packet of papers, one of many which occupied the end of his table. He slipped from it a rubber band which held the documents together.

"The first act of the drama, if we may call it so, began at the Duchess of Chiselhurst's ball."

"The Duchess of Chiselhurst's ball!" echoed Jennie, with a shudder. "Oh, dear!"

The detective looked up at her.

"Why do you say 'Oh, dear'?" he asked.

"Because," said the girl wearily, "I am tired hearing of the Duchess of Chiselhurst's ball; there seems to have been nothing else in the papers for weeks past."

"It has excited a great deal of comment," assented the detective; "and, by the way, the Daily Bugle had one of the best accounts of it that was printed in any newspaper."

"So I have heard," said Jennie carelessly, "but I most confess that I didn't read that copy of the Bugle."

"You amaze me! I should have thought that would have been the first part of the paper to which any lady would turn. However, the report of the ball has nothing to do with what we have in hand. Now, you remember the Princess von Steinheimer, at whose castle I first had the pleasure of meeting you?"

"You had the pleasure of meeting me before that," said Jennie, speaking without giving thought to what she said.

"Really!" cried the detective, dropping his papers on the table; "and where was that?"

"Oh, well, as you have just said—it has nothing to do with this case. Perhaps I was wrong in saying you saw me; it would be more correct to say that I saw you. You must remember that you are a public character, Mr. Taylor."

"Ah, quite so," said the detective complacently, turning to his documents again. "Now, the Princess von Steinheimer was invited to the Duchess of Chiselhurst's ball, but she did not attend it."

"Are you sure of that?" said the girl. "I thought her name was among the list of those present."

"It was in the list, and that is just where our mystery begins. Someone else attended the ball as the Princess von Steinheimer; it is this person that I wish to find."

"Ah, then you are employed by the Duke of Chiselhurst?"

"No, I am not, for, strangely enough, I believe the Duke thinks it was actually the Princess who attended the ball. Only one man knows that the Princess was not present, one man and two women. Of the latter, one is the Princess von Steinheimer, and the other, the lady who impersonated her. The one man is Lord Donal Stirling, of the Diplomatic Service, whose name is no doubt familiar to you. Lord Donal has done me the honour to place the case in my hands."

"Why does his lordship wish to find this—this—fraudulent person?" asked Jennie, speaking slowly and with difficulty.

"Because," said the detective, with the air of a man who knows whereof he speaks, "he is in love with her."

"What makes you think that?"

"I don't think it, I know it. Listen to his description of her."

The detective chose a paper from among his pile of documents, folded, labelled, and docketed for reference.

"'The girl is of average height, or perhaps a trifle taller than the average; carries herself superbly, like a born duchess. Her eyes are of a deep, velvety black—'"

"Dear me!" cried the girl, "he describes her as if she were a cat!"

"Wait a moment," said the detective.

"I don't see much trace of love in that," continued Jennie breathlessly.

"Wait a moment," repeated the detective. "'They light up and sparkle with merriment, and they melt into the most entrancing tenderness.'"

"Good gracious!" cried Jennie, rising, "the conceit of the man is illimitable. Does he mean to intimate that he saw tenderness for himself in the eyes of a woman he had met for an hour or two?"

"That's just it," said the detective, laughing. "You see the man is head over ears in love. Please sit down again, Miss Baxter, and listen. I know this sentimental kind of writing must be irksome to a practical woman like yourself, but in our business we cannot neglect even the slightest detail. Let's see, where was I?—'tenderness,' oh, yes. 'Her hair is of midnight darkness, inclined to ripple, with little whiffs of curls imperiously defying restraint about her temples. Her complexion is as pure as the dawn, touched now and then with a blush as delicate as the petal of a rose.'"

"Absurd!" cried Jennie impatiently. "The complexion of a woman at a ball! Of course, she put it on for the occasion."

"Of course," agreed the detective. "But that merely shows you how deeply in love he is. Lord Donal is quite a young man. He came up to this room to consult with me, and certainly he doesn't know the difference between a complexion developed in a Surrey lane and one purchased in New Bond Street."

"Still, the blushing would seem to indicate that the complexion was genuine," retorted Jennie, apparently quite unflattered by Mr. Taylor's agreement with the theory she herself had put forward.

"Oh, I don't know about that. I believe modern science enables an enamelled woman to blush at will; I wouldn't be sure of it, because it is outside of my own line of investigation, but I have understood such is the case."

"Very likely," assented Jennie. "What is that you have at the bottom of your packet?"

"That," said the detective, drawing it forth and handing it to the girl, "is her glove."

Jennie picked up the glove—which, alas! she had paid for and only worn on one occasion—and smoothed it out between her fingers. It was docketed "G; made by Gaunt et Cie, Boulevard Hausmann; purchased in Paris by one alleging herself to be the Princess von Steinheimer."

"You have found out all about it," said Jennie, as she finished reading the label.

"Yes, it is our business to do so; but the glove has not been of much assistance to us."

"How did he say he became possessed of the glove?" asked the girl innocently. "Did she give it to him?"

"No; he tore it from her hand as she was leaving him in the carriage. It seemed to me a most ungentlemanly thing to do, but of course it was not my business to tell Lord Donal that."

"So the glove has not been of much assistance to you. Tell me, then, what you have done, and perhaps I shall be the better able to advise you."

"We have done everything that suggested itself. We traced the alleged Princess from the Hotel Bristol in Pans to Claridge's in London. I have a very clever woman in Paris who assisted me, and she found where the gloves were bought and where the dress was made. Did I read you Lord Donal's description of the lady's costume?"

"No, never mind that; go on with your story."

"Well, Claridge's provided carriage, coachman and footman to take her to the ball, and this returned with her sometime about midnight. Now, here a curious thing happened. The lady ordered a hansom as she passed the night-porter and shortly after packed off her maid in the cab."

"Her maid!" echoed Jennie.

"Yes. The maid came down in ordinary street dress shortly after, deeply veiled, and drove away in the hansom; the lady paid her bill next morning and went to the eight o'clock Paris express, with carriage and pair, coachman and footman. Of course it struck me that it might be the lady herself who had gone off in the cab, but a moment's reflection showed me that she was not likely to leave the hotel in a cab at midnight, and allow her maid to take the carriage in state next morning."

"That doesn't appear reasonable," murmured Jennie. "You made no attempt, then, to trace the maid?"

"Oh yes, we did. We found the cabman who took her from Claridge's, and he left her at Charing Cross Station, but there all trace of her vanishes. She probably left on one of the late trains—there are only a few after midnight—to some place out in the country. The lady took a first-class ticket to Paris, and departed alone next morning by the eight o'clock Continental express. My assistant discovered her and took a snapshot of her as she was walking down the boulevard; here is the picture."

The detective handed Miss Baxter an instantaneous view of one of the boulevards taken in bright sunshine. The principal figure in the foreground Jennie had no difficulty in recognizing as her own maid, dressed in that chic fashion which Parisian women affect.

"She seems to answer the description," said Jennie.

"So I thought," admitted the detective, "and I sent the portrait to Lord Donal. See what he has written on the back."

Jennie turned the picture over, and there under the inscription, "H. Supposed photo of the missing woman," was written in a bold hand, "Bosh! Read my description of the girl; this is evidently some Paris lady's maid."

"Well, what did you do when you got this picture back?" asked Jennie.

"I remembered you, and went to the office of the Daily Bugle. This brings us to the present moment. You have now the whole story, and I shall be very pleased to listen to any suggestions you are good enough to offer."

The girl sat where she was for a few moments and pondered over the situation. The detective, resting his elbow on the table and his chin in his hand, regarded her with eager anticipation. The more Jennie thought over the matter, the more she was amazed at the man before her, who seemed unable to place two and two together. He had already spoken of the account of the ball which had appeared in the Daily Bugle; of its accuracy and its excellence; he knew that she was a member of the Bugle staff, yet it had never occurred to him to inquire who wrote that description; he knew also that she had been a guest at the Schloss Steinheimer when the invitation to the ball must have reached the Princess. These facts were so plainly in evidence that the girl was afraid to speak lest some chance word would form the connecting link between the detective's mind and the seemingly palpable facts. At last she looked up, the colour coming and going in her cheeks, as Lord Donal had so accurately described it.

"I don't think I can be of any assistance to you in this crisis, Mr. Taylor. You have already done everything that human ingenuity can suggest."

"Yes, I have—everything that my human ingenuity can suggest. But does nothing occur to you? have you no theory to put forward?"

"None that would be of any practical advantage. Is Lord Donal certain that it was not the Princess herself whom he met? Are you thoroughly convinced that there was really an impersonation?"

"What do you mean, Miss Baxter?"

"Well, you met Prince von Steinheimer; what do you think of him?"

"I thought him an overbearing bully, if you ask me. I can't imagine what English or American girls see in those foreigners to cause them to marry. It is the titles, I suppose. The Prince was very violent—practically ordered me out of the Castle, spoke to his father-in-law in the most peremptory manner, and I could easily see the Princess was frightened out of her wits."

"A very accurate characterization of his Highness, Mr. Taylor. Now, of course, the Princess being a woman—and a young woman—would naturally be very anxious to attend the Duchess of Chiselhurst's ball, wouldn't she?"

"One would think so."

"And, as you have just said, she has a bear of a husband, a good deal older than herself, who does not in the least care for such functions as that to which the Princess was invited. Is it not quite possible that the Princess actually attended the ball, but, for reasons of her own, desired to keep the fact of her presence there a secret; and you must remember that Lord Donal Stirling had not seen the Princess for five years."

"For five years?" said the detective sharply. "How did you learn that, Miss Baxter?"

"Well, you know," murmured the girl, with a gasp, "he met her last in Washington, and the Princess has not been in America for five years; so you see—"

"Oh, I was not aware that he had met her in America at all; in fact, Lord Donal said nothing much about the Princess—all his talk had reference to this lady who impersonated her."

Jennie leaned back in her chair, closed her eyes for a moment, and breathed quickly.

"I am afraid," she said at last, "that I do not remember with sufficient minuteness the details you have given me, to be able to advise. I can only suggest that Lord Donal met the Princess herself at the Duchess of Chiselhurst's ball. The Princess, naturally, would wish to mislead him regarding her identity; and so, if he had not met her for some time—say two years, or three years, or five years, or whatever the period may be—it is quite possible that the Princess has changed greatly in the interval, and perhaps she was not reluctant to carry on a flirtation with the young man—your client. Of course, she could not allow it to go further than the outside of the door of the Duke of Chiselhurst's town house, for you must remember there was her husband in the background—a violent man, as you have said; and Lord Donal must have thoroughly angered the Princess by what you term his rudeness in tearing off her glove; and now the Princess will never admit that she was at the ball, so it seems to me that you are wasting your time in a wild goose chase. Why, it is absurd to think, if there had been a real disappearing woman, that you, with all your experience and all your facilities, should not have unearthed her long ago. You said at the beginning that nothing was more difficult than to disappear. Very well, then—why have you been baffled? Simply because the Princess herself attended the ball, and there has been no disappearing lady at all."

The detective, with great vehemence, brought down his fist on the table.

"By Jove!" he cried, "I believe you are right. I have been completely blinded, the more so that I have the clue to the mystery right here under my own eyes."

He fumbled for a moment and brought forth a letter from his pile of documents.

"Here is a note from St. Petersburg, written by Lord Donal himself, saying the Princess had sent him the companion glove to the one you now have in your hand. He says he is sure the Princess knows who her impersonator was, but that she won't tell; and, although I had read this note, it never struck me that the Princess herself was the woman. Miss Baxter, you have solved the puzzle!"

"I should be glad to think so," replied the girl, rising, "and I am very happy if I have enabled you to give up a futile chase."

"It is as plain as daylight," replied the detective. "Lord Donal's description fits the Princess exactly, and yet I never thought of her before."

Jennie hurried away from the detective's office, happy in the belief that she had not betrayed herself, although she was not blind to the fact that her escape was due more to good luck than to any presence of mind of her own, which had nearly deserted her at one or two points in the conversation. When Mr. Hardwick saw her, he asked how much space he should have to reserve for the romance in high life; but she told him there was nothing in the case, so far as she could see, to interest any sane reader.

Here matters rested for a fortnight; then the girl received an urgent note from Cadbury Taylor, asking her to call at his office next day promptly at four o'clock. It was very important, he said, and he hoped she would on no account disappoint him. Jennie's first impulse was not to go, but she was so anxious to learn what progress the detective had made in the case, fearing that at last he might have got on the right track, that she felt it would be unwise to take the risk of not seeing him. If his suspicions were really aroused, her absence might possibly serve to confirm them. Exactly at four o'clock next afternoon she entered his office and found him, to her relief, alone. He sprang up from his table on seeing her, and said in a whisper, "I am so glad you have come. I am in rather a quandary. Lord Donal Stirling is in London on a flying visit. He called here yesterday."

The girl caught her breath, but said nothing.

"I explained to him the reasons I have for believing that it was actually the Princess von Steinheimer whom he met at the Duchess of Chiselhurst's ball. He laughed at me; there was no convincing him. He said that theory was more absurd than the sending him a picture of a housemaid as that of the lady he met at the ball. I used all the arguments which you had used, but he brushed them aside as of no consequence, and somehow the case did not appear to be as clear as when you propounded your theory."

"Well, what then?" asked the girl.

"Why, then I asked him to come up here at four o'clock and hear what an assistant of mine would say about the case."

"At four o'clock!" cried the girl in terror; "then he may be here at any moment."

"He is here now; he is in the next room. Come in, and I will introduce you, and then I want you to tell him all the circumstances which lead you to believe that it was the Princess herself whom he met. I am sure you can place all the points before him so tersely that you will succeed in bringing him round to your own way of thinking. You will try, won't you, Miss Baxter? It will be a very great obligement to me."

"Oh, no, no, no!" cried the girl; "I am not going to admit to anyone that I have been acting as a detective's assistant. You had no right to bring me here. I must go at once. If I had known this I would not have come."

"It won't take you five minutes," pleaded Cadbury Taylor. "He is at this moment waiting for you; I told him you would be here at four."

"I can't help that; you had no right to make an appointment for me without my knowledge and consent."

Taylor was about to speak when the door-handle of the inner room turned.

"I say, detective," remarked Lord Donal, in a voice of some irritation, "you should have assistants who are more punctual. I am a very busy man, and must leave for St. Petersburg to-night, so I can't spend all my time in your office, you know."

"I am sure I beg your pardon, my lord," said the detective with great obsequiousness. "This young lady has some objections to giving her views, but I am sure you will be able to persuade her—"

He turned, but the place at his side was vacant. The door to the hall was open, and the girl had escaped as she saw the handle of the inner door turn. Taylor looked blankly at his client with dropped jaw. Lord Donal laughed.

"Your assistant seems to have disappeared as completely as did the lady at the ball. Why not set your detectives on her track? Perhaps she will prove to be the person I am in search of."

"I am very sorry, my lord," stammered the detective.

"Oh, don't mention it. I am sure you have done all that could be done with the very ineffective clues which unfortunately are our only possession, but you are quite wrong in thinking it was the Princess herself who attended the ball, and I don't blame your assistant for refusing to bolster up an impossible case. We will consider the search ended, and if you will kindly let me have your bill at the Diplomatic Club before six o'clock to-night, I will send you a cheque. Good afternoon, Mr. Taylor."

CHAPTER XI. JENNIE ELUDES AN OFFER OF MARRIAGE.

As Jennie rapidly hurried away from the office of Mr. Cadbury Taylor, there arose in her mind some agitation as to what the detective would think of her sudden flight. She was convinced that, up to the moment of leaving him so abruptly, he had not the slightest suspicion she herself, to whom he was then talking, was the person he had been searching for up and down Europe. What must he think of one who, while speaking with him, suddenly, without a word of leave-taking, disappeared as if the earth had opened and swallowed her, and all because the handle of the door to the inner room had turned? Then the excuse she had given for not wishing to meet Lord Donal must have struck him as ridiculously inadequate. When she reached her desk and reflected with more calmness over the situation, she found no cause to censure herself for her hasty departure; although she had acted on impulse, she saw there had been nothing else to do; another moment and she would have been face to face with Lord Donal himself.

Next day brought a note from the detective which went far to reassure her. He apologized for having made the appointment without her permission, and explained that Lord Donal's unexpected arrival in London, and his stubborn unbelief that it had been the Princess herself whom he met at the ball, seemingly left the detective no alternative out to call on the person who had so persistently advanced the theory, to explain it to the one most intimately concerned. It had not occurred to him at the time to think that Miss Baxter might object to meet Lord Donal, who was an entire stranger to her; but now he saw that he was wrong, etc., etc., etc. This note did much to convince Jennie that, after all, the detective had not seen the clues which appeared to be spread so plainly before his eyes. Cadbury Taylor, however, said nothing about the search being ended, and a few days later Jennie received a disquieting letter from the Princess von Steinheimer.

"My dear Jennie," her Highness wrote, "I am sure the detectives are after you, and so I thought it best to send you a word of warning. Of course it is only surmise on my part, but for days there has been a woman hovering about the castle, trying to get information from my servants. My maid came directly to me and told me what she knew. The woman detective had spoken to her. This inquisitive person, who had come from Paris, wished particularly to know whether I had been seen about the castle during the week in which the Duchess of Chiselhurst's ball took place; and so this leads me to suppose that some one is making inquiries for you. It must be either Lord Donal Stirling or the Duke of Chiselhurst, but I rather think it is the former. I have written an indignant letter to Lord Donal, accusing him of having caused detectives to haunt the castle. I have not yet received a reply, but Lord Donal is a truthful person, and in a day or two I expect to find out whether or not he has a hand in this business. Meanwhile, Jennie, be on your guard, and I will write you again as soon as I have something further to tell."

The reading of this letter greatly increased Jennie's fears, for she felt assured that, stupid as the men undoubtedly were, they verged so closely on the brink of discovery, they were almost certain to stumble upon the truth if the investigation was continued. She wrote a hurried note to the Princess, imploring her to be cautious, and not inadvertently give any clue that would lead to her discovery. Her letter evidently crossed one from the Princess herself. Lord Donal had confessed, said the letter, and promised never, never to do it again. "He says that before my letter was received he had stopped the detectives, who were doing no good and apparently only annoying innocent people. He says the search is ended, as far as the detective is concerned, and that I need fear no more intrusions from inquiry agents, male or female. He apologized very handsomely, but says he has not given up hopes of finding the lady who disappeared. And now, Jennie, I trust that you will admit my cleverness. You see that I had only a word or two from my maid as a clue, but I unravelled the whole plot and at once discovered who was the instigator of it, so I think I wouldn't make a bad detective myself. I am tremendously interested in episodes like this. I believe if I had known nothing of the impersonation, and if the case had been put in my hands, I should have discovered you long ago. Can't you think of some way in which my undoubted talent for research may be made use of? You don't know how much I envy you in your newspaper office, always with an absorbing mystery on hand to solve. It must be like being the editor of a puzzle department. I wish you would let me help you next time you have anything important to do. Will you promise?

"When you write again, please send your letter to Vienna, as we are going into residence there, my husband having been unexpectedly called to the capital. He holds an important position in the Government, as perhaps you remember."

Jennie was delighted to know that all inquiry had ceased, and she wrote a long letter of gratitude to the Princess. She concluded her epistle by saying: "It is perfectly absurd of you to envy one who has to work as hard as I. You are the person to be envied. It is not all beer and skittles in a newspaper office, which is a good thing, for I don't like beer, and I don't know what skittles is or are. But I promise you that the next time I have an interesting case on hand I shall write and give you full particulars, and I am sure that together we shall be invincible."

But one trouble leaves merely to give place to another in this life. Jennie was disturbed to notice that Mr. Hardwick was becoming more and more confidential with her. He sat down by her desk whenever there was a reasonable excuse for doing so, and he consulted her on matters important and on matters trivial. An advance of salary came to her, and she knew it was through his influence with the board of directors. Although Mr. Hardwick was sharp and decisive in business matters, he proved an awkward man where his affections were concerned, and he often came and sat by the girl's desk, evidently wishing to say something, and yet quite as evidently having nothing to say; and thus the situation became embarrassing. Jennie was a practical girl and had no desire to complicate the situation by allowing her employer to fall in love with her, yet it was impossible to go to him and ask that his attentions might be limited strictly to a business basis. The crisis, however, was brought on by Mr. Hardwick himself. One day, when they were alone together, he said abruptly,—

"That romance in high life which you were investigating with Mr. Cadbury Taylor did not come to anything?"

"No, Mr. Hardwick."

"Then don't you think we might enact a romance in high life in this very room; it is high enough from the street to entitle it to be called a romance in high life," and the editor grinned uneasily, like an unready man who hopes to relieve a dilemma by a poor joke.

Jennie, however, did not laugh and did not look up at him, but continued to scribble shorthand notes on the paper before her.

"Ah, Mr. Hardwick!" she said with a sigh, "I see you have discovered my secret, although I had hoped to conceal it even from your alert eyes. I am, indeed, in the situation of Ralph Rackstraw in 'Pinafore,' 'I love, and love, alas! above my station,' and now that you know half, you may as well know all. It arose out of that unfortunate ball given by the Duchess of Chiselhurst which will haunt me all the rest of my life, I fear," said Jennie, still without looking up. Mr. Hardwick smothered an ejaculation and was glad that the girl's eyes were not upon him. There was a pause of a few moments' duration between them. He took the path which was left open to him, fondly flattering himself that, while he had stumbled inadvertently upon her romance, he had kept his own secret safe.

"I—I have no right to intrude on your confidences, Miss Baxter," he said finally with an effort, "and I hope you will excuse me for—for———"

"Oh! I have been sure for some days you knew it," interrupted the girl, looking up, but not at him. "I have been neglecting my work, I fear, and so you were quite right in speaking."

"No, your work is all right; it wasn't that exactly—but never mind, we won't speak of this any more, for I see it embarrasses you."

"Thank you, Mr. Hardwick," said Jennie, again bending her eyes on the desk before her.

The man saw the colour come and go in her cheeks, and thought he had never beheld anyone so entrancing. He rose quickly, without making further attempt at explanation, and left the room. One or two tear drops stained the paper on which the girl was scribbling. She didn't like giving pain to anyone, but could not hold herself to blame for what had happened. She made up her mind to leave the Daily Bugle and seek employment elsewhere, but next day Mr. Hardwick showed no trace of disappointment, and spoke to her with that curt imperiousness which had heretofore been his custom.

"Miss Baxter," he said, "have you been reading the newspapers with any degree of attention lately?"

"Yes, Mr. Hardwick."

"Have you been watching the drift of foreign politics?"

"Do you refer to that speech by the Prime Minister of Austria a week or two ago?"

"Yes, that is what I have in my mind. As you know, then, it amounted almost to a declaration of war against England—almost, but not quite. It was a case of saying too much or of not saying enough; however, it was not followed up, and the Premier has been as dumb as a graven image ever since. England has many enemies in different parts of the world, but I must confess that this speech by the Austrian Premier came as a surprise. There must have been something hidden, which is not visible from the outside. The Premier is too astute a man not to know exactly what his words meant, and he was under no delusion as to the manner in which England would take them. It is a case, then, of, 'When I was so quickly done for, I wonder what I was begun for'—that is what all Europe is asking."

"Is it not generally supposed, Mr. Hardwick, that his object was to consolidate Austria and Hungary? I understood that local politics were at the bottom of his fiery speech."

"Quite so, but the rousing of the war spirit in Austria and Hungary was useless unless that spirit is given something to do. It needs a war, not a threat of war, to consolidate Austria and Hungary. If the speech had been followed up by hostile action, or by another outburst that would make war inevitable, I could understand it. The tone of the speech indicates that the Prime Minister meant business at the time he gave utterance to it. Something has occurred meanwhile to change the situation, and what that something is, all the newspapers in Europe have been trying to find out. We have had our regular Vienna representative at work ever since the words were uttered, and for the past two weeks he has been assisted by one of the cleverest men I could send him from London; but up to date, both have failed. Now I propose that you go quietly to Vienna; I shall not let either of the men know you are investigating the affair at which they have laboured with such little success; for both are good men, and I do not want to discourage either of them; still, above all things, I wish to have the solution of this mystery. So it occurred to me last night that you might succeed where others had failed. What do you think of it?"

"I am willing to try," said Miss Baxter, as there flashed across her mind an idea that here was a case in which the Princess von Steinheimer could be of the greatest assistance to her.

"It has been thought," went on the editor, "that the Emperor is extremely adverse to having trouble with England or any other country. Still, if that were the case, a new Cabinet would undoubtedly have been formed after this intemperate address of the Premier; but this man still holds his office, and there has been neither explanation nor apology from Court or Cabinet. I am convinced that there is something behind all this, a wheel within a wheel of some sort, because, the day after the speech, there came a rumour from Vienna that an attempt had been made on the life of the Emperor or of the Premier; it was exceedingly vague, but it was alleged that a dynamite explosion had taken place in the palace. This was promptly contradicted, but we all know what official contradictions amount to. There is internal trouble of some kind at the Court of Vienna, and if we could publish the full details, such an article would give us a European reputation. When could you be ready to begin your journey, Miss Baxter?"

"I am ready now."

"Well, in an affair like this it is best to lose no time; you can go to-morrow morning, then?"

"Oh, certainly, but I must leave the office at once, and you should get someone to finish the work I am on."

"I will attend to that," said the editor.

Thus relieved, Jennie betook herself to a telegraph office. She knew that if she wrote a letter to the Princess, who was now in Vienna, she would probably herself reach that city as soon as her note, so she telegraphed that something important was on hand which would take her to Vienna by next day's Orient express, and intimated that it was a matter in which she might need the assistance of the Princess. Then she hastened to her rooms to pack up. That evening there came an answering telegram from Vienna. The Princess asked her to bring her ball dress and all the rest of her finery. The lady added that she herself would be at the railway station, and asked Jennie to telegraph to her, en route, the time of her arrival. It was evident that her Highness was quite prepared to engage in whatever scheme there was on hand, and this fact encouraged Jennie to hope that success perhaps awaited her.

CHAPTER XII. JENNIE TOUCHES THE EDGE OF A GOVERNMENT SECRET.

True to her promise, the Princess von Steinheimer was waiting at the immense railway station of Vienna, and she received her friend with gushing effusion. Jennie left the train as neat as when she had entered it, for many women have the faculty of taking long journeys without showing the dishevelled effect which protracted railway travelling seems to have upon the masculine, and probably more careless, portion of humanity.

"Oh, you dear girl!" cried the Princess; "you cannot tell how glad I am to see you. I was just yearning for someone to talk English to. I am so tired of French and German, although they flatter me by saying that I speak those two languages extremely well; yet English is my own tongue, and it is so delightful to talk with one who can understand every blessed word you say, which you can easily see those who pretend to speak English in Vienna do not. What long chats we shall have! And now come this way to the carriage. There is a man here to look after your luggage. You are coming right home with me and are going to stay with me as long as you are in Vienna. Don't say, 'No,' nor make any excuse, nor talk of going to an hotel, for a suite of rooms is all ready for you, and your luggage will be there before we are. Now let us enter the carriage, for I am just pining to hear what it is you have on hand. Some delicious scandal, I hope."

"No," answered Jennie; "it pertains to Government matters."

"Oh, dear!" cried the Princess; "how tiresome! Politics are so dull."

"I don't think this case is dull," said Jennie; "because it has brought Austria and England to the verge of war."

"What a dreadful idea! I hadn't heard anything of it. When did this happen?"

"Less than a month ago," and Jennie related the whole circumstance, giving a synopsis of the Premier's speech.

"But I see nothing in that speech to cause war," protested the Princess. "It is as mild as new milk."

"I don't pretend to understand diplomacy," continued Jennie, blushing slightly as she remembered Lord Donal; and it seemed that the same thought struck the Princess at the same moment, for she looked quizzically at Jennie and burst out into a laugh.

"You may laugh," cried the girl; "but I tell you that this is a serious business. They say it only needed a second 'new milk' speech from the Premier to have England answer most politely in words of honey, and next instant the two countries would have been at each other's throats."

"Suppose we write to Lord Donal in St. Petersburg," suggested the Princess, still laughing, "and ask him to come to Vienna and help us? He understands all about diplomacy. By the way, Jennie, did Lord Donal ever find out whom he met at the ball that night?"

"No, he didn't," answered Miss Baxter shortly.

"Don't you ever intend to let him know? Are you going to leave the romance unfinished, like one of Henry James's novels?"

"It isn't a romance; it is simply a very distressing incident which I have been trying to forget ever since. It is all very well for you to laugh, but if you ever mention the subject again I'll leave you and go to an hotel."

"Oh, no, you won't," chirruped the Princess brightly; "you daren't. You know I hold all the trump cards; at any time I can send a letter to Lord Donal and set the poor young man's mind at rest. So you see, Miss Jennie, you will have to talk very sweetly and politely to me and not make any threats, because I am like those dreadful persons in the sensational plays who possess the guilty secrets of other people and blackmail them. But you are a nice girl, and I won't say anything you don't want to hear said. Now, what is it you wish to find out about this political crisis?"

"I want to discover why the Premier did not follow up his speech with another. He must have known when he spoke how his words would be taken in England; therefore it is thought that he had some plans which unforeseen circumstances intervening have nullified. I want to know what those unforeseen circumstances were, and what these plans were. For the past fortnight the Daily Bugle has had two men here in Vienna trying to throw some light on the dark recesses of diplomacy. Up to date they have failed, but at any moment they may succeed; it was because they failed that I am sent here. Now, have you anything to suggest, Madame la Princesse?"

"I suggest, Jennie, that we put our heads together and learn all that those diplomatists wish to hide. Have you no plans yourself?"

"I have no very definite plan, but I have a general scheme. These men I spoke of are trying to discover what other men are endeavouring to conceal. All the officials are on their guard; they are highly placed, and are not likely to be got at by bribery. They are clever, alert men of the world, so hoodwinking them is out of the question; therefore I think my two fellow journalists have a difficult task before them."

"But it is the same task that you have before you; why is it not as difficult for you, Jennie, as for them?"

"Because I propose to work with people who are not on their guard, and there is where you can help me, if you are not shocked at my proposal. Each official has a wife, or at least most of them have. Some of these wives, in all probability, possess the information that we would like to get. Women will talk more freely with women than men will with men. Now, I propose to leave the officials severely alone and to interview their wives."

The Princess clapped her hands.

"Excellent!" she cried. "The women of Vienna are the greatest gossips you ever heard chattering together. I have never taken any interest in politics, otherwise I suppose I might have become possessed of some important Government secrets. Now, Jennie, I'll tell you what I propose doing. I shall give a formal tea next Thursday afternoon. I shall invite to that tea a dozen, or two dozen, or three dozen wives of influential officials about the Court. My husband will like that, because he is always complaining that I do not pay enough attention to the ladies of the political circle of Vienna. He takes a great interest in politics, you know. If we discover nothing at the first tea-meeting, we will have another, and another, and another, until we do. We are sure to invite the right woman on one of those occasions, and when we find her I'll warrant the secret will soon belong to us. Ah, here we are at home, and we will postpone the discussion of our delightful conspiracy until you have had something to eat and are rested a bit."

The carriage drew up at the magnificent palace, well known in Vienna, which belongs to the Prince von Steinheimer; and shortly afterwards Jennie Baxter found herself in possession of the finest suite of rooms she had ever beheld in her life. Jennie laughed as she looked round her apartment and noted its luxuriant appointments.

"These are not exactly what we should call 'diggings' in London, are they?" she said to the Princess, who stood by her side, delighted at the pleasure of her friend. "We often read of poor penny-a-liners in their garrets; but I don't think any penny-a-liner ever had such a garret as this placed at his disposal."

"I knew you would like the rooms," cried the Princess gaily. "I like them myself, and I hope they will help to induce you to stay in Vienna as long as you can. I have given you my own maid Gretlich, and I assure you it isn't every friend I would lend her to; she is a model servant."

"Oh, but you mustn't do that," said Jennie. "I cannot rob you of your maid and also be selfish enough to monopolize these rooms."

"You are not robbing me; in fact, I am, perhaps, a little artful in giving you Gretlich, for she is down in the dumps this last week or two, and I don't know what in the world is the matter with her. I suspect it is some love affair; but she will say nothing, although I have asked her time and again what is the trouble. Now, you are such a cheery, consoling young woman that I thought if Gretlich were in your service for a time she might brighten up and be her own self again. So you see, instead of robbing me, I am really taking advantage of your good nature."

"I am afraid you are just saying that to make it easier for me to be selfish;

still, you are so generous, Princess, that I am not going to object to anything you do, but just give myself up to luxury while I stay in Vienna."

"That is right. Ah, here is Gretlich. Now, Gretlich, I want you to help make Miss Baxter's stay here so pleasant that she will never want to leave us."

"I shall do my best, your Highness," said the girl, with quiet deference.

The Princess left the two alone together, and Jennie saw that Gretlich was not the least ornamental appendage to the handsome suite of rooms. Gretlich was an excellent example of that type of fair women for which Vienna is noted; but she was, as the Princess had said, extremely downcast, and Jennie, who had a deep sympathy for all who worked, spoke kindly to the girl and endeavoured to cheer her. There was something of unaccustomed tenderness in the compassionate tones of Jennie's voice that touched the girl, for, after a brief and ineffectual effort at self-control, she broke down and wept. To her pitying listener she told her story. She had been betrothed to a soldier whose regiment was stationed in the Burg. When last the girl saw her lover he was to be that night on guard in the Treasury. Before morning a catastrophe of some kind occurred. The girl did not know quite what had happened. Some said there had been a dreadful explosion and her lover had lost his life. Neither the soldier's relatives nor his betrothed were allowed to see him after the disaster. He had been buried secretly, and it appeared to be the intention of the authorities to avoid all publicity. The relatives and the betrothed of the dead soldier had been warned to keep silence and seek no further information. It was not till several days after her lover's death that Gretlich, anxious because he did not keep his appointment with her, and not hearing from him, fearing that he was ill, began to make inquiries; then she received together the information and the caution.

In the presence of death all consolers are futile, and Jennie realized this as she endeavoured as well as she could to comfort the girl. Her heart was so much enlisted in this that perhaps her intellect was the less active; but here she stood on the very threshold of the secret she had come to Vienna to discover, and yet had not the slightest suspicion that the girl's tragedy and her own mission were interwoven. Jennie had wondered at the stupidity of

Cadbury Taylor, who failed to see what seemed so plainly before him, yet here was Jennie herself come a thousand miles, more or less, to obtain certain information, and here a sobbing girl was narrating the very item of news that she had come so far to learn—all of which would seem to show that none of us are so bright and clever as we imagine ourselves to be.

In the afternoon the Princess entered Jennie's sitting-room carrying in her hand a bunch of letters.

"There!" she cried, "while you have been resting I have been working, and we are not going to allow any time to be lost. I have written with my own hand invitations to about two dozen people to our tea on Thursday; among others, the wife of the Premier, Countess Stron. I expect you to devote yourself to that lady and tell me the result of the conversation after it is over. Have you been talking consolation to Gretlich? I came up here half an hour ago, and it seemed to me I heard the sound of crying in this room."

"Oh, yes," said Jennie, "she has been telling me all her trouble. It seems she had a lover in the army, and he has been killed in some accident in the Treasury."

"What kind of an accident?"

"Gretlich said there had been an explosion there."

"Dear me! I never heard of it. It is a curious thing that one must come from London to tell us our own news. An explosion in the Treasury! and so serious that a soldier was killed! That arouses my curiosity, so I shall just sit down and write another invitation to the wife of the Master of the Treasury."

"I wish you would, because I should like to know something further about this myself. Gretlich seems to have had but scant information regarding the occurrence, and I should like to know more about it so that I might tell her."

"We shall learn all about it from madame, and I must write that note at once for fear I forget it."

CHAPTER XIII. JENNIE INDULGES IN TEA AND GOSSIP.

On Thursday afternoon there was a brilliant assemblage in the spacious salon of the Princess von Steinheimer. The rich attire of the ladies formed a series of kinetographic pictures that were dazzling, for Viennese women are adepts in the art of dress, as are their Parisian sisters. Tea was served, not in cups and saucers, as Jennie had been accustomed to seeing it handed round, but in goblets of clear, thin Venetian glass, each set in a holder of encrusted filigree gold. There were all manner of delicious cakes, for which the city is celebrated. The tea itself had come overland through Russia from China and had not suffered the deterioration which an ocean voyage produces. The decoction was served clear, with sugar if desired, and a slice of lemon, and Jennie thought it the most delicious brew she had ever tasted.

"I am so sorry," whispered the Princess to Jennie when an opportunity occurred, "but the Countess Stron has sent a messenger to say that she cannot be present this afternoon. It seems her husband, the Premier, is ill, and she, like a good wife, remains at home to nurse him. This rather upsets our plans, doesn't it?"

"Oh, I don't know," replied Jennie. "It is more than likely that the wife of the Premier would be exceedingly careful not to discuss any political question in this company. I have counted more upon the wife of a lesser official than upon the Countess Stron."

"You are right," said the Princess, "and now come with me. I want to introduce you to the wife of the Master of the Treasury, and from her, perhaps, you can learn something of the accident that befell the lover of poor Gretlich."

The wife of the Master of the Treasury proved to be a garrulous old lady who evidently prided herself on knowing everything that was taking place about her. Jennie and she became quite confidential over their goblets of tea, a beverage of which the old lady seemed inordinately fond. As the conversation between them drifted on, Jennie saw that here was a person who would take a delight in telling everything she knew, and the only question which now arose was whether she knew anything Jennie wished to learn. But before she tried her on high politics the girl determined to find out more about the disaster that had made such an abrupt ending to Gretlich's young dream.

"I have been very much interested," she said, "in one of the maids here who lost her lover some weeks ago in an accident that occurred in the Treasury. The maid doesn't seem to know very much about what happened, and was merely told that her lover, a soldier who had been on guard there that night, was dead."

"Oh, dear, yes!" whispered the old lady, lowering her voice, "what a dreadful thing that was, four men killed and eight or nine now in the hospital. My poor husband has had hardly a wink of sleep since the event, and the Premier is ill in bed through the worry."

"Because of the loss of life?" asked Jennie innocently.

"Oh, no, no! the loss of life wouldn't matter; it is the loss of the money that is the serious thing, and how they are going to replace it or account for its disappearance I am sure I don't know. The deficiency is something over two hundred million florins. Was it not awful?"

"Was the building shattered to such an extent?" inquired Jennie, who did not stop to think that such a sum would replace any edifice in Vienna, even if it had been wiped off the face of the earth.

"The Treasury was damaged, of course, but the cost of repairs will not be great. No, my child, it is a much more disturbing affair than the destruction of any state house in the Empire. What has made the Premier ill, and what is worrying my poor husband into an untimely grave, is nothing less than the loss of the war chest."

"The war chest!" echoed Jennie, "what is that?"

"My dear, every great nation has a war chest. England has one, so has France, Germany, Russia—no matter how poor a nation may be, or how difficult it is to collect the taxes, that nation must have a war chest. If war were to break out suddenly, even with the most prosperous country, there would be instant financial panic; ready money would be difficult to obtain; a loan would be practically impossible; and what war calls for the very instant it is declared is money—not promises of money, not paper money, not silver money even, but gold; therefore, every nation which is in danger of war has a store of gold coin. This store is not composed mainly, or even largely, of the coins of the nation which owns the store; it consists of the sovereigns of England, the louis of France, the Willems d'or of Holland, the eight-florin pieces of Austria, the double-crown of Germany, the half-imperials of Russia, the double-Frederics of Denmark, and so on. All gold, gold, gold! I believe that in the war chest of Austria there were deposited coins of different nations to the value of something like two hundred million florins. My husband never told me exactly how much was there, but sometimes when things looked peaceable there was less money in the war chest than when there was imminent danger of the European outbreak which we all fear. The war chest of Austria was in a stone-vaulted room, one of the strongest dungeons in the Treasury. The public are admitted into several rooms of the Treasury, but no stranger is ever allowed into that portion of the building which houses the war chest. This room is kept under guard night and day. For what happened, my husband feels that he is in no way to blame, and I don't think his superiors are inclined to charge him with neglect of duty. It is a singular thing that the day before the disaster took place he of his own accord doubled the guard that watched over the room and also the approaches to it. The war chest was at its fullest. Never, so he tells me, was there so much money in the war chest as at that particular time. Something had occurred that in his opinion called for extra watchfulness, and so he doubled the guard. But about midnight there was a tremendous explosion. The strong door communicating with the passage was wrenched from its hinges and flung outwards into the hallway. It is said that dynamite must have been used, and that in a very large quantity. Not a vestige of the chest remained but a few splintered pieces of iron. The four soldiers in the room were blown literally to pieces, and those in the passage-way were stunned by the shock. The fact that they were unconscious for some minutes seems to have given the criminal, whoever he was, his chance of escape. For, although an instant alarm was sent out, and none but those who had a right to be on the premises were allowed out of or in the Treasury, yet no one was caught, nor has anyone been caught up to this day."

"But the gold, the gold?" cried Jennie eagerly.

"There was not a florin of it left. Every piece has disappeared. It is at once the most clever and the most gigantic robbery of money that has taken place within our knowledge."

"But such a quantity of gold," said Jennie, "must have been of enormous weight. Two hundred million florins! Why, that is twenty million pounds, isn't it? It would take a regiment of thieves to carry so much away. How has that been done? And where is the gold concealed?"

"Ah, my child, if you can answer your own questions the Austrian Government will pay you almost any sum you like to name. The police are completely baffled. Of course, nothing has been said of this gigantic robbery; but every exit from Vienna is watched, and not only that, but each frontier is guarded. What the Government wants, of course, is to get back its gold, the result of years of taxation, which cannot very easily be re-levied."

"And when did this robbery take place?" asked Jennie.

"On the night of the 17th."

"On the night of the 17th," repeated the girl, more to herself than to the voluble old woman; "and it was on the 16th that the Premier made his war speech."

"Exactly," said the old lady, who overheard the remark not intended for her ears; "and don't you think there was something striking in the coincidence?"

"I don't quite understand. What coincidence?"

"Well, you know the speech of the Premier was against England. It was not a speech made on the spur of the moment, but was doubtless the result of many consultations, perhaps with Russia, perhaps with Germany, or with

France—who knows? We have been growing very friendly with Russia of late; and as England has spies all over the world, doubtless her Government knew before the speech was made that it was coming; so the police appear to think that the whole resources of the British Government were set at the task of crippling Austria at a critical moment."

"Surely you don't mean, madame, that the Government of England would descend to burglary, robbery—yes, and murder, even, for the poor soldiers who guarded the treasure were as effectually murdered as if they had been assassinated in the street? You don't imagine that the British Government would stoop to such deeds as these?"

The old lady shook her head wisely.

"By the time you are my age, my dear, and have seen as much of politics as I have, you will know that Governments stop at nothing to accomplish their ends. No private association of thieves could have laid such plans as would have done away with two hundred millions of florins in gold, unless they had not only ample resources, but also a master brain to direct them. Nations hesitate at nothing where their interests are concerned. It was to the interest of no other Empire but England to deplete Austria at this moment, and see how complete her machinations are. No nation trusts another, and if Austria had proof that England is at the bottom of this robbery, she dare not say anything, because her war chest is empty. Then, again, she cannot allow either Germany or Russia to know how effectually she has been robbed, for no one could tell what either of these nations might do under the circumstances. The Government fears to let even its own people know what has happened. It is a stroke of vengeance marvellous in its finality. Austria is crippled for years to come, unless she finds the stolen gold on her own territory."

The old lady had worked herself up into such a state of excitement during her recital that she did not notice that most of her companion visitors had taken their leave, and when the Princess approached the two, she arose with some trepidation.

"My dear Princess," she said, "your tea has been so good, and the company of your young compatriot has been so charming, that I have done nothing but chatter, chatter, chatter away about things which should only be spoken of under one's breath, and now I must hurry away. May I venture to hope that you will honour me with your presence at one of my receptions if I send you a card?"

"I shall be delighted to do so," replied the Princess, with that gracious condescension which became her so well.

The garrulous old lady was the last to take her leave, and when the Princess was left alone with her guest, she cried,—

"Jennie, I have found out absolutely nothing, what have you discovered?"

"Everything!" replied the girl, walking up and down the floor in excitement over the unearthing of such a bonanza of news.

"You don't tell me so! Now do sit down and let me know the full particulars at once."

When Jennie's exciting story was finished she said,—

"You see, this robbery explains why the Premier did not follow up his warlike speech. The police seem to think that England has had a hand in this robbery, but of course that is absurd."

"I am not so sure of that," replied the Princess, taking as she spoke, the Chicago point of view, and forgetting for the moment her position among the aristocracy of Europe. "England takes most things it can get its hands on, and she is not too slow to pick up a gold mine here and there, so why should she hesitate when the gold is already minted for her?"

"It is too absurd for argument," continued Jennie calmly, "so we won't talk of that phase of the subject. I must get away to England instantly. Let us find out when the first train leaves."

"Nonsense!" protested the Princess; "what do you need to go to England for? You have seen nothing of Vienna."

"Oh, I can see Vienna another time; I must get to England with this account of the robbery."

"Won't your paper pay for telegraphing such an important piece of news?

"Oh, yes; there would be no difficulty about that, but I dare not trust either the post or the telegraph in a case like this. The police are on the watch."

"But couldn't you send it through by a code? My father always used to do his cabling by code; it saved a lot of money and also kept other people from knowing what his business was."

"I have a code, but I hesitate about trusting even to that."

"I'll tell you what we'll do," said the Princess. "I want you to stay in Vienna."

"Oh, I shall return," said Jennie. "I've only just had a taste of this delightful city. I'll come right back."

"I can't trust you to do anything of the kind. When you get to London you will stay there. Now here is what I propose, and it will have the additional advantage of saving your paper a day. We will run down together into Italy—to Venice; then you can take along your code and telegraph from there in perfect safety. When that is done you will return here to Vienna with me. And another thing, you may be sure your editor will want you to stay right here on the spot to let him know of any outcome of this sensational dénouement."

"That isn't a bad idea," murmured Jennie. "How long will it take us to get to Venice?"

"I don't know, but I am sure it will save you hours compared with going to London. I shall get the exact time for you in a moment."

Jennie followed the suggestion of the Princess, and together the two went to the ever-entrancing city of Venice. By the time they reached there, Jennie had her account written and coded. The long message was handed in at the telegraph office as soon as the two arrived in Venice. Jennie also sent the editor a private despatch giving her address in Venice, and also telling him the reason for sending the telegram from Italy rather than from Austria or Germany. In the evening she received a reply from Mr. Hardwick. "This is magnificent," the telegram said. "I doubt if anything like it has ever been done before. We will startle the world to-morrow morning. Please return to Vienna, for, as you have discovered this much, I am perfectly certain that you will be able to capture the robbers. Of course all the police and all the papers of Europe will be on the same scent, but I am sure that you will prove a match for the whole combination."

"Oh, dear!" cried Jennie, as she handed the message to her friend. "What a bothersome world this is; there is no finality about anything. One piece of work simply leads to another. Here I thought I had earned at least a good month's rest, but, instead of that, a further demand is made upon me. I am like the genii in fairy tales: no sooner is one apparently impossible task accomplished than another is set."

"But what a magnificent thing it would be if you could discover the robber or robbers."

"Magnificent enough, yes; but that isn't to be done by inviting a lot of old women to tea, is it?"

"True, so we shall have to set our wits together in another direction. I tell you, Jennie, I know I have influence enough to have you made a member of the special police. Shall I introduce you as from America, and say that you have made a speciality of solving mysteries? An appointment to the special police would allow you to have unrestricted entrance to the secret portion of the Treasury building. You would see the rooms damaged by the explosion, and you would learn what the police have discovered. With that knowledge to begin with, we might then do something towards solving the problem."

"Madame la Princesse," cried Jennie enthusiastically, "you are inspired! The very thing. Let us get back to Vienna." And accordingly the two conspirators left Italy by the night train for Austria.

CHAPTER XIV. JENNIE BECOMES A SPECIAL POLICE OFFICER.

When Jennie returned to Vienna, and was once more installed in her luxurious rooms at the Palace Steinheimer, she received in due time a copy of the Daily Bugle, sent to her under cover as a registered letter. The girl could not complain that the editor had failed to make the most of the news she had sent him. As she opened out the paper she saw the great black headlines that extended across two columns, and the news itself dated not from Venice, but from Vienna, was in type much larger than that ordinarily used in the paper, and was double-leaded. The headings were startling enough:—

PHANTOM GOLD.

THE MOST GIGANTIC ROBBERY OF MODERN TIMES.

THE AUSTRIAN WAR CHEST DYNAMITED.

TWENTY MILLION POUNDS IN COIN LOOTED.

APPALLING DISASTER AT THE TREASURY IN VIENNA.

FOUR MEN KILLED, AND SIXTEEN OTHERS MORE OR LESS SERIOUSLY INJURED.

"Dear me!" the Princess cried, peering over Jennie's shoulder at these amazing headings, "how like home that looks. The Bugle doesn't at all resemble a London journal; it reminds me of a Chicago paper's account of a baseball match; a baseball match when Chicago was winning, of course, and when Anson had lined out the ball from the plate to the lake front, and brought three men in on a home run at a critical point in the game."

"Good gracious!" cried Jennie, "what language are you speaking? Is it slang, or some foreign tongue?"

"It is pure Chicagoese, Jennie, into which I occasionally lapse even here in prim Vienna. I would like to see a good baseball match, with the Chicago nine going strong. Let us abandon this effete monarchy, Jennie, and pay a visit to America."

"I'll go with pleasure if you will tell me first who robbed the war chest. If you can place your dainty forefinger on the spot that conceals two hundred million florins in gold, I'll go anywhere with you."

"Oh, yes, that reminds me. I spoke to my husband this morning, and asked him if he could get you enrolled as a special detective, and he said there would be some difficulty in obtaining such an appointment for a woman. Would you have any objection to dressing up as a nice young man, Jennie?"

"I would very much rather not; I hope you didn't suggest that to the Prince."

The Princess laughed merrily and shook her head.

"No, I told him that I believed that you would solve the mystery if anyone could, and, remembering what you had done in that affair of my diamonds, my husband has the greatest faith in your powers as an investigator; but he fears the authorities here will be reluctant to allow a woman to have any part in the search. They have very old-fashioned ideas about women in Austria, and think her proper place is presiding over a tea-table."

"Well, if they only knew it," said Jennie archly, "some things have been discovered over a teacup within our own memories."

"That is quite true," replied the Princess, "but we can hardly give the incident as a recommendation to the Austrian authorities. By the way, have you noticed that no paper in Vienna has said a single word about the robbery of the war chest?"

"It must have been telegraphed here very promptly from London, and yet they do not even deny it, which is the usual way of meeting the truth."

While they were talking, a message came from his Highness, asking if he might take the liberty of breaking in upon their conference. A few moments after, the Prince himself entered the apartment and bowed with courtly deference to the two ladies.

"I have succeeded," he said, "beyond my expectations. It seems that a newspaper in London has published an account of the whole affair, and the police, who were at their wits end before, are even more flustered now that the account of the robbery has been made public. By the way, how did you learn anything about this robbery? It did not strike me at the time you spoke about Miss Baxter's commission this morning, but I have been wondering ever since."

"Jennie received a paper from London," said the Princess hurriedly, "which said the war chest of Austria had been robbed of two hundred million florins, but there is nothing about it in the Vienna Press."

"No," replied the Prince; "nor is there likely to be. The robbery is now known to all the world except Austria, and I imagine nothing will be said about it here."

"Is there, then, any truth in the report?" asked the Princess innocently.

"Truth! It's all truth; that is just where the trouble is. There is little use of our denying it, because this London paper is evidently well informed, and to deny it we should have to publish something about the robbery itself, which we are not inclined to do. It is known, however, who the two correspondents of this London paper are, and I believe the police are going to make it so interesting for those two gentlemen that they will be glad to leave Vienna, for a time at least. Of course, nothing can be done openly, because Englishmen make such a fuss when their liberties are encroached upon. One of the young men has been lured across the frontier by a bogus telegram, and I think the authorities will see that he does not get back in a hurry; the other we expect to be rid of before long. Of course, we could expel him, but if we did, it would be thought that we had done so because he had found out the truth about the explosion."

"How did you learn of the explosion?" asked the Princess.

"Oh, I have known all about the affair ever since it happened."

The Princess gave Jennie a quick look, which said as plainly as words, "Here was the news that we wanted in our household, and we never suspected it." "Why didn't you tell me?" cried the Princess indignantly.

"Well, you see, my dear, you never took much interest in politics, and I did not think the news would have any attraction for you; besides," he added, with a smile, "we were all cautioned to keep the matter as secret as possible."

"And wonderfully well you have managed it!" exclaimed the Princess. "That shows what comes of trusting a secret to a lot of men; here it is, published to all the world."

"Not quite all the world my dear. As I have said, Austria will know nothing regarding it."

"The Princess tells me," said Jennie, "that you were kind enough to endeavour to get me permission to make some investigation into this mystery. Have you succeeded?"

"Yes, Miss Baxter, as I said, I have succeeded quite beyond my expectations, for the lady detective is comparatively an innovation in Vienna. However, the truth is, the police are completely in a fog, and they are ready to welcome help from whatever quarter it comes. Here is a written permit from the very highest authority, which you do not need to use except in a case of emergency. Here is also an order from the Chief of Police, which will open for you every door in Vienna; and finally, here is a badge which you can pin on some not too conspicuous portion of your clothing. This badge, I understand, is rarely given out. It is partly civil and partly military. You can show it to any guard, who will, on seeing it, give you the right-of-way. In case he does not, appeal to his superior officer, and allow him to read your police permit. Should that fail, then play your trump card, which is this highly important document. The Director of the Police, who is a very shrewd man, seemed anxious to make your acquaintance before you began your investigation. He asked me if you would call upon him, but seemed taken aback when I told him you were my wife's friend and a guest at our house, so he suggested that you would in all probability wish first to see the scene of the explosion, and proposed that he should call here with his carriage and accompany you to the Treasury. He wished to know if four o'clock in the afternoon would suit your convenience!"

"Oh, yes!" replied Jennie. "I am eager to begin at once, and, of course,

I shall be much obliged to him if he will act as my guide in the vaults of the Treasury, and tell me how much they have already discovered."

"You must not expect much information from the police—in fact, I doubt if they have discovered anything. Still, if they have, they are more than likely to keep it to themselves; and I imagine they will hold a pretty close watch on you, being more anxious to learn what you discover, and thus take the credit if they can, than to furnish you with any knowledge of the affair they may happen to possess."

"That is quite natural, and only what one has a right to expect. I don't wish to rob the police of whatever repute there is to be gained from this investigation, and I am quite willing to turn over to them any clues I may happen to chance upon."

"Well, if you can convince the Director of that, you will have all the assistance he can give you. It wouldn't be bad tactics to let him know that you are acting merely in an amateur way, and that you have no desire to rob the police of their glory when it comes to the solving of the problem." Promptly at four o'clock the Director of the Police put in an appearance at the Palace Steinheimer. He appeared to be a most obsequious, highly decorated old gentleman, in a very resplendent uniform, and he could hardly conceal his surprise at learning that the lady detective was a woman so young and so pretty. Charmed as he was to find himself in the company of one so engaging, it was nevertheless evident to Jennie that he placed no very high estimate on the assistance she might be able to give in solving the mystery of the Treasury. This trend of mind, she thought, had its advantages, for the Director would be less loth to give her full particulars of what had already been accomplished by the police.

Jennie accompanied the Director to that extensive mass of buildings of which the Treasury forms a part. The carriage drew up at a doorway, and here the Director and his companion got out. He led the way into the edifice, then, descending a stair, entered an arched corridor, at the door of which two soldiers stood on guard, who saluted as the Chief passed them.

"Does this lead to the room where the explosion took place?" asked

Jennie. "Yes." "And is this the only entrance?" "The only entrance, madame." "Were the men on guard in this doorway injured by the explosion?" "Yes. They were not seriously injured, but were rendered incapable for a time of attending to their duties." "Then a person could have escaped without their seeing him?" "A whole regiment of persons might have escaped. You will understand the situation exactly if I compare this corridor to a long cannon, the room at the end being the breech-loading chamber. Two guards were inside the room, and two others stood outside the door that communicated with this corridor. These four men were killed instantly. Of the guards inside the room not a vestige has been found. The door, one of the strongest that can be made, somewhat similar to the door of a safe, was flung outward and crushed to the floor the two guards who stood outside it in the corridor. Between the chamber in which the chest lay and the outside entrance were sixteen men on guard. Every one of these was flung down, for the blast, if I may call it so, travelled through this straight corridor like the charge along the inside of the muzzle of a gun. The guards nearest the treasure chamber were, of course, the more seriously injured, but those further out did not escape the shock, and the door by which we entered this corridor, while not blown from its hinges, was nevertheless forced open, its strong bolts snapping like matches. So when you see the great distance that intervened between the chamber and that door, you will have some idea of the force of the explosion."

"There is no exit, then, from the treasure chamber except along this corridor?"

"No, madame. The walls at the outside of the chamber are of enormous strength, because, of course, it was expected that if an attempt at robbery were ever made, it would be made from the outside, and it is scarcely possible that even the most expert of thieves could succeed in passing two guards at the door, sixteen officers and soldiers along the corridor, two outside the Treasury door, and two in the chamber itself. Such a large number of soldiers were kept here so that any attempt at bribery would be impossible. Among such a number one or two were sure to be incorruptible, and the guards were constantly changed. Seldom was either officer or man twice on duty here during the month. With such a large amount at stake every precaution was taken."

"Are there any rooms at the right or left of this corridor in which the thieves could have concealed themselves while they fired the mine?"

"No, the corridor leads to the treasure chamber alone."

"Then," said Jennie, "I can't see how it was possible for a number of men to have made away with the treasure in such circumstances as exist here."

"Nevertheless, my dear young lady, the treasure is gone. We think that the mine was laid with the connivance of one or more officers on duty here. You see the amount at stake was so large that a share of it would tempt any nine human beings out of any ten. Our theory is that the train was laid, possibly electric wires being used, which would be unnoticed along the edge of the corridor, and that the bribed officer exploded the dynamite by bringing the ends of the wires into contact. We think the explosion was a great deal more severe than was anticipated. Probably, it was expected that the shock would break a hole from the treasure chamber to the street, but so strong were the walls that no impression was made upon them, and a cabman who was driving past at the time heard nothing of the sound of the explosion, though he felt a trembling of the ground, and thought for a moment there had been a shock of earthquake."

"You think, then, that the thieves were outside?"

"That seems the only possible opinion to hold."

"The outside doors were locked and bolted, of course?"

"Oh, certainly; but if they had a confederate or two in the large hallway upstairs, these traitors would see to it that there was no trouble about getting in. Once inside the large hallway, with guards stunned by the shock, the way to the treasure chamber was absolutely clear."

"There were sentries outside the building, I suppose?"

"Yes."

"Did they see any vehicle driving near the Treasury?"

"No, except the cab I spoke of, and the driver has accounted satisfactorily for his time that night. The absence of any conveyance is the strange part of it; and, moreover, the sentries, although pacing outside the walls of this building, heard nothing of the concussion beyond a low rumble, and those who thought of the matter at all imagined an explosion had occurred in some distant part of the city."

"Then the outside doors in the large hall above were not blown open?"

"No; the officer reports that they were locked and bolted when he examined them, which was some minutes, of course, after the disaster had taken place; for he, the officer in charge, had been thrown down and stunned, seemingly by the concussion of air which took place."

As Jennie walked down the corridor, she saw more and more of the evidences of the convulsion. The thick iron-bound door lay where it had fallen, and it had not been moved since it was lifted to get the two men from under it. Its ponderous hinges were twisted as if they had been made of glue, and its massive bolts were snapped across like bits of glass. All along the corridor on the floor was a thick coating of dust and débris, finely powdered, growing deeper and deeper until they came to the entrance of the room. There was no window either in corridor or chamber, and the way was lit by candles held by soldiers who accompanied them. The scoria crunched under foot as they walked, and in the chamber itself great heaps of dust, sand and plaster, all pulverized into minute particles, lay in the corners of the room, piled up on one side higher than a man's head. There seemed to be tons of this débris, and, as Jennie looked up at the arched ceiling, resembling the roof of a vaulted dungeon, she saw that the stone itself had been ground to fine dust with the tremendous force of the blast.

"Where are the remnants of the treasure chest?" she asked.

The Director shook his head. "There are no remnants; not a vestige of it is to be found."

"Of what was it made?"

"We used to have an old treasure chest here made of oak, bound with iron; but some years ago, a new receptacle being needed, one was especially built of hardened steel, constructed on the modern principles of those burglar-proof and fire-proof safes."

"And do you mean to say that there is nothing left of this?"

"Nothing that we have been able to discover."

"Well, I have seen places where dynamite explosions have occurred, but I know of nothing to compare with this. I am sure that if dynamite has been used, or any explosive now generally obtainable, there would have been left, at least, some remnant of the safe. Hasn't this pile of rubbish been disturbed since the explosion?"

"Yes, it has been turned over; we made a search for the two men, but we found no trace of them."

"And you found no particles of iron or steel?"

"The heap throughout is just as you see it on the surface—a fine, almost impalpable dust. We had to exercise the greatest care in searching through it, for the moment it was disturbed with a shovel it filled the air with suffocating clouds. Of course we shall have it removed by-and-by, and carted away, but I considered it better to allow it to remain here until we had penetrated somewhat further into the mystery than we have already done."

Jennie stooped and picked up a handful from the heap, her action caused a mist to rise in the air that made them both choke and cough, and yet she was instantly struck by the fact that her handful seemed inordinately heavy for its bulk.

"May I take some of this with me?" she asked.

"Of course," replied the Director. "I will have a packet of it put up for you."

"I would like to take it with me now," said Jennie. "I have curiosity to know exactly of what it is composed. Who is the Government analyst? or have you such an official?"

"Herr Feltz, in the Graubenstrasse, is a famous analytical chemist; you cannot do better than go to him."

"Do you think he knows anything about explosives?"

"I should suppose so, but if not, he will certainly be able to tell you who the best man is in that line."

The Director ordered one of the soldiers who accompanied him to find a small paper bag, and fill it with some dust from the treasure chamber. When this was done, he handed the package to Jennie, who said, "I shall go at once and see Herr Feltz."

"My carriage is at your disposal, madame."

"Oh, no, thank you, I do not wish to trouble you further. I am very much obliged to you for devoting so much time to me already. I shall take a fiacre."

"My carriage is at the door," persisted the Director, "and I will instruct the driver to take you directly to the shop of Herr Feltz; then no time will be lost, and I think if I am with you, you will be more sure of attention from the chemist, who is a very busy man."

Jennie saw the Director did not wish to let her out of his sight, and although she smiled at his suspicion, she answered politely,—

"It is very kind of you to take so much trouble and devote so much of your time to me. I shall be glad of your company if you are quite certain I am not keeping you from something more important."

"There is nothing more important than the investigation we have on hand," replied the Chief grimly.

CHAPTER XV. JENNIE BESTOWS INFORMATION UPON THE CHIEF OF POLICE.

A few minutes after leaving the Treasury building the carriage of the Chief stopped in front of the shop of Herr Feltz in the wide Graubenstrasse. The great chemist himself waited upon them and conducted them to an inner and private room.

"I should be obliged to you if you would tell me the component parts of the mixture in this package," said Jennie, as she handed the filled paper bag to the chemist.

"How soon do you wish to know the result?" asked the man of chemicals.

"As soon as possible," replied Jennie.

"Could you give me until this hour to-morrow?"

"That will do very nicely," replied Jennie, looking up at the Director of Police, who nodded his head.

With that the two took their leave, and once more the Director of Police politely handed the girl into his carriage, and they drove to the Palace Steinheimer. Here she again thanked him cordially for his attentions during the day. The Director answered, with equal suavity, that his duty had on this occasion been a pleasure, and asked her permission to call at the same hour the next afternoon and take her to the chemist. To this Jennie assented, and cheerily bade him good-evening. The Princess was waiting for her, wild with curiosity to know what had happened.

"Oh, Jennie!" she cried, "who fired the mine, and who robbed the Government?"

Jennie laughed merrily as she replied,—

"Dear Princess, what a compliment you are paying me! Do you think that in one afternoon I am able to solve a mystery that has defied the combined talents of all the best detectives in Austria? I wish the Director of Police had such faith in me as you have."

"And hasn't he, Jennie?"

"Indeed he has not. He watched me every moment he was with me, as if he feared I would disappear into thin air, as the treasure had done."

"The horrid man. I shall have my husband speak to him, and rid you of this annoyance."

"Oh, no, Princess, you mustn't do anything of the kind. I don't mind it in the least; in fact, it rather amuses me. One would think he had some suspicion that I stole the money myself."

"A single word from the Prince will stop all that, you know."

"Yes, I know. But I really want to help the Director; he is so utterly stupid."

"Now, Jennie, take off your hat and sit down here, and tell me every incident of the afternoon. Don't you see I am just consumed with curiosity? I know you have discovered something. What is it?"

"I will not take off my hat, because I am going out again directly; but, if you love me, get me a cup of that delicious tea of yours."

"I shall order it at once, but dinner will be served shortly. You are surely not going out alone to-night?"

"I really must. Do not forget that I have been used to taking care of myself in a bigger city than Vienna is, and I shall be quite safe. You will please excuse my absence from the dinner-table to-night."

"Nonsense, Jennie! You cannot be allowed to roam round Vienna in that Bohemian way."

"Then, Princess, I must go to an hotel, for this roaming round is strictly necessary, and I don't want to bring the Palace Steinheimer into disrepute."

"Jennie, I'll tell you what we will do; we'll both bring it into disrepute.

The Prince is dining at his club to-night with some friends, so I shall order the carriage, and you and I will roam round together. You will let me come, won't you? Where are you going?"

"I am going to the Graubenstrasse to see Herr Feltz."

"Oh, I know Herr Feltz, and a dear old man he is; he will do anything for me. If you want a favour from Herr Feltz, you had better take me with you."

"I shall be delighted. Ah, here comes the tea! But what is the use of ordering the carriage? we can walk there in a very few minutes."

"I think we had better have the carriage. The Prince would be wild if he heard that we two went walking about the streets of Vienna at night. So, Jennie, we must pay some respect to conventionality, and we will take the carriage. Now, tell me where you have been, and what you have seen, and all about it." Over their belated decoction of tea Jennie related everything that had happened.

"And what do you expect to learn from the analysis at the chemist's, Jennie?"

"I expect to learn something that will startle the Director of Police."

"And what is that? Jennie, don't keep me on tenterhooks in this provoking way. How can you act so? I shall write to Lord Donal and tell him that you are here in Vienna, if you don't mind."

"Well, under such a terrible threat as that, I suppose I must divulge all my suspicions. But I really don't know anything yet; I merely suspect. The weight of that dust, when I picked up a handful of it, seemed to indicate that the gold is still there in the rubbish heap."

"You don't mean to say so! Then there has been no robbery at all?"

"There may have been a robbery planned, but I do not think any thief got a portion of the gold. The chances are that they entirely underestimated the force of the explosive they were using, for, unless I am very much mistaken, they were dealing with something a hundred times more powerful than dynamite."

"And will the chemical analysis show what explosive was used?"

"No; it will only show of what the débris is composed. It will settle the question whether or not the gold is in that dust-heap. If it is, then I think the Government will owe me some thanks, because the Director of Police talked of carting the rubbish away and dumping it out of sight somewhere. If the Government gets back its gold, I suppose the question of who fired the mine is merely of academic interest."

"The carriage is waiting, your Highness," was the announcement made to the Princess, who at once jumped up, and said,—

"I'll be ready in five minutes. I'm as anxious now as you are to hear what the chemist has to say; but I thought you told me he wouldn't have the analysis ready until four o'clock to-morrow. What is the use of going there to-night?".

"Because I am reasonably certain that the Director of Police will see him early to-morrow morning, and I want to get the first copy of the analysis myself."

With that the Princess ran away and presently reappeared with her wraps on. The two drove to the shop of Herr Feltz in the Graubenstrasse, and were told that the chemist could not be seen in any circumstances. He had left orders that he was not to be disturbed.

"Disobey those orders and take in my card," said the Princess.

A glance at the card dissolved the man's doubts, and he departed to seek his master.

"He is working at the analysis now, I'll warrant," whispered the Princess to her companion. In a short time Herr Feltz himself appeared. He greeted the Princess with most deferential respect, but seemed astonished to find in her company the young woman who had called on him a few hours previously with the Director of the Police.

"I wanted to ask you," said Jennie, "to finish your analysis somewhat earlier than four o'clock to-morrow. I suppose it can be done?"

The man of science smiled and looked at her for a moment, but did not reply. "You will oblige my friend, I hope," said the Princess.

"I should be delighted to oblige any friend of your Highness," answered the chemist slowly, "but, unfortunately, in this instance I have orders from an authority not to be disputed."

"What orders?" demanded the Princess.

"I promised the analysis at four o'clock to-morrow, and at that hour it will be ready for the young lady. I am ordered not to show the analysis to anyone before that time."

"Those orders came from the Director of Police, I suppose?" The chemist bowed low, but did not speak.

"I understand how it is, Jennie; he came here immediately after seeing you home. I suppose he visited you again within the hour after he left with this young lady—is that the case, Herr Feltz?"

"Your Highness distresses me by asking questions that I am under pledge not to answer."

"Is the analysis completed?"

"That is another question which I sincerely hope your Highness will not press."

"Very well, Herr Feltz, I shall ask you a question or two of which you will not be so frightened. I have told my friend here that you would do anything for me, but I see I have been mistaken."

The chemist made a deprecatory motion of his hands, spreading them out and bowing. It was plainly apparent that his seeming discourtesy caused him deep regret. He was about to speak, but the Princess went impetuously on.

"Is the Director of Police a friend of yours, Herr Feltz? I don't mean merely an official friend, but a personal friend?"

"I am under many obligations to him, your Highness, and besides that, like any other citizen of Vienna, I am compelled to obey him when he commands."

"What I want to learn," continued the Princess, her anger visibly rising at this unexpected opposition, "is whether you wish the man well or not?"

"I certainly wish him well, your Highness."

"In that case know that if my friend leaves this shop without seeing the analysis of the material she brought to you, the Director of Police will be dismissed from his office to-morrow. If you doubt my influence with my husband to have that done, just try the experiment of sending us away unsatisfied."

The old man bowed his white head.

"Your Highness," he said, "I shall take the responsibility of refusing to obey the orders of the Director of Police. Excuse me for a moment."

He retired into his den, and presently emerged with a sheet of paper in his hand.

"It must be understood," he said, addressing Jennie, "that the analysis is but roughly made. I intended to devote the night to a more minute scrutiny."

"All I want at the present moment," said Jennie, "is a rough analysis."

"There it is," said the chemist, handing her the paper. She read,——

Calcium	*29*
Iron	*4*
Quartz]	
Feldspar]	*27*
Mica]	
Gold	*36-1/2*

Traces of other substances	*3-1/2*
———	
Total	*100*

Jennie's eyes sparkled as she looked at the figures before her. She handed the paper to the Princess saying,—

"You see, I was right in my surmise. More than one-third of that heap is pure gold."

"I should explain," said the chemist, "that I have grouped the quartz, feldspar, and mica together, without giving the respective portions of each, because it is evident that the combination represents granite."

"I understand," said Jennie; "the walls and the roof are of granite."

"I would further add," continued the chemist, "that I have never met gold so finely divided as this is."

"Have you the gold and other ingredients separated?"

"Yes, madame."

"I shall take them with me, if you please."

The chemist shortly after brought her the components, in little glass vials, labelled.

"Have you any idea, Herr Feltz, what explosive would reduce gold to such fine powder as this?"

"I have only a theoretical knowledge of explosives, and I know of nothing that would produce such results as we have here. Perhaps Professor Carl Seigfried could give you some information on that point. The science of detonation has been his life study, and he stands head and shoulders above his fellows in that department."

"Can you give me his address?"

The chemist wrote the address on a sheet of paper and handed it to the young woman.

"Do you happen to know whether Professor Seigfried or his assistants have been called in during this investigation?"

"What investigation, madame?"

"The investigation of the recent terrible explosion."

"I have heard of no explosion," replied the chemist, evidently bewildered.

Then Jennie remembered that, while the particulars of the disaster in the Treasury were known to the world at large outside of Austria, no knowledge of the catastrophe had got abroad in Vienna.

"The Professor," continued the chemist, noticing Jennie's hesitation, "is not a very practical man. He is deeply learned, and has made some great discoveries in pure science, but he has done little towards applying his knowledge to any everyday useful purpose. If you meet him, you will find him a dreamer and a theorist. But if you once succeed in interesting him in any matter, he will prosecute it to the very end, quite regardless of the time he spends or the calls of duty elsewhere."

"Then he is just the man I wish to see," said Jennie decisively, and with that they took leave of the chemist and once more entered the carriage.

"I want to drive to another place," said Jennie, "before it gets too late."

"Good gracious!" cried the Princess, "you surely do not intend to call on Professor Seigfried to-night?"

"No; but I want to drive to the office of the Director of Police."

"Oh, that won't take us long," said the Princess, giving the necessary order. The coachman took them to the night entrance of the central police station by the Hohenstaufengasse, and, leaving the Princess in the carriage, Jennie went in alone to speak with the officer in charge.

"I wish to see the Director of Police," she said.

"He will not be here until to-morrow morning. He is at home. Is it anything important?"

"Yes. Where is his residence?"

"If you will have the kindness to inform me what your business is, madame, we will have pleasure in attending to it without disturbing Herr Director."

"I must communicate with the Director in person. The Princess von Steinheimer is in her carriage outside, and I do not wish to keep her waiting." At mention of the Princess the officer bestirred himself and became tremendously polite.

"I shall call the Director at once, and he will be only too happy to wait upon you."

"Oh, have you a telephone here? and can I speak with him myself without being overheard?"

"Certainly, madame. If you will step into this room with me, I will call him up and leave you to speak with him."

This was done, and when the Chief had answered, Jennie introduced herself to him.

"I am Miss Baxter, whom you were kind enough to escort through the Treasury building this afternoon."

"Oh, yes," replied the Chief. "I thought we were to postpone further inquiry until to-morrow."

"Yes, that was the arrangement; but I wanted to say that if my plans are interfered with; if I am kept under surveillance, I shall be compelled to withdraw from the search."

A few moments elapsed before the Chief replied, and then it was with some hesitation.

"I should be distressed to have you withdraw; but, if you wish to do so, that must be a matter entirely for your own consideration. I have my own duty to perform, and I must carry it out to the best of my poor ability."

"Quite so. I am obliged to you for speaking so plainly. I rather surmised this afternoon that you looked upon my help in the light of an interference."

"I should not have used the word interference," continued the Chief; "but I must confess that I never knew good results to follow amateur efforts, which could not have been obtained much more speedily and effectually by the regular force under my command."

"Well, the regular force under your command has been at work several weeks and has apparently not accomplished very much. I have devoted part of an afternoon and evening to the matter, so before I withdraw I should like to give you some interesting information which you may impart to the Government, and I am quite willing that you should take all the credit for the discovery, as I have no wish to appear in any way as your competitor. Can you hear me distinctly?"

"Perfectly, madame," replied the Chief.

"Then, in the first place, inform the Government that there has been no robbery."

"No robbery? What an absurd statement, if you will excuse me speaking so abruptly! Where is the gold if there was no robbery?"

"I am coming to that. Next inform the Government that their loss will be but trifling. That heap of débris which you propose to cart away contains practically the whole of the missing two hundred million florins. More than one-third of the heap is pure gold. If you want to do a favour to a good friend of yours, and at the same time confer a benefit upon the Government itself, you will advise the Government to secure the services of Herr Feltz, so that the gold may be extracted from the rubbish completely and effectually. I put in a word for Herr Feltz, because I am convinced that he is a most competent man. To-night his action saved you from dismissal to-morrow, therefore you should be grateful to him. And now I have the honour to wish you good-night."

"Wait—wait a moment!" came in beseeching tones through the

telephone. "My dear young lady, pray pardon any fault you have to find with me, and remain for a moment or two longer. Who, then, caused the explosion, and why was it accomplished?"

"That I must leave for you to find out, Herr Director. You see, I am giving you the results of merely a few hours' inquiry, and you cannot expect me to discover everything in that time. I don't know how the explosion was caused, neither do I know who the criminals are or were. It would probably take me all day to-morrow to find that out; but as I am leaving the discovery in such competent hands as yours, I must curb my impatience until you send me full particulars. So, once again, good-night, Herr Director."

"No, no, don't go yet. I shall come at once to the station, if you will be kind enough to stop there until I arrive."

"The Princess von Steinheimer is waiting for me in her carriage outside, and I do not wish to delay her any longer."

"Then let me implore you not to give up your researches."

"Why? Amateur efforts are so futile, you know, when compared with the labours of the regular force."

"Oh, my dear young lady, you must pardon an old man for what he said in a thoughtless moment. If you knew how many useless amateurs meddle in our very difficult business you would excuse me. Are you quite convinced of what you have told me, that the gold is in the rubbish heap?"

"Perfectly. I will leave for you at the office here the analysis made by Herr Feltz, and if I can assist you further, it must be on the distinct understanding that you are not to interfere again with whatever I may do. Your conduct in going to Herr Feltz to-night after you had left me, and commanding him not to give me any information, I should hesitate to characterize by its right name. When I have anything further to communicate, I will send for you."

"Thank you; I shall hold myself always at your command." This telephonic interview being happily concluded, Jennie hurried to the Princess, stopping on her way to give the paper containing the analysis to the official in charge, and telling him to hand it to the Director when he returned to his desk. This done, she passed out into the night, with the comfortable consciousness that the worries of a busy day had not been without their compensation.

CHAPTER XVI. JENNIE VISITS A MODERN WIZARD IN HIS MAGIC ATTIC.

When Jennie entered the carriage in which her friend was waiting, the other cried, "Well, have you seen him?" apparently meaning the Director of Police.

"No, I did not see him, but I talked with him over the telephone. I wish you could have heard our conversation; it was the funniest interview I ever took part in. Two or three times I had to shut off the instrument, fearing the Director would hear me laugh. I am afraid that before this business is ended you will be very sorry I am a guest at your house. I know I shall end by getting myself into an Austrian prison. Just think of it! Here have I been 'holding up' the Chief of Police in this Imperial city as if I were a wild western brigand. I have been terrorizing the man, brow-beating him, threatening him, and he the person who has the liberty of all Vienna in his hands; who can have me dragged off to a dungeon-cell any time he likes to give the order."

"Not from the Palace Steinheimer," said the Princess, with decision.

"Well, he might hesitate about that; yet, nevertheless, it is too funny to think that a mere newspaper woman, coming into a city which contains only one or two of her friends, should dare to talk to the Chief of Police as I have done to-night, and force him actually to beg that I shall remain in the city and continue to assist him."

"Tell me what you said," asked the Princess eagerly; and Jennie related all that had passed between them over the telephone.

"And do you mean to say calmly that you are going to give that man the right to use the astounding information you have acquired, and allow him to accept complacently all the kudos that such a discovery entitles you to?"

"Why, certainly," replied Jennie. "What good is the kudos to me? All the credit I desire I get in the office of the Daily Bugle in London."

"But, you silly girl, holding such a secret as you held, you could have made your fortune," insisted the practical Princess, for the principles which had been instilled into her during a youth spent in Chicago had not been entirely eradicated by residence in Vienna. "If you had gone to the Government and said, 'How much will you give me if I restore to you the missing gold?' just imagine what their answer would be."

"Yes, I suppose there was money in the scheme if it had really been a secret. But you forget that to-morrow morning the Chief of Police would have known as much as he knows to-night. Of course, if I had gone alone to the Treasury vault and kept my discovery to myself, I might, perhaps, have 'held up' the Government of Austria-Hungary as successfully as I 'held up' the Chief of Police to-night. But with the Director watching everything I did, and going with me to the chemist, there was no possibility of keeping the matter a secret."

"Well, Jennie, all I can say is that you are a very foolish girl. Here you are, working hard, as you said in one of your letters, merely to make a living, and now, with the greatest nonchalance, you allow a fortune to slip through your fingers. I am simply not going to allow this. I shall tell my husband all that has happened, and he will make the Government treat you honestly; if not generously. I assure you, Jennie, that Lord Donal—no, I won't mention his name, since you protest so strenuously—but the future young man, whoever he is, will not think the less of you because you come to him with a handsome dowry. But here we are at home; and I won't say another word on the subject if it annoys you."

When Jennie reached her delightful apartments—which looked even more luxuriantly comfortable bathed in the soft radiance that now flooded them from quiet-toned shaded lamps than they did in the more garish light of day—she walked up and down her sitting-room in deep meditation. She was in a quandary—whether or not to risk sending a coded telegram to her paper was the question that presented itself to her. If she were sure that no one else would learn the news, she would prefer to wait until she had further particulars of the Treasury catastrophe. A good deal would depend on whether or not the Director of Police took anyone into his confidence that night. If he did not, he would be aware that only he and the girl possessed this important piece of news. If a full account of the discovery appeared in the next morning's Daily Bugle, then, when that paper arrived in Vienna, or even before, if a synopsis were telegraphed to the Government, as it was morally certain to be, the Director would know at once that she was the correspondent of the newspaper whom he was so anxious to frighten out of Vienna. On the other hand, her friendship with the Princess von Steinheimer gave her such influence with the Chief's superiors, that, after the lesson she had taught him, he might hesitate to make any move against her. Then, again, the news that to-night belonged to two persons might on the morrow come to the knowledge of all the correspondents in Vienna, and her efforts, so far as the Bugle was concerned, would have been in vain. This consideration decided the girl, and, casting off all sign of hesitation, she sat down at her writing table and began the first chapter of the solution of the Vienna mystery. Her opening sentence was exceedingly diplomatic: "The Chief of Police of Vienna has made a most startling discovery." Beginning thus, she went on to details of the discovery she had that day made. When her account was finished and codified, she went down to her hostess and said,—

"Princess, I want a trustworthy man, who will take a long telegram to the central telegraph office, pay for it, and come away quickly before anyone can ask him inconvenient questions."

"Would it not be better to call a Dienstmanner?"

"A Dienstmanner? That is your commissionaire, or telegraph messenger? No, I think not. They are all numbered and can be traced."

"Oh, I know!" cried the Princess; "I will send our coachman. He will be out of his livery now, and he is a most reliable man; he will not answer inconvenient questions, or any others, even if they are asked."

To her telegram for publication Jennie had added a private despatch to the editor, stating that it would be rather inconvenient for her if he published the account next morning, but she left the decision entirely with him. Here was the news, and if he thought it worth the risk, he might hold it over; if not, he was to print it regardless of consequences.

As a matter of fact, the editor, with fear and trembling, held the news for a day, so that he might not embarrass his fair representative, but so anxious was he, that he sat up all night until the other papers were out, and he heaved a sigh of relief when, on glancing over them, he found that not one of them contained an inkling of the information locked up in his desk. And so he dropped off to sleep when the day was breaking. Next night he had nearly as much anxiety, for although the Bugle would contain the news, other papers might have it as well, and thus for the second time he waited in his office until the other sheets, wet from the press, were brought to him. Again fortune favoured him, and the triumph belonged to the Bugle alone.

The morning after her interview with the Director of Police, Jennie, taking a small hand-satchel, in which she placed the various bottles containing the different dusts which the chemist had separated, went abroad alone, and hailing a fiacre, gave the driver the address of Professor Carl Seigfried. The carriage of the Princess was always at the disposal of the girl, but on this occasion she did not wish to be embarrassed with so pretentious an equipage. The cab took her into a street lined with tall edifices and left her at the number she had given the driver. The building seemed to be one let out in flats and tenements; she mounted stair after stair, and only at the very top did she see the Professor's name painted on a door. Here she rapped several times without any attention being paid to her summons, but at last the door was opened partially by a man whom she took, quite accurately, to be the Professor himself. His head was white; and his face deeply wrinkled. He glared at her through his glasses, and said sharply, "Young lady, you have made a mistake; these are the rooms of Professor Carl Seigfried."

"It is Professor Carl Seigfried that I wish to see," replied the girl hurriedly, as the old man was preparing to shut the door.

"What do you want with him?"

"I want some information from him about explosives. I have been told that he knows more about explosives than any other man living."

"Quite right—he does. What then?"

"An explosion has taken place producing the most remarkable results.

They say that neither dynamite nor any other known force could have had such an effect on metals and minerals as this power has had."

"Ah, dynamite is a toy for children!" cried the old man, opening the door a little further and exhibiting an interest which had, up to that moment, been absent from his manner. "Well, where did this explosion take place? Do you wish me to go and see it?"

"Perhaps so, later on. At present I wish to show you some of its effects, but I don't propose to do this standing here in the passageway."

"Quite right—quite right," hastily ejaculated the old scientist, throwing the door wide open. "Of course, I am not accustomed to visits from fashionable young ladies, and I thought at first there had been a mistake; but if you have any real scientific problem, I shall be delighted to give my attention to it. What may appear very extraordinary to the lay mind will doubtless prove fully explainable by scientists. Come in, come in."

The old man shut the door behind her, and led her along a dark passage, into a large apartment, whose ceiling was the roof of the building. At first sight it seemed in amazing disorder. Huge as it was, it was cluttered with curious shaped machines and instruments. A twisted conglomeration of glass tubing, bent into fantastic tangles, stood on a central table, and had evidently been occupying the Professor's attention at the time he was interrupted. The place was lined with shelving, where the walls were not occupied by cupboards, and every shelf was burdened with bottles and apparatus of different kinds. Whatever care Professor Seigfried took of his apparatus, he seemed to have little for his furniture. There was hardly a decent chair in the room, except one deep arm-chair, covered with a tiger's skin, in which the Professor evidently took his ease while meditating or watching the progress of an experiment. This chair he did not offer to the young lady; in fact, he did not offer her a seat at all, but sank down on the tiger's skin himself, placed the tips of his fingers together, and glared at her through his glittering glasses.

"Now, young woman," he said abruptly, "what have you brought for me? Don't begin to chatter, for my time is valuable. Show me what you have brought, and I will tell you all about it; and most likely a very simple thing it is."

Jennie, interested in so rude a man, smiled, drew up the least decrepit bench she could find, and sat down, in spite of the angry mutterings of her irritated host. Then she opened her satchel, took out the small bottle of gold, and handed it to him without a word. The old man received it somewhat contemptuously, shook it backward and forward without extracting the cork, adjusted his glasses, then suddenly seemed to take a nervous interest in the material presented to him. He rose and went nearer the light. Drawing out the cork with trembling hands, he poured some of the contents into his open palm. The result was startling enough. The old man flung up his hands, letting the vial crash into a thousand pieces on the floor. He staggered forward, shrieking, "Ah, mein Gott—mein Gott!"

Then, to the consternation of Jennie, who had already risen in terror from her chair, the scientist plunged forward on his face. The girl had difficulty in repressing a shriek. She looked round hurriedly for a bell to ring, but apparently there was none. She tried to open the door and cry for help, but in her excitement could neither find handle nor latch. It seemed to be locked, and the key, doubtless, was in the Professor's pocket. She thought at first that he had dropped dead, but the continued moaning as he lay on the floor convinced her of her error. She bent over him anxiously and cried, "What can I do to help you?"

With a struggle he muttered, "The bottle, the bottle, in the cupboard behind you."

She hurriedly flung open the doors of the cupboard indicated, and found a bottle of brandy, and a glass, which she partly filled. The old man had with an effort struggled into a sitting posture, and she held the glass of fiery liquid to his pallid lips. He gulped down the brandy, and gasped, "I feel better now. Help me to my chair."

Assisting him to his feet, she supported him to his arm-chair, when he shook himself free, crying angrily, "Let me alone! Don't you see I am all right again?"

The girl stood aside, and the Professor dropped into his chair, his nervous hands vibrating on his knees. For a long interval nothing was said by either, and the girl at last seated herself on the bench she had formerly occupied. The next words the old man spoke were, "Who sent you here?"

"No one, I came of my own accord. I wished to meet someone who had a large knowledge of explosives, and Herr Feltz, the chemist, gave me your address."

"Herr Feltz! Herr Feltz!" he repeated. "So he sent you here?"

"No one sent me here," insisted the girl. "It is as I tell you. Herr Feltz merely gave me your address."

"Where did you get that powdered gold?"

"It came from the débris of an explosion."

"I know, you said that before. Where was the explosion? Who caused it?"

"That I don't know."

"Don't you know where the explosion was?"

"Yes, I know where the explosion was, but I don't know who caused it."

"Who sent you here?"

"I tell you no one sent me here."

"That is not true, the man who caused the explosion sent you here. You are his minion. What do you expect to find out from me?"

"I expect to learn what explosive was used to produce the result that seemed to have such a remarkable effect on you."

"Why do you say that? It had no effect on me. My heart is weak. I am subject to such attacks, and I ward them off with brandy. Some day they will kill me. Then you won't learn any secrets from a dead man, will you?"

"I hope, Professor Seigfried, that you have many years yet to live, and I must further add that I did not expect such a reception as I have received from a man of science, as I was told you were. If you have no information to give to me, very well, that ends it; all you have to do is to say so."

"Who sent you here?"

"No one, as I have repeated once or twice. If anyone had, I would give him my opinion of the errand when I got back. You refuse, then, to tell me anything about the explosive that powdered the gold?"

"Refuse? Of course I refuse! What did you expect? I suppose the man who sent you here thought, because you were an engaging young woman and I an old dotard, I would gabble to you the results of a life's work. Oh, no, no, no; but I am not an old dotard. I have many years to live yet."

"I hope so. Well, I must bid you good morning. I shall go to someone else."

The old man showed his teeth in a forbidding grin.

"It is useless. Your bottle is broken, and the material it contained is dissipated. Not a trace of it is left."

He waved his thin, emaciated hand in the air as he spoke.

"Oh, that doesn't matter in the least," said Jennie. "I have several other bottles here in my satchel."

The Professor placed his hands on the arms of his chair, and slowly raised himself to his feet.

"You have others," he cried, "other bottles? Let me see them—let me see them!"

"No," replied Jennie, "I won't."

With a speed which, after his recent collapse, Jennie had not expected, the Professor ambled round to the door and placed his back against it. The glasses over his eyes seemed to sparkle as if with fire. His talon-like fingers crooked rigidly. He breathed rapidly, and was evidently labouring under intense excitement.

"Who knows you came up to see me?" he whispered hoarsely, glaring at her.

Jennie, having arisen, stood there, smoothing down her perfectly fitting glove, and answered with a calmness she was far from feeling,—

"Who knows I am here? No one but the Director of Police."

"Oh, the Director of Police!" echoed the Professor, quite palpably abashed by the unexpected answer. The rigidity of his attitude relaxed, and he became once more the old man he had appeared as he sat in a heap in his chair. "You will excuse me," he muttered, edging round towards the chair again; "I was excited."

"I noticed that you were, Professor. But before you sit down again, please unlock that door."

"Why?" he asked, pausing on his way to the chair.

"Because I wish it open."

"And I," he said in a higher tone, "wish it to remain locked until we have come to some understanding. I can't let you go out now; but I shall permit you to go unmolested as soon as you have made some explanation to me."

"If you do not unlock the door immediately I shall take this machine and fling it through the front window out on the street. The crashing glass on the pavement will soon bring someone to my rescue, Professor, and, as I have a voice of my own and small hesitation about shouting, I shall have little difficulty in directing the strangers where to come."

As Jennie spoke she moved swiftly towards the table on which stood the strange aggregation of reflectors and bent glass tubing.

"No, no, no!" screamed the Professor, springing between her and the table. "Touch anything but that—anything but that. Do not disturb it an inch—there is danger—death not only to you and me, but perhaps to the whole city. Keep away from it!"

"Very well, then," said Jennie, stepping back in spite of her endeavour to maintain her self-control; "open the door. Open both doors and leave them so. After that, if you remain seated in your chair, I shall not touch the machine, nor shall I leave until I make the explanations you require, and you have answered some questions that I shall ask. But I must have a clear way to the stair, in case you should become excited again."

"I'll unlock the doors; I'll unlock both doors," replied the old man tremulously, fumbling about in his pockets for his keys. "But keep away from that machine, unless you want to bring swift destruction on us all."

With an eagerness that retarded his speed, the Professor, constantly looking over his shoulder at his visitor, unlocked the first door, then hastily he flung open the second, and tottered back to his chair, where he collapsed on the tiger skin, trembling and exhausted.

"We may be overheard," he whined. "One can never tell who may sneak quietly up the stair. I am surrounded by spies trying to find out what I am doing."

"Wait a moment," said Jennie.

She went quickly to the outer door, found that it closed with a spring latch, opened and shut it two or three times until she was perfectly familiar with its workings, then she closed it, drew the inner door nearly shut, and sat down.

"There," she said, "we are quite safe from interruption, Professor Seigfried; but I must request you not to move from your chair."

"I have no intention of doing so," murmured the old man. "Who sent you? You said you would tell me. I think you owe me an explanation."

"I think you owe me one," replied the girl. "As I told you before, no one sent me. I came here entirely of my own accord, and I shall endeavour to make clear to you exactly why I came. Some time ago there occurred in this city a terrific explosion—"

"Where? When?" exclaimed the old man, placing his hands on the arms of his chair, as if he would rise to his feet.

"Sit where you are," commanded Jennie firmly, "and I shall tell you all I can about it. The Government, for reasons of its own, desires to keep the fact of this explosion a secret, and thus very few people outside of official circles know anything about it. I am trying to discover the cause of that disaster."

"Are you—are you working on behalf of the Government?" asked the old man eagerly, a tremor of fear in his quavering voice.

"No. I am conducting my investigations quite independently of the Government."

"But why? But why? That is what I don't understand."

"I would very much rather not answer that question."

"But that question—everything is involved in that question. I must know why you are here. If you are not in the employ of the Government, in whose employ are you?"

"If I tell you," said Jennie with some hesitation, "will you keep what I say a secret?"

"Yes, yes, yes!" cried the scientist impatiently.

"Well, I am in the service of a London daily newspaper."

"I see, I see; and they have sent you here to publish broadcast over the world all you can find out of my doings. I knew you were a spy the moment I saw you. I should never have let you in."

"My dear sir, the London paper is not even aware of your existence. They have not sent me to you at all. They have sent me to learn, if possible, the cause of the explosion I spoke of. I took some of the débris to Herr Feltz to analyze it, and he said he had never seen gold, iron, feldspar, and all that, reduced to such fine, impalpable grains as was the case with the sample I left with him. I then asked him who in Vienna knew most about explosives, and he gave me your address. That is why I am here."

"But the explosion—you have not told me when and where it occurred!"

"That, as I have said, is a Government secret."

"But you stated you are not in the Government employ, therefore it can be no breach of confidence if you let me have full particulars."

"I suppose not. Very well, then, the explosion occurred after midnight on the seventeenth in the vault of the Treasury."

The old man, in spite of the prohibition, rose uncertainly to his feet.

Jennie sprang up and said menacingly, "Stay where you are!"

"I am not going to touch you. If you are so suspicious of every move I make, then go yourself and bring me what I want. There is a map of Vienna pinned against the wall yonder. Bring it to me."

Jennie proceeded in the direction indicated. It was an ordinary map of the city of Vienna, and as Jennie took it down she noticed that across the southern part of the city a semi-circular line in pencil had been drawn. Examining it more closely, she saw that the stationary part of the compass had been placed on the spot where stood the building which contained the Professor's studio. She paid closer attention to the pencil mark and observed that it passed through the Treasury building.

"Don't look at that map!" shrieked the Professor, beating the air with his hands. "I asked you to bring it to me. Can't you do a simple action like that without spying about?"

Jennie rapidly unfastened the paper from the wall and brought it to him. The scientist scrutinized it closely, adjusting his glasses the better to see, then deliberately tore the map into fragments, numerous and minute. He rose—and this time Jennie made no protest—went to the window, opened it, and flung the fluttering bits of paper out into the air, the strong wind carrying them far over the roofs of Vienna. Closing the casement, he came back to his chair.

"Was—was anyone hurt at this explosion?" he asked presently.

"Yes, four men were killed instantly, a dozen were seriously injured and are now in hospital."

"Oh, my God—my God!" cried the old man, covering his face with his hands, swaying from side to side in his chair like a man tortured with agony and remorse. At last he lifted a face that had grown more pinched and yellow within the last few minutes.

"I can tell you nothing," he said, moistening his parched lips.

"You mean that you will tell me nothing, for I see plainly that you know everything."

"I knew nothing of any explosion until you spoke of it. What have I to do with the Treasury or the Government?"

"That is just what I want to know."

"It is absurd. I am no conspirator, but a man of learning."

"Then you have nothing to fear, Herr Seigfried. If you are innocent, why are you so loth to give me any assistance in this matter?"

"It has nothing to do with me. I am a scientist—I am a scientist. All I wish is to be left alone with my studies. I have nothing to do with governments or newspapers, or anything belonging to them."

Jennie sat tracing a pattern on the dusty floor with the point of her parasol. She spoke very quietly:—

"The pencilled line which you drew on the map of Vienna passed through the Treasury building; the centre of the circle was this garret. Why did you draw that pencilled semi-circle? Why were you anxious that I should not see you had done so? Why did you destroy the map?"

Professor Seigfried sat there looking at her with dropped jaw, but he made no reply.

"If you will excuse my saying so," the girl went on, "you are acting very childishly. It is evident to me that you are no criminal, yet if the Director of Police had been in my place he would have arrested you long ago, and that merely because of your own foolish actions."

"The map proved nothing," he said at last, haltingly, "and besides, both you and the Director will now have some difficulty in finding it."

"That is further proof of your folly. The Director doesn't need to find it. I am here to testify that I saw the map, saw the curved line passing through the Treasury, and saw you destroy what you thought was an incriminating piece of evidence. It would be much better if you would deal as frankly with me as I have done with you. Then I shall give you the best advice I can—if my advice will be of any assistance to you."

"Yes, and publish it to all the world."

"It will have to be published to all the world in any case, for, if I leave here without full knowledge, I will simply go to the police office and there tell what I have learned in this room."

"And if I do speak, you will still go to the Director of the Police and tell him what you have discovered."

"No, I give you my word that I will not."

"What guarantee have I of that?" asked the old man suspiciously.

"No guarantee at all except my word!"

"Will you promise not to print in your paper what I tell you?"

"No, I cannot promise that!"

"Still, the newspaper doesn't matter," continued the scientist. "The story would be valueless to you, because no one would believe it. There is little use in printing a story in a newspaper that will be laughed at, is there? However, I think you are honest, otherwise you would have promised not to print a line of what I tell you, and then I should have known you were lying. It was as easy to promise that as to say you would not tell the Director of Police. I thought at first some scientific rival had sent you here to play the spy on me, and learn what I was doing. I assure you I heard nothing about the explosion you speak of, yet I was certain it had occurred somewhere along that line which I drew on the map. I had hoped it was not serious, and begun to believe it was not. The anxiety of the last month has nearly driven me insane, and, as you say quite truly, my actions have been childish." The old man in his excitement had risen from his chair and was now pacing up and down the room, running his fingers distractedly through his long white hair, and talking more to himself than to his auditor.

Jennie had edged her chair nearer to the door, and had made no protest against his rising, fearing to interrupt his flow of talk and again arouse his suspicions.

"I have no wish to protect my inventions. I have never taken out a patent in my life. What I discover I give freely to the world, but I will not be robbed of my reputation as a scientist. I want my name to go down to posterity among those of the great discoverers. You talked just now of going to the police and telling them what you knew. Foolish creature! You could no more have gone to the central police office without my permission, or against my will, than you could go to the window and whistle back those bits of paper I scattered to the winds. Before you reached the bottom of the stairs I could have laid Vienna in a mass of ruins. Yes, I could in all probability have blown up the entire Empire of Austria. The truth is, that I do not know the limit of my power, nor dare I test it."

"Oh, this is a madman!" thought Jennie, as she edged still nearer to the door. The old man paused in his walk and turned fiercely upon her.

"You don't believe me?" he said.

"No, I do not," she answered, the colour leaving her cheeks.

The aged wizard gave utterance to a hideous chuckle. He took from one of his numerous shelves a hammer-head without the handle, and for a moment Jennie thought he was going to attack her; but he merely handed the metal to her and said,—

"Break that in two. Place it between your palms and grind it to powder."

"You know that is absurd; I cannot do it."

"Why can't you do it?"

"Because it is of steel."

"That is no reason. Why can't you do it?"

He glared at her fiercely over his glasses, and she saw in his wild eye all the enthusiasm of an instructor enlightening a pupil.

"I'll tell you why you can't do it; because every minute particle of it is held together by an enormous force. It may be heated red-hot and beaten into this shape and that, but still the force hangs on as tenaciously as the grip of a giant. Now suppose I had some substance, a drop of which, placed on that piece of iron, would release the force which holds the particles together—what would happen?"

"I don't know," replied Jennie.

"Oh, yes you do!" cried the Professor impatiently; "but you are like every other woman—you won't take the trouble to think. What would happen is this. The force that held the particles together would be released, and the hammer would fall to powder like that gold you showed me. The explosion that followed, caused by the sudden release of the power, would probably wreck this room and extinguish both our lives. You understand that, do you not?"

"Yes, I think I do."

"Well, here is something you won't understand, and probably won't believe when you hear it. There is but one force in this world and but one particle of matter. There is only one element, which is the basis of everything. All the different shapes and conditions of things that we see are caused by a mere variation of that force in conjunction with numbers of that particle. Am I getting beyond your depth?"

"I am afraid you are, Professor."

"Of course; I know what feeble brains the average woman is possessed of; still, try and keep that in your mind. Now listen to this. I have discovered how to disunite that force and that particle. I can, with a touch, fling loose upon this earth a giant whose strength is irresistible and immeasurable."

"Then why object to making your discovery public?"

"In the first place, because there are still a thousand things and more to be learned along such a line of investigation. The moment a man announces his discoveries, he is first ridiculed, then, when the truth of what he affirms is proven, there rise in every part of the world other men who say that they knew all about it ten years ago, and will prove it too—at least, far enough to delude a gullible world; in the second because I am a humane man, I hesitate to spread broadcast a knowledge that would enable any fool to destroy the universe. Then there is a third reason. There is another who, I believe, has discovered how to make this force loosen its grip on the particle—that is Keely, of Philadelphia, in the United States—"

"What! You don't mean the Keely motor man?" cried Jennie, laughing. "That arrant humbug! Why, all the papers in the world have exposed his ridiculous pretensions; he has done nothing but spend other people's money."

"Yes, the newspapers have ridiculed him. Human beings have, since the beginning of the world, stoned their prophets. Nevertheless, he has liberated a force that no gauge made by man can measure. He has been boastful, if you like, and has said that with a teacupful of water he would drive a steamship across the Atlantic. I have been silent, working away with my eye on him, and he has been working away with his eye on me, for each knows what the other is doing. If either of us discovers how to control this force, then that man's name will go down to posterity for ever. He has not yet been able to do it; neither have I. There is still another difference between us. He appears to be able to loosen that force in his own presence; I can only do it at a distance. All my experiments lately have been in the direction of making modifications with this machine, so as to liberate the force within the compass, say, of this room; but the problem has baffled me. The invisible rays which this machine sends out, and which will penetrate stone, iron, wood, or any other substance, must unite at a focus, and I have not been able to bring that focus nearer me than something over half a mile. Last summer I went to an uninhabited part of Switzerland and there continued my experiments. I blew up at will rocks and boulders on the mountain sides, the distances varying from a mile to half a mile. I examined the results of the disintegration, and when you came in and showed me that gold, I recognized at once that someone had discovered the secret I have been trying to fathom for the last ten years. I thought that perhaps you had come from Keely. I am now convinced that the explosion you speak of in the Treasury was caused by myself. This machine, which you so recklessly threatened to throw out of the window, accidentally slipped from its support when I was working here some time after midnight on the seventeenth. I placed it immediately as you see it now, where it throws its rays into mid-air, and is consequently harmless; but I knew an explosion must have taken place in Vienna somewhere within the radius of half a mile. I drew the pencilled semi-circle that you saw on the map of Vienna, for in my excitement in placing the machine upright I had not noticed exactly where it had pointed, but I knew that, along the line I had drawn, an explosion must have occurred, and could only hope that it had not been a serious one, which it seems it was. I waited and waited, hardly daring to leave my attic, but hearing no news of any disaster, I was torn between the anxiety that would naturally come to any humane man in my position who did not wish to destroy life, and the fear that, if nothing had occurred, I had not actually made the discovery I thought I had made. You spoke of my actions being childish; but when I realized that I had myself been the cause of the explosion, a fear of criminal prosecution came over me. Not that I should object to imprisonment if they would allow me to continue my experiments; but that, doubtless, they would not do, for the authorities know nothing of science, and care less."

In spite of her initial scepticism, Jennie found herself gradually coming to believe in the efficiency of the harmless-looking mechanism of glass and iron which she saw on the table before her, and a sensation of horror held her spellbound as she gazed at it. Its awful possibilities began slowly to develop in her mind, and she asked breathlessly,—"What would happen if you were to turn that machine and point it towards the centre of the earth?"

"I told you what would happen. Vienna would lie in ruins, and possibly the whole Austrian Empire, and perhaps some adjoining countries would become a mass of impalpable dust. It may be that the world itself would dissolve. I cannot tell what the magnitude of the result might be, for I have not dared to risk the experiment."

"Oh, this is too frightful to think about," she cried. "You must destroy the machine, Professor, and you must never make another."

"What! And give up the hope that my name will descend to posterity?"

"Professor Seigfried, when once this machine becomes known to the world, there will be no posterity for your name to descend to. With the present hatred of nation against nation, with different countries full of those unimprisoned maniacs whom we call Jingoes—men preaching the hatred of one people against another—how long do you think the world will last when once such knowledge is abroad in it?"

The Professor looked longingly at the machine he had so slowly and painfully constructed.

"It would be of much use to humanity if it were but benevolently employed. With the coal fields everywhere diminishing, it would supply a motive force for the universe that would last through the ages."

"Professor Seigfried," exclaimed Jennie earnestly, "when the Lord permits a knowledge of that machine to become common property, it is His will that the end of the world shall come."

The Professor said nothing, but stood with deeply wrinkled brow, gazing earnestly at the mechanism. In his hand was the hammer-head which he had previously given to the girl; his arm went up and down as if he were estimating its weight; then suddenly, without a word of warning, he raised it and sent it crashing through the machine, whose splintering glass fell with a musical tinkle on the floor.

Jennie gave a startled cry, and with a low moan the Professor struggled to his chair and fell, rather than sat down, in it. A ghastly pallor overspread his face, and the girl in alarm ran again to the cupboard, poured out some brandy and offered it to him, then tried to pour it down his throat, but his tightly set teeth resisted her efforts. She chafed his rigid hands, and once he opened his eyes, slowly shaking his head.

"Try to sip this brandy," she said, seeing his jaws relax.

"It is useless," he murmured with difficulty. "My life was in the instrument, as brittle as the glass. I have—"

He could say no more. Jennie went swiftly downstairs to the office of a physician, on the first floor, which she had noticed as she came up.

The medical man, who knew of the philosopher, but was not personally acquainted with him, for the Professor had few friends, went up the steps three at a time, and Jennie followed him more slowly. He met the girl at the door of the attic.

"It is useless," he said. "Professor Seigfried is dead; and it is my belief that in his taking away Austria has lost her greatest scientist."

"I am sure of it," answered the girl, with trembling voice; "but perhaps after all it is for the best."

"I doubt that," said the doctor. "I never feel so like quarrelling with Providence as when some noted man is removed right in the midst of his usefulness."

"I am afraid," replied Jennie solemnly, "that we have hardly reached a state of development that would justify us in criticizing the wisdom of Providence. In my own short life I have seen several instances where it seemed that Providence intervened for the protection of His creatures; and even the sudden death of Professor Seigfried does not shake my belief that Providence knows best."

She turned quickly away and went down the stairs in some haste. At the outer door she heard the doctor call down, "I must have your name and address, please."

But Jennie did not pause to answer. She had no wish to undergo cross-examination at an inquest, knowing that if she told the truth she would not be believed, while if she attempted to hide it, unexpected personal inconvenience might arise from such a course. She ran rapidly to the street corner, hailed a fiacre and drove to a distant part of the city; then she dismissed the cab, went to a main thoroughfare, took a tramcar to the centre of the town, and another cab to the Palace.

CHAPTER XVII. JENNIE ENGAGES A ROOM IN A SLEEPING CAR.

Jennie had promised Professor Seigfried not to communicate with the Director of Police, and she now wondered whether it would be breaking her word, or not, if she let that official know the result of her investigation, when it would make no difference, one way or the other, to the Professor. If Professor Seigfried could have foreseen his own sudden death, would he not, she asked herself, have preferred her to make public all she knew of him? for had he not constantly reiterated that fame, and the consequent transmission of his name to posterity, was what he worked for? Then there was this consideration: if the Chief of Police was not told how the explosion had been caused, his fruitless search would go futilely on, and, doubtless, in the course of police inquiry, many innocent persons would be arrested, put to inconvenience and expense, and there was even a chance that one or more, who had absolutely nothing to do with the affair, might be imprisoned for life. She resolved, therefore, to tell the Director of the Police all she knew, which she would not have done had Professor Seigfried been alive. She accordingly sent a messenger for the great official, and just as she had begun to relate to the impatient Princess what had happened, he was announced. The three of them held convention in Jennie's drawing-room with locked doors.

"I am in a position," began Jennie, "to tell you how the explosion in the Treasury was caused and who caused it; but before doing so you must promise to grant me two favours, each of which is in your power to bestow without inconvenience."

"What are they?" asked the Director of Police cautiously.

"To tell what they are is to tell part of my story. You must first promise blindly, and afterwards keep your promise faithfully."

"Those are rather unusual terms, Miss Baxter," said the Chief; "but I accede to them, the more willingly as we have found that all the gold is still in the Treasury, as you said it was."

"Very well, then, the first favour is that I shall not be called to give testimony when an inquest is held on the body of Professor Carl Seigfried."

"You amaze me!" cried the Director; "how did you know he was dead? I had news of it only a moment before I left my office."

"I was with him when he died," said Jennie simply, which statement drew forth an exclamation of surprise from both the Princess and the Director. "My next request is that you destroy utterly a machine which stands on a table near the centre of the Professor's room. Perhaps the instrument is already disabled—I believe it is—but, nevertheless, I shall not rest content until you have seen that every vestige of it is made away with, because the study of what is left of it may enable some other scientist to put it in working order again. I entreat you to attend to this matter yourself. I will go with you, if you wish me to, and point out the instrument in case it has been moved from its position."

"The room is sealed," said the Director, "and nothing will be touched until I arrive there. What is the nature of this instrument?"

"It is of a nature so deadly and destructive that, if it got into the hands of an anarchist, he could, alone, lay the city of Vienna in ruins."

"Good heavens!" cried the horrified official, whose bane was the anarchist, and Jennie, in mentioning this particular type of criminal, had builded better than she knew. If she had told him that the Professor's invention might enable Austria to conquer all the surrounding nations, there is every chance that the machine would have been carefully preserved.

"The explosion in the Treasury vaults," continued Jennie, "was accidentally caused by this instrument, although the machine at the moment was in a garret half a mile away. You saw the terrible effect of that explosion; imagine, then, the destruction it would cause in the hands of one of those anarchists who are so reckless of consequences."

"I shall destroy the instrument with my own hands," asserted the Director fervently, mopping his pallid brow.

Jennie then went on, to the increasing astonishment of the Princess and the Director, and related every detail of her interview with the late professor Carl Seigfried.

"I shall go at once and annihilate that machine," said the Director, rising when the recital was finished. "I shall see to that myself. Then, after the inquest, I shall give an order that everything in the attic is to be destroyed. I wish that every scientific man on the face of the earth could be safely placed behind prison bars."

"I am afraid that wouldn't do much good," replied Jennie, "unless you could prevent chemicals being smuggled in. The scientists would probably reduce your prison to powder, and walk calmly out through the dust."

Mr. Hardwick had told Jennie that if she solved the Vienna mystery she would make a European reputation for the Daily Bugle. Jennie did more than was expected of her, yet the European reputation which the Bugle established was not one to be envied. It is true that the account printed of the cause of the explosion, dramatically completed with the Professor's tragically sudden death, caused a great sensation in London. The comic papers of the week were full of illustrations showing the uses to which the Professor's instrument might be put. To say that any sane man in England believed a word of the article would be to cast an undeserved slight upon the intelligence of the British public. No one paused to think that if a newspaper had published an account of what could be done by the Röentgen rays, without being able to demonstrate practically the truth of the assertions made, the contribution would have been laughed at. If some years ago a newspaper had stated that a man in York listened to the voice of a friend at that moment standing in London, and was not only able to hear what his friend said, but could actually recognize the voice speaking in an ordinary tone, and then if the paper had added that, unfortunately, the instrument which accomplished this had been destroyed, people would have denounced the sensational nature of modern journalism.

Letters poured in upon the editor, saying that while, as a general rule, the writers were willing to stand the ordinary lie of commerce daily printed in the sheet, there was a limit to their credulity and they objected to be taken for drivelling imbeciles. To complete the discomfiture of the Daily Bugle, the Government of Austria published an official statement, which Reuter and the special correspondents scattered broadcast over the earth. The statement was written in that calm, serious, and consistent tone which diplomatists use when uttering a falsehood of more than ordinary dimensions.

Irresponsible rumours had been floating about (the official proclamation began) to the effect that there had been an explosion in the Treasury at Vienna. It had been stated that a large quantity of gold had been stolen, and that a disaster of some kind had occurred in the Treasury vaults. Then a ridiculous story had been printed which asserted that Professor Seigfried, one of Austria's honoured dead, had in some manner that savoured of the Black Art, encompassed this wholesale destruction. The Government now begged to make the following declarations: First, not a penny had been stolen out of the Treasury; second, the so-called war-chest was intact; third, the two hundred million florins reposed securely within the bolted doors of the Treasury vaults; fourth, the coins were not, as had been alleged, those belonging to various countries, which was a covert intimation that Austria had hostile intent against one or the other of those friendly nations. The whole coinage in this falsely named war-chest, which was not a war-chest at all, but merely the receptacle of a reserve fund which Austria possessed, was entirely in Austrian coinage; fifth, in order that these sensational and disquieting scandals should be set at rest, the Government announced that it intended to weigh this gold upon a certain date, and it invited representatives of the Press, from Russia, Germany, France, and England to witness this weighing.

The day after this troy-weight function had taken place in Vienna, long telegraphic accounts of it appeared in the English press, and several solemn leading articles were put forward in the editorial columns, which, without mentioning the name of the Daily Bugle, deplored the voracity of the sensational editor, who respected neither the amity which should exist between friendly nations, nor the good name of the honoured and respected dead, in his wolfish hunt for the daily scandal. Nothing was too high-spiced or improbable for him to print. He traded on the supposed gullibility of a fickle public. But, fortunately, in the long run, these staid sheets asserted, such actions recoiled upon the head of him who promulgated them. Sensational journals merited and received the scathing contempt of all honest men. Later on, one of the reviews had an article entitled "Some Aspects of Modern Journalism," which battered in the head of the Daily Bugle as with a sledge hammer, and in one of the quarterlies a professor at Cambridge showed the absurdity of the alleged invention from a scientific point of view.

"I swear," cried Mr. Hardwick, as he paced up and down his room, "that I shall be more careful after this in the handling of truth; it is a most dangerous thing to meddle with. If you tell the truth about a man, you are mulcted in a libel suit, and if you tell the truth about a nation, the united Press of the country are down upon you. Ah, well, it makes the battle of life all the more interesting, and we are baffled to fight better, as Browning says."

The editor had sent for Miss Baxter, and she now sat by his desk while he paced nervously to and fro. The doors were closed and locked so that they might not be interrupted, and she knew by the editor's manner that something important was on hand. Jennie had returned to London after a month's stay in Vienna, and had been occupied for a week at her old routine work in the office.

"Now, Miss Baxter," said the editor, when he had proclaimed his distrust of the truth as a workable material in journalism, "I have a plan to set before you, and when you know what it is, I am quite prepared to hear you refuse to have anything to do with it. And, remember, if you do undertake it, there is but one chance in a million of your succeeding. It is on this one chance that I propose now to send you to St. Petersburg—"

"To St. Petersburg!" echoed the girl in dismay.

"Yes," said the editor, mistaking the purport of her ejaculation, "it is a very long trip, but you can travel there in great comfort, and I want you to spare no expense in obtaining for yourself every luxury that the various railway lines afford during your journey to St. Petersburg and back."

"And what am I to go to St. Petersburg for?" murmured Jennie faintly.

"Merely for a letter. Here is what has happened, and what is happening.

I shall mention no names, but at present a high and mighty personage in Russia, who is friendly to Great Britain, has written a private letter, making some proposals to a certain high and mighty personage in England, who is friendly to Russia. This communication is entirely unofficial; neither Government is supposed to know anything at all about it. As a matter of fact, the Russian Government have a suspicion, and the British Government have a certainty, that such a document will shortly be in transit. Nothing may come of it, or great things may come of it. Now on the night of the 21st, in one of the sleeping cars leaving St. Petersburg by the Nord Express for Berlin, there will travel a special messenger having this letter in his possession. I want you to take passage by that same train and secure a compartment near the messenger, if possible. This messenger will be a man in whom the respective parties to the negotiation have implicit confidence. I wish I knew his name, but I don't; still, the chances are that he is leaving London for St. Petersburg about this time, and so you might keep your eyes open on your journey there, for, if you discovered him to be your fellow-passenger, it might perhaps make the business that comes after easier. You see this letter," continued the editor, taking from a drawer in his desk a large envelope, the flap of which was secured by a great piece of stamped sealing-wax. "This merely contains a humble ordinary copy of to-day's issue of the Bugle, but in outside appearance it might be taken for a duplicate of the letter which is to leave St. Petersburg on the 21st. Now, what I would like you to do is to take this envelope in your hand-bag, and if, on the journey back to London, you have an opportunity of securing the real letter, and leaving this in its place, you will have accomplished the greatest service you have yet done for the paper."

"Oh!" cried Jennie, rising, "I couldn't think of that, Mr. Hardwick—I couldn't think of doing it. It is nothing short of highway robbery!"

"I know it looks like that," pleaded Hardwick; "but listen to me. If I were going to open the letter and use its contents, then you might charge me with instigating theft. The fact is, the letter will not be delayed; it will reach the hands of the high and mighty personage in England quite intact. The only difference is that you will be its bearer instead of the messenger they send for it."

"You expect to open the letter, then, in some surreptitious way—some way that will not be noticed afterwards? Oh, I couldn't do it, Mr. Hardwick."

"My dear girl, you are jumping at conclusions. I shall amaze you when I tell you that I know already practically what the contents of that letter are."

"Then what is the use of going to all this expense and trouble trying to steal it?"

"Don't say 'steal it,' Miss Baxter. I'll tell you what my motive is. There is an official in England who has gone out of his way to throw obstacles in mine. This is needless and irritating, for generally I manage to get the news I am in quest of; but in several instances, owing to his opposition, I have not only not got the news, but other papers have. Now, since the general raking we have had over this Austrian business, quite aside from the fact that we published the exact truth, this stupid old official duffer has taken it upon himself to be exceedingly sneering and obnoxious to me, and I confess I want to take him down a peg. He hasn't any idea that I know as much about this business as I do—in fact, he thinks it is an absolute secret; yet, if I liked, I could to-morrow nullify all the arrangements by simply publishing what is already in my possession, which action on my part would create a furore in this country, and no less of a furore in Russia. For the sake of amity between nations, which I am accused of disregarding, I hold my hand.

"Now, if you get possession of that communication, I want you to telegraph to me while you are en route for London, and I will meet you at the terminus; then I shall take the document direct to this official, even before the regular messenger has time to reach him. I shall say to the official, 'There is the message from the high personage in Russia to the high personage in England. If you want the document, I will give it to you, but it must be understood that you are to be a little less friendly to certain other newspapers, and a little more friendly to mine, in future.'"

"And suppose he refuses your terms?"

"He won't refuse them; but if he does I shall hand him the envelope just the same."

"Well, honestly, Mr. Hardwick, I don't think your scheme worth the amount of money it will cost, and, besides, the chance of my getting hold of the packet, which will doubtless be locked safely within a despatch box, and constantly under the eye of the messenger, is most remote."

"I am more than willing to risk all that if you will undertake the journey. You speak lightly of my scheme, but that is merely because you do not understand the situation. Everything you have heretofore done has been of temporary advantage to the paper; but if you carry this off, I expect the benefit to the Bugle will be lasting. It will give me a standing with certain officials that I have never before succeeded in getting. In the first place, it will make them afraid of me, and that of itself is a powerful lever when we are trying to get information which they are anxious to give to some other paper."

"Very well, Mr. Hardwick, I will try; though I warn you to expect nothing but failure. In everything else I have endeavoured to do, I have felt confident of success from the beginning. In this instance I am as sure I shall fail."

"As I told you, Miss Baxter, the project is so difficult that your failure, if you do fail, will merely prove it to have been impossible, because I am sure that if anyone on earth could carry the project to success, you are that person; and, furthermore, I am very much obliged to you for consenting to attempt such a mission."

And thus it was that Jennie Baxter found herself in due time in the great capital of the north, with a room in the Hotel de l'Europe overlooking the Nevski Prospect. In ordinary circumstances she would have enjoyed a visit to St. Petersburg; but now she was afraid to venture out, being under the apprehension that at any moment she might meet Lord Donal Stirling face to face, and that he would recognize her; therefore she remained discreetly in her room, watching the strange street scenes from her window. She found herself scrutinizing everyone who had the appearance of being an Englishman, and she had to confess to a little qualm of disappointment when the person in question proved to be some other than Lord Donal; in fact, during her short stay at St. Petersburg she saw nothing of the young man.

Jennie went, on the evening of her arrival, to the offices of the Sleeping Car Company, to secure a place in one of the carriages that left at six o'clock on the evening of the 21st. Her initial difficulty met her when she learned there were several sleeping cars on that train, and she was puzzled to know which to select. She stood there, hesitating, with the plans of the carriages on the table before her.

"You have ample choice," said the clerk; "seats are not usually booked so long in advance, and only two places have been taken in the train, so far."

"I should like to be in a carriage containing some English people," said the girl, not knowing what excuse to give for her hesitation.

"Then let me recommend this car, for one compartment has been taken by the British Embassy—Room C, near the centre, marked with a cross."

"Ah, well, I will take the compartment next to it—Room D, isn't it?" said Jennie.

"Oh, I am sorry to say that also has been taken. Those are the two which are bespoken. I will see under what name Room D has been booked. Probably its occupant is English also. But I can give you Room B, on the other side of the one reserved by the Embassy. It is a two-berth room, Nos. 5 and 6."

"That will do quite as well," said Jennie.

The clerk looked up the order book, and then said,—

"It is not recorded here by whom Room D was reserved. As a usual thing," he continued, lowering his voice almost to a whisper and looking furtively over his shoulder, "when no name is marked down, that means the Russian police. So, you see, by taking the third room you will not only be under the shadow of the British Embassy, but also under the protection of Russia. Do you wish one berth only, or the whole room? It is a two-berth compartment."

"I desire the whole room, if you please."

She paid the price and departed, wondering if the other room had really been taken by the police, and whether the authorities were so anxious for the safety of the special messenger that they considered it necessary to protect him to the frontier. If, in addition to the natural precautions of the messenger, there was added the watchfulness of one or two suspicious Russian policemen, then would her difficult enterprise become indeed impossible. On the other hand, the ill-paid policemen might be amenable to the influence of money, and as she was well supplied with the coin of the realm, their presence might be a help rather than a hindrance. All in all, she had little liking for the task she had undertaken, and the more she thought of it, the less it commended itself to her. Nevertheless, having pledged her word to the editor, if failure came it would be through no fault of hers.

CHAPTER XVIII. JENNIE ENDURES A TERRIBLE NIGHT JOURNEY.

Jennie went early to the station on the night of the 21st and entered the sleeping car as soon as she was allowed to do so. The conductor seemed unaccountably flustered at her anxiety to get to her room, and he examined her ticket with great care; then, telling her to follow him, brought her to Room B, in which were situated berths 5 and 6, upper and lower. The berths were not made up, and the room showed one seat, made to accommodate two persons. The conductor went out on the platform again, and Jennie, finding herself alone in the carriage, walked up and down the narrow passage-way at the side, to get a better idea of her surroundings.

Room C, next to her own, was the one taken by the British Embassy. Room D, still further on, was the one that appeared to have been retained by the police. She stood for a few moments by the broad plate-glass window that lined the passage and looked out at the crowded platform. For a time she watched the conductor, who appeared to be gazing anxiously towards the direction from which passengers streamed, as if looking for someone in particular. Presently a big man, a huge overcoat belted round him, with a stern bearded face—looking, the girl thought, typically Russian—strode up to the conductor and spoke earnestly with him. Then the two turned to the steps of the car, and Jennie fled to her narrow little room, closing the door all but about an inch. An instant later the two men came in, speaking together in French. The larger man had a gruff voice and spoke the language in a way that showed it was not native to him.

"When did you learn that he had changed his room?" asked the man with the gruff voice.

"Only this afternoon," replied the conductor.

"Did you bore holes between that and the adjoining compartment?"

"Yes, Excellency; but Azof did not tell me whether you wanted the holes at the top or the bottom."

"At the bottom, of course," replied the Russian. "Any fool might have known that. The gas must rise, not fall; then when he feels its effect and tumbles down, he will be in a denser layer of it, whereas, if we put it in the top, and he fell down, he would come into pure air, and so might make his escape. You did not bore the hole over the top berth, I hope?"

"Yes, Excellency, but I bored one at the bottom also."

"Oh, very well, we can easily stop the one at the top. Have you fastened the window? for the first thing these English do is to open a window."

"The window is securely fastened, your Excellency, unless he breaks the glass."

"Oh, he will not think of doing that until it is too late. The English are a law-abiding people. How many other passengers are there in the car?"

"Oh, I forgot to tell you, Excellency, the Room B has been taken by an English lady, who is there now."

"Ten thousand devils!" cried the Russian in a hoarse whisper. "Why did you not say that before?"

The voices now fell to so low a murmur that Jennie could not distinguish the words spoken. A moment later there was a rap at her door, and she had presence of mind enough to get in the further corner, and say in a sleepy voice,—

"Come in!"

The conductor opened the door.

"Votre billet, s'il vous plaît, madame."

"Can't you speak English?" asked Jennie.

The conductor merely repeated his question, and as Jennie was shaking her head the big Russian looked over the conductor's shoulder and said in passable English,—

"He is asking for your ticket, madam. Do you not speak French?" In answer to this direct question Jennie, fumbling in her purse for her ticket, replied,—

"I speak English, and I have already shown him my ticket." She handed her broad-sheet sleeping-car ticket to the Russian, who had pushed the conductor aside and now stood within the compartment.

"There has been a mistake," he said. "Room C is the one that has been reserved for you."

"I am sure there isn't any mistake," said Jennie. "I booked berths 5 and 6. See, there are the numbers," pointing to the metallic plates by the door, "and here are the same numbers on the ticket."

The Russian shook his head.

"The mistake has been made at the office of the Sleeping Car Company. I am a director of the Company."

"Oh, are you?" asked Jennie innocently. "Is Room C as comfortable as this one?"

"It is a duplicate of this one, madam, and is more comfortable, because it is nearer the centre of the car."

"Well, there is no mistake about my reserving the two berths, is there?"

"Oh, no, madam, the room is entirely at your disposal."

"Well, then, in that case," said Jennie, "I have no objection to making a change."

She knew that she would be compelled to change, no matter what her ticket recorded, so she thought it best to play the simple maiden abroad, and make as little fuss as possible about the transfer. She had to rearrange the car in her mind. She was now in Room C, which had been first reserved by the British Embassy. It was evident that at the last moment the messenger had decided to take Room A, a four-berth compartment at the end of the car. The police then would occupy Room B, which she had first engaged, and, from the bit of conversation she had overheard, Jennie was convinced that they intended to kill or render insensible the messenger who bore the important letter. The police were there not to protect, but to attack. This amazing complication in the plot concentrated all the girl's sympathies on the unfortunate man who was messenger between two great personages, even though he travelled apparently under the protection of the British Embassy at St. Petersburg. The fact, to put it baldly, that she had intended to rob him herself, if opportunity occurred, rose before her like an accusing ghost. "I shall never undertake anything like this again," she cried to herself, "never, never," and now she resolved to make reparation to the man she had intended to injure. She would watch for him until he came down the passage, and then warn him by relating what she had heard. She had taken off her hat on entering the room; now she put it on hurriedly, thrusting a long pin through it. As she stood up, there was a jolt of the train that caused her to sit down again somewhat hurriedly. Passing her window she saw the lights of the station; the train was in motion. "Thank Heaven!" she cried fervently, "he is too late. Those plotting villains will have all their trouble for nothing."

She glanced upwards towards the ceiling and noticed a hole about an inch in diameter bored in the thin wooden partition between her compartment and the next. Turning to the wall behind her she saw that another hole had been bored in a similar position through to Room B. The car had been pretty thoroughly prepared for the work in hand, and Jennie laughed softly to herself as she pictured the discomfiture of the conspirators. The train was now rushing through the suburbs of St. Petersburg, when Jennie was startled by hearing a stranger's voice say in French,—

"Conductor, I have Room A; which end of the car is that?"

"This way, Excellency," replied the conductor. Everyone seemed to be "Excellency" with him. A moment later, Jennie, who had again risen to her feet, horrified to learn that, after all, the messenger had come, heard the door of his room click. Everything was silent save the purring murmur of the swiftly moving train. She stood there for a few moments tense with excitement, then bethought herself of the hole between her present compartment and the one she had recently left. She sprang up on the seat, and placing her eye with some caution at the hole, peered through. First she thought the compartment was empty, then noticed there had been placed at the end by the window a huge cylinder that reached nearly to the ceiling of the room. The lamp above was burning brightly, and she could see every detail of the compartment, except towards the floor. As she gazed a man's back slowly rose; he appeared to have been kneeling on the floor, and he held in his hand the loop of a rubber tube. Peering downwards, she saw that it was connected with the cylinder, and that it was undoubtedly pouring whatever gas the cylinder contained through the hole into Room A. For a moment she had difficulty in repressing a shriek; but realizing how perfectly helpless she was, even if an alarm were raised, she fought down all exclamation. She saw that the man who was regulating the escape of gas was not the one who had spoken to the conductor. Then, fearing that he might turn his head and see her eye at the small aperture, she reached up and covered the lamp, leaving her own room in complete darkness. The double covering, which closed over the semi-globular lamp like an eyelid, kept every ray of light from penetrating into the compartment she occupied.

As Jennie turned to her espionage again, she heard a blow given to the door in Room A that made it chatter, then there was a sound of a heavy fall on the floor. The door of Room B was flung open, the head of the first Russian was thrust in, and he spoke in his own language a single gruff word. His assistant then turned the cock and shut off the gas from the cylinder. The door of Room B was instantly shut again, and Jennie heard the rattle of the key as Room A was being unlocked.

Jennie jumped down from her perch, threw off her hat, and, with as little noise as possible, slid her door back an inch or two. The conductor had unlocked the door of Room A, the tall Russian standing beside him saying in a whisper,—

"Never mind the man, he'll recover the moment you open the door and window; get the box. Hold your nose with your fingers and keep your mouth shut. There it is, that black box in the corner."

The conductor made a dive into the room, and came out with an ordinary black despatch-box.

The policeman seemed well provided with the materials for his burglarious purpose. He selected a key from a jingling bunch, tried it; selected another; then a third, and the lid of the despatch-box was thrown back. He took out a letter so exactly the duplicate of the one Jennie possessed that she clutched her own document to see if it were still in her pocket. The Russian put the envelope between his knees and proceeded to lock the box. His imagination had not gone to any such refinement as the placing of a dummy copy where the original had been. Quick as thought Jennie acted. She slid open the door quietly and stepped out into the passage. So intent were the two men on their work that neither saw her. The tall man gave the box back to the conductor, then took the letter from between his knees, holding it in his right hand, when Jennie, as if swayed by the motion of the car, lurched against him, and, with a sleight of hand that would have made her reputation on a necromantic stage, she jerked the letter from the amazed and frightened man; at the same moment allowing the bogus document to drop on the floor of the car from her other hand. The conductor had just emerged from Room A, holding his nose and looking comical enough as he stood there in that position, amazed at the sudden apparition of the lady. The Russian struck down the conductor's fingers with his right hand, and by a swift motion of the left closed the door of Compartment A, all of which happened in a tenth of the time taken to tell it.

"Oh, pardon me!" cried Jennie in English, "I'm afraid a lurch of the car threw me against you."

The Russian, before answering, cast a look at the floor and saw the large envelope lying there with its seal uppermost. He quietly placed his huge foot upon it, and then said, with an effort at politeness,—

"It is no matter, madam. I fear I am so bulky that I have taken up most of the passage."

"It is very good of you to excuse me," said Jennie; "I merely came out to ask the conductor if he would make up my berth. Would you be good enough to translate that to him?"

The Russian surlily told the conductor to attend to the wants of the lady. The conductor muttered a reply, and that reply the Russian translated.

"He will be at your service in a few moments, madam. He must first make up the berth of the gentleman in Room A."

"Oh, thank you very much," returned Jennie. "I am in no hurry; any time within the hour will do."

With that she retired again into her compartment, the real letter concealed in the folds of her dress, the bogus one on the floor under the Russian's foot. She closed the door tightly, then, taking care that she was not observed through either of the holes the conductor had bored in the partition, she swiftly placed the important document in a deep inside pocket of her jacket. As a general rule, women have inside pockets in their capes, and outside pockets in their jackets; but Jennie, dealing as she did with many documents in the course of her profession, had had this jacket especially made, with its deep and roomy inside pocket. She sat on a corner of the sofa, wondering what was to be the fate of the unfortunate messenger, for, in spite of the sudden shutting of the door by the Russian, she caught a glimpse of the man lying face downwards on the floor of his stifling room. She also had received a whiff of the sweet, heavy gas which had been used, that seemed now to be tincturing the whole atmosphere of the car, especially in the long narrow passage. It was not likely they intended to kill the man, for his death would cause an awkward investigation, while his statement that he had been rendered insensible might easily be denied. As she sat there, the silence disturbed only by the low, soothing rumble of the train, she heard the ring of the metal cylinder against the woodwork of the next compartment. The men were evidently removing their apparatus. A little later the train slowed, finally coming to a standstill, and looking out of the window into the darkness, she found they were stopping at an ill-lighted country station. Covering the light in the ceiling again, the better to see outside, herself, unobserved, she noted the conductor and another man place the bulky cylinder on the platform, without the slightest effort at concealment. The tall Russian stood by and gave curt orders. An instant later the train moved on again, and when well under way there was a rap at her door. When she opened it, the conductor said that he would make up her berth now, if it so pleased her. She stood out in the corridor while this was deftly and swiftly done. She could not restrain her curiosity regarding the mysterious occupant of Room A, and to satisfy it she walked slowly up and down the corridor, her hands behind her, passing and repassing the open door of her room, and noticing that ever and anon the conductor cast a suspicious eye in her direction.

The door of Room A was partly open, but the shaded lamp in the ceiling left the interior in darkness. There was now no trace of the intoxicating gas in the corridor, and as she passed Room A she noticed that a fresh breeze was blowing through the half open doorway, therefore the window must be up. Once as she passed her own door she saw the conductor engaged in a task which would keep him from looking into the corridor for at least a minute, and in that interval she set her doubts at rest by putting her head swiftly into Room A, and as swiftly withdrawing it. The man had been lifted on to his sofa, and lay with his face towards the wall, his head on a pillow. The despatch-box rested on a corner of the sofa, where, doubtless, he had left it. He was breathing heavily like a man in a drunken sleep; but the air of the room was sweet and fresh, and he would doubtless recover.

Jennie still paced up and down, pondering deeply over what had happened. At first, when she had secured the important document, she had made up her mind to return it to the messenger; but further meditation induced her to change her mind. The messenger had been robbed by the Russian police; he would tell his superiors exactly what had happened, and yet the letter would reach its destination as speedily as if he had brought it himself—as if he had never been touched. Knowing the purpose which Mr. Hardwick had in his mind, Jennie saw that the letter now was of tenfold more value to him than it would have been had she taken it from the messenger. It was evident that the British Embassy, or the messenger himself, had suspicions that an attempt was to be made to obtain the document, otherwise Room C of the sleeping car would not have been changed for Room A at the very last moment. If, then, the editor could say to the official, "The Russian police robbed your messenger in spite of all the precautions that could be taken, and my emissary cozened the Russians; so, you see, I have accomplished what the whole power of the British Government was powerless to effect; therefore it will be wisdom on your part to come to terms with me."

Jennie resolved to relate to Hardwick exactly how she came into possession of the document, and she knew his alert nature well enough to be sure he would make the most of the trump card dealt to him.

"Your room is ready for you," said the conductor in French.

She had the presence of mind enough not to comprehend his phrase until, with a motion of his hand, he explained his meaning. She entered her compartment and closed the door.

Having decided what disposal to make of the important document, there now arose in her mind the disquieting problem whether or not it would be allowed to remain with her. She cogitated over the situation and tried to work out the mental arithmetic of it. Trains were infrequent on the Russian railways, and she had no means of estimating when the burly ruffian who had planned and executed the robbery would get back to St. Petersburg. There was no doubt that he had not the right to open the letter and read its contents; that privilege rested with some higher official in St. Petersburg. The two men had got off at the first stopping place. It was quite possible that they would not reach the capital until next morning, when the Berlin express would be well on its way to the frontier. Once over the frontier she would be safe; but the moment it was found that the purloined envelope merely contained a copy of an English newspaper, what might not happen? Would the Russian authorities dare telegraph to the frontier to have her searched, or would the big official who had planned the robbery suspect that she, by legerdemain, had become possessed of the letter so much sought for? Even if he did suspect her, he would certainly have craft enough not to admit it. His game would rather be to maintain that this was the veritable document found in the Englishman's despatch-box; and it was more than likely, taking into consideration the change of room at the last moment, which would show the officials the existence of suspicion in the messenger's mind, or in the minds of those who sent him, the natural surmise would be that another messenger had gone with the real document, and that the robbed man was merely a blind to delude the Russian police. In any case, Jennie concluded, there was absolutely nothing to do but to remain awake all night and guard the treasure which good luck had bestowed upon her. She stood up on her bed, about to stuff her handkerchief into the hole bored in the partition, but suddenly paused and came down to the floor again. No, discomforting as it was to remain in a room under possible espionage, she dared not stop the openings, as that would show she had cognisance of them, and arouse the conductor's suspicion that, after all, she had understood what had been said; whereas, if she left them as they were, the fact of her doing so would be strong confirmation of her ignorance. She took from her bag a scarf, tied one end round her wrist and the other to the door, so that it could not be opened, should she fall asleep, without awakening her. Before entrenching herself thus, she drew the eyelids down over the lamp, and left her room in darkness. Then, if anyone did spy upon her they would not see the dark scarf which united her wrist with the door.

In spite of the danger of her situation she had the utmost difficulty in keeping awake. The rumble of the train had a very somnolent effect, and once or twice she started up, fearing that she had been slumbering. Once she experienced a tightening sensation in her throat, and sprang to the floor, seeing the rising gas somehow made visible, the colour of blood. The scarf drew her to her knees, and for a moment she thought someone clutched her wrist. Panting, she undid the scarf and flooded the room with light. Her heart was beating wildly, but all was still, save the ever-present rumble of the train rushing through the darkness over the boundless plains of Russia. She looked at her tiny watch, it was two o'clock in the morning. She knew then that she must have fallen asleep in spite of her strong resolutions. The letter was still in the inside pocket of her jacket, and all was well at two in the morning. No eye appeared at either of the apertures, so she covered up the light once more and lay down again, sighing to think how rumpled her dainty costume would look in the morning. Now she was resolved not to go to sleep, if force of will could keep her awake. A moment later she was startled by someone beating down the partition with an axe. She sprang up, and again the scarf pulled her back. She untied it from her wrist and noticed that daylight flooded the compartment. This amazed her; how could it be daylight so soon? Had she been asleep again, and was the fancied battering at the door with an axe merely the conclusion of a dream caused by the conductor's knock? After a breathless pause there came a gentle rap on her door, and the voice of the conductor said,—

"Breakfast at Luga, madame, in three-quarters of an hour."

"Very good," she replied in English, her voice trembling with fear. Slowly she untied the scarf from the door and placed it in her handbag. She shivered notwithstanding her effort at self-control, for she knew she had slept through the night, and far into the morning. In agitation she unbuttoned her jacket. Yes; there was the letter, just where she had placed it. She dare not take it out and examine it, fearing still that she might be watched from some unseen quarter, but "Thank God," she said to herself fervently, "this horrible night is ended. Once over the frontier I am safe." She smoothed and brushed down her dress as well as she was able, and was greatly refreshed by her wash in cold water, which is one of the luxuries, not the least acceptable, on a sleeping car.

CHAPTER XIX. JENNIE EXPERIENCES THE SURPRISE OF HER LIFE.

At nine o'clock the long train came to a standstill, seventeen minutes late at Luga, and ample time was allowed for a leisurely breakfast in the buffet of the station. The restaurant was thronged with numerous passengers, most of whom seemed hardly yet awake, while many were unkempt and dishevelled, as if they had had little sleep during the night.

Jennie found a small table and sat down beside it, ordering her coffee and rolls from the waiter who came to serve her. Looking round at the cosmopolitan company, and listening to the many languages, whose clash gave a Babel air to the restaurant, Jennie fell to musing on the strange experiences she had encountered since leaving London. It seemed to her she had been taking part in some ghastly nightmare, and she shuddered as she thought of the lawlessness, under cover of law, of this great and despotic empire, where even the ruler was under the surveillance of his subordinates, and could not get a letter out of his own dominion in safety, were he so minded. In her day-dream she became conscious, without noting its application to herself, that a man was standing before her table; then a voice which made her heart stop said,—

"Ah, lost Princess!"

She placed her hand suddenly to her throat, for the catch in her breath seemed to be suffocating her, then looked up and saw Lord Donal Stirling, in the ordinary everyday dress of an English gentleman, as well groomed as if he had come, not from a train, but from his own house. There was a kindly smile on his lips and a sparkle in his eyes, but his face was of ghastly pallor.

"Oh, Lord Donal!" she cried, regarding him with eyes of wonder and fear, "what is wrong with you?"

"Nothing," the young man replied, with an attempt at a laugh; "nothing, now that I have found you, Princess. I have been making a night of it, that's all, and am suffering the consequences in the morning. May I sit down?"

He dropped into a chair on the other side of the table, like a man thoroughly exhausted, unable to stand longer, and went on,—

"Like all dissipated men, I am going to break my fast on stimulants. Waiter," he said, "bring me a large glass of your best brandy."

"And, waiter," interjected Jennie in French, "bring two breakfasts. I suppose it was not a meal that you ordered just now, Lord Donal?"

"I have ordered my breakfast," he said; "still, it pleads in my favour that I do not carry brandy with me, as I ought to do, and so must drink the vile stuff they call their best here."

"You should eat as well," she insisted, taking charge of him as if she had every right to do so.

"All shall be as you say, now that I have the happiness of seeing you sitting opposite me, but don't be surprised if I show a most unappreciative appetite."

"What is the matter?" she asked breathlessly. "You certainly look very ill."

"I have been drugged and robbed," he replied, lowering his voice. "I imagine I came to close quarters with death itself. I have spent a night in Hades, and this morning am barely able to stagger; but the sight of you, Princess—Ah, well, I feel once more that I belong to the land of the living!"

"Please do not call me Princess," said the girl, looking down at the tablecloth.

"Then what am I to call you, Princess?"

"My name is Jennie Baxter," she said in a low voice.

"Miss Jennie Baxter?" he asked eagerly, with emphasis on the first word.

"Miss Jennie Baxter," she answered, still not looking up at him.

He leaned back in his chair and said,—

"Well, this is not such a bad world, after all. To think of meeting you here in Russia! Have you been in St. Petersburg, then?"

"Yes. I am a newspaper woman," explained Jennie hurriedly. "When you met me before, I was there surreptitiously—fraudulently, if you like; I was there to—to write a report of it for my paper. I can never thank you enough, Lord Donal, for your kindness to me that evening."

"Your thanks are belated," said the young man, with a visible attempt at gaiety. "You should have written and acknowledged the kindness you are good enough to say I rendered to you. You knew my address, and etiquette demanded that you should make your acknowledgments."

"I was reluctant to write," said Jennie, a smile hovering round her lips, "fearing my letter might act as a clue. I had no wish to interfere with the legitimate business of Mr. Cadbury Taylor."

"Great heavens!" cried the young man, "how came you to know about that? But of course the Princess von Steinheimer told you of it. She wrote to me charging me with all sorts of wickedness for endeavouring to find you."

"No, Lord Donal, I did not learn it from her. In fact, if you had opened the door of the inner room at Mr. Cadbury Taylor's a little quicker, you would have come upon me, for I was the assistant who tried to persuade him that you really met the Princess von Steinheimer."

Lord Donal, for the first time, laughed heartily.

"Well, if that doesn't beat all! And I suppose Cadbury Taylor hasn't the slightest suspicion that you are the person he was looking for?"

"No, not the slightest."

"I say! that is the best joke I have heard in ten years," said Lord Donal; and here, breakfast arriving, Jennie gave him his directions.

"You are to drink a small portion of that brandy," she said, "and then put the rest in your coffee. You must eat a good breakfast, and that will help you to forget your troubles,—that is, if you have any real troubles."

"Oh, my troubles are real enough," said the young man. "When I met you before, Princess, I was reasonably successful. We even talked about ambassadorships, didn't we, in spite of the fact that ambassadors were making themselves unnecessarily obtrusive that night? Now you see before you a ruined man. No, I am not joking; it is true. I was given a commission, or, rather, knowing the danger there was in it, I begged that the commission might be given me. It was merely to take a letter from St. Petersburg to London. I have failed, and when that is said, all is said."

"But surely," cried the girl, blushing guiltily as she realized that this was the man she had been sent to rob, "you could not be expected to ward off such a lawless attempt at murder as you have been the victim of?"

"That is just what I expected, and what I supposed I could ward off. In my profession—which, after all has a great similarity to yours, except that I think we have to do more lying in ours—there must be no such word as fail. The very best excuses are listened to with tolerance, perhaps, and a shrug of the shoulders; but failure, no matter from what cause, is fell doom. I have failed. I shall not make any excuses. I will go to London and say merely, 'The Russian police have robbed me.' Oh, I know perfectly well who did the trick, and how it was done. Then I shall send in my resignation. They will accept it with polite words of regret, and will say to each other, 'Poor fellow, he had a brilliant career before him, but he got drunk, or something, and fell into the ditch.' Ah, well, we won't talk any more about it."

"Then you don't despise the newspaper profession, Lord Donal?"

"Despise it! Bless you, no: I look up to it. Belonging myself to a profession very much lower down in the scale of morality, as I have said. But, Princess," he added, leaning towards her, "will you resign from the newspaper if I resign from diplomacy?"

The girl slowly shook her head, her eyes on the tablecloth before her.

"I will telegraph my resignation," he said impetuously, "if you will telegraph yours to your paper."

"You are feeling ill and worried this morning, Lord Donal, and so you take a pessimistic view of life. You must not resign."

"Oh, but I must. I have failed, and that is enough."

"It isn't enough. You must do nothing until you reach London."

"I like your word must, Jennie," said the young man audaciously. "It implies something, you know."

"What does it imply, Lord Donal?" she asked, glancing up at him.

"It implies that you are going to leave the 'Lord' off my name."

"That wouldn't be very difficult," replied Jennie.

"I am delighted to hear you say so," exclaimed his lordship; "and now, that I may know how it sounds from your dear lips, call me Don."

"No; if I ever consented to omit the title, I should call you Donal. I like the name in its entirety."

He reached his hand across the table. "Are you willing then, to accept a man at the very lowest ebb of his fortunes? I know that if I were of the mould that heroes are made of, I would hesitate to proffer you a blighted life. But I loved you the moment I saw you; and, remembering my fruitless search for you, I cannot run the risk of losing you again; I have not the courage."

She placed her hand in his and looked him, for the first time, squarely in the eyes.

"Are you sure, Donal," she said, "that I am not a mere effigy on which you are hanging the worn-out garments of a past affection? You thought I was the Princess at first."

"No, I didn't," he protested. "As soon as I heard you speak, I knew you were the one I was destined to meet."

"Ah, Donal, Donal, at lovers' perjuries they say Jove laughs. I don't think you were quite so certain as all that. But I, too, am a coward, and I dare not refuse you."

Lord Donal glanced quickly about him; the room was still crowded. Even the Berlin Express gave them a long time for breakfast, and was in no hurry to move westward. His hurried gaze returned to her and he sighed.

"What an unholy spot for a proposal!" he whispered; "and yet they call Russia the Great Lone Land. Oh, that we had a portion of it entirely to ourselves!"

The girl sat there, a smile on her pretty lips that Lord Donal thought most tantalizing. A railway official announced in a loud voice that the train was about to resume its journey. There was a general shuffling of feet as the passengers rose to take their places.

"Brothers and sisters kiss each other, you know, on the eve of a railway journey," said Lord Donal, taking advantage of the confusion.

Jennie Baxter made no protest.

"There is plenty of time," he whispered. "I know the leisurely nature of Russian trains. Now I am going to the telegraph office, to send in my resignation, and I want you to come with me and send in yours."

"No, Lord Donal," said the girl.

"Aren't you going to resign?" he asked, in surprise.

"Yes, all in good time; but you are not."

"Oh, I say," he cried, "it is really imperative. I'll tell you all about it when we get on the train."

"It is really imperative that you should not send in your resignation. Indeed, Donal, you need not look at me with that surprised air. You may as well get accustomed to dictation at once. You did it yourself, you know. You can't say that I encouraged you. I eluded the vigilant Cadbury Taylor as long as I could. But, if there is time, go to the telegraph office and send a message to the real Princess, Palace Steinheimer, Vienna. Say you are engaged to be married to Jennie Baxter, and ask her to telegraph you her congratulations at Berlin."

"I'll do it," replied the young man with gratifying alacrity.

When Lord Donal came out of the telegraph office, Jennie said to him, “Wait a moment while I go into the sleeping car and get my rugs and handbag.”

“I’ll go for them,” he cried impetuously.

“Oh, no,” she said. “I’ll tell you why, later. The conductor is a villain and was in collusion with the police.”

“Oh, I know that,” said Lord Donal. “Poor devil, he can’t help himself; he must do what the police order him to do, while he is in Russia.”

“I’ll get my things and go into an ordinary first class carriage. When I pass this door, you must get your belongings and come and find me. There is still time, and I don’t want the conductor to see us together.”

“Very well,” said the young man with exemplary obedience.

CHAPTER XX. JENNIE CONVERSES WITH A YOUNG MAN SHE THINKS MUCH OF.

When the train started, they were seated together in a carriage far forward.

"One of my failings," said the girl, "is to act first, and think afterwards. I am sorry now that I asked you to send that telegram to the Princess."

"Why?"

"Because I have a great deal to tell you, and perhaps you may wish to withdraw from the rash engagement you have undertaken."

"A likely thing!" cried the ardent lover. "Indeed, Miss Princess, if you think you can get rid of me as easily as all that, you are very much mistaken."

"Well, I want to tell you why I did not allow you to resign."

Slowly she undid the large buttons of her jacket, then, taking it by the lapel and holding it so that no one else could see, she drew partly forth from the inside pocket the large envelope, until the stamp of the Embassy was plainly visible. Lord Donal's eyes opened to their widest capacity, and his breath seemed to stop.

"Great heavens!" he gasped at last, "do you mean to say you have it?"

"Yes," she said, buttoning up her jacket again. "I robbed the robbers. Listen, and I will tell you all that happened. But, first, are you armed?"

"Yes," he replied, "I have a trumpery revolver in my pocket; little good it did me last night."

"Very well, we shall be across the frontier by noon to-day. If the Russian authorities find before that time how they have been checkmated, and if they have any suspicion that I am the cause of it, is it not likely that they will have me stopped and searched on some pretence or other?" Lord Donal pondered for a moment. "They are quite capable of it," he said; "but, Jennie, I will fight for you against the whole Russian Empire, and somebody will get hurt if you are meddled with. The police will hesitate, however, before interfering with a messenger from the Embassy, or anyone in his charge in broad daylight on a crowded train. We will not go back into that car, but stay here, where some of our fellow-countrymen are."

"That is what I was going to propose," said Jennie. "And now listen to the story I have to tell you, and then you will know exactly why I came to Russia."

"Don't tell me anything you would rather not," said the young man hurriedly.

"I would rather not, but it must be told," answered the girl.

The story lasted a long time, and when it was ended the young man cried enthusiastically in answer to her question,—

"Blame you? Why, of course I don't blame you in the slightest. It wasn't Hardwick who sent you here at all, but Providence. Providence brought us together, Jennie, and my belief in it hereafter will be unshaken."

Jennie laughed a contented little laugh, and said she was flattered at being considered an envoy of Providence.

"It is only another way of saying you are an angel, Jennie," remarked the bold young man.

They crossed the frontier without interference, and, once in Germany, Jennie took the object of so much contention and placed it in the hands of her lover.

"There," she whispered, with a tiny sigh, for she was giving up the fruits of her greatest achievement, "put that in your despatch box, and see that it doesn't leave that receptacle until you reach London. I hope the Russians will like the copy of the Daily Bugle they find in their envelope."

The two chatted together throughout the long ride to Berlin, and when

11 p.m. and the Schleischer station came at last, they still seemed only to have begun their conversation, so much more remained to be told.

The telegram from the Princess was handed to Lord Donal at Berlin.

"I congratulate you most sincerely," she wired; "and tell Jennie the next time you see her"—Lord Donal laughed as he read this aloud—"that the Austrian Government has awarded her thirty thousand pounds for her share in enabling them to recover their gold, and little enough I think it is, considering what she has done."

"Now, I call that downright handsome of the Austrian Government," cried Lord Donal. "I thought they were going to fight us when I read the speech of their Prime Minister, but, instead of that, they are making wedding presents to our nice girls."

"Ah, that comes through the good-heartedness of the Princess, and the kindness of the Prince," said Jennie. "He has managed it."

"But what in the world did you do for the Austrian Government, Jennie?"

"That is a long story, Donal, and I think a most interesting one."

"Well, let us thank heaven that we have a long journey for you to tell it and me to listen."

And saying this, the unabashed, forward young man took the liberty of kissing his fair companion good-night, right there amidst all the turmoil and bustle of the Schleischer Bahnhof in Berlin.

It was early in the morning when the two met again in the restaurant car. The train had passed Cologne and was now rushing up that picturesque valley through which runs the brawling little river Vesdre. Lord Donal and Jennie had the car to themselves, and they chose a table near the centre of it and there ordered their breakfast. The situation was a most picturesque one. The broad, clear plate glass windows on each side displayed, in rapid succession, a series of landscapes well worth viewing; the densely wooded hills, the cheerful country houses, the swift roaring stream lashing itself into fleecy foam; now and then a glimpse of an old ruined castle on the heights, and, in the deep valley, here and there a water mill.

It was quite evident that Jennie had slept well, and, youth being on her side, her rest had compensated for the nightmare of the Russian journey. She was simply but very effectively dressed, and looked as fresh and pretty and cool and sweet as a snowdrop. The enchanted young man found it impossible to lure his eyes away from her, and when, with a little laugh, Jennie protested that he was missing all the fine scenery, he answered that he had something much more beautiful to look upon; whereat Jennie blushed most enticingly, smiled at him, but made no further protest. Whether it was his joy in meeting Jennie, or the result of his night's sleep, or his relief at finding that his career was not wrecked, as he had imagined, or all three together, Lord Donal seemed his old self again, and was as bright, witty, and cheerful as a boy home for the holidays. They enjoyed their breakfast with the relish that youth and a healthy appetite gives to a dainty meal well served. The rolls were brown and toothsome, the butter, in thick corrugated spirals, was of a delicious golden colour, cold and crisp. The coffee was all that coffee should be, and the waiter was silent and attentive. Russia, like an evil vision, was far behind, and the train sped through splendid scenery swiftly towards England and home.

The young man leaned back in his chair, interlaced his fingers behind his head, and gazed across at Jennie, drawing a sigh of deep satisfaction.

"Well, this is jolly," he said.

"Yes," murmured Jennie, "it's very nice. I always did enjoy foreign travel, especially when it can be done in luxury; but, alas! luxury costs money, doesn't it?"

"Oh, you don't need to mind, you are rich."

"That is true; I had forgotten all about it."

"I hope, Jennie, that the fact of my travelling on a train de luxe has not deluded you regarding my wealth. I should have told you that I usually travel third class when I am transporting myself in my private capacity. I am wringing this pampered elegance from the reluctant pockets of the British taxpayer. When I travel for the British Government I say, as Pooh Bah said to Koko in the 'Mikado,' 'Do it well, my boy,' or words to that effect."

"Indeed," laughed Jennie, "I am in a somewhat similar situation; the newspaper is paying all the expenses of this trip, but I shall insist on returning the money to the Bugle now that I have failed in my mission."

"Dear me, how much more honest the newspaper business is than diplomacy! The idea of returning any money never even occurred to me. The mere suggestion freezes my young blood and makes each particular hair to stand on end like quills upon the fretful porcupine. Our motto in the service is, Get all you can, and keep all you get."

"But then, you see, your case differs from mine; you did your best to succeed, and I failed through my own choice; and thus I sit here a traitor to my paper."

"Well, Jennie," said the young man, picking up the despatch-box, which he never allowed to leave his sight, and placing it on the table, "you've only to say the word, and this contentious letter is in your possession again. Do you regret your generosity?"

"Oh, no, no, no, no, I would not have it back on any account. Even looking at the matter in the most materialistic way, success means far more to you than it does to me. As you say, I am rich, therefore I am going to give up my newspaper career. I suppose that is why women very rarely make great successes of their lives. A woman's career so often is merely of incidental interest to her; a man's career is his whole life."

"What a pity it is," mused the young man, "that one person's success usually means another person's failure. If I were the generous, whole-souled person I sometimes imagine myself to be, I should refuse to accept success at the price of your failure. You have actually succeeded, while I have actually failed. With a generosity that makes me feel small and mean, you hand over your success to me, and I selfishly accept it. But I compound with my conscience in this way. You and I are to be married; then we will be one. That one shall be heir to all the successes of each of us and shall disclaim all the failures of each. Isn't that a good idea?"

"Excellent," replied Jennie; "nevertheless, I cannot help feeling just a little sorry for poor Mr. Hardwick."

"Who is he—the editor?"

"Yes. He did have such faith in me that it seems almost a pity to disappoint him."

"You mustn't trouble your mind about Hardwick. Don't think of him at all; think of me instead."

"I am afraid I do, and have done so for some time past; nevertheless, I shall get off at Liege and telegraph to him that I am not bringing the document to London."

"I will send the telegram for you when we reach there; but, if I remember rightly what you told me of his purpose, he can't be very deeply disappointed. I understood you to say that he did not intend to publish the document, even if he got it."

"That is quite true. He wished to act as the final messenger himself, and was to meet me at Charing Cross Station, secure the envelope, and take it at once to its destination."

"I must confess," said the young man, with a bewildered expression, "that I don't see the object of that. Are you sure he told you the truth?"

"Oh, yes. The object was this. It seems that there is in the Foreign Office some crusty old curmudgeon who delights in baffling Mr. Hardwick. This official—I forget his name; in fact, I don't think Mr. Hardwick told me who he was—seems to forget the Daily Bugle when important items of news are to be given out, and Mr. Hardwick says that he favours one of the rival papers, and the Bugle has been unable, so far, to receive anything like fair treatment from him; so Mr. Hardwick wanted to take the document to him, and thus convince him there was danger in making an enemy of the Daily Bugle. As I understood his project, which didn't commend itself very much to me, Hardwick had no intention of making a bargain, but simply proposed to hand over the document, and ask the Foreign Office man to give the Bugle its fair share in what was going."

"Do you mean to say that the official in question is the man to whom I am to give this letter?"

"Yes."

"Oh, my prophetic soul, my uncle! Why, that is Sir James Cardiff, the elder brother of my mother; he is a dear old chap, but I can well understand an outsider thinking him gruff and uncivil. If the editor really means what he says, then there will be no difficulty and no disappointment. If all that is needed is the winning over of old Jimmy to be civil to Hardwick, I can guarantee that. I am the especial protégé of my uncle. Everything I know I have learned from him. He cannot understand why the British Government does not appoint me immediately Ambassador to France; Jimmy would do it to-morrow if he had the power. It was through him that I heard of this letter, and I believe his influence had a good deal to do with my getting the commission of special messenger. It was the chagrin that my uncle Jimmy would have felt, had I failed, that put the final drop of bitterness in my cup of sorrow when I came to my senses after my encounter with the Russian police. That would have been a stunning blow to Sir James Cardiff. We shall reach Charing Cross about 7.30 to-night, and Sir James will be there with his brougham to take charge of me when I arrive. Now, what do you say to our settling all this under the canopy of Charing Cross Station? If you telegraph Mr. Hardwick to meet us there, I will introduce him to Sir James, and he will never have any more trouble in that quarter."

"I think," said the girl, looking down at the tablecloth, "that I'd rather not have Mr. Hardwick meet us."

"Of course not," answered the young man quickly. "What was I thinking about? It will be a family gathering, and we don't want any outsiders about, do we?"

Jennie laughed, but made no reply.

CHAPTER XXI. JENNIE KEEPS STEP WITH THE WEDDING MARCH.

They had a smooth and speedy passage across from Calais to Dover, and the train drew in at Charing Cross Station exactly on time. Lord Donal recognized his uncle's brougham waiting for him, and on handing the young lady out of the railway carriage he espied the old man himself closely scrutinizing the passengers. Sir James, catching sight of him, came eagerly forward and clasped both his nephew's hands.

"Donal," he cried, "I am very glad indeed to see you. Is everything right?"

"As right as can be, uncle."

"Then I am glad of that, too, for we have had some very disquieting hints from the East."

"They were quite justified, as I shall tell you later on; but meanwhile, uncle, allow me to introduce to you Miss Baxter, who has done me the honour of promising to be my wife."

Jennie blushed in the searching rays of the electric light as the old man turned quickly towards her. Sir James held her hand in his for some moments before he spoke, gazing intently at her. Then he said slowly, "Ah, Donal, Donal, you always had a keen eye for the beautiful."

"Oh, I say," cried the young man, abashed at his uncle's frankness, "I don't call that a diplomatic remark at all, you know."

"Indeed, Sir James," said the girl, laughing merrily, "it is better than diplomatic, it is complimentary, and I assure you I appreciate it. The first time he met me he took me for quite another person."

"Then, whoever that person is, my dear," replied the old man, "I'll guarantee she is a lovely woman. And you mustn't mind what I say; nobody else does, otherwise my boy Donal here would be much higher in the service than the present moment finds him; but I am pleased to tell you that the journey he has now finished will prove greatly to his advantage."

"Indeed, uncle, that is true," said the young man, looking at his betrothed, "for on this journey I met again Miss Baxter, whom, to my great grief, I had lost for some time. And now, uncle, I want you to do me a great favour. Do you know Mr. Hardwick, editor of the Daily Bugle?"

"Yes, I know him; but I don't like him, nor his paper either."

"Well, neither do the Russians, for that matter, by this time, and I merely wish to tell you that if it hadn't been for his action, and for the promptness of a member of his staff, I should have failed in this mission. I was drugged by the Russian police and robbed. Miss Baxter, who was on the train, saw something of what was going forward, and succeeded, most deftly, in despoiling the robbers. I was lying insensible at the time and helpless. She secured the document and handed it back to me when we had crossed the frontier, leaving in the hands of the Russians a similar envelope containing a copy of the Daily Bugle; therefore, uncle, if in future you can do anything to oblige Mr. Hardwick, you will help in a measure to cancel the obligation which our family owes to him."

"My dear boy, I shall be delighted to do so. I am afraid I have been rather uncivil to him. If you wish it, I will go at once and apologize to him."

"Oh, no," cried Jennie, "you must not do that; but if you can help him without jeopardizing the service, I, for one, will be very glad."

"So shall I," said Donal.

The old man took out his card-case, and on the back of his card scribbled a most cordial invitation to Hardwick, asking him to call on him. He handed this to Jennie, and said,—

"Tell Mr. Hardwick that I shall be pleased to see him at any time."

"And now," said Lord Donal, "you must let us both escort you home in the carriage."

"No, no. I shall take a hansom, and will go directly to the office of the

Bugle, for Mr. Hardwick will be there by this time."

"But we can drive you there."

"No, please."

She held out her hand to Sir James and said, with the least bit of hesitation before uttering the last word, "Good night—uncle."

"Good night, my dear," said the old man, "and God bless you," he added with a tenderness which his appearance, so solemn and stately, left one unprepared for.

Lord Donal saw his betrothed into a hansom, protesting all the while at thus having to allow her to go off unprotected.

"What an old darling he is," murmured Jennie, ignoring his protests. "I think if Mr. Hardwick had allowed me to look after the interests of the paper at the Foreign Office, Sir James would not have snubbed me."

"If the Foreign Office dared to do such a thing, it would hear of something not to its advantage from the Diplomatic Service; and so, goodnight, my dear." And, with additions, the nephew repeated the benediction of the uncle.

Jennie drove directly to the office of the Daily Bugle, and, for the last time, mounting the stairs, entered the editorial rooms. She found Mr. Hardwick at his desk, and he sprang up quickly on seeing who his visitor was. "Ah, you have returned," he cried. "You didn't telegraph to me, so I suppose that means failure."

"I don't know, Mr. Hardwick. It all depends on whether or not your object was exactly what you told me it was."

"And what was that? I think I told you that my desire was to get possession of the document which was being transmitted from St. Petersburg to London."

"No; you said the object was the mollifying of old Sir James Cardiff, of the Foreign Office."

"Exactly; that was the ultimate object, of course."

"Very well. Read this card. Sir James gave it to me at Charing Cross Station less than half an hour ago."

The editor took the card, turned it over in his hands once or twice, and read the cordial message which the old man had scribbled on the back of it.

"Then you have succeeded," cried Hardwick. "You got the document; but why did you give it to Sir James yourself, instead of letting me hand it to him?"

"That is a long story. To put it briefly, it was because the messenger carrying the document was Lord Donal Stirling, who is—who is—an old friend of mine. Sir James is his uncle, and Lord Donal promised that he would persuade the old man to let other newspapers have no advantages which he refused to the Daily Bugle. I did not give the document to Sir James, I gave it back to Lord Donal."

"Lord Donal Stirling—Lord Donal Stirling," mused the editor. "Where have I heard that name before?"

"He is a member of the British Embassy at St. Petersburg, so you may have seen his name in the despatches."

"No. He is not so celebrated as all that comes to. Ah, I remember now. I met the detective the other night and asked him if anything had come of that romance in high life, to solve which he had asked your assistance. He said the search for the missing lady had been abandoned, and mentioned the name of Lord Donal Stirling as the foolish young man who had been engaged in the pursuit of the unknown."

Jennie coloured at this and drew herself up indignantly.

"Before you say anything further against Lord Donal," she cried hotly, "I wish to inform you that he and I are to be married."

"Oh, I beg your pardon," said the editor icily. "Then, having failed to find the other girl, he has speedily consoled himself by—"

"There was no other girl. I was the person of whom Mr. Cadbury Taylor was in search. I willingly gave him valuable assistance in the task of failing to find myself. Having only a stupid man to deal with, I had little difficulty in accomplishing my purpose. Neither Mr. Taylor nor Mr. Hardwick ever suspected that the missing person was in their own employ."

"Well, I'm blessed!" ejaculated Hardwick. "So you baffled Cadbury Taylor in searching for yourself, as you baffled me in getting hold of the Russian letter. It seems to me, Miss Baxter, that where your own inclinations do not coincide with the wishes of your employers, the interests of those who pay you fall to the ground."

"Mr. Cadbury Taylor didn't pay me anything for my services as amateur detective, and he has, therefore, no right to grumble. As for the St. Petersburg trip, I shall send you a cheque for all expenses incurred as soon as I reach home."

"Oh, you mistake me," asserted Mr. Hardwick earnestly. "I had no thought of even hinting that you have not earned over and over again all the money the Daily Bugle has paid you; besides, I was longing for your return, for I want your assistance in solving a mystery that has rather puzzled us all. Paris is in a turmoil just now over the—"

Jennie's clear laugh rang out.

"I am going over to Paris in a day or two, Mr. Hardwick, to solve the mystery of dressmaking, and I think, from what I know of it already, it will require my whole attention. I must insist on returning to you the cost of the St. Petersburg journey, for, after all, it proved to be rather a personal excursion, and I couldn't think of allowing the paper to pay for it. I merely came in to-night to hand you this card from Sir James Cardiff, and I also desired to tender to you personally my resignation. And so I must bid you good-bye, Mr. Hardwick," said the girl holding out her hand; "and I thank you very much indeed for having given me a chance to work on your paper."

Before the editor could reply, she was gone, and that good man sat down in his chair bewildered by the suddenness of it all, the room looking empty and dismal, lacking her presence.

"Confound Lord Donal Stirling!" he muttered under his breath, and then, as an editor should he went on impassively with his night's work.

It was intended that the wedding should be rather a quiet affair, but circumstances proved too strong for the young people. Lord Donal was very popular and the bride was very beautiful. Sir James thought it necessary to invite a great many people, and he intimated to Lord Donal that a highly placed personage desired to honour the function with his presence. And thus the event created quite a little flutter in the smart set. The society papers affirmed that this elevated personage had been particularly pleased by some diplomatic service which Lord Donal had recently rendered him; but then, of course, one can never believe what one reads in the society press. However, the man of exalted rank was there, and so people said that perhaps there might be something in the rumour. Naturally there was a great turn-out of ambassadors and ministers, and their presence gave colour and dignity to the crush at St. George's, Hanover Square. The Princess von Steinheimer made a special journey from Vienna to attend, and on this occasion she brought the Prince with her. The general opinion was that the bridegroom was a very noble-looking fellow, and that the bride, in her sumptuous wedding apparel, was quite too lovely for anything.

The Princess was exceedingly bright and gay, and she chatted with her old friends the Ambassadors from Austria and America.

"I'm so sorry," she said to the Ambassador from America, "that I did not have time to speak with you at the Duchess of Chiselhurst's ball, but I was compelled to leave early. You should have come to me sooner. The Count here was much more gallant. We had a most delightful conversation, hadn't we, Count? I was with Lord Donal, you remember."

"Oh, yes," replied the aged Austrian, bowing low; "I shall not soon forget the charming conversation I had with your Highness, and I hope you, on your part, have not forgotten the cordial invitation you gave me to visit again your castle at Meran."

"Indeed, Count, you know very well how glad I am to see you at any time, either in Vienna or at Meran."

The American Ambassador remained silent, and glanced alternately from the bride to the Princess with a puzzled expression on his face.

The mystery of the Duchess of Chiselhurst's Ball proved too much for him, as the search for the missing lady had proved too much for Mr. Cadbury Taylor.

THE END

IN THE MIDST OF ALARMS:
A NOVEL

CHAPTER I.

In the marble-floored vestibule of the Metropolitan Grand Hotel in Buffalo, Professor Stillson Renmark stood and looked about him with the anxious manner of a person unused to the gaudy splendor of the modern American house of entertainment. The professor had paused halfway between the door and the marble counter, because he began to fear that he had arrived at an inopportune time, that something unusual was going on. The hurry and bustle bewildered him.

An omnibus, partly filled with passengers, was standing at the door, its steps backed over the curbstone, and beside it was a broad, flat van, on which stalwart porters were heaving great square, iron-bound trunks belonging to commercial travelers, and the more fragile, but not less bulky, saratogas, doubtless the property of the ladies who sat patiently in the omnibus. Another vehicle which had just arrived was backing up to the curb, and the irate driver used language suitable to the occasion; for the two restive horses were not behaving exactly in the way he liked.

A man with a stentorian, but monotonous and mournful, voice was filling the air with the information that a train was about to depart for Albany, Saratoga, Troy, Boston, New York, and the East. When he came to the words "the East," his voice dropped to a sad minor key, as if the man despaired of the fate of those who took their departure in that direction. Every now and then a brazen gong sounded sharply; and one of the negroes who sat in a row on a bench along the marble-paneled wall sprang forward to the counter, took somebody's handbag, and disappeared in the direction of the elevator with the newly arrived guest following him. Groups of men stood here and there conversing, heedless of the rush of arrival and departure around them.

Before the broad and lofty plate-glass windows sat a row of men, some talking, some reading, and some gazing outside, but all with their feet on the brass rail which had been apparently put there for that purpose. Nearly everybody was smoking a cigar. A lady of dignified mien came down the hall to the front of the counter, and spoke quietly to the clerk, who bent his well-groomed head deferentially on one side as he listened to what she had to say. The men instantly made way for her. She passed along among them as composedly as if she were in her own drawing room, inclining her head slightly to one or other of her acquaintances, which salutation was gravely acknowledged by the raising of the hat and the temporary removal of the cigar from the lips.

All this was very strange to the professor, and he felt himself in a new world, with whose customs he was not familiar. Nobody paid the slightest attention to him as he stood there among it all with his satchel in his hand. As he timidly edged up to the counter, and tried to accumulate courage enough to address the clerk, a young man came forward, flung his handbag on the polished top of the counter, metaphorically brushed the professor aside, pulled the bulky register toward him, and inscribed his name on the page with a rapidity equaled only by the illegibility of the result.

"Hello, Sam!" he said to the clerk. "How's things? Get my telegram?"

"Yes," answered the clerk; "but I can't give you 27. It's been taken for a week. I reserved 85 for you, and had to hold on with my teeth to do that."

The reply of the young man was merely a brief mention of the place of torment.

"It is hot," said the clerk blandly. "In from Cleveland?"

"Yes. Any letters for me?"

"Couple of telegrams. You'll find them up in 85."

"Oh, you were cocksure I'd take that room?"

"I was cocksure you'd have to. It is that or the fifth floor. We're full. Couldn't give a better room to the President if he came."

"Oh, well, what's good enough for the President I can put up with for a couple of days."

The hand of the clerk descended on the bell. The negro sprang forward and took the “grip.”

“Eighty-five,” said the clerk; and the drummer and the Negro disappeared.

“Is there any place where I could leave my bag for a while?” the professor at last said timidly to the clerk.

“Your bag?”

The professor held it up in view.

“Oh, your grip. Certainly. Have a room, sir?” And the clerk’s hand hovered over the bell.

“No. At least, not just yet. You see, I’m——”

“All right. The baggage man there to the left will check it for you.”

“Any letters for Bond?” said a man, pushing himself in front of the professor. The clerk pulled out a fat bunch of letters from the compartment marked “B,” and handed the whole lot to the inquirer, who went rapidly over them, selected two that appeared to be addressed to him, and gave the letters a push toward the clerk, who placed them where they were before.

The professor paused a moment, then, realizing that the clerk had forgotten him, sought the baggage man, whom he found in a room filled with trunks and valises. The room communicated with the great hall by means of a square opening whose lower ledge was breast high. The professor stood before it, and handed the valise to the man behind this opening, who rapidly attached one brass check to the handle with a leather thong, and flung the other piece of brass to the professor. The latter was not sure but there was something to pay, still he quite correctly assumed that if there had been the somewhat brusque man would have had no hesitation in mentioning the fact; in which surmise his natural common sense proved a sure guide among strange surroundings. There was no false delicacy about the baggage man.

Although the professor was to a certain extent bewildered by the condition of things, there was still in his nature a certain dogged persistence that had before now stood him in good stead, and which had enabled him to distance, in the long run, much more brilliant men. He was not at all satisfied with his brief interview with the clerk. He resolved to approach that busy individual again, if he could arrest his attention. It was some time before he caught the speaker's eye, as it were, but when he did so, he said:

"I was about to say to you that I am waiting for a friend from New York who may not yet have arrived. His name is Mr. Richard Yates of the——"

"Oh, Dick Yates! Certainly. He's here." Turning to the negro, he said: "Go down to the billiard room and see if Mr. Yates is there. If he is not, look for him at the bar."

The clerk evidently knew Mr. Dick Yates. Apparently not noticing the look of amazement that had stolen over the professor's face, the clerk said:

"If you wait in the reading room, I'll send Yates to you when he comes. The boy will find him if he's in the house; but he may be uptown."

The professor, disliking to trouble the obliging clerk further, did not ask him where the reading room was. He inquired, instead, of a hurrying porter, and received the curt but comprehensive answer:

"Dining room next floor. Reading, smoking, and writing rooms up the hall. Billiard room, bar, and lavatory downstairs."

The professor, after getting into the barber shop and the cigar store, finally found his way into the reading room. Numerous daily papers were scattered around on the table, each attached to a long, clumsy cleft holder made of wood; while other journals, similarly encumbered, hung from racks against the wall. The professor sat down in one of the easy leather-covered chairs, but, instead of taking up a paper, drew a thin book from his pocket, in which he was soon so absorbed that he became entirely unconscious of his strange surroundings. A light touch on the shoulder brought him up from his book into the world again, and he saw, looking down on him, the stern face of a heavily mustached stranger.

"I beg your pardon, sir, but may I ask if you are a guest of this house?"

A shade of apprehension crossed the professor's face as he slipped the book into his pocket. He had vaguely felt that he was trespassing when he first entered the hotel, and now his doubts were confirmed.

"I—I am not exactly a guest," he stammered.

"What do you mean by not exactly a guest?" continued the other, regarding the professor with a cold and scrutinizing gaze. "A man is either a guest or he is not, I take it. Which is it in your case?"

"I presume, technically speaking, I am not."

"Technically speaking! More evasions. Let me ask you, sir, as an ostensibly honest man, if you imagine that all this luxury—this—this elegance—is maintained for nothing? Do you think, sir, that it is provided for any man who has cheek enough to step out of the street and enjoy it? Is it kept up, I ask, for people who are, technically speaking, not guests?"

The expression of conscious guilt deepened on the face of the unfortunate professor. He had nothing to say. He realized that his conduct was too flagrant to admit of defense, so he attempted none. Suddenly the countenance of his questioner lit up with a smile, and he smote the professor on the shoulder.

"Well, old stick-in-the-mud, you haven't changed a particle in fifteen years! You don't mean to pretend you don't know me?"

"You can't—you can't be Richard Yates?"

"I not only can, but I can't be anybody else. I know, because I have often tried. Well, well, well, well! Stilly we used to call you; don't you remember? I'll never forget that time we sang 'Oft in the stilly night' in front of your window when you were studying for the exams. You always were a quiet fellow, Stilly. I've been waiting for you nearly a whole day. I was up just now with a party of friends when the boy brought me your card—a little philanthropic gathering—sort of mutual benefit arrangement, you know: each of us contributed what we could spare to a general fund, which was given to some deserving person in the crowd."

"Yes," said the professor dryly. "I heard the clerk telling the boy where he would be most likely to find you."

"Oh, you did, eh?" cried Yates, with a laugh. "Yes, Sam generally knows where to send for me; but he needn't have been so darned public about it. Being a newspaper man, I know what ought to go in print and what should have the blue pencil run through it. Sam is very discreet, as a general thing; but then he knew, of course, the moment he set eyes on you, that you were an old pal of mine."

Again Yates laughed, a very bright and cheery laugh for so evidently wicked a man.

"Come along," he said, taking the professor by the arm. "We must get you located."

They passed out into the hall, and drew up at the clerk's counter.

"I say, Sam," cried Yates, "can't you do something better for us than the fifth floor? I didn't come to Buffalo to engage in ballooning. No sky parlors for me, if I can help it."

"I'm sorry, Dick," said the clerk; "but I expect the fifth floor will be gone when the Chicago express gets in."

"Well, what can you do for us, anyhow?"

"I can let you have 518. That's the next room to yours. Really, they're the most comfortable rooms in the house this weather. Fine lookout over the lake. I wouldn't mind having a sight of the lake myself, if I could leave the desk."

"All right. But I didn't come to look at the lake, nor yet at the railroad tracks this side, nor at Buffalo Creek either, beautiful and romantic as it is, nor to listen to the clanging of the ten thousand locomotives that pass within hearing distance for the delight of your guests. The fact is that, always excepting Chicago, Buffalo is more like—for the professor's sake I'll say Hades, than any other place in America."

"Oh, Buffalo's all right," said the clerk, with that feeling of local loyalty which all Americans possess. "Say, are you here on this Fenian snap?"

"What Fenian snap?" asked the newspaper man.

"Oh! don't you know about it? I thought, the moment I saw you, that you were here for this affair. Well, don't say I told you, but I can put you on to one of the big guns if you want the particulars. They say they're going to take Canada. I told 'em that I wouldn't take Canada as a gift, let alone fight for it. I've been there."

Yates' newspaper instinct thrilled him as he thought of the possible sensation. Then the light slowly died out of his eyes when he looked at the professor, who had flushed somewhat and compressed his lips as he listened to the slighting remarks on his country.

"Well, Sam," said the newspaper man at last, "it isn't more than once in a lifetime that you'll find me give the go-by to a piece of news, but the fact is I'm on my vacation just now. About the first I've had for fifteen years; so, you see, I must take care of it. No, let the Argus get scooped, if it wants to. They'll value my services all the more when I get back. No. 518, I think you said?"

The clerk handed over the key, and the professor gave the boy the check for his valise at Yates' suggestion.

"Now, get a move on you," said Yates to the elevator boy. "We're going right through with you."

And so the two friends were shot up together to the fifth floor.

CHAPTER II.

The sky parlor, as Yates had termed it, certainly commanded a very extensive view. Immediately underneath was a wilderness of roofs. Farther along were the railway tracks that Yates objected to; and a line of masts and propeller funnels marked the windings of Buffalo Creek, along whose banks arose numerous huge elevators, each marked by some tremendous letter of the alphabet, done in white paint against the somber brown of the big building. Still farther to the west was a more grateful and comforting sight for a hot day. The blue lake, dotted with white sails and an occasional trail of smoke, lay shimmering under the broiling sun. Over the water, through the distant summer haze, there could be seen the dim line of the Canadian shore.

"Sit you down," cried Yates, putting both hands on the other's shoulders, and pushing him into a chair near the window. Then, placing his finger on the electric button, he added: "What will you drink?"

"I'll take a glass of water, if it can be had without trouble," said Renmark.

Yates' hand dropped from the electric button hopelessly to his side, and he looked reproachfully at the professor.

"Great Heavens!" he cried, "have something mild. Don't go rashly in for Buffalo water before you realize what it is made of. Work up to it gradually. Try a sherry cobbler or a milk shake as a starter."

"Thank you, no. A glass of water will do very well for me. Order what you like for yourself."

"Thanks, I can be depended on for doing that." He pushed the button, and, when the boy appeared, said: "Bring up an iced cobbler, and charge it to Professor Renmark, No. 518. Bring also a pitcher of ice water for Yates, No. 520. There," he continued gleefully, "I'm going to have all the drinks, except the ice water, charged to you. I'll pay the bill, but I'll keep the account to hold over your head in the future. Professor Stillson Renmark, debtor to Metropolitan Grand—one sherry cobbler, one gin sling, one whisky cocktail, and so on. Now, then, Stilly, let's talk business. You're not married, I take it, or you wouldn't have responded to my invitation so promptly." The professor shook his head. "Neither am I. You never had the courage to propose to a girl; and I never had the time."

"Lack of self-conceit was not your failing in the old days, Richard," said Renmark quietly.

Yates laughed. "Well, it didn't hold me back any, to my knowledge. Now I'll tell you how I've got along since we attended old Scragmore's academy together, fifteen years ago. How time does fly! When I left, I tried teaching for one short month. I had some theories on the education of our youth which did not seem to chime in with the prejudices the school trustees had already formed on the subject."

The professor was at once all attention. Touch a man on his business, and he generally responds by being interested.

"And what were your theories?" he asked.

"Well, I thought a teacher should look after the physical as well as the mental welfare of his pupils. It did not seem to me that his duty to those under his charge ended with mere book learning."

"I quite agree with you," said the professor cordially.

"Thanks. Well, the trustees didn't. I joined the boys at their games, hoping my example would have an influence on their conduct on the playground as well as in the schoolroom. We got up a rattling good cricket club. You may not remember that I stood rather better in cricket at the academy than I did in mathematics or grammar. By handicapping me with several poor players, and having the best players among the boys in opposition, we made a pretty evenly matched team at school section No. 12. One day, at noon, we began a game. The grounds were in excellent condition, and the opposition boys were at their best. My side was getting the worst of it. I was very much interested; and, when one o'clock came, I thought it a pity to call school and spoil so good and interesting a contest. The boys were unanimously of the same opinion. The girls were happy, picnicking under the trees. So we played cricket all the afternoon."

"I think that was carrying your theory a little too far," said the professor dubiously.

"Just what the trustees thought when they came to hear of it. So they dismissed me; and I think my leaving was the only case on record where the pupils genuinely mourned a teacher's departure. I shook the dust of Canada from my feet, and have never regretted it. I tramped to Buffalo, continuing to shake the dust off at every step. (Hello! here's your drinks at last, Stilly. I had forgotten about them—an unusual thing with me. That's all right, boy; charge it to room 518. Ah! that hits the spot on a hot day.) Well, where was I? Oh, yes, at Buffalo. I got a place on a paper here, at just enough to keep life in me; but I liked the work. Then I drifted to Rochester at a bigger salary, afterward to Albany at a still bigger salary, and of course Albany is only a few hours from New York, and that is where all newspaper men ultimately land, if they are worth their salt. I saw a small section of the war as special correspondent, got hurt, and rounded up in the hospital. Since then, although only a reporter, I am about the top of the tree in that line, and make enough money to pay my poker debts and purchase iced drinks to soothe the asperities of the game. When there is anything big going on anywhere in the country, I am there, with other fellows to do the drudgery; I writing the picturesque descriptions and interviewing the big men. My stuff goes red-hot over the telegraph wire, and the humble postage stamp knows my envelopes no more. I am acquainted with every hotel clerk that amounts to anything from New York to San Francisco. If I could save money, I should be rich, for I make plenty; but the hole at the top of my trousers pocket has lost me a lot of cash, and I don't seem to be able to get it mended. Now, you've listened with your customary patience in order to give my self-esteem, as you called it, full sway. I am grateful. I will reciprocate. How about yourself?"

The professor spoke slowly. "I have had no such adventurous career," he began. "I have not shaken Canadian dust from my feet, and have not made any great success. I have simply plodded; and am in no danger of becoming rich, although I suppose I spend as little as any man. After you were expel—after you left the aca——"

"Don't mutilate the good old English language, Stilly. You were right in the first place. I am not thin-skinned. You were saying after I was expelled. Go on."

"I thought perhaps it might be a sore subject. You remember, you were very indignant at the time, and——"

"Of course I was—and am still, for that matter. It was an outrage!"

"I thought it was proved that you helped to put the pony in the principal's room."

"Oh, certainly. That. Of course. But what I detested was the way the principal worked the thing. He allowed that villain Spink to turn evidence against us, and Spink stated I originated the affair, whereas I could claim no such honor. It was Spink's own project, which I fell in with, as I did with every disreputable thing proposed. Of course the principal believed at once that I was the chief criminal. Do you happen to know if Spink has been hanged yet?"

"I believe he is a very reputable business man in Montreal, and much respected."

"I might have suspected that. Well, you keep your eye on the respected Spink. If he doesn't fail some day, and make a lot of money, I'm a Dutchman. But go on. This is digression. By the way, just push that electric button. You're nearest, and it is too hot to move. Thanks. After I was expelled——"

"After your departure I took a diploma, and for a year or two taught a class in the academy. Then, as I studied during my spare time, I got a chance as master of a grammar school near Toronto, chiefly, as I think, though the recommendation of Principal Scragmore. I had my degree by this time. Then——"

There was a gentle tap at the door.

"Come in!" shouted Yates. "Oh, it's you. Just bring up another cooling cobbler, will you? and charge it, as before, to Professor Renmark, room 518. Yes; and then——"

"And then there came the opening in University College, Toronto. I had the good fortune to be appointed. There I am still, and there I suppose I shall stay. I know very few people, and am better acquainted with books than with men. Those whom I have the privilege of knowing are mostly studious persons, who have made, or will make, their mark in the world of learning. I have not had your advantage, of meeting statesmen who guide the destinies of a great empire.

"No; you always were lucky, Stilly. My experience is that the chaps who do the guiding are more anxious about their own pockets, or their own political advancement, than they are of the destinies. Still, the empire seems to take its course westward just the same. So old Scragmore's been your friend, has he?"

"He has, indeed."

"Well, he insulted me only the other day."

"You astonish me. I cannot imagine so gentlemanly and scholarly a man as Principal Scragmore insulting anybody."

"Oh, you don't know him as I do. It was like this: I wanted to find out where you were, for reasons that I shall state hereafter. I cudgeled my brains, and then thought of old Scrag. I wrote him, and enclosed a stamped and addressed envelope, as all unsought contributors should do. He answered—But I have his reply somewhere. You shall read it for yourself."

Yates pulled from his inside pocket a bundle of letters, which he hurriedly fingered over, commenting in a low voice as he did so: "I thought I answered that. Still, no matter. Jingo! haven't I paid that bill yet? This pass is run out. Must get another." Then he smiled and sighed as he looked at a letter in dainty handwriting; but apparently he could not find the document he sought.

"Oh, well, it doesn't matter. I have it somewhere. He returned me the prepaid envelope, and reminded me that United States stamps were of no use in Canada, which of course I should have remembered. But he didn't pay the postage on his own letter, so that I had to fork out double. Still, I don't mind that, only as an indication of his meanness. He went on to say that, of all the members of our class, you—you!—were the only one who had reflected credit on it. That was the insult. The idea of his making such a statement, when I had told him I was on the New York Argus! Credit to the class, indeed! I wonder if he ever heard of Brown after he was expelled. You know, of course. No? Well, Brown, by his own exertions, became president of the Alum Bank in New York, wrecked it, and got off to Canada with a clear half million. Yes, sir. I saw him in Quebec not six months ago. Keeps the finest span and carriage in the city, and lives in a palace. Could buy out old Scragmore a thousand times, and never feel it. Most liberal contributor to the cause of education that there is in Canada. He says education made him, and he's not a man to go back on education. And yet Scragmore has the cheek to say that you were the only man in the class who reflects credit on it!"

The professor smiled quietly as the excited journalist took a cooling sip of the cobbler.

"You see, Yates, people's opinions differ. A man like Brown may not be Principal Scragmore's ideal. The principal may be local in his ideals of a successful man, or of one who reflects credit on his teaching."

"Local? You bet he's local. Too darned local for me. It would do that man good to live in New York for a year. But I'm going to get even with him. I'm going to write him up. I'll give him a column and a half; see if I don't. I'll get his photograph, and publish a newspaper portrait of him. If that doesn't make him quake, he's a cast-iron man. Say, you haven't a photograph of old Scrag that you can lend me, have you?"

"I have; but I won't lend it for such a purpose. However, never mind the principal. Tell me your plans. I am at your disposal for a couple of weeks, or longer if necessary."

"Good boy! Well, I'll tell you how it is. I want rest and quiet, and the woods, for a week or two. This is how it happened: I have been steadily at the grindstone, except for a while in the hospital; and that, you will admit, is not much of a vacation. The work interests me, and I am always in the thick of it. Now, it's like this in the newspaper business: Your chief is never the person to suggest that you take a vacation. He is usually short of men and long on things to do, so if you don't worry him into letting you off, he won't lose any sleep over it. He's content to let well enough alone every time. Then there is always somebody who wants to get away on pressing business,—grandmother's funeral, and that sort of thing,—so if a fellow is content to work right along, his chief is quite content to let him. That's the way affairs have gone for years with me. The other week I went over to Washington to interview a senator on the political prospects. I tell you what it is, Stilly, without bragging, there are some big men in the States whom no one but me can interview. And yet old Scrag says I'm no credit to his class! Why, last year my political predictions were telegraphed all over this country, and have since appeared in the European press. No credit! By Jove, I would like to have old Scrag in a twenty-four-foot ring, with thin gloves on, for about ten minutes!"

"I doubt if he would shine under those circumstances. But never mind him. He spoke, for once, without due reflection, and with perhaps an exaggerated remembrance of your school-day offenses. What happened when you went to Washington?"

"A strange thing happened. When I was admitted to the senator's library, I saw another fellow, whom I thought I knew, sitting there. I said to the senator: 'I will come when you are alone.' The senator looked up in surprise, and said: 'I am alone.' I didn't say anything, but went on with my interview; and the other fellow took notes all the time. I didn't like this, but said nothing, for the senator is not a man to offend, and it is by not offending these fellows that I can get the information I do. Well, the other fellow came out with me, and as I looked at him I saw that he was myself. This did not strike me as strange at the time, but I argued with him all the way to New York, and tried to show him that he wasn't treating me fairly. I wrote up the interview, with the other fellow interfering all the while, so I compromised, and half the time put in what he suggested, and half the time what I wanted in myself. When the political editor went over the stuff, he looked alarmed. I told him frankly just how I had been interfered with, and he looked none the less alarmed when I had finished. He sent at once for a doctor. The doctor metaphorically took me to pieces, and then said to my chief: 'This man is simply worked to death.

He must have a vacation, and a real one, with absolutely nothing to think of, or he is going to collapse, and that with a suddenness which will surprise everybody.' The chief, to my astonishment, consented without a murmur, and even upbraided me for not going away sooner. Then the doctor said to me: 'You get some companion—some man with no brains, if possible, who will not discuss politics, who has no opinion on anything that any sane man would care to talk about, and who couldn't say a bright thing if he tried for a year. Get such a man to go off to the woods somewhere. Up in Maine or in Canada. As far away from post offices and telegraph offices as possible. And, by the way, don't leave your address at the Argus office.' Thus it happened, Stilly, when he described this man so graphically, I at once thought of you."

"I am deeply gratified, I am sure," said the professor, with the ghost of a smile, "to be so promptly remembered in such a connection, and if I can be of service to you, I shall be very glad. I take it, then, that you have no intention of stopping in Buffalo?"

"You bet I haven't. I'm in for the forest primeval, the murmuring pines and the hemlock, bearded with moss and green in the something or other—I forget the rest. I want to quit lying on paper, and lie on my back instead, on the sward or in a hammock. I'm going to avoid all boarding houses or delightful summer resorts, and go in for the quiet of the forest."

"There ought to be some nice places along the lake shore."

"No, sir. No lake shore for me. It would remind me of the Lake Shore Railroad when it was calm, and of Long Branch when it was rough. No, sir. The woods, the woods, and the woods. I have hired a tent and a lot of cooking things. I'm going to take that tent over to Canada to-morrow; and then I propose we engage a man with a team to cart it somewhere into the woods, fifteen or twenty miles away. We shall have to be near a farmhouse, so that we can get fresh butter, milk, and eggs. This, of course, is a disadvantage; but I shall try to get near someone who has never even heard of New York."

"You may find that somewhat difficult."

"Oh, I don't know. I have great hopes of the lack of intelligence in the

Canadians."

"Often the narrowest," said the professor slowly, "are those who think themselves the most cosmopolitan."

"Right you are," cried Yates, skimming lightly over the remark, and seeing nothing applicable to his case in it. "Well, I've laid in about half a ton, more or less, of tobacco, and have bought an empty jug."

"An empty one?"

"Yes. Among the few things worth having that the Canadians possess, is good whisky. Besides, the empty jar will save trouble at the customhouse. I don't suppose Canadian rye is as good as the Kentucky article, but you and I will have to scrub along on it for a while. And, talking of whisky, just press the button once again."

The professor did so, saying:

"The doctor made no remark, I suppose, about drinking less or smoking less, did he?"

"In my case? Well, come to think of it, there was some conversation in that direction. Don't remember at the moment just what it amounted to; but all physicians have their little fads, you know. It doesn't do to humor them too much. Ah, boy, there you are again. Well, the professor wants another drink. Make it a gin fizz this time, and put plenty of ice in it; but don't neglect the gin on that account. Certainly; charge it to room 518."

CHAPTER III.

"What's all this tackle?" asked the burly and somewhat red-faced customs officer at Fort Erie.

"This," said Yates, "is a tent, with the poles and pegs appertaining thereto. These are a number of packages of tobacco, on which I shall doubtless have to pay something into the exchequer of her Majesty. This is a jug used for the holding of liquids. I beg to call your attention to the fact that it is at present empty, which unfortunately prevents me making a libation to the rites of good-fellowship. What my friend has in that valise I don't know, but I suspect a gambling outfit, and would advise you to search him."

"My valise contains books principally, with some articles of wearing apparel," said the professor, opening his grip.

The customs officer looked with suspicion on the whole outfit, and evidently did not like the tone of the American. He seemed to be treating the customs department in a light and airy manner, and the officer was too much impressed by the dignity of his position not to resent flippancy. Besides, there were rumors of Fenian invasion in the air, and the officer resolved that no Fenian should get into the country without paying duty.

"Where are you going with this tent?"

"I'm sure I don't know. Perhaps you can tell us. I don't know the country about here. Say, Stilly, I'm off uptown to attend to the emptiness in this stone utensil. I've been empty too often myself not to sympathize with its condition. You wrestle this matter out about the tent. You know the ways of the country, whereas I don't."

It was perhaps as well that Yates left negotiations in the hands of his friend. He was quick enough to see that he made no headway with the officer, but rather the opposite. He slung the jar ostentatiously over his shoulder, to the evident discomfort of the professor, and marched up the hill to the nearest tavern, whistling one of the lately popular war tunes.

"Now," he said to the barkeeper, placing the jar tenderly on the bar, "fill that up to the nozzle with the best rye you have. Fill it with the old familiar juice, as the late poet Omar saith."

The bartender did as he was requested.

"Can you disguise a little of that fluid in any way, so that it may be taken internally without a man suspecting what he is swallowing?"

The barkeeper smiled. "How would a cocktail fill the vacancy?"

"I can suggest nothing better," replied Yates. "If you are sure you know how to make it."

The man did not resent this imputation of ignorance. He merely said, with the air of one who gives an incontrovertible answer:

"I am a Kentucky man myself."

"Shake!" cried Yates briefly, as he reached his hand across the bar. "How is it you happened to be here?"

"Well, I got in to a little trouble in Louisville, and here I am, where I can at least look at God's country."

"Hold on," protested Yates. "You're making only one cocktail."

"Didn't you say one?" asked the man, pausing in the compounding.

"Bless you, I never saw one cocktail made in my life. You are with me on this."

"Just as you say," replied the other, as he prepared enough for two.

"Now I'll tell you my fix," said Yates confidentially. "I've got a tent and some camp things down below at the customhouse shanty, and I want to get them taken into the woods, where I can camp out with a friend. I want a place where we can have absolute rest and quiet. Do you know the country round here? Perhaps you could recommend a spot."

"Well, for all the time I've been here, I know precious little about the back country. I've been down the road to Niagara Falls, but never back in the woods. I suppose you want some place by the lake or the river?"

"No, I don't. I want to get clear back into the forest—if there is a forest."

"Well, there's a man in to-day from somewhere near Ridgeway, I think. He's got a hay rack with him, and that would be just the thing to take your tent and poles. Wouldn't be very comfortable traveling for you, but it would be all right for the tent, if it's a big one."

"That will suit us exactly. We don't care a cent about the comfort. Roughing it is what we came for. Where will I find him?"

"Oh, he'll be along here soon. That's his team tied there on the side street. If he happens to be in good humor, he'll take your things, and as like as not give you a place to camp in his woods. Hiram Bartlett's his name. And, talking of the old Nick himself, here he is. I say, Mr. Bartlett, this gentleman was wondering if you couldn't tote out some of his belongings. He's going out your way."

Bartlett was a somewhat uncouth and wiry specimen of the Canadian farmer who evidently paid little attention to the subject of dress. He said nothing, but looked in a lowering way at Yates, with something of contempt and suspicion in his glance.

Yates had one receipt for making the acquaintance of all mankind. "Come in, Mr. Bartlett," he said cheerily, "and try one of my friend's excellent cocktails."

"I take mine straight," growled Bartlett gruffly, although he stepped inside the open door. "I don't want no Yankee mixtures in mine. Plain whisky's good enough for any man, if he is a man. I don't take no water, neither. I've got trouble enough."

The bartender winked at Yates as he shoved the decanter over to the newcomer.

"Right you are," assented Yates cordially.

The farmer did not thaw out in the least because of this prompt agreement with him, but sipped his whisky gloomily, as if it were a most disagreeable medicine.

"What did you want me to take out?" he said at last.

"A friend and a tent, a jug of whisky and a lot of jolly good tobacco."

"How much are you willing to pay?"

"Oh, I don't know. I'm always willing to do what's right. How would five dollars strike you?"

The farmer scowled and shook his head.

"Too much," he said, as Yates was about to offer more. "'Taint worth it. Two and a half would be about the right figure. Don'no but that's too much. I'll think on it going home, and charge you what it's worth. I'll be ready to leave in about an hour, if that suits you. That's my team on the other side of the road. If it's gone when you come back, I'm gone, an' you'll have to get somebody else."

With this Bartlett drew his coat sleeve across his mouth and departed.

"That's him exactly," said the barkeeper. "He's the most cantankerous crank in the township. And say, let me give you a pointer. If the subject of 1812 comes up,—the war, you know,—you'd better admit that we got thrashed out of our boots; that is, if you want to get along with Hiram. He hates Yankees like poison."

"And did we get thrashed in 1812?" asked Yates, who was more familiar with current topics than with the history of the past.

"Blessed if I know. Hiram says we did. I told him once that we got what we wanted from old England, and he nearly hauled me over the bar. So I give you the warning, if you want to get along with him."

"Thank you. I'll remember it. So long."

This friendly hint from the man in the tavern offers a key to the solution of the problem of Yates' success on the New York press. He could get news when no other man could. Flippant and shallow as he undoubtedly was, he somehow got into the inner confidences of all sorts of men in a way that made them give him an inkling of anything that was going on for the mere love of him; and thus Yates often received valuable assistance from his acquaintances which other reporters could not get for money.

The New Yorker found the professor sitting on a bench by the customhouse, chatting with the officer, and gazing at the rapidly flowing broad blue river in front of them.

"I have got a man," said Yates, "who will take us out into the wilderness in about an hour's time. Suppose we explore the town. I expect nobody will run away with the tent till we come back."

"I'll look after that," said the officer; and, thanking him, the two friends strolled up the street. They were a trifle late in getting back, and when they reached the tavern, they found Bartlett just on the point of driving home. He gruffly consented to take them, if they did not keep him more than five minutes loading up. The tent and its belongings were speedily placed on the hay rack, and then Bartlett drove up to the tavern and waited, saying nothing, although he had been in such a hurry a few moments before. Yates did not like to ask the cause of the delay; so the three sat there silently. After a while Yates said as mildly as he could:

"Are you waiting for anyone, Mr. Bartlett?"

"Yes," answered the driver in a surly tone. "I'm waiting for you to go in fur that jug. I don't suppose you filled it to leave it on the counter."

"By Jove!" cried Yates, springing off, "I had forgotten all about it, which shows the extraordinary effect this country has on me already." The professor frowned, but Yates came out merrily, with the jar in his hand, and Bartlett started his team. They drove out of the village and up a slight hill, going for a mile or two along a straight and somewhat sandy road. Then they turned into the Ridge Road, as Bartlett called it, in answer to a question by the professor, and there was no need to ask why it was so termed. It was a good highway, but rather stony, the road being, in places, on the bare rock. It paid not the slightest attention to Euclid's definition of a straight line, and in this respect was rather a welcome change from the average American road. Sometimes they passed along avenues of overbranching trees, which were evidently relics of the forest that once covered all the district. The road followed the ridge, and on each side were frequently to be seen wide vistas of lower lying country. All along the road were comfortable farmhouses; and it was evident that a prosperous community flourished along the ridge.

Bartlett spoke only once, and then to the professor, who sat next to him.

"You a Canadian?"

"Yes."

"Where's he from?"

"My friend is from New York," answered the innocent professor.

"Humph!" grunted Bartlett, scowling deeper than ever, after which he became silent again. The team was not going very fast, although neither the load nor the road was heavy. Bartlett was muttering a good deal to himself, and now and then brought down his whip savagely on one or the other of the horses; but the moment the unfortunate animals quickened their pace he hauled them in roughly. Nevertheless, they were going quickly enough to be overtaking a young woman who was walking on alone. Although she must have heard them coming over the rocky road she did not turn her head, but walked along with the free and springy step of one who is not only accustomed to walking, but who likes it. Bartlett paid no attention to the girl; the professor was endeavoring to read his thin book as well as a man might who is being jolted frequently; but Yates, as soon as he recognized that the pedestrian was young, pulled up his collar, adjusted his necktie with care, and placed his hat in a somewhat more jaunty and fetching position.

"Are you going to offer that girl a ride?" he said to Bartlett.

"No, I'm not."

"I think that is rather uncivil," he added, forgetting the warning he had had.

"You do, eh? Well, you offer her a ride. You hired the team."

"By Jove! I will," said Yates, placing his hand on the outside of the rack, and springing lightly to the ground.

"Likely thing," growled Bartlett to the professor, "that she's going to ride with the like of him."

The professor looked for a moment at Yates, politely taking off his hat to the apparently astonished young woman, but he said nothing.

"Fur two cents," continued Bartlett, gathering up the reins, "I'd whip up the horses, and let him walk the rest of the way."

"From what I know of my friend," answered the professor slowly, "I think he would not object in the slightest."

Bartlett muttered something to himself, and seemed to change his mind about galloping his horses.

Meanwhile, Yates, as has been said, took off his hat with great politeness to the fair pedestrian, and as he did so he noticed, with a thrill of admiration, that she was very handsome. Yates always had an eye for the beautiful.

"Our conveyance," he began, "is not as comfortable as it might be, yet I shall be very happy if you will accept its hospitalities."

The young woman flashed a brief glance at him from her dark eyes, and for a moment Yates feared that his language had been rather too choice for her rural understanding, but before he could amend his phrase she answered briefly:

"Thank you. I prefer to walk."

"Well, I don't know that I blame you. May I ask if you have come all the way from the village?"

"Yes."

"That is a long distance, and you must be very tired." There was no reply; so Yates continued. "At least, I thought it a long distance; but perhaps that was because I was riding on Bartlett's hay rack. There is no 'downy bed of ease' about his vehicle."

As he spoke of the wagon he looked at it, and, striding forward to its side, said in a husky whisper to the professor:

"Say, Stilly, cover up that jug with a flap of the tent."

"Cover it up yourself," briefly replied the other; "it isn't mine."

Yates reached across and, in a sort of accidental way, threw the flap of the tent over the too conspicuous jar. As an excuse for his action he took up his walking cane and turned toward his new acquaintance. He was flattered to see that she was loitering some distance behind the wagon, and he speedily rejoined her. The girl, looking straight ahead, now quickened her pace, and rapidly shortened the distance between herself and the vehicle. Yates, with the quickness characteristic of him, made up his mind that this was a case of country diffidence, which was best to be met by the bringing down of his conversation to the level of his hearer's intelligence.

"Have you been marketing?" he asked.

"Yes."

"Butter and eggs, and that sort of thing?"

"We are farmers," she answered, "and we sell butter and eggs"—a pause—"and that sort of thing."

Yates laughed in his light and cheery way. As he twirled his cane he looked at his pretty companion. She was gazing anxiously ahead toward a turn in the road. Her comely face was slightly flushed, doubtless with the exercise of walking.

"Now, in my country," continued the New Yorker, "we idolize our women. Pretty girls don't tramp miles to market with butter and eggs."

"Aren't the girls pretty—in your country?"

Yates made a mental note that there was not as much rurality about this girl as he had thought at first. There was a piquancy about the conversation which he liked. That she shared his enjoyment was doubtful, for a slight line of resentment was noticeable on her smooth brow.

"You bet they're pretty! I think all American girls are pretty. It seems their birthright. When I say American, I mean the whole continent, of course. I'm from the States myself—from New York." He gave an extra twirl to his cane as he said this, and bore himself with that air of conscious superiority which naturally pertains to a citizen of the metropolis. "But over in the States we think the men should do all the work, and that the women should—well, spend the money. I must do our ladies the justice to say that they attend strictly to their share of the arrangement."

"It should be a delightful country to live in—for the women."

"They all say so. We used to have an adage to the effect that America was paradise for women, purgatory for men, and—well, an entirely different sort of place for oxen."

There was no doubt that Yates had a way of getting along with people. As he looked at his companion he was gratified to note just the faintest suspicion of a smile hovering about her lips. Before she could answer, if she had intended to do so, there was a quick clatter of hoofs on the hard road ahead, and next instant an elegant buggy, whose slender jet-black polished spokes flashed and twinkled in the sunlight, came dashing past the wagon. On seeing the two walking together the driver hauled up his team with a suddenness that was evidently not relished by the spirited dappled span he drove.

"Hello, Margaret!" he cried; "am I late? Have you walked in all the way?"

"You are just in good time," answered the girl, without looking toward Yates, who stood aimlessly twirling his cane. The young woman put her foot on the buggy step, and sprang lightly in beside the driver. It needed no second glance to see that he was her brother, not only on account of the family resemblance between them, but also because he allowed her to get into the buggy without offering the slightest assistance, which, indeed, was not needed, and graciously permitted her to place the duster that covered his knees over her own lap as well. The restive team trotted rapidly down the road for a few rods, until they came to a wide place in the highway, and then whirled around, seemingly within an ace of upsetting the buggy; but the young man evidently knew his business, and held them in with a firm hand. The wagon was jogging along where the road was very narrow, and Bartlett kept his team stolidly in the center of the way.

"Hello, there, Bartlett!" shouted the young man in the buggy; "half the road, you know—half the road."

"Take it," cried Bartlett over his shoulder.

"Come, come, Bartlett, get out of the way, or I'll run you down."

"You just try it."

Bartlett either had no sense of humor or his resentment against his young neighbor smothered it, since otherwise he would have recognized that a heavy wagon was in no danger of being run into by a light and expensive buggy. The young man kept his temper admirably, but he knew just where to touch the elder on the raw. His sister's hand was placed appealingly on his arm. He smiled, and took no notice of her.

"Come, now, you move out, or I'll have the law on you."

"The law!" roared Bartlett; "you just try it on."

"Should think you'd had enough of it by this time."

"Oh, don't, don't, Henry!" protested the girl in distress.

"There aint no law," yelled Bartlett, "that kin make a man with a load move out fur anything."

"You haven't any load, unless it's in that jug."

Yates saw with consternation that the jar had been jolted out from under its covering, but the happy consolation came to him that the two in the buggy would believe it belonged to Bartlett. He thought, however, that this dog-in-the-manger policy had gone far enough. He stepped briskly forward, and said to Bartlett:

"Better drive aside a little, and let them pass."

"You 'tend to your own business," cried the thoroughly enraged farmer.

"I will," said Yates shortly, striding to the horses' heads. He took them by the bits and, in spite of Bartlett's maledictions and pulling at the lines, he drew them to one side, so that the buggy got by.

"Thank you!" cried the young man. The light and glittering carriage rapidly disappeared up the Ridge Road.

Bartlett sat there for one moment the picture of baffled rage. Then he threw the reins down on the backs of his patient horses, and descended.

"You take my horses by the head, do you, you good-fur-nuthin' Yank? You do, eh? I like your cheek. Touch my horses an' me a-holdin' the lines! Now you hear me? Your traps comes right off here on the road. You hear me?"

"Oh, anybody within a mile can hear you."

"Kin they? Well, off comes your pesky tent."

"No, it doesn't."

"Don't it, eh? Well, then, you'll lick me fust; and that's something no Yank ever did nor kin do."

"I'll do it with pleasure."

"Come, come," cried the professor, getting down on the road, "this has gone far enough. Keep quiet, Yates. Now, Mr. Bartlett, don't mind it; he means no disrespect."

"Don't you interfere. You're all right, an' I aint got nothin' ag'in you. But I'm goin' to thrash this Yank within an inch of his life; see if I don't. We met 'em in 1812, an' we fit 'em an' we licked 'em, an' we can do it ag'in. I'll learn ye to take my horses by the head."

"Teach," suggested Yates tantalizingly.

Before he could properly defend himself, Bartlett sprang at him and grasped him round the waist. Yates was something of a wrestler himself, but his skill was of no avail on this occasion. Bartlett's right leg became twisted around his with a steel-like grip that speedily convinced the younger man he would have to give way or a bone would break. He gave way accordingly, and the next thing he knew he came down on his back with a thud that seemed to shake the universe.

"There, darn ye!" cried the triumphant farmer; "that's 1812 and Queenstown Heights for ye. How do you like 'em?"

Yates rose to his feet with some deliberation, and slowly took off his coat.

"Now, now, Yates," said the professor soothingly, "let it go at this. You're not hurt, are you?" he asked anxiously, as he noticed how white the young man was around the lips.

"Look here, Renmark; you're a sensible man. There is a time to interfere and a time not to. This is the time not to. A certain international element seems to have crept into this dispute. Now, you stand aside, like a good fellow, for I don't want to have to thrash both of you."

The professor stood aside, for he realized that, when Yates called him by his last name, matters were serious.

"Now, old chucklehead, perhaps you would like to try that again."

"I kin do it a dozen times, if ye aint satisfied. There aint no Yank ever raised on pumpkin pie that can stand ag'in that grapevine twist."

"Try the grapevine once more."

Bartlett proceeded more cautiously this time, for there was a look in the young man's face he did not quite like. He took a catch-as-catch-can attitude, and moved stealthily in a semi-circle around Yates, who shifted his position constantly so as to keep facing his foe. At last Bartlett sprang forward, and the next instant found himself sitting on a piece of the rock of the country, with a thousand humming birds buzzing in his head, while stars and the landscape around joined in a dance together. The blow was sudden, well placed, and from the shoulder.

"That," said Yates, standing over him, "is 1776—the Revolution—when, to use your own phrase, we met ye, fit ye, and licked ye. How do you like it? Now, if my advice is of any use to you, take a broader view of history than you have done. Don't confine yourself too much to one period. Study up the War of the Revolution a bit."

Bartlett made no reply. After sitting there for a while, until the surrounding landscape assumed its normal condition, he arose leisurely, without saying a word. He picked the reins from the backs of the horses and patted the nearest animal gently. Then he mounted to his place and drove off. The professor had taken his seat beside the driver, but Yates, putting on his coat and picking up his cane, strode along in front, switching off the heads of Canada thistles with his walking stick as he proceeded.

CHAPTER IV.

Bartlett was silent for a long time, but there was evidently something on his mind, for he communed with himself, his mutterings growing louder and louder, until they broke the stillness; then he struck the horses, pulled them in, and began his soliloquy over again. At last he said abruptly to the professor:

"What's this Revolution he talked about?"

"It was the War of Independence, beginning in 1776."

"Never heard of it. Did the Yanks fight us?"

"The colonies fought with England."

"What colonies?"

"The country now called the United States."

"They fit with England, eh? Which licked?"

"The colonies won their independence."

"That means they licked us. I don't believe a word of it. 'Pears to me I'd 'a' heard of it; fur I've lived in these parts a long time."

"It was a little before your day."

"So was 1812; but my father fit in it, an' I never heard him tell of this Revolution. He'd 'a' known, I sh'd think. There's a nigger in the fence somewheres."

"Well, England was rather busy at the time with the French."

"Ah, that was it, was it? I'll bet England never knew the Revolution was a-goin' on till it was over. Old Napoleon couldn't thrash 'em, and it don't stand to reason that the Yanks could. I thought there was some skullduggery. Why, it took the Yanks four years to lick themselves. I got a book at home all about Napoleon. He was a tough cuss."

The professor did not feel called upon to defend the character of Napoleon, and so silence once more descended upon them. Bartlett seemed a good deal disturbed by the news he had just heard of the Revolution, and he growled to himself, while the horses suffered more than usual from the whip and the hauling back that invariably followed the stroke. Yates was some distance ahead, and swinging along at a great rate, when the horses, apparently of their own accord, turned in at an open gateway and proceeded, in their usual leisurely fashion, toward a large barn, past a comfortable frame house with a wide veranda in front.

"This is my place," said Bartlett shortly.

"I wish you had told me a few minutes ago," replied the professor, springing off, "so that I might have called to my friend."

"I'm not frettin' about him," said Bartlett, throwing the reins to a young man who came out of the house.

Renmark ran to the road and shouted loudly to the distant Yates. Yates apparently did not hear him, but something about the next house attracted the pedestrian's attention, and after standing for a moment and gazing toward the west he looked around and saw the professor beckoning to him. When the two men met, Yates said:

"So we have arrived, have we? I say, Stilly, she lives in the next house. I saw the buggy in the yard."

"She? Who?"

"Why, that good-looking girl we passed on the road. I'm going to buy our supplies at that house, Stilly, if you have no objections. By the way, how is my old friend 1812?"

"He doesn't seem to harbor any harsh feelings. In fact, he was more troubled about the Revolution than about the blow you gave him."

"News to him, eh? Well, I'm glad I knocked something into his head."

"You certainly did it most unscientifically."

"How do you mean—unscientifically?"

"In the delivery of the blow. I never saw a more awkwardly delivered undercut."

Yates looked at his friend in astonishment. How should this calm, learned man know anything about undercuts or science in blows?

"Well, you must admit I got there just the same."

"Yes, by brute force. A sledge hammer would have done as well. But you had such an opportunity to do it neatly and deftly, without any display of surplus energy, that I regretted to see such an opening thrown away."

"Heavens and earth, Stilly, this is the professor in a new light! What do you teach in Toronto University, anyhow? The noble art of self-defense?"

"Not exactly; but if you intend to go through Canada in this belligerent manner, I think it would be worth your while to take a few hints from me."

"With striking examples, I suppose. By Jove! I will, Stilly."

As the two came to the house they found Bartlett sitting in a wooden rocking chair on the veranda, looking grimly down the road.

"What an old tyrant that man must be in his home!" said Yates. There was no time for the professor to reply before they came within earshot.

"The old woman's setting out supper," said the farmer gruffly, that piece of information being apparently as near as he could get toward inviting them to share his hospitality. Yates didn't know whether it was meant for an invitation or not, but he answered shortly:

"Thanks, we won't stay."

"Speak fur yourself, please," snarled Bartlett.

"Of course I go with my friend," said Renmark; "but we are obliged for the invitation."

"Please yourselves."

"What's that?" cried a cheery voice from the inside of the house, as a stout, rosy, and very good-natured-looking woman appeared at the front door. "Won't stay? Who won't stay? I'd like to see anybody leave my house hungry when there's a meal on the table! And, young men, if you can get a better meal anywhere on the Ridge than what I'll give you, why, you're welcome to go there next time, but this meal you'll have here, inside of ten minutes. Hiram, that's your fault. You always invite a person to dinner as if you wanted to wrastle with him!"

Hiram gave a guilty start, and looked with something of mute appeal at the two men, but said nothing.

"Never mind him," continued Mrs. Bartlett. "You're at my house; and, whatever my neighbors may say ag'in me, I never heard anybody complain of the lack of good victuals while I was able to do the cooking. Come right in and wash yourselves, for the road between here and the fort is dusty enough, even if Hiram never was taken up for fast driving. Besides, a wash is refreshing after a hot day."

There was no denying the cordiality of this invitation, and Yates, whose natural gallantry was at once aroused, responded with the readiness of a courtier. Mrs. Bartlett led the way into the house; but as Yates passed the farmer the latter cleared his throat with an effort, and, throwing his thumb over his shoulder in the direction his wife had taken, said in a husky whisper:

"No call to—to mention the Revolution, you know."

"Certainly not," answered Yates, with a wink that took in the situation. "Shall we sample the jug before or after supper?"

"After, if it's all the same to you;" adding, "out in the barn."

Yates nodded, and followed his friend into the house.

The young men were shown into a bedroom of more than ordinary size, on the upper floor. Everything about the house was of the most dainty and scrupulous cleanliness, and an air of cheerful comfort pervaded the place.

Mrs. Bartlett was evidently a housekeeper to be proud of. Two large pitchers of cool, soft water awaited them, and the wash, as had been predicted, was most refreshing.

"I say," cried Yates, "it's rather cheeky to accept a man's hospitality after knocking him down."

"It would be for most people, but I think you underestimate your cheek, as you call it."

"Bravo, Stilly! You're blossoming out. That's repartee, that is. With the accent on the rap, too. Never you mind; I think old 1812 and I will get on all right after this. It doesn't seem to bother him any, so I don't see why it should worry me. Nice motherly old lady, isn't she?"

"Who? 1812?"

"No; Mrs. 1812. I'm sorry I complimented you on your repartee. You'll get conceited. Remember that what in the newspaper man is clever, in a grave professor is rank flippancy. Let's go down."

The table was covered with a cloth as white and spotless as good linen can well be. The bread was genuine homemade, a term so often misused in the cities. It was brown as to crust, and flaky and light as to interior. The butter, cool from the rock cellar, was of a refreshing yellow hue. The sight of the well-loaded table was most welcome to the eyes of hungry travelers. There was, as Yates afterward remarked, "abundance, and plenty of it."

"Come, father!" cried Mrs. Bartlett, as the young men appeared; they heard the rocking chair creak on the veranda in prompt answer to the summons.

"This is my son, gentlemen," said Mrs. Bartlett, indicating the young man who stood in a noncommittal attitude near a corner of the room. The professor recognized him as the person who had taken charge of the horses when his father came home. There was evidently something of his father's demeanor about the young man, who awkwardly and silently responded to the recognition of the strangers.

"And this is my daughter," continued the good woman. "Now, what might your names be?"

"My name is Yates, and this is my friend Professor Renmark of T'ronto," pronouncing the name of the fair city in two syllables, as is, alas! too often done. The professor bowed, and Yates cordially extended his hand to the young woman. "How do you do, Miss Bartlett?" he said, "I am happy to meet you."

The girl smiled very prettily, and said she hoped they had a pleasant trip out from Fort Erie.

"Oh, we had," said Yates, looking for a moment at his host, whose eyes were fixed on the tablecloth, and who appeared to be quite content to let his wife run the show. "The road's a little rocky in places, but it's very pleasant."

"Now, you sit down here, and you here," said Mrs. Bartlett; "and I do hope you have brought good appetites with you."

The strangers took their places, and Yates had a chance to look at the younger member of the family, which opportunity he did not let slip. It was hard to believe that she was the daughter of so crusty a man as Hiram Bartlett. Her cheeks were rosy, with dimples in them that constantly came and went in her incessant efforts to keep from laughing. Her hair, which hung about her plump shoulders, was a lovely golden brown. Although her dress was of the cheapest material, it was neatly cut and fitted; and her dainty white apron added that touch of wholesome cleanliness which was so noticeable everywhere in the house. A bit of blue ribbon at her white throat, and a pretty spring flower just below it, completed a charming picture, which a more critical and less susceptible man than Yates might have contemplated with pleasure.

Miss Bartlett sat smilingly at one end of the table, and her father grimly at the other. The mother sat at the side, apparently looking on that position as one of vantage for commanding the whole field, and keeping her husband and her daughter both under her eye. The teapot and cups were set before the young woman. She did not pour out the tea at once, but seemed to be waiting instructions from her mother. That good lady was gazing with some sternness at her husband, he vainly endeavoring to look at the ceiling or anywhere but at her. He drew his open hand nervously down his face, which was of unusual gravity even for him. Finally he cast an appealing glance at his wife, who sat with her hands folded on her lap, but her eyes were unrelenting. After a moment's hopeless irresolution Bartlett bent his head over his plate and murmured:

"For what we are about to receive, oh, make us truly thankful. Amen."

Mrs. Bartlett echoed the last word, having also bowed her head when she saw surrender in the troubled eyes of her husband.

Now, it happened that Yates, who had seen nothing of this silent struggle of the eyes, being exceedingly hungry, was making every preparation for the energetic beginning of the meal. He had spent most of his life in hotels and New York boarding houses, so that if he ever knew the adage, "Grace before meat," he had forgotten it. In the midst of his preparations came the devout words, and they came upon him as a stupefying surprise. Although naturally a resourceful man, he was not quick enough this time to cover his confusion. Miss Bartlett's golden head was bowed, but out of the corner of her eye she saw Yates' look of amazed bewilderment and his sudden halt of surprise. When all heads were raised, the young girl's still remained where it was, while her plump shoulders quivered. Then she covered her face with her apron, and the silvery ripple of a laugh came like a smothered musical chime trickling through her fingers.

"Why, Kitty!" cried her mother in astonishment, "whatever is the matter with you?"

The girl could no longer restrain her mirth. "You'll have to pour out the tea, mother!" She exclaimed, as she fled from the room.

"For the land's sake!" cried the astonished mother, rising to take her frivolous daughter's place, "what ails the child? I don't see what there is to laugh at."

Hiram scowled down the table, and was evidently also of the opinion that there was no occasion for mirth. The professor was equally in the dark.

"I am afraid, Mrs. Bartlett," said Yates, "that I am the innocent cause of Miss Kitty's mirth. You see, madam—it's a pathetic thing to say, but really I have had no home life. Although I attend church regularly, of course," he added with jaunty mendacity, "I must confess that I haven't heard grace at meals for years and years, and—well, I wasn't just prepared for it. I have no doubt I made an exhibition of myself, which your daughter was quick to see."

"It wasn't very polite," said Mrs. Bartlett with some asperity.

"I know that," pleaded Yates with contrition, "but I assure you it was unintentional on my part."

"Bless the man!" cried his hostess. "I don't mean you. I mean Kitty. But that girl never could keep her face straight. She always favored me more than her father."

This statement was not difficult to believe, for Hiram at that moment looked as if he had never smiled in his life. He sat silent throughout the meal, but Mrs. Bartlett talked quite enough for two.

"Well, for my part," she said, "I don't know what farming's coming to! Henry Howard and Margaret drove past here this afternoon as proud as Punch in their new covered buggy. Things is very different from what they was when I was a girl. Then a farmer's daughter had to work. Now Margaret's took her diploma at the ladies' college, and Arthur he's begun at the university, and Henry's sporting round in a new buggy. They have a piano there, with the organ moved out into the back room."

"The whole Howard lot's a stuck-up set," muttered the farmer.

But Mrs. Bartlett wouldn't have that. Any detraction that was necessary she felt competent to supply, without help from the nominal head of the house.

"No, I don't go so far as to say that. Neither would you, Hiram, if you hadn't lost your lawsuit about the line fence; and served you right, too, for it wouldn't have been begun if I had been at home at the time. Not but what

Margaret's a good housekeeper, for she wouldn't be her mother's daughter if she wasn't that; but it does seem to me a queer way to raise farmers' children, and I only hope they can keep it up. There were no pianos nor French and German in my young days."

"You ought to hear her play! My lands!" cried young Bartlett, who spoke for the first time. His admiration for her accomplishment evidently went beyond his powers of expression.

Bartlett himself did not relish the turn the conversation had taken, and he looked somewhat uneasily at the two strangers. The professor's countenance was open and frank, and he was listening with respectful interest to Mrs. Bartlett's talk. Yates bent over his plate with flushed face, and confined himself strictly to the business in hand.

"I am glad," said the professor innocently to Yates, "that you made the young lady's acquaintance. I must ask you for an introduction."

For once in his life Yates had nothing to say, but he looked at his friend with an expression that was not kindly. The latter, in answer to Mrs. Bartlett's inquiries, told how they had passed Miss Howard on the road, and how Yates, with his usual kindness of heart, had offered the young woman the hospitalities of the hay rack. Two persons at the table were much relieved when the talk turned to the tent. It was young Hiram who brought about this boon. He was interested in the tent, and he wanted to know. Two things seemed to bother the boy: First, he was anxious to learn what diabolical cause had been at work to induce two apparently sane men to give up the comforts of home and live in this exposed manner, if they were not compelled to do so. Second, he desired to find out why people who had the privilege of living in large cities came of their own accord into the uninteresting country, anyhow. Even when explanations were offered, the problem seemed still beyond him.

After the meal they all adjourned to the veranda, where the air was cool and the view extensive. Mrs. Bartlett would not hear of the young men pitching the tent that night. "Goodness knows, you will have enough of it, with the rain and the mosquitoes. We have plenty of room here, and you will have one comfortable night on the Ridge, at any rate. Then in the morning you can find a place in the woods to suit you, and my boy will take an ax and cut stakes for you, and help to put up your precious tent. Only remember that when it rains you are to come to the house, or you will catch your deaths with cold and rheumatism. It will be very nice till the novelty wears off; then you are quite welcome to the front rooms upstairs, and Hiram can take the tent back to Erie the first time he goes to town."

Mrs. Bartlett had a way of taking things for granted. It never seemed to occur to her that any of her rulings might be questioned. Hiram sat gazing silently at the road, as if all this was no affair of his.

Yates had refused a chair, and sat on the edge of the veranda, with his back against one of the pillars, in such a position that he might, without turning his head, look through the open doorway into the room. where Miss Bartlett was busily but silently clearing away the tea things. The young man caught fleeting glimpses of her as she moved airily about her work. He drew a cigar from his case, cut off the end with his knife, and lit a match on the sole of his boot, doing this with an easy automatic familiarity that required no attention on his part; all of which aroused the respectful envy of young Hiram, who sat on a wooden chair, leaning forward, eagerly watching the man from New York.

"Have a cigar?" said Yates, offering the case to young Hiram.

"No, no; thank you," gasped the boy, aghast at the reckless audacity of the proposal.

"What's that?" cried Mrs. Bartlett. Although she was talking volubly to the professor, her maternal vigilance never even nodded, much less slept. "A cigar? Not likely! I'll say this for my husband and my boy: that, whatever else they may have done, they have never smoked nor touched a drop of liquor since I've known them, and, please God, they never will."

"Oh, I guess it wouldn't hurt them," said Yates, with a lack of tact that was not habitual. He fell several degrees in the estimation of his hostess.

"Hurt 'em?" cried Mrs. Bartlett indignantly. "I guess it won't get a chance to." She turned to the professor, who was a good listener—respectful and deferential, with little to say for himself. She rocked gently to and fro as she talked.

Her husband sat unbendingly silent, in a sphinxlike attitude that gave no outward indication of his mental uneasiness. He was thinking gloomily that it would be just his luck to meet Mrs. Bartlett unexpectedly in the streets of Fort Erie on one of those rare occasions when he was enjoying the pleasures of sin for a season. He had the most pessimistic forebodings of what the future might have in store for him. Sometimes, when neighbors or customers "treated" him in the village, and he felt he had taken all the whisky that cloves would conceal, he took a five-cent cigar instead of a drink. He did not particularly like the smoking of it, but there was a certain devil-may-care recklessness in going down the street with a lighted cigar in his teeth, which had all the more fascination for him because of its manifest danger. He felt at these times that he was going the pace, and that it is well our women do not know of all the wickedness there is in this world. He did not fear that any neighbor might tell his wife, for there were depths to which no person could convince Mrs. Bartlett he would descend. But he thought with horror of some combination of circumstances that might bring his wife to town unknown to him on a day when he indulged. He pictured, with a shudder, meeting her unexpectedly on the uncertain plank sidewalk of Fort Erie, he smoking a cigar. When this nightmare presented itself to him, he resolved never to touch a cigar again; but he well knew that the best resolutions fade away if a man is excited with two or three glasses of liquor.

When Mrs. Bartlett resumed conversation with the professor, Yates looked up at young Hiram and winked. The boy flushed with pleasure under the comprehensiveness of that wink. It included him in the attractive halo of crime that enveloped the fascinating personality of the man from New York. It seemed to say:

"That's all right, but we are men of the world. We know."

Young Hiram's devotion to the Goddess Nicotine had never reached the altitude of a cigar. He had surreptitiously smoked a pipe in a secluded corner behind the barn in days when his father was away. He feared both his father and his mother, and so was in an even more embarrassing situation than old Hiram himself. He had worked gradually up to tobacco by smoking cigarettes of cane made from abandoned hoop-skirts. Crinoline was fashionable, even in the country, in those days, and ribs of cane were used before the metallic distenders of dresses came in. One hoop-skirt, whose usefulness as an article of adornment was gone, would furnish delight and smoking material for a company of boys for a month. The cane smoke made the tongue rather raw, but the wickedness was undeniable. Yates' wink seemed to recognize young Hiram as a comrade worthy to offer incense at the shrine, and the boy was a firm friend of Yates from the moment the eyelid of the latter drooped.

The tea things having been cleared away, Yates got no more glimpses of the girl through the open door. He rose from his lowly seat and strolled toward the gate, with his hands in his pockets. He remembered that he had forgotten something, and cudgeled his brains to make out what it was. He gazed down the road at the house of the Howards, which naturally brought to his recollection his meeting with the young girl on the road. There was a pang of discomfiture in this thought when he remembered the accomplishments attributed to her by Mrs. Bartlett. He recalled his condescending tone to her, and recollected his anxiety about the jar. The jar! That was what he had forgotten. He flashed a glance at old Hiram, and noted that the farmer was looking at him with something like reproach in his eyes. Yates moved his head almost imperceptibly toward the barn, and the farmer's eyes dropped to the floor of the veranda. The young man nonchalantly strolled past the end of the house.

"I guess I'll go to look after the horses," said the farmer, rising.

"The horses are all right, father. I saw to them," put in his son, but the old man frowned him down, and slouched around the corner of the house. Mrs. Bartlett was too busy talking to the professor to notice. So good a listener did not fall to her lot every day.

"Here's looking at you," said Yates, strolling into the barn, taking a telescopic metal cup from his pocket, and clinking it into receptive shape by a jerk of the hand. He offered the now elongated cup to Hiram, who declined any such modern improvement.

"Help yourself in that thing. The jug's good enough for me."

"Three fingers" of the liquid gurgled out into the patented vessel, and the farmer took the jar, after a furtive look over his shoulder.

"Well, here's luck." The newspaper man tossed off the potion with the facility of long experience, shutting up the dish with his thumb and finger, as if it were a metallic opera hat.

The farmer drank silently from the jar itself. Then he smote in the cork with his open palm.

"Better bury it in the wheat bin," he said morosely. "The boy might find it if you put it among the oats—feedin' the horses, ye know."

"Mighty good place," assented Yates, as the golden grain flowed in a wave over the submerged jar. "I say, old man, you know the spot; you've been here before."

Bartlett's lowering countenance indicated resentment at the imputation, but he neither affirmed nor denied. Yates strolled out of the barn, while the farmer went through a small doorway that led to the stable. A moment later he heard Hiram calling loudly to his son to bring the pails and water the horses.

"Evidently preparing an alibi," said Yates, smiling to himself, as he sauntered toward the gate.

CHAPTER V.

"What's up? what's up?" cried Yates drowsily next morning, as a prolonged hammering at his door awakened him.

"Well, you're not, anyhow." He recognized the voice of young Hiram. "I say, breakfast's ready. The professor has been up an hour."

"All right; I'll be down shortly," said Yates, yawning, adding to himself: "Hang the professor!" The sun was streaming in through the east window, but Yates never before remembered seeing it such a short distance above the horizon in the morning. He pulled his watch from the pocket of his vest, hanging on the bedpost. It was not yet seven o'clock. He placed it to his ear, thinking it had stopped, but found himself mistaken.

"What an unearthly hour," he said, unable to check the yawns. Yates' years on a morning newspaper had made seven o'clock something like midnight to him. He had been unable to sleep until after two o'clock, his usual time of turning in, and now this rude wakening seemed thoughtless cruelty. However, he dressed, and yawned himself downstairs.

They were all seated at breakfast when Yates entered the apartment, which was at once dining room and parlor.

"Waiting for you," said young Hiram humorously, that being one of a set of jokes which suited various occasions. Yates took his place near Miss Kitty, who looked as fresh and radiant as a spirit of the morning.

"I hope I haven't kept you waiting long," he said.

"No fear," cried Mrs. Bartlett. "If breakfast's a minute later than seven o'clock, we soon hear of it from the men-folks. They get precious hungry by that time."

"By that time?" echoed Yates. "Then do they get up before seven?"

"Laws! what a farmer you would make, Mr. Yates!" exclaimed Mrs.

Bartlett, laughing.

"Why, everything's done about the house and barn; horses fed, cows milked—everything. There never was a better motto made than the one you learned when you were a boy, and like as not have forgotten all about:

"'Early to bed and early to rise

Makes a man healthy, wealthy, and wise.'

I'm sorry you don't believe in it, Mr. Yates."

"Oh, that's all right," said Yates with some loftiness; "but I'd like to see a man get out a morning paper on such a basis. I'm healthy enough, quite as wealthy as the professor here, and everyone will admit that I'm wiser than he is; yet I never go to bed until after two o'clock, and rarely wake before noon."

Kitty laughed at this, and young Hiram looked admiringly at the New Yorker, wishing he was as clever.

"For the land's sake!" cried Mrs. Bartlett, with true feminine profanity, "What do you do up so late as that?"

"Writing, writing," said Yates airily; "articles that make dynasties tremble next morning, and which call forth apologies or libel suits afterward, as the case may be."

Young Hiram had no patience with one's profession as a topic of conversation. The tent and its future position was the burning question with him. He mumbled something about Yates having slept late in order to avoid the hearing of the words of thankfulness at the beginning of the meal. What his parents caught of this remark should have shown them how evil communications corrupt good manners; for, big as he was, the boy had never before ventured even to hint at ridicule on such a subject. He was darkly frowned upon by his silent father, and sharply reprimanded by his voluble mother. Kitty apparently thought it rather funny, and would like to have laughed. As it was, she contented herself with a sly glance at Yates, who, incredible as it may seem, actually blushed at young Hiram's allusion to the confusing incident of the day before.

The professor, who was a kind-hearted man, drew a herring across the scent.

"Mr. Bartlett has been good enough," said he, changing the subject, "to say we may camp in the woods at the back of the farm. I have been out there this morning, and it certainly is a lovely spot."

"We're awfully obliged, Mr. Bartlett," said Yates. "Of course Renmark went out there merely to show the difference between the ant and the butterfly. You'll find out what a humbug he is by and by, Mrs. Bartlett. He looks honest; but you wait."

"I know just the spot for the tent," cried young Hiram—"down in the hollow by the creek. Then you won't need to haul water."

"Yes, and catch their deaths of fever and ague," said Mrs. Bartlett. Malaria had not then been invented. "Take my advice, and put your tent—if you will put it up at all—on the highest ground you can find. Hauling water won't hurt you."

"I agree with you, Mrs. Bartlett. It shall be so. My friend uses no water—you ought to have seen his bill at the Buffalo hotel. I have it somewhere, and am going to pin it up on the outside of the tent as a warning to the youth of this neighborhood—and what water I need I can easily carry up from the creek."

The professor did not defend himself, and Mrs. Bartlett evidently took a large discount from all that Yates said. She was a shrewd woman.

After breakfast the men went out to the barn. The horses were hitched to the wagon, which still contained the tent and fittings. Young Hiram threw an ax and a spade among the canvas folds, mounted to his place, and drove up the lane leading to the forest, followed by Yates and Renmark on foot, leaving the farmer in his barnyard with a cheery good-by, which he did not see fit to return.

First, a field of wheat; next, an expanse of waving hay that soon would be ready for the scythe; then, a pasture field, in which some young horses galloped to the fence, gazing for a moment at the harnessed horses, whinnying sympathetically, off the next with flying heels wildly flung in the air, rejoicing in their own contrast of liberty, standing at the farther corner and snorting defiance to all the world; last, the cool shade of the woods into which the lane ran, losing its identity as a wagon road in diverging cow paths. Young Hiram knew the locality well, and drove direct to an ideal place for camping. Yates was enchanted. He included all that section of the country in a sweeping wave of his hand, and burst forth:

"'This is the spot, the center of the grove:

There stands the oak, the monarch of the wood.

In such a place as this, at such an hour,

We'll raise a tent to ward off sun and shower.'

Shakespeare improved."

"I think you are mistaken," said Renmark.

"Not a bit it. Couldn't be a better camping ground."

"Yes; I know that. I picked it out two hours ago. But you were wrong in your quotation. It is not by Shakespeare and yourself, as you seem to think."

"Isn't it? Some other fellow, eh? Well, if Shake is satisfied, I am. Do you know, Renny, I calculate that, line for line, I've written about ten times as much as Shakespeare. Do the literati recognize that fact? Not a bit of it. This is an ungrateful world, Stilly."

"It is, Dick. Now, what are you going to do toward putting up the tent?"

"Everything, my boy, everything. I know more about putting up tents than you do about science, or whatever you teach. Now, Hiram, my boy, you cut me some stakes about two feet long—stout ones. Here, professor, throw off that coat and négligé manner, and grasp this spade. I want some trenches dug."

Yates certainly made good his words. He understood the putting up of tents, his experience in the army being not yet remote. Young Hiram gazed with growing admiration at Yates' deftness and evident knowledge of what he was about, while his contempt for the professor's futile struggle with a spade entangled in tree roots was hardly repressed.

"Better give me that spade," he said at length; but there was an element of stubbornness in Renmark's character. He struggled on.

At last the work was completed, stakes driven, ropes tightened, trenches dug.

Yates danced, and gave the war whoop of the country.

"Thus the canvas tent has risen,

All the slanting stakes are driven,

Stakes of oak and stakes of beechwood:

Mops his brow, the tired professor;

Grins with satisfaction, Hiram;

Dances wildly, the reporter—

Calls aloud for gin and water.

Longfellow, old man, Longfellow. Bet you a dollar on it!" And the frivolous Yates poked the professor in the ribs.

"Richard," said the latter, "I can stand only a certain amount of this sort of thing. I don't wish to call any man a fool, but you act remarkably like one."

"Don't be mealy-mouthed, Renny; call a spade a spade. By George! young Hiram has gone off and forgotten his—And the ax, too! Perhaps they're left for us. He's a good fellow, is young Hiram. A fool? Of course I'm a fool. That's what I came for, and that's what I'm going to be for the next two weeks. 'A fool—a fool, I met a fool i' the forest'—just the spot for him. Who could be wise here after years of brick and mortar?

"Where are your eyes, Renny," he cried, "that you don't grow wild when you look around you? See the dappled sunlight filtering through the leaves; listen to the murmur of the wind in the branches; hear the trickle of the brook down there; notice the smooth bark of the beech and the rugged covering of the oak; smell the wholesome woodland scents. Renmark, you have no soul, or you could not be so unmoved. It is like paradise. It is—Say, Renny, by Jove, I've forgotten that jug at the barn!"

"It will be left there."

"Will it? Oh, well, if you say so."

"I do say so. I looked around for it this morning to smash it, but couldn't find it."

"Why didn't you ask old Bartlett?"

"I did; but he didn't know where it was."

Yates threw himself down on the moss and laughed, flinging his arms and legs about with the joy of living.

"Say, Culture, have you got any old disreputable clothes with you? Well, then, go into the tent and put them on; then come out and lie on your back and look up at the leaves. You're a good fellow, Renny, but decent clothes spoil you. You won't know yourself when you get ancient duds on your back. Old clothes mean freedom, liberty, all that our ancestors fought for. When you come out, we'll settle who's to cook and who to wash dishes. I've settled it already in my own mind, but I am not so selfish as to refuse to discuss the matter with you."

When the professor came out of the tent, Yates roared. Renmark himself smiled; he knew the effect would appeal to Yates.

"By Jove! old man, I ought to have included a mirror in the outfit. The look of learned respectability, set off with the garments of a disreputable tramp, makes a combination that is simply killing. Well, you can't spoil that suit, anyhow. Now sprawl."

"I'm very comfortable standing up, thank you."

"Get down on your back. You hear me?"

"Put me there."

"You mean it?" asked Yates, sitting up.

"Certainly."

"Say, Renny, beware. I don't want to hurt you."

"I'll forgive you for once."

"On your head be it."

"On my back, you mean."

"That's not bad, Renny," cried Yates, springing to his feet. "Now, it will hurt. You have fair warning. I have spoken."

The young men took sparring attitudes. Yates tried to do it gently at first, but, finding he could not touch his opponent, struck out more earnestly, again giving a friendly warning. This went on ineffectually for some time, when the professor, with a quick movement, swung around his foot with the airy grace of a dancing master, and caught Yates just behind the knee, at the same time giving him a slight tap on the breast. Yates was instantly on his back.

"Oh, I say, Renny, that wasn't fair. That was a kick."

"No, it wasn't. It is merely a little French touch. I learned it in Paris. They do kick there, you know; and it is good to know how to use your feet as well as your fists if you are set on by three, as I was one night in the Latin Quarter."

Yates sat up.

"Look here, Renmark; when were you in Paris?"

"Several times."

Yates gazed at him for a few moments, then said:

"Renny, you improve on acquaintance. I never saw a Bool-var in my life.

You must teach me that little kick."

"With pleasure," said Renmark, sitting down, while the other sprawled at full length. "Teaching is my business, and I shall be glad to exercise any talents I may have in that line. In endeavoring to instruct a New York man the first step is to convince him that he doesn't know everything. That is the difficult point. Afterward everything is easy."

"Mr. Stillson Renmark, you are pleased to be severe. Know that you are forgiven. This delicious sylvan retreat does not lend itself to acrimonious dispute, or, in plain English, quarreling. Let dogs delight, if they want to; I refuse to be goaded by your querulous nature into giving anything but the soft answer. Now to business. Nothing is so conducive to friendship, when two people are camping out, as a definition of the duties of each at the beginning. Do you follow me?"

"Perfectly. What do you propose?"

"I propose that you do the cooking and I wash the dishes. We will forage for food alternate days."

"Very well. I agree to that."

Richard Yates sat suddenly upright, looking at his friend with reproach in his eyes. "See here, Renmark; are you resolved to force on an international complication the very first day? That's no fair show to give a man."

"What isn't?"

"Why, agreeing with him. There are depths of meanness in your character, Renny, that I never suspected. You know that people who camp out always object to the part assigned them by their fellow-campers. I counted on that. I'll do anything but wash dishes."

"Then why didn't you say so?"

"Because any sane man would have said 'no' when I suggested cooking, merely because I suggested it. There is no diplomacy about you, Renmark. A man doesn't know where to find you when you act like that. When you refused to do the cooking, I would have said: 'Very well, then, I'll do it,' and everything would have been lovely; but now——"

Yates lay down again in disgust. There are moments in life when language fails a man.

"Then it's settled that you do the cooking and I wash the dishes?" said the professor.

"Settled? Oh yes, if you say so; but all the pleasure of getting one's own way by the use of one's brains is gone. I hate to be agreed with in that objectionably civil manner."

"Well, that point being arranged, who begins the foraging—you or I?"

"Both, Herr Professor, both. I propose to go to the house of the Howards, and I need an excuse for the first visit; therefore I shall forage to a limited extent. I go ostensibly for bread. As I may not get any, you perhaps should bring some from whatever farmhouse you choose as the scene of your operations. Bread is always handy in the camp, fresh or stale. When in doubt, buy more bread. You can never go wrong, and the bread won't."

"What else should I get? Milk, I suppose?"

"Certainly; eggs, butter—anything. Mrs. Bartlett will give you hints on what to get that will be more valuable than mine."

"Have you all the cooking utensils you need?"

"I think so. The villain from whom I hired the outfit said it was complete. Doubtless he lied; but we'll manage, I think."

"Very well. If you wait until I change my clothes, I'll go with you as far as the road."

"My dear fellow, be advised, and don't change. You'll get everything twenty per cent. cheaper in that rig-out. Besides, you are so much more picturesque. Your costume may save us from starvation if we run short of cash. You can get enough for both of us as a professional tramp. Oh, well, if you insist, I'll wait. Good advice is thrown away on a man like you."

CHAPTER VI.

Margaret Howard stood at the kitchen table kneading dough. The room was called the kitchen, which it was not, except in winter. The stove was moved out in spring to a lean-to, easily reached through the open door leading to the kitchen veranda.

When the stove went out or came in, it marked the approach or the departure of summer. It was the heavy pendulum whose swing this way or that indicated the two great changes of the year. No job about the farm was so much disliked by the farmer and his boys as the semiannual removal of the stove. Soot came down, stovepipes gratingly grudged to go together again; the stove was heavy and cumbersome, and many a pain in a rural back dated from the journey of the stove from outhouse to kitchen.

The kitchen itself was a one-story building, which projected back from the two-story farmhouse, giving the whole a T-shape. There was a veranda on each side of the kitchen, as well as one along the front of the house itself.

Margaret's sleeves were turned back nearly to her elbows, showing a pair of white and shapely arms. Now and then she deftly dusted the kneading board with flour to prevent the dough sticking, and as she pressed her open palms into the smooth, white, spongy mass, the table groaned protestingly. She cut the roll with a knife into lumps that were patted into shape, and placed side by side, like hillocks of snow, in the sheet-iron pan.

At this moment there was a rap at the open kitchen door, and Margaret turned round, startled, for visitors were rare at that hour of the day; besides, neighbors seldom made such a concession to formality as to knock. The young girl flushed as she recognized the man who had spoken to her the day before. He stood smiling in the doorway, with his hat in his hand. She uttered no word of greeting or welcome, but stood looking at him, with her hand on the floury table.

"Good-morning, Miss Howard," said Yates blithely; "may I come in? I have been knocking for some time fruitlessly at the front door, so I took the liberty of coming around."

"I did not hear you knock," answered Margaret. She neglected to invite him in, but he took the permission for granted and entered, seating himself as one who had come to stay. "You must excuse me for going on with my work," she added; "bread at this stage will not wait."

"Certainly, certainly. Please do not let me interrupt you. I have made my own bread for years, but not in that way. I am glad that you are making bread, for I have come to see if I can buy some."

"Really? Perhaps I can sell you some butter and eggs as well."

Yates laughed in that joyous, free-hearted manner of his which had much to do with his getting on in the world. It was difficult to remain long angry with so buoyant a nature.

"Ah, Miss Howard, I see you haven't forgiven me for that remark. You surely could not have thought I meant it. I really intended it for a joke, but I am willing to admit, now that I look back on it, that the joke was rather poor; but, then, most of my jokes are rather shopworn."

"I am afraid I lack a sense of humor."

"All women do," said Yates with easy confidence. "At least, all I've ever met."

Yates was sitting in a wooden chair, which he now placed at the end of the table, tilting it back until his shoulders rested against the wall. His feet were upon the rung, and he waved his hat back and forth, fanning himself, for it was warm. In this position he could look up at the face of the pretty girl before him, whose smooth brow was touched with just the slightest indication of a faint frown. She did not even glance at the self-confident young man, but kept her eyes fixed resolutely on her work. In the silence the table creaked as Margaret kneaded the dough. Yates felt an unaccustomed sensation of embarrassment creeping over him, and realized that he would have to re-erect the conversation on a new basis. It was manifestly absurd that a resourceful New Yorker, who had conversed unabashed with presidents, senators, generals, and other great people of a great nation, should be put out of countenance by the unaccountable coldness of a country girl in the wilds of Canada.

"I have not had an opportunity of properly introducing myself," he said at last, when the creaking of the table, slight as it was, became insupportable. "My name is Richard Yates, and I come from New York. I am camping out in this neighborhood to relieve, as it were, a mental strain—the result of years of literary work."

Yates knew from long experience that the quickest and surest road to a woman's confidence was through her sympathy. "Mental strain" struck him as a good phrase, indicating midnight oil and the hollow eye of the devoted student.

"Is your work mental, then?" asked Margaret incredulously, flashing, for the first time, a dark-eyed look at him.

"Yes," Yates laughed uneasily. He had manifestly missed fire. "I notice by your tone that you evidently think my equipment meager. You should not judge by appearances, Miss Howard. Most of us are better than we seem, pessimists to the contrary notwithstanding. Well, as I was saying, the camping company consists of two partners. We are so different in every respect that we are the best of friends. My partner is Mr. Stillson Renmark, professor of something or other in University College, Toronto."

For the first time Margaret exhibited some interest in the conversation.

"Professor Renmark? I have heard of him."

"Dear me! I had no idea the fame of the professor had penetrated beyond the precincts of the university—if a university has precincts. He told me it had all the modern improvements, but I suspected at the time that was merely Renny's brag."

The frown on the girl's brow deepened, and Yates was quick to see that he had lost ground again, if, indeed, he had ever gained any, which he began to doubt. She evidently did not relish his glib talk about the university. He was just about to say something deferentially about that institution, for he was not a man who would speak disrespectfully of the equator if he thought he might curry favor with his auditor by doing otherwise, when it occurred to him that Miss Howard's interest was centered in the man, and not in the university.

"In this world, Miss Howard," he continued, "true merit rarely finds its reward; at least, the reward shows some reluctance in making itself visible in time for man to enjoy it. Professor Renmark is a man so worthy that I was rather astonished to learn that you knew of him. I am glad for his sake that it is so, for no man more thoroughly deserves fame than he."

"I know nothing of him," said Margaret, "except what my brother has written. My brother is a student at the university."

"Is he really? And what is he going in for?"

"A good education."

Yates laughed.

"Well, that is an all-round handy thing for a person to have about him. I often wish I had had a university training. Still, it is not valued in an American newspaper office as much as might be. Yet," he added in a tone that showed he did not desire to be unfair to a man of education, "I have known some university men who became passably good reporters in time."

The girl made no answer, but attended strictly to the work in hand. She had the rare gift of silence, and these intervals of quiet abashed Yates, whose most frequent boast was that he could outtalk any man on earth. Opposition, or even abuse, merely served as a spur to his volubility, but taciturnity disconcerted him.

"Well," he cried at length, with something like desperation, "let us abandon this animated discussion on the subject of education, and take up the more practical topic of bread. Would you believe, Miss Howard, that I am an expert in bread making?"

"I think you said already that you made your bread."

"Ah, yes, but I meant then that I made it by the sweat of my good lead pencil. Still, I have made bread in my time, and I believe that some of those who subsisted upon it are alive to-day. The endurance of the human frame is something marvelous, when you come to think of it. I did the baking in a lumber camp one winter. Used to dump the contents of a sack of flour into a trough made out of a log, pour in a pail or two of melted snow, and mix with a hoe after the manner of a bricklayer's assistant making mortar. There was nothing small or mean about my bread making. I was in the wholesale trade."

"I pity the unfortunate lumbermen."

"Your sympathy is entirely misplaced, Miss Howard. You ought to pity me for having to pander to such appetites as those men brought in from the woods with them. They never complained of the quality of the bread, although there was occasionally some grumbling about the quantity. I have fed sheaves to a threshing machine and logs to a sawmill, but their voracity was nothing to that of a big lumberman just in from felling trees. Enough, and plenty of it, is what he wants. No 'tabbledote' for him. He wants it all at once, and he wants it right away. If there is any washing necessary, he is content to do it after the meal. I know nothing, except a morning paper, that has such an appetite for miscellaneous stuff as the man of the woods."

The girl made no remark, but Yates could see that she was interested in his talk in spite of herself. The bread was now in the pans, and she had drawn out the table to the middle of the floor; the baking board had disappeared, and the surface of the table was cleaned. With a light, deft motion of her two hands she had whisked over its surface the spotlessly white cloth, which flowed in waves over the table and finally settled calmly in its place like the placid face of a pond in the moonlight. Yates realized that the way to success lay in keeping the conversation in his own hands and not depending on any response. In this way a man may best display the store of knowledge he possesses, to the admiration and bewilderment of his audience, even though his store consists merely of samples like the outfit of a commercial traveler; yet a commercial traveler who knows his business can so arrange his samples on the table of his room in a hotel that they give the onlooker an idea of the vastness and wealth of the warehouses from which they are drawn.

"Bread," said Yates with the serious air of a very learned man, "is a most interesting subject. It is a historical subject—it is a biblical subject. As an article of food it is mentioned oftener in the Bible than any other. It is used in parable and to point a moral. 'Ye must not live on bread alone.'"

From the suspicion of a twinkle in the eye of his listener he feared he had not quoted correctly. He knew he was not now among that portion of his samples with which he was most familiar, so he hastened back to the historical aspect of his subject. Few people could skate over thinner ice than Richard Yates, but his natural shrewdness always caused him to return to more solid footing.

"Now, in this country bread has gone through three distinct stages, and although I am a strong believer in progress, yet, in the case of our most important article of food, I hold that the bread of to-day is inferior to the bread our mothers used to make, or perhaps, I should say, our grandmothers. This is, unfortunately, rapidly becoming the age of machinery—and machinery, while it may be quicker, is certainly not so thorough as old-fashioned hand work. There is a new writer in England named Ruskin who is very bitter against machinery. He would like to see it abolished—at least, so he says. I will send for one of his books, and show it to you, if you will let me."

"You, in New York, surely do not call the author of 'Modern Painters' and 'The Seven Lamps of Architecture' a new man. My father has one of his books which must be nearly twenty years old."

This was the longest speech Margaret had made to him, and, as he said afterward to the professor in describing its effects, it took him right off his feet. He admitted to the professor, but not to the girl, that he had never read a word of Ruskin in his life. The allusion he had made to him he had heard someone else use, and he had worked it into an article before now with telling effect. "As Mr. Ruskin says" looked well in a newspaper column, giving an air of erudition and research to it. Mr. Yates, however, was not at the present moment prepared to enter into a discussion on either the age or the merits of the English writer.

"Ah, well," he said, "technically speaking, of course, Ruskin is not a new man. What I meant was that he is looked on—ah—in New York as—that is—you know—as comparatively new—comparatively new. But, as I was saying about bread, the old log-house era of bread, as I might call it, produced the most delicious loaf ever made in this country. It was the salt-rising kind, and was baked in a round, flat-bottomed iron kettle. Did you ever see the baking kettle of other days?"

"I think Mrs. Bartlett has one, although she never uses it now. It was placed on the hot embers, was it not?"

"Exactly," said Yates, noting with pleasure that the girl was thawing, as he expressed it to himself. "The hot coals were drawn out and the kettle placed upon them. When the lid was in position, hot coals were put on he top of it. The bread was firm and white and sweet inside, with the most delicious golden brown crust all around. Ah, that was bread! but perhaps I appreciated it because I was always hungry in those days. Then came the alleged improvement of the tin Dutch oven. That was the second stage in the evolution of bread in this country. It also belonged to the log-house and open-fireplace era. Bread baked by direct heat from the fire and reflected heat from the polished tin. I think our present cast-iron stove arrangement is preferable to that, although not up to the old-time kettle."

If Margaret had been a reader of the New York Argus, she would have noticed that the facts set forth by her visitor had already appeared in that paper, much elaborated, in an article entitled "Our Daily Bread." In the pause that ensued after Yates had finished his dissertation on the staff of life the stillness was broken by a long wailing cry. It began with one continued, sustained note, and ended with a wail half a tone below the first. The girl paid no attention to it, but Yates started to his feet.

"In the name of—What's that?"

Margaret smiled, but before she could answer the stillness was again broken by what appeared to be the more distant notes of a bugle.

"The first," she said, "was Kitty Bartlett's voice calling the men home from the field for dinner. Mrs. Bartlett is a very good housekeeper and is usually a few minutes ahead of the neighbors with the meals. The second was the sound of a horn farther up the road. It is what you would deplore as the age of tin applied to the dinner call, just as your tin oven supplanted the better bread maker. I like Kitty's call much better than the tin horn. It seems to me more musical, although it appeared to startle you."

"Oh, you can talk!" cried Yates with audacious admiration, at which the girl colored slightly and seemed to retire within herself again. "And you can make fun of people's historical lore, too. Which do you use—the tin horn or the natural voice?"

"Neither. If you will look outside, you will see a flag at the top of a pole. That is our signal."

It flashed across the mind of Yates that this was intended as an intimation that he might see many things outside to interest him. He felt that his visit had not been at all the brilliant success he had anticipated. Of course the quest for bread had been merely an excuse. He had expected to be able to efface the unfavorable impression he knew he had made by his jaunty conversation on the Ridge Road the day before, and he realized that his position was still the same. A good deal of Yates' success in life came from the fact that he never knew when he was beaten. He did not admit defeat now, but he saw he had, for some reason, not gained any advantage in a preliminary skirmish. He concluded it would be well to retire in good order, and renew the contest at some future time. He was so unused to anything like a rebuff that all his fighting qualities were up in arms, and he resolved to show this unimpressionable girl that he was not a man to be lightly valued.

As he rose the door from the main portion of the house opened, and there entered a woman hardly yet past middle age, who had once been undoubtedly handsome, but on whose worn and faded face was the look of patient weariness which so often is the result of a youth spent in helping a husband to overcome the stumpy stubbornness of an American bush farm. When the farm is conquered, the victor is usually vanquished. It needed no second glance to see that she was the mother from whom the daughter had inherited her good looks. Mrs. Howard did not appear surprised to see a stranger standing there; in fact, the faculty of being surprised at anything seemed to have left her. Margaret introduced them quietly, and went about her preparation for the meal. Yates greeted Mrs. Howard with effusion. He had come, he said, on a bread mission. He thought he knew something about bread, but he now learned he came too early in the day. He hoped he might have the privilege of repeating his visit.

"But you are not going now?" said Mrs. Howard with hospitable anxiety.

"I fear I have already stayed too long," answered Yates lingeringly. "My partner, Professor Renmark, is also on a foraging expedition at your neighbors', the Bartletts. He is doubtless back in camp long ago, and will be expecting me."

"No fear of that. Mrs. Bartlett would never let anyone go when there is a meal on the way."

"I am afraid I shall be giving extra trouble by staying. I imagine there is quite enough to do in every farmhouse without entertaining any chance tramp who happens along. Don't you agree with me for once, Miss Howard?"

Yates was reluctant to go, and yet he did not wish to stay unless Margaret added her invitation to her mother's. He felt vaguely that his reluctance did him credit, and that he was improving. He could not remember a time when he had not taken without question whatever the gods sent, and this unaccustomed qualm of modesty caused him to suspect that there were depths in his nature hitherto unexplored. It always flatters a man to realize that he is deeper than he thought.

Mrs. Howard laughed in a subdued manner because Yates likened himself to a tramp, and Margaret said coldly:

"Mother's motto is that one more or less never makes any difference."

"And what is your motto, Miss Howard?"

"I don't think Margaret has any," said Mrs. Howard, answering for her daughter. "She is like her father. She reads a great deal and doesn't talk much. He would read all the time, if he did not have to work. I see Margaret has already invited you, for she has put an extra plate on the table."

"Ah, then," said Yates, "I shall have much pleasure in accepting both the verbal and the crockery invitation. I am sorry for the professor at his lonely meal by the tent; for he is a martyr to duty, and I feel sure Mrs. Bartlett will not be able to keep him."

Before Mrs. Howard could reply there floated in to them, from the outside, where Margaret was, a cheery voice which Yates had no difficulty in recognizing as belonging to Miss Kitty Bartlett.

"Hello, Margaret!" she said. "Is he here?"

The reply was inaudible.

"Oh, you know whom I mean. That conceited city fellow."

There was evidently an admonition and a warning.

"Well, I don't care if he does. I'll tell him so to his face. It might do him good."

Next moment there appeared a pretty vision in the doorway. On the fair curls, which were flying about her shoulders, had been carelessly placed her brother's straw hat, with a broad and torn brim. Her face was flushed with running; and of the fact that she was a very lovely girl there was not the slightest doubt.

"How de do?" she said to Mrs. Howard, and, nodding to Yates, cried: "I knew you were here, but I came over to make sure. There's going to be war in our house. Mother's made a prisoner of the professor already, but he doesn't know it. He thinks he's going back to the tent, and she's packing up the things he wanted, and doing it awfully slow, till I get back. He said you would be sure to be waiting for him out in the woods. We both told him there was no fear of that. You wouldn't leave a place where there was good cooking for all the professors in the world."

"You are a wonderful judge of character, Miss Bartlett," said Yates, somewhat piqued by her frankness.

"Of course I am. The professor knows ever so much more than you, but he doesn't know when he's well off, just the same. You do. He's a quiet, stubborn man."

"And which do you admire the most, Miss Bartlett—a quiet, stubborn man, or one who is conceited?"

Miss Kitty laughed heartily, without the slightest trace of embarrassment. "Detest, you mean. I'm sure I don't know. Margaret, which is the most objectionable?"

Margaret looked reproachfully at her neighbor on being thus suddenly questioned, but said nothing.

Kitty, laughing again, sprang toward her friend, dabbed a little kiss, like the peck of a bird, on each cheek, cried: "Well, I must be off, or mother will have to tie up the professor to keep him," and was off accordingly with the speed and lightness of a young fawn.

"Extraordinary girl," remarked Yates, as the flutter of curls and calico dress disappeared.

"She is a good girl," cried Margaret emphatically.

"Bless me, I said nothing to the contrary. But don't you think she is somewhat free with her opinions about other people?" asked Yates.

"She did not know that you were within hearing when she first spoke, and after that she brazened it out. That's her way. But she's a kind girl and good-hearted, otherwise she would not have taken the trouble to come over here merely because your friend happened to be surly."

"Oh, Renny is anything but surly," said Yates, as quick to defend his friend as she was to stand up for hers. "As I was saying a moment ago, he is a martyr to duty, and if he thought I was at the camp, nothing would keep him. Now he will have a good dinner in peace when he knows I am not waiting for him, and a good dinner is more than he will get when I take to the cooking."

By this time the silent signal on the flagpole had done its work, and Margaret's father and brother arrived from the field. They put their broad straw hats on the roof of the kitchen veranda, and, taking water in a tin basin from the rain barrel, placed it on a bench outside and proceeded to wash vigorously.

Mr. Howard was much more interested in his guest than his daughter had apparently been. Yates talked glibly, as he could always do if he had a sympathetic audience, and he showed an easy familiarity with the great people of this earth that was fascinating to a man who had read much of them, but who was, in a measure, locked out of the bustling world. Yates knew many of the generals in the late war, and all of the politicians. Of the latter there was not an honest man among them, according to the reporter; of the former there were few who had not made the most ghastly mistakes. He looked on the world as a vast hoard of commonplace people, wherein the men of real genius were buried out of sight, if there were any men of genius, which he seemed to doubt, and those on the top were there either through their own intrigues or because they had been forced up by circumstances. His opinions sometimes caused a look of pain to cross the face of the older man, who was enthusiastic in his quiet way, and had his heroes. He would have been a strong Republican if he had lived in the States; and he had watched the four-years' struggle, through the papers, with keen and absorbed interest. The North had been fighting, in his opinion, for the great and undying principle of human liberty, and had deservedly won. Yates had no such delusion. It was a politicians' war, he said. Principle wasn't in it. The North would have been quite willing to let slavery stand if the situation had not been forced by the firing on Fort Sumter. Then the conduct of the war did not at all meet the approval of Mr. Yates.

"Oh, yes," he said, "I suppose Grant will go down into history as a great general. The truth is that he simply knew how to subtract. That is all there is in it. He had the additional boon of an utter lack of imagination. We had many generals who were greater than Grant, but they were troubled with imaginations. Imagination will ruin the best general in the world. Now, take yourself, for example. If you were to kill a man unintentionally, your conscience would trouble you all the rest of your life. Think how you would feel, then, if you were to cause the death of ten thousand men all in a lump. It would break you down. The mistake an ordinary man makes may result in the loss of a few dollars, which can be replaced; but if a general makes a mistake, the loss can never be made up, for his mistakes are estimated by the lives of men. He says 'Go' when he should have said 'Come.' He says 'Attack' when he should have said 'Retreat.' What is the result? Five, ten, or fifteen thousand men, many of them better men than he is, left dead on the field. Grant had nothing of this feeling. He simply knew how to subtract, as I said before. It is like this: You have fifty thousand men and I have twenty-five thousand. When I kill twenty-five thousand of your men and you kill twenty-five thousand of my men, you have twenty-five thousand left and I have none. You are the victor, and the thoughtless crowd howls about you, but that does not make you out the greatest general by a long shot. If Lee had had Grant's number, and Grant had Lee's, the result would have been reversed. Grant set himself to do this little sum in subtraction, and he did it—did it probably as quickly as any other man would have done it, and he knew that when it was done the war would have to stop. That's all there was to it."

The older man shook his head. "I doubt," he said, "if history will take your view either of the motives of those in power or of the way the war was carried on. It was a great and noble struggle, heroically fought by those deluded people who were in the wrong, and stubbornly contested at immense self-sacrifice by those who were in the right."

"What a pity it was," said young Howard to the newspaper man, with a rudeness that drew a frown from his father, "that you didn't get to show 'em how to carry on the war."

"Well," said Yates, with a humorous twinkle in his eye, "I flatter myself that I would have given them some valuable pointers. Still, it is too late to bemoan their neglect now."

"Oh, you may have a chance yet," continued the unabashed young man. "They say the Fenians are coming over here this time sure. You ought to volunteer either on our side or on theirs, and show how a war ought to be carried on."

"Oh, there's nothing in the Fenian scare! They won't venture over. They fight with their mouths. It's the safest way."

"I believe you," said the youth significantly.

Perhaps it was because the boy had been so inconsiderate as to make these remarks that Yates received a cordial invitation from both Mr. and Mrs. Howard to visit the farm as often as he cared to do so. Of this privilege Yates resolved to avail himself, but he would have prized it more if Miss Margaret had added her word—which she did not, perhaps because she was so busy looking after the bread. Yates knew, however, that with a woman apparent progress is rarely synonymous with real progress. This knowledge soothed his disappointment.

As he walked back to the camp he reviewed his own feelings with something like astonishment. The march of events was rapid even for him, who was not slow in anything he undertook.

"It is the result of leisure," he said to himself. "It is the first breathing time I have had for fifteen years. Not two days of my vacation gone, and here I am hopelessly in love!"

CHAPTER VII.

Yates had intended to call at the Bartletts' and escort Renmark back to the woods; but when he got outside he forgot the existence of the professor, and wandered somewhat aimlessly up the side road, switching at the weeds that always grow in great profusion along the ditches of a Canadian country thoroughfare. The day was sunny and warm, and as Yates wandered on in the direction of the forest he thought of many things. He had feared that he would find life deadly dull so far from New York, without even the consolation of a morning-paper, the feverish reading of which had become a sort of vice with him, like smoking. He had imagined that he could not exist without his morning paper, but he now realized that it was not nearly so important a factor in life as he had supposed; yet he sighed when he thought of it, and wished he had one with him of current date. He could now, for the first time in many years, read a paper without that vague fear which always possessed him when he took up an opposition sheet, still damp from the press. Before he could enjoy it his habit was to scan it over rapidly to see if it contained any item of news which he himself had missed the previous day. The impending "scoop" hangs over the head of the newspaper man like the sword so often quoted. Great as the joy of beating the opposition press is, it never takes the poignancy of the sting away from a beating received. If a terrible disaster took place, and another paper gave fuller particulars than the Argus did, Yates found himself almost wishing the accident had not occurred, although he recognized such a wish as decidedly unprofessional.

Richard's idea of the correct spirit in a reporter was exemplified by an old broken-down, out-of-work morning newspaper man, who had not long before committed suicide at an hour in the day too late for the evening papers to get the sensational item. He had sent in to the paper for which he formerly worked a full account of the fatality, accurately headed and sub-headed; and, in his note to the city editor, he told why he had chosen the hour of 7 P.M. as the time for his departure from an unappreciative world.

"Ah, well," said Yates under his breath, and suddenly pulling himself together, "I mustn't think of New York if I intend to stay here for a couple of weeks. I'll be city-sick the first thing I know, and then I'll make a break for the metropolis. This will never do. The air here is enchanting, it fills a man with new life. This is the spot for me, and I'll stick to it till I'm right again. Hang New York! But I mustn't think of Broadway or I'm done for."

He came to the spot in the road where he could see the white side of the tent under the dark trees, and climbed up on the rail fence, sitting there for a few moments. The occasional call of a quail from a neighboring field was the only sound that broke the intense stillness. The warm smell of spring was in the air. The buds had but recently broken, and the woods, intensely green, had a look of newness and freshness that was comforting to the eye and grateful to the other senses. The world seemed to be but lately made. The young man breathed deeply of the vivifying air, and said: "No, there's nothing the matter with this place, Dick. New York's a fool to it." Then, with a sigh, he added: "If I can stand it for two weeks. I wonder how the boys are getting on without me."

In spite of himself his thoughts kept drifting back to the great city, although he told himself that it wouldn't do. He gazed at the peaceful, spreading landscape, but his eyes were vacant and he saw nothing. The roar of the streets was in his ears. Suddenly his reverie was broken by a voice from the forest.

"I say, Yates, where's the bread?"

Yates looked quickly around, somewhat startled, and saw the professor coming toward him.

"The bread? I forgot all about it. No; I didn't either. They were baking—that was it. I am to go for it later in the day. What loot did you rake in, professor?"

"Vegetables mostly."

"That's all right. Have a good dinner?"

"Excellent."

"So did I. Renny, when you interrupted me, I was just counting the farmhouses in sight. What do you say to boarding round among them? You are a schoolmaster, and ought to know all about it. Isn't education in this country encouraged by paying the teacher as little as possible, and letting him take it out in eating his way from one house to another? Ever board around, Renny?"

"Never. If the custom once existed in Canada, it is out of date now."

"That's a pity. I hate to face my own cooking, Renmark. We become less brave as we grow older. By the way, how is old man Bartlett? As well as could be expected?"

"He seemed much as usual. Mrs. Bartlett has sent out two chairs to the tent; she fears we will get rheumatism if we sit on the ground."

"She is a kind woman, Renny, and a thoughtful. And that reminds me: I have a hammock somewhere among my belongings. I will swing it up. Chairs are comfortable, but a hammock is luxury."

Yates slid down from the fence top, and together the two men walked to the tent. The hammock was unfurled and slung between two trees. Yates tested it cautiously, and finally trusted himself to its restful folds of network. He was swaying indolently several feet from the ground when he said to Renmark:

"I call this paradise—paradise regained; but it will be paradise lost next month. Now, professor, I am ready to do the cooking, but I have a fancy for doing it by proxy. The general directs, and the useful prosaic man executes. Where are your vegetables, Renny? Potatoes and carrots, eh? Very good. Now, you may wash them, Renny; but first you must bring some water from the spring."

The professor was a patient man, and he obeyed. Yates continued to swing in the hammock alternating directions with rhapsodies on the beauties of the day and the stillness of the woods. Renmark said but little, and attended strictly to the business in hand. The vegetables finished, he took a book from his valise, tilted a chair back against a tree, and began to read.

"I'm depending upon you for the bread," he said to the drowsy man in the hammock.

"Right you are, Renny. Your confidence is not misplaced. I shall presently journey down into the realms of civilization, and fill the long-felt want. I shall go to the Howards by way of the Bartlett homestead, but I warn you that if there is a meal on, at either place, you will not have me here to test your first efforts at cooking. So you may have to wait until breakfast for my opinion."

Yates extricated himself slowly and reluctantly from the hammock, and looked regretfully at it when he stood once more on the ground.

"This mad struggle for bread, professor, is the curse of life here below. It is what we are all after. If it were not for the necessity of bread and clothing, what a good time a fellow might have. Well, my blessing, Renny. Good-by."

Yates strolled slowly through the woods, until he came to the beginning of a lane which led to the Bartlett homestead. He saw the farmer and his son at work in the back fields. From between the distant house and barn there arose, straight up into the still air, a blue column of smoke, which, reaching a certain height, spread out like a thin, hazy cloud above the dwelling. At first Yates thought that some of the outhouses were on fire, and he quickened his pace to a run; but a moment's reflection showed him that the column was plainly visible to the workers in the fields, and that if anything were wrong they would not continue placidly at their labor. When he had walked the long length of the lane, and had safely rounded the corner of the barn, he saw, in the open space between that building and the house, a huge camp fire blazing. From a pole, upheld by two crotched supports, hung a big iron kettle over the flames. The caldron was full nearly to the brim, and the steam was already beginning to rise from its surface, although the fire had evidently been but recently kindled. The smoke was not now so voluminous, but Kitty Bartlett stood there with a big-brimmed straw hat in her hands, fanning it away from her face, while the hat at the same time protected her rosy countenance from the fire. She plainly was not prepared to receive visitors, and she started when the young man addressed her, flushing still more deeply, apparently annoyed at his unwelcome appearance.

"Good-afternoon," he said cordially. "Preparing for washing? I thought Monday was washing day."

"It is."

"Then I have not been misinformed. And you are not preparing for washing?"

"We are."

Yates laughed so heartily that Kitty, in spite of herself, had to permit a smile to brighten her own features. She always found it difficult remain solemn for any length of time.

"This is obviously a conundrum," said Yates, ticking off the items on his four fingers. "First, Monday is washing day. Second, this is not Monday. Third, neither is to-morrow. Fourth, we are preparing for washing. I give it up, Miss Bartlett. Please tell me the answer."

"The answer is that I am making soap; soft soap, if you know what that is."

"Practically, I don't know what it is; but I have heard the term used in a political connection. In the States we say that if a man is very diplomatic he uses soft soap, so I suppose it has lubricating qualities. Sam Slick used the term 'soft sawder' in the same way; but what sawder is, soft or hard, I haven't the slightest idea."

"I thought you knew everything, Mr. Yates."

"Me? Bless you, no. I'm a humble gleaner in the field of knowledge. That's why I brought a Toronto professor with me. I want to learn something. Won't you teach me how to make soap?"

"I'm very busy just now. When I said that we were preparing for washing, I should perhaps have told you there was something else we are not prepared for to-day."

"What is that?"

"A visitor."

"Oh, I say, Miss Bartlett, you are a little hard on me. I'm not a visitor. I'm a friend of the family. I want to help. You will find me a most diligent student. Won't you give me a chance?"

"All the hard work's done. But perhaps you knew that before you came."

Yates looked at her reproachfully, and sighed deeply.

"That's what it is to be a misunderstood man. So you think, among other bad qualities, I have the habit of shirking work? Let me tell you, Miss Bartlett, that the reason I am here is because I have worked too hard. Now, confess that you are sorry for what you said—trampling on an already downtrodden man."

Kitty laughed merrily at this, and Yates laughed also, for his sense of comradeship was strong.

"You don't look as if you had ever worked in your life; I don't believe you know what work is."

"But there are different kinds of labor. Don't you call writing work?"

"No."

"That's just where you're mistaken. It is, and hard work, too. I'll tell you about the newspaper business if you'll tell me about soap making. Fair exchange. I wish you would take me as a pupil, Miss Bartlett; you would find me quick at picking up things."

"Well, then, pick up that pail and draw a pailful of water."

"I'll do it," cried Yates sternly; "I'll do it, though it blast me."

Yates picked up the wooden pail, painted blue on the outside, with a red stripe near the top for ornament, and cream-colored inside. It was called a "patent pail" in those days, as it was a comparatively recent innovation, being cheaper, lighter, and stronger than the tin pail which it was rapidly replacing. At the well was a stout pole, pinned through the center to the upright support on which it swung, like the walking-beam of an engine. The thick end, which rested on the ground, was loaded with heavy stones; while from the thin end, high in the air, there dangled over the mouth of the well a slim pole with a hook. This hook was ingeniously furnished with a spring of hickory, which snapped when the handle of the pail was placed on the hook, and prevented the "patent" utensil from slipping off when it was lowered to the surface of the water. Yates speedily recognized the usefulness of this contrivance, for he found that the filling of a wooden pail in a deep well was not the simple affair it looked. The bucket bobbed about on the surface of the water. Once he forgot the necessity of keeping a stout grip on the pole, and the next instant the pail came up to the sunlight with a suddenness that was terrifying. Only an equally sudden backward jump on Yates' part saved his head. Miss Bartlett was pleased to look upon this incident as funny. Yates was so startled by the unexpected revolt of the pail that his native courtesy did not get a chance to prevent Kitty from drawing up the water herself. She lowered the vessel, pulling down the pole in a hand-over-hand manner that the young man thought decidedly fetching, and then she gave an almost imperceptible twist to the arrangement that resulted in instant success. The next thing Yates knew the full pail was resting on the well curb, and the hickory spring had given the click that released the handle.

"There," said Kitty, suppressing her merriment, "that's how it's done."

"I see the result, Miss Bartlett; but I'm not sure I can do the trick. These things are not so simple as they seem. What is the next step?"

"Pour the water into the leach."

"Into the what?"

"Into the leach, I said. Where else?"

"Oh, I'm up a tree again. I see I don't even know the A B C of this business. In the old days the leech was a physician. You don't mean I'm to drown a doctor?"

"This is the leach," said Kitty, pointing to a large, yellowish, upright wooden cylinder, which rested on some slanting boards, down the surface of which ran a brownish liquid that dripped into a trough.

As Yates stood on a bench with the pail in his hand he saw that the cylinder was filled nearly to the top with sodden wood ashes. He poured in the water, and it sank quickly out of sight.

"So this is part of the soap-making equipment?" he said, stepping down; "I thought the iron kettle over the fire was the whole factory. Tell me about the leach."

"That is where the hard work of soap making comes in," said Kitty, stirring the contents of the iron kettle with a long stick. "Keeping the leach supplied with water at first is no fun, for then the ashes are dry. If you put in five more pails of water, I will tell you about it."

"Right!" cried Yates, pleased to see that the girl's evident objection to his presence at first was fast disappearing. "Now you'll understand how energetic I am. I'm a handy man about a place."

When he had completed his task, she was still stirring the thickening liquid in the caldron, guarding her face from the fire with her big straw hat. Her clustering, tangled fair hair was down about her shoulders; and Yates, as he put the pail in its place, when it had been emptied the fifth time, thought she formed a very pretty picture standing there by the fire, even if she were making soft soap.

"The wicked genii has finished the task set him by the fairy princess. Now for the reward. I want all the particulars about the leach. In the first place, where do you get this huge wooden cylinder that I have, without apparent effect, been pouring water into? Is it manufactured or natural?"

"Both. It is a section of the buttonwood tree."

"Buttonwood? I don't think I ever heard of that. I know the beech and the maple, and some kinds of oak, but there my wood lore ends. Why the buttonwood?"

"The buttonwood happens to be exactly suited to the purpose. It is a tree that is very fine to look at. It seems all right, but it generally isn't. It is hollow or rotten within, and, even when sound, the timber made from it is of little value, as it doesn't last. Yet you can't tell until you begin to chop whether it is of any use or not." Kitty shot a quick glance at the young man, who was sitting on a log watching her.

"Go on, Miss Bartlett; I see what you mean. There are men like the buttonwood tree. The woods are full of them. I've met lots of that kind, fair to look upon, but hollow. Of course you don't mean anything personal; for you must have seen my worth by the way I stuck to the water hauling. But go on."

"Dear me, I never thought of such a thing; but a guilty conscience, they say——" said Kitty, with a giggle.

"Of course they say; but it's wrong, like most other things they say. It's the man with the guilty conscience who looks you straight in the eye. Now that the buttonwood is chopped down, what's the next thing to be done?"

"It is sawn off at the proper length, square at one end and slanting at the other."

"Why slanting?"

"Don't you see, the foundation of plank on which it rests is inclined, so the end of the leach that is down must be slantingly cut, otherwise it would not stand perpendicularly. It would topple over in the first windstorm."

"I see, I see. Then they haul it in and set it up?"

"Oh, dear no; not yet. They build a fire in it when it gets dry enough."

"Really? I think I understand the comprehensive scheme, but I slip up on the details, as when I tried to submerge that wooden pail. What's the fire for?"

"To burn out what remains of the soft inside wood, so as to leave only the hard outside shell. Then the charring of the inner surface is supposed to make the leach better—more water-tight, perhaps."

"Quite so. Then it is hauled in and set up?"

"Yes; and gradually filled with ashes. When it is full, we pour the water in it, and catch the lye as it drips out. This is put in the caldron with grease, pigskins, and that sort of thing, and when it boils long enough, the result is soft soap."

"And if you boil it too long, what is the result?"

"Hard soap, I suppose. I never boil it too long."

The conversation was here interrupted by a hissing in the fire, caused by the tumultuous boiling over of the soap. Kitty hurriedly threw in a basin of cold lye, and stirred the mixture vigorously.

"You see," she said reproachfully, "the result of keeping me talking nonsense to you. Now you will have to make up for it by bringing in some wood and putting more water into the leach."

"With the utmost pleasure," cried Yates, springing to his feet. "It is a delight to atone for a fault by obeying your commands."

The girl laughed. "Buttonwood," she said. Before Yates could think of anything to say in reply Mrs. Bartlett appeared at the back door.

"How is the soap getting on, Kitty?" she asked. "Why, Mr. Yates, are you here?"

"Am I here? I should say I was. Very much here. I'm the hired man. I'm the hewer of wood and the hauler of water, or, to speak more correctly, I'm the hauler of both. And, besides, I've been learning how to make soap, Mrs. Bartlett."

"Well, it won't hurt you to know how."

"You bet it won't. When I get back to New York, the first thing I shall do will be to chop down a buttonwood tree in the park, if I can find one, and set up a leach for myself. Lye comes useful in running a paper."

Mrs. Bartlett's eyes twinkled, for, although she did not quite understand his nonsense, she knew it was nonsense, and she had a liking for frivolous persons, her own husband being so somber-minded.

"Tea is ready," she said. "Of course you will stay, Mr. Yates."

"Really, Mrs. Bartlett, I cannot conscientiously do so. I haven't earned a meal since the last one. No; my conscience won't let me accept, but thank you all the same."

"Nonsense; my conscience won't let you go away hungry. If nobody were to eat but those who earn their victuals, there would be more starving people in the world than there are. Of course you'll stay."

"Now, that's what I like, Mrs. Bartlett. I like to have a chance of refusing an invitation I yearn for, and then be forced to accept. That's true hospitality." Then in a whisper he added to Kitty; "If you dare to say 'buttonwood,' Miss Bartlett, you and I will quarrel."

But Kitty said nothing, now that her mother had appeared on the scene, but industriously stirred the contents of the iron kettle.

"Kitty," said the mother, "you call the men to supper."

"I can't leave this," said Kitty, flushing; "it will boil over. You call, mother."

So Mrs. Bartlett held her open palms on each side of her mouth, and gave the long wailing cry, which was faintly answered from the fields, and Yates, who knew a thing or two, noted with secret satisfaction that Kitty had refused doubtless because he was there.

CHAPTER VIII.

"I tell you what it is, Renny," said Yates, a few days after the soap episode, as he swung in his hammock at the camp, "I'm learning something new every day."

"Not really?" asked the professor in surprise.

"Yes, really. I knew it would astonish you. My chief pleasure in life, professor, is the surprising of you. I sometimes wonder why it delights me; it is so easily done."

"Never mind about that. What have you been learning?"

"Wisdom, my boy; wisdom in solid chunks. In the first place, I am learning to admire the resourcefulness of these people around us. Practically, they make everything they need. They are the most self-helping people that I was ever thrown among. I look upon theirs as the ideal life."

"I think you said something like that when we first came here."

"I said that, you ass, about camping out. I am talking now about farm life. Farmers eliminate the middleman pretty effectually, and that in itself is going a long way toward complete happiness. Take the making of soap, that I told you about; there you have it, cheap and good. When you've made it, you know what is in it, and I'll be hanged if you do when you pay a big price for it in New York. Here they make pretty nearly everything they need, except the wagon and the crockery; and I'm not sure but they made them a few years back. Now, when a man with a good sharp ax and a jack-knife can do anything from building his house to whittling out a chair, he's the most independent man on earth. Nobody lives better than these people do. Everything is fresh, sweet, and good. Perhaps the country air helps; but it seems to me I never tasted such meals as Mrs. Bartlett, for instance, gets up. They buy nothing at the stores except the tea, and I confess I prefer milk myself. My tastes were always simple."

"And what is the deduction?"

"Why, that this is the proper way to live. Old Hiram has an anvil and an amateur forge. He can tinker up almost anything, and that eliminates the blacksmith. Howard has a bench, saws, hammers, and other tools, and that eliminates the carpenter. The women eliminate the baker, the soap boiler, and a lot of other parasites. Now, when you have eliminated all the middlemen, then comes independence, and consequently complete happiness. You can't keep happiness away with a shotgun then."

"But what is to become of the blacksmith, the carpenter, and all the rest?"

"Let them take up land and be happy too; there's plenty of land. The land is waiting for them. Then look how the master is eliminated. That's the most beautiful riddance of all. Even the carpenter and blacksmith usually have to work under a boss; and if not, they have to depend on the men who employ them. The farmer has to please nobody but himself. That adds to his independence. That's why old Hiram is ready to fight the first comer on the slightest provocation. He doesn't care whom he offends, so long as it isn't his wife. These people know how to make what they want, and what they can't make they do without. That's the way to form a great nation. You raise, in this way, a self-sustaining, resolute, unconquerable people. The reason the North conquered the South was because we drew our armies mostly from the self-reliant farming class, while we had to fight a people accustomed for generations to having things done for them."

"Why don't you buy a farm, Yates?"

"Several reasons. I am spoiled for the life here. I am like the drunkard who admires a temperate life, yet can't pass a ginshop. The city virus is in my blood. And then, perhaps, after all, I am not quite satisfied with the tendency of farm life; it is unfortunately in a transition state. It is at the frame-house stage, and will soon blossom into the red-brick stage. The log-house era is what I yearn for. Then everything a person needed was made on the farm. When the brick-house era sets in, the middleman will be rampant. I saw the other day at the Howards' a set of ancient stones that interested me as much as an Assyrian marble would interest you. They were old, home-made millstones, and they have not been used since the frame house was built. The grist mill at the village put them out of date. And just here, notice the subtlety of the crafty middleman. The farmer takes his grist to the mill, and the miller does not charge him cash for grinding it. He takes toll out of the bags, and the farmer has a vague idea that he gets his grinding for almost nothing. The old way was the best, Renny, my boy. The farmer's son won't be as happy in the brick house which the mason will build for him as his grandfather was in the log house he built for himself. And fools call this change the advance of civilization."

"There is something to be said for the old order of things," admitted Renmark. "If a person could unite the advantages of what we call civilization with the advantages of a pastoral life, he would inaugurate a condition of things that would be truly idyllic."

"That's so, Renmark, that's so!" cried Yates enthusiastically. "A brownstone mansion on Fifth Avenue, and a log hut on the shores of Lake Superior! That would suit me down to the ground. Spend half the year in each place."

"Yes," said the professor meditatively; "a log hut on the rocks and under the trees, with the lake in front, would be very nice if the hut had a good library attached."

"And a daily paper. Don't forget the press."

"No. I draw the line there. The daily paper would mean the daily steamer or the daily train. The one would frighten away the fish, and the other would disturb the stillness with its whistle."

Yates sighed. "I forgot about the drawbacks," he said. "That's the trouble with civilization. You can't have the things you want without bringing in their trail so many things you don't want. I shall have to give up the daily paper."

"Then there is another objection, worse than either steamer or train."

"What's that?"

"The daily paper itself."

Yates sat up indignantly.

"Renmark!" he cried, "that's blasphemy. For Heaven's sake, man, hold something sacred. If you don't respect the press, what do you respect? Not my most cherished feelings, at any rate, or you wouldn't talk in that flippant manner. If you speak kindly of my daily paper, I'll tolerate your library."

"And that reminds me: Have you brought any books with you, Yates? I have gone through most of mine already, although many of them will bear going over again; still, I have so much time on my hands that I think I may indulge in a little general reading. When you wrote asking me to meet you in Buffalo, I thought you perhaps intended to tramp through the country, so I did not bring as many books with me as I should have done if I had known you were going to camp out."

Yates sprang from the hammock.

"Books? Well, I should say so! Perhaps you think I don't read anything but the daily papers. I'd have you know that I am something of a reader myself. You mustn't imagine you monopolize all the culture in the township, professor."

The young man went into the tent, and shortly returned with an armful of yellow-covered, paper-bound small volumes, which he flung in profusion at the feet of the man from Toronto. They were mostly Beadle's Dime Novels, which had a great sale at the time.

"There," he said, "you have quantity, quality, and variety, as I have before remarked. 'The Murderous Sioux of Kalamazoo;' that's a good one. A hair-raising Indian story in every sense of the word. The one you are looking at is a pirate story, judging by the burning ship on the cover. But for first-class highwaymen yarns, this other edition is the best. That's the 'Sixteen String Jack set.' They're immense, if they do cost a quarter each. You must begin at the right volume, or you'll be sorry. You see, they never really end, although every volume is supposed to be complete in itself. They leave off at the most exciting point, and are continued in the next volume. I call that a pretty good idea, but it's rather exasperating if you begin at the last book. You'll enjoy this lot. I'm glad I brought them along."

"It is a blessing," said Renmark, with the ghost of a smile about his lips. "I can truthfully say that they are entirely new to me."

"That's all right, my boy," cried Yates loftily, with a wave of his hand. "Use them as if they were your own."

Renmark arose leisurely and picked up a quantity of the books.

"These will do excellently for lighting our morning camp fire," he said. "And if you will allow me to treat them as if they were my own, that is the use to which I will put them. You surely do not mean to say that you read such trash as this, Yates?"

"Trash?" exclaimed Yates indignantly. "It serves me right. That's what a man gets for being decent to you, Renny. Well, you're not compelled to read them; but if you put one of them in the fire, your stupid treatises will follow, if they are not too solid to burn. You don't know good literature when you see it."

The professor, buoyed up, perhaps, by the conceit which comes to a man through the possession of a real sheepskin diploma, granted by a university of good standing, did not think it necessary to defend his literary taste. He busied himself in pruning a stick he had cut in the forest, and finally he got it into the semblance of a walking cane. He was an athletic man, and the indolence of camp life did not suit him as it did Yates. He tested the stick in various ways when he had trimmed it to his satisfaction.

"Are you ready for a ten-mile walk?" he asked of the man in the hammock.

"Good gracious, no. Man wants but little walking here below, and he doesn't want it ten miles in length either. I'm easily satisfied. You're off, are you? Well, so long. And I say, Renny, bring back some bread when you return to camp. It's the one safe thing to do."

CHAPTER IX.

Renmark walked through the woods and then across the fields, until he came to the road. He avoided the habitations of man as much as he could, for he was neither so sociably inclined nor so frequently hungry as was his companion. He strode along the road, not caring much where it led him. Everyone he met gave him "Good-day," after the friendly custom of the country. Those with wagons or lighter vehicles going in his direction usually offered him a ride, and went on, wondering that a man should choose to walk when it was not compulsory. The professor, like most silent men, found himself good company, and did not feel the need of companionship in his walks. He had felt relieved rather than disappointed when Yates refused to accompany him. And Yates, swinging drowsily in his hammock, was no less gratified. Even where men are firm and intimate friends, the first few days of camping out together is a severe strain on their regard for each other. If Damon and Pythias had occupied a tent together for a week, the worst enemy of either, or both, might at the end of that time have ventured into the camp in safety, and would have been welcome.

Renmark thought of these things as he walked along. His few days' intimacy with Yates had shown him how far apart they had managed to get by following paths that diverged more and more widely the farther they were trodden. The friendship of their youth had turned out to be merely ephemeral. Neither would now choose the other as an intimate associate. Another illusion had gone.

"I have surely enough self-control," said Renmark to himself, as he walked on, "to stand his shallow flippancy for another week, and not let him see what I think of him."

Yates at the same time was thoroughly enjoying the peaceful silence of the camp. "That man is an exaggerated schoolmaster, with all the faults of the species abnormally developed. If I once open out on him, he will learn more truth about himself in ten minutes than he ever heard in his life before. What an unbearable prig he has grown to be." Thus ran Yates' thoughts as he swung in his hammock, looking up at the ceiling of green leaves.

Nevertheless, the case was not so bad as either of them thought. If it had been, then were marriage not only a failure, but a practical impossibility. If two men can get over the first few days in camp without a quarrel, life becomes easier, and the tension relaxes.

Renmark, as he polished off his ten miles, paid little heed to those he met; but one driver drew up his horse and accosted him.

"Good-day," he said. "How are you getting on in the tent?"

The professor was surprised at the question. Had their tenting-out eccentricity gone all over the country? He was not a quick man at recognizing people, belonging, as he did, to the "I-remember-your-face-but-can't-recall-your-name" fraternity. It had been said of him that he never, at any one time, knew the names of more than half a dozen students in his class; but this was an undergraduate libel on him. The young man who had accosted him was driving a single horse, attached to what he termed a "democrat"—a four-wheeled light wagon, not so slim and elegant as a buggy, nor so heavy and clumsy as a wagon. Renmark looked up at the driver with confused unrecognition, troubled because he vaguely felt that he had met him somewhere before. But his surprise at being addressed speedily changed into amazement as he looked from the driver to the load. The "democrat" was heaped with books. The larger volumes were stuck along the sides with some regularity, and in this way kept the miscellaneous pile from being shaken out on the road. His eye glittered with a new interest as it rested on the many-colored bindings; and he recognized in the pile the peculiar brown covers of the "Bohn" edition of classic translations, that were scattered like so many turnips over the top of this ridge of literature. He rubbed his eyes to make sure he was not dreaming. How came a farmer's boy to be driving a wagon load of books in the wilds of the country as nonchalantly as if they were so many bushels of potatoes?

The young driver, who had stopped his horse, for the load was heavy and the sand was deep, saw that the stranger not only did not recognize him, but that from the moment he saw the books he had forgotten everything else. It was evidently necessary to speak again.

"If you are coming back, will you have a ride?" he asked.

"I—I think I will," said the professor, descending to earth again and climbing up beside the boy.

"I see you don't remember me," said the latter, starting his horse again. "My name is Howard. I passed you in my buggy when you were coming in with your tent that day on the Ridge. Your partner—what's his name—Yates, isn't it?—had dinner at our house the other day."

"Ah, yes. I recollect you now. I thought I had seen you before; but it was only for a moment, you know. I have a very poor memory so far as people are concerned. It has always been a failing of mine. Are these your books? And how do you happen to have such a quantity?"

"Oh, this is the library," said young Howard.

"The library?"

"Yes, the township library, you know."

"Oh! The township has a library, then? I didn't know."

"Well, it's part of it. This is a fifth part. You know about township libraries, don't you? Your partner said you were a college man."

Renmark blushed at his own ignorance, but he was never reluctant to admit it.

"I ought to be ashamed to confess it, but I know nothing of township libraries. Please, tell me about them."

Young Howard was eager to give information to a college man, especially on the subject of books, which he regarded as belonging to the province of college-bred men. He was pleased also to discover that city people did not know everything. He had long had the idea that they did, and this belief had been annoyingly corroborated by the cocksureness of Yates. The professor evidently was a decent fellow, who did not pretend to universal knowledge.

This was encouraging. He liked Renmark better than Yates, and was glad he had offered him a ride, although, of course, that was the custom; still, a person with one horse and a heavy load is exempt on a sandy road.

"Well, you see," he said in explanation, "it's like this: The township votes a sum of money, say a hundred dollars, or two hundred, as the case may be. They give notice to the Government of the amount voted, and the Government adds the same amount to the township money. It's like the old game: you think of a number, and they double it. The Government has a depository of books, in Toronto, I think, and they sell them cheaper than the bookstores do. At any rate, the four hundred dollars' worth are bought, or whatever the amount is, and the books are the property of the township. Five persons are picked out in the township as librarians, and they have to give security. My father is librarian for this section. The library is divided into five parts, and each librarian gets a share. Once a year I go to the next section and get all their books. They go to the next section, again, and get all the books at that place. A man comes to our house to-day and takes all we have. So we get a complete change every year, and in five years we get back the first batch, which by that time we have forgotten all about. To-day is changing day all around."

"And the books are lent to any person in each section who wishes to read them?" asked the professor.

"Yes. Margaret keeps a record, and a person can have a book out for two weeks; after that time there is a fine, but Margaret never fines anyone."

"And do people have to pay to take out the books?"

"Not likely!" said Howard with fine contempt. "You wouldn't expect people to pay for reading books; would you, now?"

"No, I suppose not. And who selected the volumes?"

"Well, the township can select the books if it likes, or it can send a committee to select them; but they didn't think it worth the trouble and expense. People grumbled enough at wasting money on books as it was, even if they did buy them at half price. Still, others said it was a pity not to get the money out of the Government when they had the chance. I don't believe any of them cared very much about the books, except father and a few others. So the Government chose the books. They'll do that if you leave it to them. And a queer lot of trash they sent, if you take my word for it. I believe they shoved off on us all the things no one else would buy. Even when they did pick out novels, they were just as tough as the history books. 'Adam Bede' is one. They say that's a novel. I tried it, but I would rather read the history of Josephus any day. There's some fighting in that, if it is a history. Then there's any amount of biography books. They're no good. There's a 'History of Napoleon.' Old Bartlett's got that, and he won't give it up. He says he was taxed for the library against his will. He dares them to go to law about it, and it aint worth while for one book. The other sections are all asking for that book; not that they want it, but the whole country knows that old Bartlett's a-holding on to it, so they'd like to see some fun. Bartlett's read that book fourteen times, and it's all he knows. I tell Margaret she ought to fine him, and keep on fining, but she won't do it. I guess Bartlett thinks the book belongs to him by this time. Margaret likes Kitty and Mrs. Bartlett,—so does everybody,—but old Bartlett's a seed. There he sits now on his veranda, and it's a wonder he's not reading the 'History of Napoleon.'"

They were passing the Bartlett house, and young Howard raised his voice and called out:

"I say, Mr. Bartlett, we want that Napoleon book. This is changing day, you know. Shall I come up for it, or will you bring it down? If you fetch it to the gate, I'll cart it home now."

The old man paid no heed to what was said to him; but Mrs. Bartlett, attracted by the outcry, came to the door.

"You go along with your books, you young rascal!" she cried, coming down to the gate when she saw the professor. "That's a nice way to carry bound books, as if they were a lot of bricks. I'll warrant you have lost a dozen between Mallory's and here. But easy come, easy go. It's plain to be seen they didn't cost you anything. I don't know what the world's a-coming to when the township spends its money in books, as if taxes weren't heavy enough already.

Won't you come in, Mr. Renmark? Tea's on the table."

"Mr. Renmark's coming with me this trip, Mrs. Bartlett," young Howard said before the professor had time to reply; "but I'll come over and take tea, if you'll invite me, as soon as I have put the horse up."

"You go along with your nonsense," she said; "I know you." Then in a lower voice she asked: "How is your mother, Henry—and Margaret?"

"They're pretty well, thanks."

"Tell them I'm going to run over to see them some day soon, but that need not keep them from coming to see me. The old man's going to town to-morrow," and with this hint, after again inviting the professor to a meal, she departed up the path to the house.

"I think I'll get down here," said Renmark, halfway between the two houses. "I am very much obliged to you for the ride, and also for what you told me about the books. It was very interesting."

"Nonsense!" cried young Howard; "I'm not going to let you do anything of the sort. You're coming home with me. You want to see the books, don't you? Very well, then, come along, Margaret is always impatient on changing day, she's so anxious to see the books, and father generally comes in early from the fields for the same reason."

As they approached the Howard homestead they noticed Margaret waiting for them at the gate; but when the girl saw that a stranger was in the wagon, she turned and walked into the house. Renmark, seeing this retreat, regretted he had not accepted Mrs. Bartlett's invitation. He was a sensitive man, and did not realize that others were sometimes as shy as himself. He felt he was intruding, and that at a sacred moment—the moment of the arrival of the library. He was such a lover of books, and valued so highly the privilege of being alone with them, that he fancied he saw in the abrupt departure of Margaret the same feeling of resentment he would himself have experienced if a visitor had encroached upon him in his favorite nook in the fine room that held the library of the university.

When the wagon stopped in the lane, Renmark said hesitatingly:

"I think I'll not stay, if you don't mind. My friend is waiting for me at the camp, and will be wondering what has become of me."

"Who? Yates? Let him wonder. I guess he never bothers about anybody else as long as he is comfortable himself. That's how I sized him up, at any rate. Besides, you're never going back on carrying in the books, are you? I counted on your help. I don't want to do it, and it don't seem the square thing to let Margaret do it all alone; does it, now?"

"Oh, if I can be of any assistance, I shall——"

"Of course you can. Besides, I know my father wants to see you, anyhow. Don't you, father?"

The old man was coming round from the back of the house to meet them.

"Don't I what?" he asked.

"You said you wanted to see Professor Renmark when Margaret told you what Yates had said to her about him."

Renmark reddened slightly at finding so many people had made him the subject of conversation, rather suspecting at the same time that the boy was making fun of him. Mr. Howard cordially held out his hand.

"So this is Professor Renmark, is it? I am very pleased to see you. Yes, as Henry was saying, I have been wanting to see you ever since my daughter spoke of you. I suppose Henry told you that his brother is a pupil of yours?"

"Oh! is Arthur Howard your son?" cried Renmark, warming up at once. "I did not know it. There are many young men at the college, and I have but the vaguest idea from what parts of the country they all come. A teacher should have no favorites, but I must confess to a strong liking for your son. He is a good boy, which cannot be said about every member of my class."

"Arthur was always studious, so we thought we would give him a chance. I am glad to hear he behaves himself in the city. Farming is hard work, and I hope my boys will have an easier time than I had. But come in, come in. The missus and Margaret will be glad to see you, and hear how the boy is coming on with his studies."

So they went in together.

CHAPTER X.

"Hello! Hello, there! Wake up! Breakfa-a-a-st! I thought that would fetch you. Gosh! I wish I had your job at a dollar a day!"

Yates rubbed his eyes, and sat up in the hammock. At first he thought the forest was tumbling down about his ears, but as he collected his wits he saw that it was only young Bartlett who had come crashing through the woods on the back of one horse, while he led another by a strap attached to a halter. The echo of his hearty yell still resounded in the depths of the woods, and rang in Yates' ears as he pulled himself together.

"Did you—ah—make any remarks?" asked Yates quietly.

The boy admired his gift of never showing surprise.

"I say, don't you know that it's not healthy to go to sleep in the middle of the day?"

"Is it the middle of the day? I thought it was later. I guess I can stand it, if the middle of the day can. I've a strong constitution. Now, what do you mean by dashing up on two horses into a man's bedroom in that reckless fashion?"

The boy laughed.

"I thought perhaps you would like a ride. I knew you were alone, for I saw the professor go mooning up the road a little while ago."

"Oh! Where was he going?"

"Hanged if I know, and he didn't look as if he knew himself. He's a queer fish, aint he?"

"He is. Everybody can't be as sensible and handsome as we are, you know. Where are you going with those horses, young man?"

"To get them shod. Won't you come along? You can ride the horse I'm on. It's got a bridle. I'll ride the one with the halter."

"How far away is the blacksmith's shop?"

"Oh, a couple of miles or so; down at the Cross Roads."

"Well," said Yates, "there's merit in the idea. I take it your generous offer is made in good faith, and not necessarily for publication."

"I don't understand. What do you mean?"

"There is no concealed joke, is there? No getting me on the back of one of those brutes to make a public exhibition of me? Do they bite or kick or buck, or playfully roll over a person?"

"No," cried, young Bartlett indignantly. "This is no circus. Why, a baby could ride this horse."

"Well, that's about the style of horse I prefer. You see, I'm a trifle out of practice. I never rode anything more spirited than a street car, and I haven't been on one of them for a week."

"Oh, you can ride all right. I guess you could do most things you set your mind to."

Yates was flattered by this evidently sincere tribute to his capacity, so he got out of the hammock. The boy, who had been sitting on the horse with both feet on one side, now straightened his back and slipped to the ground.

"Wait till I throw down the fence," he said.

Yates mounted with some difficulty, and the two went trotting down the road. He managed to hold his place with some little uncertainty, but the joggling up and down worried him. He never seemed to alight in quite the same place on the horse's back, and this gave an element of chance to his position which embarrassed him. He expected to come down some time and find the horse wasn't there. The boy laughed at his riding, but Yates was too much engaged in keeping his position to mind that very much.

"D-d-dirt is s-s-said to b-b-be matter out of place, and that's what's the m-m-mat-matter w-w-with me." His conversation seemed to be shaken out of him by the trotting of the horse. "I say, Bartlett, I can't stand this any longer. I'd rather walk."

"You're all right," said the boy; "we'll make him canter."

He struck the horse over the flank with the loose end of the halter rein.

"Here!" shouted Yates, letting go the bridle and grasping the mane. "Don't make him go faster, you young fiend. I'll murder you when I get off—and that will be soon."

"You're all right," repeated young Bartlett, and, much to his astonishment, Yates found it to be so. When the horse broke into a canter, Yates thought the motion as easy as swinging in a hammock, and as soothing as a rocking chair.

"This is an improvement. But we've got to keep it up, for if this brute suddenly changes to a trot, I'm done for."

"We'll keep it up until we come in sight of the Corners, then we'll slow down to a walk. There's sure to be a lot of fellows at the blacksmith's shop, so we'll come in on them easy like."

"You're a good fellow, Bartlett," said Yates. "I suspected you of tricks at first. I'm afraid, if I had got another chap in such a fix, I wouldn't have let him off as easily as you have me. The temptation would have been too great."

When they reached the blacksmith's shop at the Corners, they found four horses in the building ahead of them. Bartlett tied his team outside, and then, with his comrade, entered the wide doorway of the smithy. The shop was built of rough boards, and the inside was blackened with soot. It was not well lighted, the two windows being obscured with much smoke, so that they were useless as far as their original purpose was concerned; but the doorway, as wide as that of a barn, allowed all the light to come in that the smith needed for his work. At the far end and darkest corner of the place stood the forge, with the large bellows behind it, concealed, for the most part, by the chimney. The forge was perhaps six feet square and three or four feet high, built of plank and filled in with earth. The top was covered with cinders and coal, while in the center glowed the red core of the fire, with blue flames hovering over it. The man who worked the bellows chewed tobacco, and now and then projected the juice with deadly accuracy right into the center of the fire, where it made a momentary hiss and dark spot. All the frequenters of the smithy admired Sandy's skill in expectoration, and many tried in vain to emulate it. The envious said it was due to the peculiar formation of his front teeth, the upper row being prominent, and the two middle teeth set far apart, as if one were missing. But this was jealousy; Sandy's perfection in the art was due to no favoritism of nature, but to constant and long-continued practice. Occasionally with his callous right hand, never removing his left from the lever, Sandy pulled an iron bar out of the fire and examined it critically. The incandescent end of the bar radiated a blinding white light when it was gently withdrawn, and illuminated the man's head, making his beardless face look, against its dark background, like the smudged countenance of some cynical demon glowing with a fire from within. The end of the bar which he held must have been very hot to an ordinary mortal, as everyone in the shop knew, all of them, at their initiation to the country club, having been handed a black piece of iron from Sandy's hand, which he held unflinchingly, but which the innocent receiver usually dropped with a yell. This was Sandy's favorite joke, and made life worth living for him. It was perhaps not so good as the blacksmith's own bit of humor, but public opinion was divided on that point. Every great man has his own particular set of admirers; and there were some who said,—under their breaths, of course,—that Sandy could turn a horseshoe as well as Macdonald himself. Experts, however, while admitting Sandy's general genius, did not go so far as this.

About half a dozen members of the club were present, and most of them stood leaning against something with hands deep in their trousers pockets; one was sitting on the blacksmith's bench, with his legs dangling down. On the bench tools were scattered around so thickly that he had had to clear a place before he could sit down; the taking of this liberty proved the man to be an old and privileged member. He sat there whittling a stick, aimlessly bringing it to a fine point, examining it frequently with a critical air, as if he were engaged in some delicate operation which required great discrimination.

The blacksmith himself stooped with his back to one of the horses, the hind hoof of the animal, between his knees, resting on his leathern apron. The horse was restive, looking over its shoulder at him, not liking what was going on. Macdonald swore at it fluently, and requested it to stand still, holding the foot as firmly as if it were in his own iron vise, which was fixed to the table near the whittler. With his right hand he held a hot horseshoe, attached to an iron punch that had been driven into one of the nail holes, and this he pressed against the upraised hoof, as though sealing a document with a gigantic seal. Smoke and flame rose from the contact of the hot iron with the hoof, and the air was filled with the not unpleasant odor of burning horn. The smith's tool box, with hammer, pinchers, and nails, lay on the earthern floor within easy reach. The sweat poured from his grimy brow; for it was a hot job, and Macdonald was in the habit of making the most of his work. He was called the hardest working man in that part of the country, and he was proud of the designation. He was a standing reproach to the loafers who frequented his shop, and that fact gave him pleasure in their company. Besides, a man must have an audience when he is an expert in swearing. Macdonald's profanity was largely automatic,—a natural gift, as it were,—and he meant nothing wrong by it. In fact, when you got him fighting angry, he always forgot to swear; but in his calm moments oaths rolled easily and picturesquely from his lips, and gave fluency to his conversation. Macdonald enjoyed the reputation round about of being a wicked man, which he was not; his language was against him, that was all. This reputation had a misty halo thrown around it by Macdonald's unknown doings "down East," from which mystical region he had come. No one knew just what Macdonald had done, but it was admitted on all sides that he must have had some terrible experiences, although he was still a young man and unmarried. He used to say: "When you have come through what I have, you won't be so ready to pick a quarrel with a man."

This must have meant something significant, but the blacksmith never took anyone into his confidence; and "down East" is a vague place, a sort of indefinite, unlocalized no-man's-land, situated anywhere between Toronto and Quebec. Almost anything might have happened in such a space of country. Macdonald's favorite way of crushing an opponent was to say: "When you've had some of my experiences, young man, you'll know better'n to talk like that." All this gave a certain fascination to friendship with the blacksmith; and the farmers' boys felt that they were playing with fire when in his company, getting, as it were, a glimpse of the dangerous side of life. As for work, the blacksmith reveled in it, and made it practically his only vice. He did everything with full steam on, and was, as has been said, a constant reproach to loafers all over the country. When there was no work to do, he made work. When there was work to do, he did it with a rush, sweeping the sweat from his grimy brow with his hooked fore finger, and flecking it to the floor with a flirt of the right hand, loose on the wrist, in a way that made his thumb and fore finger snap together like the crack of a whip. This action was always accompanied with a long-drawn breath, almost a sigh, that seemed to say: "I wish I had the easy times you fellows have." In fact, since he came to the neighborhood the current phrase, "He works like a steer" had given way to, "He works like Macdonald," except with the older people, who find it hard to change phrases. Yet everyone liked the blacksmith, and took no special offense at his untiring industry, looking at it rather as an example to others.

He did not look up as the two newcomers entered, but industriously pared down the hoof with a curiously formed knife turned like a hook at the point, burned in the shoe to its place, nailed it on, and rasped the hoof into shape with a long, broad file. Not till he let the foot drop on the earthen floor, and slapped the impatient horse on the flank, did he deign to answer young Bartlett's inquiry.

"No," he said, wringing the perspiration from his forehead, "all these horses aint ahead of you, and you won't need to come next week. That's the last hoof of the last horse. No man needs to come to my shop and go away again, while the breath of life is left in me. And I don't do it, either, by sitting on a bench and whittling a stick."

"That's so. That's so," said Sandy, chuckling, in the admiring tone of one who intimated that, when the boss spoke, wisdom was uttered. "That's one on you, Sam."

"I guess I can stand it, if he can," said the whittler from the bench; which was considered fair repartee.

"Sit it, you mean," said young Bartlett, laughing with the others at his own joke.

"But," said the blacksmith severely, "we're out of shoes, and you'll have to wait till we turn some, that is, if you don't want the old ones reset. Are they good enough?"

"I guess so, if you can find 'em; but they're out in the fields. Didn't think I'd bring the horses in while they held on, did you?" Then, suddenly remembering his duties, he said by, way of general introduction: "Gentlemen, this is my friend Mr. Yates from New York."

The name seemed to fall like a wet blanket on the high spirits of the crowd. They had imagined from the cut of his clothes that he was a storekeeper from some village around, or an auctioneer from a distance, these two occupations being the highest social position to which a man might attain. They were prepared to hear that he was from Welland, or perhaps St. Catherines; but New York! that was a crusher. Macdonald, however, was not a man to be put down in his own shop and before his own admirers. He was not going to let his prestige slip from him merely because a man from New York had happened along. He could not claim to know the city, for the stranger would quickly detect the imposture and probably expose him; but the slightly superior air which Yates wore irritated him, while it abashed the others. Even Sandy was silent.

"I've met some people from New York down East," he said in an offhand manner, as if, after all, a man might meet a New Yorker and still not sink into the ground.

"Really?" said Yates. "I hope you liked them."

"Oh, so-so," replied the blacksmith airily. "There's good and bad among them, like the rest of us."

"Ah, you noticed that," said Yates. "Well, I've often thought the same myself. It's a safe remark to make; there is generally no disputing it."

The condescending air of the New Yorker was maddening, and

Macdonald realized that he was losing ground. The quiet insolence of Yates' tone was so exasperating to the blacksmith that he felt any language at his disposal inadequate to cope with it. The time for the practical joke had arrived. The conceit of this man must be taken down. He would try Sandy's method, and, if that failed, it would at least draw attention from himself to his helper.

"Being as you're from New York, maybe you can decide a little bet Sandy here wants to have with somebody."

Sandy, quick to take the hint, picked up the bar that always lay near enough the fire to be uncomfortably warm.

"How much do you reckon that weighs?" he said, with critical nicety estimating its ounces in his swaying hand. Sandy had never done it better. There was a look of perfect innocence on his bland, unsophisticated countenance, and the crowd looked on in breathless suspense.

Bartlett was about to step forward and save his friend, but a wicked glare from Macdonald restrained him; besides, he felt, somehow, that his sympathies were with his neighbors, and not with the stranger he had brought among them. He thought resentfully that Yates might have been less high and mighty. In fact, when he asked him to come he had imagined his brilliancy would be instantly popular, and would reflect glory on himself. Now he fancied he was included in the general scorn Yates took such little pains to conceal.

Yates glanced at the piece of iron and, without taking his hands from his pockets, said carelessly:

"Oh, I should imagine it weighed a couple of pounds."

"Heft it," said Sandy beseechingly, holding it out to him.

"No, thank you," replied Yates, with a smile. "Do you think I have never picked up a hot horseshoe before? If you are anxious to know its weight, why don't you take it over to the grocery store and have it weighed?"

"'Taint hot," said Sandy, as he feebly smiled and flung the iron back on the forge. "If it was, I couldn't have held it s'long."

"Oh, no," returned Yates, with a grin, "of course not. I don't know what a blacksmith's hands are, do I? Try something fresh."

Macdonald saw there was no triumph over him among his crowd, for they all evidently felt as much involved in the failure of Sandy's trick as he did himself; but he was sure that in future some man, hard pushed in argument, would fling the New Yorker at him. In the crisis he showed the instinct of a Napoleon.

"Well, boys," he cried, "fun's fun, but I've got to work. I have to earn my living, anyhow."

Yates enjoyed his victory; they wouldn't try "getting at" him again, he said to himself.

Macdonald strode to the forge and took out the bar of white-hot iron. He gave a scarcely perceptible nod to Sandy, who, ever ready with tobacco juice, spat with great directness on the top of the anvil. Macdonald placed the hot iron on the spot, and quickly smote it a stalwart blow with the heavy hammer. The result was appalling. An instantaneous spreading fan of apparently molten iron lit up the place as if it were a flash of lightning. There was a crash like the bursting of a cannon. The shop was filled for a moment with a shower of brilliant sparks, that flew like meteors to every corner of the place. Everyone was prepared for the explosion except Yates. He sprang back with a cry, tripped, and, without having time to get the use of his hands to ease his fall, tumbled and rolled to the horses' heels. The animals, frightened by the report, stamped around; and Yates had to hustle on his hands and knees to safer quarters, exhibiting more celerity than dignity. The blacksmith never smiled, but everyone else roared. The reputation of the country was safe. Sandy doubled himself up in his boisterous mirth.

"There's no one like the old man!" he shouted. "Oh, lordy! lordy! He's all wool, and a yard wide."

Yates picked himself up and dusted himself off, laughing with the rest of them.

"If I ever knew that trick before, I had forgotten it. That's one on me, as this youth in spasms said a moment ago. Blacksmith, shake! I'll treat the crowd, if there's a place handy."

CHAPTER XI.

People who have but a superficial knowledge of the life and times here set down may possibly claim that the grocery store, and not the blacksmith's shop, used to be the real country club—the place where the politics of the country were discussed; where the doings of great men were commended or condemned, and the government criticised. It is true that the grocery store was the club of the village, when a place like the Corners grew to be a village; but the blacksmith's shop was usually the first building erected on the spot where a village was ultimately to stand. It was the nucleus. As a place grew, and enervating luxury set in, the grocery store slowly supplanted the blacksmith's shop, because people found a nail keg, or a box of crackers, more comfortable to sit on than the limited seats at their disposal in a smithy; moreover, in winter the store, with its red-hot box stove, was a place of warmth and joy, but the reveling in such an atmosphere of comfort meant that the members of the club had to live close at hand, for no man would brave the storms of a Canadian winter night, and journey a mile or two through the snow, to enjoy even the pleasures of the store. So the grocery was essentially a village club, and not a rural club.

Of course, as civilization advanced, the blacksmith found it impossible to compete with the grocer. He could not offer the same inducements. The grocery approached more nearly than the smithy the grateful epicurism of the Athenaeum, the Reform, or the Carlton. It catered to the appetite of man, besides supplying him with the intellectual stimulus of debate. A box of soda crackers was generally open, and, although such biscuits were always dry, they were good to munch, if consumed slowly. The barrel of hazel nuts never had a lid on. The raisins, in their square box, with blue-tinted paper, setting forth the word "Malaga" under the colored picture of joyous Spanish grape pickers, stood on the shelves behind the counter, at an angle suited to display the contents to all comers, requiring an exceptionally long reach, and more than an ordinary amount of cheek, before they were got at; but the barrel of Muscavado brown sugar was where everyone could dip his hand in; while the man on the keg of tenpenny nails might extend his arm over into the display window, where the highly colored candies exhibited themselves, although the person who meddled often with them was frowned upon, for it was etiquette in the club not to purloin things which were expensive. The grocer himself drew the line at the candies, and a second helping usually brought forth the mild reproof:

"Shall I charge that, Sam; or would you rather pay for it now?"

All these delicacies were taken in a somewhat surreptitious way, and the takers generally wore an absent-minded look, as if the purloining was not quite intentional on their part. But they were all good customers of the grocer, and the abstractions were doubtless looked on by him as being in the way of trade; just as the giving of a present with a pound of tea, or a watch with a suit of clothes, became in later days. Be that as it may, he never said anything unless his generosity was taken advantage of, which was rarely the case.

Very often on winter nights there was a hilarious feast, that helped to lighten the shelves and burden the till. This ordinarily took the form of a splurge in cove oysters. Cove oysters came from Baltimore, of course, in round tins; they were introduced into Canada long before the square tin boxes that now come in winter from the same bivalvular city. Cove oysters were partly cooked before being tinned, so that they would, as the advertisements say, keep in any climate. They did not require ice around them, as do the square tins which now contain the raw oysters. Someone present would say:

"What's the matter with having a feed of cove oysters?"

He then collected a subscription of ten cents or so from each member, and the whole was expended in several cans of oysters and a few pounds of crackers. The cooking was done in a tin basin on the top of the hot stove. The contents of the cans were emptied into this handy dish, milk was added, and broken crackers, to give thickness and consistency to the result. There were always plenty of plates, for the store supplied the crockery of the neighborhood. There were also plenty of spoons, for everything was to be had at the grocery. What more could the most exacting man need? On a particularly reckless night the feast ended with several tins of peaches, which needed no cooking, but only a sprinkling of sugar. The grocer was always an expert at cooking cove oysters and at opening tins of peaches.

There was a general feeling among the members that, by indulging in these banquets, they were going the pace rather; and some of the older heads feebly protested against the indulgence of the times, but it was noticed that they never refrained from doing their share when it came to spoon work.

"A man has but one life to live," the younger and more reckless would say, as if that excused the extravagance; for a member rarely got away without being fifteen cents out of pocket, especially when they had peaches as well as oysters.

The grocery at the Corners had been but recently established and as yet the blacksmith's shop had not looked upon it as a rival. Macdonald was monarch of all he surveyed, and his shop was the favorite gathering place for miles around. The smithy was also the patriotic center of the district, as a blacksmith's shop must be as long as anvils can take the place of cannon for saluting purposes. On the 24th of May, the queen's birthday, celebrated locally as the only day in the year, except Sundays, when Macdonald's face was clean and when he did no work, the firing of the anvils aroused the echoes of the locality. On that great day the grocer supplied the powder, which was worth three York shillings a pound—a York shilling being sixpence halfpenny. It took two men to carry an anvil, with a good deal of grunting; but Macdonald, if the crowd were big enough, made nothing of picking it up, hoisting it on his shoulder, and flinging it down on the green in front of his shop. In the iron mass there is a square hole, and when the anvil was placed upside down, the hole was uppermost. It was filled with powder, and a wooden plug, with a notch cut in it, was pounded in with a sledge hammer. Powder was sprinkled from the notch over the surface of the anvil, and then the crowd stood back and held its breath. It was a most exciting moment. Macdonald would come running out of the shop bareheaded, holding a long iron bar, the wavering, red-hot end of which descended on the anvil, while the blacksmith shouted in a terrifying voice: "Look out, there!" The loose powder hissed and spat for a moment, then bang went the cannon, and a great cloud of smoke rolled upward, while the rousing cheers came echoing back from the surrounding forests. The helper, with the powder-horn, would spring to the anvil and pour the black explosive into the hole, while another stood ready with plug and hammer. The delicious scent of burned gunpowder filled the air, and was inhaled by all the youngsters with satisfaction, for now they realized what real war was. Thus the salutes were fired, and thus the royal birthday was fittingly celebrated.

Where two anvils were to be had, the cannonade was much brisker, as then a plug was not needed. The hole in the lower anvil was filled with powder, and the other anvil was placed over it. This was much quicker than pounding in a plug, and had quite as striking and detonating an effect. The upper anvil gave a heave, like Mark Twain's shot-laden frog, and fell over on its side. The smoke rolled up as usual, and the report was equally gratifying.

Yates learned all these things as he sat in the blacksmith's shop, for they were still in the month of May, and the smoke of the echoing anvils had hardly yet cleared away. All present were eager to tell him of the glory of the day. One or two were good enough to express regret that he had not been there to see. After the disaster which had overturned Yates things had gone on very smoothly, and he had become one of the crowd, as it were. The fact that he was originally a Canadian told in his favor, although he had been contaminated by long residence in the States.

Macdonald worked hard at the turning of horseshoes from long rods of iron. Usually an extended line of unfinished shoes bestrode a blackened scantling, like bodiless horsemen, the scantling crossing the shop overhead, just under the roof. These were the work of Macdonald's comparatively leisure days, and they were ready to be fitted to the hoofs of any horse that came to be shod, but on this occasion there had been such a run on his stock that it was exhausted, a depletion the smith seemed to regard as a reproach on himself, for he told Yates several times that he often had as many as three dozen shoes up aloft for a rainy day.

When the sledge hammer work was to be done, one of those present stepped forward and swung the heavy sledge, keeping stroke for stroke with

Macdonald's one-handed hammer, all of which required a nice ear for time. This assistance was supposed to be rendered by Sandy; but, as he remarked, he was no hog, and anyone who wished to show his skill was at liberty to do so. Sandy seemed to spend most of his time at the bellows, and when he was not echoing the sentiments of the boss, as he called him, he was commending the expertness of the pro tem. amateur, the wielder of the sledge. It was fun to the amateur, and it was an old thing with Sandy, so he never protested against this interference with his duty, believing in giving everyone a chance, especially when it came to swinging a heavy hammer. The whole scene brought back to Yates the days of his youth, especially when Macdonald, putting the finishing strokes to his shoe, let his hammer periodically tinkle with musical clangor on the anvil, ringing forth a tintinnabulation that chimed melodiously on the ear—a sort of anvil-chorus accompaniment to his mechanical skill. He was a real sleight-of-hand man, and the anvil was his orchestra.

Yates soon began to enjoy his visit to the rural club. As the members thawed out he found them all first-rate fellows, and, what was more, they were appreciative listeners. His stories were all evidently new to them, and nothing puts a man into a genial frame of mind so quickly as an attentive, sympathetic audience. Few men could tell a story better than Yates, but he needed the responsive touch of interested hearers. He hated to have to explain the points of his anecdotes, as, indeed, what story-teller does not? A cold and critical man like the professor froze the spring of narration at its source. Besides, Renmark had an objectionable habit of tracing the recital to its origin; it annoyed Yates to tell a modern yarn, and then discover that Aristophanes, or some other prehistoric poacher on the good things men were to say, had forestalled him by a thousand years or so. When a man is quick to see the point of your stories, and laughs heartily at them, you are apt to form a high opinion of his good sense, and to value his companionship.

When the horses were shod, and young Bartlett, who was delighted at the impression Yates had made, was preparing to go, the whole company protested against the New Yorker's departure. This was real flattery.

"What's your hurry, Bartlett?" asked the whittler. "You can't do anything this afternoon, if you do go home. It's a poor time this to mend a bad day's work. If you stay, he'll stay; won't you, Mr. Yates? Macdonald is going to set tires, and he needs us all to look on and see that he does it right; don't you, Mac?"

"Yes; I get a lot of help from you while there's a stick to whittle," replied the smith.

"Then there's the protracted meeting to-night at the schoolhouse," put in another, anxious that all the attractions of the place should be brought forward.

"That's so," said the whittler; "I had forgotten about that. It's the first night, so we must all be there to encourage old Benderson. You'll be on hand to-night, won't you, Macdonald?"

The blacksmith made no answer, but turned to Sandy and asked him savagely what in —— and —-nation he was standing gawking there for. Why didn't he go outside and get things ready for the tire setting? What in thunder was he paying him for, anyhow? Wasn't there enough loafers round, without him joining the ranks?

Sandy took this rating with equanimity, and, when the smith's back was turned, he shrugged his shoulders, took a fresh bite of tobacco from the plug which he drew from his hip pocket, winking at the others as he did so. He leisurely followed Macdonald out of the shop, saying in a whisper as he passed the whittler:

"I wouldn't rile the old man, if I were you."

The club then adjourned to the outside, all except those who sat on the bench. Yates asked:

"What's the matter with Macdonald? Doesn't he like protracted meetings? And, by the way, what are protracted meetings?"

"They're revival meetings—religious meetings, you know, for converting sinners."

"Really?" said Yates. "But why protracted? Are they kept on for a week or two?"

"Yes; I suppose that's why, although, to tell the truth, I never knew the reason for the name. Protracted meetings always stood for just the same thing ever since I was a boy, and we took it as meaning that one thing, without thinking why."

"And doesn't Macdonald like them?"

"Well, you see, it's like this: He never wants to go to a protracted meeting, yet he can't keep away. He's like a drunkard and the corner tavern. He can't pass it, and he knows if he goes in he will fall. Macdonald's always the first one to go up to the penitent bench. They rake him in every time. He has religion real bad for a couple of weeks, and then he backslides. He doesn't seem able to stand either the converting or the backsliding. I suppose some time they will gather him in finally, and he will stick and become a class leader, but he hasn't stuck up to date."

"Then he doesn't like to hear the subject spoken of?"

"You bet he don't. It isn't safe to twit him about it either. To tell the truth, I was pleased when I heard him swear at Sandy; then I knew it was all right, and Sandy can stand it. Macdonald is a bad man to tackle when he's mad. There's nobody in this district can handle him. I'd sooner get a blow from a sledge hammer than meet Mac's fist when his dander is up. But so long as he swears it's all right. Say, you'll stay down for the meeting, won't you?"

"I think I will. I'll see what young Bartlett intends to do. It isn't very far to walk, in any case."

"There will be lots of nice girls going your way to-night after the meeting. I don't know but I'll jog along in that direction myself when it's over. That's the principal use I have for the meetings, anyhow."

The whittler and Yates got down from the bench, and joined the crowd outside. Young Bartlett sat on one of the horses, loath to leave while the tire setting was going on.

"Are you coming, Yates?" he shouted, as his comrade appeared.

"I think I'll stay for the meeting," said Yates, approaching him and patting the horse. He had no desire for mounting and riding away in the presence of that critical assemblage.

"All right," said young Bartlett. "I guess I'll be down at the meeting, too; then I can show you the way home."

"Thanks," said Yates; "I'll be on the lookout for you."

Young Bartlett galloped away, and was soon lost to sight in a cloud of dust. The others had also departed with their shod horses; but there were several new arrivals, and the company was augmented rather than diminished. They sat around on the fence, or on the logs dumped down by the wayside.

Few smoked, but many chewed tobacco. It was a convenient way of using the weed, and required no matches, besides being safer for men who had to frequent inflammable barns.

A circular fire burned in front of the shop, oak bark being the main fuel used. Iron wagon tires lay hidden in this burning circle. Macdonald and Sandy bustled about making preparations, their faces, more hideous in the bright sunlight than in the comparative obscurity of the shop, giving them the appearance of two evil spirits about to attend some incantation scene of which the circular fire was the visible indication. Crosstrees, of four pieces of squared timber, lay near the fire, with a tireless wheel placed flat upon them, the hub in the square hole at the center. Shiftless farmers always resisted having tires set until they would no longer stay on the wheel. The inevitable day was postponed, time and again, by a soaking of the wheels overnight in some convenient puddle of water; but as the warmer and dryer weather approached this device, supplemented by wooden wedges, no longer sufficed, and the tires had to be set for summer work. Frequently the tire rolled off on the sandy highway, and the farmer was reluctantly compelled to borrow a rail from the nearest fence, and place it so as to support the axle; he then put the denuded wheel and its tire on the wagon, and drove slowly to the nearest blacksmith's shop, his vehicle "trailing like a wounded duck," the rail leaving a snake's track behind it on the dusty road.

The blacksmith had previously cut and welded the tire, reducing its circumference, and when it was hot enough, he and Sandy, each with a pair of tongs, lifted it from the red-hot circle of fire. It was pressed and hammered down on the blazing rim of the wheel, and instantly Sandy and Macdonald, with two pails of water that stood handy, poured the cold liquid around the red-hot zone, enveloping themselves in clouds of steam, the quick contraction clamping the iron on the wood until the joints cracked together. There could be no loitering; quick work was necessary, or a spoiled wheel was the result. Macdonald, alternately spluttering through fire and steam, was in his element. Even Sandy had to be on the keen jump, without a moment to call his plug of tobacco his own. Macdonald fussed and fussed, but got through an immense amount of work in an incredibly short space of time, cursing Sandy pretty much all the while; yet that useful man never replied in kind, contenting himself with a wink at the crowd when he got the chance, and saying under his breath:

"The old man's in great fettle to-day."

Thus everybody enjoyed himself: Macdonald, because he was the center figure in a saturnalia of work; Sandy, because no matter how hard a man has to work he can chew tobacco all the time; the crowd, because the spectacle of fire, water, and steam was fine, and they didn't have to do anything but sit around and look on. The sun got lower and lower as, one by one, the spectators departed to do their chores, and prepare for the evening meeting. Yates at the invitation of the whittler went home with him, and thoroughly relished his evening meal.

CHAPTER XII.

Margaret had never met any man but her father who was so fond of books as Professor Renmark. The young fellows of her acquaintance read scarcely anything but the weekly papers; they went with some care through the yellow almanac that was given away free, with the grocer's name printed on the back. The marvelous cures the almanac recorded were of little interest, and were chiefly read by the older folk, but the young men reveled in the jokes to be found at the bottom of every page, their only drawback being that one could never tell the stories at a paring-bee or other social gathering, because everyone in the company had read them. A few of the young men came sheepishly round to get a book out of the library, but it was evident that their interest was not so much in the volume as in the librarian, and when that fact became apparent to the girl, she resented it. Margaret was thought to be cold and proud by the youth of the neighborhood, or "stuck-up," as they expressed it.

To such a girl a man like Renmark was a revelation. He could talk of other things than the weather, live stock, and the prospects for the crops. The conversation at first did not include Margaret, but she listened to every word of it with interest. Her father and mother were anxious to hear about their boy; and from that engrossing subject the talk soon drifted to university life, and the differences between city and country. At last the farmer, with a sigh, arose to go. There is little time for pleasant talk on a farm while daylight lasts. Margaret, remembering her duties as librarian, began to take in the books from the wagon to the front room. Renmark, slow in most things, was quick enough to offer his assistance on this occasion; but he reddened somewhat as he did so, for he was unused to being a squire of dames.

"I wish you would let me do the porterage," he said. "I would like to earn the right to look at these books sometimes, even though I may not have the privilege of borrowing, not being a taxable resident of the township."

"The librarian," answered Margaret, with a smile, "seems to be at liberty to use her own discretion in the matter of lending. No one has authority to look over her accounts, or to censure her if she lends recklessly. So, if you wish to borrow books, all you have to do is to ask for them."

"You may be sure I shall avail myself of the permission. But my conscience will be easier if I am allowed to carry them in."

"You will be permitted to help. I like carrying them. There is no more delicious armful than books."

As Renmark looked at the lovely girl, her face radiant with enthusiasm, the disconcerting thought came suddenly that perhaps her statement might not be accurate. No such thought had ever suggested itself to him before, and it now filled him with guilty confusion. He met the clear, honest gaze of her eyes for a moment, then he stammered lamely:

"I—I too am very fond of books."

Together they carried in the several hundred volumes, and then began to arrange them.

"Have you no catalogue?" he asked.

"No. We never seem to need one. People come and look over the library, and take out whatever book they fancy."

"Yes, but still every library ought to be catalogued. Cataloguing is an art in itself. I have paid a good deal of attention to it, and will show you how it is done, if you care to know."

"Oh, I wish you would."

"How do you keep a record of the volumes that are out?"

"I just write the name of the person, the title, and the date in this blank book. When the volume is returned, I score out the record."

"I see," said Renmark dubiously.

"That isn't right, is it? Is there a better way?"

"Well, for a small library, that ought to do; but if you were handling many books, I think confusion might result."

"Do tell me the right way. I should like to know, even if it is a small library."

"There are several methods, but I am by no means sure your way is not the simplest, and therefore the best in this instance."

"I'm not going to be put off like that," said Margaret, laughing. "A collection of books is a collection of books, whether large or small, and deserves respect and the best of treatment. Now, what method is used in large libraries?"

"Well, I should suggest a system of cards, though slips of paper would do. When any person wants to take out a book, let him make out a card, giving the date and the name or number of the book; he then must sign the card, and there you are. He cannot deny having had the book, for you have his own signature to prove it. The slips are arranged in a box according to dates, and when a book is returned, you tear up the recording paper."

"I think that is a very good way, and I will adopt it."

"Then let me send to Toronto and get you a few hundred cards. We'll have them here in a day or two."

"Oh, I don't want to put you to that trouble."

"It is no trouble at all. Now, that is settled, let us attack the catalogue. Have you a blank book anywhere about? We will first make an alphabetical list; then we will arrange them under the heads of history, biography, fiction, and so on."

Simple as it appeared, the making of a catalogue took a long time. Both were absorbed in their occupation. Cataloguing in itself is a straight and narrow path, but in this instance there were so many delightful side excursions that rapid progress could not be expected. To a reader the mere mention of a book brings up recollections. Margaret was reading out the names; Renmark, on slips of paper, each with a letter on it, was writing them down.

"Oh, have you that book?" he would say, looking up as a title was mentioned. "Have you ever read it?"

"No; for, you see, this part of the library is all new to me. Why, here is one of which the leaves are not even cut. No one has read it. Is it good?"

"One of the best," Renmark would say, taking the volume. "Yes, I know this edition. Let me read you one passage."

And Margaret would sit in the rocking while he cut the leaves and found the place. One extract was sure to suggest another, and time passed before the title of the book found its way to the proper slip of paper. These excursions into literature were most interesting to both excursionists, but they interfered with cataloguing. Renmark read and read, ever and anon stopping to explain some point, or quote what someone else had said on the same subject, marking the place in the book, as he paused, with inserted fore finger. Margaret swayed back and forth in the comfortable rocking chair, and listened intently, her large dark eyes fixed upon him so earnestly that now and then, when he met them, he seemed disconcerted for a moment. But the girl did not notice this. At the end of one of his dissertations she leaned her elbow on the arm of the chair, with her cheek resting against her hand, and said:

"How very clear you make everything, Mr. Renmark."

"Do you think so?" he said with a smile. "It's my business, you know."

"I think it's a shame that girls are not allowed to go to the university; don't you?"

"Really, I never gave any thought to the subject, and I am not quite prepared to say."

"Well, I think it most unfair. The university is supported by the Government, is it not? Then why should half of the population be shut out from its advantages?"

"I'm afraid it wouldn't do, you know."

"Why?"

"There are many reasons," he replied evasively.

"What are they? Do you think girls could not learn, or are not as capable of hard study as well as——"

"It isn't that," he interrupted; "there are plenty of girls' schools in the country, you know. Some very good ones in Toronto itself, for that matter."

"Yes; but why shouldn't I go to the university with my brother? There are plenty of boys' schools, too, but the university is the university. I suppose my father helps to support it. Why, then, should one child be allowed to attend and the other not? It isn't at all just."

"It wouldn't do," said the professor more firmly, the more he thought about it.

"Would you take that as a satisfying reason from one or your students?"

"What?"

"The phrase, 'It wouldn't do.'"

Renmark laughed.

"I'm afraid not," he said; "but, then, I'm very exacting in class. Now, if you want to know, why do you not ask your father?"

"Father and I have discussed the question, often, and he quite agrees with me in thinking it unfair."

"Oh, does he?" said Renmark, taken aback; although, when he reflected, he realized that the father doubtless knew as little about the dangers of the city as the daughter did.

"And what does your mother say?"

"Oh, mother thinks if a girl is a good housekeeper it is all that is required. So you will have to give me a good reason, if there is one, for nobody else in this house argues on your side of the question."

"Well," said Renmark in an embarrassed manner, "if you don't know by the time you are twenty-five, I'll promise to discuss the whole subject with you."

Margaret sighed as she leaned back in her chair.

"Twenty-five?" she cried, adding with the unconscious veracity of youth: "That will be seven years to wait. Thank you, but I think I'll find out before that time."

"I think you will," Renmark answered.

They were interrupted by the sudden and unannounced entrance of her brother.

"Hello, you two!" he shouted with the rude familiarity of a boy. "It seems the library takes a longer time to arrange than usual."

Margaret rose with dignity.

"We are cataloguing," she said severely.

"Oh, that's what you call it, is it? Can I be of any assistance, or is two company when they're cataloguing? Have you any idea what time it is?"

"I'm afraid I must be off," said the professor, rising. "My companion in camp won't know what has become of me."

"Oh, he's all right!" said Henry. "He's down at the Corners, and is going to stay there for the meeting to-night. Young Bartlett passed a while ago; he was getting the horses shod, and your friend went with him. I guess Yates can take care of himself, Mr. Renmark. Say, sis, will you go to the meeting? I'm going. Young Bartlett's going, and so is Kitty. Won't you come, too, Mr. Renmark? It's great fun."

"Don't talk like that about a religious gathering, Henry," said his sister, frowning.

"Well, that's what it is, anyhow."

"Is it a prayer meeting?" asked the professor, looking at the girl.

"You bet it is!" cried Henry enthusiastically, giving no one a chance to speak but himself. "It's a prayer meeting, and every other kind of meeting all rolled into one. It's a revival meeting; a protracted meeting, that's what it is.

You had better come with us, Mr. Renmark, and then you can see what it is like. You can walk home with Yates."

This attractive dénouement did not seem to appeal so strongly to the professor as the boy expected, for he made no answer.

"You will come, sis; won't you?" urged the boy.

"Are you sure Kitty is going?"

"Of course she is. You don't think she'd miss it, do you? They'll soon be here, too; better go and get ready."

"I'll see what mother says," replied Margaret as she left the room. She shortly returned, dressed ready for the meeting, and the professor concluded he would go also.

CHAPTER XIII.

Anyone passing the Corners that evening would have quickly seen that something important was on. Vehicles of all kinds lined the roadway, drawn in toward the fence, to the rails of which the horses were tied. Some had evidently come from afar, for the fame of the revivalist was widespread. The women, when they arrived, entered the schoolhouse, which was brilliantly lighted with oil lamps. The men stood around outside in groups, while many sat in rows on the fences, all conversing about every conceivable topic except religion. They apparently acted on the theory that there would be enough religion to satisfy the most exacting when they went inside. Yates sat on the top rail of the fence with the whittler, whose guest he had been. It was getting too dark for satisfactory whittling, so the man with the jack-knife improved the time by cutting notches in the rail on which he sat. Even when this failed, there was always a satisfaction in opening and shutting a knife that had a powerful spring at the back of it, added to which was the pleasurable danger of cutting his fingers. They were discussing the Fenian question, which at that time was occupying the minds of Canadians to some extent. Yates was telling them what he knew of the brotherhood in New York, and the strength of it, which his auditors seemed inclined to underestimate. Nobody believed that the Fenians would be so foolhardy as to attempt an invasion of Canada; but Yates held that if they did they would give the Canadians more trouble than was expected.

"Oh, we'll turn old Bartlett on them, if they come over here. They'll be glad enough to get back if he tackles them."

"With his tongue," added another.

"By the way," said the whittler, "did young Bartlett say he was coming to-night? I hope he'll bring his sister if he does. Didn't any of you fellows ask him to bring her? He'd never think of it if he wasn't told. He has no consideration for the rest of us."

"Why didn't you ask him? I hear you have taken to going in that direction yourself."

"Who? Me?" asked the whittler, quite unconcerned. "I have no chance in that quarter, especially when the old man's around."

There was a sound of singing from the schoolhouse. The double doors were wide open, and as the light streamed out the people began to stream in.

"Where's Macdonald?" asked Yates.

"Oh, I guess he's taken to the woods. He washes his face, and then he hides. He has the sense to wash his face first, for he knows he will have to come. You'll see him back before they start the second hymn."

"Well, boys!" said one, getting down from the fence and stretching his arms above his head with a yawn, "I guess, if we're going in, it's about time."

One after another they got down from the fence, the whittler shutting his knife with a reluctant snap, and putting it in his pocket with evident regret. The schoolhouse, large as it was, was filled to its utmost capacity—women on one side of the room, and men on the other; although near the door there was no such division, all the occupants of the back benches being men and boys. The congregation was standing, singing a hymn, when Yates and his comrades entered, so their quiet incoming was not noticed. The teacher's desk had been moved from the platform on which it usually stood, and now occupied a corner on the men's side of the house. It was used as a seat by two or three, who wished to be near the front, and at the same time keep an eye on the rest of the assemblage. The local preacher stood on the edge of the platform, beating time gently with his hymn book, but not singing, as he had neither voice nor ear for music, and happily recognized the fact. The singing was led by a man in the middle of the room.

At the back of the platform, near the wall, were two chairs, on one of which sat the Rev. Mr. Benderson, who was to conduct the revival. He was a stout, powerful-looking man, but Yates could not see his face, for it was buried in his hands, his head being bowed in silent prayer. It was generally understood that he had spent a youth of fearful wickedness, and he always referred to himself as a brand snatched from the burning. It was even hinted that at one time he had been a card player, but no one knew this for a fact. Many of the local preachers had not the power of exhortation, therefore a man like the Rev. Mr. Benderson, who had that gift abnormally developed, was too valuable to be localized; so he spent the year going from place to place, sweeping, driving, coaxing, or frightening into the fold those stray sheep that hovered on the outskirts; once they were within the religious ring-fence the local minister was supposed to keep them there. The latter, who had given out the hymn, was a man of very different caliber. He was tall, pale, and thin, and his long black coat hung on him as if it were on a post. When the hymn was finished; and everyone sat down, Yates, and those with him, found seats as best they could at the end near the door. This was the portion of the hall where the scoffers assembled, but it was also the portion which yielded most fruit, if the revival happened to be a successful one. Yates, seeing the place so full, and noticing two empty benches up at the front, asked the whittler why they were not occupied.

"They'll be occupied pretty soon."

"Who are they being kept for?"

"Perhaps you, perhaps me, perhaps both of us. You never can tell. That's the penitents' bench."

The local preacher knelt on the platform, and offered up a prayer. He asked the Lord to bless the efforts of the brother who was with them there that night, and to crown his labors with success; through his instrumentality to call many wandering sinners home. There were cries of "Amen" and "Bless the Lord" from different parts of the hall as the prayer was being made. On rising, another hymn was given out:

"Joy to the world, the Lord is come.

Let earth receive her King."

The leader of the singing started it too low. The tune began high, and ran down to the bottom of the scale by the time it reached the end of the first line. When the congregation had got two-thirds of the way down, they found they could go no farther, not even those who sang bass. The leader, in some confusion, had to pitch the tune higher, and his miscalculation was looked upon as exceedingly funny by the reckless spirits at the back of the hall. The door opened quietly; and they all turned expecting to see Macdonald, but it was only Sandy. He had washed his face with but indifferent success, and the bulge in his cheek, like a wen, showed that he had not abandoned tobacco on entering the schoolhouse. He tiptoed to a place beside his friends.

"The old man's outside," he whispered to the youth who sat nearest him, holding his hand to the side of his mouth so that the sound would not travel. Catching sight of Yates, he winked at him in a friendly sort of way.

The hymn gathered volume and spirit as it went on, gradually recovering from the misadventure at starting. When it was finished, the preacher sat down beside the revivalist. His part of the work was done, as there was no formal introduction of speaker to audience to be gone through. The other remained as he was with bowed head, for what appeared to be a long time.

A deep silence fell on all present. Even the whisperings among the scoffers ceased.

At last Mr. Benderson slowly raised his head, arose, and came to the front of the platform. He had a strong, masterful, clean-shaven face, with the heavy jaw of a stubborn man—a man not easily beaten. "Open the door," he said in a quiet voice.

In the last few meetings he had held he had found this an effective beginning. It was new to his present audience. Usually a knot of people stood outside, and if they were there, he made an appeal to them, through the open door, to enter. If no one was there, he had a lesson to impart, based on the silence and the darkness. In this instance it was hard to say which was the more surprised, the revivalist or the congregation. Sandy, being on his feet, stepped to the door, and threw it open. He was so astonished at what he saw that he slid behind the open door out of sight. Macdonald stood there, against the darkness beyond, in a crouching attitude, as if about to spring. He had evidently been trying to see what was going on through the keyhole; and, being taken unawares by the sudden opening of the door, had not had time to recover himself. No retreat was now possible. He stood up with haggard face, like a man who has been on a spree, and, without a word, walked in. Those on the bench in front of Yates moved together a little closer, and the blacksmith sat down on the vacant space left at the outside. In his confusion he drew his hand across his brow, and snapped his fingers loudly in the silence. A few faces at the back wore a grin, and would have laughed had not Sandy, closing the door quietly, given them one menacing look which quelled their merriment. He was not going to have the "old man" made fun of in his extremity; and they all had respect enough for Sandy's fist not to run the risk of encountering it after the meeting was over. Macdonald himself was more to be dreaded in a fight; but the chances were that for the next two or three weeks, if the revival were a success, there would be no danger from that quarter. Sandy, however, was permanently among the unconverted, and therefore to be feared, as being always ready to stand up for his employer, either with voice or blow. The unexpected incident Mr. Benderson had witnessed suggested no remarks at the time, so, being a wise man, he said nothing. The congregation wondered how he had known Macdonald was at the door, and none more than Macdonald himself. It seemed to many that the revivalist had a gift of divination denied to themselves, and this belief left them in a frame of mind more than ever ready to profit by the discourse they were about to hear.

Mr. Benderson began in a low monotone, that nevertheless penetrated to every part of the room. He had a voice of peculiar quality, as sweet as the tones of a tenor, and as pleasant to hear as music; now and then there was a manly ring in it which thrilled his listeners. "A week ago to-night," he said, "at this very hour, I stood by the deathbed of one who is now among the blessed. It is four years since he found salvation, by the mercy of God, through the humble instrumentality of the least of his servants. It was my blessed privilege to see that young man—that boy almost—pledge his soul to Jesus. He was less than twenty when he gave himself to Christ, and his hopes of a long life were as strong as the hopes of the youngest here to-night. Yet he was struck down in the early flush of manhood—struck down almost without warning. When I heard of his brief illness, although knowing nothing of its seriousness, something urged me to go to him, and at once. When I reached the house, they told me that he had asked to see me, and that they had just sent a messenger to the telegraph office with a dispatch for me. I said: 'God telegraphed to me.' They took me to the bedside of my young friend, whom I had last seen as hearty and strong as anyone here."

Mr. Benderson then, in a voice quivering with emotion, told the story of the deathbed scene. His language was simple and touching, and it was evident to the most callous auditor that he spoke from the heart, describing in pathetic words the scene he had witnessed. His unadorned eloquence went straight home to every listener, and many an eye dimmed as he put before them a graphic picture of the serenity attending the end of a well-spent life.

"As I came through among you to-night," he continued, "as you stood together in groups outside this building, I caught a chance expression that one of you uttered. A man was speaking of some neighbor who, at this busy season of the year, had been unable to get help. I think the one to whom this man was speaking had asked if the busy man were here, and the answer was: 'No; he has not a minute to call his own.' The phrase has haunted me since I heard it, less than an hour ago. 'Not a minute to call his own!' I thought of it as I sat before you. I thought of it as I rose to address you. I think of it now. Who has a minute to call his own?" The soft tones of the preacher's voice had given place to a ringing cry that echoed from the roof down on their heads. "Have you? Have I? Has any king, any prince, any president, any ruler over men, a minute or a moment he can call his own? Not one. Not one of all the teeming millions on this earth. The minutes that are past are yours. What use have you made of them? All your efforts, all your prayers, will not change the deeds done in any one of those minutes that are past, and those only are yours. The chiseled stone is not more fixed than are the deeds of the minutes that are past. Their record is for you or against you. But where now are those minutes of the future—those minutes that, from this time onward, you will be able to call your own when they are spent? They are in the hand of God—in his hand to give or to withhold. And who can count them in the hand of God? Not you, not I, not the wisest man upon the earth. Man may number the miles from here to the farthest visible star; but he cannot tell you,—you; I don't mean your neighbor, I mean you,—he cannot tell YOU whether your minutes are to be one or a thousand. They are doled out to you, and you are responsible for them. But there will come a moment,—it may be to-night, it may be a year hence,—when the hand of God will close, and you will have had your sum. Then time will end for you, and eternity begin. Are you prepared for that awful moment—that moment when the last is given you, and the next withheld? What if it came now? Are you prepared for it? Are you ready to welcome it, as did our brother who died at this hour one short week ago? His was not the only deathbed I have attended. Some scenes have been so seared into my brain that I can never forget them. A year ago I was called to the bedside of a dying man, old in years and old in sin. Often had he been called, but he put Christ away from him, saying: 'At a more convenient season.' He knew the path, but he walked not therein. And when at last God's patience ended, and this man was stricken down, he, foolish to the last, called for me, the servant, instead of to God, the Master. When I reached his side, the stamp of death was on his face. The biting finger of agony had drawn lines upon his haggard brow. A great fear was upon him, and he gripped my hand with the cold grasp of death itself. In that darkened room it seemed to me I saw the angel of peace standing by the bed, but it stood aloof, as one often offended. It seemed to me at the head of the bed the demon of eternal darkness bent over, whispering to him: 'It is too late! it is too late!' The dying man looked at me—oh, such a look! May you never be called upon to witness its like. He gasped: 'I have lived—I have lived a sinful life. Is it too late?' 'No,' I said, trembling. 'Say you believe.' His lips moved, but no sound came. He died as he had lived. The one necessary minute was withheld. Do you hear? It—was—withheld! He had not the minute to call his own. Not that minute in which to turn from everlasting damnation. He—went—down—into—hell, dying as he had lived."

The preacher's voice rose until it sounded like a trumpet blast. His eyes shone, and his face flushed with the fervor of his theme. Then followed, as rapidly as words could utter, a lurid, awful picture of hell and the day of judgment. Sobs and groans were heard in every part of the room. "Come—now—now!" he cried, "Now is the appointed time, now is the day of salvation. Come now; and as you rise pray God that in his mercy he may spare you strength and life to reach the penitent bench."

Suddenly the preacher ceased talking. Stretching out his hands, he broke forth, with his splendid tenor voice, into the rousing hymn, with its spirited marching time:

[Musical score: Come ye sinners, poor and needy,

Weak and wounded, sick and sore;

Jesus ready stands to save you.

Full of pity, love, and power.]

The whole congregation joined him. Everyone knew the words and the tune. It seemed a relief to the pent-up feelings to sing at the top of the voice. The chorus rose like a triumphal march:

[Musical score: Turn to the Lord, and seek salvation,

Sound the praise of His dear name;

Glory, honour, and salvation,

Christ the Lord has come to reign.]

As the congregation sang the preacher in stentorian tones urged sinners to seek the Lord while he was yet to be found.

Yates felt the electric thrill in the air, and he tugged at his collar, as if he were choking. He could not understand the strange exaltation that had come over him. It seemed as if he must cry aloud. All those around him were much moved. There were now no scoffers at the back of the room. Most of them seemed frightened, and sat looking one at the other. It only needed a beginning, and the penitent bench would be crowded. Many eyes were turned on Macdonald. His face was livid, and great beads of perspiration stood on his brow. His strong hand clutched the back of the seat before him, and the muscles stood out on the portion of his arm that was bare. He stared like a hypnotized man at the preacher. His teeth were set, and he breathed hard, as would a man engaged in a struggle. At last the hand of the preacher seemed to be pointed directly at him. He rose tremblingly to his feet and staggered down the aisle, flinging himself on his knees, with his head on his arms, beside the penitent bench, groaning aloud.

"Bless the Lord!" cried the preacher.

It was the starting of the avalanche. Up the aisle, with pale faces, many with tears streaming from their eyes, walked the young men and the old. Mothers, with joy in their hearts and a prayer on their lips, saw their sons fall prostrate before the penitent bench. Soon the contrite had to kneel wherever they could. The ringing salvation march filled the air, mingled with cries of joy and devout ejaculations.

"God!" cried Yates, tearing off his collar, "what is the matter with me? I never felt like this before. I must get into the open air."

He made for the door, and escaped unnoticed in the excitement of the moment. He stood for a time by the fence outside, breathing deeply of the cool, sweet air. The sound of the hymn came faintly to him. He clutched the fence, fearing he was about to faint. Partially recovering himself at last, he ran with all his might up the road, while there rang in his ears the marching words:

[Musical score: Turn to the Lord, and seek salvation,

Sound the praise of His dear Name.

Glory, honour and salvation,

Christ the Lord has come to reign.]

CHAPTER XIV.

When people are thrown together, especially when they are young, the mutual relationship existing between them rarely remains stationary. It drifts toward like or dislike; and cases have been known where it progressed into love or hatred.

Stillson Renmark and Margaret Howard became at least very firm friends. Each of them would have been ready to admit this much. These two had a good foundation on which to build up an acquaintance in the fact that Margaret's brother was a student in the university of which the professor was a worthy member. They had also a subject of difference, which, if it leads not to heated argument, but is soberly discussed, lends itself even more to the building of friendship than subjects of agreement. Margaret held, as has been indicated in a previous chapter, that the university was wrong in closing its doors to women. Renmark, up to the time of their first conversation on the subject, had given the matter but little thought; yet he developed an opinion contrary to that of Margaret, and was too honest a man, or too little of a diplomatist, to conceal it. On one occasion Yates had been present, and he threw himself, with the energy that distinguished him, into the woman side of the question—cordially agreeing with Margaret, citing instances, and holding those who were against the admission of women up to ridicule, taunting them with fear of feminine competition. Margaret became silent as the champion of her cause waxed the more eloquent; but whether she liked Richard Yates the better for his championship who that is not versed in the ways of women can say? As the hope of winning her regard was the sole basis of Yates' uncompromising views on the subject, it is likely that he was successful, for his experiences with the sex were large and varied. Margaret was certainly attracted toward Renmark, whose deep scholarship even his excessive self-depreciation could not entirely conceal; and he, in turn, had naturally a schoolmaster's enthusiasm over a pupil who so earnestly desired advancement in knowledge. Had he described his feelings to Yates, who was an expert in many matters, he would perhaps have learned that he was in love;

but Renmark was a reticent man, not much given either to introspection or to being lavish with his confidences. As to Margaret, who can plummet the depth of a young girl's regard until she herself gives some indication? All that one is able to record is that she was kinder to Yates than she had been at the beginning.

Miss Kitty Bartlett probably would not have denied that she had a sincere liking for the conceited young man from New York. Renmark fell into the error of thinking Miss Kitty a frivolous young person, whereas she was merely a girl who had an inexhaustible fund of high spirits, and one who took a most deplorable pleasure in shocking a serious man. Even Yates made a slight mistake regarding her on one occasion, when they were having an evening walk together, with that freedom from chaperonage which is the birthright of every American girl, whether she belongs to a farmhouse or to the palace of a millionaire.

In describing the incident afterward to Renmark, (for Yates had nothing of his comrade's reserve in these matters) he said:

"She left a diagram of her four fingers on my cheek that felt like one of those raised maps of Switzerland. I have before now felt the tap of a lady's fan in admonition, but never in my life have I met a gentle reproof that felt so much like a censure from the paw of our friend Tom Sayers."

Renmark said with some severity that he hoped Yates would not forget that he was, in a measure, a guest of his neighbors.

"Oh, that's all right," said Yates. "If you have any spare sympathy to bestow, keep it for me. My neighbors are amply able, and more than willing, to take care of themselves."

And now as to Richard Yates himself. One would imagine that here, at least, a conscientious relater of events would have an easy task. Alas! such is far from being the fact. The case of Yates was by all odds the most complex and bewildering of the four. He was deeply and truly in love with both of the girls. Instances of this kind are not so rare as a young man newly engaged to an innocent girl tries to make her believe. Cases have been known where a chance meeting with one girl, and not with another, has settled who was to be a young man's companion during a long life. Yates felt that in multitude of counsel there is wisdom, and made no secret of his perplexity to his friend. He complained sometimes that he got little help toward the solution of the problem, but generally he was quite content to sit under the trees with Renmark and weigh the different advantages of each of the girls. He sometimes appealed to his friend, as a man with a mathematical turn of mind, possessing an education that extended far into conic sections and algebraic formulae, to balance up the lists, and give him a candid and statistical opinion as to which of the two he should favor with serious proposals. When these appeals for help were coldly received, he accused his friend of lack of sympathy with his dilemma, said that he was a soulless man, and that if he had a heart it had become incrusted with the useless debris of a higher education, and swore to confide in him no more. He would search for a friend, he said, who had something human about him. The search for the sympathetic friend, however, seemed to be unsuccessful; for Yates always returned to Renmark, to have, as he remarked, ice water dashed upon his duplex-burning passion.

It was a lovely afternoon in the latter part of May, 1866, and Yates was swinging idly in the hammock, with his hands clasped under his head, gazing dreamily up at the patches of blue sky seen through the green branches of the trees overhead, while his industrious friend was unromantically peeling potatoes near the door of the tent.

"The human heart, Renny," said the man in the hammock reflectively, "is a remarkable organ, when you come to think of it. I presume, from your lack of interest, that you haven't given the subject much study, except, perhaps, in a physiological way. At the present moment it is to me the only theme worthy of a man's entire attention. Perhaps that is the result of spring, as the poet says; but, anyhow, it presents new aspects to me each hour. Now, I have made this important discovery: that the girl I am with last seems to me the most desirable. That is contrary to the observation of philosophers of bygone days. Absence makes the heart grow fonder, they say. I don't find it so. Presence is what plays the very deuce with me. Now, how do you account for it, Stilly?"

The professor did not attempt to account for it, but silently attended to the business in hand. Yates withdrew his eyes from the sky, and fixed them on the professor, waiting for the answer that did not come.

"Mr. Renmark," he drawled at last, "I am convinced that your treatment of the potato is a mistake. I think potatoes should not be peeled the day before, and left to soak in cold water until to-morrow's dinner. Of course I admire the industry that gets work well over before its results are called for. Nothing is more annoying than work left untouched until the last moment, and then hurriedly done. Still, virtue may be carried to excess, and a man may be too previous."

"Well, I am quite willing to relinquish the work into your hands. You may perhaps remember that for two days I have been doing your share as well as my own."

"Oh, I am not complaining about that, at all," said the hammock magnanimously. "You are acquiring practical knowledge, Renny, that will be of more use to you than all the learning taught at the schools. My only desire is that your education should be as complete as possible, and to this end I am willing to subordinate my own yearning desire for scullery work. I should suggest that, instead of going to the trouble of entirely removing the covering of the potato in that laborious way, you should merely peel a belt around its greatest circumference. Then, rather than cook the potatoes in the slow and soggy manner that seems to delight you, you should boil them quickly, with some salt placed in the water. The remaining coat would then curl outward, and the resulting potato would be white and dry and mealy, instead of being in the condition of a wet sponge."

"The beauty of a precept, Yates, is the illustrating of it. If you are not satisfied with my way of boiling potatoes, give me a practical object lesson."

The man in the hammock sighed reproachfully.

"Of course an unimaginative person like you, Renmark, cannot realize the cruelty of suggesting that a man as deeply in love as I am should demean himself by attending to the prosaic details of household affairs. I am doubly in love, and much more, therefore, as that old bore Euclid used to say, is your suggestion unkind and uncalled for."

"All right, then; don't criticise."

"Yes, there is a certain sweet reasonableness in your curt suggestion. A man who is unable, or unwilling, to work in the vineyard should not find fault with the pickers. And now, Renny, for the hundredth time of asking, add to the many obligations already conferred, and tell me, like the good fellow you are, what you would do if you were in my place. To which of those two charming, but totally unlike, girls would you give the preference?"

"Damn!" said the professor quietly.

"Hello, Renny!" cried Yates, raising his head. "Have you cut your finger? I should have warned you about using too sharp a knife."

But the professor had not cut his finger. His use of the word given above is not to be defended; still, as it was spoken by him, it seemed to lose all relationship with swearing. He said it quietly, mildly, and, in a certain sense, innocently. He was astonished at himself for using it, but there had been moments during the past few days when the ordinary expletives used in the learned volumes of higher mathematics did not fit the occasion.

Before anything more could be said there was a shout from the roadway near them.

"Is Richard Yates there?" hailed the voice.

"Yes. Who wants him?" cried Yates, springing out of the hammock.

"I do," said a young fellow on horseback. He threw himself off a tired horse, tied the animal to a sapling,—which, judging by the horse's condition, was an entirely unnecessary operation,—jumped over the rail fence, and approached through the woods. The young men saw, coming toward them, a tall lad in the uniform of the telegraph service.

"I'm Yates. What is it?"

"Well," said the lad, "I've had a hunt and a half for you. Here's a telegram."

"How in the world did you find out where I was? Nobody has my address."

"That's just the trouble. It would have saved somebody in New York a pile of money if you had left it. No man ought to go to the woods without leaving his address at a telegraph office, anyhow." The young man looked at the world from a telegraph point of view. People were good or bad according to the trouble they gave a telegraph messenger. Yates took the yellow envelope, addressed in lead pencil, but, without opening it, repeated his question:

"But how on earth did you find me?"

"Well, it wasn't easy;" said the boy. "My horse is about done out. I'm from Buffalo. They telegraphed from New York that we were to spare no expense; and we haven't. There are seven other fellows scouring the country on horseback with duplicates of that dispatch, and some more have gone along the lake shore on the American side. Say, no other messenger has been here before me, has he?" asked the boy with a touch of anxiety in his voice.

"No; you are the first."

"I'm glad of that. I've been 'most all over Canada. I got on your trail about two hours ago, and the folks at the farmhouse down below said you were up here. Is there any answer?"

Yates tore open the envelope. The dispatch was long, and he read it with a deepening frown. It was to this effect:

"Fenians crossing into Canada at Buffalo. You are near the spot; get there as quick as possible. Five of our men leave for Buffalo to-night. General O'Neill is in command of Fenian army. He will give you every facility when you tell him who you are. When five arrive, they will report to you. Place one or two with Canadian troops. Get one to hold the telegraph wire, and send over all the stuff the wire will carry. Draw on us for cash you need; and don't spare expense."

When Yates finished the reading of this, he broke forth into a line of language that astonished Renmark, and drew forth the envious admiration of the Buffalo telegraph boy.

"Heavens and earth and the lower regions! I'm here on my vacation. I'm not going to jump into work for all the papers in New York. Why couldn't those fools of Fenians stay at home? The idiots don't know when they're well off. The Fenians be hanged!"

"Guess that's what they will be," said the telegraph boy. "Any answer, sir?"

"No. Tell 'em you couldn't find me."

"Don't expect the boy to tell a lie," said the professor, speaking for the first time.

"Oh, I don't mind a lie!" exclaimed the boy, "but not that one. No, sir. I've had too much trouble finding you. I'm not going to pretend I'm no good. I started out for to find you, and I have. But I'll tell any other lie you like, Mr. Yates, if it will oblige you."

Yates recognized in the boy the same emulous desire to outstrip his fellows that had influenced himself when he was a young reporter, and he at once admitted the injustice of attempting to deprive him of the fruits of his enterprise.

"No," he said, "that won't do. No; you have found me, and you're a young fellow who will be president of the telegraph company some day, or perhaps hold the less important office of the United States presidency. Who knows? Have you a telegraph blank?"

"Of course," said the boy, fishing out a bundle from the leathern wallet by his side. Yates took the paper, and flung himself down under the tree.

"Here's a pencil," said the messenger.

"A newspaper man is never without a pencil, thank you," replied Yates, taking one out of his inside pocket. "Now, Renmark, I'm not going to tell a lie on this occasion," he continued.

"I think the truth is better on all occasions."

"Right you are. So here goes for the solid truth."

Yates, as he lay on the ground, wrote rapidly on the telegraph blank. Suddenly he looked up and said to the professor: "Say, Renmark, are you a doctor?"

"Of laws," replied his friend.

"Oh, that will do just as well." And he finished his writing.

"How is this?" he cried, holding the paper at arm's length:

"L. F. SPENCER,

"Managing Editor 'Argus,' New York:

"I'm flat on my back. Haven't done a hand's turn for a week. Am under the constant care, night and day, of one of the most eminent doctors in Canada, who even prepares my food for me. Since leaving New York trouble of the heart has complicated matters, and at present baffles the doctor. Consultations daily. It is impossible for me to move from here until present complications have yielded to treatment.

"Simson would be a good man to take charge in my absence."

"YATES.

"There," said Yates, with a tone of satisfaction, when he had finished the reading. "What do you think of that?"

The professor frowned, but did not answer. The boy, who partly saw through it, but not quite, grinned, and said: "Is it true?"

"Of course it's true!" cried Yates, indignant at the unjust suspicion. "It is a great deal more true than you have any idea of. Ask the doctor, there, if it isn't true. Now, my boy, will you give this in when you get back to the office? Tell 'em to rush it through to New York. I would mark it 'rush' only that never does any good, and always makes the operator mad."

The boy took the paper, and put it in his wallet.

"It's to be paid for at the other end," continued Yates.

"Oh, that's all right," answered the messenger with a certain condescension, as if he were giving credit on behalf of the company. "Well, so long," he added. "I hope you'll soon be better, Mr. Yates."

Yates sprang to his feet with a laugh, and followed him to the fence.

"Now, youngster, you are up to snuff, I can see that. They'll perhaps question you when you get back. What will you say?"

"Oh, I'll tell 'em what a hard job I had to find you, and let 'em know nobody else could 'a' done it, and I'll say you're a pretty sick man. I won't tell 'em you gave me a dollar!"

"Right you are, sonny; you'll get along. Here's five dollars, all in one bill. If you meet any other of the messengers, take them back with you. There's no use of their wasting valuable time in this little neck of the woods."

The boy stuffed the bill into his vest pocket as carelessly as if it represented cents instead of dollars, mounted his tired horse, and waved his hand in farewell to the newspaper man. Yates turned and walked slowly back to the tent. He threw himself once more into the hammock. As he expected, the professor was more taciturn than ever, and, although he had been prepared for silence, the silence irritated him. He felt ill used at having so unsympathetic a companion.

"Look here, Renmark; why don't you say something?"

"There is nothing to say."

"Oh, yes, there is. You don't approve of me, do you?"

"I don't suppose it makes any difference whether I approve or not."

"Oh, yes, it does. A man likes to have the approval of even the humblest of his fellow-creatures. Say, what will you take in cash to approve of me? People talk of the tortures of conscience, but you are more uncomfortable than the most cast-iron conscience any man ever had. One's own conscience one can deal with, but a conscience in the person of another man is beyond one's control. Now, it is like this: I am here for quiet and rest. I have earned both, and I think I am justified in——"

"Now, Mr. Yates, please spare me any cheap philosophy on the question. I am tired of it."

"And of me, too, I suppose?"

"Well, yes, rather—if you want to know."

Yates sprang out of the hammock. For the first time since the encounter with Bartlett on the road Renmark saw that he was thoroughly angry. The reporter stood with clenched fists and flashing eyes, hesitating. The other, his heavy brows drawn, while not in an aggressive attitude, was plainly ready for an attack. Yates concluded to speak, and not to strike. This was not because he was afraid, for he was not a coward. The reporter realized that he had forced the conversation, and remembered he had invited Renmark to accompany him. Although this recollection stayed his hand, it had no effect on his tongue.

"I believe," he said slowly, "that it would do you good for once to hear a straight, square, unbiased opinion of yourself. You have associated so long with pupils, to whom your word is law, that it may interest you to know what a man of the world thinks of you. A few years of schoolmastering is enough to spoil an archangel. Now, I think, of all the——"

The sentence was interrupted by a cry from the fence:

"Say, do you gentlemen know where a fellow named Yates lives?"

The reporter's hand dropped to his side. A look of dismay came over his face, and his truculent manner changed with a suddenness that forced a smile even to the stern lips of Renmark.

Yates backed toward the hammock like a man who had received an unexpected blow.

"I say, Renny," he wailed, "it's another of those cursed telegraph messengers. Go, like a good fellow, and sign for the dispatch. Sign it 'Dr. Renmark, for R. Yates.' That will give it a sort of official, medical-bulletin look. I wish I had thought of that when the other boy was here. Tell him

I'm lying down." He flung himself into the hammock, and Renmark, after a moment's hesitation, walked toward the boy at the fence, who had repeated his question in a louder voice. In a short time he returned with the yellow envelope, which he tossed to the man in the hammock. Yates seized it savagely, tore it into a score of pieces, and scattered the fluttering bits around him on the ground. The professor stood there for a few moments in silence.

"Perhaps," he said at last, "you'll be good enough to go on with your remarks."

"I was merely going to say," answered Yates wearily, "that you are a mighty good fellow, Renny. People who camp out always have rows. That is our first; suppose we let it be the last. Camping out is something like married life, I guess, and requires some forbearance on both sides. That philosophy may be cheap, but I think it is accurate. I am really very much worried about this newspaper business. I ought, of course, to fling myself into the chasm like that Roman fellow; but, hang it! I've been flinging myself into chasms for fifteen years, and what good has it done? There's always a crisis in a daily newspaper office. I want them to understand in the Argus office that I am on my vacation."

"They will be more apt to understand from the telegram that you're on your deathbed."

Yates laughed. "That's so," he said; "but, you see, Renny, we New Yorkers live in such an atmosphere of exaggeration that if I did not put it strongly it wouldn't have any effect. You've got to give a big dose to a man who has been taking poison all his life. They will take off ninety per cent. from any statement I make, anyhow; so, you see, I have to pile it up pretty high before the remaining ten per cent. amounts to anything."

The conversation was interrupted by the crackling of the dry twigs behind them, and Yates, who had been keeping his eye nervously on the fence, turned round. Young Bartlett pushed his way through the underbrush. His face was red; he had evidently been running.

"Two telegrams for you, Mr. Yates," he panted. "The fellows that brought 'em said they were important; so I ran out with them myself, for fear they wouldn't find you. One of them's from Port Colborne, the other's from Buffalo."

Telegrams were rare on the farm, and young Bartlett looked on the receipt of one as an event in a man's life. He was astonished to see Yates receive the double event with a listlessness that he could not help thinking was merely assumed for effect. Yates held them in his hand, and did not tear them up at once out of consideration for the feelings of the young man, who had had a race to deliver them.

"Here's two books they wanted you to sign. They're tired out, and mother's giving them something to eat."

"Professor, you sign for me, won't you?" said Yates.

Bartlett lingered a moment, hoping that he would hear something of the contents of the important messages; but Yates did not even open the envelopes, although he thanked the young man heartily for bringing them.

"Stuck-up cuss!" muttered young Bartlett to himself, as he shoved the signed books into his pocket and pushed his way through the underbrush again. Yates slowly and methodically tore the envelopes and their contents into little pieces, and scattered them as before.

"Begins to look like autumn," he said, "with the yellow leaves strewing the ground."

CHAPTER XV.

Before night three more telegraph boys found Yates, and three more telegrams in sections helped to carpet the floor of the forest. The usually high spirits of the newspaper man went down and down under the repeated visitations. At last he did not even swear, which, in the case of Yates, always indicated extreme depression. As night drew on he feebly remarked to the professor that he was more tired than he had ever been in going through an election campaign. He went to his tent bunk early, in a state of such utter dejection that Renmark felt sorry for him, and tried ineffectually to cheer him up.

"If they would all come together," said Yates bitterly, "so that one comprehensive effort of malediction would include the lot and have it over, it wouldn't be so bad; but this constant dribbling in of messengers would wear out the patience of a saint."

As he sat in his shirt sleeves on the edge of his bunk Renmark said that things would look brighter in the morning—which was a safe remark to make, for the night was dark.

Yates sat silently, with his head in his hands, for some moments. At last he said slowly: "There is no one so obtuse as the thoroughly good man. It is not the messenger I am afraid of, after all. He is but the outward symptom of the inward trouble. What you are seeing is an example of the workings of conscience where you thought conscience was absent. The trouble with me is that I know the newspaper depends on me, and that it will be the first time I have failed. It is the newspaper man's instinct to be in the center of the fray. He yearns to scoop the opposition press. I will get a night's sleep if I can, and to-morrow, I know, I shall capitulate. I will hunt out General O'Neill, and interview him on the field of slaughter. I will telegraph pages. I will refurbish my military vocabulary, and speak of deploying and massing and throwing out advance guards, and that sort of thing. I will move detachments and advance brigades, and invent strategy. We will have desperate fighting in the columns of the Argus, whatever there is on the fields of Canada. But to a man who has seen real war this opéra-bouffe masquerade of fighting——I don't want to say anything harsh, but to me it is offensive."

He looked up with a wan smile at his partner, sitting on the bottom of an upturned pail, as he said this. Then he reached for his hip pocket and drew out a revolver, which he handed, butt-end forward, to the professor, who, not knowing his friend carried such an instrument, instinctively shrank from it.

"Here, Renny, take this weapon of devastation and soak it with the potatoes. If another messenger comes in on me to-night, I know I shall riddle him if I have this handy. My better judgment tells me he is innocent, and I don't want to shed the only blood that will be spilled during this awful campaign."

How long they had been asleep they did not know, as the ghost-stories have it, but both were suddenly awakened by a commotion outside. It was intensely dark inside the tent, but as the two sat up they noticed a faint moving blur of light, which made itself just visible through the canvas.

"It's another of those fiendish messengers," whispered Yates. "Gi' me that revolver."

"Hush!" said the other below his breath. "There's about a dozen men out there, judging by the footfalls. I heard them coming."

"Let's fire into the tent and be done with it," said a voice outside.

"No, no," cried another; "no man shoot. It makes too much noise, and there must be others about. Have ye all got yer bayonets fixed?"

There was a murmur, apparently in the affirmative.

"Very well, then. Murphy and O'Rourick, come round to this side. You three stay where you are. Tim, you go to that end; and, Doolin, come with me."

"The Fenian army, by all the gods!" whispered Yates, groping for his clothes. "Renny, give me that revolver, and I'll show you more fun than a funeral."

"No, no. They're at least three to our one. We're in a trap here, and helpless."

"Oh, just let me jump out among 'em and begin the fireworks. Those I didn't shoot would die of fright. Imagine scouts scouring the woods with a lantern—with a lantern, Renny! Think of that! Oh, this is pie! Let me at 'em."

"Hush! Keep quiet! They'll hear you."

"Tim, bring the lantern round to this side." The blur of light moved along the canvas. "There's a man with his back against the wall of the tent. Just touch him up with your bayonet, Murphy, and let him know we're here."

"There may be twenty in the tent," said Murphy cautiously.

"Do what I tell you," answered the man in command.

Murphy progged his bayonet through the canvas, and sunk the deadly point of the instrument into the bag of potatoes.

"Faith, he sleeps sound," said Murphy with a tremor of fear in his voice, as there was no demonstration on the part of the bag.

The voice of Yates rang out from the interior of the tent:

"What the old Harry do you fellows think you're doing, anyhow? What's the matter with you? What do you want?"

There was a moment's silence, broken only by a nervous scuffling of feet and the clicking of gun-locks.

"How many are there of you in there?" said the stern voice of the chief.

"Two, if you want to know, both unarmed, and one ready to fight the lot of you if you are anxious for a scrimmage."

"Come out one by one," was the next command.

"We'll come out one by one," said Yates, emerging in his shirt sleeves, "but you can't expect us to keep it up long, as there are only two of us."

The professor next appeared, with his coat on. The situation certainly did not look inviting. The lantern on the ground threw up a pallid glow on the severe face of the commander, as the footlights might illuminate the figure of a brigand in a wood on the stage. The face of the officer showed that he was greatly impressed with the importance and danger of his position. Yates glanced about him with a smile, all his recent dejection gone now that he was in the midst of a row.

"Which is Murphy," he said, "and which is Doolin? Hello, alderman!" he cried, as his eyes rested on one tall, strapping, red-haired man who held his bayonet ready to charge, with a fierce determination in his face that might have made an opponent quail. "When did you leave New York? and who's running the city now that you're gone?"

The men had evidently a sense of humor, in spite of their bloodthirsty business, for a smile flickered on their faces in the lantern light, and several bayonets were unconsciously lowered. But the hard face of the commander did not relax.

"You are doing yourself no good by your talk," he said solemnly. "What you say will be used against you."

"Yes, and what you do will be used against you; and don't forget that fact. It's you who are in danger—not I. You are, at this moment, making about the biggest ass of yourself there is in Canada."

"Pinion these men!" cried the captain gruffly.

"Pinion nothing!" shouted Yates, shaking off the grasp of a man who had sprung to his side. But both Yates and Renmark were speedily overpowered; and then an unseen difficulty presented itself. Murphy pathetically remarked that they had no rope. The captain was a man of resource.

"Cut enough rope from the tent to tie them."

"And when you're at it, Murphy," said Yates, "cut off enough more to hang yourself with. You'll need it before long. And remember that any damage you do to that tent you'll have to pay for. It's hired."

Yates gave them all the trouble he could while they tied his elbows and wrists together, offering sardonic suggestions and cursing their clumsiness. Renmark submitted quietly. When the operation was finished, the professor said with the calm confidence of one who has an empire behind him and knows it:

"I warn you, sir, that this outrage is committed on British soil; and that I, on whom it is committed, am a British subject."

"Heavens and earth, Renmark, if you find it impossible to keep your mouth shut, do not use the word 'subject' but 'citizen.'"

"I am satisfied with the word, and with the protection given to those who use it."

"Look here, Renmark; you had better let me do the talking. You will only put your foot in it. I know the kind of men I have to deal with; you evidently don't."

In tying the professor they came upon the pistol in his coat pocket. Murphy held it up to the light.

"I thought you said you were unarmed?" remarked the captain severely, taking the revolver in his hand.

"I was unarmed. The revolver is mine, but the professor would not let me use it. If he had, all of you would be running for dear life through the woods."

"You admit that you are a British subject?" said the captain to Renmark, ignoring Yates.

"He doesn't admit it, he brags of it," said the latter before Renmark could speak. "You can't scare him; so quit this fooling, and let us know how long we are to stand here trussed up like this."

"I propose, captain," said the red-headed man, "that we shoot these men where they stand, and report to the general. They are spies. They are armed, and they denied it. It's according to the rules of war, captain."

"Rules of war? What do you know of the rules of war, you red-headed Senegambian? Rules of Hoyle! Your line is digging sewers, I imagine. Come, captain, undo these ropes, and make up your mind quickly. Trot us along to General O'Neill just as fast as you can. The sooner you get us there the more time you will have for being sorry over what you have done."

The captain still hesitated, and looked from one to the other of his men, as if to make up his mind whether they would obey him if he went to extremities. Yates' quick eye noted that the two prisoners had nothing to hope for, even from the men who smiled. The shooting of two unarmed and bound men seemed to them about the correct way of beginning a great struggle for freedom.

"Well," said the captain at length, "we must do it in proper form, so I suppose we should have a court-martial. Are you agreed?"

They were unanimously agreed.

"Look here," cried Yates, and there was a certain impressiveness in his voice in spite of his former levity; "this farce has gone just as far as it is going. Go inside the tent, there, and in my coat pocket you will find a telegram, the first of a dozen or two received by me within the last twenty-four hours. Then you will see whom you propose to shoot."

The telegram was found, and the captain read it, while Tim held the lantern. He looked from under his knitted brows at the newspaper man.

"Then you are one of the Argus staff."

"I am chief of the Argus staff. As you see, five of my men will be with General O'Neill to-morrow. The first question they will ask him will be: 'Where is Yates?' The next thing that will happen will be that you will be hanged for your stupidity, not by Canada nor by the State of New York, but by your general, who will curse your memory ever after. You are fooling not with a subject this time, but with a citizen; and your general is not such an idiot as to monkey with the United States Government; and, what is a blamed sight worse, with the great American press. Come, captain, we've had enough of this. Cut these cords just as quickly as you can, and take us to the general. We were going to see him in the morning, anyhow."

"But this man says he is a Canadian."

"That's all right. My friend is me. If you touch him, you touch me. Now, hurry up, climb down from your perch. I shall have enough trouble now, getting the general to forgive all the blunders you have made to-night, without your adding insult to injury. Tell your men to untie us, and throw the ropes back into the tent. It will soon be daylight. Hustle, and let us be off."

"Untie them," said the captain, with a sigh.

Yates shook himself when his arms regained their freedom.

"Now, Tim," he said, "run into that tent and bring out my coat. It's chilly here."

Tim did instantly as requested, and helped Yates on with the coat.

"Good boy!" said, Yates. "You've evidently been porter in a hotel."

Tim grinned.

"I think," said Yates meditatively, "that if I you look under the right-hand bunk, Tim, you will find a jug. It belongs to the professor, although he has hidden it under my bed to divert suspicion from himself. Just fish it out and bring it here. It is not as full as it was, but there's enough to go round, if the professor does not take more than his share."

The gallant troop smacked their lips in anticipation, and Renmark looked astonished to see the jar brought forth. "You first, professor," said Yates; and Tim innocently offered him the vessel. The learned man shook his head. Yates laughed, and took it himself.

"Well, here's to you, boys," he said. "And may you all get back as safely to New York as I will." The jar passed down along the line, until Tim finished its contents.

"Now, then, for the camp of the Fenian army," cried Yates, taking Renmark's arm; and they began their march through the woods. "Great Caesar! Stilly," he continued to his friend, "this is rest and quiet with a vengeance, isn't it?"

CHAPTER XVI.

The Fenians, feeling that they had to put their best foot foremost in the presence of their prisoners, tried at first to maintain something like military order in marching through the woods. They soon found, however, that this was a difficult thing to do. Canadian forests are not as trimly kept as English parks. Tim walked on ahead with the lantern, but three times he tumbled over some obstruction, and disappeared suddenly from view, uttering maledictions. His final effort in this line was a triumph. He fell over the lantern and smashed it. When all attempts at reconstruction failed, the party tramped on in go-as-you-please fashion, and found they did better without the light than with it. In fact, although it was not yet four o'clock, daybreak was already filtering through the trees, and the woods were perceptibly lighter.

"We must be getting near the camp," said the captain.

"Will I shout, sir?" asked Murphy.

"No, no; we can't miss it. Keep on as you are doing."

They were nearer the camp than they suspected. As they blundered on among the crackling underbrush and dry twigs the sharp report of a rifle echoed through the forest, and a bullet whistled above their heads.

"Fat the divil are you foiring at, Mike Lynch?" cried the alderman, who recognized the shooter, now rapidly falling back.

"Oh, it's you, is it?" said the sentry, stopping in his flight. The captain strode angrily toward him.

"What do you mean by firing like that? Don't you know enough to ask for the counter-sign before shooting?"

"Sure, I forgot about it, captain, entirely. But, then, ye see, I never can hit anything; so it's little difference it makes."

The shot had roused the camp, and there was now wild commotion, everybody thinking the Canadians were upon them.

A strange sight met the eye of Yates and Renmark. Both were astonished to see the number of men that O'Neill had under his command. They found a motley crowd. Some tattered United States uniforms were among them, but the greater number were dressed as ordinary individuals, although a few had trimmings of green braid on their clothes. Sleeping out for a couple of nights had given the gathering the unkempt appearance of a great company of tramps. The officers were indistinguishable from the men at first, but afterward Yates noticed that they, mostly in plain clothes and slouch hats, had sword belts buckled around them; and one or two had swords that had evidently seen service in the United States cavalry.

"It's all right, boys," cried the captain to the excited mob. "It was only that fool Lynch who fired at us. There's nobody hurt. Where's the general?"

"Here he comes," said half a dozen voices at once, and the crowd made way for him.

General O'Neill was dressed in ordinary citizen's costume, and did not wear even a sword belt. On his head of light hair was a black soft felt hat. His face was pale, and covered with freckles. He looked more like a clerk from a grocery store than the commander of an army. He was evidently somewhere between thirty-five and forty years of age.

"Oh, it's you, is it?" he said. "Why are you back? Any news?"

The captain saluted, military fashion, and replied:

"We took two prisoners, sir. They were encamped in a tent in the woods. One of them says he is an American citizen, and says he knows you, so I brought them in."

"I wish you had brought in the tent, too," said the general with a wan smile. "It would be an improvement on sleeping in the open air. Are these the prisoners? I don't know either of them."

"The captain makes a mistake in saying that I claimed a personal acquaintance with you, general. What I said was that you would recognize, somewhat quicker than he did, who I was, and the desirability of treating me with reasonable decency. Just show the general that telegram you took from my coat pocket, captain."

The paper was produced, and O'Neill read it over once or twice.

"You are on the New York Argus, then?"

"Very much so, general."

"I hope you have not been roughly used?"

"Oh, no; merely tied up in a hard knot, and threatened with shooting—that's all."

"Oh, I'm sorry to hear that. Still, you must make some allowance at a time like this. If you will come with me, I will write you a pass which will prevent any similar mistake happening in the future." The general led the way to a smoldering camp fire, where, out of a valise, he took writing materials and, using the valise as a desk, began to write. After he had written "Headquarters of the Grand Army of the Irish Republic" he looked up, and asked Yates his Christian name. Being answered, he inquired the name of his friend.

"I want nothing from you," interposed Renmark. "Don't put my name on the paper."

"Oh, that's all right," said Yates. "Never mind him, general. He's a learned man who doesn't know when to talk and when not to. As you march up to our tent, general, you will see an empty jug, which will explain everything. Renmark's drunk, not to put too fine a point upon it; and he imagines himself a British subject."

The Fenian general looked up at the professor.

"Are you a Canadian?" he asked.

"Certainly I am."

"Well, in that case, if I let you leave camp, you must give me your word that, should you fall in with the enemy, you will give no information to them of our position, numbers, or of anything else you may have seen while with us."

"I shall not give my word. On the contrary, if I should fall in with the Canadian troops, I will tell them where you are, that you are from eight hundred to one thousand strong, and the worst looking set of vagabonds I have ever seen out of jail."

General O'Neill frowned, and looked from one to the other.

"Do you realize that you confess to being a spy, and that it becomes my duty to have you taken out and shot?"

"In real war, yes. But this is mere idiotic fooling. All of you that don't escape will be either in jail or shot before twenty-four hours."

"Well, by the gods, it won't help you any. I'll have you shot inside of ten minutes, instead of twenty-four hours."

"Hold on, general, hold on!" cried Yates, as the angry man rose and confronted the two. "I admit that he richly deserves shooting, if you were the fool killer, which you are not. But it won't do, I will be responsible for him. Just finish that pass for me, and I will take care of the professor. Shoot me if you like, but don't touch him. He hasn't any sense, as you can see; but I am not to blame for that, nor are you. If you take to shooting everybody who is an ass, general, you won't have any ammunition left with which to conquer Canada."

The general smiled in spite of himself, and resumed the writing of the pass. "There," he said, handing the paper to Yates. "You see, we always like to oblige the press. I will risk your belligerent friend, and I hope you will exercise more control over him, if you meet the Canadians, than you were able to exert here. Don't you think, on the whole, you had better stay with us? We are going to march in a couple of hours, when the men have had a little rest." He added in a lower voice, so that the professor could not hear: "You didn't see anything of the Canadians, I suppose?"

"Not a sign. No, I don't think I'll stay. There will be five of our fellows here some time to-day, I expect, and that will be more than enough. I'm really here on a vacation. Been ordered rest and quiet. I'm beginning to think I have made a mistake in location."

Yates bade good-by to the commander, and walked with his friend out of the camp. They threaded their way among sleeping men and groups of stacked guns. On the top of one of the bayonets was hung a tall silk hat, which looked most incongruous in such a place.

"I think," said Yates, "that we will make for the Ridge Road, which must lie somewhere in this direction. It will be easier walking than through the woods; and, besides, I want to stop at one of the farmhouses and get some breakfast. I'm as hungry as a bear after tramping so long."

"Very well," answered the professor shortly.

The two stumbled along until they reached the edge of the wood; then, crossing some open fields, they came presently upon the road, near the spot where the fist fight had taken place between Yates and Bartlett. The comrades, now with greater comfort, walked silently along the road toward the west, with the reddening east behind them. The whole scene was strangely quiet and peaceful, and the recollection of the weird camp they had left in the woods seemed merely a bad dream. The morning air was sweet, and the birds were beginning to sing. Yates had intended to give the professor a piece of his mind regarding the lack of tact and common sense displayed by Renmark in the camp, but, somehow, the scarcely awakened day did not lend itself to controversy, and the serene stillness soothed his spirit. He began to whistle softly that popular war song, "Tramp, tramp, tramp, the boys are marching," and then broke in with the question:

"Say, Renny, did you notice that plug hat on the bayonet?"

"Yes," answered the professor; "and I saw five others scattered around the camp."

"Jingo! you were observant. I can imagine nothing quite so ridiculous as a man going to war in a tall silk hat."

The professor made no reply, and Yates changed his whistling to "Rally round the flag."

"I presume," he said at length, "there is little use in attempting to improve the morning hour by trying to show you, Renmark, what a fool you made of yourself in the camp? Your natural diplomacy seemed to be slightly off the center."

"I do not hold diplomatic relations with thieves and vagabonds."

"They may be vagabonds; but so am I, for that matter. They may also be well-meaning, mistaken men; but I do not think they are thieves."

"While you were talking with the so-called general, one party came in with several horses that had been stolen from the neighboring farmers, and another party started out to get some more."

"Oh, that isn't stealing, Renmark; that's requisitioning. You mustn't use such reckless language. I imagine the second party has been successful; for here are three of them all mounted."

The three horsemen referred to stopped their steeds at the sight of the two men coming round the bend of the road, and awaited their approach. Like so many of the others, they wore no uniform, but two of them held revolvers in their hands ready for action. The one who had no visible revolver moved his horse up the middle of the road toward the pedestrians, the other two taking positions on each side of the wagon way.

"Who are you? Where do you come from, and where are you going?" cried the foremost horseman, as the two walkers came within talking distance.

"It's all right, commodore," said Yates jauntily, "and the top of the morning to you. We are hungry pedestrians. We have just come from the camp, and we are going to get something to eat."

"I must have a more satisfactory answer than that."

"Well, here you have it, then," answered Yates, pulling out his folded pass, and handing it up to the horseman. The man read it carefully. "You find that all right, I expect?"

"Right enough to cause your immediate arrest."

"But the general said we were not to be molested further. That is in his own handwriting."

"I presume it is, and all the worse for you. His handwriting does not run quite as far as the queen's writ in this country yet. I arrest you in the name of the queen. Cover these men with your revolvers, and shoot them down if they make any resistance." So saying, the rider slipped from his horse, whipped out of his pocket a pair of handcuffs joined by a short, stout steel chain, and, leaving his horse standing, grasped Renmark's wrist.

"I'm a Canadian," said the professor, wrenching his wrist away. "You mustn't put handcuffs on me."

"You are in very bad company, then. I am a constable of this county; if you are what you say, you will not resist arrest."

"I will go with you, but you mustn't handcuff me."

"Oh, mustn't I?" And, with a quick movement indicative of long practice with resisting criminals, the constable deftly slipped on one of the clasps, which closed with a sharp click and stuck like a burr.

Renmark became deadly pale, and there was a dangerous glitter in his eyes. He drew back his clinched fist, in spite of the fact that the cocked revolver was edging closer and closer to him, and the constable held his struggling manacled hand with grim determination.

"Hold on!" cried Yates, preventing the professor from striking the representative of the law. "Don't shoot," he shouted to the man on horseback; "it is all a little mistake that will be quickly put right. You are three armed and mounted men, and we are only two, unarmed and on foot. There is no need of any revolver practice. Now, Renmark, you are more of a rebel at the present moment than O'Neill. He owes no allegiance, and you do. Have you no respect for the forms of law and order? You are an anarchist at heart, for all your professions. You would sing 'God save the Queen!' in the wrong place a while ago, so now be satisfied that you have got her, or, rather, that she has got you. Now, constable, do you want to hitch the other end of that arrangement on my wrist? or have you another pair for my own special use?

"I'll take your wrist, if you please."

"All right; here you are." Yates drew back his coat sleeve, and presented his wrist. The dangling cuff was speedily clamped upon it. The constable mounted the patient horse that stood waiting for him, watching him all the while with intelligent eye. The two prisoners, handcuffed together, took the middle of the road, with a horseman on each side of them, the constable bringing up the rear; thus they marched on, the professor gloomy from the indignity put upon them, and the newspaper man as joyous as the now thoroughly awakened birds. The scouts concluded to go no farther toward the enemy, but to return to the Canadian forces with their prisoners. They marched down the road, all silent except Yates, who enlivened the morning air with the singing of "John Brown."

"Keep quiet," said the constable curtly.

"All right, I will. But look here; we shall pass shortly the house of a friend. We want to go and get something to eat."

"You will get nothing to eat until I deliver you up to the officers of the volunteers."

"And where, may I ask, are they?"

"You may ask, but I will not answer."

"Now, Renmark," said Yates to his companion, "the tough part of this episode is that we shall have to pass Bartlett's house, and feast merely on the remembrance of the good things which Mrs. Bartlett is always glad to bestow on the wayfarer. I call that refined cruelty."

As they neared the Bartlett homestead they caught sight of Miss Kitty on the veranda, shading her eyes from the rising sun, and gazing earnestly at the approaching squad. As soon as she recognized the group she disappeared, with a cry, into the house. Presently there came out Mrs. Bartlett, followed by her son, and more slowly by the old man himself.

They all came down to the gate and waited.

"Hello, Mrs. Bartlett!" cried Yates cheerily. "You see, the professor has got his desserts at last; and I, being in bad company, share his fate, like the good dog Tray."

"What's all this about?" cried Mrs. Bartlett.

The constable, who knew both the farmer and his wife, nodded familiarly to them. "They're Fenian prisoners," he said.

"Nonsense!" cried Mrs. Bartlett—the old man, as usual, keeping his mouth grimly shut when his wife was present to do the talking—"they're not Fenians. They've been camping on our farm for a week or more."

"That may be," said the constable firmly, "but I have the best of evidence against them; and, if I'm not very much mistaken, they'll hang for it."

Miss Kitty, who had been partly visible through the door, gave a cry of anguish at this remark, and disappeared again.

"We have just escaped being hanged by the Fenians themselves, Mrs. Bartlett, and I hope the same fate awaits us at the hands of the Canadians."

"What! hanging?"

"No, no; just escaping. Not that I object to being hanged,—I hope I am not so pernickety as all that,—but, Mrs. Bartlett, you will sympathize with me when I tell you that the torture I am suffering from at this moment is the remembrance of the good things to eat which I have had in your house. I am simply starved to death, Mrs. Bartlett, and this hard-hearted constable refuses to allow me to ask you for anything."

Mrs. Bartlett came out through the gate to the road in a visible state of indignation.

"Stoliker," she exclaimed, "I'm ashamed of you! You may hang a man if you like, but you have no right to starve him. Come straight in with me," she said to the prisoners.

"Madam," said Stoliker severely, "you must not interfere with the course of the law."

"The course of stuff and nonsense!" cried the angry woman. "Do you think I am afraid of you, Sam Stoliker? Haven't I chased you out of this very orchard when you were a boy trying to steal my apples? Yes, and boxed your ears, too, when I caught you, and then was fool enough to fill your pockets with the best apples on the place, after giving you what you deserved. Course of the law, indeed! I'll box your ears now if you say anything more. Get down off your horse, and have something to eat yourself. I dare say you need it."

"This is what I call a rescue," whispered Yates to his linked companion.

What is a stern upholder of the law to do when the interferer with justice is a determined and angry woman accustomed to having her own way? Stoliker looked helplessly at Hiram, as the supposed head of the house, but the old man merely shrugged his shoulders, as much as to say: "You see how it is yourself. I am helpless."

Mrs. Bartlett marched her prisoners through the gate and up to the house.

"All I ask of you now," said Yates, "is that you will give Renmark and me seats together at the table. We cannot bear to be separated, even for an instant."

Having delivered her prisoners to the custody of her daughter, at the same time admonishing her to get breakfast as quickly as possible, Mrs. Bartlett went to the gate again. The constable was still on his horse. Hiram had asked, by way of treating him to a noncontroversial subject, if this was the colt he had bought from old Brown, on the second concession, and Stoliker had replied that it was. Hiram was saying he thought he recognized the horse by his sire when Mrs. Bartlett broke in upon them.

"Come, Sam," she said, "no sulking, you know. Slip off the horse and come in. How's your mother?"

"She's pretty well, thank you," said Sam sheepishly, coming down on his feet again.

Kitty Bartlett, her gayety gone and her eyes red, waited on the prisoners, but absolutely refused to serve Sam Stoliker, on whom she looked with the utmost contempt, not taking into account the fact that the poor young man had been merely doing his duty, and doing it well.

"Take off these handcuffs, Sam," said Mrs. Bartlett, "until they have breakfast, at least."

Stoliker produced a key and unlocked the manacles, slipping them into his pocket.

"Ah, now!" said Yates, looking at his red wrist, "we can breathe easier; and I, for one, can eat more."

The professor said nothing. The iron had not only encircled his wrist, but had entered his soul as well. Although Yates tried to make the early meal as cheerful as possible, it was rather a gloomy festival. Stoliker began to feel, poor man, that the paths of duty were unpopular. Old Hiram could always be depended upon to add somberness and taciturnity to a wedding feast; the professor, never the liveliest of companions, sat silent, with clouded brow, and vexed even the cheerful Mrs. Bartlett by having evidently no appetite. When the hurried meal was over, Yates, noticing that Miss Kitty had left the room, sprang up and walked toward the kitchen door. Stoliker was on his feet in an instant, and made as though to follow him.

"Sit down," said the professor sharply, speaking for the first time. "He is not going to escape. Don't be afraid. He has done nothing, and has no fear of punishment. It is always the innocent that you stupid officials arrest. The woods all around you are full of real Fenians, but you take excellent care to keep out of their way, and give your attention to molesting perfectly inoffensive people."

"Good for you, professor!" cried Mrs. Bartlett emphatically. "That's the truth, if ever it was spoken. But are there Fenians in the woods?"

"Hundreds of them. They came on us in the tent about three o'clock this morning,—or at least an advance guard did,—and after talking of shooting us where we stood they marched us to the Fenian camp instead. Yates got a pass, written by the Fenian general, so that we should not be troubled again. That is the precious document which this man thinks is deadly evidence. He never asked us a question, but clapped the handcuffs on our wrists, while the other fools held pistols to our heads."

"It isn't my place to ask questions," retorted Stoliker doggedly. "You can tell all this to the colonel or the sheriff; if they let you go, I'll say nothing against it."

Meanwhile, Yates had made his way into the kitchen, taking the precaution to shut the door after him. Kitty Bartlett looked quickly round as the door closed. Before she could speak the young man caught her by the plump shoulders—a thing which he certainly had no right to do.

"Miss Kitty Bartlett," he said, "you've been crying."

"I haven't; and if I had, it is nothing to you."

"Oh, I'm not so sure about that. Don't deny it. For whom were you crying? The professor?"

"No, nor for you either, although I suppose you have conceit enough to think so."

"Me conceited? Anything but that. Come, now, Kitty, for whom were you crying? I must know."

"Please let me go, Mr. Yates," said Kitty, with an effort at dignity.

"Dick is my name, Kit."

"Well, mine is not Kit.

"You're quite right. Now that you mention it, I will call you Kitty, which is much prettier than the abbreviation."

"I did not 'mention it.' Please let me go. Nobody has the right to call me anything but Miss Bartlett; that is, you haven't, anyhow."

"Well, Kitty, don't you think it is about time to give somebody the right? Why won't you look up at me, so that I can tell for sure whether I should have accused you of crying? Look up—Miss Bartlett."

"Please let me go, Mr. Yates. Mother will be here in a minute."

"Mother is a wise and thoughtful woman. We'll risk mother. Besides, I'm not in the least afraid of her, and I don't believe you are. I think she is at this moment giving poor Mr. Stoliker a piece of her mind; otherwise, I imagine, he would have followed me. I saw it in his eye."

"I hate that man," said Kitty inconsequently.

"I like him, because he brought me here, even if I was handcuffed. Kitty, why don't you look up at me? Are you afraid?"

"What should I be afraid of?" asked Kitty, giving him one swift glance from her pretty blue eyes. "Not of you, I hope."

"Well, Kitty, I sincerely hope not. Now, Miss Bartlett, do you know why I came out here?"

"For something more to eat, very likely," said the girl mischievously.

"Oh, I say, that to a man in captivity is both cruel and unkind. Besides, I had a first-rate breakfast, thank you. No such motive drew me into the kitchen. But I will tell you. You shall have it from my own lips. That was the reason!"

He suited the action to the word, and kissed her before she knew what was about to happen. At least, Yates, with all his experience, thought he had taken her unawares. Men often make mistakes in little matters of this kind. Kitty pushed him with apparent indignation from her, but she did not strike him across the face, as she had done before, when he merely attempted what he had now accomplished. Perhaps this was because she had been taken so completely by surprise.

"I shall call my mother," she threatened.

"Oh, no, you won't. Besides, she wouldn't come." Then this frivolous young man began to sing in a low voice the flippant refrain, "Here's to the girl that gets a kiss, and runs and tells her mother," ending with the wish that she should live and die an old maid and never get another. Kitty should not have smiled, but she did; she should have rebuked his levity, but she didn't.

"It is about the great and disastrous consequences of living and dying an old maid that I want to speak to you. I have a plan for the prevention of such a catastrophe, and I would like to get your approval of it."

Yates had released the girl, partly because she had wrenched herself away from him, and partly because he heard a movement in the dining room, and expected the entrance of Stoliker or some of the others. Miss Kitty stood with her back to the table, her eyes fixed on a spring flower, which she had unconsciously taken from a vase standing on the window-ledge. She smoothed the petals this way and that, and seemed so interested in botanical investigation that Yates wondered whether she was paying attention to what he was saying or not. What his plan might have been can only be guessed; for the Fates ordained that they should be interrupted at this critical moment by the one person on earth who could make Yates' tongue falter.

The outer door to the kitchen burst open, and Margaret Howard stood on the threshold, her lovely face aflame with indignation, and her dark hair down over her shoulders, forming a picture of beauty that fairly took Yates' breath away. She did not notice him.

"O Kitty," she cried, "those wretches have stolen all our horses! Is your father here?"

"What wretches?" asked Kitty, ignoring the question, and startled by the sudden advent of her friend.

"The Fenians. They have taken all the horses that were in the fields, and your horses as well. So I ran over to tell you."

"Have they taken your own horse, too?"

"No. I always keep Gypsy in the stable. The thieves did not come near the house. Oh, Mr. Yates! I did not see you." And Margaret's hand, with the unconscious vanity of a woman, sought her disheveled hair, which Yates thought too becoming ever to be put in order again.

Margaret reddened as she realized, from Kitty's evident embarrassment, that she had impulsively broken in upon a conference of two.

"I must tell your father about it," she said hurriedly, and before Yates could open the door she had done so for herself. Again she was taken aback to see so many sitting round the table.

There was a moment's silence between the two in the kitchen, but the spell was broken.

"I—I don't suppose there will be any trouble about getting back the horses," said Yates hesitatingly. "If you lose them, the Government will have to pay."

"I presume so," answered Kitty coldly; then: "Excuse me, Mr. Yates; I mustn't stay here any longer." So saying, she followed Margaret into the other room.

Yates drew a long breath of relief. All his old difficulties of preference had arisen when the outer door burst open. He felt that he had had a narrow escape, and began to wonder if he had really committed himself. Then the fear swept over him that Margaret might have noticed her friend's evident confusion, and surmised its cause. He wondered whether this would help him or hurt him with Margaret, if he finally made up his mind to favor her with his serious attentions. Still, he reflected that, after all, they were both country girls, and would no doubt be only too eager to accept a chance to live in New York. Thus his mind gradually resumed its normal state of self-confidence; and he argued that, whatever Margaret's suspicions were, they could not but make him more precious in her eyes. He knew of instances where the very danger of losing a man had turned a woman's wavering mind entirely in the man's favor. When he had reached this point, the door from the dining room opened, and Stoliker appeared.

"We are waiting for you," said the constable.

"All right. I am ready."

As he entered the room he saw the two girls standing together talking earnestly.

"I wish I was a constable for twenty-four hours," cried Mrs. Bartlett. "I would be hunting horse thieves instead of handcuffing innocent men."

"Come along," said the impassive Stoliker, taking the handcuffs from his pocket.

"If you three men," continued Mrs. Bartlett, "cannot take those two to camp, or to jail, or anywhere else, without handcuffing them, I'll go along with you myself and protect you, and see that they don't escape. You ought to be ashamed of yourself, Sam Stoliker, if you have any manhood about you—which I doubt."

"I must do my duty."

The professor rose from his chair. "Mr. Stoliker," he said with determination, "my friend and myself will go with you quietly. We will make no attempt to escape, as we have done nothing to make us fear investigation. But I give you fair warning that if you attempt to put a handcuff on my wrist again I will smash you."

A cry of terror from one of the girls, at the prospect of a fight, caused the professor to realize where he was. He turned to them and said in a contrite voice:

"Oh! I forgot you were here. I sincerely beg your pardon."

Margaret, with blazing eyes, cried:

"Don't beg my pardon, but—smash him."

Then a consciousness of what she had said overcame her, and the excited girl hid her blushing face on her friend's shoulder, while Kitty lovingly stroked her dark, tangled hair.

Renmark took a step toward them, and stopped. Yates, with his usual quickness, came to the rescue, and his cheery voice relieved the tension of the situation.

"Come, come, Stoliker, don't be an idiot. I do not object in the least to the handcuffs; and, if you are dying to handcuff somebody, handcuff me. It hasn't struck your luminous mind that you have not the first tittle of evidence against my friend, and that, even if I were the greatest criminal in America, the fact of his being with me is no crime. The truth is, Stoliker, that I wouldn't be in your shoes for a good many dollars. You talk a great deal about doing your duty, but you have exceeded it in the case of the professor. I hope you have no property; for the professor can, if he likes, make you pay sweetly for putting the handcuffs on him without a warrant, or even without one jot of evidence. What is the penalty for false arrest, Hiram?" continued Yates, suddenly appealing to the old man. "I think it is a thousand dollars."

Hiram said gloomily that he didn't know. Stoliker was hit on a tender spot, for he owned a farm.

"Better apologize to the professor and let us get along. Good-by, all. Mrs. Bartlett, that breakfast was the very best I ever tasted."

The good woman smiled and shook hands with him.

"Good-by, Mr. Yates; and I hope you will soon come back to have another."

Stoliker slipped the handcuffs into his pocket again, and mounted his horse. The girls, from the veranda, watched the procession move up the dusty road. They were silent, and had even forgotten the exciting event of the stealing of the horses.

CHAPTER XVII.

When the two prisoners, with their three captors, came in sight of the Canadian volunteers, they beheld a scene which was much more military than the Fenian camp. They were promptly halted and questioned by a picket before coming to the main body; the sentry knew enough not to shoot until he had asked for the countersign. Passing the picket, they came in full view of the Canadian force, the men of which looked very spick and span in uniforms which seemed painfully new in the clear light of the fair June morning. The guns, topped by a bristle of bayonets which glittered as the rising sun shone on them, were stacked with neat precision here and there. The men were preparing their breakfast, and a temporary halt had been called for that purpose. The volunteers were scattered by the side of the road and in the fields. Renmark recognized the colors of the regiment from his own city, and noticed that there was with it a company that was strange to him. Although led to them a prisoner, he felt a glowing pride in the regiment and their trim appearance—a pride that was both national and civic. He instinctively held himself more erect as he approached.

"Renmark," said Yates, looking at him with a smile, "you are making a thoroughly British mistake."

"What do you mean? I haven't spoken."

"No, but I see it in your eye. You are underestimating the enemy. You think this pretty company is going to walk over that body of unkempt tramps we saw in the woods this morning."

"I do indeed, if the tramps wait to be walked over—which I very much doubt."

"That's just where you make a mistake. Most of these are raw boys, who know all that can be learned of war on a cricket field. They will be the worst whipped set of young fellows before night that this part of the country has ever seen. Wait till they see one of their comrades fall, with the blood gushing out of a wound in his breast. If they don't turn and run, then I'm a Dutchman. I've seen raw recruits before. They should have a company of older men here who have seen service to steady them. The fellows we saw this morning were sleeping like logs, in the damp woods, as we stepped over them. They are veterans. What will be but a mere skirmish to them will seem to these boys the most awful tragedy that ever happened. Why, many of them look as if they might be university lads."

"They are," said Renmark, with a pang of anguish.

"Well, I can't see what your stupid government means by sending them here alone. They should have at least one company of regulars with them."

"Probably the regulars are on the way."

"Perhaps; but they will have to put in an appearance mighty sudden, or the fight will be over. If these boys are not in a hurry with their meal, the Fenians will be upon them before they know it. If there is to be a fight, it will be before a very few hours—before one hour passes, you are going to see a miniature Bull Run."

Some of the volunteers crowded around the incomers, eagerly inquiring for news of the enemy. The Fenians had taken the precaution to cut all the telegraph wires leading out of Fort Erie, and hence those in command of the companies did not even know that the enemy had left that locality. They were now on their way to a point where they were to meet Colonel Peacocke's force of regulars—a point which they were destined never to reach. Stoliker sought an officer and delivered up his prisoners, together with the incriminating paper that Yates had handed to him. The officer's decision was short and sharp, as military decisions are generally supposed to be. He ordered the constable to take both the prisoners and put them in jail at Port Colborne. There was no time now for an inquiry into the case,—that could come afterward,—and, so long as the men were safe in jail, everything would be all right. To this the constable mildly interposed two objections. In the first place, he said, he was with the volunteers not in his capacity as constable, but in the position of guide and man who knew the country. In the second place, there was no jail at Port Colborne.

"Where is the nearest jail?"

"The jail of the county is at Welland, the county town," replied the constable.

"Very well; take them there."

"But I am here as guide," repeated Stoliker.

The officer hesitated for a moment. "You haven't handcuffs with you, I presume?"

"Yes, I have," said Stoliker, producing the implements.

"Well, then, handcuff them together, and I will send one of the company over to Welland with them. How far is it across country?"

Stoliker told him.

The officer called one of the volunteers, and said to him:

"You are to make your way across country to Welland, and deliver these men up to the jailer there. They will be handcuffed together, but you take a revolver with you, and if they give you any trouble, shoot them."

The volunteer reddened, and drew himself up. "I am not a policeman," he said. "I am a soldier."

"Very well, then your first duty as a soldier is to obey orders. I order you to take these men to Welland."

The volunteers had crowded around as this discussion went on, and a murmur rose among them at the order of the officer. They evidently sympathized with their comrade's objection to the duties of a policeman. One of them made his way through the crowd, and cried:

"Hello! this is the professor. This is Mr. Renmark. He's no Fenian." Two or three more of the university students recognized Renmark, and, pushing up to him, greeted him warmly. He was evidently a favorite with his class. Among others young Howard pressed forward.

"It is nonsense," he cried, "talking about sending Professor Renmark to jail! He is no more a Fenian than Governor-General Monck. We'll all go bail for the professor."

The officer wavered. "If you know him," he said, "that is a different matter. But this other man has a letter from the commander of the Fenians, recommending him to the consideration of all friends of the Fenian cause. I can't let him go free."

"Are you the chief in command here?" asked Renmark.

"No, I am not."

"Mr. Yates is a friend of mine who is here with me on his vacation. He is a New York journalist, and has nothing in common with the invaders. If you insist on sending him to Welland, I must demand that we be taken before the officer in command. In any case, he and I stand or fall together. I am exactly as guilty or innocent as he is."

"We can't bother the colonel about every triviality."

"A man's liberty is no triviality. What, in the name of common sense, are you fighting for but liberty?"

"Thanks, Renmark, thanks," said Yates; "but I don't care to see the colonel, and I shall welcome Welland jail. I am tired of all this bother. I came here for rest and quiet, and I am going to have them, if I have to go to jail for them. I'm coming reluctantly to the belief that jail's the most comfortable place in Canada, anyhow."

"But this is an outrage," cried the professor indignantly.

"Of course it is," replied Yates wearily; "but the woods are full of them. There's always outrages going on, especially in so-called free countries; therefore one more or less won't make much difference. Come, officer, who's going to take me to Welland? or shall I have to go by myself? I'm a Fenian from 'way back, and came here especially to overturn the throne and take it home with me. For Heaven's sake, know your own mind one way or other, and let us end this conference."

The officer was wroth. He speedily gave the order to Stoliker to handcuff the prisoner to himself, and deliver him to the jailer at Welland.

"But I want assistance," objected Stoliker. "The prisoner is a bigger man than I am." The volunteers laughed as Stoliker mentioned this self-evident fact.

"If anyone likes to go with you, he can go. I shall give no orders."

No one volunteered to accompany the constable.

"Take this revolver with you," continued the officer, "and if he attempts to escape, shoot him. Besides, you know the way to Welland, so I can't send anybody in your place, even if I wanted to."

"Howard knows the way," persisted Stoliker. That young man spoke up with great indignation: "Yes, but Howard isn't constable, and Stoliker is. I'm not going."

Renmark went up to his friend.

"Who's acting foolishly now, Yates?" he said. "Why don't you insist on seeing the colonel? The chances are ten to one that you would be allowed off."

"Don't make any mistake. The colonel will very likely be some fussy individual who magnifies his own importance, and who will send a squad of volunteers to escort me, and I want to avoid that. These officers always stick by each other; they're bound to. I want to go alone with Stoliker. I have a score to settle with him."

"Now, don't do anything rash. You've done nothing so far; but if you assault an officer of the law, that will be a different matter."

"Satan reproving sin. Who prevented you from hitting Stoliker a short time since?"

"Well, I was wrong then. You are wrong now."

"See here, Renny," whispered Yates; "you get back to the tent, and see that everything's all right. I'll be with you in an hour or so. Don't look so frightened. I won't hurt Stoliker. But I want to see this fight, and I won't get there if the colonel sends an escort. I'm going to use Stoliker as a shield when the bullets begin flying."

The bugles sounded for the troops to fall in, and Stoliker very reluctantly attached one clasp of the handcuff around his own left wrist, while he snapped the other on the right wrist of Yates, who embarrassed him with kindly assistance. The two manacled men disappeared down the road, while the volunteers rapidly fell in to continue their morning's march.

Young Howard beckoned to the professor from his place in the ranks. "I say, professor, how did you happen to be down this way?"

"I have been camping out here for a week or more with Yates, who is an old schoolfellow of mine."

"What a shame to have him led off in that way! But he seemed to rather like the idea. Jolly fellow, I should say. How I wish I had known you were in this neighborhood. My folks live near here. They would only have been too glad to be of assistance to you."

"They have been of assistance to me, and exceedingly kind as well."

"What? You know them? All of them? Have you met Margaret?"

"Yes," said the professor slowly, but his glance fell as it encountered the eager eyes of the youth. It was evident that Margaret was the brother's favorite.

"Fall back, there!" cried the officer to Renmark.

"May I march along with them? or can you give me a gun, and let me take part?"

"No," said the officer with some hauteur; "this is no place for civilians." Again the professor smiled as he reflected that the whole company, as far as martial experience went, were merely civilians dressed in uniform; but he became grave again when he remembered Yates' ominous prediction regarding them.

"I say, Mr. Renmark," cried young Howard, as the company moved off, "if you see any of them, don't tell them I'm here—especially Margaret. It might make them uneasy. I'll get leave when this is over, and drop in on them."

The boy spoke with the hopeful confidence of youth, and had evidently no premonition of how his appointment would be kept. Renmark left the road, and struck across country in the direction of the tent.

Meanwhile, two men were tramping steadily along the dusty road toward Welland: the captor moody and silent, the prisoner talkative and entertaining—indeed, Yates' conversation often went beyond entertainment, and became, at times, instructive. He discussed the affairs of both countries, showed a way out of all political difficulties, gave reasons for the practical use of common sense in every emergency, passed opinions on the methods of agriculture adopted in various parts of the country, told stories of the war, gave instances of men in captivity murdering those who were in charge of them, deduced from these anecdotes the foolishness of resisting lawful authority lawfully exercised, and, in general, showed that he was a man who respected power and the exercise thereof. Suddenly branching to more practical matters, he exclaimed:

"Say, Stoliker, how many taverns are there between here and Welland?"

Stoliker had never counted them.

"Well, that's encouraging, anyhow. If there are so many that it requires an effort of the memory to enumerate them, we will likely have something to drink before long."

"I never drink while on duty," said Stoliker curtly.

"Oh, well, don't apologize for it. Every man has his failings. I'll be only too happy to give you some instructions. I have acquired the useful practice of being able to drink both on and off duty. Anything can be done, Stoliker, if you give your mind to it. I don't believe in the word 'can't,' either with or without the mark of elision."

Stoliker did not answer, and Yates yawned wearily.

"I wish you would hire a rig, constable. I'm tired of walking. I've been on my feet ever since three this morning."

"I have no authority to hire a buggy."

"But what do you do when a prisoner refuses to move?"

"I make him move," said Stoliker shortly.

"Ah, I see. That's a good plan, and saves bills at the livery stable."

They came to a tempting bank by the roadside, when Yates cried:

"Let's sit down and have a rest. I'm done out. The sun is hot, and the road dusty. You can let me have half an hour: the day's young, yet."

"I'll let you have fifteen minutes."

They sat down together. "I wish a team would come along," said Yates with a sigh.

"No chance of a team, with most of the horses in the neighborhood stolen, and the troops on the roads."

"That's so," assented Yates sleepily.

He was evidently tired out, for his chin dropped on his breast, and his eyes closed. His breathing came soft and regular, and his body leaned toward the constable, who sat bolt upright. Yates' left arm fell across the knees of Stoliker, and he leaned more and more heavily against him. The constable did not know whether he was shamming or not, but he took no risks. He kept his grasp firm on the butt of the revolver. Yet, he reflected, Yates could surely not meditate an attempt on his weapon, for he had, a few minutes before, told him a story about a prisoner who escaped in exactly that way. Stoliker was suspicious of the good intentions of the man he had in charge; he was altogether too polite and good-natured; and, besides, the constable dumbly felt that the prisoner was a much cleverer man than he.

"Here, sit up," he said gruffly. "I'm not paid to carry you, you know."

"What's that? What's that? What's that?" cried Yates rapidly, blinking his eyes and straightening up. "Oh, it's only you, Stoliker. I thought it was my friend Renmark. Have I been asleep?"

"Either that or pretending—I don't know which, and I don't care."

"Oh! I must have been pretending," answered Yates drowsily; "I can't have dropped asleep. How long have we been here?"

"About five minutes."

"All right." And Yates' head began to droop again.

This time the constable felt no doubt about it. No man could imitate sleep so well. Several times Yates nearly fell forward, and each time saved himself, with the usual luck of a sleeper or a drunkard. Nevertheless, Stoliker never took his hand from his revolver. Suddenly, with a greater lurch than usual, Yates pitched head first down the bank, carrying the constable with him. The steel band of the handcuff nipped the wrist of Stoliker, who, with an oath and a cry of pain, instinctively grasped the links between with his right hand, to save his wrist. Like a cat, Yates was upon him, showing marvelous agility for a man who had just tumbled in a heap. The next instant he held aloft the revolver, crying triumphantly:

"How's that, umpire? Out, I expect."

The constable, with set teeth, still rubbed his wounded wrist, realizing the helplessness of a struggle.

"Now, Stoliker," said Yates, pointing the pistol at him, "what have you to say before I fire?"

"Nothing," answered the constable, "except that you will be hanged at Welland, instead of staying a few days in jail."

Yates laughed. "That's not bad, Stoliker; and I really believe there's some grit in you, if you are a man-catcher. Still, you were not in very much danger, as perhaps you knew. Now, if you should want this pistol again, just watch where it alights." And Yates, taking the weapon by the muzzle, tossed it as far as he could into the field.

Stoliker watched its flight intently, then, putting his hand into his pocket, he took out some small object and flung it as nearly as he could to the spot where the revolver fell.

"Is that how you mark the place?" asked Yates; "or is it some spell that will enable you to find the pistol?"

"Neither," answered the constable quietly. "It is the key of the handcuffs. The duplicate is at Welland."

Yates whistled a prolonged note, and looked with admiration at the little man. He saw the hopelessness of the situation. If he attempted to search for the key in the long grass, the chances were ten to one that Stoliker would stumble on the pistol before Yates found the key, in which case the reporter would be once more at the mercy of the law.

"Stoliker, you're evidently fonder of my company than I am of yours. That wasn't a bad strategic move on your part, but it may cause you some personal inconvenience before I get these handcuffs filed off. I'm not going to Welland this trip, as you may be disappointed to learn. I have gone with you as far as I intend to. You will now come with me."

"I shall not move," replied the constable firmly.

"Very well, stay there," said Yates, twisting his hand around so as to grasp the chain that joined the cuffs. Getting a firm grip, he walked up the road, down which they had tramped a few minutes before. Stoliker set his teeth and tried to hold his ground, but was forced to follow. Nothing was said by either until several hundred yards were thus traversed. Then Yates stopped.

"Having now demonstrated to you the fact that you must accompany me, I hope you will show yourself a sensible man, Stoliker, and come with me quietly. It will be less exhausting for both of us, and all the same in the end. You can do nothing until you get help. I am going to see the fight, which I feel sure will be a brief one, so I don't want to lose any more time in getting back. In order to avoid meeting people, and having me explain to them that you are my prisoner, I propose we go through the fields."

One difference between a fool and a wise man is that the wise man always accepts the inevitable. The constable was wise. The two crossed the rail fence into the fields, and walked along peaceably together—Stoliker silent, as usual, with the grim confidence of a man who is certain of ultimate success, who has the nation behind him, with all its machinery working in his favor; Yates talkative, argumentative, and instructive by turns, occasionally breaking forth into song when the unresponsiveness of the other rendered conversation difficult.

"Stoliker, how supremely lovely and quiet and restful are the silent, scented, spreading fields! How soothing to a spirit tired of the city's din is this solitude, broken only by the singing of the birds and the drowsy droning of the bee, erroneously termed 'bumble'! The green fields, the shady trees, the sweet freshness of the summer air, untainted by city smoke, and over all the eternal serenity of the blue unclouded sky—how can human spite and human passion exist in such a paradise? Does it all not make you feel as if you were an innocent child again, with motives pure and conscience white?"

If Stoliker felt like an innocent child, he did not look it. With clouded brow he eagerly scanned the empty fields, hoping for help. But, although the constable made no reply, there was an answer that electrified Yates, and put all thought of the beauty of the country out of his mind. The dull report of a musket, far in front of them, suddenly broke the silence, followed by several scattering shots, and then the roar of a volley. This was sharply answered by the ring of rifles to the right. With an oath, Yates broke into a run.

"They're at it!" he cried, "and all on account of your confounded obstinacy I shall miss the whole show. The Fenians have opened fire, and the Canadians have not been long in replying."

The din of the firing now became incessant. The veteran in Yates was aroused. He was like an old war horse who again feels the intoxicating smell of battle smoke. The lunacy of gunpower shone in his gleaming eye.

"Come on, you loitering idiot!" he cried to the constable, who had difficulty in keeping pace with him; "come on, or, by the gods! I'll break your wrist across a fence rail and tear this brutal iron from it."

The savage face of the prisoner was transformed with the passion of war, and, for the first time that day, Stoliker quailed before the insane glare of his eyes. But if he was afraid, he did not show his fear to Yates.

"Come on, you!" he shouted, springing ahead, and giving a twist to the handcuffs well known to those who have to deal with refractory criminals. "I am as eager to see the fight as you are."

The sharp pain brought Yates to his senses again. He laughed, and said: "That's the ticket, I'm with you. Perhaps you would not be in such a hurry if you knew that I am going into the thick the fight, and intend to use you as a shield from the bullets."

"That's all right," answered the little constable, panting. "Two sides are firing. I'll shield you on one side, and you'll have to shield me on the other."

Again Yates laughed, and they ran silently together. Avoiding the houses, they came out at the Ridge Road. The smoke rolled up above the trees, showing where the battle was going on some distance beyond. Yates made the constable cross the fence and the road, and take to the fields again, bringing him around behind Bartlett's house and barn. No one was visible near the house except Kitty Bartlett, who stood at the back watching, with pale and anxious face, the rolling smoke, now and then covering her ears with her hands as the sound of an extra loud volley assailed them. Stoliker lifted up his voice and shouted for help.

"If you do that again," cried Yates, clutching him by the throat, "I'll choke you!"

But he did not need to do it again. The girl heard the cry, turned with a frightened look, and was about to fly into the house when she recognized the two. Then she came toward them. Yates took his hand away from the constable's throat.

"Where is your father or your brother?" demanded the constable.

"I don't know."

"Where is your mother?"

"She is over with Mrs. Howard, who is ill."

"Are you all alone?"

"Yes."

"Then I command you, in the name of the Queen, to give no assistance to this prisoner, but to do as I tell you."

"And I command you, in the name of the President," cried Yates, "to keep your mouth shut, and not to address a lady like that. Kitty," he continued in a milder tone, "could you tell me where to get a file, so that I may cut these wrist ornaments? Don't you get it. You are to do nothing. Just indicate where the file is. The law mustn't have any hold on you, as it seems to have on me."

"Why don't you make him unlock them?" asked Kitty.

"Because the villain threw away the key in the fields."

"He couldn't have done that."

The constable caught his breath.

"But he did. I saw him."

"And I saw him unlock them at breakfast. The key was on the end of his watch chain. He hasn't thrown that away."

She made a move to take out his watch chain but Yates stopped her.

"Don't touch him. I'm playing a lone hand here." He jerked out the chain, and the real key dangled from it.

"Well, Stoliker," he said, "I don't know which to admire most—your cleverness and pluck, my stupidity, or Miss Bartlett's acuteness of observation. Can we get into the barn, Kitty?"

"Yes; but you mustn't hurt him."

"No fear. I think too much of him. Don't you come in. I'll be out in a moment, like the medium from a spiritualistic dark cabinet."

Entering the barn, Yates forced the constable up against the square oaken post which was part of the framework of the building, and which formed one side of the perpendicular ladder that led to the top of the hay mow.

"Now, Stoliker," he, said solemnly, "you realize, of course, that I don't want to hurt you yet you also realize that I must hurt you if you attempt any tricks. I can't take any risks, please remember that; and recollect that, by the time you are free again, I shall be in the State of New York. So don't compel me to smash your head against this post." He, with some trouble, unlocked the clasp on his own wrist; then, drawing Stoliker's right hand around the post, he snapped the same clasp on the constable's hitherto free wrist. The unfortunate man, with his cheek against the oak, was in the comical position of lovingly embracing the post.

"I'll get you a chair from the kitchen, so that you will be more comfortable—unless, like Samson, you can pull down the supports. Then I must bid you good-by."

Yates went out to the girl, who was waiting for him.

"I want to borrow a kitchen chair, Kitty," he said, "so that poor Stoliker will get a rest."

They walked toward the house. Yates noticed that the firing had ceased, except a desultory shot here and there across the country.

"I shall have to retreat over the border as quickly as I can," he continued. "This country is getting too hot for me."

"You are much safer here," said the girl, with downcast eyes. "A man has brought the news that the United States gunboats are sailing up and down the river, making prisoners of all who attempt to cross from this side."

"You don't say! Well, I might have known that. Then what am I to do with Stoliker? I can't keep him tied up here. Yet the moment he gets loose I'm done for."

"Perhaps mother could persuade him not to do anything more. Shall I go for her?"

"I don't think it would be any use. Stoliker's a stubborn animal. He has suffered too much at my hands to be in a forgiving mood. We'll bring him a chair anyhow, and see the effect of kindness on him."

When the chair was placed at Stoliker's disposal, he sat down upon it, still hugging the post with an enforced fervency that, in spite of the solemnity of the occasion, nearly made Kitty laugh, and lit up her eyes with the mischievousness that had always delighted Yates.

"How long am I to be kept here?" asked the constable.

"Oh, not long," answered Yates cheerily; "not a moment longer than is necessary. I'll telegraph when I'm safe in New York State; so you won't be here more than a day or two."

This assurance did not appear to bring much comfort to Stoliker.

"Look here," he said; "I guess I know as well as the next man when I'm beaten. I have been thinking all this over. I am under the sheriff's orders, and not under the orders of that officer. I don't believe you've done anything, anyhow, or you wouldn't have acted quite the way you did. If the sheriff had sent me, it would have been different. As it is, if you unlock those cuffs, I'll give you my word I'll do nothing more unless I'm ordered to. Like as not they've forgotten all about you by this time; and there's nothing on record, anyhow."

"Do you mean it? Will you act square?"

"Certainly I'll act square. I don't suppose you doubt that. I didn't ask any favors before, and I did what I could to hold you."

"Enough said," cried Yates. "I'll risk it."

Stoliker stretched his arms wearily above his head when he was released.

"I wonder," he said, now that Kitty was gone, "if there is anything to eat in the house?"

"Shake!" cried Yates, holding out his hand to him. "Another great and mutual sentiment unites us, Stoliker. Let us go and see."

CHAPTER XVIII.

The man who wanted to see the fight did not see it, and the man who did not want to see it saw it. Yates arrived on the field of conflict when all was over; Renmark found the battle raging around him before he realized that things had reached a crisis.

When Yates reached the tent, he found it empty and torn by bullets. The fortunes of war had smashed the jar, and the fragments were strewn before the entrance, probably by some disappointed man who had tried to sample the contents and had found nothing.

"Hang it all!" said Yates to himself, "I wonder what the five assistants that the Argus sent me have done with themselves? If they are with the Fenians, beating a retreat, or, worse, if they are captured by the Canadians, they won't be able to get an account of this scrimmage through to the paper. Now, this is evidently the biggest item of the year—it's international, by George! It may involve England and the United States in a war, if both sides are not extra mild and cautious. I can't run the chance of the paper being left in the lurch. Let me think a minute. Is it my tip to follow the Canadians or the Fenians? I wonder is which is running the faster? My men are evidently with the Fenians, if they were on the ground at all. If I go after the Irish Republic, I shall run the risk of duplicating things; but if I follow the Canadians, they may put me under arrest. Then we have more Fenian sympathizers among our readers than Canadians, so the account from the invasion side of the fence will be the more popular. Yet a Canadian version would be a good thing, if I were sure the rest of the boys got in their work, and the chances are that the other papers won't have any reporters among the Canucks. Heavens! What is a man to do? I'll toss up for it. Heads, the Fenians."

He spun the coin in the air, and caught it. "Heads it is! The Fenians are my victims. I'm camping on their trail, anyhow. Besides, it's safer than following the Canadians, even though Stoliker has got my pass."

Tired as he was, he stepped briskly through the forest. The scent of a big item was in his nostrils, and it stimulated him like champagne. What was temporary loss of sleep compared to the joy of defeating the opposition press?

A blind man might have followed the trail of the retreating army. They had thrown away, as they passed through the woods, every article that impeded their progress. Once he came on a man lying with his face in the dead leaves. He turned him over.

"His troubles are past, poor devil," said Yates, as he pushed on.

"Halt! Throw up your hands!" came a cry from in front of him.

Yates saw no one, but he promptly threw up his hands, being an adaptable man.

"What's the trouble?" he shouted. "I'm retreating, too."

"Then retreat five steps farther. I'll count the steps. One."

Yates strode one step forward, and then saw that a man behind a tree was covering him with a gun. The next step revealed a second captor, with a huge upraised hammer, like a Hercules with his club. Both men had blackened faces, and resembled thoroughly disreputable fiends of the forest. Seated on the ground, in a semicircle, were half a dozen dejected prisoners. The man with the gun swore fearfully, but his comrade with the hammer was silent.

"Come," said the marksman, "you blank scoundrel, and take a seat with your fellow-scoundrels. If you attempt to run, blank blank you, I'll fill you full of buckshot!"

"Oh, I'm not going to run, Sandy," cried Yates, recognizing him. "Why should I? I've always enjoyed your company, and Macdonald's. How are you, Mac? Is this a little private raid of your own? For which side are you fighting? And I say, Sandy, what's the weight of that old-fashioned bar of iron you have in your hands? I'd like to decide a bet. Let me heft it, as you said in the shop."

"Oh, it's you, is it?" said Sandy in a disappointed tone, lowering his gun. "I thought we had raked in another of them. The old man and I want to make it an even dozen."

"Well, I don't think you'll capture any more. I saw nobody as I came through the woods. What are you going to do with this crowd?"

"Brain 'em," said Macdonald laconically, speaking for the first time. Then he added reluctantly: "If any of 'em tries to escape."

The prisoners were all evidently too tired and despondent to make any attempt at regaining their liberty. Sandy winked over Macdonald's shoulder at Yates, and by a slight side movement of his head he seemed to indicate that he would like to have some private conversation with the newspaper man.

"I'm not your prisoner, am I?" asked Yates.

"No," said Macdonald. "You may go if you like, but not in the direction the Fenians have gone."

"I guess I won't need to go any farther, if you will give me permission to interview your prisoners. I merely want to get some points about the fight."

"That's all right," said the blacksmith, "as long as you don't try to help them. If you do, I warn you there will be trouble."

Yates followed Sandy into the depths of the forest, out of hearing of the others, leaving Macdonald and his sledge-hammer on guard.

When at a safe distance, Sandy stopped and rested his arms on his gun, in a pathfinder attitude.

"Say," he began anxiously, "you haven't got some powder and shot on you by any chance?"

"Not an ounce. Haven't you any ammunition?"

"No, and haven't had all through the fight. You see, we left the shop in such a hurry we never thought about powder and ball. As soon as a man on horseback came by shouting that there was a fight on, the old man he grabbed his sledge, and I took this gun that had been left at the shop for repairs, and off we started. I'm not sure that it would shoot if I had ammunition, but I'd like to try. I've scared some of them Fee-neens nigh to death with it, but I was always afraid one of them would pull a real gun on me, and then I don't know just what I'd 'a' done."

Sandy sighed, and added, with the air of a man who saw his mistake, but was somewhat loath to acknowledge it: "Next battle there is you won't find me in it with a lame gun and no powder. I'd sooner have the old man's sledge. It don't miss fire." His eye brightened as he thought of Macdonald. "Say," he continued, with a jerk of his head back over his shoulder, "the boss is on the warpath in great style, aint he?"

"He is," said Yates, "but, for that matter, so are you. You can swear nearly as well as Macdonald himself. When did you take to it?"

"Oh, well, you see," said Sandy apologetically, "it don't come as natural to me as chewing, but, then, somebody's got to swear. The old man's converted, you know."

"Ah, hasn't he backslid yet?"

"No, he hasn't. I was afraid this scrimmage was going to do for him, but it didn't; and now I think that if somebody near by does a little cussing,—not that anyone can cuss like the boss,—he'll pull through. I think he'll stick this time. You'd ought to have seen him wading into them d—d Fee-neens, swinging his sledge, and singing 'Onward, Christian soldiers.' Then, with me to chip in a cuss word now and again when things got hot, he pulled through the day without ripping an oath. I tell you, it was a sight. He bowled 'em over like nine-pins. You ought to 'a' been there."

"Yes," said Yates regretfully. "I missed it, all on account of that accursed Stoliker. Well, there's no use crying over spilled milk, but I'll tell you one thing, Sandy: although I have no ammunition, I'll let you know what I have got. I have, in my pocket, one of the best plugs of tobacco that you ever put your teeth into."

Sandy's eyes glittered. "Bless you!" was all he could say, as he bit off a corner of the offered plug.

"You see, Sandy, there are compensations in this life, after all; I thought you were out."

"I haven't had a bite all day. That's the trouble with leaving in a hurry."

"Well, you may keep that plug, with my regards. Now, I want to get back and interview those fellows. There's no time to be lost."

When they reached the group, Macdonald said:

"Here's a man says he knows you, Mr. Yates. He claims he is a reporter, and that you will vouch for him."

Yates strode forward, and looked anxiously at the prisoners, hoping, yet fearing, to find one of his own men there. He was a selfish man, and wanted the glory of the day to be all his own. He soon recognized one of the prisoners as Jimmy Hawkins of the staff of a rival daily, the New York Blade. This was even worse than he had anticipated.

"Hello, Jimmy!" he said, "how did you get here?"

"I was raked in by that adjective fool with the unwashed face."

"Whose a—fool?" cried Macdonald in wrath, and grasping his hammer. He boggled slightly as he came to the "adjective," but got over it safely. It was evidently a close call, but Sandy sprang to the rescue, and cursed Hawkins until even the prisoners turned pale at the torrent of profanity. Macdonald looked with sad approbation at his pupil, not knowing that he was under the stimulus of newly acquired tobacco, wondering how he had attained such proficiency in malediction; for, like all true artists, he was quite unconscious of his own merit in that direction.

"Tell this hammer wielder that I'm no anvil. Tell him that I'm a newspaper man, and didn't come here to fight. He says that if you guarantee that I'm no Fenian he'll let me go."

Yates sat down on a fallen log, with a frown on his brow. He liked to do a favor to a fellow-creature when the act did not inconvenience himself, but he never forgot the fact that business was business.

"I can't conscientiously tell him that, Jimmy," said Yates soothingly. "How am I to know you are not a Fenian?"

"Bosh!" cried Hawkins angrily. "Conscientiously? A lot you think of conscience when there is an item to be had."

"We none of us live up to our better nature, Jimmy," continued Yates feelingly. "We can but do our best, which is not much. For reasons that you might fail to understand, I do not wish to run the risk of telling a lie. You appreciate my hesitation, don't you, Mr. Macdonald? You would not advise me to assert a thing I was not sure of, would you?"

"Certainly not," said the blacksmith earnestly.

"You want to keep me here because you are afraid of me," cried the indignant Blade man. "You know very well I'm not a Fenian."

"Excuse me, Jimmy, but I know nothing of the kind. I even suspect myself of Fenian leanings. How, then, can I be sure of you?"

"What's your game?" asked Hawkins more calmly, for he realized that he himself would not be slow to take advantage of a rival's dilemma.

"My game is to get a neat little account of this historical episode sent over the wires to the Argus. You see, Jimmy, this is my busy day. When the task is over, I will devote myself to your service, and will save you from being hanged, if I can; although I shall do so without prejudice, as the lawyers say, for I have always held that that will be the ultimate end of all the Blade staff.

"Look here, Yates; play fair. Don't run in any conscientious guff on a prisoner. You see, I have known you these many years."

"Yes, and little have you profited by a noble example. It is your knowledge of me that makes me wonder at your expecting me to let you out of your hole without due consideration."

"Are you willing to make a bargain?

"Always—when the balance of trade is on my side."

"Well, if you give me a fair start, I'll give you some exclusive information that you can't get otherwise."

"What is it?"

"Oh, I wasn't born yesterday, Dick."

"That is interesting information, Jimmy, but I knew it before. Haven't you something more attractive to offer?"

"Yes, I have. I have the whole account of the expedition and the fight written out, all ready to send, if I could get my clutches on a telegraph wire. I'll hand it over to you, and allow you to read it, if you will get me out of this hole, as you call it. I'll give you permission to use the information in any way you choose, if you will extricate me, and all I ask is a fair start in the race for a telegraph office."

Yates pondered over the proposition for some moments.

"I'll tell you what I'll do, Jimmy," he finally said. "I'll buy that account from you, and give you more money than the Blade will. And when I get back to New York I'll place you on the staff of the Argus at a higher salary than the Blade gives you—taking your own word for the amount."

"What! And leave my paper in the lurch? Not likely."

"Your paper is going to be left in the lurch, anyhow."

"Perhaps. But it won't be sold by me. I'll burn my copy before I will let you have a glimpse of it. That don't need to interfere with your making me an offer of a better position when we get back to New York; but while my paper depends on me, I won't go back on it."

"Just as you please, Jimmy. Perhaps I would do the same myself. I always was weak where the interests of the Argus were concerned. You haven't any blank paper you could lend me, Jimmy?"

"I have, but I won't lend it."

Yates took out his pencil, and pulled down his cuff.

"Now, Mac," he said, "tell me all you saw of this fight."

The blacksmith talked, and Yates listened, putting now and then a mark on his cuff. Sandy spoke occasionally, but it was mostly to tell of sledge-hammer feats or to corroborate something the boss said. One after another Yates interviewed the prisoners, and gathered together all the materials for that excellent full-page account "by an eyewitness" that afterward appeared in the columns of the Argus. He had a wonderful memory, and simply jotted down figures with which he did not care to burden his mind. Hawkins laughed derisively now and then at the facts they were giving Yates, but the Argus man said nothing, merely setting down in shorthand some notes of the information Hawkins sneered at, which Yates considered was more than likely accurate and important. When he had got all he wanted, he rose.

"Shall I send you help, Mac?" he asked.

"No," said the smith; "I think I'll take these fellows to the shop, and hold them there till called for. You can't vouch for Hawkins, then, Mr. Yates?"

"Good Heavens, no! I look on him as the most dangerous of the lot. These half-educated criminals, who have no conscientious scruples, always seem to me a greater menace to society than their more ignorant co-conspirators. Well, good-by, Jimmy. I think you'll enjoy life down at Mac's shop. It's the best place I've struck since I've been in the district. Give my love to all the boys, when they come to gaze at you. I'll make careful inquiries into your opinions, and as soon as I am convinced that you can be set free with safety to the community I'll drop in on you and do all I can. Meanwhile, so long."

Yates' one desire now was to reach a telegraph office, and write his article as it was being clicked off on the machine. He had his fears about the speed of a country operator, but he dared not risk trying to get through to Buffalo in the then excited state of the country. He quickly made up his mind to go to the Bartlett place, borrow a horse, if the Fenians had not permanently made off with them all, and ride as rapidly as he could for the nearest telegraph office. He soon reached the edge of the woods, and made his way across the fields to the house. He found young Bartlett at the barn.

"Any news of the horses yet?" was the first question he asked.

"No," said young Bartlett gloomily; "guess they've rode away with them."

"Well, I must get a horse from somewhere to ride to the telegraph office.

Where is the likeliest place to find one?"

"I don't know where you can get one, unless you steal the telegraph boy's nag; it's in the stable now, having a feed."

"What telegraph boy?"

"Oh, didn't you see him? He went out to the tent to look for you, and I thought he had found you."

"No, I haven't been at the tent for ever so long. Perhaps he has some news for me. I'm going to the house to write, so send him in as soon as he gets back. Be sure you don't let him get away before I see him."

"I'll lock the stable," said young Bartlett, "and then he won't get the horse, at any rate."

Yates found Kitty in the kitchen, and he looked so flurried that the girl cried anxiously:

"Are they after you again, Mr. Yates?"

"No, Kitty; I'm after them. Say, I want all the blank paper you have in the house. Anything will do, so long as it will hold a lead-pencil mark."

"A copy book—such as the children use in school?"

"Just the thing."

In less than a minute the energetic girl had all the materials he required ready for him in the front room. Yates threw off his coat, and went to work as if he were in his own den in the Argus building.

"This is a —— of a vacation," he muttered to himself, as he drove his pencil at lightning speed over the surface of the paper. He took no note of the time until he had finished; then he roused himself and sprang to his feet.

"What in thunder has become of that telegraph boy?" he cried. "Well, it doesn't matter; I'll take the horse without his permission."

He gathered up his sheets, and rushed for the kitchen. He was somewhat surprised to see the boy sitting there, gorging himself with the good things which that kitchen always afforded.

"Hello, youngster! how long have you been here?"

"I wouldn't let him go in to disturb you while you were writing," said Kitty, the boy's mouth being too full to permit of a reply.

"Ah, that was right. Now, sonny, gulp that down and come in here; I want to talk to you for a minute."

The boy followed him into the front room.

"Well, my son, I want to borrow your horse for the rest of the day."

"You can't have it," said the boy promptly.

"Can't have it? I must have it. Why, I'll take it. You don't imagine you can stop me, do you?"

The boy drew himself up, and folded his arms across his breast.

"What do you want with the horse, Mr. Yates?" he asked.

"I want to get to the nearest telegraph office. I'll pay you well for it."

"And what am I here for?"

"Why, to eat, of course. They'll feed you high while you wait."

"Canadian telegraph office?"

"Certainly."

"It's no good, Mr. Yates. Them Canadians couldn't telegraph all you've written in two weeks. I know 'em," said the boy with infinite scorn. "Besides, the Government has got hold of all the wires, and you can't get a private message through till it gets over its fright."

"By George!" cried Yates, taken aback, "I hadn't thought of that. Are you sure, boy?"

"Dead certain."

"Then what's to be done? I must get through to Buffalo."

"You can't. United States troops won't let you. They're stopping everybody—except me," he added, drawing himself up, as if he were the one individual who stood in with the United States Government.

"Can you get this dispatch through?"

"You bet! That's why I came back. I knew, as soon as I looked at you that you would write two or three columns of telegraph; and your paper said 'Spare no expense,' you remember. So says I to myself: 'I'll help Mr. Yates to spare no expense. I'll get fifty dollars from that young man, seeing I'm the only person who can get across in time.'"

"You were mighty sure of it, weren't you?"

"You just bet I was. Now, the horse is fed and ready, I'm fed and ready, and we're losing valuable time waiting for that fifty dollars."

"Suppose you meet another newspaper man who wants to get his dispatch through to another paper, what will you do?"

"Charge him the same as I do you. If I meet two other newspaper men, that will be one hundred and fifty dollars; but if you want to make sure that I won't meet any more newspaper men, let us call it one hundred dollars, and I'll take the risk of the odd fifty for the ready cash; then if I meet a dozen newspaper men, I'll tell them I'm a telegraph boy on a vacation."

"Quite so. I think you will be able to take care of yourself in a cold and callous world. Now, look here, young man; I'll trust you if you'll trust me. I'm not a traveling mint, you know. Besides, I pay by results. If you don't get this dispatch through, you don't get anything. I'll give you an order for a hundred dollars, and as soon as I get to Buffalo I'll pay you the cash. I'll have to draw on the Argus when I get to Buffalo; if my article has appeared, you get your cash; if it hasn't, you're out. See?"

"Yes, I see. It won't do, Mr. Yates."

"Why won't it do?"

"Because I say it won't. This is a cash transaction. Money down, or you don't get the goods. I'll get it through all right, but if I just miss, I'm not going to lose the money."

"Very well, I'll take it to the Canadian telegraph office."

"All right, Mr. Yates. I'm disappointed in you. I thought you were some good. You aint got no sense, but I wish you luck. When I was at your tent, there was a man with a hammer taking a lot of men out of the woods. When one of them sees my uniform, he sings out he'd give me twenty-five dollars to take his stuff. I said I'd see him later, and I will. Good-by, Mr. Yates."

"Hold on, there! You're a young villain. You'll end in state's prison yet, but here's your money. Now, you ride like a house a-fire."

After watching the departing boy until he was out of sight Yates, with a feeling of relief, started back to the tent. He was worried about the interview the boy had had with Hawkins, and he wondered, now that it was too late, whether, after all, he had not Hawkins' manuscript in his pocket. He wished he had searched him. That trouble, however, did not prevent him from sleeping like the dead the moment he lay down in the tent.

CHAPTER XIX.

The result of the struggle was similar in effect to an American railway accident of the first class. One officer and five privates were killed on the Canadian side, one man was missing, and many were wounded. The number of the Fenians killed will probably never be known. Several were buried on the field of battle, others were taken back by O'Neill's brigade when they retreated.

Although the engagement ended as Yates had predicted, yet he was wrong in his estimate of the Canadians. Volunteers are invariably underrated by men of experience in military matters. The boys fought well, even when they saw their ensign fall dead before them. If the affair had been left entirely in their hands, the result might have been different—as was shown afterward, when the volunteers, unimpeded by regulars, quickly put down a much more formidable rising in the Northwest. But in the present case they were hampered by their dependence on the British troops, whose commander moved them with all the ponderous slowness of real war, and approached O'Neill as if he had been approaching Napoleon. He thus managed to get in a day after the fair on every occasion, being too late for the fight at Ridgeway, and too late to capture any considerable number of the flying Fenians at Fort Erie. The campaign, on the Canadian side, was magnificently planned and wretchedly carried out. The volunteers and regulars were to meet at a point close to where the fight took place, but the British commander delayed two hours in starting, which fact the Canadian colonel did not learn until too late. These blunders culminated in a ghastly mistake on the field. The Canadian colonel ordered his men to charge across an open field, and attack the Fenian force in the woods—a brilliant but foolish move. To the command the volunteers gallantly responded, but against stupidity the gods are powerless. In the field they were appalled to hear the order given to form square and receive cavalry. Even the schoolboys knew the Fenians could have no cavalry.

Having formed their square, the Canadians found themselves the helpless targets of the Fenians in the woods. If O'Neill's forces had shot with reasonable precision, they must have cut the volunteers to pieces. The latter were victorious, if they had only known it; but, in this hopeless square, panic seized them, and it was every man for himself; at the same time, the Fenians were also retreating as fast as they could. This farce is known as the battle of Ridgeway, and would have been comical had it not been that death hovered over it. The comedy, without the tragedy, was enacted a day or two before at a bloodless skirmish which took place near a hamlet called Waterloo, which affray is dignified in Canadian annals as the second battle of that name.

When the Canadian forces retreated, Renmark, who had watched the contest with all the helpless anxiety of a noncombatant, sharing the danger, but having no influence upon the result, followed them, making a wide detour to avoid the chance shots which were still flying. He expected to come up with the volunteers on the road, but was not successful. Through various miscalculations he did not succeed in finding them until toward evening. At first they told him that young Howard was with the company, and unhurt, but further inquiry soon disclosed the fact that he had not been seen since the fight. He was not among those who were killed or wounded, and it was nightfall before Renmark realized that opposite his name on the roll would be placed the ominous word "missing." Renmark remembered that the boy had said he would visit his home if he got leave; but no leave had been asked for. At last Renmark was convinced that young Howard was either badly wounded or dead. The possibility of his desertion the professor did not consider for a moment, although he admitted to himself that it was hard to tell what panic of fear might come over a boy who, for the first time in his life, found bullets flying about his ears.

With a heavy heart Renmark turned back and made his way to the fatal field. He found nothing on the Canadian side. Going over to the woods, he came across several bodies lying where they fell; but they were all those of strangers. Even in the darkness he would have had no difficulty in recognizing the volunteer uniform which he knew so well. He walked down to the Howard homestead, hoping, yet fearing, to hear the boy's voice—the voice of a deserter. Everything was silent about the house, although a light shone through an upper window, and also through one below. He paused at the gate, not knowing what to do. It was evident the boy was not here, yet how to find the father or brother, without alarming Margaret or her mother, puzzled him. As he stood there the door opened, and he recognized Mrs. Bartlett and Margaret standing in the light. He moved away from the gate, and heard the older woman say:

"Oh, she will be all right in the morning, now that she has fallen into a nice sleep. I wouldn't disturb her to-night, if I were you. It is nothing but nervousness and fright at that horrible firing. It's all over now, thank God. Good-night, Margaret."

The good woman came through the gate, and then ran, with all the speed of sixteen, toward her own home. Margaret stood in the doorway, listening to the retreating footsteps. She was pale and anxious, but Renmark thought he had never seen anyone so lovely; and he was startled to find that he had a most un-professor-like longing to take her in his arms and comfort her. Instead of bringing her consolation, he feared it would be his fate to add to her anxiety; and it was not until he saw she was about to close the door that he found courage to speak.

"Margaret," he said.

The girl had never heard her name pronounced in that tone before, and the cadence of it went direct to her heart, frightening her with an unknown joy. She seemed unable to move or respond, and stood there, with wide eyes and suspended breath, gazing into the darkness. Renmark stepped into the light, and she saw his face was haggard with fatigue and anxiety.

"Margaret," he said again, "I want to speak with you a moment. Where is your brother?"

"He has gone with Mr. Bartlett to see if he can find the horses. There is something wrong," she continued, stepping down beside him. "I can see it in your face. What is it?"

"Is your father in the house?"

"Yes, but he is worried about mother. Tell me what it is. It is better to tell me."

Renmark hesitated.

"Don't keep me in suspense like this," cried the girl in a low but intense voice. "You have said too much or too little. Has anything happened to Henry?"

"No. It is about Arthur I wanted to speak. You will not be alarmed?"

"I am alarmed. Tell, me quickly." And the girl in her excitement laid her hands imploringly on his.

"Arthur joined the volunteers in Toronto some time ago. Did you know that?"

"He never told me. I understand—I think so, but I hope not. He was in the battle today. Is he—has he been—hurt?"

"I don't know. I'm afraid so," said Renmark hurriedly, now that the truth had to come out; he realized, by the nervous tightening of the girl's unconscious grasp, how clumsily he was telling it. "He was with the volunteers this morning. He is not with them now. They don't know where he is. No one saw him hurt, but it is feared he was, and that he has been left behind. I have been all over the ground."

"Yes, yes?"

"But I could not find him. I came here hoping to find him."

"Take me to where the volunteers were," she sobbed. "I know what has happened. Come quickly."

"Will you not put something on your head?"

"No, no. Come at once." Then, pausing, she said: "Shall we need a lantern?"

"No; it is light enough when we get out from the shadow of the house."

Margaret ran along the road so swiftly that Renmark had some trouble in keeping pace with her. She turned at the side road, and sped up the gentle ascent to the spot where the volunteers had crossed it.

"Here is the place," said Renmark.

"He could not have been hit in the field," she cried breathlessly, "for then he might have reached the house at the corner without climbing a fence. If he was badly hurt, he would have been here. Did you search this field?"

"Every bit of it. He is not here."

"Then it must have happened after he crossed the road and the second fence. Did you see the battle?"

"Yes."

"Did the Fenians cross the field after the volunteers?"

"No; they did not leave the woods."

"Then, if he was struck, it could not have been far from the other side of the second fence. He would be the last to retreat; and that is why the others did not see him," said the girl, with confident pride in her brother's courage.

They crossed the first fence; the road, and the second fence, the girl walking ahead for a few paces. She stopped, and leaned for a moment against a tree. "It must have been about here," she said in a voice hardly audible. "Have you searched on this side?"

"Yes, for half a mile farther into the fields and woods."

"No, no, not there; but down along the fence. He knew every inch of this ground. If he were wounded here, he would at once try to reach our house. Search down along the fence. I—I cannot go."

Renmark walked along the fence, peering into the dark corners made by the zigzag of the rails; and he knew, without looking back, that Margaret, with feminine inconsistency, was following him. Suddenly she darted past him, and flung herself down in the long grass, wailing out a cry that cut Renmark like a knife.

The boy lay with his face in the grass, and his outstretched hand grasping the lower rail of the fence. He had dragged himself this far, and reached an insurmountable obstacle.

Renmark drew the weeping girl gently away, and rapidly ran his hand over the prostrate lad. He quickly opened his tunic, and a thrill of joy passed over him as he felt the faint beating of the heart.

"He is alive!" he cried. "He will get well, Margaret." A statement somewhat premature to make on so hasty an examination.

He rose, expecting a look of gratitude from the girl he loved. He was amazed to see her eyes almost luminous in the darkness, blazing with wrath.

"When did you know he was with the volunteers?"

"This morning—early," said the professor, taken aback.

"Why didn't you tell me?"

"He asked me not to do so."

"He is a mere boy. You are a man, and ought to have a man's sense. You had no right to mind what a boy said. It was my right to know, and your duty to tell me. Through your negligence and stupidity my brother has lain here all day—perhaps dying," she added with a break in her angry voice.

"If you had known—I didn't know anything was wrong until I saw the volunteers. I have not lost a moment since."

"I should have known he was missing, without going to the volunteers."

Renmark was so amazed at the unjust accusation, from a girl whom he had made the mistake of believing to be without a temper of her own, that he knew not what to say. He was, however, to have one more example of inconsistency.

"Why do you stand there doing nothing, now that I have found him?" she demanded.

It was on his tongue to say: "I stand here because you stand there unjustly quarreling with me," but he did not say it. Renmark was not a ready man, yet he did, for once, the right thing.

"Margaret," he said sternly, "throw down that fence."

This curt command, delivered in his most schoolmastery manner, was instantly obeyed. Such a task may seem a formidable one to set to a young woman, but it is a feat easily accomplished in some parts of America. A rail fence lends itself readily to demolition. Margaret tossed a rail to the right, one to the left, and to the right again, until an open gap took the place of that part of the fence. The professor examined the young soldier in the meantime, and found his leg had been broken by a musket ball. He raised him up tenderly in his arms, and was pleased to hear a groan escape his lips. He walked through the open gap and along the road toward the house, bearing the unconscious form of his pupil. Margaret silently kept close to his side, her fingers every now and then unconsciously caressing the damp, curly locks of her brother.

"We shall have to get a doctor?" Her assertion was half an inquiry.

"Certainly."

"We must not disturb anyone in the house. It is better that I should tell you what to do now, so that we need not talk when we reach there."

"We cannot help disturbing someone."

"I do not think it will be necessary. If you will stay with Arthur, I will go for the doctor, and no one need know."

"I will go for the doctor."

"You do not know the way. It is five or six miles. I will ride Gypsy, and will soon be back."

"But there are prowlers and stragglers all along the roads. It is not safe for you to go alone."

"It is perfectly safe. No horse that the stragglers have stolen can overtake Gypsy. Now, don't say anything more. It is best that I should go. I will run on ahead, and enter the house quietly. I will take the lamp to the room at the side, where the window opens to the floor. Carry him around there. I will be waiting for you at the gate, and will show you the way."

With that the girl was off, and Renmark carried his burden alone. She was waiting for him at the gate, and silently led the way round the house, to where the door-window opened upon the bit of lawn under an apple tree. The light streamed out upon the grass. He placed the boy gently upon the dainty bed. It needed no second glance to tell Renmark whose room he was in. It was decorated with those pretty little knickknacks so dear to the heart of a girl in a snuggery she can call her own.

"It is not likely you will be disturbed here," she whispered, "until I come back. I will tap at the window when I come with the doctor."

"Don't you think it would be better and safer for me to go? I don't like the thought of your going alone."

"No, no. Please do just what I tell you. You do not know the way. I shall be very much quicker. If Arthur should—should—wake, he will know you, and will not be alarmed, as he might be if you were a stranger."

Margaret was gone before he could say anything more, and Renmark sat down, devoutly hoping no one would rap at the door of the room while he was there.

CHAPTER XX.

Margaret spoke caressingly to her horse, when she opened the stable door, and Gypsy replied with that affectionate, low guttural whinny which the Scotch graphically term "nickering." She patted the little animal; and if Gypsy was surprised at being saddled and bridled at that hour of the night, no protest was made, the horse merely rubbing its nose lovingly up and down Margaret's sleeve as she buckled the different straps. There was evidently a good understanding between the two.

"No, Gyp," she whispered, "I have nothing for you to-night—nothing but hard work and quick work. Now, you mustn't make a noise till we get past the house."

On her wrist she slipped the loop of a riding whip, which she always carried, but never used. Gyp had never felt the indignity of the lash, and was always willing to do what was required merely for a word.

Margaret opened the big gate before she saddled her horse, and there was therefore no delay in getting out upon the main road, although the passing of the house was an anxious moment. She feared that if her father heard the steps or the neighing of the horse he might come out to investigate. Halfway between her own home and Bartlett's house she sprang lightly into the saddle.

"Now, then, Gyp!"

No second word was required. Away they sped down the road toward the east, the mild June air coming sweet and cool and fresh from the distant lake, laden with the odors of the woods and the fields. The stillness was intense, broken only by the plaintive cry of the whippoorwill, America's one-phrased nightingale, or the still more weird and eerie note of a distant loon.

The houses along the road seemed deserted; no lights were shown anywhere. The wildest rumors were abroad concerning the slaughter of the day; and the population, scattered as it was, appeared to have retired into its shell. A spell of silence and darkness was over the land, and the rapid hoof beats of the horse sounded with startling distinctness on the harder portions of the road, emphasized by intervals of complete stillness, when the fetlocks sank in the sand and progress was more difficult for the plucky little animal. The only thrill of fear that Margaret felt on her night journey was when she entered the dark arch of an avenue of old forest trees that bordered the road, like a great, gloomy cathedral aisle, in the shadow of which anything might be hidden. Once the horse, with a jump of fear, started sideways and plunged ahead: Margaret caught her breath as she saw, or fancied she saw, several men stretched on the roadside, asleep or dead. Once in the open again she breathed more freely, and if it had not been for the jump of the horse, she would have accused her imagination of playing her a trick. Just as she had completely reassured herself a shadow moved from the fence to the middle of the road, and a sharp voice cried:

"Halt!"

The little horse, as if it knew the meaning of the word, planted its two front hoofs together, and slid along the ground for a moment, coming so quickly to a standstill that it was with some difficulty Margaret kept her seat. She saw in front of her a man holding a gun, evidently ready to fire if she attempted to disobey his command.

"Who are you, and where are you going?" he demanded.

"Oh, please let me pass!" pleaded Margaret with a tremor of fear in her voice. "I am going for a doctor—for my brother; he is badly wounded, and will perhaps die if I am delayed."

The man laughed.

"Oho!" he cried, coming closer; "a woman, is it? and a young one, too, or I'm a heathen. Now, miss or missus, you get down. I'll have to investigate this. The brother business won't work with an old soldier. It's your lover you're riding for at this time of the night, or I'm no judge of the sex. Just slip down, my lady, and see if you don't like me better than him; remember that all cats are black in the dark. Get down, I tell you."

"If you are a soldier, you will let me go. My brother is badly wounded.

I must get to the doctor."

"There's no 'must' with a bayonet in front of you. If he has been wounded, there's plenty of better men killed to-day. Come down, my dear."

Margaret gathered up the bridle rein, but, even in the darkness, the man saw her intention.

"You can't escape, my pretty. If you try it, you'll not be hurt, but I'll kill your horse. If you move, I'll put a bullet through him."

"Kill my horse?" breathed Margaret in horror, a fear coming over her that she had not felt at the thought of danger to herself.

"Yes, missy," said the man, approaching nearer, and laying his hand on Gypsy's bridle. "But there will be no need of that. Besides, it would make too much noise, and might bring us company, which would be inconvenient. So come down quietly, like the nice little girl you are."

"If you will let me go and tell the doctor, I will come back here and be your prisoner."

The man laughed again in low, tantalizing tones. This was a good joke.

"Oh, no, sweetheart. I wasn't born so recently as all that. A girl in the hand is worth a dozen a mile up the road. Now, come off that horse, or I'll take you off. This is war time, and I'm not going to waste any more pretty talk on you."

The man, who, she now saw, was hatless, leered up at her, and something in his sinister eyes made the girl quail. She had been so quiet that he apparently was not prepared for any sudden movement. Her right hand, hanging down at her side, had grasped the short riding whip, and, with a swiftness that gave him no chance to ward off the blow, she struck him one stinging, blinding cut across the eyes, and then brought down the lash on the flank of her horse, drawing the animal round with her left over her enemy. With a wild snort of astonishment, the horse sprang forward, bringing man and gun down to the ground with a clatter that woke the echoes; then, with an indignant toss of the head, Gyp sped along the road like the wind. It was the first time he had ever felt the cut of a whip, and the blow was not forgiven. Margaret, fearing further obstruction on the road, turned her horse's head toward the rail fence, and went over it like a bird. In the field, where fast going in the dark had dangers, Margaret tried to slacken the pace, but the little horse would not have it so. He shook his head angrily whenever he thought of the indignity of that blow, while Margaret leaned over and tried to explain and beg pardon for her offense. The second fence was crossed with a clean-cut leap, and only once in the next field did the horse stumble, but quickly recovered and went on at the same breakneck gait. The next fence, gallantly vaulted over, brought them to the side road, half a mile up which stood the doctor's house. Margaret saw the futility of attempting a reconciliation until the goal was won. There, with difficulty, the horse was stopped, and the girl struck the panes of the upper window, through which a light shone, with her riding whip. The window was raised, and the situation speedily explained to the physician.

"I will be with you in a moment," he said.

Then Margaret slid from the saddle, and put her arms around the neck of the trembling horse. Gypsy would have nothing to do with her, and sniffed the air with offended dignity.

"It was a shame, Gyp," she cried, almost tearfully, stroking the glossy neck of her resentful friend; "it was, it was, and I know it; but what was I to do, Gyp? You were the only protector I had, and you did bowl him over beautifully; no other horse could have done it so well. It's wicked, but I do hope you hurt him, just because I had to strike you."

Gypsy was still wrathful, and indicated by a toss of the head that the wheedling of a woman did not make up for a blow. It was the insult more than the pain; and from her—there was the sting of it.

"I know—I know just how you feel, Gypsy dear; and I don't blame you for being angry. I might have spoken to you, of course, but there was no time to think, and it was really him I was striking. That's why it came down so hard. If I had said a word, he would have got out of the way, coward that he was, and then would have shot you—you, Gypsy! Think of it!"

If a man can be molded in any shape that pleases a clever woman, how can a horse expect to be exempt from her influence. Gypsy showed signs of melting, whinnying softly and forgivingly.

"And it will never happen again, Gypsy—never, never. As soon as we are safe home again I will burn that whip. You little pet, I knew you wouldn't——"

Gypsy's head rested on Margaret's shoulder, and we must draw a veil over the reconciliation. Some things are too sacred for a mere man to meddle with. The friends were friends once more, and on the altar of friendship the unoffending whip was doubtless offered as a burning sacrifice.

When the doctor came out, Margaret explained the danger of the road, and proposed that they should return by the longer and northern way—the Concession, as it was called.

They met no one on the silent road, and soon they saw the light in the window.

The doctor and the girl left their horses tied some distance from the house, and walked together to the window with the stealthy steps of a pair of housebreakers. Margaret listened breathlessly at the closed window, and thought she heard the low murmur of conversation. She tapped lightly on the pane, and the professor threw back the door-window.

"We were getting very anxious about you," he whispered.

"Hello, Peggy!" said the boy, with a wan smile, raising his head slightly from the pillow and dropping it back again.

Margaret stooped over and kissed him.

"My poor boy! what a fright you have given me!"

"Ah, Margery, think what a fright I got myself. I thought I was going to die within sight of the house."

The doctor gently pushed Margaret from the room. Renmark waited until the examination was over, and then went out to find her.

She sprang forward to meet him.

"It is all right," he said. "There is nothing to fear. He has been exhausted by loss of blood, but a few days' quiet will set that right. Then all you will have to contend against will be his impatience at being kept to his room, which may be necessary for some weeks."

"Oh, I am so glad! and—and I am so much obliged to you, Mr. Renmark!"

"I have done nothing—except make blunders," replied the professor with a bitterness that surprised and hurt her.

"How can you say that? You have done everything. We owe his life to you."

Renmark said nothing for a moment. Her unjust accusation in the earlier part of the night had deeply pained him, and he hoped for some hint of disclaimer from her. Belonging to the stupider sex, he did not realize that the words were spoken in a state of intense excitement and fear, that another woman would probably have expressed her condition of mind by fainting instead of talking, and that the whole episode had left absolutely no trace on the recollection of Margaret. At last Renmark spoke:

"I must be getting back to the tent, if it still exists. I think I had an appointment there with Yates some twelve hours ago, but up to this moment I had forgotten it. Good-night."

Margaret stood for a few moments alone, and wondered what she had done to offend him. He stumbled along the dark road, not heeding much the direction he took, but automatically going the nearest way to the tent. Fatigue and the want of sleep were heavy upon him, and his feet were as lead. Although dazed, he was conscious of a dull ache where his heart was supposed to be, and he vaguely hoped he had not made a fool of himself. He entered the tent, and was startled by the voice of Yates:

"Hello! hello! Is that you, Stoliker?"

"No; it is Renmark. Are you asleep?"

"I guess I have been. Hunger is the one sensation of the moment. Have you provided anything to eat within the last twenty-four hours?"

"There's a bag full of potatoes here, I believe. I haven't been near the tent since early morning."

"All right; only don't expect a recommendation from me as cook. I'm not yet hungry enough for raw potatoes. What time has it got to be?"

"I'm sure I don't know."

"Seems as if I had been asleep for weeks. I'm the latest edition of Rip Van Winkle, and expect to find my mustache gray in the morning. I was dreaming sweetly of Stoliker when you fell over the bunk."

"What have you done with him?"

"I'm not wide enough awake to remember. I think I killed him, but wouldn't be sure. So many of my good resolutions go wrong that very likely he is alive at this moment. Ask me in the morning. What have you been prowling after all night?"

There was no answer. Renmark was evidently asleep.

"I'll ask you in the morning," muttered Yates drowsily—after which there was silence in the tent.

CHAPTER XXI.

Yates had stubbornly refused to give up his search for rest and quiet in spite of the discomfort of living in a leaky and battered tent. He expressed regret that he had not originally camped in the middle of Broadway, as being a quieter and less exciting spot than the place he had chosen; but, having made the choice, he was going to see the last dog hung, he said. Renmark had become less and less of a comrade. He was silent, and almost as gloomy as Hiram Bartlett himself. When Yates tried to cheer him up by showing him how much worse another man's position might be, Renmark generally ended the talk by taking to the wood.

"Just reflect on my position," Yates would say. "Here I am dead in love with two lovely girls, both of whom are merely waiting for the word. To one of them I have nearly committed myself, which fact, to a man of my temperament, inclines me somewhat to the other. Here I am anxious to confide in you, and yet I feel that I risk a fight every time I talk about the complication. You have no sympathy for me, Renny, when I need sympathy; while I am bubbling over with sympathy for you, and you won't have it. Now, what would you do if you were in my fix? If you would take five minutes and show me clearly which of the two girls I really ought to marry, it would help me ever so much, for then I would be sure to settle on the other. It is the indecision that is slowly but surely sapping my vitality."

By this time, Renmark would have pulled his soft felt hat over his eyes, and, muttering words that would have echoed strangely in the silent halls of the university building, would plunge into the forest. Yates generally looked after his retreating figure without anger, but with mild wonder.

"Well, of all cantankerous cranks he is the worst," he would say with a sigh. "It is sad to see the temple of friendship tumble down about one's ears in this way." At their last talk of this kind Yates resolved not to discuss the problem again with the professor, unless a crisis came. The crisis came in the form of Stoliker, who dropped in on Yates as the latter lay in the hammock, smoking and enjoying a thrilling romance. The camp was strewn with these engrossing, paper-covered works, and Yates had read many of them, hoping to came across a case similar to his own, but up to the time of Stoliker's visit he had not succeeded.

"Hello, Stoliker! how's things? Got the cuffs in your pocket? Want to have another tour across country with me?"

"No. But I came to warn you. There will be a warrant out to-morrow or next day, and, if I were you, I would get over to the other side; though you need never say I told you. Of course, if they give the warrant to me, I shall have to arrest you; and although nothing may be done to you, still, the country is in a state of excitement, and you will at least be put to some inconvenience."

"Stoliker," cried Yates, springing out of the hammock, "you are a white man! You're a good fellow, Stoliker, and I'm ever so much obliged. If you ever come to New York, you call on me at the Argus office,—anybody will show you where it is,—and I'll give you the liveliest time you ever had in your life. It won't cost you a cent, either."

"That's all right," said the constable. "Now, if I were you, I would light out to-morrow at the latest."

"I will," said Yates.

Stoliker disappeared quietly among the trees, and Yates, after a moment's thought, began energetically to pack up his belongings. It was dark before he had finished, and Renmark returned.

"Stilly," cried the reporter cheerily, "there's a warrant out for my arrest. I shall have to go to-morrow at the latest!"

"What! to jail?" cried his horrified friend, his conscience now troubling him, as the parting came, for his lack of kindness to an old comrade.

"Not if the court knows herself. But to Buffalo, which is pretty much the same thing. Still, thank goodness, I don't need to stay there long. I'll be in New York before I'm many days older. I yearn to plunge into the arena once more. The still, calm peacefulness of this whole vacation has made me long for excitement again, and I'm glad the warrant has pushed me into the turmoil."

"Well, Richard, I'm sorry you have to go under such conditions. I'm afraid I have not been as companionable a comrade as you should have had."

"Oh, you're all right, Renny. The trouble with you is that you have drawn a little circle around Toronto University, and said to yourself: 'This is the world.' It isn't, you know. There is something outside of all that."

"Every man, doubtless, has his little circle. Yours is around the Argus office."

"Yes, but there are special wires from that little circle to all the rest of the world, and soon there will be an Atlantic cable."

"I do not hold that my circle is as large as yours; still, there is something outside of New York, even."

"You bet your life there is; and, now that you are in a more sympathetic frame of mind, it is that I want to talk with you about. Those two girls are outside my little circle, and I want to bring one of them within it. Now, Renmark, which of those girls would you choose if you were me?"

The professor drew in his breath sharply, and was silent for a moment. At last he said, speaking slowly:

"I am afraid, Mr. Yates, that you do not quite appreciate my point of view. As you may think I have acted in an unfriendly manner, I will try for the first and final time to explain it. I hold that any man who marries a good woman gets more than he deserves, no matter how worthy he may be. I have a profound respect for all women, and I think that your light chatter about choosing between two is an insult to both of them. I think either of them is infinitely too good for you—or for me either."

"Oh, you do, do you? Perhaps you think that you would make a much better husband than I. If that is the case, allow me to say you are entirely wrong. If your wife was sensitive, you would kill her with your gloomy fits. I wouldn't go off in the woods and sulk, anyhow."

"If you are referring to me, I will further inform you that I had either to go off in the woods or knock you down. I chose the less of two evils."

"Think you could do it, I suppose? Renny, you're conceited. You're not the first man who has made such a mistake, and found he was barking up the wrong tree when it was too late for anything but bandages and arnica."

"I have tried to show you how I feel regarding this matter. I might have known I should not succeed. We will end the discussion, if you please."

"Oh, no. The discussion is just beginning. Now, Renny, I'll tell you what you need. You need a good, sensible wife worse than any man I know. It is not yet too late to save you, but it soon will be. You will, before long, grow a crust on you like a snail, or a lobster, or any other cold-blooded animal that gets a shell on itself. Then nothing can be done for you. Now, let me save you, Renny, before it is too late. Here is my proposition: You choose one of those girls and marry her. I'll take the other. I'm not as unselfish as I may seem in this, for your choice will save me the worry of making up my own mind. According to your talk, either of the girls is too good for you, and for once I entirely agree with you. But let that pass. Now, which one is it to be?"

"Good God! man, do you think I am going to bargain with you about my future wife?"

"That's right, Renny. I like to hear you swear. It shows you are not yet the prig you would have folks believe. There's still hope for you, professor. Now, I'll go further with you. Although I cannot make up my mind just what to do myself, I can tell instantly which is the girl for you, and thus we solve both problems at one stroke. You need a wife who will take you in hand. You need one who will not put up with your tantrums, who will be cheerful, and who will make a man of you. Kitty Bartlett is the girl. She will tyrannize over you, just as her mother does over the old man. She will keep house to the queen's taste, and delight in getting you good things to eat. Why, everything is as plain as a pikestaff. That shows the benefit of talking over a thing. You marry Kitty, and I'll marry Margaret. Come, let's shake hands over it." Yates held up his right hand, ready to slap it down on the open palm of the professor, but there was no response. Yates' hand came down to his side again, but he had not yet lost the enthusiasm of his proposal. The more he thought of it the more fitting it seemed.

"Margaret is such a sensible, quiet, level-headed girl that, if I am as flippant as you say, she will be just the wife for me. There are depths in my character, Renmark, that you have not suspected."

"Oh, you're deep."

"I admit it. Well, a good, sober-minded woman would develop the best that is in me. Now, what do you say, Renny?"

"I say nothing. I am going into the woods again, dark as it is."

"Ah, well," said Yates with a sigh, "there's no doing anything with you or for you. I've tried my best; that is one consolation. Don't go away. I'll let fate decide. Here goes for a toss-up."

And Yates drew a silver half dollar from his pocket. "Heads for Margaret!" he cried. Renmark clinched his fist, took a step forward, then checked himself, remembering that this was his last night with the man who had at least once been his friend.

Yates merrily spun the coin in the air, caught it in one hand, and slapped the other over it.

"Now for the turning point in the lives of two innocent beings." He raised the covering hand, and peered at the coin in the gathering gloom. "Heads it is. Margaret Howard becomes Mrs. Richard Yates. Congratulate me, professor."

Renmark stood motionless as a statue, an object lesson in self-control. Yates set his hat more jauntily on his head, and slipped the epoch-making coin into his trousers pocket.

"Good-by, old man," he said. "I'll see you later, and tell you all the particulars."

Without waiting for the answer, for which he probably knew there would have been little use in delaying, Yates walked to the fence and sprang over it, with one hand on the top rail. Renmark stood still for some minutes, then, quietly gathering underbrush and sticks large and small, lighted a fire, and sat down on a log, with his head in his hands.

CHAPTER XXII.

Yates walked merrily down the road, whistling "Gayly the troubadour." Perhaps there is no moment in a man's life when he feels the joy of being alive more keenly than when he goes to propose to a girl of whose favorable answer he is reasonably sure—unless it be the moment he walks away an accepted lover. There is a magic about a June night, with its soft, velvety darkness and its sweet, mild air laden with the perfumes of wood and field. The enchantment of the hour threw its spell over the young man, and he resolved to live a better life, and be worthy of the girl he had chosen, or, rather, that fate had chosen for him. He paused a moment, leaning over the fence near the Howard homestead, for he had not yet settled in his own mind the details of the meeting. He would not go in, for in that case he knew he would have to talk, perhaps for hours, with everyone but the person he wished to meet. If he announced himself and asked to see Margaret alone, his doing so would embarrass her at the very beginning. Yates was naturally too much of a diplomat to begin awkwardly. As he stood there, wishing chance would bring her out of the house, there appeared a light in the door-window of the room where he knew the convalescent boy lay. Margaret's shadow formed a silhouette on the blind. Yates caught up a handful of sand, and flung it lightly against the pane. Its soft patter evidently attracted the attention of the girl, for, after a moment's pause, the window opened carefully, while Margaret stepped quickly out and closed it, quietly standing there.

"Margaret," whispered Yates hardly above his breath.

The girl advanced toward the fence.

"Is that you?" she whispered in return, with an accent on the last word that thrilled her listener. The accent told plainly as speech that the word represented the one man on earth to her.

"Yes," answered Yates, springing over the fence and approaching her.

"Oh!" cried Margaret, starting back, then checking herself, with a catch in her voice. "You—you startled me—Mr. Yates."

"Not Mr. Yates any more, Margaret, but Dick. Margaret, I wanted to se you alone. You know why I have come." He tried to grasp both her hands, bu she put them resolutely behind her, seemingly wishing to retreat, yet standin her ground.

"Margaret, you must have seen long ago how it is with me. I love you Margaret, loyally and truly. It seems as if I had loved you all my life. I certainl have since the first day I saw you."

"Oh, Mr. Yates, you must not talk to me like this."

"My darling, how else can I talk to you? It cannot be a surprise to you Margaret. You must have known it long ago."

"I did not, indeed I did not—if you really mean it."

"Mean it? I never meant anything as I mean this. It is everything to me and nothing else is anything. I have knocked about the world a good deal, admit, but I never was in love before—never knew what love was until I me you. I tell you that——"

"Please, please, Mr. Yates, do not say anything more. If it is really true, cannot tell you how sorry I am. I hope nothing I have said or done has mad you believe that—that—Oh, I do not know what to say! I never thought you could be in earnest about anything."

"You surely cannot have so misjudged me, Margaret. Others have, but did not expect it of you. You are far and away better than I am. No one knows that so well as I. I do not pretend to be worthy of you, but I will be a devoted husband to you. Any man who gets the love of a good woman," continued Yates earnestly, plagiarizing Renmark, "gets more than he deserves; but surely such love as mine is not given merely to be scornfully trampled underfoot."

"I do not treat your—you scornfully. I am only sorry if what you say is true."

"Why do you say if it is true? Don't you know it is true?"

"Then I am very sorry—very, very sorry, and I hope it is through no fault of mine. But you will soon forget me. When you return to New York——"

"Margaret," said the young man bitterly, "I shall never forget you. Think what you are doing before it is too late. Think how much this means to me. If you finally refuse me, you will wreck my life. I am the sort of man that a woman can make or mar. Do not, I beg of you, ruin the life of the man who loves you."

"I am not a missionary," cried Margaret with sudden anger. "If your life is to be wrecked, it will be through your own foolishness, and not from any act of mine. I think it cowardly of you to say that I am to be held responsible. I have no wish to influence your future one way or another."

"Not for good, Margaret?" asked Yates with tender reproach.

"No. A man whose good or bad conduct depends on anyone but himself is not my ideal of a man."

"Tell me what your ideal is, so that I may try to attain it."

Margaret was silent.

"You think it will be useless for me to try?"

"As far as I am concerned, yes."

"Margaret, I want to ask you one more question. I have no right to, but I beg you to answer me. Are you in love with anyone else?"

"No!" cried Margaret hotly. "How dare you ask me such a question?"

"Oh, it is not a crime—that is, being in love with someone else is not. I'll tell you why I dare ask. I swear, by all the gods, that I shall win you—if not this year, then next; and if not next, then the year after. I was a coward to talk as I did; but I love you more now than I did even then. All I want to know is that you are not in love with another man.

"I think you are very cruel in persisting as you do, when you have had your answer. I say no. Never! never! never!—this year nor any other year. Is not that enough?"

"Not for me. A woman's 'no' may ultimately mean 'yes.'"

"That is true, Mr. Yates," replied Margaret, drawing herself up as one who makes a final plunge. "You remember the question you asked me just now?—whether I cared for anyone else? I said 'no.' That 'no' meant 'yes.'"

He was standing between her and the window, so she could not escape by the way she came. He saw she meditated flight, and made as though he would intercept her, but she was too quick for him. She ran around the house, and he heard a door open and shut.

He knew he was defeated. Dejectedly he turned to the fence, climbing slowly over where he had leaped so lightly a few minutes before, and walked down the road, cursing his fate. Although he admitted he was a coward for talking to her as he had done about his wrecked life, yet he knew now that every word he had spoken was true. What did the future hold out to him? Not even the incentive to live. He found himself walking toward the tent, but, not wishing to meet Renmark in his present frame of mind, he turned and came out on the Ridge Road. He was tired and broken, and resolved to stay in camp until they arrested him. Then perhaps she might have some pity on him. Who was the other man she loved? or had she merely said that to give finality to her refusal? In his present mood he pictured the worst, and imagined her the wife of some neighboring farmer—perhaps even of Stoliker. These country girls, he said to himself, never believed a man was worth looking at unless he owned a farm. He would save his money, and buy up the whole neighborhood; then she would realize what she had missed. He climbed up on the fence beside the road, and sat on the top rail, with his heels resting on a lower one, so that he might enjoy his misery without the fatigue of walking. His vivid imagination pictured himself as the owner in a few years' time of a large section of that part of the country, with mortgages on a good deal of the remainder, including the farm owned by Margaret's husband. He saw her now, a farmer's faded wife, coming to him and begging for further time in which to pay the seven per cent. due. He knew he would act magnanimously on such an occasion, and grandly give her husband all the time he required. Perhaps then she would realize the mistake she had made. Or perhaps fame, rather than riches, would be his line. His name would ring throughout the land. He might become a great politician, and bankrupt Canada with a rigid tariff law. The unfairness of making the whole innocent people suffer for the inconsiderate act of one of them did not occur to him at the moment, for he was humiliated and hurt. There is no bitterness like that which assails the man who has been rejected by the girl he adores—while it lasts. His eye wandered toward the black mass of the Howard house. It was as dark as his thoughts. He turned his head slowly around, and, like a bright star of hope, there glimmered up the road a flickering light from the Bartletts' parlor window. Although time had stopped as far as he was concerned, he was convinced it could not be very late, or the Bartletts would have gone to bed. It is always difficult to realize that the greatest of catastrophes are generally over in a few minutes. It seemed an age since he walked so hopefully away from the tent. As he looked at the light the thought struck him that perhaps Kitty was alone in the parlor. She at least would not have treated him so badly as the other girl; and—and she was pretty, too, come to think of it. He always did like a blonde better than a brunette.

A fence rail is not a comfortable seat. It is used in some parts of the country in such a manner as to impress the sitter with the fact of its extreme discomfort, and as a gentle hint that his presence is not wanted in that immediate neighborhood. Yates recollected this, with a smile, as he slid off and stumbled into the ditch by the side of the road. His mind had been so preoccupied that he had forgotten about the ditch. As he walked along the road toward the star that guided him he remembered he had recklessly offered Miss Kitty to the callous professor. After all, no one knew about the episode of a short time before except himself and Margaret, and he felt convinced she was not a girl to boast of her conquests. Anyhow, it didn't matter. A man is surely master of himself.

As he neared the window he looked in. People are not particular about lowering the blinds in the country. He was rather disappointed to see Mrs. Bartlett sitting there knitting, like the industrious woman she was. Still it was consoling to note that none of the men-folks were present, and that Kitty, with her fluffy hair half concealing her face, sat reading a book he had lent to her. He rapped at the door, and it was opened by Mrs. Bartlett, with some surprise.

"For the land's sake! is that you, Mr. Yates?"

"It is."

"Come right in. Why, what's the matter with you? You look as if you had lost your best friend. Ah, I see how it is,"—Yates started,—"you have run out of provisions, and are very likely as hungry as a bear."

"You've hit it first time, Mrs. Bartlett. I dropped around to see if I could borrow a loaf of bread. We don't bake till to-morrow."

Mrs. Bartlett laughed.

"Nice baking you would do if you tried it. I'll get you a loaf in a minute. Are you sure one is enough?"

"Quite enough, thank you."

The good woman bustled out to the other room for the loaf, and Yates made good use of her temporary absence.

"Kitty," he whispered, "I want to see you alone for a few minutes. I'll wait for you at the gate. Can you slip out?"

Kitty blushed very red and nodded.

"They have a warrant out for my arrest, and I'm off to-morrow before they can serve it. But I couldn't go without seeing you. You'll come, sure?"

Again Kitty nodded, after looking up at him in alarm when he spoke of the warrant. Before anything further could be said Mrs. Bartlett came in, and Kitty was absorbed in her book.

"Won't you have something to eat now before you go back?"

"Oh, no, thank you, Mrs. Bartlett. You see, the professor is waiting for me."

"Let him wait, if he didn't have sense enough to come."

"He didn't. I offered him the chance."

"It won't take us a moment to set the table. It is not the least trouble."

"Really, Mrs. Bartlett, you are very kind. I am not in the slightest degree hungry now. I am merely taking some thought of the morrow. No; I must be going, and thank you very much."

"Well," said Mrs. Bartlett, seeing him to the door, "if there's anything you want, come to me, and I will let you have it if it's in the house."

"You are too good to me," said the young man with genuine feeling, "and I don't deserve it; but I may remind you of your promise—to-morrow."

"See that you do," she answered. "Good-night."

Yates waited at the gate, placing the loaf on the post, where he forgot it, much to the astonishment of the donor in the morning. He did not have to wait long, for Kitty came around the house somewhat shrinkingly, as one who was doing the most wicked thing that had been done since the world began. Yates hastened to meet her, clasping one of her unresisting hands in his.

"I must be off to-morrow," he began.

"I am very sorry," answered Kitty in a whisper.

"Ah, Kitty, you are not half so sorry as I am. But I intend to come back, if you will let me. Kitty, you remember that talk we had in the kitchen, when we—when there was an interruption, and when I had to go away with our friend Stoliker?"

Kitty indicated that she remembered it.

"Well, of course you know what I wanted to say to you. Of course you know what I want to say to you now."

It seemed, however, that in this he was mistaken, for Kitty had not the slightest idea, and wanted to go into the house, for it was late, and her mother would miss her.

"Kitty, you darling little humbug, you know that I love you. You must know that I have loved you ever since the first day I saw you, when you laughed at me. Kitty, I want you to marry me and make something of me, if that is possible. I am a worthless fellow, not half good enough for a little pet like you; but, Kitty, if you will only say 'yes,' I will try, and try hard, to be a better man than I have ever been before."

Kitty did not say "yes" but she placed her disengaged hand, warm and soft, upon his, and Yates was not the man to have any hesitation about what to do next. To practical people it may seem an astonishing thing that, the object of the interview being happily accomplished, there should be any need of prolonging it; yet the two lingered there, and he told her much of his past life, and of how lonely and sordid it had been because he had no one to care for him—at which her pretty eyes filled with tears. She felt proud and happy to think she had won the first great love of a talented man's life, and hoped she would make him happy, and in a measure atone for the emptiness of the life that had gone before. She prayed that he might always be as fond of her as he was then, and resolved to be worthy of him if she could.

Strange to say, her wishes have been amply fulfilled, and few wives are as happy or as proud of their husbands as Kitty Yates. The one woman who might have put the drop of bitterness in her cup of life merely kissed her tenderly when Kitty told her of the great joy that had come to her, and said she was sure she would be happy; and thus for the second time Margaret told the thing that was not, but for once Margaret was wrong in her fears.

Yates walked to the tent a glorified man, leaving his loaf on the gatepost behind him. Few realize that it is quite as pleasant to be loved as to love. The verb "to love" has many conjugations. The earth he trod was like no other ground he had ever walked upon. The magic of the June night was never so enchanting before. He strode along with his head and his thoughts in the clouds, and the Providence that cares for the intoxicated looked after him, and saw that the accepted lover came to no harm. He leaped the fence without even putting his hand to it, and then was brought to earth again by the picture of a man sitting with his head in his hands beside a dying fire.

CHAPTER XXIII.

Yates stood for a moment regarding the dejected attitude of his friend.

"Hello, old man!" he cried, "you have the most 'hark-from-the-tombs' appearance I ever saw. What's the matter?"

Renmark looked up.

"Oh, it's you, is it?"

"Of course it's I. Been expecting anybody else?"

"No. I have been waiting for you, and thinking of a variety of things."

"You look it. Well, Renny, congratulate me, my boy. She's mine, and I'm hers—which are two ways of stating the same delightful fact. I'm up in a balloon, Renny. I'm engaged to the prettiest, sweetest, and most delightful girl there is from the Atlantic to the Pacific. What d'ye think of that? Say, Renmark, there's nothing on earth like it. You ought to reform and go in for being in love. It would make a man of you. Champagne isn't to be compared to it. Get up here and dance, and don't sit there like a bear nursing a sore paw. Do you comprehend that I am to be married to the darlingest girl that lives?"

"God help her!"

"That's what I say. Every day of her life, bless her! But I don't say it quite in that tone, Renmark. What's the matter with you? One would think you were in love with the girl yourself, if such a thing were possible."

"Why is it not possible?"

"If that is a conundrum, I can answer it the first time. Because you are a fossil. You are too good, Renny; therefore dull and uninteresting. Now, there is nothing a woman likes so much as to reclaim a man. It always annoys a woman to know that the man she is interested in has a past with which she has had nothing to do. If he is wicked and she can sort of make him over, like an old dress, she revels in the process. She flatters herself she makes a new man of him, and thinks she owns that new man by right of manufacture. We owe it to the sex, Renny, to give 'em a chance at reforming us. I have known men who hated tobacco take to smoking merely to give it up joyfully for the sake of the women they loved. Now, if a man is perfect to begin with, what is a dear, ministering angel of a woman to do with him? Manifestly nothing. The trouble with you, Renny, is that you are too evidently ruled by a good and well-trained conscience, and naturally all women you meet intuitively see this, and have no use for you. A little wickedness would be the making of you."

"You think, then, that if a man's impulse is to do what his conscience tells him is wrong, he should follow his impulse, and not his conscience?"

"You state the case with unnecessary seriousness. I believe that an occasional blow-out is good for a man. But if you ever have an impulse of that kind, I think you should give way to it for once, just to see how it feels. A man who is too good gets conceited about himself."

"I half believe you are right, Mr. Yates," said the professor, rising. "I will act on your advice, and, as you put it, see how it feels. My conscience tells me that I should congratulate you, and wish you a long and happy life with the girl you have—I won't say chosen, but tossed up for. The natural man in me, on the other hand, urges me to break every bone in your worthless body. Throw off your coat, Yates."

"Oh, I say, Renmark, you're crazy."

"Perhaps so. Be all the more on your guard, if you believe it. A lunatic is sometimes dangerous."

"Oh, go away. You're dreaming. You're talking in your sleep. What! Fight? Tonight? Nonsense!"

"Do you want me to strike you before you are ready?"

"No, Renny, no. My wants are always modest. I don't wish to fight at all, especially to-night. I'm a reformed man, I tell you. I have no desire to bid good-by to my best girl with a black eye to-morrow."

"Then stop talking, if you can, and defend yourself."

"It's impossible to fight here in the dark. Don't flatter yourself for a moment that I am afraid. You just spar with yourself and get limbered up, while I put some wood on the fire. This is too ridiculous."

Yates gathered some fuel, and managed to coax the dying embers into a blaze.

"There," he said, "that's better. Now, let me have a look at you. In the name of wonder, Renny, what do you want to fight me for to-night?"

"I refuse to give my reason."

"Then I refuse to fight. I'll run, and I can beat you in a foot race any day in the week. Why, you're worse than her father. He at least let me know why he fought me."

"Whose father?"

"Kitty's father, of course—my future father-in-law. And that's another ordeal ahead of me. I haven't spoken to the old man yet, and I need all my fighting grit for that."

"What are you talking about?"

"Isn't my language plain? It usually is."

"To whom are you engaged? As I understand your talk, it is to Miss Bartlett. Am I right?"

"Right as rain, Renny. This fire is dying down again. Say, can't we postpone our fracas until daylight? I don't want to gather any more wood. Besides, one of us is sure to be knocked into the fire, and thus ruin whatever is left of our clothes. What do you say?"

"Say? I say I am an idiot."

"Hello! reason is returning, Renny. I perfectly agree with you."

"Thank you. Then you did not propose to Mar—to Miss Howard?"

"Now, you touch upon a sore spot, Renmark, that I am trying to forget. You remember the unfortunate toss-up; in fact, I think you referred to it a moment ago, and you were justly indignant about it at the time. Well, I don't care to talk much about the sequel; but, as you know the beginning, you will have to know the end, because I want to wring a sacred promise from you. You are never to mention this episode of the toss-up, or of my confession, to any living soul. The telling of it might do harm, and it couldn't possibly do any good. Will you promise?"

"Certainly. But do not tell me unless you wish to."

"I don't exactly yearn to talk about it, but it is better you should understand how the land lies, so you won't make any mistake. Not on my account, you know, but I would not like it to come to Kitty's ears. Yes, I proposed to Margaret—first. She wouldn't look at me. Can you credit that?"

"Well, now that you mention it, I——"

"Exactly. I see you can credit it. Well, I couldn't at first; but Margaret knows her own mind, there's no question about that. Say! she's in love with some other fellow. I found out that much."

"You asked her, I presume."

"Well, it's my profession to find out things; and, naturally, if I do that for my paper, it is not likely I am going to be behindhand when it comes to myself. She denied it at first, but admitted it afterward, and then bolted."

"You must have used great tact and delicacy."

"See here, Renmark; I'm not going to stand any of your sneering. I told you this was a sore subject with me. I'm not telling you because I like to, but because I have to. Don't put me in fighting humor, Mr. Renmark. If I talk fight, I won't begin for no reason and then back out for no reason. I'll go on."

"I'll be discreet, and beg to take back all I said. What else?"

"Nothing else. Isn't that enough? It was more than enough for me—at the time. I tell you, Renmark, I spent a pretty bad half hour sitting on the fence and thinking about it."

"So long as that?"

Yates rose from the fire indignantly.

"I take that back, too," cried the professor hastily. "I didn't mean it."

"It strikes me you've become awfully funny all of a sudden. Don't you think it's about time we took to our bunks? It's late."

Renmark agreed with him but did not turn in. He walked to the friendly fence, laid his arms along the top rail, and gazed at the friendly stars. He had not noticed before how lovely the night was, with its impressive stillness, as if the world had stopped, as a steamer stops in mid-ocean. After quieting his troubled spirit with the restful stars he climbed the fence and walked down the road, taking little heed of the direction. The still night was a soothing companion. He came at last to a sleeping village of wooden houses, and through the center of the town ran a single line of rails, an iron link connecting the unknown hamlet with all civilization. A red and a green light glimmered down the line, giving the only indication that a train ever came that way. As he went a mile or two farther the cool breath of the great lake made itself felt, and after crossing a field he suddenly came upon the water, finding all further progress in that direction barred. Huge sand dunes formed the shore, covered with sighing pines. At the foot of the dunes stretched a broad beach of firm sand, dimly visible in contrast with the darker water; and at long intervals fell the light ripple of the languid summer waves, running up the beach with a half-asleep whisper, that became softer and softer until it was merged in the silence beyond. Far out on the dark waters a point of light, like a floating star, showed where a steamer was slowly making her way; and so still was the night that he felt rather than heard her pulsating engines. It was the only sign of life visible from that enchanted bay—the bay of the silver beach.

Renmark threw himself down on the soft sand at the foot of a dune. The point of light gradually worked its way to the west, following, doubtless unconsciously, the star of empire, and disappeared around the headland, taking with it a certain vague sense of companionship. But the world is very small, and a man is never quite as much alone as he thinks he is. Renmark heard the low hoot of an owl among the trees, which cry he was astonished to hear answered from the water. He sat up and listened. Presently there grated on the sand the keel of a boat, and someone stepped ashore. From the woods there emerged the shadowy forms of three men. Nothing was said, but they got silently into the boat, which might have been Charon's craft for all he could see of it. The rattle of the rowlocks and the plash of oars followed, while a voice cautioned the rowers to make less noise. It was evident that some belated fugitives were eluding the authorities of both countries. Renmark thought, with a smile, that if Yates were in his place he would at least give them a fright. A sharp command to an imaginary company to load and fire would travel far on such a night, and would give the rowers a few moments of great discomfort. Renmark, however, did not shout, but treated the episode as part of the mystical dream, and lay down on the sand again. He noticed that the water in the east seemed to feel the approach of morning even before the sky. Gradually the day dawned, a slowly lightening gray at first, until the coming sun spattered a filmy cloud with gold and crimson. Renmark watched the glory of the sunrise, took one lingering look at the curved beauty of the bay shore, shook the sand from his clothing, and started back for the village and the camp beyond.

The village was astir when he reached it. He was surprised to see Stoliker on horseback in front of one of the taverns. Two assistants were with him, also seated on horses. The constable seemed disturbed by the sight of Renmark, but he was there to do his duty.

"Hello!" he cried, "you're up early. I have a warrant for the arrest of your friend: I suppose you won't tell me where he is?"

"You can't expect me to give any information that will get a friend into trouble, can you? especially as he has done nothing."

"That's as may turn out before a jury," said one of the assistants gravely.

"Yes," assented, Stoliker, winking quietly at the professor. "That is for judge and jury to determine—not you."

"Well," said Renmark, "I will not inform about anybody, unless I am compelled to do so, but I may save you some trouble by telling where I have been and what I have seen. I am on my way back from the lake. If you go down there, you will still see the mark of a boat's keel on the sand, and probably footprints. A boat came over from the other shore in the night, and a man got on board. I don't say who the man was, and I had nothing to do with the matter in any way except as a spectator. That is all the information I have to give."

Stoliker turned to his assistants, and nodded. "What did I tell you?" he asked. "We were right on his track."

"You said the railroad," grumbled the man who had spoken before.

"Well, we were within two miles of him. Let us go down to the lake and see the traces. Then we can return the warrant."

Renmark found Yates still asleep in the tent. He prepared breakfast without disturbing him. When the meal was ready, he roused the reporter and told him of his meeting with Stoliker, advising him to get back to New York without delay.

Yates yawned sleepily.

"Yes," he said, "I've been dreaming it all out. I'll get father-in-law to tote me out to Fort Erie to-night."

"Do you think it will be safe to put it off so long?"

"Safer than trying to get away during the day. After breakfast I'm going down to the Bartlett homestead. Must have a talk with the old folks, you know. I'll spend the rest of the day making up for that interview by talking with Kitty. Stoliker will never search for me there, and, now that he thinks I'm gone, he will likely make a visit to the tent. Stoliker is a good fellow, but his strong point is duty, you know; and if he's certain I'm gone, he'll give his country the worth of its money by searching. I won't be back for dinner, so you can put in your time reading my Dime Novels. I make no reflections on your cooking, Renny, now that the vacation is over; but I have my preferences, and they incline toward a final meal with the Bartletts. If I were you, I'd have a nap. You look tired out."

"I am," said the professor.

Renmark intended to lie down for a few moments until Yates was clear of the camp, after which he determined to pay a visit; but Nature, when she got him locked up in sleep, took her revenge. He did not hear Stoliker and his satellites search the premises, just as Yates had predicted they would; and when he finally awoke, he found to his astonishment that it was nearly dark. But he was all the better for his sleep, and he attended to his personal appearance with more than ordinary care.

Old Hiram Bartlett accepted the situation with the patient and grim stolidity of a man who takes a blow dealt him by a Providence known by him to be inscrutable. What he had done to deserve it was beyond his comprehension. He silently hitched up his horses, and, for the first time in his life, drove into Fort Erie without any reasonable excuse for going there. He tied his team at the usual corner, after which he sat at one of the taverns and drank strong waters that had no apparent effect on him. He even went so far as to smoke two native cigars; and a man who can do that can do anything. To bring up a daughter who would deliberately accept a man from "the States," and to have a wife who would aid and abet such an action, giving comfort and support to the enemy, seemed to him traitorous to all the traditions of 1812, or any other date in the history of the two countries. At times wild ideas of getting blind full, and going home to break every breakable thing in the house, rose in his mind; but prudence whispered that he had to live all the rest of his life with his wife, and he realized that this scheme of vengeance had its drawbacks. Finally, he untied his patient team, after paying his bill, and drove silently home, not having returned, even by a nod, any of the salutations tendered to him that day. He was somewhat relieved to find no questions were asked, and that his wife recognized the fact that he was passing through a crisis. Nevertheless, there was a steely glitter in her eye under which he uneasily quailed, for it told him a line had been reached which it would not be well for him to cross. She forgave, but it must not go any further.

When Yates kissed Kitty good-night at the gate, he asked her, with some trepidation, whether she had told anyone of their engagement.

"No one but Margaret," said Kitty.

"And what did she say?" asked Yates, as if, after all, her opinion was of no importance.

"She said she was sure I should be happy, and she knew you would make a good husband."

"She's rather a nice girl, is Margaret," remarked Yates, with the air of a man willing to concede good qualities to a girl other than his own, but indicating, after all, that there was but one on earth for him.

"She is a lovely girl," said Kitty enthusiastically. "I wonder, Dick, when you knew her, why you ever fell in love with me."

"The idea! I haven't a word to say against Margaret; but, compared with my girl——"

And he finished his sentence with a practical illustration of his frame of mind.

As he walked alone down the road he reflected that Margaret had acted very handsomely, and he resolved to drop in and wish her good-by. But as he approached the house his courage began to fail him, and he thought it better to sit on the fence, near the place where he had sat the night before, and think it over. It took a good deal of thinking. But as he sat there it was destined that Yates should receive some information which would simplify matters. Two persons came slowly out of the gate in the gathering darkness. They strolled together up the road past him, absorbed in themselves. When directly opposite the reporter, Renmark put his arm around Margaret's waist, and Yates nearly fell off the fence. He held his breath until they were safely out of hearing, then slid down and crawled along in the shadow until he came to the side road, up which he walked, thoughtfully pausing every few moments to remark: "Well, I'll be——" But speech seemed to have failed him; he could get no further.

He stopped at the fence and leaned against it, gazing for the last time at the tent, glimmering white, like a misshapen ghost, among the somber trees. He had no energy left to climb over.

"Well, I'm a chimpanzee," he muttered to himself at last. "The highest bidder can have me, with no upset price. Dick Yates, I wouldn't have believed it of you. You a newspaper man? You a reporter from 'way back? You up to snuff? Yates, I'm ashamed to be seen in your company! Go back to New York, and let the youngest reporter in from a country newspaper scoop the daylight out of you. To think that this thing has been going on right under your well-developed nose, and you never saw it—worse, never had the faintest suspicion of it; that it was thrust at you twenty times a day—nearly got your stupid head smashed on account of it; yet you bleated away like the innocent little lamb that you are, and never even suspected! Dick, you're a three-sheet-poster fool in colored ink. And to think that both of them know all about the first proposal! Both of them! Well, thank Heaven, Toronto is a long way from New York."

THE END.

About Author

Robert Barr (16 September 1849 – 21 October 1912) was a Scottish-Canadian short story writer and novelist.

Early years in Canada

Robert Barr was born in Barony, Lanark, Scotland to Robert Barr and Jane Watson. In 1854, he emigrated with his parents to Upper Canada at the age of four years old. His family settled on a farm near the village of Muirkirk. Barr assisted his father with his job as a carpenter, and developed a sound work ethic. Robert Barr then worked as a steel smelter for a number of years before he was educated at Toronto Normal School in 1873 to train as a teacher.

After graduating Toronto Normal School, Barr became a teacher, and eventually headmaster/principal of the Central School of Windsor, Ontario in 1874. While Barr worked as head master of the Central School of Windsor, Ontario, he began to contribute short stories—often based on personal experiences, and recorded his work. On August 1876, when he was 27, Robert Barr married Ontario-born Eva Bennett, who was 21. According to the 1891 England Census, the couple appears to have had three children, Laura, William, and Andrew.

In 1876, Barr quit his teaching position to become a staff member of publication, and later on became the news editor for the Detroit Free Press. Barr wrote for this newspaper under the pseudonym, "Luke Sharp." The idea for this pseudonym was inspired during his morning commute to work when Barr saw a sign that read "Luke Sharp, Undertaker." In 1881, Barr left Canada to return to England in order to start a new weekly version of "The Detroit Free Press Magazine."

London years

In 1881 Barr decided to "vamoose the ranch", as he called the process of immigration in search of literary fame outside of Canada, and relocated to London to continue to write/establish the weekly English edition of the Detroit Free Press. During the 1890s, he broadened his literary works, and started writing novels from the popular crime genre. In 1892 he founded the magazine The Idler, choosing Jerome K. Jerome as his collaborator (wanting, as Jerome said, "a popular name"). He retired from its co-editorship in 1895.

In London of the 1890s Barr became a more prolific author—publishing a book a year—and was familiar with many of the best-selling authors of his day, including :Arnold Bennett, Horatio Gilbert Parker, Joseph Conrad, Bret Harte, Rudyard Kipling, H. Rider Haggard, H. G. Wells, and George Robert Gissing. Barr was well-spoken, well-cultured due to travel, and considered a "socializer."

Because most of Barr's literary output was of the crime genre, his works were highly in vogue. As Sherlock Holmes stories were becoming well-known, Barr wrote and published in the Idler the first Holmes parody, "The Adventures of "Sherlaw Kombs" (1892), a spoof that was continued a decade later in another Barr story, "The Adventure of the Second Swag" (1904). Despite those jibes at the growing Holmes phenomenon, Barr remained on very good terms with its creator Arthur Conan Doyle. In Memories and Adventures, a serial memoir published 1923–24, Doyle described him as "a volcanic Anglo—or rather Scot-American, with a violent manner, a wealth of strong adjectives, and one of the kindest natures underneath it all".

In 1904, Robert Barr completed an unfinished novel for Methuen & Co. by the recently deceased American author Stephen Crane entitled The O'Ruddy, a romance.Despite his reservations at taking on the project, Barr reluctantly finished the last eight chapters due to his longstanding friendship with Crane and his common-law wife, Cora, the war correspondent and bordello owner.

Death

The 1911 census places Robert Barr, "a writer of fiction," at Hillhead, Woldingham, Surrey, a small village southeast of London, living with his wife, Eva, their son William, and two female servants. At this home, the author died from heart disease on 21 October 1912.

Writing Style

Barr's volumes of short stories were often written with an ironic twist in the story with a witty, appealing narrator telling the story. Barr's other works also include numerous fiction and non-fiction contributions to periodicals. A few of his mystery stories and stories of the supernatural were put in anthologies, and a few novels have been republished. His writings have also attracted scholarly attention. His narrative personae also featured moral and editorial interpolations within their tales. Barr's achievements were recognized by an honorary degree from the University of Michigan in 1900.

His protagonists were journalists, princes, detectives, deserving commercial and social climbers, financiers, the new woman of bright wit and aggressive accomplishment, and lords. Often, his characters were stereotypical and romanticized.

Barr wrote fiction in an episode-like format. He developed this style when working as an editor for the newspaper Detroit Press. Barr developed his skill with the anecdote and vignette; often only the central character serves to link the nearly self-contained chapters of the novels. (Source: Wikipedia)

NOTABLE WORKS

In a Steamer Chair and Other Stories (Thirteen short stories by one of the most famous writers in his day -1892)

"The Face And The Mask" (1894) consists of twenty-four delightful short stories.

In the Midst of Alarms (1894, 1900, 1912), a story of the attempted Fenian invasion of Canada in 1866.

From Whose Bourne (1896) Novel in which the main character, William Brenton, searches for truth to set his wife free.

One Day's Courtship (1896)

Revenge! (Collection of 20 short stories, Alfred Hitchcock-like style, thriller with a surprise ending)

The Strong Arm

A Woman Intervenes (1896), a story of love, finance, and American journalism.

Tekla: A Romance of Love and War (1898)

Jennie Baxter, Journalist (1899)

The Unchanging East (1900)

The Victors (1901)

A Prince of Good Fellows (1902)

Over The Border: A Romance (1903)

The O'Ruddy, A Romance, with Stephen Crane (1903)

A Chicago Princess (1904)

The Speculations of John Steele (1905)

The Tempestuous Petticoat (1905–12)

A Rock in the Baltic (1906)

The Triumphs of Eugène Valmont (1906)

The Measure of the Rule (1907)

Stranleigh's Millions (1909)

The Sword Maker (Medieval action/adventure novel, genre: Historical Fiction-1910)

The Palace of Logs (1912)

"The Ambassadors Pigeons" (1899)

"And the Rigor of the Game" (1892)

"Converted" (1896)

"Count Conrad's Courtship" (1896)

"The Count's Apology" (1896)

"A Deal on Change " (1896)

"The Exposure of Lord Stanford" (1896)

"Gentlemen: The King!"

"The Hour-Glass" (1899)

"An invitation" (1892)

" A Ladies Man"

"The Long Ladder" (1899)

"Mrs. Tremain" (1892)

" Transformation" (1896)

"The Understudy" (1896)

" The Vengeance of the Dead" (1896)

"The Bromley Gibbert's Story" (1896)

" Out of Thun" (1896)

"The Shadow of Greenback" (1896)

"Flight of the Red Dog" (fiction)

"Lord Stranleigh Abroad" (1913)

"One Day's Courtship and the Herald's of Fame" (1896)

"Cardillac"

"Dr. Barr's Tales"

"The Triumphs of Eugene Valmont"

CPSIA information can be obtained
at www.ICGtesting.com
Printed in the USA
LVHW041023300720
661936LV00003B/565